I0788786

Moongrove Academy

Wicked Spells

Complete Series

Flutterbye Trail Press
797 Sam Bass Road #2541
Round Rock, TX 78681

First edition

Chapter Art by Etheric Tales
Cover Design by Covers by Methyss Art
Editing by Red Loop Editing
Hardback Case Design by Olga Sauchenia
Published by Flutterbye Trail Press

ISBN: 978-1-954582-56-9 (E-book)
ISBN: 978-1-954582-57-6 (Hardback)

Feedback: Encounter a problem with this book? Let us know at
ellahendricksauthor@gmail.com

BOOKS BY ELLA HENDRICKS

THE ARCANE ALLIANCES UNIVERSE

House of the Sanguine
with Nicole LaBrocca
Dark Vampire Romantasy (RH)

Thirst

MOONGROVE ACADEMY: WICKED SPELLS

COMPLETE SERIES

ELLA HENDRICKS

LIBRARIAN WITCH
MOONGROVE ACADEMY: WICKED SPELLS BOOK 1

Librarian Witch

CONTENT OVERVIEW

This is a paranormal RH romance, meaning that the main female character does not need to choose between love interests. There are graphic sex scenes (some including more than one partner) between consenting adults. *Librarian Witch* is book one of a trilogy with a cliffhanger ending.

Please be aware that this book includes a death (murder) of a friend and depictions of grief because of it. Also contained within are fight sequences that include death, gore, and magical violence. This trilogy is classified as dark academia because the main antagonists have magic that affects the souls of others.

This trilogy does not include a pregnancy for the FMC or MM content.

If you find anything in the contents of this book that should be added to this page, please let me know at ellahendricksauthor@gmail.com.

1

CRESS

THIRTY-SOME WITCHES SAT in a dimly lit classroom with auditorium-style seating. Gum snapped, and young women giggled quietly, paying little heed to the elderly figure at the front projecting her raspy voice over the group via a tiny microphone taped to one ear. She had one gnarled hand resting on the surface of what looked like a pure-black tabletop. "This device will determine what you study at our esteemed university. It will tell you which branch of witchcraft you are best suited for."

I shot a glare over my shoulder as a girl said a little too loudly, "Can we hurry this up?"

I'd met her at orientation, learning that she was one of many legacy witches attending this university like their parents had in the past. Unlike her and a disruptive handful of her friends, I didn't come from an established witch family who'd specialized in one kind of magic for generations. Every word from the venerated Dr. Evanora Heartwood was news to me. That was why I was one of three people who'd sat themselves in the front row.

While today was a formality for most of the students here, it was vital for me. I couldn't stop my fidgeting as I waited to learn what kind of magic was the right fit for me. Today was my stepping stone into the supernatural world, which I'd just learned about a couple short months ago.

Dr. Heartwood acted like she hadn't heard the pointed question. Considering that she was at least two decades past retirement age, maybe her aging ears made her immune to the impatience of the younger generation. "I hope you are ready to learn your affinity! Even those of you who have already bonded your magic to a chosen affinity will be required to step forward and confirm it for the university's records," she said. She perched a tiny pair of eyeglasses on the tip of her nose before consulting a clipboard. "Merrill Blackwood, you're up first."

A guy with shaggy, clay-colored corkscrew hair descended the steps. He wore a polo and a pair of khaki shorts, looking for all the world like a normal college student.

That's what was still so surreal about Moongrove Academy. To me, witches were supposed to be green-skinned crones bent over bubbling cauldrons of goop, who rode brooms across the night sky and owned irritable black cats. They weren't guys like Merrill, who had the good looks and swagger of a future popular man on campus.

"The Blackwoods are a verdant witch family," the girl next to me whispered behind her hand. She was the only witch I'd talked to in depth since I'd arrived two days ago. I hadn't connected with any other witches, who all seemed to scoff when they realized I knew next to nothing about being one of them.

Luckily, I had a roommate who didn't mind I was completely new to magic. Lanie Graygazer had greeted me with an enthusiastic wave and an effusive, "Hi, Cress! I've seen we're going to be best friends." There was just something candy sweet and earnest about her, so I listened to her explain how she'd already known my name. Which, of course, involved magic.

Lanie was from a big family of augury witches that traveled all over helping others, sometimes before they realized they needed help. She'd come into her powers at fourteen, which was incredibly impressive by witch standards. While I was angsting over boys and pimples in eighth grade, she'd been busy viewing the future.

Lanie had already spent half her life in Europe and Asia, learning from her parents about how to use her augury magic. She could speak several languages fluently, starting with her family's native Korean, due to being homeschooled all that time. She'd learned everything she needed to know by doing it. Next to her, I felt like a talentless potato.

She took her family's calling to heart—she helped answer some of my questions before I asked them. "That thing up there looks like it's a table, but there's a machine in the center that'll prick your finger with a tiny needle. Inside it, a computer will read all the bits in your blood and then will turn on a light under the symbol for your affinity," she explained since Merrill had his back to us while he completed the process. A fresh-faced assistant had popped up out of nowhere to ask him a few questions first, recording his responses by tapping on a tablet.

After a few minutes, Dr. Heartwood announced his affinity. "A verdant witch. Congratulations, Mr. Blackwood." She led the group in a smattering round of applause.

One by one, the other witches completed the process. I started to sweat as the group went in alphabetical order. Usually, my last name, Rollins, meant I was comfortably in the last third when it came to roll calls and classroom assignments. I'd never complained about it until the minutes crawled and the walls pushed in around me.

"Are you sure you can't tell me what my affinity is?" I asked Lanie.

She shook her head rapidly, flapping the dark hair of her bob. A reassuring smile crossed her face. "It's not my place to say. You'll like it, though," she said.

My lips formed a nervous twist, and I rubbed my clammy palms over my thighs. What would happen if I went up there and the machine couldn't find any potential in my blood? Other than my cats, I had no proof I was someone special and supernatural.

Cats don't just say "hello" to you. Not like Milo had when I'd walked by his cage at the shelter.

If that hadn't been enough, the brown tabby in the cage under him had pawed at the metal bars that separated us. "Get me out of here!" she'd howled.

I had two cats now. They talked. What explanation did I have for it if I wasn't a witch?

Lanie, too, had a cat for a familiar. Just one, though, an opinionated scrap of black fur. I couldn't understand what she mewed, only that she squeaked a lot for attention and food. I wondered if we were matched as roommates due to our familiars, considering how I'd seen a few of my witch peers walking around with wolves by their sides or falcons on their wrists. How many familiars fought one another despite their tamer natures? I had more questions than answers.

I drew myself out of my reverie to watch the different personalities come take their affinity test. The way someone walked up to that machine told me a lot about them. I looked at the slope of their shoulders and the fit of their clothes, drawing on years of people watching from the other side of a cash register as an ex-fast-food worker.

A slim brunette approached the podium like a timid mouse, her hands clutched before her. She took nearly five minutes with the assistant, whispering her answers and hunching her shoulders further when it looked like there was about to be an argument between them. Dr. Heartwood stepped in and announced the girl as Willow Frost, oceanic witch. I made sure to applaud more sincerely for her.

"Those without compound last names are new witches," Lanie told me. "They're probably going to try renaming you, too."

I scowled, my mouth forming a reply, when Lanie was called up to test next. It was brief, so she was soon skipping back to sit beside me again.

"And if I don't want a witchy last name?" I asked in an undertone.

"Oh, c'mon. There's no harm in it," she said. "It means you're one of us. And we don't go by the whole thing around humans. Like, my family introduces ourselves as the Grays, not the Graygazers."

I crossed my arms, not about to budge on my opinion. We would've argued had the double doors into this room not shot open and another woman who looked about our age walked in casually.

She had a post-workout glow on her tanned complexion. A towel hung around her neck, and she'd elevated a wavy mass of red hair into a springy high tail, highlighting a face with strong features and a constellation of freckles. She was muscular in a way most women weren't, with obvious pride in her body, which was barely covered by a neon pink pair of shorts and a matching crop top with the word "Tuff" in white lettering between two cartoon flexing arms.

She glanced around and announced loudly, "Sorry I'm late! Lost track of time."

Dr. Heartwood and her assistant were deep in conversation the moment the redhead appeared. The professor beckoned. "You must be Miss Ashbough. Let's test you next, then."

"Eh, no need. I'll go last. It's only fair," the redhead replied. She crossed the room to sit on my other side, her muscular arm scooting mine off the armrest.

To my shock, Dr. Heartwood nodded and called the next witch in line rather than make this girl respect her judgment. I glanced at the newcomer in disbelief, and she jerked her chin up. "Sup?"

Lanie came to my rescue, leaning past me to say, "Roe, this is Cress. She's a new witch."

A toothy white grin split the newcomer's face. "No way? Just learned about your powers?" she asked me. I nodded. "Coulda fooled me with that hair!"

I twirled a lock of hair self-consciously. The box color was "radiant orchid," but I wasn't sure such a bold change suited me yet. My little sister and I had dyed our hair in different intense shades before I'd left for college, and my palms were still purplish with lingering pigment.

"Yeah, I just thought it was a nice color," I said. Plus, purple was Carly's favorite color, and every time I looked in the mirror, I remember the joy on her face when I pulled out "radiant orchid" from the shopping bag. Carly was getting ready for her senior year of high school with a head of electric blue locks as we spoke.

"Cool, cool. Nice to meet you, new witch. I'm Rowena Ashbough, but you can call me Roe. My family is *ooooooold* witch blood, so there's no real surprises here." She hitched a thumb toward her chest. "Ninety-nine percent chance I'm a guardian witch."

I asked something that'd been burning a hole in my thoughts. "How can you be so sure? Like, if you haven't bonded to your affinity yet, couldn't you be something else?"

"In that case, I'd ask to be bonded to the earth anyway," Roe said. "I'd embarrass my family if I didn't come home a guardian witch, no matter what."

"Right, you could do that." I nodded to myself.

I already knew this, sort of. The university had sent me a welcome package that included an informative video on the seven affinities, which were the official and safe wells of power witches could draw from. Generation after generation had honed down what worked and what didn't.

Along with the video, the university sent a thousand-page tome with details on the supernatural world. The kind of things the other witches in this room learned in their special supernatural-only private schools. It was *a lot*. Since I'd been busy working all summer to help support my family, I hadn't had a chance to read it in depth yet.

Witches could be any affinity they wanted to be, but the purpose of having our blood tested first was to find the best fit. Our magic was naturally drawn to just one of the seven sources we can safely pull from.

"But don't follow my lead. If your magic wants you to be a blood witch and you get afraid of that and pick the verdant path instead, then it's unlikely you're going to be a successful witch," Roe continued. "The moment you tap into a well of power for the first time, you're locked to that kind of magic for life."

I felt myself sweat. The fact that this was a permanent choice still made me quite nervous. I had enough trouble choosing what to eat for dinner, and I was soon expected to pledge myself to one of the seven affinities for life. No pressure at all!

"Whatever the machine shows you, you should accept it," Lanie agreed more quietly on my other side.

Easy enough for these two witches from established families to say. But I kept my lips clamped on that thought. "Blood magic seems dangerous," I pointed out.

Roe shrugged. "It's bad in the wrong hands. But it's regulated as tightly as vampires are, and many great witches have been blood witches. I won't think any less of you if you turn out to be one too."

I held back from saying that she barely even knew me yet to form an opinion, locking it behind a practiced customer service smile. "Great, but what if—?"

"Next up, Cressida Rollins," Dr. Heartwood announced.

"Hey, that's you!" Roe exclaimed. There was a twinkle in her bright green eyes.

Lanie flashed me a knowing smile. "Good luck."

I took a deep breath and stood, feeling like the whole auditorium had its attention on me. Wiping my forehead, I told myself I was imagining things.

The attendant consulted her tablet as I came to a stop before her expectantly. "Hi, Cressida. Just a couple questions before we find out what your affinity is," she said. "We update the SPDI registry on all our witches regularly, in accordance with supernatural law. Your file is mostly blank right now."

I licked my dry lips as she launched into the first question. "Do you have any supernatural relatives that you know of? We can link your file to theirs, and it'll save you time at the SPDI office later when you change your license."

"I wouldn't know. I'm adopted," I answered.

She nodded rapidly and tapped on her screen. "How were your talents first identified?"

"One of my teachers was secretly a supernatural. He was a talent scout and recognized a change in something about me after I found my cats." He'd also convinced me that I wasn't a total loony for being able to converse with a pair of felines.

"Of course." She drew out the words out as she documented what I'd said. "You found your familiars. How many cats do you have?"

"Two."

"Okay, Cressida. That's it for now. Best of luck," she said, gesturing to the machine next to us, which still resembled a black tabletop.

Dr. Heartwood beckoned me over. For the first time, I got a good look at the machine, seeing that it was mostly gears and wires underneath a black varnish. There was a raised lump in the center, and seven symbols were spread in an arc around it.

"I know you must be very excited," the professor said in an undertone. "May I give you a generic last name based on your affinity to begin your witch line?"

"No thank you," I said stiffly.

"Very well. Put your hand on that knob. You'll feel a little pinch, and then the machine will do its work and identify where you belong." She gave me a warm, grandmotherly smile.

This was the moment of truth, and my heartbeat roared in my ears. I had an understanding of the affinities and what kind of witch came from each, but up until this moment, I'd considered myself an imposter, a "normal" human who'd accidentally gotten an invitation to the university. When was I going to wake up and realize I'd never heard a cat talk and there were no such thing as supernaturals?

I needed a sign that this was real. I needed to know my affinity.

Swallowing past the lump in my throat, I studied the seven symbols as my hand descended toward my destiny.

Half of all witches were verdant witches, powered by the green things out in untamed nature. They mixed potions and healed even the direst of wounds. The verdant symbol, a wand intertwined with a patch of flowers, was the first one to the left of my hand.

Immediately to the right was the second most common type, guardian. Drawing from the solid strength of the earth, they were tough as stone, with the magic to fight for and protect what they believed in. They were represented by an image of a rocky shield and a jagged cluster of crystals.

Third was the symbol for oceanic witches, a wave and trident together. They commanded control of the weather and summoned ice to defend themselves. Of the seven, I least wanted this one. Despite living in chilly Massachusetts my whole life, I hated the cold.

My hand closed around the knob on the table. I waited a few anxiety-filled seconds before a little needle poked the center of my thumb.

Would the machine read that I was a blood witch, the most feared affinity? They could steal power from almost any supernatural if they got their hands on a single drop of blood. I watched the dagger and cup symbol on the machine, hoping that one wouldn't light up either.

I knew the least about the last three affinities, the rarest ones. The tarot symbol was for augury witches like Lanie, wielding the kind of power only a chosen few should have.

The librarian witch's symbol of an open book and unsheathed sword also remained dark opposite of the augury mark. All I could remember was that librarians tapped power beyond mere mortal understanding. The witches with this affinity weren't busy filing away books, but instead dealing with darker powers.

And finally was the strongest affinity, that of celestial witches, who channeled the raw power of the sun and moon. Its crescent moon and staff symbol only lit for the privileged few that ruled witchkind, or so I'd heard.

My expression began to fall as the seconds ticked away and nothing happened. Maybe I really was dreaming, or this was all one big, elaborate mistake. I glanced at Dr. Heartwood, whose smile was rapidly shading toward pity. Then, a patch of brightness lit up in the corner of my eye with a mechanical *ding*.

2

BEN

I KNEW it was going to be a bad day when a politician visited. The strutting and puffing and doublespeak. Exhausting. Master Garroway inevitably gained the upper hand every time, fleecing eye-watering amounts from his clients in exchange for his discreet services.

Garroway required that his whole "coven" of blood witches attend every meeting when he negotiated with clients, if we weren't out on missions. Today, oddly enough, there was an actual coven of seven lining the far wall, standing in order of seniority. From Seth, the tough old salt who'd served here the longest, to my little brother, Lucas, who'd recently joined us with his blood witch affinity. He was only sixteen, with a boyish tousle of blond hair atop his head and soft cheek-bones that'd never grown more than a bit of fuzz. Too young to be called an assassin, in my opinion.

We were the muscle and the reminder of which spider owned this parlor. Today, the fly was none other than Blaize Starsurge, a middle-aged celestial witch. He was an old client who'd wised up to some of Garroway's tricks. He'd left his steaming cup of tea untouched on the low table between them and angled his chair away from the seven of us assassins without a single nervous glance in our direction.

The man was a member of the Crown Coven, the ruling body of witchkind. He had the air of old money about him, clear in the crisp cut of his suit and his fair hair professionally styled to comb over the balding patch creeping across his head.

After only ten minutes of pleasantries, however, Crown Starsurge seemed tired of avoiding the subject of his appointment. "Do you remember the Darkmore job, Garroway?"

I watched my vampire master as he calmly sipped from his cup of tea, eyeing the man opposite of him from over the rim. He placed the priceless china back on its dish with a little hum. "That was many years ago." As always, Garroway spoke in a hypnotic cadence, soft and precise. His deep voice had lost its power over me, but many female clients relaxed utterly in his presence.

"I paid you a fortune to send your best man to kill the Darkmore family."

"It rings a few bells," Garroway said smoothly. "Did you call on me to reminisce over your successes?"

"No," Starsurge muttered. He slapped a folder on the table between them, scattering a few glossy photos. "Whomever you sent on the job half-assed it. One of them survived."

My brother shot me a worried glance. Lucas had attended maybe two of these meetings. He didn't know yet that we were easy scape-goats should anything go wrong. "Accidents happen," I murmured.

Garroway, with his inhumanly good hearing, shot me a quick warning look.

He shuffled through the contents of the folder. "And what makes you believe that this girl is a Darkmore?" the vampire asked.

Starsurge flipped an impatient hand. "Without a genetic test, it's all the evidence you're holding. Orphan witches with potential like hers don't just *appear*. You were supposed to take out the whole Darkmore family for me. Four people! Eris Darkmore, her husband, sister, and baby."

Garroway covered his lips with a hand, glancing through the folder a second time. "So, you believe this girl is the baby, miraculously returned to life. Well. You have certainly done your homework on her, Crown Starsurge. Her adoption papers, plus an augury reading that says she'll be a celestial witch." His cunning blood-red gaze flashed toward the politician's face. "But this doesn't tell me why you're here."

"Isn't it obvious?"

"I do not operate on assumptions. They are bad for business."

"Your best assassin *failed*. I want what I paid for." Now he flashed a sneer over his shoulder at us, his gaze fixed on Seth. As one, the seven of us tensed, muscles flexing, hands drifting for weapons. I drew one of the knives at my belt. He raised an unimpressed brow and turned back to Garroway. "I want the last Darkmore dead before she can inherit the full might of her family line. For free."

"Free," Garroway echoed with a low chuckle.

"I have a contact in the university who will sabotage her affinity test. She will be an easy target for you." Starsurge sniffed.

My fingers tensed on the hilt of my knife. I couldn't stand the superior smirk in his words. It was like if the girl wasn't a celestial witch, she was a defenseless nobody. He must not have been paying attention during his own schooling.

Celestial witches didn't wield offensive magic until they learned complicated astrology and some of the most laborious runes. They were insanely powerful when fully trained, but the drawback was slow casting speed. If his proposed mark became a blood or guardian witch, she'd be able to fight back much more effectively.

All seven of us were trained by the same playbook. Even my little brother shook his head with a little snort. We knew how best to fight most anything in the supernatural world.

"And if you're wrong about her? What happens then?" Garroway asked.

Starsurge lifted his shoulder. "People die every day."

The vampire threw his head back and laughed. "Very well. Due to our long friendship, I shall send someone to remove your little enemy for free."

With a nod, Starsurge got to his feet and pointed. "I do not trust your best anymore. I want her for the job."

We weren't actually lined up in order of age, but price. Next to Seth stood the woman he pointed to, Bianca. She flashed her signature vicious smile.

Bianca had dressed in her femme fatale wannabe leather today, posing sexily on the wall. Male clients liked her, and she loved going on missions. I was past worrying for her. We were about the same age, but she'd taken to her blood witchery much faster than me. Master Garroway usually picked her for one of the other services he provided, monster hunting. She was adept at killing man and unnatural alike. Just give her a blade, and let her go.

"Very well. Will this conclude your visit, Crown Starsurge?" Garroway asked, getting to his feet as well. When the politician nodded, our vampire master led him out.

Lucas gave a soft breath of relief, but the rest of us knew not to relax yet. Garroway's smile was nonexistent when he returned alone and swept up the folder and all its contents so quickly the paper made a snapping noise. His long face was drawn in an irritated snarl, fangs pearly white underneath the dark shadow of his mustache.

My heart drummed at double time as his bloody gaze swept over us. It landed on the boy standing next to me. "Lucas," he barked. "It's time for your first mission."

"But Master, he wanted *me* to do it," Bianca whined.

He shot her a look that could boil her blood. Her pouty red lips snapped closed, and she bowed her head in acknowledgment. Mollified, Garroway dismissed us with a wave of his hand, leaving an eager Lucas. I remained at his side, feet planted, waiting to receive the same treatment as Bianca.

"May I attend my brother's first briefing?" I placed a hand on Lucas's shoulder and flashed my best smile, earning a sullen look from him.

I squeezed him more firmly, trying to express my urgency with a single glance. He hadn't been old enough to see what had happened to some of the older witches in Garroway's employ, but I could still see their faces. They'd been caught. Executed. Our blood runes wouldn't leave us alive long enough to share Garroway's name and whereabouts. The most dangerous time for him was now, with his first assignment, especially since it was supposed to be "easy."

Garroway watched this brief exchange far too keenly. Somehow, some way, he'd use my concern for Lucas against me. But for now, he gestured us back to the living room where he'd been negotiating with Crown Starsurge. "By all means," he said.

Lucas jerked out of my hold and sat on one side of an unused couch, closest to Garroway's favorite chair, and I settled next to him. Everything in this room was handcrafted to resemble antiques, just as the vampire liked it, with upholstery in red and black patterns.

I didn't know exactly how old he was, but Garroway seemed ancient beyond any measure of understanding. He liked things only in his exacting way, and that included the position of the furniture down to the angle and the flavor of the black tea he sipped on that never had even a wink of sugar.

"Little Lucas. Finally earning his keep," Garroway said, a hint of mockery in his precise cadence. "You are to remove a new enrollee in the Moongrove Academy division of the Northern Supernatural University. Here's what she looks like. Hard to miss."

He passed Lucas a few photos of a young woman from several angles. Discreet, paparazzi-style snaps of her that my brother let me see over his shoulder. "She's hot," Lucas commented.

Garroway flipped the folder over Lucas's knuckles. "You're going to kill her, not fuck her. Focus."

"Yes, Master," he grumbled.

Secretly, I agreed with my brother. Her most striking feature was a head of dark purple hair, freshly dyed by the looks of it. Since these pictures had been taken without her noticing, she wasn't smiling in any of them. Even with a serious case of resting bitch face, she was a looker with soulful brown eyes and a heart-shaped face.

The only time she looked happier was a photo with her walking next to a petite girl with a dark bob. I took that picture from Lucas for further inspection, happy I didn't get this mission. I'd only gone on a few missions and could justify taking out all of my marks by twisted logic. It was hard to validate killing this woman, though.

"Her name is Cressida Rollins. She's an upcoming freshman with signs of great potential already," Garroway said. "Before you make a plan, find out which affinity she picks. If it's blood, I want you to bring her back to me alive, Starsurge be damned. We will find out together if she gains the Darkmore hereditary power."

From the glimmer in his eyes, I could tell he was dreaming of having control of a witch with access to the Darkmores' power. She'd be dead-lier than Bianca, maybe even Seth. I shuddered to think of what Garroway would do with her. He made most of his money in lending, but it was the threat of his deadliest agents that kept a flow of income pouring into his pockets.

"And if she doesn't pick blood, I kill her," Lucas confirmed.

"That's right. Don't get yourself caught. Any other creative details are at your discretion." The vampire bared his fangs with a bloodthirsty smile. "See, isn't that an easy job? Go earn your place here, Lucas."

"Yes, Master," he said eagerly. "I won't let you down."

My brother didn't turn to see the concern flashing over my features. The easy jobs rarely ended that way.

3
CRESS

THE LIGHT FLICKERED under one mark before switching to another. I waited, my brow drawn, to see if the machine would change its mind again about what kind of witch I should be. For the barest moment, I swore it'd said I'd be a celestial witch, but now the light held steady under a different mark.

The book and sword of a librarian shimmered before me. I could hardly believe it. Not only was I a confirmed witch, but I was one of the rarest three types. Dr. Heartwood peered at it before nodding to her assistant, who tapped on her screen to record the results.

"Everyone, welcome Cressida Rollins, a new librarian witch," the elderly professor announced, and I received a smattering of applause. Even though the group's enthusiasm was flagging at this point, I still grinned like I'd received a standing ovation as I crossed the room to take my seat again.

My gaze caught on a reflection of light, and I realized there was a phone camera pointed at me from one of the back rows. Elation turned to a scowl immediately, aimed toward a blonde girl popping gum as she looked down at her screen.

Roe clapped me on the shoulder as the testing continued. "Congrats, librarian! One of the coolest affinities, if you ask me. Right behind being a guardian."

"You might be biased," Lanie teased.

"Girl, I've watched my mama juggle boulders as a pre-workout. Tell me guardians aren't cool," Roe said with a belly laugh.

"Sure, but my parents have saved hundreds of lives just by slightly altering the timeline of fate," Lanie replied.

I was barely listening. The blonde was called up to test next, and I stared daggers into her back as she approached the table with an obnoxious snap of her gum. Her name was Wren Starsurge, and my eyebrows rose in surprise when she was announced as a celestial witch. She was the second one in this whole session of affinity testing.

On her way back to her seat, I noticed Wren walked confidently in the kind of stiletto heels that would break a lesser woman's ankles. Her satiny dress was a deep blue, matching the shade of her eyes as our gazes locked. It was only a fraction of a second before her attention flicked over my two companions and her lips twisted into a smirk. She flipped a wave of thick hair over her shoulder and moved on, leaving only a lingering hint of sweet perfume behind.

Roe's elbow nudged my side, bringing my attention back to her. "You wanna grab some food after this?" she invited.

"I guess," I said noncommittally. "Shouldn't we be getting started with our affinities, though?"

"That's after orientation. Two days from now," Lanie supplied. Well, the augur would know. "Dr. Heartwood will share this too, but we get time to think things over before committing to our affinities. If we have any lingering questions over what the test said, there's time to test again and seek answers."

I chewed thoughtfully on my lower lip. Not that I'd question a good thing, but the flickering symbol of celestial magic came to mind. Was it normal for the machine to change its mind like that? Or perhaps being a celestial witch was a viable option for me as well?

"Makes sense," I said mostly to myself.

Roe tested last and was quickly announced as a guardian witch. She pumped her fists in the air like she'd won a huge prize. I applauded for her like she had for me, surprising myself. I didn't make friends easily, but I could see myself hanging out with Roe.

As soon as Dr. Heartwood finished telling us what came next, which echoed Lanie's wisdom exactly, we were released to acclimate to campus life for our last two days free of the pressures of classes and deadlines. "Take us to the best grub, Graygazer," Roe said, flanking the petite girl as we walked out into the late afternoon sunshine.

"I know just the place," Lanie said, a skip to her step as she picked a direction.

I soon gained a skip too, smiling to myself. I knew my affinity now, doubts notwithstanding. I was a real witch, soon to bond to whatever "dimensional energy" was, and had the opportunity to stay here and study magic alongside a more normal college major. Giddy bubbles floated in my belly as we crossed the campus together.

Northern Supernatural University was a massive complex, and I kept my head on a swivel as we headed toward a corner I hadn't explored yet. The air gained a salty tang, and the path we took wound its way around a massive grassy field and ended at a roadway, where we waited for a red light to cross.

Everything seemed ordinary until we passed a marina and I realized some of the buildings along the lakeside were actually deeper in the water than any human would design. Sidewalks ended with lapping, green water where they submerged and presumably continued the campus underwater, if the gleaming spires of a few buildings further into the lake were any indication.

We'd entered the mer side of campus, where the merfolk and oceanic witches had class. I tried not to gape too much. I hadn't had enough time to have it sink in that nobody here would be hiding their true natures. My introduction to NSU had been walking through a gate that was apparently a portal or a seam in reality. My guide had called it both. One moment, we'd been in Salem, Massachusetts, and the next, we were on the other side of the gate leading to this campus. It was a safe place for supernaturals to be themselves.

Lanie led us to a building with a brightly painted sign declaring it Poseidon's Kitchen. "Here it is, the kind of food you were craving," she said to Roe.

The redhead licked her lips. "I love your magic."

We were seated quickly, and Lanie was sure to ask for a lakeside table. The back of the building was a massive deck with a water-level bar. With only a railing between me and a dunking in the green lake, I leaned over to get my first look at a group of giggling mermaids cracking oysters below us.

"Wow," I murmured. They were mostly what I was expecting, except instead of wearing shells and seaweed, they had flowy shirts that covered the seam in their bodies where human torso met flexible, iridescent fish tail. They were every shade of the rainbow, with scales and fins lining their arms and cheeks.

I sat up straight before any mermaid could notice me gawking. When I'd worked in fast food, I'd learned when and where to make eye contact and how long was considered uncomfortable. Customers started getting weird if you stared at them, unblinking, while they complained about something.

Roe glanced my way. "Takes a minute to get used to it all," she said. "I get it. I just saw my first cupid the other day."

Self-conscious, I turned my gaze down to the menu. I'd just confirmed for her that I was a gaping newcomer compared to most of the people on this campus. Hopefully she wasn't judging like some of the other witches I'd already met.

It was an honor to be here, like I'd fallen into one of my favorite books, where the most incredible creatures and magic both existed and thrived just under the nose of humanity. At the same time, I was one of the only supernaturals here who'd grown up with no clue about this secret world. I had so many misconceptions to correct.

I cleared my throat, searching for any topic other than my own ignorance. "So, uh, how do you two know each other?" I asked.

Lanie and Roe exchanged a glance. They'd both sat across from me. "Our parents go back a long way," Lanie answered. "The Ashboughs guard some of the Graygazer family's relics in exchange for our augury services."

"She's told me a lot about my future. Good and bad," Roe added. "Including that we'd be close friends."

"You too?" I laughed.

She nodded, pausing to put her order in with the waiter. He was obviously merfolk of some kind, with shiny green scales lining his hands and face, complete with a set of flapping fins under his aquamarine hair instead of ears. When his slitted pupils turned my way to take my order, I was momentarily catching flies.

Don't ask him what he is. Don't be weird, I told myself.

I ordered the first special on the menu, ignoring the snickers coming from Roe until he walked away.

"As I was going to say, it must be nice to know your friends before you meet them," she said instead of teasing me, nudging Lanie in the side.

"Can you tell me about someone, actually?" I asked suddenly. "Wren Starsurge? I think she was recording me earlier."

The smiles erased from both of their faces. "Yeah. She's from another old bloodline. Her dad's a member of the ruling coven of witch-es," Roe answered. "My pops runs security for some of their family arti-facts, and he hates working with the Starsurges. They've got money and entitlement, and Wren's no different. I only know her by reputa-tion, and it's the same as the rest of her family. I wouldn't mess with her."

My frown deepened. "And if *she* messes with *me*?"

There was no immediate answer, as I expected. When a girl had power and money, there was no stopping her if you were an ordinary person. And a nobody like me might as well have a target on my back for someone like her.

"Gotta play it cool for now. Let's see if she tries something, and then maybe Lanie and I can help," Roe offered.

The waiter returned, dropping off a basket of seaweed chips. We took a moment to sample them, and I pulled a face at how salty they were. I let Lanie and Roe have them.

"What majors are you picking?" I asked. The university's piles of information had suggested that it wasn't common to get a degree in magic unless one was good at it and intended to stay exclusively in a supernatural community. That was the kind of thing I couldn't plan for yet.

Roe rolled her eyes. "Business," she answered in a grumble.

"You already know this, but I'm in world cultural studies," Lanie said, glancing to Roe. "Your dad won that argument, huh?"

"Yeah," she sighed, glancing at my puzzled expression. "I'm the eldest kid, so I get to inherit the family business. Means I get to babysit other people's important things for the rest of my life."

I tried to look sympathetic, but there were worse fates than getting a successful business from one's parents. "What would you do other-wise?" I asked.

She started to brighten again. "I was thinking physiotherapy. Don't you know how hard it is to find help if you have an injury in your wings or tail? It's not like you can walk in to see a human doctor for things like that."

"Yeah. Limited clients, though," I said.

"Please. The supernatural world is *huge*. There's a need for a super-natural physiotherapist somewhere." From the way she puffed up, I imagined she'd argued this point before with less sympathetic ears. "What about you? What are you majoring in?"

A tinge of pink lit my cheeks. "Well, I picked fashion design. The professors are still reviewing my portfolio and 'extenuating circum-stances,'" I said, making air quotes. "But all my designs were for humans. They're looking for, like, more creativity."

I still hoped to hear back from the committee making the decision soon. Attending a university wasn't even in my five-year plan, not when I'd been gainfully employed and helping support my mother and sister.

Yet life had thrown me a curve ball, so here I was, trying to get accepted into one of the more competitive degree tracks at NSU. From the moment I'd been identified as a supernatural and ordered to attend a school to properly develop my powers, the authorities had made it clear this could be a two-year deal if I wasn't feeling the college envi-ronment.

So, if the committee didn't accept me, I would just leave in two years. There was nothing I wanted more than to bring my sketches to life. Mermaids, winged fae, and other assorted supernaturals needed to wear clothes, too.

I know most people my age would sneer at the decision to leave NSU two years early, considering that I'd been put on a full-ride schol-arship. Newcomers to the supernatural world all received the same perk. If we *had* to be here and had no means to pay, it was the least the university could do.

"Do you have any designs on you?" Roe asked curiously. "How about it, Lanie? Is she going to make it?"

Lanie's dark eyes twinkled. "I can't give away everything, can I?"

"C'mon, the suspense is killing me!"

While I was busy thumbing through my phone for a photo of a recent sketch, the two girls leaned together and whispered behind their hands. "Hey, if you're going to tell her, tell me too," I complained.

The huge grin on Roe's face seemed to be answer enough, though she tried to hide it by cramming more seaweed chips in her mouth. I showed her what was on my screen before I could regret it. I was so worried about offending other races that I hadn't started drawing clothes for their varied body shapes yet, so I'd made a design I wanted to bring to life for myself. It was a little black dress with an empire waist and elbow-length sleeves. What made it unique was the insert of spider-web-shaped lace to expose shoulders and collarbone. Simple, sleek, and witchy.

Well, my conception of witchy. So far, none of the witches I'd met seemed like the type to keep spiders and other creepy crawlies.

"Cress, this is super cool," Roe said. "You drew that yourself?"

"Yeah. I have a whole sketchbook full," I said, wishing I could show her some of the more whimsical designs I'd drawn before ever knowing of the supernatural world. I dreamed in flowing dresses and beautiful fabrics, all the premium kinds my adopted family couldn't afford.

But I didn't share with my two new friends that I'd learned to make my own clothes out of necessity. I didn't need pity, just a place for myself in this supernatural world.

4
CRESS

THE NEXT MORNING, a tiny sprite thumped against my dorm's door at eight sharp. Bleary eyed, I opened the door to see a floating person at eye level, holding the edge of an envelope three times its size. I scrubbed my eyeballs and then confirmed, yup, normal-sized envelope, mini-sized person.

"Thanks," I said, taking the letter it offered. A feline chirp behind me turned into the quiet chattering of a cat who'd spotted something it wanted to hunt. With a squeak, the tiny person zoomed off on its diminutive wings. I closed the door before Bella could run after it.

"That was a friend," I said, plopping back onto my nest of blankets, all thrown askew in my rush to get the door. I gathered up one corner and pulled them off Milo, my black and white boy cat, who licked the fur prickling against his side in disgruntlement at getting buried.

Bella, the brown tabby girl cat, paced the doorway as if the sprite would come inside at any moment. "I just wanted to play," she complained.

Where anyone else would hear meowing, I heard a high-pitch voice as she whined her frustration at losing access to what must've seemed like a living, flying toy.

"Was it food?" Milo asked, his voice only a little lower than my other familiar's. He looked at me, eyes rounded expectantly. As he grew to adult size, his black spots had been engulfed in white fluff. I was probably feeding him too much, as he was developing a chubby belly.

"No," I giggled. I tore open the envelope and scanned its contents before releasing a sound somewhere in the octaves of a dog whistle. Milo and Bella scattered.

My dorm room was set up like a cinderblock box. There was barely enough room for two beds, two desks, and two closets for Lanie and me to share. So when I popped up and screamed, Lanie, sitting a couple feet away at her desk, earphones on so loud that I could hear the beat of her music, still startled.

"What happened?" she asked, resting a pale hand over her chest. She was already showered and ready for the day, while I'd been passed out with no alarm set.

"Don't you already know?" I laughed and passed the letter to her.

She rolled her eyes before reading it. "My magic doesn't tell me *everything*," she said, brightening and turning a smile my way. "Congratulations!"

She gave me my acceptance letter back. I was officially in the fashion design major and invited to the building where classes were held for a little meet and greet at lunchtime. "Everything okay?" Milo squeaked, peeking out from under my bed.

"Definitely," I answered, making kissy noises until he hopped up onto the bed and barreled into my lap for a snuggle. Bella settled at the foot of the bed, curling up into a loaf. She resumed her favorite pastime, staring daggers at Lanie's cat, Jin. Her cat was barely bigger than a kitten, but she was apparently three years old. She didn't seem bothered at all by Bella's stink eye.

"Are you going to the event?" Lanie asked. I realized again that I was assuming she already knew the answer and was just asking to talk me out of my decision. I cast her a side glance and a shrug. "It'd be a great opportunity. See the campus, meet some non-witches that share your major..."

I groaned and flopped back on the bed.

"Plus, you can take your familiars out! I bet they're dying to see the campus too," Lanie added.

My heart rate stuttered. "Out? But have you *seen* the other familiars walking around? It's dangerous for a little cat out there."

Jin let out an opinionated meow. "She's right, we can take care of ourselves," Milo agreed with the other cat. Both he and Bella turned pleading faces my way, complete with him making soft pats of my arm when I tried to avert my gaze.

"You could even take Jin. She's already explored," Lanie offered.

Bella released a little growl. "Sounds good," I said just to watch her fur lift. I couldn't feel any emotions from her and Milo like other witches do with their familiars. That was supposed to come after I attained my magic, apparently.

I spent the time until then showering and sipping on an energy drink while reading over the massive book the university had sent as a welcome gift. It was the third time I'd reread the requirements to be a celestial or a librarian witch. It wasn't too late to ask for a redo of the affinity test and see if the machine really meant for me to be the former. But did I want that?

The more I read over what celestial witches had to learn, the less I wanted to be one. They had the most rituals of the seven affinities. Though it was possible a celestial witch could call down the full wrath of the sun to scorch away her opponents, her day-to-day life involved preparing for hours to be able to unleash that kind of power.

When would I have use for magic like that? Honestly, the more I thought about it, the less the decision seemed to matter in the end. I was a confirmed witch with the need to train in one of the seven affinities, but I wanted to design clothes, not read star charts or fight the dangerous supernatural creatures called unnaturals that plagued our world in secret.

On the other hand for my decision, though, librarian witches handled artifacts and beings from other dimensions. They wielded silver swords instead of decimal systems, even though, for the most part, the job still involved books. Books of occult knowledge that might drive the reader insane, but books nonetheless.

It sounded really *cool*, and that cemented the decision for me. I was going for the affinity the test had decided on and becoming a librarian witch. As I pet Milo, I daydreamed about the kind of outfits a proper librarian wore. Maybe it was tweed jackets and polish, or tank tops and grit. Depended on how much they actually used the swords associated with the affinity, I decided.

When a distant clock chimed eleven o'clock, I set the book aside and took the cat trio outside on a walk. I occasionally glanced behind me to make sure they were still around...they were. Sniffing flowers, rolling in the grass, or giving strangers' ankles a brush of soft fur, but still following me.

I smiled to myself at their antics and consulted a paper map several times. The campus was shaped like a big egg from above, with the center serving as a multicultural center where most races studied together. But on the outskirts, there were sections of space for each individual race. Witches had the largest space, actually, labeled "Moongrove Academy." Considering we were located in Salem, Moongrove was first built as a haven for witches and still had the biggest enrollment of them of all the supernatural universities.

But we shared space with vampires, shifters, and fae, with smaller sections for cupids, merfolk, and dimensionals. Each race had their own academy to learn the ins and outs of their place in the supernatural world. Considering how our individual spaces were pushed to the outskirts of the university grounds, I could tell we were meant to mingle and learn from each other just as much as we were here for magical training and our degrees.

I stopped briefly at the Voidbinder Building, a three-story structure where the witch professors had their offices and most witch-related classes were held. Dr. Heartwood was in there somewhere with the affinity-testing machine. This was my chance to change my mind and get tested again...but I was pretty sure of my decision, so I kept walking.

I kept my eyes peeled for the Margot E. Frederick Building, and along the way, my phone vibrated in my back pocket. I fumbled it out and answered, "Hello?"

"Cress!" It was my sister, Carly. I felt my expression stretch into a big smile. "You don't text, you don't call. I was wondering if they'd turned you into a frog or something!"

"Sorry," I said quickly. "It's just...it's been a wild ride already."

Truth be told, I was waiting for something concrete to tell her and Mom. But now I knew what kind of witch I was going to be and what my major was. Her call couldn't be better timing. "Well, you won't believe who asked me out," she practically squealed.

I listened and made encouraging noises, glad to hear her voice again. She babbled on about her new guy as I finally spotted the building I was looking for. It was as modern as any other human campus would have, with a front of smoky glass and chrome. The double doors were thrown open, a banner over the threshold to welcome all the newbies like myself.

I ducked to the side of the stairs and leaned against their cool surface. "How's witch school?" she was asking, a teasing lit to the question.

"I made it into the fashion design major." This time, we squealed together. It felt like I'd never left home.

"Are you going to be making, like..." She dropped her voice to an awed hush. "...*magic* clothes?"

Due to my circumstances, the first people who'd learned I was actually a supernatural were Mom and Carly. It was heavily frowned upon to have "normal" people made aware of this kind of thing, but I trusted my adopted family. They knew everything I did about NSU and the students who attended it.

"If I do, I'll let you try them on first," I promised her.

We giggled together before I let her go, heading up the steps in high spirits. Just on the inside of the building stood a statuesque woman. She was straight out of an earlier era, wearing a billowing maroon ball gown and classic, understated makeup with gently curled brunette hair. Her red lips spread and...she flashed a fanged smile my way.

I stopped short of shaking her hand for a split second before realizing...of course. A vampire. Yeah. "So pleased you could make it," she said politely as I gave myself a mental slap and closed the gap between us to shake her hand. "Dr. Margot Fredrick, at your service."

My mouth hung. "Like...*the*..."

"One in the same," she drawled. "Who might you be, darling?"

I shared my name, and she nodded. Her long, pale fingers tweezed a lock of my hair, and she turned it with a curious eye. "This will fade in a couple weeks. If you have a verdant witch friend, I know the most delightful potion recipe for vibrant, long-lasting colors."

"Oh, um, thank you, ma'am," I said.

"Please, come inside. We have refreshments." She gestured me into the lobby, where a few clusters of students were already chatting away happily. I went a few yards in and stood, a little petrified to join in somewhere. I wished I had more of Carly's bubbly personality right about now, since she was capable of wading into the middle of a crowded room and joining any conversation.

An upperclassman came to my rescue and looped her finned arm through mine, sweeping me off for a big round of introductions. She was an amethyst-toned mer woman, but ordinary legs replaced her tail for now. She wore a tunic and the tiniest shorts possible, which seemed to be a common style amongst the mostly female crowd getting to know each other.

With a lemonade in one hand and the other free for handshakes, I dare say I was having a good time until I heard a pointed voice say, "What is *she* doing here?"

I turned and made eye contact with a smirking blonde, dressed up from the college casual the rest of us sported. She'd spoken in a loud aside to the umber-skinned witch next to her, who I recognized from the affinity test as a fellow freshman and the other girl to reveal an affinity for celestial magic.

I quietly cursed my luck. Really? Wren Starsurge had to have the same major as me?

Well, this just confirmed that she had some chip on her shoulder. She and her friend moved into the crowd to start socializing too, but the draw for me was gone. I said my goodbyes, ducking away from confrontation before it could get ugly. But something told me I was making a mistake showing my vulnerable back to a girl like her.

BESIDES THE BRIEF unpleasantness of realizing I might have several classes with Wren, I enjoyed the time learning my way around the NSU campus and hanging out with Lanie and Roe. We sat together toward the front of the double-tiered auditorium waiting for Convocation to begin. We'd gotten here early since the whole place was due to fill with all manner of supernatural students.

Roe, it turned out, lived in a multi-race dorm. She'd brought her roommate, a slender fae who might be about five feet tall if her horns grew in more. She had the upper body of a woman, which met the furry hindquarters of an animal, complete with dainty cloven hooves painted with silvery sparkles.

Her skin was a warm, earthy brown, complimenting curly auburn hair woven with a myriad of fresh pink flowers. Two bell-shaped deer ears poked out of either side of her head, flickering toward any loud noise. A pair of two-inch-long horns were starting to grow upward from her forehead, and her nose took on a blunted slope and ended in a damp, textured button that connected to her lips by a thick cupid's bow.

The fae gal, Áine, didn't tell me what kind of fae she was, and I didn't ask. That seemed super rude. She did clarify that her name was pronounced "Anya" and spelled it out for me, accent mark included. When she learned my major, she'd turned around and showed off how the flag of her deer-like tail stuck out awkwardly above the line of her shorts. "Remember to make more comfortable clothes for your tailed sisters."

"Of course," I'd said, too surprised to have a fae shake her tail at me to have a better response. But my mind turned around a few ideas as we waited. I'd noticed how her fur puffed out under the cuff of her shorts, brown with white spots like a fawn's.

Convocation began with a speech by the Dean of Magical Studies, an ordinary-seeming gentleman. Lanie leaned over and shared that he was a shifter. "How can you tell?" I asked behind my hand.

"He has an aura of magic. You'll see it too when you bond to your affinity," she promised.

The Dean spoke briefly before gesturing off stage. "It is my greatest honor to welcome our esteemed University President, Dr. Melinda Aurina, to the stage. For nearly fifty years, Dr. Aurina has seen to the modernization and continued privacy of NSU and its esteemed academies of magic." He led the crowd in a round of applause as a winged woman joined him at the microphone.

There was an audible murmur of awe from the audience as the spotlight caused her rose gold feathers to shine. Dr. Aurina didn't look like she'd even reached fifty, let alone earned a doctorate and clawed her way up the academic ladder to helm a university the size of NSU. Her pink hair flowed around her to waist length, lending her a nearly ethereal beauty.

An elbow jabbed my side hard. It was Roe, and the moment I glared at her, I wondered why I was angry. "Rule number, like, five hundred of the supernatural world…never look at a cupid for too long," she whispered.

"I wasn't," I said defensively.

She bent and placed the program we'd all gotten at the door back into my hands, flipping it over to a section I hadn't bothered to read before putting it under my chair. I scanned it, and my eyebrows rose. "She's a demigoddess?" I gasped. "That's possible?"

"It means she's got *very* strong emotional magic. Any of us can get to demigod or demigoddess status if we get enough power, so…don't look at her directly," Roe said. The audience was listening in silently as Dr. Aurina's flute-like voice and beautiful looks kept them spellbound.

"Show me your schedule again," Lanie suggested when I started fidgeting. We'd just picked up our schedules from a small army of upperclassmen outside who'd had the documents separated in alphabetical order by last name.

We exchanged schedules. Regrettably, I only had one class with my two friends, Introduction to Witchcraft. Lanie hadn't been happy to see it on her schedule, considering how she was the furthest from a newcomer, but I was just happy she'd be there too.

On Mondays, Wednesdays, and Fridays, I had Introduction to Witchcraft, Drawing for Fashion, and Library Science 101. Tuesdays and Thursdays were dominated by Introduction to Supernatural Society and Beginning Fashion. And then there was the class I wasn't thrilled with…Latin I, my foreign language requirement. Apparently, all librarian witches were required to take Latin, and the first semester of it was hosted bright and early every day.

It was a full schedule, and Roe's was bursting too. Oh well. If we took eighteen hours in our first semesters, we would have less to do by the time we were in our later years here.

By the time I was done reviewing Lanie's schedule, Dr. Aurina was saying goodbye to us and bidding that we go do well in our first semester at NSU. She received a standing ovation on her way out. I glanced at Roe, and she shrugged. "Want to go hit the gym?"

5
CRESS

On Monday, I'd already gone and gotten my Latin I class syllabus by the time I glanced up from my campus map and beheld Moongrove Library for the first time. It was right in the middle of the general campus, accented by a strip of garden paths and a fountain of geometric shapes where a pair of students were already sitting and chatting.

I hoisted my backpack higher on my shoulders, stopping just past those students so they weren't watching me awkwardly as I took a moment to admire my destination. I was a little starstruck. It was the biggest library I'd seen in my life, with gothic towers framing an arched entryway. Even from a distance, the shiny panes high above reflected colored light in circular mosaics or tall, skinny windows.

It was the oldest-looking building on campus, and as I shook off my awe and neared it, I noted crouching figures along the high eaves. Gargoyles. Shading my eyes, I tried to view the ugly, snarling face of one, just to realize it was a little too human-looking for my taste. Whoever was in charge of this library must've added the gargoyles in later. They weren't worn down by the elements yet.

I consulted the email I had up on my phone. The instructor, a man named Lars Eriksson, wanted us to meet in the foyer to begin our tour of the library. My heart raced faster as I read the last line a few times.

We were also bonding to the magic of the library today, so I would officially be a librarian witch when I walked back down these steps. The moment I'd been waiting for. I would have magic soon!

One of the wooden double doors into the library was propped open by a block of concrete. Cool air conditioning blew my purple-hued hair back as I stepped into a modern foyer complete with a coffee shop and bank of computers. A group milled by the circulation desk, so I assumed that was where I needed to be.

The desk had a barcode scanner flashing steadily and a little gate blocking anyone from coming and going into the heart of the library. Leaning against the gate was a pale man with fine, feathered platinum hair. He had a clipboard jammed into his armpit, flashing a white grin when some of my fellow students giggled at something he'd been saying.

My attention flashed to the sword he held. This must be our instructor, considering his business casual clothing. He didn't seem much older than me, but there was no mistaking he had magic of some sort when he pulled the sword a few inches out of its sheath. Its metal glowed from within, throwing off a silvery aura.

"In two years, you'll have yours too," he said to the students closest to him. His voice held a generous accent.

The girl next to me released a dreamy sigh, masking the sound of disappointment I uttered at the same time. It would really take two years before I could have a sword of my own? That sucked. I hoped that meant we'd be practicing in the library for those two years before we were trusted to take a sword out of its confines. I'd be okay with that.

Our instructor started counting the group with one finger extended. "This looks like everyone," he said cheerfully. "Welcome to Library Science 101, my students. Or as you're called in my country...my pages."

I fought a losing battle for being a respectful listener at that point, rolling my eyes.

"I am Lars Eriksson, this year's Distinguished Guest Professor at Moongrove Library. Here to teach you all the way from Sweden. You are my first group of pages ever." He flashed his bright smile proudly over the group. "Every year, many compete for the chance to teach and work in this position, but I was the lucky victor this year due to my many accomplishments. We can talk about those later.

"NSU has the largest dimensional powercore in North America. You will draw from it several times over the course of your first month here to nurture your affinity in pure power. Under my care and guidance, you will discover your potential as librarian witches. Who's ready?" He drew out a cheer from the class, and I waited for a cliché librarian shush to come. Yet, the only librarian around was Mr. Eriksson himself.

He scanned his ID to unlock the gate barring us from going deeper into the library before laughing and smacking his forehead. "I need to take attendance." He drew the clipboard and its battered sheet of paper from his armpit and quickly checked us off.

A cramp rolled through my belly as the group started moving. I placed a hand over it, willing it to wait. I wanted to see the powercore and get my magic, and a trip to the bathroom wasn't going to stop me.

"The Moongrove Library has existed in one form or another since the Salem Witch Trials," Mr. Eriksson said at the head of our group. He led us like ducklings down a grand hall with a vaulted ceiling. I craned my neck upward to catch glimpses of the colored glass far above us.

I needed to come back here on my own and really take in the art lining the walls as well. Expensive, authentic pieces captured the history of this place and what I presumed were the exploits of past librarian witches.

"It is built atop a seam of power invisible to human eyes, otherwise known as a ley line. Only with a partnership with the beings from beyond our world was it possible for us witches to find it," my instructor continued. For a moment, I thought he was mentioning aliens and was halfway to accepting it. Aliens, no problem. Just like vampires, cupids, and mer. "I'm talking about dimensions, of course. It is only possible to have a library and a dimensional powercore with the permission of the dimensional travelers who have come to call our planet home."

Our group reached the end of the hallway, where it joined the kind of library I was expecting. Endless stacks lined each direction I looked, momentarily distracting me from Mr. Eriksson's explanation. I inhaled the scent of aging paper and ink with a wide smile.

The instructor took a sharp left turn. I swiveled on my heels and noticed a pair of brightly polished elevators at severe odds with the aged, austere environment of this part of the library. "We go down," he said simply.

My belly gave another grumble, and I crossed my legs impatiently. I didn't want to miss a second of this and raised my hand, trying to butt in before he continued talking. "Yes?" he said, pointing toward me.

"Can you explain what a dimensional is? It sounds like you're saying they come from another planet," I asked, hoping I didn't sound too stupid. A few of my classmates stilled and glanced my way. One guy hid a smile by glancing down at his phone.

"We will talk about dimensionals in great detail over the course of this semester." Mr. Eriksson gave me a patient smile. "Most humans know them by a different name: demons. They first traveled to our lands evading creatures spawned in the darkness of their world. But in the process of meeting humans, many were hunted and feared by us for how closely their likenesses evoke our own ideas of evil."

The elevator arrived behind him with a bell tone. "Half of us will go down at a time," he continued as if he hadn't just blown my mind. There were real demons around somewhere? But they came from another world? Perhaps sensing that I was bursting with more questions, Mr. Eriksson waved me into the first group to head into the heart of the library...thirty floors down.

The bay of buttons went down to negative fifty, however. A scanner sat prominently next to the buttons, implying that not everyone could go down fifty floors into the earth, even if they wanted to. The elevator started descending smoothly, taking me and nine other students down.

"I've seen a dimensional once." A guy interrupted the rules of elevator etiquette by talking and glancing my way instead of at the wall. "There's, like, a lot of them on campus."

"But you've only seen one?" I asked.

"Yeah. They hide in shadows with their magic. It's pretty cool, actually."

I hummed, pondering this mysterious race that hid on an open, accepting campus like NSU. Could it be that even supernaturals feared their demon-like appearance?

We stepped off the elevator and waited quietly for the other one to deliver Mr. Eriksson and the other half of our class. The lights were dim overhead and the air here felt...different. Static charged each breath, tingling in my lungs and over my skin.

"Okay, my pages," Mr. Eriksson said as soon as he joined us and clapped his hands. "It is time for you to touch the powercore for the first time and take its magic into yourself."

My heart leapt with excitement. I was one of the first people to follow him through a door he unlocked. On the other side, there was a huge open space. Stone columns straight out of another era supported the ceiling. Instead of manmade lights, the air was lit by the eerie purple-black glow thrown off by a massive orb at the center of it all.

A set of stairs led up its side, so someone could place their hands on it where it was suspended a few feet above the ground by a stone loop. I inched closer, squinting to get a better look. As I watched, tiny white strikes of lightning zapped the underside of the core.

"All true libraries have a powercore, which fills its librarians with magic to keep its day-to-day functions running," Mr. Eriksson explained. "In becoming a librarian witch, you take in dimensional power. It makes you much more resistant to the charms of danger-ous, unknowable magic and able to fight back against the monsters that followed our dimensional friends to our world. Now, who's first?"

He fumbled out the battered attendance roster and answered his own question...calling on the first name in alphabetical order. I barely concealed a groan of dismay. I'd need to watch about two-thirds of the class go before me and touch that thing. Curse my last name. I should've let Dr. Heartwood name me Cressida Book-something.

At least on the sidelines, I could watch how this actually worked. My peers didn't touch the surface of the powercore...they stuck their hands inside it. Purple mist swirled around the newly anointed librari-ans, and the powercore pushed their hands back out when they'd had enough.

Since it was reasonably fast, my turn was up sooner rather than later. I regretted not using the restroom before coming down with the group, though, because every second was becoming agonizing.

I approached the powercore with caution, hearing it crackle with electricity. If I wasn't worthy, what would it do? Electrocute me? I hadn't even cleared the steps before I felt a tug on my arms. The power-core drew me forward like we were magnetized. It felt like jelly when my hands submerged into it to the wrist. Cold and wiggly.

Static crawled over my skin, setting every hair straight up. The other students had mentioned the powercore talking to them, but I only understood when it whispered into my mind.

"Hmm. Stars and shine."

I tried to open my mouth, to somehow converse with this object of magic. However, I was frozen, only able to breathe shallowly.

"My, my, aren't you a special one?"

I got the feeling it was inspecting me. Its magical eye peered into my very being, turning over the bits of fluffy dreams and jagged emotional edges. Nothing was private between us...but it wasn't malicious, either. I felt it rummaging around with gentle fingers, picking up memories like mementos and turning them over with care.

"Such a bright soul has found its way to me. Tell me, why do you want to be a librarian witch?"

It read my thoughts like we were conversing. Of course, thinking it was cool and fitting for me was my answer. I felt both vain and vapid standing before the powercore. I had the impression I was touching something ancient beyond comprehension. Immobile but precious, in need of librarians as much as they needed it.

Tinkling, almost feminine laughter echoed in my ears. *"Perhaps you will find a more serious reason than fashion, with time. My librarians are, without a doubt, more polished appearances and tweed jackets, by the way."*

I nodded slowly. I did prefer that look myself.

"You have the potential for greatness, once you shake your more youthful endeavors. I gladly accept you into my service if you will pledge to defend this library."

No sound escaped my lips, but it must've sensed the agreement in me past the embarrassment of this conversation. At least it'd called me out in a private way.

"There is no judgment here, only power. Accept this gift and thrive."

Electricity flowed over my palms, sending numbness up my arms and through my body. It was over within a split second, and the core left me panting and looking down at my unmarked palms as its mysterious magic sizzled its way through my every pore. I stumbled away from it, soon filled with giddiness I could barely express. The powercore had accepted me...I was a real witch now!

Another student took my place at the core while I drifted to Mr.

Eriksson's side. He glanced my way and raised a brow. "I need to use the restroom," I whispered.

"Oh." He gave a careless wave. "Go back up to the first floor for that. We'll go back up when everyone's done."

"Okay, sure." I nodded and forced feeling back into my numb legs by making them move back to the elevator bay. An uncomfortable pins and needles sensation followed, which I tried to shake off as one of the elevators arrived.

I went into it and faced the buttons, labeled from three to negative fifty. My inner child wanted to press every single button. I was alone, after all, with just the pressing need of my bladder to suggest that it was a bad idea. So instead, I indulged my curiosity with a single button press. Negative fifty. I expected it wouldn't depress since I didn't have a staff ID or any sort of authority in the library.

The elevator started descending instead.

"Shit," I muttered. This was a golden opportunity to figure out what was on the bottommost level, though, because I bet Mr. Eriksson would never take us that far into the library. Considering it served as a place to store dangerous magic and creatures, the worst had to be chained up at the bottom.

I was probably a moron. But I still stepped out of the elevator when it opened on the bottom floor. It began with another small, dim foyer, just like on the thirtieth floor, but this time there was already someone here. I stopped dead in my tracks as he turned and canted his head in my direction.

"At last, a librarian," he said softly. He paced my way with the silent, fluid manner of a predator. Before he'd turned around, I'd caught sight of his tail, a long and whip-thin appendage. I tried to tamp down the panic making my heart race. A half-naked demon was coming my way, and the elevator doors had already closed behind me with a telltale whirr of machinery suggesting it was on its way upward.

Not a demon. A dimensional, I reminded myself.

"Greetings, librarian," he said formally, stopping far too close. He had a good foot on me in height, putting my eyes level with his naked pecs. Did dimensionals not believe in clothing? His smooth skin was a cool gray, with undertones of purple veins. I couldn't help but notice he had muscle tone like any human man, with defined ridges down to the pair of dusty pants he wore.

Blushing hard, I edged back from him and craned my neck to meet his eyes. I almost regretted it. His eyes were a shocking yellow color and glimmered like well-cut topaz. Catlike slits marked his pupils, which drilled into my skull with unsettling intensity. "I apologize for my state of undress." He had the smooth, deep voice of a devil to match the hint of fangs I noticed behind his lips. "Something terrible has occurred to wake me from stasis. I have been trapped here, unable to escape. Might you be able to assist me?"

He tilted his head with the request, sending a sheet of glossy black hair free from the trap of his horn. Two of them framed his face, curved into spirals. When his gray lips spread into a smile, my heart skipped a beat. His angular face may not be human, but it wasn't hard on the eyes either.

I wetted my lips. *Focus, Cress.* "Um, you want help with what, exactly?" I asked. Hopefully I could escape this situation without Mr. Eriksson knowing about it. I'd just been curious...I hadn't expected to actually meet a dimensional, let alone one who needed something from me.

"The library has changed in my absence," he murmured. "Yours is the first living face I've seen. Can you take me to the surface?"

"Like, the first floor?" A breathy note wove into my question when he slid even closer. I could feel the heat of his naked chest from here. He had the most attractive figure I'd seen in person, and now he was a breath away while fixing me with the heat of an otherworldly smolder. "Y-yeah, I was just going that way." I pawed blindly at the cold metal behind me until my fingertips found the call elevator button.

"I am in your debt..." His dark brows rose expectantly, like he wanted me to finish his sentence.

"Cress," I offered.

Two vampire-like fangs peeked out from his top lip as his smile widened. "Cress," he repeated in a low purr. I startled when his hand closed around mine and he shifted back just enough to lift my fingertips to his lips for a delicate kiss. "I am Phaeron Sudair, Prince of..." He inhaled sharply when the elevator made a bell tone and the doors opened. "...Well, it matters not."

I backed into the elevator, and my finger landed squarely on the first floor button. Hopefully the class wasn't done with the powercore; otherwise, it'd be seriously awkward to arrive after everyone else. Especially alongside a huge, half-naked dimensional man. As the elevator lurched upward, I stopped inspecting the wall to ask, "So, you're a prince...?"

But no one was next to me. I made the elevator trip alone, wondering what the hell had just happened. That man was *real*, but he'd disappeared, and I was still flushed from just how close we'd been.

Fortunately, I arrived at the first floor before Mr. Eriksson and the rest of my class. As my head swiveled, trying to spot the closest bathroom, air drifted into my ear.

It felt like the hot breath of a man leaning right over my shoulder. "Thank you for my freedom, Cress," whispered Phaeron's disembodied voice. I yelped and turned, but there was no one there, again.

As the seconds ticked away with no further sign of him, I had the sinking feeling I'd made a horrible mistake.

6

CRESS

I WAITED for several days in utter paranoia. I didn't tell Mr. Eriksson, or anyone else for that matter, about my surreal meeting with a dimensional prince in the bottom floor foyer of Moongrove Library. Surely there were cameras, though, capturing my blushing perusal of the half-naked man who'd gotten me to free him.

Because that's what he'd said. I'd freed him.

I was so, *so* stupid. What if that guy had been imprisoned there? I weighed opening up to Mr. Eriksson or simply leaving a note somewhere, but I cared too much for my own ass. NSU was like a dream come true, and I didn't want to get expelled within a week of starting classes. How fucking embarrassing that would be.

I kept my mouth shut and ears open, trying to catch any inkling that a mega dangerous dimensional was free and terrorizing the supernatural world. By Friday after Library Science 101, four days after "the incident," I started to relax. Maybe Phaeron wasn't some villain I'd let escape from his eternal prison. Dimensionals were an accepted supernatural race, so maybe he'd just gotten lost in the library or something.

After class, I dropped my backpack off in a corner and splayed on my bed facedown. Bella took the opportunity to curl up on the small of my back. Lanie, seated at her computer and bobbing along to her music, lifted one headphone cuff. "Rough day?" she asked.

"Long week," I said honestly. "I have, like, three essays and five chapters to read this weekend too. High school wasn't this intense!"

I watched her expression, wondering if she'd seen Phaeron somewhere in my future. She hadn't given off any hints that she knew my secret yet and just flashed a reassuring smile at me now. "Yeah, it's a lot, isn't it? I bet we'll get used to it fast."

"As long as we don't have special meetings every weekend, I'll be happy," I grumbled into my comforter.

All the freshman witches were to attend an event this Sunday evening, and I dreaded it. We'd heard about the news through Introduction to Witchcraft alongside a lesson about covens. Witches came in groups of seven, with early covens assembled carefully so each member represented one of the seven witch affinities. The strongest rituals were performed in groups of varied individuals, apparently.

In modern times, the university staff decided who was in your first coven, and their "careful considerations" were probably just random. It was normal now to double up on affinities, especially the more common ones.

"It won't be bad at all! Your coven is supposed to be made up of your closest friends, bonded by magic," Lanie said.

I muffled a groan. "Sounds like a bunch of sugar and rainbows to me."

"Okay, Negative Nancy. Know what I think you need?" She drew out the question, and when I peeked over at her, she had her hand to her chin in a thoughtful pose. There was a twinkle in her eye, and for a moment, I could tell her augury magic was actively working.

Now that I had my magic, I was starting to pick up on auras, mostly by accident. Aura reading was a touch too advanced for a newbie like me, but it came and went mostly without my input. Lanie's reading of my fate created a halo around her head and a sparkle in her eyes. Suddenly, her last name made perfect sense. Augury magic made a steely gray aura.

Her magic faded, and an excited smile crossed her face. "Ah! Tomorrow, I'm taking you into town. My treat."

I perked up quickly. "Like, New Salem?" I asked.

During the whirlwind of moving into NSU, I'd gotten a full map of the land I'd entered by portal. Though I still didn't understand exactly how I'd arrived in this magical slice of the world, I understood that there was more than just the university here. Many supernaturals entered, went through NSU, and settled in the supernatural-only city of New Salem that thrived past its gates. I'd longed to go when I wasn't so busy, to see if it was as much a multi-race paradise as my new school.

"Yup! Just you and me. What do you say?" Lanie offered.

"I'd love to," I answered. Much like magic, our plan for tomorrow gave me the motivation to coax Bella off me so I could sit down at my own desk and start plinking away at the hill of work I'd accumulated to finish this weekend. Lanie returned to her work too, typing away rapidly at whatever caught her attention.

With a covert glance behind me, I felt I had enough privacy to place a quick call to my mom. While I'd heard from Carly a few times as she updated me on her high school experience, Mom let me call her. She was too busy working for casual calls anyway.

"Hi, baby," she answered on the first ring. She sounded exhausted.

I smiled at the wall, where I'd pinned a few pictures of my little family. "Hey, Mom." I imagined her kindly face just as it had to look after a long shift at the hospital. Dark half-moons under her blue eyes, creases along the bridge of her nose and cheeks where a tight mask held her skin for hours on end.

"Did I catch you at a bad time?" I asked in concern. She worked too much, even when she was married to Carly's sperm donor. The bills piled up too fast, and I knew things had to be tight without me working at the fast-food place up the street anymore.

"No, no. It's nice to hear from you. How are you doing? Carly's told me you've got magic now," she said.

"I do. I'm a librarian." After a short pause, it occurred to me that that didn't sound all that witchy to someone who wasn't supernatural. "That means my magic is made to help me contain dangerous spells, books, and creatures that don't quite come from our world."

"Wow," she breathed. I'd gotten my love of reading from her, so I knew she had to be imagining what kind of things I was getting into. I wish I had something even cooler to tell her, like if I'd held a book of black magic or something, but so far, Mr. Eriksson hadn't let us get a sniff of anything even remotely dangerous outside of the classroom tucked into the corner of floor negative one.

"And I also made it into the fashion design major," I added.

"Are you going to be a fashionable librarian, then?"

I stifled a giggle. "Well, no. I still want to design clothes. The supernatural world requires everyone get trained in their unique magic for two years, but I doubt I'm going to do more with it. Most witches do normal human things after university," I explained.

She hummed, and I imagined her tilting her head back and forth as she considered more deeply. "Never say no to opportunity," she replied.

"I know, Mom."

I mouthed her response, I'd heard it so much. "That's how I got you, and I've never regretted it," she said.

"You did a few times when I was in high school," I joked.

"Never," she repeated firmly.

When I'd been surrendered by my birth parents as an infant, it'd been my mom who'd immediately wanted me. She'd been as surprised as I was when I suddenly developed the ability to speak to my two cats, but like in all things, she was supportive of who I was. My gaze traced the outline of her in one of my family photos, and for the first time, I missed the normalcy of home.

I stuck out from Mom and Carly in every picture. While they were both fair and pale, I had a complexion a few shades darker and chestnut brown hair when it wasn't dyed. Mom was five-foot-nothing and naturally slim, Carly not much taller, while I'd been blessed with curves and above-average height. But with the two of them, I had acceptance and love. For me, there was no other family.

And if I wasn't a witch...I wouldn't be the odd one out again, nearly alone on a campus full of mythical beings straight from fairy tales and the imaginations of paranormal romance authors. I'd never wonder if I'd made a grave mistake meeting and releasing a dimension prince named Phaeron.

As I caught her up on what'd happened so far at NSU, I skirted mentioning anything about him. I didn't want to hear her warm voice go stiff with disapproval. So, when I let her go, I nursed a quiet tinge of shame. If I couldn't tell the woman who'd raised me what I'd done, I knew deep down that it was truly wrong.

I blew out a breath and resolved to tell Mr. Eriksson about Phaeron after class on Monday.

LANIE and I took the shuttle into New Salem the next morning. She let me take the window seat, knowing I'd be pressing my nose almost to the glass to watch the supernatural world scroll by.

"There is a distinct lack of puns," I commented after a few blocks. "Like, why isn't the blood delicacy store called 'Fangs for Everything'?"

"Most supernaturals don't take places like that seriously," Lanie said, shrugging. "This is one of the only cities where we don't have to hide what we are behind clever puns and a wink."

"Well, when you put it that way..." I just felt my lack of experience again.

"You're in for a treat. Promise," she said.

I looked over at her to see if her gray magic aura was flaring up again, to see if she was viewing my future with a statement like that. A smile creased the skin around her dark eyes, but if she was using her magic, my sense of auras was too weak to spot it.

She must've realized where my thoughts went and nudged me with an elbow, Roe-style. "I just know that. I love New Salem," she clarified.

The shuttle dropped us off in the heart of it, several buildings looming around us. Lanie set off in what seemed like a random direction, passing a couple parking garages with storefronts lining the ground level. I counted three pubs and a sandwich shop that leaked the scent of garlic and herbs when someone exited with a brown paper bag.

In other words, completely ordinary until it wasn't. The next block held a few stores we browsed, from a general store for merfolk, selling enchanted seashells and pearls alongside clothing tailored for their unique body shape, to a witch-run shop with tools for all witch affinities.

I spent a lot of time in the latter building, exploring at length with Lanie there to explain what was useful and what to do with it. Verdant witches had the biggest section, with candles of several colors and an expansive selection of dried herbs and pickled bits from various animals. "Ugh," I muttered upon picking up a bottle just to see a frog's eyeball staring back.

"Come over here," Lanie practically giggled. She directed me to the section for librarians, which was quite short, covering half a row. It had some stuff I expected to be junk, like talismans against malicious and dark magic, but I stopped to scan the spines of the books lining one shelf.

I pulled one, surprised to see the pages it bore were battered with use. It was a hardback with no jacket, dark brown leather with golden letters embossed on the front and spine. "Is this something I need?" I asked Lanie, showing her the title: *The Librarian Witch's Handbook.* Cute little symbols surrounded the title in the same embossment. It was the only copy here, and someone had committed the grave sin of putting a discount sticker on it.

Lanie brightened and nodded. "Open it and see if it speaks to you!" she said.

"It talks?" I echoed uncertainly, getting a vivid flashback to the powercore I'd touched and how it'd somehow seen into me and spoken to my mind.

Still, I cracked it open to the first page. It was completely blank, and I skimmed through the rest with a thumb. Nothing, just cream-colored paper. "Weird," I said. "It doesn't even have lines like a jour—"

I cut myself off abruptly as color leaked onto the page where I'd stopped. A thin band of cursive ink darkened to read "Henceforth and Always."

I said it out loud, glancing at Lanie in confusion. "You should buy it," she said immediately.

"Because I see words on the page?" I asked. The book flipped a page on its own.

A new line of cursive text appeared in the middle of the new page. *Just do what the augur says.*

"I've heard about books like it. A strong librarian will hold on to it through his or her travels, and it records everything they learn," Lanie explained. "When another librarian gets it, the book is there to help them. It can give advice and continue to learn as it's passed from witch to witch."

"Like a hardback Wikipedia," I said mostly to myself. "I wonder why it's here, then. Surely these kinds of things are a family heirloom." This one was discounted, no less.

The book flipped another page on its own. *Are you going to buy me, or what?*

"Ask it who its former owners were," my friend suggested.

I echoed her, and it flipped another page. *Don't you want to know?* wrote its ink.

My eyes narrowed. "Yes, that's why I asked."

Maybe do something of note with your magic and I'll tell you.

"It's kind of...sarcastic," I said, shutting it with a huff.

"That's cool, it's got a personality! It must've had a lot of owners," she said cheerfully.

In the end, I bought the snarky magical book. The cashier stuck the receipt right under the front cover and told me I could return it, no questions asked, within a month.

The moment we walked outside, the cover flipped up, and I scrambled to catch the receipt before the wind could snatch it away. *Only $19.99?* the book wrote out.

"You were on sale," I informed it. I closed the cover again to remove the sticker on its front.

It opened again of its own volition. *Hey, that tickles.*

"You're a book. How could it tickle?" I asked.

It flipped another page. Instead of answering, it asked a question of its own: *You got a name, toots?*

"It's Cress."

Watercress?

"Cressida. Do *you* have a name?"

The Librarian Witch's Handbook. Duh.

Rolling my eyes, I snapped it closed and tucked it under my elbow to end the conversation.

Lanie took me to a spa next and covered a special for us both with a swipe of the Graygazer family's credit card. One relaxing massage later, and we were next to each other in pedicure chairs, our feet submerged in hot water.

"Thank you for this," I said, humbled by her generosity. A pair of shifter women wheeled over carts of tools to start our pedicures. This time, there was no questioning what they were since they both had fluffy white tails and softly rounded ears poking out of their fur-like hair. With the sly tilt of their eyes, they resembled arctic foxes quite heavily.

"Of course. I could tell you needed to relax and see more of the supernatural world than the university," Lanie said.

"You were spot-on, of course. I bet your magic helps a lot with that."

For a moment, Lanie's expression fell. Gray magic swirled around her head and sparkled in her eyes. It was over before I could even blink. She shook herself off with a heavy sigh, her shoulders slumping like they held a weight too heavy for her to bear. "What? What is it?" I practically demanded.

She smiled. "Hmm? Nothing happened. Just enjoy the moment," she said. "You never know exactly when life will throw you another challenge, even as an augury witch."

No matter how I phrased the question, she didn't explain that statement further and assured me she meant nothing by it.

AFTER SPENDING MOST of Saturday in town with Lanie, I devoted my Sunday to catching up on my studies. We stayed in most of the day, with Lanie practically chained to her laptop, typing away rapidly while her cat pawed at her for attention. I sat on my bed, my lap crowded with both Milo and Bella forming a warm pile as I studied my textbooks.

It was a peaceful time, only broken by quick trips to the dorm cafeteria for food and the special evening event in the Voidbinder Building. I didn't dress up for it, and to my surprise, neither did Lanie. Since the evening was unseasonably chilly, I popped on a pair of jeans and a hoodie.

"We match!" my roommate announced, sliding on a hooded jacket of the same navy blue shade.

"Nice," I said with a laugh.

The sun was setting as we left our dorm and headed to the three-story building along with a shuffle of other freshman witches. "Remember, this isn't your only coven ever," Lanie said.

"Good. I hate the idea that we're slapped with a random group of people," I muttered. I would've been much happier without a coven at all and just keeping my head down and passing my time at NSU with only a couple close friends. Being forced to socialize with the expectation of friendship just didn't sit well with me.

"It's not quite random," she said. "The augury professors get together and see who would work best together for coven spells and events."

I grumbled to myself as we came up to the Voidbinder Building, which was alive with activity. In the front office, upperclassmen were running back and forth, making sure everyone received an envelope with their name on it. Elderly Dr. Heartwood directed us to check the letter inside and head to the room it indicated.

Lanie and I both had the same room: 204. We entered together to see two different circles of eight desks, each with an upperclassman wearing a Moongrove Academy t-shirt and a few freshman witches already seated.

"Over here," one of the upperclassmen called, a dark-haired witch who was all smiles. She checked off a list of names and indicated that we sit down in her circle.

To either side of our upperclassman, who introduced herself as Yasmin, sat what I supposed were two other members of my new coven. I slipped into the desk next to the girl who I recognized from affinity testing as Willow Frost, the mousy oceanic witch who looked as uncomfortable to be here as I felt.

The other person introduced himself as Heath Storm, another oceanic witch. He was tall and obviously built, barely fitting into the desk to Yasmin's left. He had rich, tawny skin and a big grin that offset his skin tone with a sparkle of white. "Hello, ladies. Looks like I'm a lucky witch if this is my coven."

I was prepared to ask if it was because we were all women when another guy joined our ranks. "Grant Norwood, of the verdant Norwood line," he introduced himself, immediately looking bored with our company.

Two more empty seats. I craned my neck to watch the door and felt myself pale when in clicked the designer heels of Wren Starsurge, her hair perfectly coifed for this event. Her closest friend followed her like a shadow. "There has to be some mistake," I heard her tell Yasmin as the upperclassman gestured for her to join the rest of my coven. "I don't see Sanna's name on that list!"

"Here, then!" the other upperclassman called, motioning for Wren's friend to come over.

Wren's face reddened. "I won't join a coven without—"

"Hey, guys, am I too late?" burst out a loud voice from the doorway. Roe came in with a big smile and narrowed in on the two empty seats in the circle where my coven was. She turned to Yasmin. "Rowena Ashbough—is this my coven?"

Yasmin checked the list and confirmed with a nod. I breathed a huge sigh of relief that transformed to a grin as the big redhead practically squealed and came over to pull Lanie and me into an enthusiastic hug that felt more like a headlock. "We're in the same coven!" Roe exclaimed.

In the echo of her excitement, I heard Wren mutter, "Please switch me into the other coven."

"I'm sorry, Wren. The university wants you here," Yasmin replied, gesturing for the sour-faced girl to take a seat.

"Don't you know who my father is?" she practically growled.

"Can you just sit, please?" the upperclassman answered impatiently.

When Roe and Wren took their seats, my coven was completely in attendance. It was great to have both my friends in this circle, but there was Wren too, and she was glowering over at me like this was somehow my fault.

Lanie went rigid and clutched at her face. "I...I need to go," she said, turning to Yasmin. She pointed to her own forehead. "I saw something with my familiar. Forgive me, but I need to go now."

"Do I need to come too?" I asked, concerned. I assumed our familiars were together back in our dorm room.

"No!" she said, louder than her usual tone. I blinked in surprise, and she softened her voice, "I mean, no. It's okay. It's just Jin."

Lanie stood and rested a hand on my shoulder. "Bye, Cress. I wish you the best of luck," she said. Before I could reply, she pulled up the hood of her jacket and sped out of the room.

My jaw sat open, my hand lifted toward her retreating figure. That little doe that represented my subconscious told me something was very wrong.

Yasmin started saying something to the rest of us about our happy new coven family when I drew to my feet and left the circle too. "Hey!" I heard her protest behind me.

I didn't hesitate, instead plunging out of the room and whipping my head left and right. A little thread of doubt wove into my thoughts. Maybe I was overreacting. But *"I wish you the best of luck"* had held a weird, final note in Lanie's tone. Besides, what an odd thing to say in the first place.

I left the Voidbinder Building and started jogging toward my dorm, sure I was going to overtake Lanie at any moment. She hadn't had much of a head start, maybe a minute on me.

A woman's shrill scream pierced the night, and I stopped short, my chest icing over. Was that Lanie? I turned, realizing the sound had come from the opposite direction. Heart leaping to my throat, I tore into a serious run toward where I'd heard the scream. All the while, I catalogued how prepared I was for this.

Self-defense? I'd taken a couple classes as a kid.

Magic? I didn't know how to use it.

Weapons? None.

In short, I was hurtling myself straight into danger with no plan. I should've gone straight into the Voidbinder Building to get a trained witch to help me. But Lanie was in trouble *now,* and I didn't let anything stop me, not even the strange curls of white mist that started lapping at my ankles.

The sidewalk was coated with the glowing mist, centered thickest around a figure crouched a few yards ahead of me. I skidded to a halt when I realized that person was on their knees in front of a prone body sprawled on the cement. A hood was knocked askew from Lanie's distinctive bob of dark hair...and there was a growing puddle of blood spreading from underneath her.

The kneeling man lifted his head and met my gaze with eyes that gleamed like pure topaz. "This isn't what it looks like," Phaeron said.

7
PHAERON

I awoke somewhere into eternity with Morgana's name still on my lips. Laid out on my back, the world swam in double images, turning the array of librarian witch symbols engraved in the ceiling into an unreadable tangle.

The most important part, though, was that they were ruined. The dancing ink was black and fading, not an active violet-like color. This didn't fill me with glee, but dread instead. If I was awake, that meant something awful had happened, and indeed, when I found the strength to stand and feel my way around my former prison, I found the exit unsealed.

I felt the crumbling edges where a door should be and winced when my fingertips found the last remnants of silver that'd formed an impenetrable line to one such as me, a dimensional traveler. I sucked on the smoking wound even the touch of crumbling silver left on my skin.

Morgana was gone, I realized, crumpling to my knees mere steps into freedom. With my eyes closed, I saw one image, her face. The pain in her stark white face as she clutched the mortal wound in her gut and used the last of her magic to seal me in with a fiend.

"Why, Morgana?" I murmured, asking a specter at this point. I'd felt her death like a nightmare at the beginning of my long rest. She was no longer around to answer for locking me away with…with an unnamable creature. An "it," a true demon hiding within a race humans mistook for their monsters.

If I was free, that meant *it* was as well.

And I was truly alone. My mate had forsaken me and died, leaving me the sole hunter left that knew the devastation to come if *it* was not contained or destroyed.

The disorientation I felt was a lingering failsafe of librarian magic. I wandered alone for days, knowing my new prison was the size of a small rectangle. Over-bright lights stung my sensitive eyes and reflected off a section of the wall, which was lined with silver-like metal. Time slipped by, filling my dry mouth with the taste of frustration and lingering magic.

Things had changed in my absence. Modernized. If I could just escape this room, I'd see for myself and begin my new hunt. *It* had to have the help of another living soul to have a head start on me, else it'd be stuck and wandering like I was. We could meet in clumsy combat, claws and shadows and fangs.

I was still wandering without purpose when she arrived, the first living person since I'd opened my eyes once more.

The two swirling halves of my disoriented world swung into full focus as I turned to take her in. Weak librarian magic haloed her aura in purple and soaked into her violet locks. She was a lovely woman with the shapely figure and wide-set brown eyes.

My mind said, *Mate?* No, she wasn't Morgana. She wasn't nearly strong enough yet, but I felt the potential in her where her soul pulsed to my enhanced sight. It blazed with curious youth, shining with fractals like a diamond in the sunlight. Its brilliance was stunning to this creature of shadows and dark spaces, a shadowborn with a calling to defend the innocent and pure from their shadows.

She was my key to escaping. I nearly pushed her into the metal wall, half-seducing her to free me. The moment a bell sounded and the... shiny door opened, full clarity returned to me in a heady rush as the spell fogging my mind faded. We returned to the surface of the library in the modern contraption, Cress and I.

Cress. I memorized the taste of her name even as I fled into the stark brightness of a world changed.

In fact, the light seemed to do something to me as I drifted out of

Moongrove Library as a nearly invisible curl of shadow. Blinded by brightness, I closed my incorporeal eyes and drifted into a bank of darkness. Black winds caressed me, and then nothing.

I awoke *again* from that state, lying on my back in a stinking alleyway with rats nibbling on my toes.

"You okay, man?" asked a man sitting a few paces away, smelling pungently of alcohol.

Clutching my aching head, I sat up and fixed him with a stare. "How did I get here?" I demanded.

He put his hands up, one holding a bottle concealed in a brown paper bag. "Hey, man, this is my place. You just got here and passed out," he said.

Frustration bubbled in my gut as I took a look around. I doubted this drunkard had any idea of what else was wrong with me, but perhaps he could be of use.

"Very well. When is it?" I sighed.

He checked the bright screen of a little metal device he had concealed in his pocket. "About three o'clock."

"No," I practically growled. "*When* is it? What is the year?"

"Chill, my dude." The drunkard simply laughed and told me the date. This time, the world lurched because I swayed with disbelief rather than from any spell to confuse my mind. It'd been nearly two hundred years...

"You need something to take the edge off?" He offered the bottle across the alleyway.

I took it and drank a hard swig of the swill. It burned a path down my throat, and I nearly choked. That was strong stuff. After another sip, I passed it back with a gruff, "Thanks."

For the first time, I took a closer look at this other man. His aura held the ever-changing nature of a shifter, though it was subdued with how much alcohol was in his veins. His soul bore cracks at the edges, its existence much more understated than the brilliant spirit within Cress. Well, that didn't surprise me, if he was hiding in an alleyway with a bottle of swill. Shifters on their own were lonely, often broken creatures.

"Is this still Salem, Massachusetts?" I asked.

"New Salem, actually. Do you want directions to the portal?"

"No." I scraped myself back to my bare feet with a groan. "This is exactly where I want to be. Thank you."

I took to the shadows, looking for all the world like I'd disappeared in the span of a breath. There was a fiend to hunt and a city aged forward two hundred years for me to explore.

Thus started days of wandering the world a stranger. I spoke to no one, instead letting conversation drift over my incorporeal ears. How different the tongue of mortals sounded! And their technology was completely foreign. Perhaps the most jarring change was when I came across others of my kind being treated like ordinary supernaturals rather than suspicious demons.

I drifted in and out, waking in strange places with no rhyme or reason. Had I dreamt of finding a shop full of clothes and merchandise all emblazoned with the letters NSU?

One glance down at myself proved that was real. I'd stolen a set of clothes, the material fuzzy and impossibly soft. A bright white "NSU" stood out in the middle of my broad chest. I didn't care too much, not when I was comfortable, warm, and fully dressed for the first time since my prison was unsealed.

That evening, I picked up the first traces of *it*, the creature I hunted while my mind was sane and cooperative. Its dark presence stalked circles around one side of the university campus, where witches came and went. I found a patch of shadows and waited, invisible, for it to show its sorry face.

The witches were active tonight, all converging on the same building. I spotted Cress amongst them, a navy hood pulled up over her head and only allowing a few violet strands of hair to frame her heart-shaped face. Her laugh sounded tense as she focused her attention on another young woman with a similar hood pulled to hide her face in shadows.

My invisible brows arched. Significant augury magic blazed around the other witch, turning her into a beacon of pure power. Despite myself, my mouth watered. I wondered what a little taste of her blood would be like and whether I could borrow a hint of her magic for my cause.

Abruptly, darkness closed in around my vision. It came and went when it wished, and this time, I fought it desperately, worried what kind of nightmare I'd experience with the augury witch fixed so firmly in my mind.

I blinked and lost the battle of wills with myself, reemerging into coherency a step away from a corpse. Magic hung heavily in this area, tasting of *it*. It must've abandoned its kill upon sensing me, because the young woman it'd killed still had an intact soul.

The navy hood hung askew and for a moment, I thought I was seeing Cress lying on her back, unseeing eyes staring into the night sky. I knelt before her, taking in the messy gash in her neck where a weapon —or jagged teeth—had torn it open and left a smeared mess of crimson turning her clothing black. Her expression was permanently locked somewhere between horror and determination.

Not Cress, but her augury witch friend. I released a guilty sigh of relief that it wasn't the bright-souled woman lying dead before me. My kind believed in life debts, and I owed a measure of gratitude to the librarian who'd freed me, even if I was in no shape to repay her now.

"I'm sorry. I was a moment too late," I whispered over the dead girl. I closed her eyelids with gentle fingertips and set her soul free at the same time. It disappeared into the afterlife just as rapid footfalls approached. Through the obscuring mist left behind from the fiend's attack came Cress.

She stopped short a few yards away, her wild gaze flashing from the body to me kneeling beside it. "This isn't what it looks like," I said, knowing damn well how guilty I seemed.

"Lanie!" she cried, her pupils ballooning in horror. "Did you—? Is she—?"

"Dead, I'm afraid. But I reached her before it could consume her soul," I said, getting to my feet. There was nothing else I could do for the augury witch, but there was still a chance *it* lingered here, waiting for a second chance to feed.

Cress was going into shock, her breathing pattern erratic. "What do you mean, she's dead? She was just..." She gestured to the building behind her. When she turned back to me, something shifted in her expression. Growing realization and rage. "You killed my friend!"

Voices shifted toward us, undoubtedly drawn by her appearance and sudden scream.

"No, I had nothing to do with it," I said. "*It* did."

Her face creased further. I knew it sounded like an excuse, but if I said its name, it would come back and attack us both.

"I released you, and you killed her! Fuck you, Phaeron," she spat, stabbing a finger in my direction like a deadly silver sword.

She may have said more, but half a dozen witches were approaching, and at least four of them had the auras of experienced, powerful magic. She looked over her shoulder, and I took the opportunity to go incorporeal and sink into the shadows.

Cress broke into sobs as she explained what she'd seen to the group of witches. Surprisingly, she didn't mention me by name, just as "a dimensional with yellow eyes."

I stayed to watch them as long as I was able, to ward off the true monster from reappearing and making a feast of them.

8

GEO

SOMETHING SHIFTED in the world's bedrock, and I came back to awareness faster than the slow transference of patient rock. Had I friends or kin, I would tell the story about how one moment, I slept, and the next, my sightless eyes transformed from solid crystal to working and flesh-like.

It was so fast, actually, my senses returned before my muscles and tendons regained their mobility. I was trapped in the prison of my stone flesh, but I didn't panic. All things came around in time.

Besides, this patient rock remembered the first time it woke from sculpted perfection, animated by the soul of a witch demigoddess. I owed my very existence to her sacrifice, so I could take the care not to damage my vessel.

Unblinking, I took in my surroundings. I'd entered stasis guarding the eaves of Moongrove Library, loyal to the same structure my witch's soul had once served. Someone had painstakingly scraped me off my resting place and relocated me to a perfumed study warmed by sandy wood, with rugs and upholstery in a rich ruby red.

I was positioned perfectly to loom over a trio of chairs facing a broad desk. Someone shifted on the other side of it, and I caught the hint of pink shining off the figure's hair. I'd spent years of rest not on standby for the defense of my library, but instead protecting this room. If I were a fleshy, irrational being, I might be angered by the audacity.

Instead, I was tolerant. I waited for sensation to return to my fingertips, toes, and wingtips. Soon, I would be able to move and explore the sensation of danger pulsing where my heart should beat. I was needed. I woke abruptly with the knowledge that somewhere beyond this pretty wooden room, my presence was desperately required. Nothing less could wake a gargoyle fatigued by a century of unceasing service.

I was still immobile but aware when there was a knock at the door. "Come in," the pink woman said, her voice hitting a sweet, musical tone.

In walked a middle-aged man, his clothes barely containing a paunchy belly. "You wanted to see me, ma'am."

"Yes." Her slender hand gestured to one of the chairs. "Callum, I need you to explain this to me." She gestured to a packet of paper that rested on her desk.

He sat and took the packet, skimming it quickly. A flush covered his face, and a fat bead of sweat formed on his temple. "What about—?"

"All of it," she snapped. Her flute-like voice turned to an angry shriek, and the man, Callum, recoiled into the backrest of his chair. "How did a dimensional creature escape the most secure library in the world?"

"A-Aurina, y-you're quite..." he struggled and wheezed. "Y-you're..."

With a feathery snap of what sounded like wings, the woman leaned out of the edge of my line of sight. "My apologies," she said stiffly.

Callum covered his chest with a hand, gasping for air. "An unusual chain of events has occurred..."

Aurina's graceful hands balled into fists, and he flinched.

"The security cameras facing floor negative fifty were caught in a loop. It was very clever, actually, since we rarely need to inspect the seals." He tugged at his collar and released a tense laugh. "We think the seal broke about two weeks ago, with assistance from someone with access to a stolen card key. All dangerous dimensional creatures are spelled with our heaviest disorientation effects, so it follows that someone else helped it escape once the seal broke."

"And your cameras caught no hint of who that person was?" Disbelief coated Aurina's voice.

"Well, no. They came and went like a shadow. Even our best cameras have a hard time capturing dimensional magic at work. They did make one teensy mistake…" He held up two fingers pinched close together. "They didn't lock the elevator after them. It's been going down to restricted levels no matter what access badge is scanned."

"I don't see how that helps us at all," she said.

"It means the access code belonged to one of my master librarians. We fixed the elevator and identified the code used… It was from a woman I trusted," he said.

There was a shuffling of paper. "The librarian witch that was found dead in a corner of level negative twenty-two yesterday?" She made a sound of disgust as she read over a report.

"Yes, ma'am." He bowed his head. "The SPDI are conducting an autopsy, but we suspect it was the same monster."

Aurina blew out a sigh coated in frustration. "How could this happen? I need you to mobilize your master librarians and bring in this dimensional *before* it tries to eat another one of my students. I can hardly believe the incompetence that's led us to this point."

"My apologies, ma'am. I'll just be going to—"

"No. We have to make an official statement to the students and the greater New Salem population, and I'll be dead before I admit to anyone that Phaeron Sudair, the goddamned Hungering Darkness himself, was set free from Moongrove Library." She stood and paced with a rustling of soft feathers. "We contained him for two hundred years, and we will re-contain him for two hundred more. Bring your most trusted librarians directly to me, and we will spell them to secrecy as to who they are truly hunting."

Callum wrung his hands. "And what do we tell everyone else?" he asked.

Aurina stopped her pacing, standing over him. She was a gorgeous cupid with rose gold wings and wore a shimmering, curve-hugging gown that displayed generous cleavage, but my stone heart was unmoved. I was needed elsewhere, not here, listening to these two scheme.

"As for your librarian witch's death, we will tell the family that it was a containment breech and an unfortunate accident. For the student, we will announce a blood witch committed the murder. The Hungering Darkness fed on the victim's blood, so anyone on the scene saw the evidence of it," she said.

"We have a witness who described a dimensional man looming over the victim." Callum flipped to a certain page in his files and stabbed his finger at the tiny text printed there.

"Well..." Aurina's lips twisted slyly. "Tell her that she was mistaken. And if she asks any more questions, send her to me."

"Yes, ma'am," he murmured.

"Dr. Callum *Voidbinder*. I sure hope you put your all into finishing this business quickly," she continued. "The legacy of your family name rests squarely on your shoulders. You know what this very dimensional monster did to your ancestor."

"I do know," he confirmed. Both of them glanced toward me.

Aurina walked out of my line of sight. "Her soul lives on. Isn't he magnificent? A demigoddess of Morgana Voidbinder's power deserved a vessel as special as she was."

"That old thing has never moved," he said.

"Do you really think I'd display a fake gargoyle?" Aurina scoffed. Her hand felt like a brand against my cold stone as she rested it on my chest. "This vessel holds Morgana's soul. Your predecessors gave her the honor of animating the Quartz Gargoyle."

Identity and thoughts filled the empty space in my mind. Quartz. My pupils were a cloudy white, but the mineral also formed the spikes lining my back and accented my finger and toenails. Were I capable of moving my lips, my teeth would flash white, also formed of it. My hair was made of sparkling smoky geodes that grew into thick tubes. The rest of me was magically formed of pure obsidian and cured to be as resilient as any ordinary granite gargoyle.

I was special, beautifully made in memorial to an exceptional woman. I remembered now.

Crack! Stone bent and moved like flesh until I was chin to forehead with Aurina. She jumped back with a startled yelp.

I rolled my shoulders with the obnoxious grind of old rock moving for the first time in ages. My wings spread with the motion, and I drew myself up from a century-long slouch to take my full height once more.

"H-hello?" For once, the cupid woman sounded meek. I took a step, knee and ankle scraping internally with the requirements of motion. My heavy foot thumped onto a rug far down. I'd been resting on a pedestal here for her entertainment for who knew how long.

My lips parted in a jerky motion, stale dust escaping on a grinding inhale and exhale. Aurina and Callum stared at me like I was a horror come to life right before their eyes. "Greetings," I said, my low voice reminiscent of grinding rock. Both of them winced. I'd need to work on loosening my lungs and vocal cords again. Each word was a struggle to utter. "I. Am. Needed. Elsewhere."

I took blocky, thudding steps toward the door. Each one slackened my body a bit more. By the time I arrived to where I was required, hopefully I would resume the smooth semi-living motions this vessel was capable of. If not...my magic would return now that I was active, and I could shift into my flesh form for everyone's benefit and comfort.

"Now, hold on. The Moongrove Library needs your help," Callum said as I reached the door. My stiff fingers struggled to turn the knob. He didn't assist me with his more flexible digits.

Rock was patient, but not for whatever this man needed from me. I heaved the considerable weight of my stony body into the door, reducing it to splinters in moments.

"We are kin. I'm a distant relative of your brother," he said in my shadow as my neck ground left to right. We were on the top floor of a building, and one end of the hallway shone with a sheet of glass. I moved in that direction.

"I. Am. Not. Your. Kin." Each word was punctuated with a step. It was true; though I held the soul of one of his family members within me, it powered the existence of a new, duty-bound being that animated when it was needed. And I could tell that, despite the plan he and the woman had created right in front of me, I was not awake because of them.

Someone else called to my waking mind. As I smashed the window and took to the sky for the first time in a century, I swore I'd go find... her. I propelled myself through the air like a fledgling bird, determined to meet the female presence that needed me.

AT LEAST, I attempted to fly to her like a storybook hero, ready to swoop in and save her with a gargoyle's flare.

Instead, I crashed, unable to carry my weight through the air further than the length of a few buildings. My body formed a crater in a small rectangle of grass, spraying dirt in every direction. "Hey, watch it!" snapped a passing fae, glaring with a draw of his leafy eyebrows.

I righted myself and clomped onward by foot, sparing the grinding of my rocky lungs as an apology. This would be considerably slower than flying, but my purpose beckoned like a beacon in the distance. I would find her one grinding step at a time.

What had happened in my absence? Roaring carriage-like monstrosities passed me on the tar-black surface beside the sidewalk. Meanwhile, supernaturals of all sorts maneuvered around me if they weren't too busy staring. A late-summer sun cast a glare overhead, heating my obsidian body considerably.

I tried to ignore it all. I was not a spectacle, and if I needed to know how Moongrove Academy gained such a medley of individuals, I would be informed along the path to serving my purpose.

At least along the way, the struggle to breathe and move smoothed out. My chest rose and fell, my stone heart beating more steadily. In this form, my heart was the soul of my honored witch, and her energy infused my limbs with magic, movement, and life.

Perhaps my long walk was a blessing in disguise, because by the time I found a four-story building with an attached garden, I was no longer moving in the short jerks that made my animation so disconcerting. My stone feet touched the ground without breaking it under my body's considerable weight.

Still, with the tug of my purpose taking me into the garden, I walked with a *thump* of each step on grass. I glanced around, not seeing any immediate danger. Instead, in the heart of the garden, I found a decorative pond filled with lazing koi and a woman seated on a bench beside it, her knees tucked up and forming a cradle for her to hide her face. The first feature I saw was an unkempt mass of dark purple hair, so I assumed she was fae of some sort.

My approach was the opposite of stealthy, so when I took a closer look, her shoulders hitched up and she lifted her head. Red-rimmed but human eyes turned toward me, and she swiped under her nose with a wet sniffle. Faint tear tracks traced down her pale cheeks. Fatigue lined her young face and marked the skin under her eyes with bruise-like shadows.

The stone heart in my chest released a pulse of recognition. *She* was my purpose and duty, the reason I'd woken ready for combat. My heart resonated on a low level. It was my reward for fulfilling the first of what may be several steps in resolving what this young woman needed from me.

She stared at me. I knelt before her, bowing my head in deference to the woman I sensed to be either a weak or inexperienced librarian witch. Taking a deep breath, I tested the dusty depths of my newly exercised lungs. "Greetings, librarian. I am here to serve you."

"You...you're..." She cleared her throat and lowered her legs to the ground.

"I am the Quartz Gargoyle, animated to your service," I stated. She must be *very* new, for she did not immediately order me to the task she required.

All she said was a faint, "Huh?"

"Your need awoke me. What do you require?" I asked.

Her lips moved soundlessly, repeating what I'd just said to herself. Her shoulders tensed. "You know what I did."

I didn't budge an inch, gazing at her unblinkingly. "I know nothing of you yet. Direct me to your service."

"So...no one sent you?" She directed her gaze over her shoulder. "Can you keep a secret?"

"As long as it does not endanger Moongrove Library, I swear myself to secrecy," I said without curiosity. It wasn't like anyone attempted to pry idle gossip from a gargoyle. Even at the height of my service, I had the autonomy to refuse answering probing questions that infringed on others' privacy.

"I..." Her eyes welled up with tears, and she hiccupped a sob. She struggled to speak past her grief. "I made...a terrible mistake."

A mortal might be able to comfort her as she cried, but I simply stared and waited for her to deliver a clear order. Where was a fellow witch to rub her shoulders and embrace her? A faint trickle of emotion echoed from my heart, but I didn't know what it was. Emotions weren't in the suite of skills given to me upon my creation. I felt them more clearly in my flesh form, but they had to be strong indeed to pierce the unfeeling shell of my stone body.

I carefully placed a hand on her knee but took it back when she winced from its heat. "What is the matter?" I asked.

"You really won't tell anyone?" she asked in a tearful whisper.

"I have the utmost integrity," I replied.

An uneasy chuckle escaped her lips. "Okay. I think I know why you were, um, activated? Is that the right word?"

"It is sufficient to describe my awakening."

"It's because a dimensional k-killed my friend last night." She rubbed away her tears impatiently. "And...it's my fault."

"It is your fault a dimensional killed another person?" I asked to clarify and brought on another wave of her grief.

"Yeah," she mumbled. "I guess that's all you really need to know. I did him a, uh, favor. And in return, he killed her last night. I-I...found him over her body."

No wonder she grieved. I waited with a stone's endurance for her to recover. I couldn't comfort her, but perhaps I could listen and provide some ease to her guilt that way.

"The supernatural police took my statement last night. They didn't seem to believe me," she said, gaze downcast. "I mean, they didn't *say* anything about it, but I got that feeling.

"But I know who killed my friend, and I'm going to get him even if the police don't. He was imprisoned in the library until...he escaped," she continued. She formed fists on her thighs. "That's where I think you come in. Will you help me kill him?"

"You seek retribution for your friend." I considered her and the conversation I'd overheard earlier. There was a chance this young witch had broken the seals and released a dangerous dimensional, and in helping her kill him, I would also assist her in erasing her crime.

At the same time, I reassessed her aura of power and how weak it was. Any dimensional that'd reached the kind of power level to be locked in Moongrove Library would annihilate her in moments if it came to a direct confrontation. It would both fulfill my eternal duty to my home library *and* my purpose for awakening in slaying the monster for her.

"I shall assist you," I promised. "Give me a physical description of my new target."

She described the dimensional's features and, in the process, started to call him "Phae—"

I hoped my new purpose wouldn't end with me turning her in as a criminal for the release of Phaeron Sudair, the Hungering Darkness. Already, I had a developing bond to her. A mortal might call it an attraction, but I thought of it more as loyalty. Her secret was now mine, and I would serve her the head of her enemy for his trespass against her.

"It shall be done," I stated. "I will protect you as well. He may come for you next."

Her face paled further. "Maybe. Thank you..." With a shake of her head, she quirked her lips. "We've made a plan together, and I don't even know your name."

"It is Geo," I replied promptly.

"Is that short for anything?"

"No."

"Oh, well, I'm Cress," she said. "And there's something I need to do before we talk anymore."

"Is it a task I can assist with?"

"No...I need to do this alone," she sighed. "Wait right here."

And like a statue in the garden, I waited motionlessly for her return.

9
CRESS

I FELT a single pebble drop off the considerable weight of guilt balanced on my shoulders as I left the garden and went back into my dorm room. The gargoyle man had seemed more like a robot than a living, breathing creature, so I'd felt more comfortable inviting him into the messed-up situation that'd become my life.

I didn't know if Geo could kill Phaeron, but at least I had an ally now who wouldn't immediately accuse me of murder. I'd sweated my way through my statement last night, knowing if I suggested I'd known the dimensional in any way, my involvement in his freedom could come to light.

What had started as a simple curiosity for what was locked up on floor negative fifty had snowballed way out of my control. I was guilty for everything that happened afterward. Lanie's murder was my fault.

It was hard to breathe. The walls leaned in toward me in the stairwell, and I clutched my chest. *Stupid. Such an idiot,* I berated through the sudden rush of tears. I hadn't slept for a moment, instead randomly assailed by the stabbing pain of my own emotions. If I could turn the clock back twenty-four hours, I would've made Lanie stay with our new coven and walked into the night instead.

Let Phaeron have my life. It wasn't like I'd accomplished a fraction of what Lanie had. She'd traveled the world, learned several languages, and saved countless lives with her augury magic. I didn't deserve her sacrifice.

Worst of all, she'd known *exactly* what was about to happen. What was *"I wish you the best of luck"* anything but an acknowledgment of a permanent goodbye?

Her computer had been unlocked when I arrived at our dorm late last night, a document up on it that included pages and pages of her frantic typing. The top of the page was "Dear Cress," and that was about all I read before I made sure the document was saved and closed it off. I'd emailed it to myself and cried like a baby when my phone pinged with one last message from Lanie.

I was going to make Phaeron pay for what he'd done. Because I had a feeling she wasn't his original target—just a clever decoy with a similar hooded jacket. She'd thrown herself on the sword for me and left answers in a way I hadn't mustered the nerve to read.

I reached my dorm room and simply stood there, listening to the sounds of shuffling within. Lanie's parents had arrived this morning, but I'd hidden in the garden rather than witness their grief and know I'd caused it.

A school official had visited and explained that the Graygazers were here to pack up Lanie's things. At first, I'd assumed they'd seen a devastating ripple in future events and set off then and there, just to arrive too late. But no...they'd arrived by portal, traversing thousands of miles with the assistance of a talented celestial witch.

If I'd known celestial witches learned how to make real-life portals, maybe I'd have chosen to become one and sidestepped this whole mess.

Instead, here I was, hesitating with my hand over the knob. *Just go in there and apologize,* I thought viciously, cursing my hesitation.

I came in to find a diminutive, dark-haired woman perched on my bed, scratching Milo's cheeks. My two cats made a harmony of purrs. On Lanie's side of the dorm, an older man looked up from packing away her laptop, sunlight glinting off his blocky glasses frames. Both of Lanie's parents turned to me at the same time.

The only tears in the room were mine. Lanie's mother placed Milo aside gently and swept me into a hug. "Poor dear. You must be Cress... Lanie spoke well of you."

"That's me," I mumbled.

"Come, have a seat." She ushered me to sit where she'd vacated, and my familiars pressed against me for comfort. "I'm glad you chose to come see us."

Spoken just like someone with the magic to see the future, who'd known there was only a slim chance I'd gather the courage to look her in the eye. I swallowed nervously, expecting her and her husband to round on me together, but instead, she settled on Lanie's bed, and he acknowledged me with a nod before continuing to pack.

"I'm so sorry about Lanie," I burst out. "Her death was so sudden. I could tell there was something wrong, but I never expected—"

"Shh. I know." A sad smile twisted her mouth.

"We knew this day was coming," Lanie's father said through a thick accent.

My jaw dropped open. "You...did?"

"We did. Maybe not the exact date, but..." Her mother spread her hands. "It's the burden of all accomplished augurs."

"We all know how we will die," her father said.

I bit into my bottom lip, chewing on this revelation. "That must be awful for you," I said quietly.

"Is it?" She tilted her head in consideration. "We had the chance to say our goodbyes with Lanie. Most don't get the opportunity for that kind of closure."

I stood and found my tissue box atop the modest dresser on my side of the room, just in time to blot out another wave of tears and sniffles. I had to say it, to apologize to Lanie's parents. That's what I came here for.

"It's not your fault," she said before I could muster up the fragments of my nerve.

"It is. I-I couldn't stop her in time..." As I said this, Bella wiggled into my lap, and I held on to her for comfort.

Lanie's mother shook her head. "Do you know what happens when a Graygazer denies their fate? Someone else dies instead. Often horrifically." She gave me a pointed look, and I felt the color draining off my face.

"Are you saying...I almost died in a way worse than Lanie did?" That wasn't reassuring at all. In my current headspace, I thought that would've been better.

But I saw the expression on her face and the look her husband flashed my way. It wasn't supposed to be comforting. Fate or not, they'd lost their daughter because of me.

"She told us of a being of shadows and teeth, with claws made of white fire. A dimensional creature beyond her mind's ability to understand," she murmured. "Her fate was to gain its attention, because someone would've died last night, no matter what. This thing...this-this *monster*, was going to target you. It would've consumed you, body and soul. Anyone else that got in its way would've suffered the same ending. But my daughter..."

"Her soul was eaten?" I asked in a horrified whisper.

She jerked her head. "No. She said the creature would be interrupted before it did more than attack her. That she would save your life, but you would save her soul."

My lips pressed together, head bowed solemnly. *Damn.* What was I supposed to say to that?

"The monster targeted me for a reason. It's my fa—"

"No," she interrupted. "Don't you see, Cress? There's a reason I'm telling you this. It was Lanie's decision, her gift to you and all the young witches there last night."

"But..." I said weakly. I didn't ask for this gift. It wasn't like I deserved it for causing the situation in the first place.

"My daughter met her fated end, but I will take the chance to gaze at what comes next." Magic bloomed around her head in the Graygazer's gray aura, but as I watched, it intensified and brightened until she had a halo of silver casting a glare over her inky hair.

I sat up straighter, a thick knot of emotion caught in my throat.

"You aren't ready for the full truth quite yet. But I see you standing over the creature who attacked my daughter, vanquishing it alongside three men who adore you. You will be the one to avenge her," she intoned, her voice echoing with power.

"Tell me what I have to do," I practically begged.

"Find a man by the name of Callum Voidbinder. Make him train you in librarian magic beyond what a beginner is allowed," she instructed. "And don't act foolishly. You won't get another chance to make this right."

"Yes, ma'am," I said, expecting the glow around her to fade as she nodded and turned her attention away from me.

She asked her husband something in another language, and he fished his wallet out of his pocket, handing her a card. She passed it to me. "Call us when you lose your way." As she spoke, the sense of otherworldliness faded from her.

"I will," I promised, looking down at the card. "Graygazer Augury Services" stood out from the creamy paper, plus a phone number and email address. I caught her name as well. Hana.

"I hope you find peace," Lanie's father said. "Our calm comes from knowing that Lanie put everyone here on the right path."

Hana raised a finger. "One more thing." She made kissy noises and leaned down, coaxing out Jin. The small black cat had puffed-out fur and the most dejected expression a cat could have, her weight completely limp as Hana picked her up. "Will you care for Jin?"

"You don't want to take her with you?" I asked, fighting a sob. My dam was about to break again, seeing how heartbroken Jin was.

She scratched behind the little cat's ears, earning a reluctant lean. "It's not that at all. I have my familiars, but there's a chance you can win her over and give her a second chance to be a witch's cat." Hana's lips twisted, betraying a flicker of deep grief before she smoothed it behind an impassive mask. "It's very hard to bind three familiars to yourself, but I think you have the potential."

"In that case...I'd love to adopt her," I said. Lanie's cat would remind me of her, but that wasn't a bad thing. I let go of Bella to accept Jin, placing her on my lap. She trembled and watched me closely all the while. In all this mess, I'd overlooked how lost and terrified Jin must be with the sudden loss of her witch. Yet she stayed and let me hold her as we watched the Graygazers finish packing what remained of Lanie's things.

I wouldn't admit to understanding either of them. They'd just lost their daughter, but it felt like they'd just talked me down from the sharpest peak of my grief. I *was* going to avenge my friend. They'd seen it in the future.

I just had to make it happen, and I couldn't wait to start sharpening a silver blade.

BUT WHEN THE Graygazers left and I was alone with the cats, my motivation guttered out immediately. It was easier to promise big things and nod along as a powerful witch told me my fate. Now that it was time to, well, get out of bed and *do it*, in rushed another overwhelming wave of emotion.

This was still all my fault. Lanie had made the best out of a bad situation, but that didn't bring her back. Her cat had retreated from my hold to stretch out on the bare mattress left over on the other side of the room. Her eyes, yellow and sad, stared in my direction when she wasn't sleeping.

I shifted onto my back and watched the play of light over the ceiling. It was a Monday, and the cheerful chatter of young women going to and from their classes filled the hall. I'd gotten a week off and a promise of grade forgiveness for what I'd seen.

It didn't seem like enough. I wasn't sure I could get out of this bed in a week and go back to normal. Nothing about my life was "normal" anymore anyway.

I was apparently destined to slay a dimensional monster and avenge my friend. I waited and waited for a more heroic spirit to possess me, to push out the coward who had hidden the fact I'd been the one to release said monster.

It wasn't until the evening light was fading to darkness when a knock sounded on my door. I released a groan, shifting to sit up slowly so I didn't disturb Milo and Bella napping against my legs. The knock sounded again, timid and light.

On the other side of the threshold stood a semi-familiar brunette. She raised a hand in a brief wave. "Hi, Cress," whispered Willow, the oceanic witch who was apparently one of my coven-mates. "Can we come in?"

We? I glanced behind her to see Roe and her petite fae roommate, Áine, standing around the corner and peeking in on this discussion. Roe in particular looked like she was holding in her brash manner, the strain making her cheeks pinker.

"Yeah, I guess," I sighed, taking a few steps back.

"Uh, your phone is off." Roe sounded like she was murmuring, but her voice was at a regular conversational level. "So I thought maybe we could talk in person."

I glanced away awkwardly. Was anything more of a "do not disturb" sign than a phone turned off?

I perched on my bed, and the two witches sat on the empty mattress while Áine said with extra cheer, "Hey, are you hungry? I brought snacks."

Her little shorts looked like they didn't have pockets, and she wasn't wearing a backpack. I shrugged, but my belly betrayed me, grumbling its discontent.

"Sounds like a yes. Good thing I have…" She stuck her hand into a patch of wavering air, and I turned to stare as she withdrew a plate stacked high with brownies, plus bowls, spoons, napkins, and finally a tub of ice cream frosted from first exposure to warm air. She passed these things to Roe and Willow, who dutifully divided them equally between the four of us.

I realized I was gawking. "How…?"

"Pocket portal." The fae winked. "I have an emergency stash, and I think this qualifies."

Willow passed me a bowl stacked high with sugar. "I don't think she knows what fae magic does," she suggested in her quiet wisp of a voice.

"So, you know how New Salem is, like, separate from the rest of the mortal world?" Áine asked.

"Sort of." I stuffed a spoonful of ice cream in my mouth. It was still delightfully cold, despite its spontaneous appearance.

"That's fae magic, with a touch of other magics for stability. We can warp nature, basically. When I reach into here…" Her hand disappeared into a patch of air that rippled like a heat mirage. "…I'm reaching into a space that only exists for me. It's a natural extension of my being. Since I'm just a faun, the stuff I store away winks out of existence until I reach inside, and sometimes it's really gone for good. Were I a stronger fae, I could allow you to access it too. I could make it bigger than a pocket so you could come and go from it and we could decorate it with streets and buildings and nature. Does that make sense?"

"So you're telling me…a strong enough fae can create an entirely new *city?*" I said, imagining it. Screw castles in the sky, create a whole space just for yourself. I hadn't even an inkling it was possible until now. "And that's what New Salem is?"

"A group of fae, sure. New Salem used to be the Fall Court, but they gave up the space after...well, you don't need all the details right now." She waved a hand dismissively. "All the fae courts are hosted in alternate dimensions like New Salem. But most of them are fae-only and thus not as big. Magic from dimensionals allows for expansion, merfolk give us stable water sources and varied weather patterns, plus verdant, oceanic, and celestial witches can help too."

"That is so cool," I said with some of my usual enthusiasm for learning about the supernatural world.

"Right?" she said brightly.

It seemed like Roe couldn't take it anymore. "I've been so worried about you!" she burst out. "Are you going to move to our dorm? Anywhere but here?"

The school official who'd visited earlier had already tried to convince me to move in with a different roommate. I thought it was standard practice, as if this room is tainted with memories. I told them the same thing I'd said to that person. "I don't want to leave. My familiars are happy in this room...and Jin might appreciate it too."

Lanie's cat was hiding under the bed right now. She hadn't even talked to my cats since we'd lost Lanie, so I wasn't sure if it was her wish or not.

"So, I convinced the school to let me have the room to myself for the rest of the year," I said. "It's going to be nice...probably."

"You're officially the host of all our dorm parties," Roe proclaimed.

"Uhhh..."

"Anyway," Willow said. "We're a coven now. If you need to talk, we're always here for you."

I glanced at Áine, who shrugged. "Roe said I'm an honorary member."

"But we have a new guy." Roe's voice turned into a grumble. "*Already!*"

"Wren attached herself to his side instantly." Willow rolled her eyes with a delicate sigh. "We're like two mini covens right now. Roe, me, and you."

"Plus me," Áine interjected.

"And the three guy witches and Wren. That girl is vicious." Willow frowned.

"You too, huh?" I said.

"Yeah," she muttered.

Roe said, "We wanted to let you know that there's another coven meeting Wednesday evening over dinner, since our first one was, uh..."

"Canceled," Willow supplied.

"And we need you to come." Roe clasped her hands, giving me her best puppy dog eyes. "I'm not about to let Wren lead my first coven."

"Me neither." I paused for a moment. "Wait. Like, are we voting on a leader? Is that more than an unofficial title?"

"Exactly. And without you there, Wren's basically guaranteed to get it," Willow said. "Can't you come and vote for Roe instead?"

I nodded slowly. "If the three guys still vote for her..."

"Well, you have to meet the new guy," Roe said quickly. She flashed me a nervous smile, the kind that came before a big request. "He came in today and, uh, seems curious about you. Maybe you could come to Introduction to Witchcraft on Wednesday and, like, convince him..."

"Curious about me how?" I asked, my eyes narrowing.

"Like, he knows you're in our coven and you're our only librarian. It's kind of a miracle he asked since Wren was shoving her boobs in his face," Roe said with a snort.

I started to laugh too. "So that's how she's getting the guys to be friends with her?"

"Yeah, well, you should meet this guy anyway." A tinge of pink touched Willow's cheeks.

"He's hot," Roe blurted.

"All right, all right. You've twisted my arm," I said wryly.

"Great!" Roe lit up. "I think you'll like him. His name's Ben."

10

BEN

Master Garroway kept me off any missions once my brother went off to assassinate the purple-haired Darkmore girl.

Days passed. I wasn't too worried. Finding the time and place to carry out a discreet mission often took time.

Then a week went by, and I would jump at any sound my phone made, hoping to see Lucas's name on the screen. It was never him.

"I suppose little Lucas is having trouble," my vampire master drawled when I brought it up at dinner that evening. He watched me without concern every night he deigned to join his coven of blood witches. Seeing him once a week was a surprise, but his uncaring remark came after his second day at the head of the table, swirling deep red blood wine in an elegant glass.

Chilled, I didn't mention Lucas to him again. All I knew was that Garroway had given Lucas a second, smaller task to complete while he was in Moongrove Library since his mark turned out to be a librarian witch. Apparently, it was a trade-off for losing money on a free deal with Crown Starsurge.

I was going crazy, though. With no missions, all I could do was sit around the manor and serve as a medic if anyone arrived injured. It was a Sunday before I got a glimmer of hope as I tended to Bianca's ears clumsily with cotton swabs and an ancient tool in the infirmary that was like a tiny water gun.

"Ow, watch it," she hissed, slapping my arm after a particularly enthusiastic squirt into her ear. Bloody water ran into the waiting basin.

"It's not my fault you didn't wear earplugs," I grunted.

"I did! And you're supposed to irrigate my ear, not blast the eardrum," she complained. "Who fucking died and made you the new medic anyway?"

"It was the master's decision," I said, applying less pressure to the trigger as I splashed water over the outside shell of her ear before digging into the crust with a swab. I'd seen a lot worse in the last week. Even though blood witches could heal most injuries on themselves with a mending rune painted on their skin in their own blood, it left a mess behind.

And I was doing a great job, thank you very much. She'd arrived deaf after hunting down a dimensional screamer, and the first thing she did after I covered her ears with mending runes to bring her hearing back was complain about me.

She made a little *tsk* noise and started scrolling her phone. "Whatever."

I made an exaggerated smack with my lips and mimicked her in a higher voice, "Whatever! Guess I'll be deaf."

Her brow furrowed hard, her death glare aimed at her device since she was forced to lean over the padded table to drain her ear into the little curved basin that fit against her shoulder.

"It got a lucky drop on me," she admitted quietly. "I usually have two bolts in one of their throats before they can make a peep."

"Sounds sloppy to me," I said.

"Shut up, Ben. Not like you've ever been tapped to hunt a screamer," she snapped. "Stuck here while—"

An ugly gasp interrupted her, and she brought the screen closer to her face. "What? What is it?" I demanded.

"Fuck. It's Lucas, I think."

I practically snatched the phone from her as she scrolled back to the top of a page. It was a news article quoting an official statement from

NSU. My gaze darted over the screen so fast I had to stop and collect myself to really let the words sink in.

It gave sparse details of a gruesome, bloody murder on campus by a "rogue blood witch." As an actual rogue, my eyebrows rose at how amateurish and sloppy the details were...almost like a first kill.

Bianca's first thought was of Lucas, and I agreed, only pausing when I saw the victim was an unnamed augury witch.

"He killed the wrong person," I muttered. "An augur."

"They're literally the worst." I could practically hear her eyes rolling. "I've been blackmailed by one before. Threatened to turn me in to the SPDI if I killed my mark."

"Do you think this one provoked my brother?" I asked.

"The fuck if I know. Probably? Why else would he have fumbled a kill so badly?" she asked.

I stared at the words on the tiny, bright screen until they ran together in a blur. No matter what, Lucas was in trouble. The SPDI didn't fuck around if they got a whiff of rogue activity. They would hunt him down like a dog.

We were specially trained in what to do if we were ever caught, but it came to one simple fact: a quick death by suicide was a much cleaner ending than having our blood boiled in our veins for even considering telling the authorities about Master Garroway or his illegal dealings. The trigger spell for a messy end was woven in through the complex blood rune all of Garroway's witches bore.

"I have to go help him," I said, handing the phone back to Bianca. "I have to find him before bounty hunters or the SPDI do."

For a moment, she turned the device over in her hands. "Do you think Garroway will give you leave to go?"

"He can always call me back," I said, shrugging. If I asked, the answer would be no. If I just slipped out, then I could make up some kind of excuse if Garroway activated my blood rune and forced me to return.

"I guess." She hesitated for a moment. "If you clean out my other ear—*gently*—I'll forge a few documents for you to get you into NSU."

"I'm not going to attend classes," I scoffed.

"You're going to look awfully suspicious, then," she pointed out.

"C'mon, at least one class. Pick an old professor; they're easy to fool. Isn't Lucas's mark a student anyway?"

"Yeah."

"She might be your only lead. You should see if she knows the dead augur," she said.

Well, she did have a point. "All right. One class alongside Lucas's mark, then. I'll start with her and search the campus for any signs of him in the meantime."

"Great. It shouldn't be too hard," she said.

I suppressed a groan. It was one constant in my life: anything that seemed easy was anything but.

Bianca didn't just forge some documents for me; she slipped her way into NSU's database and brought up a list of the Darkmore girl's classes. She was taking Latin, introductory classes to witchery and the supernatural world, plus courses in fashion design.

The thought of having to sit through anything related to fashion gave me chills, so we looked up the professors in her other classes, narrowing the options down to Introduction to Witchcraft with a septuagenarian professor, Dr. Evanora Heartwood. It was a class that met Monday, Wednesday, Friday, so I made sure I was ready to attend the next day.

I ended up scraping off the scraggly beard forming over my jaw and browsing the manor's walk-in closet for a few outfits that would make me look like a casual college dude. Rack upon rack of different clothes in various sizes waited to be used, some beaten up and others brand new designer labels with the tags still on them.

Always look like you belong was one of the first rules I'd learned here. Garroway made sure we had all the tools for the job, including prosthetics and makeup if the situation required it. His greatest gift, though, was the set of jewelry I inspected after picking out my clothes. Each piece was designed to hold a tiny vial discreetly. I flipped open the nearly invisible catch on my favorite, a heavy, dark ring with a grayish sheen in the light. I slipped my vial of blood inside it and fit the ring on my right hand, adjusting it until it warmed.

Every blood witch here received one emergency vial filled with a bit of Garroway's blood. In dire circumstances, I could break it and paint myself with runes to gain a burst of vampiric strength, agility, and regeneration. Hopefully it wouldn't come to that.

I picked up a second item, a heavy necklace with an amethyst cluster as the pendant, then selected a vial of guardian witch blood to add to it, to help me pass as one for as long as I needed to complete this personal mission.

I left the manor and Garroway's pocket dimension under the cover of a newly risen sun that Monday, traversing several miles of ordinary human Salem. The shift in weather made my sinuses ache, for Garroway preferred dry and chilly autumn weather in his bubble of privacy disguised as a dilapidated house in the suburbs, while Salem had an overcast, windy day.

I rubbed my nose as I found the seam in reality at a cemetery gate and slipped into the NSU campus by touching that magic with a bit of my own. The glare of a sunny summer day hit my eyes immediately. I soaked in its warmth as I slouched my way onto the campus, hands in my hoodie and music thumping in my wireless earbuds.

To anyone else's eyes, I was another college kid with a bag casually slung over one shoulder, unhurriedly going to class along a route I'd memorized. Once I reached the right classroom, I drew out an official-looking letter and offered it to the elderly woman who smiled in the kind of way that said she recognized me as a lost young man.

"Hello, is this Introduction to Witchcraft?" I asked.

As she scanned the letter, I felt the faintest flutter of nerves. If anything was off with Bianca's forging, this woman would notice it immediately.

"It sure is, and you're in the right place, Benjamin," she said, an odd look passing over her expression. "Do you have a coven already?"

"No, ma'am," I replied.

"Your arrival is most fortunate, then. Please sit with this row." She gestured to the far side of the room, where a couple of students sat and chatted quietly, their gazes flashing up at us more than once. "Welcome to NSU. I hope you enjoy it here."

I thanked her and went to sit at the desk at the end of the row, my back pressed to the wall. The male witch one seat up from me grinned a perfect white smile and introduced himself as Heath. He had the kind of lean muscle that suggested he was active in some sport or was the kind of fighter I'd better keep an eye on just in case.

The witch he'd been chatting with perched herself on my desk, her sparkly shirt cut to reveal a line of cleavage. She leaned just right to put me at eye level with it. "Hey there," she purred. "I'm Wren Starsurge. Celestial witch."

I met her blue gaze and smirked. Now this was awkward. I saw a hint of family resemblance between her and the blustering Blaize Starsurge, the man that was basically the reason I'd arrived here. But I doubted she knew her daddy was involved in the business of hiring my master's services.

"Ben Cross. Guardian witch," I lied, nodding to her. A bit of her interest dimmed when I didn't pull out an impressive surname. In truth, I didn't have one, just the name Cross, which all of Garroway's witches borrowed off and on.

"Where are you from, Ben?" she asked.

"Here and there." I shrugged. "Just transferred here, but I'm a little worried it was a mistake."

Her lips narrowed to a little rosebud. "So, you've already heard the news about Lanie."

"If that was her name," I said.

"Nasty business." She gave a delicate shudder. "I guess you're in my coven now. You're like, her replacement."

"Hopefully I'm not next," I said dryly.

She opened her mouth to reply when a louder woman's voice interrupted. "Hey, are you new?" A muscular redheaded woman approached, and Wren's expression turned icy in an instant.

"He's our newest coven member. We're back to seven already. Isn't that great?" the celestial witch simpered, twirling a lock of blonde hair around her finger.

The redhead recoiled as if she'd been struck. She shot a disbelieving look at the elderly professor currently deep in conversation with another student as they both looked at something on his computer screen. "It hasn't even been a day," she mumbled.

"Ben here's a guardian too, just like you. I guess you have a partner to go to the gym with now," Wren said, her judgmental gaze sweeping over the workout gear the other witch had come in wearing. I frowned to myself. Guardians were difficult opponents for a blood witch to fight due to their natural affinity for stone, and this woman looked like she was devoted to her craft, if her muscles were any indication.

The redhead made an unimpressed noise. As more of the class filed in, I was swept into a round of introductions. I memorized each name and face. The redhead, Rowena Ashbough, was the only guardian at least. Willow and Heath, both of the oceanic affinity. Grant, a verdant witch, who had a bored glaze to his eyes as he slumped into his seat. And, of course, Wren.

"Where is the last member of our group?" I asked, seeing as class was about to begin. An empty desk was bracketed in our row by Willow and Roe. Considering I hadn't seen a head of purple hair file in yet, I had my suspicions as to who was meant to sit there.

Roe turned and leaned around Heath and Wren to answer me. "Her name's Cress, and she's a librarian. I don't think we'll see her for a while," she said. A heavy sense of sadness hung over her words.

Wren rolled her eyes. "Please, save the dramatics. She knew Lanie all of a couple weeks."

"She found the *body*," Roe argued, her tone turning biting. "And they were roommates. Have some empathy."

I disguised my keen interest with a glance at my phone. Could I be so lucky? Not only did the Darkmore girl know my brother's victim, we were now in the same coven.

"I look forward to meeting her," I said.

11

CRESS

"I'm sorry I left you out here," I said when Wednesday came around. I didn't think the gargoyle had moved an inch from the kneeling position he'd settled in the last time we'd spoken.

Only a couple things betrayed that he was more than a statue placed randomly in the middle of the garden path. His chest rose and fell with slow, steady breaths. When he noticed me approaching him, his chin had tipped up with a grinding like two stones brushing off each other.

"Is. It. Time. I. Fulfilled. My. Purpose?" His voice was deep, near guttural. Each word seemed like a struggle for him to utter.

"Are you okay?" I asked uncertainly.

He drew himself off the ground and to his full height. I started assuming the grinding noises were like if I popped my knuckles or back. Once he had a good scrape, the unsettling sounds softened to the swish of sandpaper with each motion. "I am..." He blew a cloud of dust out of his mouth, aiming it away from me. "...sufficiently rested."

I supposed that was close enough and shrugged. "I need to go to class. Do you have something else you could be doing?"

"Protecting you...is my purpose," he said. "I will...accompany you."

"Suit yourself." My mind raced to explain away a seven-foot gargoyle following me, especially into the classes with limited space. I led him into the campus, taking my time. Geo kept pace with me despite his slower steps since he had a huge stride.

I snuck an appreciating look up at him while he stared ahead, his cloudy white eyes roving constantly for danger.

A woman must've sculpted Geo, because every detail was a gal's wet dream. He had the frame to match his incredibly tall stature, detailed down to a few hairline veins of silver marbling across his bulging arm muscles. In the sunlight, his pitch-black stone skin gleamed without casting a glare.

My gaze skimmed over his perfectly formed chest. The sculptor had skipped giving him a shirt, instead outlining each abdominal with painstaking care. Fortunately for my blushing perusal, he did have a pair of stone shorts on, which moved with each flex of his generously muscled thighs.

A pair of gigantic bat wings marked him for what he was, along with the six stalactite-like spears of sharpened quartz tucked into the line of his back.

Out of nowhere, I nearly ran into his arm. My gaze flashed up to his face as a car raced past. "Careful," he said, flashing white quartz teeth.

I scratched the back of my head sheepishly, wondering if he'd realized I'd nearly walked into oncoming traffic while internally complimenting the person who'd made him. His expression was as flat as ever, though. His symmetrical face had a strong jaw and thick brow, and I hadn't seen him emote with either yet. The only expression he seemed capable of making was the serious line of his obsidian lips.

"Sorry," I said a little breathlessly.

He lowered his arm, indicating I continue leading the way.

"I'm new to the supernatural world," I told him after successfully crossing the street. "So, I'm probably going to ask you a ton of dumb questions."

"Ask," he said.

I bit my lip, unsure how to even phrase this question. If I guessed correctly, though, I wouldn't be able to offend him. He hadn't shown any emotion yet, at least. "Are you a robot?" I asked.

"No."

"Are you...alive?" I asked, holding my breath as his head turned my way with the whisper of sandpaper.

"I am capable of life."

My brow furrowed. "That's usually a yes or no question."

"For me, it is yes and no." His lips dipped, threatening a frown. "I am capable of shifting. A form of flesh and blood and feeling. But I choose not to...unless it is required."

"Why not?" I asked. The Voidbinder Building was just a block away, and I felt my palms moisten with nerves. It'd only been a few days since...

"Most gargoyles forget their duty once they've experienced living again." Geo continued speaking, oblivious to the nerves churning in my belly. "We are created to serve the library, and I have always been dutiful to my purpose."

"Oh yeah?" I mumbled, distracted.

"You need not worry. I will not abandon you to pursuits of the flesh," he answered with all the earnestness of someone who didn't know I'd do a lot to see what he looked like when he wasn't a talking, moving rock.

I stopped before the steps up to the Voidbinder Building and turned to him. "Well, my class is in here," I said. I'd decided I was just going to attend Introduction to Witchcraft today. Dip my toes back into the water and slowly get into my normal schedule.

Geo watched me for a moment. "I shall wait here for you," he said. "Will you be gone for several days again?"

I flushed, still mortified I'd left him to wait for me for that long. And he *had,* without complaint. "No! Just a couple hours at most. After class, there's someone I need to find."

"I shall find you if it takes too long, then," he promised.

I checked my phone and hustled up the steps, mere minutes from being late. Heads turned when I walked in, several conversations quieting to whispers. *Great, they're gossiping about me.* I realized there was a change in seating. Roe waved to me from the farthest row, where she and Willow were sitting with Wren and a couple guys I semi-recognized, along with one I didn't.

Roe stood, leaving the desk in front of him empty, and mouthed the words "thank you" as she took her seat further up. Meaning I had to sit sandwiched between the new guy and Wren. I cursed under my breath as I slipped into that spot. The new male witch sat with his back to the wall, leg crossed in a casual figure-four.

"Hey," he said. "Nice hair."

"Oh, thanks," I mumbled, inspecting the ends of a lock. By this point, some of its vibrant purple color had faded. I was nearly shy when face to face with the guy Roe had so shamelessly called "hot."

Fuck, he was. He could give Geo a run for his money, and the gargoyle had been created by an expert's hand. He had a generous mane of honeyed brown hair and a crooked smile that could make a gal's heart stop. It lit up his whole face, taking away a predatory edge to his expression, because something about him reminded me of a lion, golden-skinned and hungry.

"I'm Ben. You must be Cress?" I realized he had a hand held out to shake, and he gripped mine with effortless strength despite having a lean build under a casual t-shirt and shorts.

"That's right. I understand you're in my coven now?" I asked. I shifted to put my back against the wall as well.

He shrugged. "Apparently. I just got here, so it seems a little sudden."

"Cress, how are you? No one was expecting you so early. Aren't you still in that room you shared with Lanie?" Wren interjected. Quiet venom lurked under the words, and I immediately turned a glare her direction. Her expression was sweet as can be. I wondered if she practiced it in the mirror. "Isn't it hard to sleep in that room after what happened?"

I held my breath, unpleasantly reminded that I'd barely left that room and had set aside my guilt for the moment to meet Ben.

He leaned around me, scowling at Wren. "That was rude. Don't you see she and I were having a conversation?"

She twirled a length of her hair between her fingers. "I was just curious," she said, laughing it off.

Ben turned his leaf-green gaze back to me, about to say something else when Dr. Heartwood started class. She reminded us that we had coven meetings tonight to get to know each other better and vote for a leader. I released a weary sigh, feeling the now-familiar malaise of exhaustion settling over my shoulders again. Lanie should be sitting behind me, not this guy, no matter what he looked like.

"Today's lesson is on aura reading. You may have noticed auras on and off after bonding to your affinity, but today I will show you how to focus your sight on them with a few different exercises," Dr. Heartwood said, then called for us to find partners.

I turned to Ben, who was fiddling with what looked like a chunk of purple geode strung onto a heavy silver chain around his neck. He flashed a hint of his killer smile. "Partners?"

"Yup," I answered.

"Well, I have to admit to cheating. I already know you're a librarian witch from your friends," he said, gesturing to Roe and Willow, who'd partnered up a few seats up from us.

"What is your magic?" I asked curiously.

"Guess you'll have to find out," he answered with a wink. My heart sped up a step.

"Every supernatural exerts an aura of magic, and witches are particularly adept at sensing them. With practice, you will be able to identify auras at a glance," Dr. Heartwood said.

She walked us through relaxing our gazes to see what color rose off our partner's skin. The slideshow she projected today had a guide for the seven witch affinities, since that's what we'd see today as we read each other's auras.

Ben rested his chin on his palm, gazing at me steadily. "Your aura is purple smoke, about an inch thick. That was easy," he remarked.

I had a harder time and ended up staring at him far longer than was polite. His expression turned to an amused smirk. "It's not funny. I usually can't do this on command," I muttered.

"It's okay to admire," he replied with an exaggerated flip of his hair. "Maybe it'll help to know that not every aura is purely one color, too. It depends on the individual, how strong their magic is, and how long they've been practicing."

"Been a...guardian a while?" I asked, finally seeing an aura raising off his skin. Patterns of spiky crystals mixed in with the brownish smoke in his aura, and only the geode tips were the neon green I was supposed to look for. It rose a good two inches around him, which implied powerful or active magic according to the chart Dr. Heartwood was displaying.

He shrugged. "Long enough to know how to do this already."

I twisted my lips. "Sounds a lot like two of my friends. Already from established witch families. One even had her magic for years, but she had to take this class anyway."

My shoulders sagged. I missed Lanie so much in that moment.

Ben eyed me for a moment, wetting his lips to speak. That was when Dr. Heartwood announced that we should change partners with someone else.

I ended up reading the auras of several other witches and saw more of what I was expecting. Roe's aura was prickly and bright green, the color complimenting her complexion. Willow had an interesting one, hers an icy blue that writhed like waves in the ocean. Compared to Heath, the other oceanic affinity in our coven, hers was chaotic, while his was a deep blue and placid.

"Maybe you're really strong," I told her.

She ducked her shoulders. "I don't know. I haven't cast any magic successfully yet," she murmured.

My last partner of the day ended up being Wren, and I suppressed a sound of dismay. Her aura was blinding, three inches of pure rays of sunlight. She smirked as she looked me over. "Pretty weak, Cress."

I clamped my jaw on suggesting that she had the strongest magic out of any of the witches I'd seen today. She didn't need a bigger head.

We soon returned to our original seats, and I realized I hadn't done a thing to convince Ben who to vote for tonight for coven leader. With Wren just a seat away, waiting with barely concealed fangs, I waited for class to dismiss and caught his eye.

He jerked his chin in acknowledgment, staying in his seat as the majority of the class filed out. "I just wanted to say welcome to the coven, such as it is," I said. "Are you coming to the meeting tonight?"

"Wouldn't miss it," he said, flashing a brief smile.

"Great, because we're supposed to vote on a leader tonight…"

I drifted off when he held up a hand. "I wouldn't miss it *because* I want to spend more time with you," he said.

"Oh." A little tinge of color lit my cheeks.

"When's your next class? Maybe we could grab a coffee," he offered.

"Not for, uh…" I considered if I wanted to admit I wasn't going to any of my other classes. It'd lead to more questions than I wanted to answer, and I was going to find the experienced librarian witch Hana Graygazer told me to seek out. "...a couple hours."

"Well then." He hopped to his feet and offered me a hand up. "Show me the way."

I led the way out of the classroom. "How new are you to NSU?"

"Got here Monday. Just in time to miss the scare, apparently."

I nearly stumbled over my two feet. "Yeah," I muttered. An innocent witch had been murdered. Of course that would scare everyone on campus.

"They say it was a rogue blood witch." He fitted his hands in his pockets casually. "To think someone like that happened in a place as safe as NSU."

Well, the university was lying, but I wasn't about to tell him that. The fewer people who snooped into the details of that night, the better, as far as I was concerned. I'd seen a couple witches patrolling the campus on my way here, silver swords drawn. Someone in charge knew who they were really looking for.

I stepped outside and nearly stopped short upon seeing sunlight reflected off Geo's obsidian skin. I turned to Ben, who eyed the gargoyle with a raised brow. "I forgot to tell you. I have a bodyguard now," I said.

Geo lifted himself out of a hunched posture. "You are early," he rumbled.

"Just going on a coffee break. You don't have to come with. It'll be fine," I said.

The gargoyle looked down at me without blinking. "You are my duty. Where you go, I follow."

I glanced at Ben with a shrug. He echoed the motion. "It's not every day I meet someone important enough to have a gargoyle bodyguard." He smirked over my head at Geo.

I told myself I'd need to get used to this as Geo trailed a few steps behind Ben and me. Until Phaeron was dead, I needed protection anyway. "His name's Geo," I supplied.

"Is that short for anything?" Ben asked.

"No," came the grinding response behind me.

"Really?" the male witch glanced over his shoulder.

"Yes."

"It's not Geology or something?"

"My response to this line of inquiry shall remain the same."

Ben whistled under his breath. "Well, anyway." He directed his attention back to me. "The library obviously wants to protect you. I'm sorry for your loss, by the way. Wren told me what happened."

"Of course she did," I muttered, my hands forming fists.

"You know how legacy witches are." He rolled his eyes. "Her daddy's got money, so she thinks she can trod on no-names like us."

I cast a curious glance aside at him. "From what I can tell, most witches have some kind of legacy."

"Not me. You?"

"Same."

He offered a fist bump to that. I pressed my fingers to his before gesturing him into the campus coffee shop. Geo took up a post just outside the doors. Ben took my order and stood in line, if I would just find us a good spot. I picked a table by a window, just within sight of Geo. Though I doubted the gargoyle could experience anxiety, I didn't want to make his "duty" any more difficult.

A giddy laugh bubbled in my throat. I couldn't believe I was actually on a coffee date with a handsome guy. Carly would eat the news of this up—

My heart sank, and I fished my phone out, powering it up. I hadn't spoken to Carly or Mom since the weekend, and my device had a seizure in my hold as it buzzed continuously with messages and voice-mails, most of which were from Carly or Roe.

"I'm fine. Talk later?" I texted Carly after skimming a line of messages from her. She thought I was angry with her. If only she knew what rollercoaster of emotion I was still on.

I put the phone away as Ben came over with two steaming cups. "Extra sugar for you," he said, passing me my white chocolate mocha.

"Black for you?" I asked with a chuckle.

"Nah. Extra extra sugar for me." He took the top off to show the light brown color of his coffee. It looked good, actually.

"So, about the meeting tonight. It's down to Wren or Roe," I said.

Ben glanced down at his drink with a slant of his lips. "I'll vote however you like. I have little stake in how it turns out," he said with a careless wave.

"Then you should vote for Roe," I said.

"Fine, you got it."

I breathed a sigh of relief while he took a cautious first sip of coffee. "So, why did you transfer to NSU?" I asked before the pause between us could get too awkward.

"I came from SSU. It's down in Texas. I got tired of burning up in hundred-degree weather."

I laughed briefly. "You're a sophomore, then?"

He shrugged. "I'm not the best student, so it's more like I'm a bonus freshman."

That would explain why he was still taking an introductory class.

He started asking questions about how I'd gotten here, and I ended up telling him my story. How I'd only known I was a witch when I met my familiars, Milo and Bella. "Being here is a dream come true. Mostly." I couldn't help a bit of bitterness with how I'd nearly ruined it within a few weeks of arriving.

"Mostly?" he echoed.

"Well, you know, my roommate..." I bit my lip, feeling my eyes well immediately. It was way too soon to talk about Lanie so casually. "And I'm afraid whatever got her is still after me."

Understanding sparkled in his green eyes. "Yeah. But the library sent you that gargoyle out there." He hitched his thumb in Geo's direction.

I glanced over my shoulder, where Geo was still slouched and waiting. "I don't really know what's up with him. It sounded more like he sent himself," I admitted.

"Hmm." He tilted his head in consideration. "It sounds like you haven't experienced the best part of being a supernatural."

"Yeah?" A slight smile lit my face.

"The shows! Real magic and sometimes, real monsters. You have to know how to access them."

"Good thing I know a guy, huh?" I offered tentatively, a sprinkling of butterflies in my belly when he snapped his fingers and pointed.

"Exactly. You're going to be so happy we met."

12

CRESS

A FEW HOURS LATER, I was beaming as I headed back up the road toward the Voidbinder Building with Geo.

Of course, he had to dump cold water on my happiness immediately. "I do not trust that boy."

"He was a nice guy," I argued, flashing an annoyed look his way.

"You are my duty. I would not lie. He does not have good intentions," he stated.

"How would you know?" I muttered. It wasn't like the gargoyle had done anything but watched Ben and I chat for hours.

"Some things, I sense. Ignore if you wish. You will know I am right someday."

I glanced away, resisting the urge to roll my eyes. "I have to catch a professor," I told him, breezing into the Voidbinder Building to look for a man with its namesake. Geo didn't follow, instead dutifully keeping watch at the door.

I stomped my way to the second floor and started scanning the signs outside each professor's door. I'd identified the man I was looking for as a professor for advanced librarian students who wanted to actually make their magic a profession. To my surprise, his door was ajar when I found his office.

"Good afternoon," he said, not glancing up from his computer screen when I knocked on the door. "Office hours will have to wait, I'm afraid. Very important business in the library."

"Dr. Voidbinder?" I said.

He glanced over his shoulder, seeming annoyed that I hadn't left yet. "Yes?"

"I was hoping you could help me. My friend, uh..." I gritted my teeth, forcing the words out before I could get emotional. "She was killed by a dimensional a few days ago."

In a blink, he was on his feet and dragging me into his office. He slammed the door after him. "You can't go saying that in public," he hissed.

I stared at him owlishly, not expecting such a spry reaction from a man who looked like he'd abandoned the gym years ago. He had a middle age paunch, and sweat sheened his shiny head where scalp peeked out between thinning strands of hair.

"I'm sorry?" I asked.

He took a deep breath and looked me over more closely. "Please, have a seat, Miss...?"

"Cress," I supplied. I sat where he indicated, in the armpit of his tiny office. At least it was a comfortable nook.

"Nice to meet you, Cress. I didn't know your name, but I know *of* you. Don't get too nervous, but..." His weight hit his swivel chair, and it creaked in complaint. "You must understand that the murder you witnessed is a sensitive matter."

My eyes narrowed. "Mmm."

He sighed deeply. "The university is not sharing specific details in the case for a reason. Can you imagine the panic if we shared that a dimensional creature is loose somewhere on campus?"

"Maybe you *should*, because it's the truth," I snipped.

His watery brown eyes fixed on me with a serious expression. "Dr. Aurina wanted to meet you personally if I caught any hint that you were talking about what you really saw."

Ice snuck its way up my spine. "What? Why?" I asked quietly.

"We have the situation under control, Miss Cress. You must have faith in the librarians that run Moongrove Library."

"But—" I nearly blurted out more than I meant to and bit off the words with effort. With a furious heave of my lungs, I regrouped and said, "That dimensional was coming after *me*. My roommate sacrificed herself because she was an augur. She saw that any other victim would've been consumed, body and soul. Thanks to the circumstances, she only lost her life. Can you sleep at night, knowing a soul-eating monster is out there, free to strike again?"

"I'm sorry for your loss," he said carefully. "I will need to call for the University President if you speak out more."

"To expel me?" I asked.

"No. To make you compliant."

An uncomfortable prickle of goosebumps raised on my arms. "With her magic. Right."

A pitying look started to form on his expression. I blurted out before he could dismiss me. "I want to help. I have a gargoyle but no way to fight alongside him."

His lips parted with shock, jaw hanging for a few seconds. "The Quartz Gargoyle?" he asked.

"Yeah. Geo. He said I was his duty."

"No way," he said under his breath. "Young lady, do you know how remarkable that is? The Quartz Gargoyle was asleep for nearly a hundred years. Most of our original gargoyles have either lived out a mortal life or gone permanently dormant."

I debated replying and ended up with an indecisive nibble of my bottom lip. He nodded and continued, "Of course not. You're practically a baby in librarian terms. A page, even, as Lars says. Come, there's something you should see." He heaved himself to his feet, and I came with him.

We entered an empty classroom, and he drew me to the far wall. "The last gargoyles were created at the end of the era of demigods. The practice came under increased scrutiny and was eventually deemed to be barbaric. Do you know what animates the Quartz Gargoyle? Has he told you?"

"No," I admitted.

"Sometime in the nineteenth century, we lost one of our last witch demigoddesses, the librarian Morgana Voidbinder. And yes, she and I are related. The building we're in was named after her and her sacrifice," he said, stopping short and gesturing to a painting hanging on the wall. It was a diminutive square covered in a layer of protective glass to save it from the touch of grubby hands.

Dozens of similar paintings decorated the wall of this classroom, but Morgana Voidbinder's was first. I scanned the labels under each and realized this was a gallery of demigod and demigoddess witches.

Morgana's portrait depicted a pale, raven-haired beauty with a mysterious curve to her rich red lips. She was posed with a leather-bound book in one hand and a silver sword in the other, her gown floor-length scarlet velvet with a slit showing her leg up to the knee. The glow thrown off her weapon illuminated the silhouettes of several horned figures kneeling before her.

I leaned in to read the little biography engraved on a plaque under her portrait.

Morgana was one of the longest-lived witch demigoddesses in recorded history. She was the first witch to discover the librarian affinity and established the guidelines for witches to create and tap dimensional powercores. It was because of her diplomacy that dimensional travelers became an accepted supernatural race and ally to witchkind. We honor her to this day for her many sacrifices, including the one that led to her untimely death in 1812 to permanently seal away an unkillable dimensional monster. Her soul elected to continue its service to mankind as the Quartz Gargoyle.

I straightened and inspected the portrait of her again with new respect. With a gasp, I pointed at one of the kneeling dimensionals. "That's him," I said, recognizing Phaeron's curled horns.

Dr. Voidbinder bent to squint at the figure. "I saw this dimensional a few nights ago," I continued in a whisper.

"Well, that would explain why the Quartz Gargoyle has returned. If he is truly targeting you...then Morgana's soul sensed it. The dimensional that attacked your friend is the same one Morgana gave her life to seal in Moongrove Library." His Adam's apple bobbed in a nervous swallow. "An evil creature that followed the dimensional travelers to Earth."

"So, Geo is actually this demigoddess?" I asked.

He sighed, shaking his head. "If only he were. We need the power of an experienced demigoddess librarian more than ever now that the Hungering Darkness is free. Geo is his own person, given life by

Morgana's choice. He is more a memorial to her than anything, but you may be lucky enough to catch peeks of her through him."

"That's...wild," I admitted. Maybe she could help me fix my huge mistake.

"One reason of many our kind eventually outlawed the creation of new gargoyles," he said.

I straightened and turned to him, taking a deep breath to gather my nerve. If this demigoddess died to lock Phaeron away, then I knew I had no chance when he came to kill me. "Dr. Voidbinder, please. I need to know how to fight back if he returns. With Geo protecting me, you know Morgana's soul expects it."

His plump lips pinched as he considered. "You will still have to attend all your classes."

"Of course," I hurried to say.

"And pass them."

I nodded rapidly.

"I could tutor you in the evenings. But you do not tell anyone what you really saw the other night." He gave me a stern look when I continued nodding in agreement.

"I promise. I'll be the best pupil you've ever had," I said. "Just teach me how to put a silver sword through the bastard's face."

"Heart. They play by vampire rules. Only a strike to the heart is immediately fatal," he corrected.

"The heart, then."

We negotiated the time and place, floor negative two at eight in the evening every weekday. Except today, of course. I still needed to get Roe elected as leader of my coven.

My coven met in a building Roe had to lead me to, uncreatively called the Witch Clubhouse. I texted directions to Ben, who sent me a couple questions when he got lost too. I felt bad for him, getting roped into extra meetings when he'd just gotten here.

And yes, I was smiling down at my phone like a loon when his name popped up on my screen. We'd exchanged numbers earlier, and I'd already tentatively put a heart next to his name. After spending most of the afternoon chatting with him, it just felt right.

The clubhouse was for coven meetings, I learned, which were apparently expected on a regular basis. It was a four-story building with several small but cozy rooms, and as freshmen, we were assigned a place in the top floor with well-loved couches and scuffed floors, but I took a look around and decided it was comfortable enough. It had a minifridge and microwave, plus a couple desks to work at. I could see myself studying here when I wanted to be social.

Implying I ever wanted to be social.

I arrived to see Wren and Heath had already claimed the couch and Willow had found a comfortable corner to settle, where her presence was hidden by the shadow of the couch. Her hand shot out of nowhere to wave, and Heath nodded before turning his attention back to Wren.

Ben and Grant came in at about the same time. The latter sat alone, as far from the rest of as possible, while Ben turned around a chair and straddled it next to me. "Hey. Miss me?" he asked, flashing a toothy grin.

I rolled my eyes playfully. "Definitely."

"Did you have a good day? For real."

We were mid-chat when Roe came in, announcing herself with a loud, "Hello, friends!"

"Late, as always," Wren answered with a low *tsk*, inspecting her pristinely manicured nails.

"Who's ready to vote for me as our leader?" Roe continued, unperturbed.

"Let's give Yasmin a minute to get here," Heath said with a low chuckle.

I wracked my brain for who Yasmin was. It'd been a long few days, but when the dark-haired upperclassman walked in, I remembered that she was our guide to setting up our coven and making it run smoothly.

"Hello, everyone. How're we doing?" Yasmin asked as she planted herself in the middle of the space like a teacher warming up a class of students.

I certainly felt the mix of interest and disillusionment like we were back in high school. Where Roe vibrated with eagerness, Grant slouched in his seat and stared off into space. Maybe he was high or something.

Instead of paying attention, Ben was looking at me. I ended up being the one to answer the upperclassman's question. "Good. It's been...a good day." I felt my gaze shift to Ben as I said it, a little flutter of butterflies starting in my belly.

He flashed one of his sideways smiles like he knew exactly the kind of effect he had on me. Maybe when a guy had the kind of leonine beauty Ben gave off with ease, drawing a blush and fumble from a gal like me was completely normal.

I didn't have a boyfriend back home, and before I dyed my hair purple and learned I was a supernatural, there was nothing about my bookish and sullen self that had turned heads.

But I was a librarian witch now and destined to slay the beast that'd taken Lanie away, with the help of not one, but three men who had feelings for me. Maybe one of them would be Ben. Perhaps I should embrace the excited but nervous feeling that buzzed in my belly every time our eyes met.

Ben blinked, and I realized Yasmin was talking. "...vote this evening. Now, who's ready?" I'd completely blanked out whatever else she'd just said.

"Must we have speeches?" Ben asked on a sigh as Wren stood.

"It's like you took the words out of my mouth," I murmured.

He checked his phone while Wren spoke, neither of us particularly paying attention. "I have maybe an hour," he said.

"Yeah?"

Some quick expression flickered over his face. "Yeah...just getting settled and all."

I toyed with a lock of my hair. "Well, I'm glad you could come," I said.

For a moment, his expression relaxed. Something sad swirled in the depths of his evergreen eyes. He wetted his lips, glancing away. "Me too," he answered quietly.

A smattering of applause told me Wren was done. Roe replaced her, and I turned my attention toward my friend. Her speech told me I knew very little of what a coven actually did, as she spoke of old rituals and named a few traditional holidays like Mabon and Samhain that she wanted to celebrate.

She promised the kind of things that stirred the aching heart in my chest: friendship and togetherness, forging the kind of bonds that were like a family.

When the time came to vote, Roe won four to three. She shook her fists over her head and whooped like she'd taken home a huge trophy, not a lukewarm vote that I didn't think many of the guys cared about.

"Now we need a name," Roe said, and inwardly I groaned. "Every good coven has a name."

"Give me some time for that one," I suggested. There was hearty agreement at last for something, so we put off the idea of a name and relaxed. Willow discovered sodas and juice in the mini fridge, so we treated it like a little party.

I did what I did best at parties, staying in one place. Ben sipped his soda and didn't move either. He checked his phone every couple of minutes.

"That's my brother," he told me after catching me glancing at his phone with him the fourth time.

It took me a moment to realize he was talking about the picture on his screen. It was a sideways shot of Ben and another guy smiling at the camera. Ben let me get a good look, his gaze on me rather than the device's screen.

"He looks just like you." I laughed. "Twins?"

"Please. He's four years younger than me. Still piles all his hair on his head like that too."

It wasn't a bad look, I thought, but I much preferred how Ben wore his down to his shoulders. After my first glance, I realized his brother had a rounder, softer face, despite sharing the same striking green eyes. He had an almost goofy, carefree air in the photo, and Ben...

Well, he looked happier on that screen than in any of the sideways smiles I'd seen from him today. It was subtle, though. I hadn't realized Ben was carrying an invisible sadness, maybe because I was still dragging my own grief behind me everywhere I went.

"He's, uh, missing," Ben blurted.

"Missing?" I echoed.

He sighed, holding his forehead. "Like, he left our house a couple weeks ago and didn't come back. I'm still looking for him."

"Is that why you transferred here?" I asked.

"Yeah. My, uh, family lives close by. I wanted to get away for, like, college." He took a shaky breath and collected himself. "But Lucas means so much to me. It'd be like ripping my heart out if anything happened to him."

Sorrow gripped me as I nodded along. No wonder he needed to leave so soon. If it were me, I wouldn't have come to this meeting. "I'd feel the same way if it were my sister," I said. "I hope you find him soon. Is there magic you can use to track him?"

He sighed. "If only." With one last check of his phone, he stood and placed his drink aside. "I'd better go."

I followed him out, and he turned to me on the sidewalk outside the busy clubhouse. "Do you want a hug?" I offered, suddenly self-conscious. I'd just met Ben; maybe he didn't want me following him like this.

I felt like I understood the weight of his uncertainty, though. In a world still bright and merry, it'd felt like everyone moved on from Lanie like her murder was a bad dream. But I still felt her loss, and it was obvious Ben was worried about the unresolved situation with his brother.

He didn't hesitate or overthink like I was doing. Within a couple steps, he swept me into his arms and rested his chin atop my head. For a few moments, my mind eased its constant stream of thought and I drifted, safe in his hold.

"I'll see you later, all right?" he murmured.

"Yeah. Good luck. I know you'll find him," I said quietly.

He released me, but not before placing a swift kiss to my cheek. "Stay safe," he said before disappearing into the night.

I watched him go, releasing a breathy laugh as I touched my fingertips to my face.

13
BEN

I'D BROKEN MORE than one of Master Garroway's core rules within the last twelve hours.

The first, never get to know your victims. Now when I thought of Cress, I didn't see my brother's latest mark, but a person with an unhappy smile and half-formed dreams of a future as a fashion designer for supernaturals. Someone who often looked over her shoulder in a crowded room. A woman with wide brown eyes that held an ocean of unspoken thoughts.

She was no longer "the Darkmore girl" to me. I'd opened myself up to the kind of pain unique to a witch trapped in my profession. Because if my brother lived, he would kill her, and all I'd have afterward would be the haunting strain of her shy laughter in my ears.

Shit, I was a mess. I paused somewhere in between pocket dimensions, holding my head in the darkness between streetlamps.

This isn't what's going to get you killed tonight, I told myself. *Cress is probably fine right now. She has a bodyguard and everything.*

I had no such benefit going back into the spider's parlor. Garroway strictly prohibited his blood witches from heading out without permission. Some of my fellows, like Bianca and Seth, lived for the freedom of missions. They charged out of the manor like rabid dogs let off the chain.

As I looked for Lucas, it'd occurred to me that it was possible he was out enjoying one of his first tastes of the outside world. If so, why wasn't he answering my calls and texts?

The only answer I came home with was that Cress, my only lead, had no idea who Lucas was. No matter how I'd phrased the questions and framed the conversation, she had no information of note about him. And after three days of independent searching and scouting, I had found nothing at all.

I was a failure of a brother. Unless Bianca succeeded in her promise to distract our vampire master, I would also have my head smashed into a wall for my defiance of a core rule.

I slumped my way home until my fingers were millimeters from activating the trigger to allow me to enter the manor's pocket dimension. *Better go into this with some pride.* I squared my sagging shoulders and straightened my spine, fixing a serious expression on my face to mask the nerves making my palms sweat.

Slipping into the stretch of space hiding in plain sight, I crossed the immaculate lawn and tried the back door. It was unlocked. I breathed a thanks to Bianca before soundlessly gliding it open and creeping beyond the threshold. Closing the door after me, I cast my gaze around and took the first steps that would take me to a relieved face-plant on my bed.

"Benjamin."

I froze mid-stride, my head whipping to the left. The breakfast nook was concealed in shadow with the curtains drawn over the bay windows, and hidden within the darkness was my vampire master. Now that I knew he was there, I could spot his blood-red eyes peering back at me.

"Where were you, boy?" He didn't sound angry, but that could change in moments. I'd walked straight into his trap, after all, ensnared by a simple question.

"I..." had no cover story. I hadn't bought anything to bring home with me, and he'd caught me in the middle of trying to sneak in anyway.

If I mentioned Cress and her coven, he'd know I was trying to interfere with Lucas's mission.

If I talked about Lucas directly, I'd confirm what he already knew.

Not knowing if my brother was okay was torture. And I had no doubt he was already aware of it.

Over the years, I'd convinced myself that Master Garroway got his sustenance through feeding on the pain of others. He made a show out of holding glasses of blood often enough, but I'd never seen him take a drink. Even now, he had to be sucking in the despair that wafted from me at being caught with no prepared excuse.

I decided not to draw this out when he looked at me like I was a full-course buffet. "I was looking for Lucas, Master," I answered.

"Ah, little Lucas comes up again." Garroway tapped his palms together, turning on several lights. I winced, not prepared for the sudden glare coming off the polished marble table that separated us. Or for the sight of the pitch-black knife resting in front of the vampire.

Two inches long at most, the blade was darker than the deepest night and inspired a shock of fear more potent than if the lights turned on to reveal Garroway pointing a loaded gun in my direction.

I swallowed audibly. "Master, I can explain—"

He closed his hand around the hilt of the tiny weapon, giving the aged leather a squeeze. He activated its magic with a murmured word, something like "*duratus*," though once the blood rune on my chest activated, all I really heard was the hiss of air as my skin sizzled.

The magic forced me to take a ready stance, my arms pointed downward to form a capital A, my legs locked and back rigid. Crimson light leaked from under my shirt in the circular shape of the rune burning against the skin over my right ribcage like a fresh brand.

Garroway stood leisurely and circled my frozen form with a soft noise of contempt. "I told you not to interfere with little Lucas's first mission," he said. The slow, precise way he spoke was extra torture as the activated blood rune seemed to burrow deeper into my flesh with each throb of my heart.

"But you've never been good at taking directions. An unfortunate trait your brother learned from you." We stood nose to nose, and even in my frozen state, I saw the pleasure creasing his mouth and eyes. My hopes for mercy blew away on a red-stained wind.

"Never forget, Benjamin. I *own* you. I bought you from your sniveling excuse of a mother, raised you by hand into the elite ranks of my witches."

I swallowed again, the only reaction I could form. He'd carved the blood rune into me by hand, too, and shared that he'd paid the incredible sum of five million to my parents for no discernable purpose. I could only assume they wanted the chance to *not* have to raise Lucas and me. I'd been four, and my little brother, a newborn.

"Now you think you can sneak away?" Garroway wagged a finger. "There's no escape for you out there, little Benjamin. Nor for you brother. He will return eventually, even if he fails his mission."

I blinked slowly. Could it be possible...?

"That's right. I didn't give Lucas a deadline."

Damn. I was a fool. Without a deadline, Lucas probably turned off his phone and slummed it far from here. It was what I would've done on my first mission, had I not had a little brother back here to protect. None of us knew if the blood rune had a maximum distance. If Lucas got far enough away, maybe he could resist the call of the magic carved in his chest.

He could never return, his old phone disposed of, his life ripe to be lived without the restrictions of Master Garroway. But...he'd left without *me*. He'd cut and run without a backward glance.

As it sank in, the vampire's grin widened. "Imagine. Years from now, I will bring him clawing and begging back here. What do you think I should do to him if he runs for that long?"

With a gesture, he unlocked my jaw. "You'd put a deadline on the original mission," I suggested, hesitant. I knew this game too well. If I offered an over-the-top, bloodthirsty punishment, sometimes I'd override whatever he was actually planning. That was how I'd gotten Bianca lashed with a whip until she passed out from blood loss once. I don't think she's ever fully forgiven me for it.

"That's hardly a punishment," he purred. "Maybe I should sever his fingers and toes, one for every month he tried to hide from my service. Do you think that would fit his crime?"

"Y-yes, Master." If I didn't agree, he'd suggest something worse.

That must've been too easy for him, though. He ran a hand down his jawline, humming. "Or perhaps you should take his punishments for him. That is your preference, isn't it?" His tone took a mocking edge. "The noble big brother, shielding his innocent kid sibling from the big, bad vampire. Let's see how much you love him after this."

I kept my mouth closed as he waited for a reaction, for begging. It wouldn't do any good. If he wanted to punish me, he would, and if he wanted to bring Lucas back to discipline him, he could at any time. I wouldn't let him taint the last bit of family I had.

Garroway's face slanted, boredom etched in each ancient line of his face. My heart stuttered to a near-stop as I recognized that look. I was no longer an interesting plaything to help him chase off the ennui of his existence. "You will stay in the manor for the next two weeks. Your toes will not even graze a blade of grass on the lawn," he instructed, holding up the black knife to weave his will into the blood rune.

My heart sank. Two weeks was an eternity, especially when it was only a matter of time before my deception at NSU was discovered when I didn't hit its official database as a student.

"After that time, perhaps I will consider you to be the errand boy for the manor. You will not go on missions until further notice, however. And now for your punishment."

He considered me for a few moments before weaving a rune midair with the point of the knife. I watched him trace the witch rune for agony and braced myself as the crimson magic of the blood rune ran through my veins, lighting me up from the inside-out with magical fire.

My body lit with pain from crown to toes, burning brighter and deeper as the magic rooted into muscle and bone. Seconds dragged into eternity as I started screaming. If he held this spell for too long, it'd turn into his favorite form of execution, a boiling of my blood and innards.

I swear I burnt to a cinder as my vision hazed with crimson light, tears and blood mingling to trace a river of pain down my face. Through it all, I sensed the master's presence, a too-close shadow drinking in every moment of my suffering.

He did release me eventually but didn't catch my limp body as it crashed to the ground in a boneless tumble. My crisped innards gave one last spasm, one that dragged me into black unconsciousness.

A FEATHERLIGHT FINGERTIP drew marks along the skin on my face. A moan stuck in my dry throat, and my eyelids were too swollen to open. On and on someone painted the same three-lined mark on my cheeks, upper and lower lip, nose, and forehead. Tiny runes of healing.

Relief radiated slowly from each rune as my blood witchery went to work repairing the damaged veins and charred muscles left behind from Garroway's agony spell.

A firm hand closed around my shoulder, drawing a hoarse shout from me as pain spiked deep under my skin. "Hold still," Seth said gruffly.

I relaxed as best as I could, giving silent thanks that it was the experienced male witch tending to me, not Bianca. Cool wind chafed over my skin. I was probably stripped to my boxers, with huge healing runes over my chest, arms, and thighs, while Seth worked on the smaller and more delicate sections of my body with care.

"Surprised you're still breathing." Straight to the point, as always. It was more of a shock that *Seth* of all the blood witches in Garroway's coven was tending to me now. He didn't need bedside manners when he was the prized assassin and the longest surviving of all of us.

"That bad?" I croaked.

A cool lip of plastic pressed to my lips. I swallowed some of the watery energy drink, knowing it had to be terrible if Seth was giving me electrolytes directly upon waking.

"The master wouldn't let anyone approach you for three days."

I almost spluttered a whole mouthful of liquid over him. Swallowing wrong and immediately choking, I tried to sit up. He forced me back down onto the bed I rested on, maintaining that hold as I struggled to breathe amidst the deep throb of pain in my chest. "Is...Lucas?" I asked between coughs.

"Still missing," he said curtly.

I nodded, letting him go back to painting runes on me. I cracked open my eyes, letting the world come slowly into focus as my damaged eyes healed themselves. Blood witchery made us nearly invincible, but this wasn't the first time I'd woken near death in the infirmary with someone else painting runes on me with my own blood.

My blood affinity meant Garroway had more of my delicious despair to feed on, too. It sank in as I lay there, healing. I couldn't leave to search for Lucas for two weeks, enough time for him to truly disappear off the face of the earth.

The only plus was that Garroway had tipped his hand about why Cress was unscathed. If I could convince her to skip town, maybe she would escape the plotting of Garroway and Starsurge after all, free to live her life without someone waiting in the shadows to end her life.

Deadlines were carved into our flesh just like the blood runes. If I had the strength to sit up, I would see the perfect circle of the rune on my right ribcage, plus a few black lines rising from it, pointed straight at my heart. Garroway made it a rite of passage to inflict new blood witches with a week-long deadline so we'd know what it felt like.

That line stopped just millimeters from my heart, a stark reminder against my skin every time I took my shirt off. Deadlines were slow agony spells, and to have one so close to my heart had felt a lot like the white-hot pain of the spell that'd dropped me unconscious for several days. If we failed at a mission or didn't complete it in time, we'd die, simple as that.

The only other way to survive a missed deadline was Master Garroway's mercy. And he had little of it.

"Seth," I rasped. I rolled my head to look at him. His salt-and-pepper hair was still fuzzy around the edges to my damaged sight, and the serious lines of his face seemed taut with fury as he took care of me.

He asked quietly, "Yes?"

I noted the sunlight streaming into the room. Only with Garroway resting would I dare to mention this subject. "You were the one sent on the Darkmore job, right?"

"Yeah."

"Is she...Cress...could she really be...?"

Seth sighed deeply. "The master ordered me to take care of the Darkmore family. That was the wording. So, I did."

A meaningful pause passed between us. Seth had been the one to teach me what being a blood witch really meant and how to interpret orders such as this. "Taking care of" something had several meanings.

"I killed the adults. I did my job," he said, a small catch to his usual baritone. "But the baby...she was so tiny and innocent."

I was still as he finished painting healing runes on my feet. He stood abruptly and went to the sink to wash his hands, putting his back between us like a barrier.

Well, shit. Cress may seriously be who Blaize Starsurge thought she was. If she lived long enough to access the well of hereditary magic every established witch family curated, there was a chance she could tap her deceased parents' memories. It wasn't just paranoia encouraging him to have her killed. If she knew what to do with the information, she could ruin his political career with a long overdue murder trial.

And I couldn't tell her a thing, because the blood rune on my chest would kill me painfully for sharing one of Garroway's secrets. *Fuck.*

"What did you do with her instead?" I murmured.

"I surrendered her to a local hospital." One of his shoulders lifted, but he didn't turn back to face me. "That's all I know. I never expected her to come back up or for Starsurge to identify her if she did."

"Of course."

Finally, he came back to my bedside. I tried not to stare at the broken expression on his face. This wasn't the solid assassin that Garroway sent without hesitation on the nastiest and most dangerous missions. "There are some things you don't do," he said. "And I draw the line at killing children."

"Principles. I remember."

In place of a father talking about the birds and the bees, I'd had Seth to take me aside and talk about principles. The lines we didn't cross unless we had to, as the puppets to a vampire master who delighted in our pain. I had no doubt that saving Cress was a glimpse of salvation for my mentor.

"I wanted a moment with you for a different reason," he said, regaining the stony expression he always wore like armor. "I suspect Lucas is in a different sort of trouble than you expect."

"Do you have a lead?" I asked. My heart immediately went into a hopeful double-time.

He gave a stiff nod. "I believe I saw him a few days ago—"

"Where?" I burst out, then regretted it as pain stirred deep in my chest.

Seth's frown deepened. "In New Salem. I only caught a glimpse of him, but he ran when I called his name. I followed and lost him around a corner. But I wanted to let you know, since the master is sure Lucas ran away."

I shook my head slowly. "Why would he run from you?" I asked.

Seth was practically my brother's idol, on the surface everything a dutiful blood witch assassin should be. If he was having trouble with his mark, he should've been falling over himself to ask Seth for advice.

"I've seen something like it before," he said slowly. "One of our brothers was caught right after completing a mission. His blood rune was altered with a second knife like the master's. He completed several high-profile assassinations before being captured and put on trial for his crimes. I remember him running from me, just like Lucas did. His rune compelled him to avoid everything from his life here, so he could not return to the master."

I turned over his words silently. I hadn't known that it was possible for someone else to change our blood runes and thus our allegiance. Garroway, at least, valued us when we were a resource to keep him rich and influential. "His life was thrown away," I said thoughtfully.

"It happens." He sighed, patting my shoulder gently. "I'm sorry, Ben. We won't know if it happened for sure unless he's compelled to kill someone else. If it's the Darkmore girl, we can be assured Lucas will return to us. But if it's anyone else, especially someone of political importance…"

I shut my eyes tightly, imagining what would happen if Lucas committed even one more sloppy kill. The SPDI would have him in the electric chair before I had permission to leave this manor again.

Something cold nudged my fingers. "This has been vibrating constantly. Any messages from Lucas?" Seth asked.

I took my phone from him, unlocking it with a glance and scanning the list of missed calls and messages. Most of them were from an unfamiliar number, and after listening to one message, I learned the unknown caller was Roe checking on me out of obligation as a concerned coven leader.

The rest of the notifications were from Cress. I shook my head up at Seth, who left me to heal and mull over my brother's uncertain fate. What could I do to save him from here?

I scrolled Cress's messages first, going back three days. She hadn't gotten angry or passive-aggressive with my long silence, only expressing concern for me and my brother in her last message…dated yesterday, the Friday we were supposed to have another class together.

I smiled to myself, feeling a little less alone in that moment. Which was stupid, really, for a list of reasons too long to count. I was the last person she should be sending sweet messages to, and I had a responsibility to somehow tell her to watch her back without getting myself killed by my blood rune.

However, she'd think I was crazy if I came out of nowhere saying, "Hi, change your name and leave Salem. Never come back." We'd work up to that.

So instead, I texted her a simple hey and rested my eyes.

My phone buzzed immediately. "Hi. You're back!" she'd texted.

My lips tugged. For better or worse, I was indeed back.

14
GEO

Time passed, and I did my duty. Cress was safe with me as we went class to class, day by day. She grew stronger in the evenings, her aura bolstered with librarian witch power after every private training session with Callum Voidbinder.

The library was the only place I was welcome to tromp into, so I watched Cress practice and practice and practice. She was given a wooden sword to use for now, much to her chagrin, until she was proficient with the basics of how to swing and block with it. I tended to let my mind turn off during these trainings, becoming a statue again in the place I felt most welcome.

There was no sign of the boy with the chameleon aura, though I suspected he was still talking to her via the little glowing box she liked to smile into. Her "cell phone," which she used to introduce me to the confusing pocket dimension called the Internet with all its jokes. Apparently, it could be used to talk to anyone, anywhere.

No matter. If he wasn't physically here, he was no danger to her.

My rock was patient. Undoubtedly, danger brewed, looming unseen. I was at my most alert at night, standing guard in the shadows of the garden outside the building where she slept.

In those moments of quiet, I asked myself whether I should let her rest and go off to find the creature she wished to slay. Was it my duty to simply watch her, or to fulfill her goal for her? The puzzle of that simple question lingered night after night, yet I didn't move to leave her.

Some part of me knew her monster would find me. And he did.

There was no warning. Just a voice echoing from the darkness. "Morgana?"

My neck ground to the left, where the voice originated. There was nothing there, just a stretch of wilting flowers wavering in a soft wind. "Identify yourself," I commanded.

"Of course you're not her." He was close, standing in the blind spot right over my shoulder. "I need to speak to my former mate, gargoyle."

I felt some foreboding from those words. "This unit may be powered by her soul, but she is not available for a discussion," I stated, trying to get him in my line of sight.

"A pity." Now he was on my other side, moving with silent speed.

I flexed my hand, manipulating the spines of pure quartz on my back. One traveled the length of my arm, its sharpened point sticking out a couple inches from my palm as I turned again, unsurprised to see that the bearer of the chilly, demanding voice was again gone. I let my opponents think I was slow and stupid purposefully, when it only took a split second to send a quartz spike through their fleshy forms.

"I will take the soul from you by force if I have to." This time, he was behind me. Claws scraped over my wing, and I held it out like a solid screen as I whirled around, spotting a crouching dimensional.

Dark hair, gray skin, curled horns, yes. The only thing about him that didn't match Cress's description were his eyes, twin pools of eerie white fire. A rumbling growl escaped his fanged maw.

"Phaeron Sudair. You are a wanted fugitive of Moongrove Library," I intoned. "I am authorized to use lethal force if you do not surrender immediately."

"Give me her soul, you misbegotten construct," he snapped. Shadows rose from his form, overlaying his arms and shaping themselves into massive, pointed talons. He leapt, crossing the space between us in a blink to impale them straight through my stone shoulder. An unfamiliar feeling echoed dully from the impossible wounds. Pain.

Were I a being of flesh and bone, the damage would be debilitating.

Instead, I cocked back my arm and fired my primed quartz spike. It grazed his neck, showering me with a spray of fuchsia blood.

He put a hand over the wound, and fury twisted his face into an animal's snarl. The shadows lining his arms became denser as I called on the five quartz spikes I had left, absorbing them back into my body.

As the magic in my body changed the extra quartz into the shape of a club, my preferred weapon, the dimensional's shadows crept up his shoulders and engulfed his head, becoming a formless knob except for a jagged maw of black teeth. The handle of my club emerged from my palm as he clamped down over my head and arm, creating dozens of pain-points where the shadows parted my craggy skin like cutting butter.

I swung at him as he tried to savage my body like a dog. Bones crunched as he endured one, two, three slams over his right side. His tail caught my wrist before I could hit him a fourth time, squeezing hard like he could make me drop the club.

He released his bite, shadows dissipating fully. One arm hung limply as he sprang off my chest with clawed feet, landing a few yards away. Gasping in pain, a rivulet of his blood stained his clothing from the neck down, darkening the bright white NSU standing out on his chest in the darkness.

"Do you surrender?" I asked. I saw the hesitation. We'd savaged each other in less than a minute, and even now, I could feel magic leaking from the wounds peppering my shoulder and chest. It looked like quicksilver, the oily magic that kept my stone animated. A dimensional of his caliber would know I grew stiffer with every moment that passed.

He held his head, shaking it rapidly, and wavered on his feet, looking moments from passing out. I waited patiently for him to drop from his injuries, but instead, he lifted his gaze and regarded me with eyes of bright yellow. His gaze flashed to the dorm behind me and then down at himself.

"Noble gargoyle," he said, dipping his chin in a bow with a clear wince. "I have never quarreled with the human practice of making your kind until today. This isn't over. Morgana betrayed me long ago by sealing me in Moongrove Library. I see her within you now. She *will* answer for what she did to me, even if I must dismantle you to get my answers."

With that, he vanished into the darkness. Defeated. I waited several long minutes before absorbing my club back into my body, letting it become the quartz spines that line my back. As I bent to retrieve the spike still coated in his unusually hued blood, a twinge of deeper pain struck my lower chest. I looked down at myself in surprise.

I must've missed him scraping his claws over my belly. The fight had begun and ended so quickly, after all. Quicksilver magic poured from the equivalent of a gut wound, and I realized the slowing in my joints was reaching a critical point. I would soon be immobilized, easy prey for the dimensional by dawn.

I absorbed my last quartz spike and lifted a few extra pebbles from the ground, turning to view the bank of windows facing the garden. There was only one person I trusted to tend to me in my weakened state. I had Cress's window memorized, but getting her attention without committing vandalism would be difficult.

With a single pebble resting in my palm, I aimed and fired it with a burst of compressed air. I was created with state-of-the-art weapons in my time, including the twin cannons in my hollow arms. They were designed to injure and maim, not toss a pebble at a woman's window. But it plinked off the glass with a sharp sound. Only a small crack resulted.

Moments later, the bottom pane lifted, and Cress stuck a disheveled head of purple hair outside, looking left to right in a daze. I waved a stiff arm up at her, fearing the shoulder joint would stick like that.

She spotted me and yelped, her head withdrawing and the window slamming after her. The minutes ticked by, and I struggled to lower my arm in the meantime.

I lumbered toward the door she always exited from, not bending my knee joints to preserve mobility. She nearly ran headlong into me. "Geo, what's wrong?" She backed away, surveying the bright silver staining my obsidian form with wide eyes.

"Assist me inside. I must take my flesh form."

She held the door for me, staring all the while. "What happened? You look really hurt."

She peppered me with questions as I bowed my head, calling on the human soul within me to facilitate the shift from rock to flesh. I'd done this so infrequently that my wings rustled and shivered with obvious discomfort before being sucked into my back, alongside the quartz spikes I'd used against Phaeron.

I staggered sideways into the stairwell's railing, hunching over as my height slimmed down and skin thinned. My hollow arms became human and solid, the trickiest part of the shift, before my stone heart started beating in earnest. It absorbed the quicksilver magic in my veins rather than dispersing it, leaving me paralyzed during this part of the transformation.

Only when I was completely a being of flesh and blood did the magic circulate again, avoiding the scrapes and punctures where I was injured. I lifted my head, trying not to flinch when soft feathers of white dreadlocks slipped down my cheeks.

Cress paused in the midst of the panic attack that'd stricken her sometime when I started shifting. Her jaw dropped. "Uh...Geo?"

"I apologize for the distress." It was easier to speak, and my voice was no longer two guttural stones clashing. "Do you have an infirmary where I may rest off my injuries?"

"I have an extra bed," she said. "That's about it."

"It will suffice."

She started scaling the stairs, going slowly as I struggled behind her. My wounds echoed pain in full definition, nearly debilitating with each step.

"What happened?" she asked more calmly, fitting herself under my armpit to help heft my weight.

Air scraped my lungs, unpleasantly wet compared to the dry breeze from my stone throat. "I shall explain," I said with effort. "Soon."

I don't know why my fellow gargoyles abandoned their duties to... this misery. It took us ten minutes to climb up to her dorm room. My mouth tasted of copper. The first actual blood my construct body produced, and I was so damaged it attempted to leak from my lips.

Furry shapes scattered when she opened her dorm room and helped me inside. She spread out a few towels for me to lie on over an otherwise bare mattress. I sat on its edge, and she helped me lie down, tucking my long legs before they could dangle over the end.

"Do not be alarmed if I leak," I told her. Her face creased, and she snorted.

"You mean bleed? Of course you're going to bleed."

"There should be very little blood," I corrected. Already, a swirl of unfamiliar feeling rose to the surface of my awareness as I lay still. I didn't like that she'd laughed. It felt mocking. In my stone form, I wouldn't care in any way. "I heal most rapidly in my flesh form. Stone does not repair like flesh, even when enchanted."

Her brow knitted. "Yeah, okay. That makes sense."

My eyelids felt like they were still solid rock, slipping down without my permission. "As you humans say." I drew in a deep breath. "You should see the other guy." Her eyes widened in surprise as I repeated the line I'd learned from one of her favorite Internet videos. I slipped into the abyss of unconsciousness on a soft sigh, knowing I was safe with her.

15

CRESS

"Girl, I don't know," Roe said from my cell as I stood over Geo's unconscious form the next morning. She was the first person I called when it was a reasonable hour. I figured if anyone knew how to tend to a gargoyle, it'd be a guardian witch.

"He's, like, alive?" she asked.

"He's breathing," I reported.

That wasn't the part that concerned me. He had several gashes over his bare chest, and each sparkled with a coating of silver liquid. It was pretty but eerie, like nothing a normal guy would have. At least he wasn't a bloody mess. Other than the pink spittle I'd cleaned from the corner of his mouth, there was no blood at all unless that's what the silver stuff was.

"Do you have any idea how I could help him?" I asked with an edge of desperation. I didn't want my gargoyle guardian to die, especially not while he lay out on Lanie's old bed.

There was a pause on her end. "I could ask one of my professors. If you wanted."

"Uh, n-no. That won't be necessary." I didn't want any authority figures at the school poking around and asking questions. Though Geo hadn't said who he'd fought, I didn't know anything capable of gouging furrows in solid rock other than my boogeyman, Phaeron. He'd had claws.

They weren't as wide as the furrows in Geo right now, but he'd still had claws.

Roe wished me good luck, and I ended the call by telling her I wouldn't be in class. Over the last two weeks, I'd worked extra hard to catch up, so it was with a bit of reluctance that I decided to stay here and make sure I was on hand to help Geo when he woke.

Still, it gave me an excuse to lie back down and rest my aching muscles. Dr. Voidbinder had me doing basic drills with a wooden version of a librarian sword Monday through Friday, saying I couldn't learn any more serious skills until I knew my weapon like it was an extension of my hand. It was clear I was out of shape, too, so I'd started going to the gym more with Roe.

I was making "great strides," though. Soon Dr. Voidbinder was going to teach me how to conduct magic down a real sword and trace witch runes with the tip. The moment I learned how to do that, I'd be officially two years ahead, with the shakiest foundational knowledge a gal could have. We hadn't even gotten to the most basic runes yet in Introduction to Witchcraft.

Ben hadn't returned to class in all this time and was likely to fail his classes soon for poor attendance. He still texted, though. I'd burned down the battery on my phone late into the night rereading his messages and reliving how they made me feel until I went to sleep with my cheeks hurting from smiling so much. I yearned to see him more and more with each day that passed.

I got by in the meantime with the support of the solid women in my life. Roe, Willow, and Áine were always around to hang out, and Mom and Carly were a phone call away. I still carried my guilt silently, unable to confide in any of them about Phaeron.

Oddly enough, the only people who knew about him were Geo, who didn't care for the details, and Dr. Voidbinder, who knew too much and could guess at my secret guilt over freeing Phaeron with one misplaced comment.

The last thing that troubled me stared at me from under Lanie's old bed. Jin's yellow eyes were accusing. I'd laid Geo down on her favorite sleeping spot, though under the bed seemed to be just fine for her too. That's where she usually retreated when I tried to go over and pet her.

She didn't want my assurances, and she *definitely* didn't want to be my familiar. I was starting to regret having her stay here when she could be free to do as she pleased with the rest of the Graygazer family.

"Let's go get some breakfast," I suggested to Milo and Bella. The boy cat was in the process of curling up next to me, while Bella watched me from the shadows under my desk, leery of the unfamiliar man in our space.

I cast one last glance over at Geo, making sure he was still breathing. He'd taken my breath away with his near angelic good looks as a human, but I couldn't find anything sexy about his injured form right now. While he was unconscious, he was off limits, so I left to go to the ground floor of my dorm and bring a big to-go box of food back up to him.

The cafeteria manager lit up when she saw my cats trailing me. I'd learned they got fed better than I did if they sought her out for some attention, so I loaded up on waffles and fruit while they became the bright spot of her day.

What did gargoyles even eat? I balanced a couple styrofoam cups of coffee and orange juice atop my box as I pondered that question. Geo hadn't eaten anything in the time he'd guarded me, but that was before he shifted into human form.

We'd find out soon, because he was awake when I got back to my dorm, his quicksilver eyes following my progression to his bedside. "Good morning. Want something to eat?" I lifted a strawberry out of the to-go box by its stem.

A little rumble rose from his belly. He blinked a few times. "It appears this form requires sustenance," he said.

I drew a chair to sit beside him since he made no move to sit up and jostle his chest wounds. I offered the berry, and he ate it without complaint. "Shouldn't you be in class?" he asked after swallowing and coughing a few times. He held his gut wound as his chest spasmed.

"I took the day off," I answered, loading up a fork with a piece of waffle freshly dipped in syrup. My gaze flicked to his fingers, which didn't come away with any silvery blood. It was like the damage was sealed with the liquid.

"That isn't a good idea," he said.

"Well, you need me more."

For a moment, he smiled. *Angelic indeed.* The features I'd admired so much in his stone form were preserved while he was human, but softened. No longer chiseled to perfection, but shaped by a loving hand. And when he smiled...his silver eyes and perfect white teeth twinkled in the morning light. Sunshine gilded the curve of his cheek, bringing out the warm highlights under his rich skin that was a shade of darkest bronze.

He hid that beautiful glimpse of himself under his usual serious expression. "I shall be fine tomorrow. We will return to your regular schedule then."

I hesitated. He'd taken wounds to the shoulder, chest, and gut that would probably kill a normal person. That wasn't something that should heal within a day. "Want to tell me what happened now?" I suggested before feeding him that bite of waffle.

I felt the blood rush from my face as he recounted his brief but awful fight with Phaeron. He described the dimensional as a creature of fangs, shadows, and claws.

But one part snagged my attention. "Mate?" I echoed. "But Morgana was the one to seal him in the library in the first place."

"I care not for the ramblings of a creature such as him," he muttered. "Next time, I will kill him for coming so close to the place where you rest."

I caught the trace of anger in his deep voice. *Emotion. Real, human emotion.* I was liking this version of him more and more.

"Let me help next time," I suggested.

His eyes flashed. "Absolutely not. I am your protector and champion. When he shows his face again, I will take care of him alone."

A thrill settled in my belly at the vehemence in his voice. Maybe if I'd trained for a while longer and had the experience of fighting lesser dimensional creatures, I would be offended by this newfound macho man streak. Instead, I acquiesced with a nod and fed him several forkfuls of waffle before he had his fill of breakfast. I ate the rest and snuck a dollop of whipped cream to Milo while Bella was having her daily stare-off with Jin.

Milo jumped onto Geo's bed with a curious chirp, sniffing the gargoyle thoroughly with his jaw propped open. "He smells like the outside," he reported. My brows rose when my familiar curled up against his uninjured side and purred quietly when Geo rubbed his flank.

"Aww, you got a little nurse." I smiled and settled my laptop at the desk closer to Geo's bedside before plopping *The Librarian Witch's Handbook* atop it.

Cracking my knuckles, I put on a confident face and opened the book's front cover. For what was supposed to be a repository of knowledge, it had stubbornly refused to share a single helpful fact with me.

It had a message already printed on its first page today: *You know, it's not too late to get your $19.99 back.*

"I don't want to return you, but I do need your help."

Moi?

"What do you know about gargoyles?"

Geo stirred, rolling his head to look at me. "Are you conversing with that book?" he asked.

Quite a bit compared to you, the book wrote.

"Kind of," I told Geo before realizing I probably didn't need him to know I was fishing for answers about the mystery that he was. I told him I'd be right back and took the book out into the hall, sitting in the stairwell with it in my lap.

I'm feeling helpful today, it'd written on a new page, above a several-page description of gargoyles. The kind of thing I'd already read in a textbook, describing them as stone constructs created from the willing soul of a deceased witch.

"But book, they're described as impervious to almost all magic. Geo got cut to bits by a dimensional last night." I worried my bottom lip between my teeth as the page flipped again.

Oh, I'm just "book" to you now?

"Sorry, *The Librarian Witch's Handbook*," I recited dutifully.

That's better. What's the dimensional's name?

"Phaeron."

The next page was blank for a long minute. Then: *Oh shit. Holy shiiii—take mushrooms. Sugar honey iced tea.*

I stifled a nervous giggle as it filled the page with every euphemism for "shit" I knew and then some. "Yeah?"

You're not panicking right now? Gods above. You really are new, huh?

I frowned down on it. From how it mocked my lack of accomplishments as a librarian witch, I figured it already knew that. "I mean, yeah?"

Why do I always get the new ones? Fuck!

It flicked to a new page before I could get too offended. *Listen, toots. We're in this together. I'm not going to let you die like my last five owners.*

Nervous sweat slicked my palms. "What happened to them?"

Well, there was Chris, and he was just stupid. Got screamed to death day one in Aventuri Library by a loose screamer. Man didn't know how to read. I told him to wear earplugs.

Then there was Tammy, who just had to touch a nightmare lily. She's probably still asleep somewhere.

Eric got tricked down an elevator shaft by an illusion imp. Sad. I liked him.

And Wendy died defending Moongrove Library from a level-five containment breach like a true badass.

Sheldon was...well, Sheldon. Nuff said.

Now I belong to you.

I blinked owlishly down at the book as it recited these things rapidly and flipped the pages before I could ask what a screamer was or what a nightmare lily looked like so I never touched one.

I wanted to ask it why the change of heart, but it was still writing, going into information I didn't know. *Read this*, it instructed, writing up a page of information on power levels. I recognized its voice throughout, like it was telling this to me as part of a casual conversation.

Every supernatural has a power level, which dictates the potential they have in their respective magics. This is a measure of offensive capability, resistance to others' magic, and how much magic they can channel through their body and/or hold on to at one time. Noobs like you don't get told all this because you'll be curious what your number is and go out and try to test it and get hurt.

"I mean, I guess," I murmured. "What does this have to do with Phaeron and Geo?"

Getting there. A construct like your gargoyle friend was created with defense in mind. They have very high power levels, but only because their defense and resistance to magic is high. The average gargoyle is created to be

PL5, for reference. Your friend might have a higher one since I think he's one of those fancy ones animated by a demigoddess.

Power levels are exponential. Someone at PL2 is double the strength of someone at PL1. But someone at PL3 is four times as powerful because they're the equivalent of two people at PL2, etc. etc.

You following this, toots? Your gargoyle has incredible defensive capabilities.

"Yeah, this all makes sense," I said, though I thought it was totally correct. I wanted to know what my power level was now.

Spells, too, have power levels, but that relates to ease of access. There are runes you might never be able to cast because you don't have the capability of holding enough magic to fuel them.

Now, take this matchup: a PL5 gargoyle comes up against a shadow dimensional.

It made two ink drawings of a winged gargoyle facing a shadowy creature. I saw Phaeron's true form for the first time as a wolf with lush locks of shadowy fur and a curling pair of ram horns protecting his skull. His tail was a spike strip of sharp spines.

To deal any damage to the gargoyle with magic, the dimensional has to be PL6 or higher.

The dimensional wolf leapt at the gargoyle, extending huge talons and opening its maw to reveal a stretch of jagged teeth. I shuddered, shocked Geo had survived this encounter at all. *That* was what I was hunting. That *thing* was what'd killed Lanie.

So with that out of the way, can we talk about how I keep hearing you whisper that you're going to kill Phaeron Sudair?

"I am. It's my fate," I said firmly.

Okay, toots. Sure.

My gaze narrowed at it. "What else do you know about him?" It'd picked out his last name and likeness in an instant.

Enough that, as your dutiful copy of The Librarian Witch's Handbook, *I must insist you stay away from him at all costs.*

"That's not helpful."

Neither is dying.

I scowled at it. With a slow, reluctant roll of its latest page, it wrote: *Learn how to cast the Lux rune, and I will tell you his last recorded power level.*

"Deal."

Deal. Now, why don't you go enjoy teasing your gargoyle or something? Don't you know that most gargoyles never return to their stone form after discovering human pleasure?

"Really?" I stood with its spine cradled in my palm.

It replied with a page-wide winky face.

16

CRESS

GEO SLEPT most of the day, leaving me at loose ends. I sketched a new outfit for my Drawing for Fashion class, purposefully copying the soft-looking waves of shadowy fur in my book's sketch of Phaeron's true form. Strips of material could mimic the effect, but only a fan could make them wave like they had a mind of their own.

My mind drifted as I beheld my creation. Was it anything like the real thing? Hopefully I'd only know when I was strong enough to put a silver sword through the heart of the murderous dimensional.

My phone pinged, and a text box from Ben appeared on the screen. Even though I hadn't seen him in two weeks, my heart always pattered a little faster when I saw his name. I held the phone to my face so I could preview his text. It was shorthand, like he always seemed to send, asking what I was doing.

I put the phone back down and took a deep breath. It was about the time he and I would be in class together. Had I really missed his return?

"Skipping class. You?" I texted back.

"Wanna hang out?"

I glanced over my shoulder at the resting gargoyle, his quicksilver wounds starting to shimmer as sunlight drifted into the room. There was no way I could leave him here alone. What bad timing!

"I can't leave my dorm right now."

"Fine lol. Works great for me. Myth-Flix?" He sent each sentence as an individual text.

I asked him what Myth-Flix was, and he helped me find a website with a convoluted URL no one would think to type in. There was a spot to click cleverly hidden on the error page the URL sent me to, and up popped a big splash screen for Myth-Flix in gaudy orange, yellow, and white.

Stifling a giggle, I made an account and put in earbuds. Ben found my new account and friended me. Soon we were streaming the same episode of a supernatural sitcom and connected in a voice chat.

"Hey, Cress," he said. I immediately smiled at hearing his light voice again, with the same teasing edge as I remembered. "I told you the shows were the best part of being a supernatural."

"Hi. You did," I said, glancing over my shoulder again. A quiet inside voice didn't seem to bother Geo. "How've you been?"

More like, *where have you been?*

There was a moment of hesitation on the other end. "I've been a little sick. And, you know, my brother." He gusted a sigh. "I've missed you, though. Doing okay?"

I got a fluttery feeling in my belly. If he missed me, I didn't feel so silly about missing him despite our brief acquaintance. "Yeah. Sore from the gym. I've got Roe working me pretty hard."

"Oh, you're sore?" There was a suggestive edge to the question.

I smacked my lips. "Not like that!"

He chuckled at my expense. "Why are you hitting the gym so hard? And don't say to lose weight."

"I have to swing a sword someday," I pointed out.

He hummed. "Sure. But didn't you want to design clothes?" he asked.

"It's smart to keep your options open," I replied. Really, it was amazing how fast my priorities had turned on their head. Rather than pouring my all into my fashion design major, my best grades were now in my witch-related classes.

"Uh huh. You going to the Mabon celebration?"

"Are *you*?" I countered.

Roe had already talked my ear off about Mabon and the gratitude ritual she wanted to do as a coven. She'd fretted we wouldn't be able to do it without our wayward seventh member.

"I'll be there," he confirmed.

The whole university had this coming Friday off for the Mabon feast and the bonfire party afterward. I'd learned it was sort of like supernatural Thanksgiving, a day to give gratitude for the abundance of the earth and feast.

"Thank goodness. Have you told Roe?" I asked, looking forward to the end of the week even more now that I knew I'd get to see him in person.

"I wanted to tell you first," he said. "Though I'm going to text her now, since she's asked me about it a couple times."

"Only a couple?"

He chuckled. "I didn't realize we were electing her mother hen of our group."

That's about right. But other than absent Ben, she'd been most worried about Grant, our verdant witch. I wasn't the only one to notice how out of it and uncaring he always seemed to be. Roe was looking into possible supernatural reasons for this in concern.

"If it were you, you'd appreciate your coven trying to help too," Roe had said.

I echoed that wisdom back to Ben, and we soon fell into a companionable silence. We watched the first episodes of a few of his favorite shows, each with real magic and no post-production effects added. Before I knew it, we were well into the afternoon. I only noticed when Ben drifted off mid-sentence and covered his microphone, talking to someone else.

"Hey, Cress, I gotta go," he sighed. "Let's do this again sometime."

I was halfway through saying goodbye when I realized he'd left the call abruptly. Rude. My lips twisted. I glanced over my shoulder to check on Geo, just to see he'd propped himself up to sit with his back against the wall. His wounds were noticeably smaller, especially the one on his lower belly, which receded to show taut muscle and flawless ochre skin.

He was also making a nearly smiling expression at my cell. Quiet sound drifted from the device, courtesy of a video he was watching. I blinked in surprise, remembering that I'd left it unlocked by his bedside and forgot about it after the conversation with my handbook. I hadn't realized he was growing Internet savvy so quickly.

He caught my gaze and lowered the device. "It sounded like you were having fun."

"You're awake," I said.

"I am."

"Did you sleep well?"

"Yes."

I should've known not to ask him a yes or no question. "You're healing really fast."

"Flesh mends," he replied.

I wished he wouldn't say "flesh" so often. I was stuck between an uncomfortable shuffle of awareness and an "ew" face every time.

"This form pleases you," he added, unbidden.

A touch of heat rushed to my cheeks. "Uh, I mean…"

"Why?" His brow knitted together.

Goddamn. The nearly emotionless gargoyle really wanted me to explain how hot he was. He waited patiently for an answer.

I cleared my throat. "I, uh, guess it's nice to see you react to things more. You're not acting like a robot."

His brow furrowed harder.

"Maybe you could stay like this for a while?" I suggested hopefully.

He lifted his hands, turning them over under his gaze and flexing them. "I will not be able to protect you as effectively in this form," he said. My shoulders began to sag in disappointment. "However, perhaps you will be able to take me into your classes and along for your other activities."

"Yes!" I jumped on the idea so quickly that his brows lifted. Surprise. Another first-time emotion, I noted. "First, you need some clothes."

He glanced down at the pair of cloth shorts that'd transitioned with him out of his stone form. "I suppose these aren't sufficient anymore," he agreed.

THE FIRST TIME I took Geo to the gym with Roe, he lifted an entire weight machine and gave it a curious shake. "This was supposed to be a challenge?" he asked. His brow furrow of confusion was becoming a new normal for him as most of the other gym-goers stared and Roe and I gestured urgently for him to put it down.

He carefully set it in the same place where it'd been resting and wandered off in search of a "challenge." I exchanged a glance with my friend. "There go my hopes of out-benching him," Roe said with a laugh. She set off after him. "Geo! Come spot me!"

Physical activity, it turned out, was totally his element. He was at his most comfortable in the loose shirt and basketball shorts that constituted his workout attire. I'd bought him three sets of clothes for now. One for working out, two for casual wear. If he wanted to stay human for longer, we'd be thrifting, because my bank account held about two pennies and a cobweb at this point.

He didn't sweat much. Apparently sweat and blood are things his construct body didn't make until he'd been in his "flesh form" for quite some time. Gargoyles were weird, man.

By Thursday, I caught a pair of witches glancing at Geo, ever-present at my side, and whispering about my boyfriend. Well...he *was* carrying my backpack and holding my phone all the way to his face as he ventured down whatever Internet rabbit hole he'd found. I accepted the gossip as my due since I couldn't explain my faithful shadow any other way.

I'd taken to picking an emotion of the day for him, and as we sat at the back of the class for another session of Introduction to Supernatural Society, I turned to him. He caught my eye and smiled automatically. I wanted to tell him he didn't have to smile every time I looked at him, but ever since I'd told him he had a nice smile, I saw it so much more. He *was* learning.

"How are you feeling right now?" I asked.

"Hmm. Content."

That was today's emotion of the day. After starting this experiment with "happy" and "sad" as the last two days, I'd printed out a chart of emotions and gave him a word to describe the patient blankness that he often displayed, even in human form.

"How about you?" he asked.

I had a much harder time answering this question, but I unpacked it for him. Eagerness to learn more about supernaturals other than witches in this class, tired from nearly a full week of classes, excited for Mabon tomorrow, and also nervous too.

A little line appeared between his brows. "You are nervous to see Ben again."

I felt myself blush. "Yeah." I hadn't talked to him much since the beginning of the week. It was a little crazy a guy I barely knew had this much of my headspace.

Geo frowned. "I do not find this pleasing."

"Yeah, I know. You don't really like him," I sighed.

"I am one call away if you need help." He reached over and covered my hand with his own, earnestness glistening in his silver eyes. "What emotion is that?"

My cheeks heated for an entirely different reason, not that I think Geo realized it was for him. Ben might give me butterflies, but Geo's steady, solid presence gave me an even greater gift: the feeling that I was safe after losing my friend so senselessly. I realized I hadn't needed to look over my shoulder since he'd joined me in his human form, sure he would be there if I needed him.

"You're feeling protective, I think," I said.

I turned my hand over and gave his a squeeze. He dipped his head before squeezing back. He held my hand without complaint through the whole lecture.

17
BEN

I was going to have a heart attack before I turned twenty-one, I decided. That line from Bianca had stuck with me for days, and I pretended to be the model blood witch after cutting off my chat with Cress. It'd been such a welcome change to hear her sweet voice again, but I'd still jammed that "end call" button on the computer without hesitation.

Anything to ensure he didn't change his mind about sending me out on a mission.

Friday dawned with a rainy chill, but I was not summoned before the master for a punishment. I dressed in casual college guy clothes with a couple daggers in strategic pockets, checking my phone several times as I waited for Bianca to get ready. At this point, looking at my lock screen was a nervous tick.

It'd been over a month since I saw Lucas. He hadn't miraculously returned in the two weeks I'd been confined to the manor. I'd been so horrifically bored and anxious I practically vibrated to finally leave. Not just to see Cress, or celebrate Mabon, or even search for Lucas anymore. Just...leave and breathe fresh air.

Bianca came charging down the stairs. "Let's go," she said, breezing past me. We walked out into a sunny day in regular Salem, our haste cutting in half the moment sunlight warmed our skin.

I put my hands in my hoodie's pocket, slouching strategically. "You ready for this?" I asked with a hint of sympathy. Garroway had given me a difficult mission, but it was nothing compared to what he'd tasked Bianca to do.

"I guess. Fuck," she blew out. "You know a client didn't ask for either of our tasks?"

"I got the impression. Not many people want to be on Dr. Aurina's bad side," I commented. If we didn't play our cards right, we most certainly would be. "Run the wording by me again."

Bianca's hands balled into fists. She rolled some of the tension out of her shoulders, scattering dozens of tiny braids. They were a recent addition, part of an elaborate getup in autumnal colors that made her look like she was a druid of old, arriving to the Mabon celebration fresh from the forest. She'd even stuck a few turning oak leaves in her hair.

"The master requires that I make Dr. Aurina's daughter bleed. I am to cut her while she celebrates Mabon with her family," she said from between gritted teeth.

"He didn't specify how big a cut," I reasoned.

"Yeah...but he wants to send a message to someone. He doesn't want a little poke," she said with a sigh. "I coated a knife with a numbing solution. I'm thinking of making it look like she cut her sleeve on a branch."

"I think that's your best bet," I agreed, relieved to hear the kid wouldn't feel it at least.

"And the wording for your mission?" she prompted.

"I am to bring him three rose gold cupid feathers with their magic intact," I said. I had a pair of gloves secreted away in my hoodie for the task.

"Well, that could be easy. I bet they'll sell them."

"The master probably intended for me to follow Dr. Aurina around. But you know she's going to have an entourage around to jump on any feather she sheds," I said.

We'd researched the Aurina family together, and I'd set my sights on a different cupid who had similar wings to the demigoddess. Her five mates were all cupids too, though only two were strong enough in their magic to sprout the distinctively hued wings of their kind. "I'm going to pluck a couple off her mate's wings instead. They'll still have a lot of magic and no chance of being a regular feather painted rose gold."

"Just don't be a dunce and give one away to your girlfriend," she said.

I rolled my eyes. "I wasn't going to." Actually, I'd been thinking an extra one would make a nice gift for Cress. But now that Bianca had called me out, maybe I'd just go above and beyond for Garroway instead and give him as many quills as I could steal.

"I mean it. It could be really bad news if it told her you're soul mates or something," she said, flashing a serious look at me. I put my hands up. Cupid feathers could lead someone to the real deal, a destined love match. And admittedly, I wanted a quill to point Cress my way. I could barely keep that woman out of my head, even with two weeks separating us.

I checked my phone as we entered New Salem and followed the trickle of new arrivals and motion on campus toward where Mabon had to be. Even though it was early, I tried texting Cress, hoping to see her and hang out as long as possible. Garroway had given us ten hours to accomplish our task, and the deadline twinged against my chest already, a little red line arrowing steadily toward my heart with every passing moment.

"Wow, they went all out this year," Bianca commented as we found a field transformed by a legion of picnic tables decorated with white cloth and clusters of small pumpkins and gourds. I recognized that we were in the fae section of campus, standing close to a carefully maintained forest many fae and their creatures enjoyed. The leaves were starting to golden and crisp, a few carpeting the grass.

There were baskets full of balls and Frisbees for the morning and afternoon, and a team of minotaur were assembling the kindling for a bonfire come nightfall. Also, more than a few witches and fae were already here, to my relief. We weren't too early.

My phone vibrated, and I checked Cress's message. Bianca glanced toward me and snickered at whatever she saw. Ignoring her, I turned and craned my neck until I saw a cluster of new arrivals coming in together. I spotted Cress's purple hair immediately and waved, a genuine smile splitting my face at seeing her again.

She walked over alongside Roe and Willow, whom I recognized, plus a deer-like fae girl and a Black man with shiny white dreadlocks who stuck close to her side. "Hey! About time you showed up!" Roe exclaimed.

"Sorry!" I called back.

"I let everyone know we're doing the ritual at ten," Roe said. She propped a wicker basket on the closest table and drew its cloth covering up to show row after row of pristine apples.

"Cool," I said with a nod, turning immediately to Cress. I held my arms out first, and we came together for a hug like I'd just seen her yesterday. We lingered a moment longer than necessary. "Hi. You change this?" I fluffed a lock of her hair. Now, I wasn't one for fashion, but it was hard to miss how much brighter it was and shot with different hues of purple to make it look more natural.

"Oh, yeah. One of the professors in my major gave me a potion for it," she said, fixing what I'd mussed with a rake of her fingers. "Plus the recipe, if Grant will make it for me."

She'd done her makeup in shades of orange and red today, with glossy crimson lips I just wanted to kiss. Add in her light blush, and she reminded me of a blooming flower. "You look lovely," I said. I vowed to myself to make the most of today and spend as much of it as possible with her. "Where's Geography?"

"Ge—oh." She turned toward the man who'd watched our reunion. His arms were crossed over his chest, the clean-shaven planes of his face creased with disapproval. "Geo's human right now."

I jerked my chin in wordless greeting. He just frowned at me more intensely. Tough crowd.

"Who, uh, was that girl with you?" Cress asked.

I glanced over my shoulder to find Bianca had already disappeared, blending in somewhere as she waited for her mark to arrive. "No one." I shrugged, enjoying the flash of relief on her face. Aww, was she a little jealous? I'd take her over Bianca any day. She didn't play with knives for fun.

"C'mon, time to be grateful," I said, offering my hand for her to take. We walked into the forest where Roe had gone with her basket of apples, hands lightly clasped. I snuck a look behind us to see Geo following at a polite distance. That damn gargoyle was going to be her purity police at this rate.

Cress loosed a nervous giggle. "Have you ever done this before?" she asked.

"Nope. If Roe explained it to you, then you're ahead of me," I said.

"She did, actually. She's going to say a few words of thanks to the elements for a good harvest, and then we're going to go around in a circle placing apples out and saying thanks for what we're grateful for."

I made a little skeptical noise. There wasn't much in my life to be grateful for right now. Even Cress herself and her presence in my life were tainted with the fact that I needed to somehow warn her to leave town. I was still drawing a blank on how, exactly, to do that when every cell in my body wanted her by my side just like this.

"Think of it like you're at the Thanksgiving table. Just say what you'd tell your family," Cress suggested.

"Yeah, okay." I'd think of something.

Roe's coven ritual was far more chill than I expected. Grant, Wren, and Heath joined us right on time, and we gathered in a circle out in the forest. Even the haughty blonde listened respectfully as Roe gave thanks and planted a few apples in the dirt to return to the elements. She passed the basket around the circle. We sounded a bit like a broken record—giving thanks for good friends and each other.

Cress placed two apples on the ground. "I want to give thanks for the friends who've supported me through the unthinkable," she said. Roe pressed her lips tightly together, looking a little emotional. "And for Geo, who's helped me find a feeling of safety again."

She passed the basket to me last. Man, I know I didn't deserve to be on her gratitude list, but her giving thanks for the gargoyle didn't feel good. He was probably watching from the tree line, listening in as he received that honor.

I placed a single apple in the dirt, bowing my head for a moment. I said to the circle that it was for my friends, but in reality, I gave silent thanks that I was still alive. Every day above ground was another chance to escape the bloody hold Garroway had on Lucas and me.

"Happy Mabon, everyone," Roe said with a big grin. "Who's in for some ultimate frisbee?"

While Cress and the others were distracted with a game, I snuck off in search of a family of cupids. In the shadows of the tree line, I spotted a flash of scarlet as a winged man landed with a giggling girl in his arms. She couldn't be more than seven, with candy pink hair tied into pigtails. She was dressed in a romper to play, and off her father shooed her, toward a mixed group of kids here to enjoy the day with their parents.

Regret twisted in my gut. Bianca wouldn't fail a mission as easy as targeting that girl, but it was wrong. *Principles.* Garroway wanted Dr. Aurina's attention, and he'd get it if someone dared to hurt her daughter. But to what purpose? A random cut on the girl's arm didn't necessarily say it was him.

Like many of my vampire master's plots, I had to wait and be unpleasantly surprised later. But I hid further in the shadows as two more shapes swooped from the sky—two cupids with nearly identical wings of rose gold. Bingo. They scattered a handful of loose feathers upon landing, which I slunk out to pick up as Dr. Aurina joined the festivities between her two mates.

"Three...four...five..." I piled up my bounty in my gloved palms, shocked at my luck. One of the feathers stuck out against the others, gleaming love-me crimson against the soft pink of the other four.

I would give Cress that one, I decided. Bianca could make fun of me later for hoping it helped me get closer to the purple-haired woman. A big part of me hoped that, should we have some sort of real connection, I could convince Garroway that she had more worth to him alive. It was probably a doomed prospect, but I had to know for sure before I encouraged Cress to go and not look back.

18
CRESS

I REJOINED Ben after a couple rounds of ultimate frisbee, energized from a pair of victories courtesy of Roe's highly competitive side. She kept playing and brought in Áine to take my place. The faun was a better player than me, springing around the field with the agility of the deer her lower half resembled.

Ben was plopped on the sidelines, watching us play. It was surreal in the best way to see him again, hanging out like he'd never been away. In the early autumn sunlight, his blond highlights and gem-green eyes seemed all the more lustrous. He still carried that tired, worried edge, but it seemed to dull whenever he met my gaze.

He was casually looking at something in his hand when I returned to his side. At first, I thought it was his phone, but instead, it was something red. He snatched it out of my line of sight before I could make out what it was. "Bet Roe would love to go against you next game," I suggested, hitching a thumb over my shoulder.

He smirked. "She couldn't handle me." He patted the grass next to him with a gloved hand. "I have something for you."

I plopped next to him. "Oh yeah?"

"Yeah, but before you touch it, know it'll bond to you the moment you do." He lifted his other hand, showing a foot-long red feather. "It's a cupid's feather. I found it..." He jerked his head toward a small gathering of people surrounding the ever-gorgeous Dr. Aurina. She held court surrounded by several men who looked at her adoringly, plus other laughing women with hair in shades of pink, red, and platinum.

They were all cupids. Most were indistinguishable from a witch who'd dyed their hair, save for a few with magnificent feathered wings.

"One of the good doctor's mates dropped it," Ben continued. "If you touch it, it'll help you find someone you connect to emotionally."

My brows rose in surprise, and I raised a finger. "Rewind for a second. Did you just say mates, as in plural?"

He shrugged. "Yeah. Fancy-ass demigods are at their most powerful with as many mates as possible. The higher their power level, the more mates they can bind to themselves. Having several is like a status symbol."

I glanced at Dr. Aurina again and started counting the adoring gazes on her.

"She has five," Ben supplied.

I whistled low. "That's...so many men. Holy shit."

His shoulder nudged mine. "Welcome to supernatural society. The more polyamorous you are, the more power you probably have," he said with a chuckle.

My gaze fell back to the feather in his hand. "So, how does this work?"

"As I understand it, the quill gets hot when you're close to someone you might have a connection with. If you offer it to them to touch, it'll use up all the magic in the feather to tell you whether you're compatible for a serious relationship. In ye olden days, royalty used cupid feathers to find their soul mates, rather than doing it the old-fashioned way." He got a mischievous look on his face as I wondered what "the old-fashioned way" was. He whispered behind his hand, "Sex."

My cheeks burned immediately. "Oh, right."

"I know you're probably not thinking about romance or anything right now. But it's worth a lot, and I thought...well, I'd offer it to you first," he said, scratching behind his head self-consciously. "It probably won't find you a soul mate or something. You know, just for fun."

I started to smile as I waited for him to finish, holding out my hand for it. "For fun," I agreed. He dropped the large feather into my palm, and a scarlet shimmer lifted from it, absorbing into my skin with a tickling sensation.

Ben watched me hopefully as I turned the feather over into my other hand, admiring its near-metallic filaments and how soft they felt against my fingertips. It was clear he wanted me to offer the feather back to him and see what the cupid magic said about us, which snatched my breath away.

I did want to know if my feelings for him were more than a crush, but I didn't know what I'd do if it turned out we were soul mates. I was definitely not ready for something super serious. But to know there was *potential* for it?

I smiled back at him. "I'm going to take this for a walk, see what it does," I said, trying not to notice the hint of disappointment that turned down the corners of his eyes.

"Okay, I'll be here," he said, lifting a hand in farewell.

I twirled the feather by its quill, not wanting to mess up its filaments. As I moved away from Ben, it became noticeably cooler, like I'd just picked it up from a chilly room.

Well, that was certainly something. The magic in it was working... and it must've been trying to tell me something about Ben. I wandered to one of the tables being loaded with covered platters of food, drawing in sweet and savory aromas as I snagged a bottle of water and took a refreshing drink.

Maybe I was just teasing Ben at this point. I didn't think there was anyone else I wanted to offer the feather to. But I wandered with the feather in hand, saying hello to a few acquaintances from my major and other librarians I recognized from class and in passing at the library. Pretty much every witch and fae at the university seemed to be here, and then some.

I started noticing family units who must've come back to campus to celebrate Mabon and enjoy the huge upcoming feast. Sometimes, families were just happy couples...but more than half the time, there were groups of three or four men with one woman, or vice versa.

Craziness. I started imagining the kind of heart attack I'd give Mom if I came home with more than one boyfriend. Stifling a laugh at the thought, I passed a fae lady at the table set up with drinks and little snacks, doing a double take when I saw the lustrous lilac mane flowing behind her. "Your hair is beautiful," I said. More varied in hues than mine, with icy undertones that veered more toward a silvery-blue.

She flashed a sweet smile. "Aw, thanks! So is yours." She had a giggle like a peal of bells, twinkling and pleasant. We went our separate ways from there.

I settled in the shade of a few trees, looking down at the feather. I'd passed within arm's distance of a lot of folks, but it was still cool to the touch. There on my own, it began to warm up again until it was like holding a sunbaked stone. I looked around in confusion, expecting to see Ben following me. Instead, I felt the sensation of a strong arm closing around my waist and yelped.

"A cupid's arrow. Where does it point your heart?" murmured a low voice in my ear. My heart just about stopped.

"Phaeron," I breathed. I'd expected our paths to cross again, but here and now? In the light of day with so many people around?

Cold sweat sheened my back instantly, and I trembled against the sensation of a warm, muscled chest pressed to my back. I was going to die and traumatize all these people on Mabon.

"Hello, Cress. Don't be afraid." I'd forgotten the smooth purr of his deep voice, like the enticing brush of silk. "I haven't had the chance to talk to you while you've been under your guardian's watchful eye."

"What's there to talk about? You killed my friend," I whispered fiercely. Something told me I shouldn't antagonize the man who'd sliced up Geo like he wasn't made of stone.

"I would not perpetrate such a heinous act," he replied. I glared over my shoulder, catching only a hint of his glowing topaz eyes in the shade. The rest of him was functionally invisible.

"And you wouldn't attack Geo either, I'm guessing?" I demanded.

His eyes narrowed to catlike slits. "That is different. I only wanted to speak to Morgana. She owes me some answers. If your guardian had cooperated, I could've done it without hurting him."

For a moment, I simply stared. Phaeron was a murderer and a monster, yet he didn't sound like one. Old fashioned, perhaps, but not evil to the point of consuming souls.

And the best serial killers are the most charismatic, I reminded myself.

"What do you want?" I asked. I spotted Geo cooling his heels at a table close by. He'd nicked my phone again and was distractedly scrolling, but he was still within shouting distance. Granted, I didn't think he was faster than Phaeron if I pissed the dimensional off.

"I understand your hostility, so I will be brief," he said. "I have been unable to properly thank you for releasing me from my prison. Allow me to award you a boon."

"A...what?"

His chuckle blew warm air over my ear. I shivered despite myself. "A gift, Cress. My possessions are meager, but I can still offer magic." I felt him lift my left arm by the wrist, turning it over. I nearly yelled out for Geo as the claw on Phaeron's thumb traced a little pattern over the delicate skin of my inner wrist, but it was done within a breath. A circular rune the size of a dime, as gray as Phaeron's skin, now stood out where he'd touched. It looked like an intricate knot.

"When you are in need, find a patch of darkness, touch the rune, and say my name. If I am able, I will come to you," he promised.

I stared at the little mark in surprise. Didn't he realize I could use this against him? "Why would I ever use this?" I breathed.

With my hair shifted to the side to look over my shoulder at him, my neck must've presented too clear a target. His grip around my waist tightened, and I clearly felt his mouth brush the rapid pulse hiding just under my skin. I bit my lip to keep a noise from escaping, swallowing it as he sent pleasure straight to my core.

Then the sharp points of his fangs grazed my neck, and I moaned out loud, followed by a flush of mortification. "Perhaps after I convince you of my innocence, you will understand why I want to protect you." His deep voice was right in my ear, turning my knees to jelly.

"S-stop. I don't want this," I said. I didn't want him turning my body against me like that.

He straightened immediately, clearing his throat. "Then I must ask you to leave this place and take any dear to your heart with you," he said. I stiffened with immediate fear at how ominous that sounded. "A dark presence nears, and I am not at my best to combat it, thanks to your guardian."

He tapped my right side, and I glanced down, shocked to see his right arm bound by white bandages and a sling. He made it disappear back into his shadows, but several questions pushed at me. I touched what I thought was his arm around my waist before realizing it was the muscled cord of his tail. Clever.

"You were the one who attacked him," I said.

"Alas, the details don't matter. The healer I saw said it will be several days before even advanced healing will repair my shattered bones. I cannot face what's coming on your behalf, so you must leave."

I chewed on my bottom lip. "*What* is coming? And why would you fight anything for me?"

"To speak of it will bring its presence. Just trust me, Cress. Go." He released me so suddenly I stumbled.

I turned around and felt for him, but it was like he'd vanished. "I don't trust you," I said to empty air.

"Then I'm sure your soul will be a delicious treat." His voice drifted down to me. I craned my neck up, spotting him fully visible in a bough of the nearest tree. His tail dangled, twitching like an agitated cat's, while his face was drawn in a look of censure. My breath froze.

Even a disapproving Phaeron was a sight. The high cheekbones and unusual skin tone that marked him as a dimensional had a sort of alien draw. A lock of glossy black hair had escaped the tie keeping it back from his curled horns. Its length fell just past his collarbone, soft compared to the masculine cut of his features. His eyes gleamed like polished topaz in the light of afternoon.

He'd found a shirt somewhere, a short-sleeved tee. My imagination reminded me of the perfect abs that hid underneath it. As I stared, his expression shifted to something nearly coy. "I do not have your trust, but perhaps I have caught your eye all the same?" he said in a low purr. "Does cupid's arrow point my way?"

The feather was pulsing urgently with heat in my palm. The last thing I needed to know was whether this man and I were compatible on a deep level...even though I feared how likely it was with the patch on my neck still tingling.

I was destined to put a silver sword through his heart, right? No matter how his presence drew more of my attention than I cared to admit. There was no sense in flirting with the enemy.

"No," I said, forcing a scowl up at him.

His smile widened. "Is that so? I await the day you change your mind." With a wink, his presence disappeared into a curl of black smoke.

I knew he was gone this time, because the feather's heat dimmed instantly. Blowing out a tense breath, I wondered what the hell had just happened. I lifted a skeptical brow at the feather as it heated again, right before Geo rested a hand on my shoulder and asked, "Who were you talking to?"

He scanned the woods, expression fiercely protective. "No one. Just taking a breather," I lied, hoping I didn't look too flushed.

"I thought I heard the dimensional's voice," Geo said. His quicksilver gaze turned to me for explanation.

I pretended I didn't know what he was talking about, wide-eyed and shrugging. But I made a quick decision as I walked him back to the celebrations. "I think I've had enough Mabon."

Geo looked increasingly confused. "As you humans say, I believe you are acting...sus." He said the half-word stiffly. "The feast hasn't started."

"People don't say 'sus' out loud, Geo. Like, you would say 'suspicious.'" I bit down on a laugh. He was still learning, after all, listening patiently to my explanation. "I just want to go early."

Man, this was going to be a hard sell to everyone else if Geo was doubting me. Roe was the center of attention at one of the tables too, having drawn most of our coven and friends. I doubted I'd be able to convince them to leave early, but I still drew Roe aside for a private moment.

"Hey, I had a bad feeling," I whispered. "Kind of like...that awful day."

She understood instantly, a look of sympathy taking over her expression. "You're leaving?" she asked.

"I think we all need to leave. Like something bad's about to happen," I said, holding my breath as she considered. It was clear she loved Mabon and the sense of community it brought together.

"I might leave a little early too. But it's probably nothing." She rubbed a couple circles into my back. "Go take the time you need. We love you, girlie."

I realized what I looked like as the wide-eyed panic set in at the idea of losing her or any of my other friends. She thought I was overreacting on some whim, and it wasn't like I could tell her the dimensional himself had told me to leave. "I just want you guys to be safe," I said. "It's not worth the free food, you know?"

She started to frown. "Would you feel better if I promised to leave after the feast, then?"

"Yeah. Definitely." It would probably still be light out when it ended, transitioning to the evening bonfire.

"Then I'll go home early too," she said.

I promised to see her later and said a round of goodbyes to the familiar faces like Willow, Áine, and Heath sitting at her table. But Ben wasn't with them. I actually found him exactly where I'd left him, but now Dr. Aurina was on her knees, consoling her crying daughter and murmuring instructions to one of her mates, who flew off in haste.

"What happened?" I asked.

Ben glanced up from his phone and shrugged. "She got hurt playing, I guess. Did you find anyone worthy of the quill?" he gestured to the red feather I twirled idly between my thumb and forefinger. It was growing hot again as I stood next to him.

"Yeah, actually." Since I was leaving, I didn't see a point of hanging on to it any longer. So I offered it back to him, holding the bottom of it.

He sat up from his slouch with a gasp. "Oh! Let's see if it really works." He closed his hand around the soft filaments, and the feather quivered before disintegrating into a puff of crimson dust. My palm itched.

Turning it over, I saw I had a different rune on my palm, this one resembling a long line with several smaller lines crossing it. Ben gasped as he revealed a matching one on his hand. "Anam cara," he said.

A gentle wind blew away a layer of red dust still clinging to the mark, and I rubbed at the red lines now crossing my skin. I wondered how permanent it was. "Do you know what this means?" I asked him.

"Yeah...you don't know the anam cara symbol?" he asked in disbelief.

"I'm still kind of a new witch," I muttered.

He breathed a little laugh, getting up to hug me tightly. He drew back with his hands on my shoulders. "It's one kind of soul mate," he said, a big grin crossing his face. His giddy happiness gave him a boyish charm, taking away that edge of worry he seemed to always carry.

"We're...soul mates?" Whoa there. I hadn't expected this at all.

"Of a sort. I'm surprised your gal friends didn't tell you all about this," he said. "Anam cara are technically soul *friends* but...it explains a lot. Everyone's supposed to have an anam cara, someone they can be so close with. They basically have the same aura. Someone they miss deeply if they're parted for too long. It's romantic and...quite intimate."

Emotion stirred in his green eyes like a play of light and shadow. There seemed to be a deep yearning there that had his fingers flexing on my shoulders, like he didn't want me to escape now that he'd found me and learned what we could be.

And I had no intentions of running. "It does explain a lot," I agreed. How after only a day of knowing him, I'd really felt connected to him. Why I'd felt his absence so much. "I was going to leave early. Maybe you want to come with?"

"Definitely. Where are we going?" he asked.

"My dorm room? I'm allowed guy visitors until, like, nine at night," I suggested, getting a little jump of butterflies.

He chuckled. "Works for me." He caught my hand as I led him away from the festivities, and we walked with our fingers entwined to my dorm room.

I snuck glances at him, so happy I'd saved the feather to offer to him. To think something like anam cara actually existed and I'd found mine within a month and change at university. I couldn't help a silly daydream. He was a freshman too, so we had four years of too-late dates over pizza and notes before major exams, dances and socials to attend, and so much more. And if I was fated to face Phaeron with the help of three men...chances were now so much higher that Ben was one of them.

I was also quite aware that Geo was following us at a polite distance, probably wearing a stony mask of disapproval. Well, I'd have to get my gargoyle guardian to come around somehow. They'd probably gotten off on the wrong foot. He had a seat in the garden as I took Ben up to my dorm room.

Ben glanced around and raised a brow at me. "Do you live alone right now?"

"Yeah. Just me and my cats," I said, closing the door after us. "I'm like a crazy cat lady. Sorry you had to learn this after the anam cara thing." I noticed neither Milo nor Bella popped up to inspect and greet the newcomer, which was unusual for them.

"It's cool you have familiars. I haven't found mine yet," he said.

It occurred to me that, for all my daydreaming, I hadn't thought through what we'd do now that we were here in my room. I turned to Ben, my offer for Myth-Flix drying up when I noticed how close he was. He reached up to toy with a bit of my purple hair; his knuckles grazed my cheek, and his smile turned tender.

"I want to kiss you. Is that all right?" he murmured.

He waited while playing with that lock of hair, running it between his fingers. Boys in the past had just taken any hint of interest as an opportunity to mash their lips against mine. But Ben wanted to cross that boundary with respect, and it magnified that quivery feeling in my belly a hundredfold. "Yes," I breathed.

He cupped my nape and drew me into a careful, testing brush of our lips. I'd read in some of my books that a first kiss should feel like a firework, a dazzling explosion of sparks within. Good enough to make a gal's toes curl. But until Ben came back to deepen the touch of our mouths, I'd felt like all those descriptions were nonsense.

Now, I thought they didn't describe it intensely enough. I wrapped my arms around his shoulders, drawing him closer, breathing in the clean and minty taste of him. Our tongues brushed, sending shock-waves of sensation down to my core. We only surfaced for air when my phone began to ring.

I stumbled away from Ben, touching my fingertips to my sensitive lips. I felt how inexperienced I was, and with a kiss of that caliber, Ben had to have a lot more familiarity with the opposite sex. He had a knowing twist to his lips.

Blushing, I checked my phone to see it was Roe calling. I nearly let it go to voicemail, but I suddenly had a queasy sensation in my belly. "Hey," I said, answering.

"Cress! Are you okay?" she exclaimed.

I lifted my gaze to Ben's, flooded with concern at my friend's frantic tone. "Yeah, I'm fine. I'm in my dorm."

"Oh, thank the gods," she sighed. "The feast is canceled. They found a body out in the woods."

I covered my mouth, feeling sick. Suddenly I felt like I was thrown into the past, standing on a sidewalk again, watching the lifeblood leave Lanie as Phaeron loomed over her like a gray reaper. "No," I whispered, nearly pitching sideways. Ben's strong hands caught me, and he helped me sit on my bed before I slumped to the ground.

"They say the girl had purple hair. I thought of you immediately," Roe was saying. My face went numb. That was an unusual enough color that I thought to the fae I'd met, with her beautiful length of purple-blue hair. "Can you come to the clubhouse? Bring Ben and Geo if they're around."

I'm sure your soul will be a delicious treat. That fucker. He'd planned on taking another victim the whole time, with a side of messing with me again, distracting me from what was important. I glared at the shadowy knot on my wrist. Phaeron wanted to play games, but I wasn't up for that. I was going to take him down.

19
PHAERON

YET AGAIN, I found myself closing a dead girl's eyes. She was a fledgling high fae, with natural hair in icy shades of purple, straight from a polar aurora borealis. She had no pupils, her body left without a life or soul and her expression etched with horror.

I'd sensed *it* somewhere at this gathering. Waiting. Watching. But it'd struck and consumed with great haste, undoubtedly knowing I was also here to stop it.

I lifted some of the fae girl's hair, watching the multicolored strands fall through my fingers. First the seer with a hood like Cress's, and now a fae with hair like hers. I was no longer convinced this was a coincidence.

Nor did I believe my blackouts were an unrelated occurrence. Another had taken my mind within moments of leaving Cress, and my wits returned just to see this latest victim of the Hungering Darkness. There was no sign of it, other than its prone victim.

With growing dread, I had to confront a terrible possibility. I'd spent significant time hunting the monster from my original world and found no trace of its corrupted white fire. It could have taken root in myself instead. Laughing within me as I turned over every rock searching for it.

It would explain why I was still constantly sensing the monster of clawed darkness and endless hunger. It could have the ability to flare its presence, toying with me and my sensibilities before using me as its jaws to fulfill its dark desire for souls.

I flexed my good hand, and the shadows wove themselves into pitch-black talons to overlay my fingers. I turned them over, inspecting for any speck of white burning at their edges, but they were pristine. My shadowborn blessing appeared to be completely intact.

Perhaps it was time to surrender myself to Moongrove Library. An experienced custodian of dimensional magic may be able to detect the evil hiding from my own senses.

However, it was more likely I'd be killed on sight. There was something I needed before I even considered that path: Morgana's soul and the answers only she could give me.

She was a gargoyle for a reason, carrying a heavy sense of duty as the first librarian witch. Perhaps her betrayal was as simple as that... She'd been doing her duty, making sure the Hungering Darkness was locked away. But duty was a cold companion when it meant I was left in containment with the monster for two hundred years.

I balled my hand into a fist and stepped away from the girl, leaving her to be discovered. It was only a matter of time.

I didn't doubt that Cress would blame me for today's murder. Without concrete proof of my innocence, I deserved her contempt. I couldn't shake thoughts of her, one gargoyle protector away from consumption. Her soul, shockingly bright compared to those around her. This creature of the night couldn't help but crawl back into the radiance rolling from her like a beacon, despite how she felt about me.

If I was harboring the Darkness, this obsession was the biggest danger to her. It was clear she was a target, but I was missing a crucial piece of this puzzle. Why Cress? Was it because she'd released me from the library? The Darkness could be seeking revenge for siccing its most fervent hunter back on its trail.

Or perhaps it sought to harm her in order to hurt me. I thought of the reluctance on Cress's face when I'd asked if we had a connection. It was clear something brewed there, made bittersweet by her hatred of me. My body responded to hers. I wanted to know her, to bask in her radiance, to serve in her shadow. It'd taken every ounce of my willpower not to bite her, to mark her as mine to others of my kind.

I'd felt the heat radiating from the feather in her hand, which had nearly melted in my presence. I knew I was growing attached, but there was just something about her. Perhaps fate wasn't so unkind to leave me mate-less and alone into the rest of eternity. But she had to see something in me as well for this to work. If only I could prove to her that I am a guardian, not a murderer, tasked as a sacred shadowborn to protect everyone I met from within the darkness that was my constant companion.

I'd failed to kill her gargoyle protector and take Morgana's soul for one last conversation. It could've been as easy as severing his head, but at a crucial moment, I'd hesitated, earning myself shattered bones and broken ribs. That moment also lingered at the forefront of my mind, because I'd considered the results of my actions a second too late.

If I killed her gargoyle and the Darkness found her, I would have personally doomed her. The danger had refreshed itself in my mind upon seeing that fae girl. How could I seek closure if my actions directly led to Cress's death and consumption, life and soul alike?

I would consider at another time what it meant, that the most important person in my life had become the young witch who despised me. If it weren't for the gargoyle and her unfortunate misunderstanding of my intentions, she would find it hard to be rid of me.

Despite how disliked I felt, at least I had one companion. He was drunk already, but that appeared to be David's general state of being. I could tell it muted the pain fracturing his soul, so I didn't comment.

"Hey, man. How's the arm?" the shifter asked as I settled on the opposite side of the alleyway.

The Moongrove librarians would never find me here in the middle of the most run-down section of New Salem. The dregs of supernatural society made their homes here, such as they were.

David didn't mind me coming and going at what must've seemed a fickle whim. I may have sweetened that pot by using my shadows to steal him more tolerable liquor. He passed me the bottle today, and it ran smooth on my tongue before searing a path down my throat. I could've finished the whole bottle to muffle the most recent memory of the fae girl's dead face and Cress's distrustful expression. My latest failures.

I gave the bottle back to him. "Fine. I have had worse."

"You're funny. Sorry you got all banged up," he said.

I hadn't expected anyone to care for my well-being, let alone someone who'd lost everything. When I'd arrived to the alleyway in the dead of night, stained with blood, he'd jumped into action immediately with a roar of, "Holy shit!"

That's how I learned he was a bear shifter under all the unshaven hair. He'd practically slung me over his shoulder and taken me to a charity place run by a verdant witch man covered head to toe with tattoos. No questions, just healing, a meal, and a new set of clothes.

Gang violence was apparently prevalent in the area. Somehow, that'd turned me into a badass in David's eyes. Though he certainly thought the story of how I'd gotten to this place in my life was a work of total fiction.

I'd tried to tell him about my home dimension and the Age of Decay that'd driven me to lead my people to a safer land not ruled by an insane goddess and her monsters.

He'd laughed. *Laughed.* Then said, "I think I played that video game!"

I decided to forgive him when he sobered up that morning and told me how his true mate had ripped his metaphorical heart out by rejecting him. The cracks in his soul had pulsed, growing worse before my eyes.

"Then she doesn't understand that she is doomed to never find someone better than you, David," I'd said. "And one day, you will find a woman who calls to your heart and soul in an entirely different way."

"You really think so, man?" he'd asked, looking down at himself.

As I shared his latest bottle with him tonight, I remembered my vow to him. I'd try to find him someone else with a compatible soul, someone kinder than the woman who'd broken him. All he needed to do was let the alcohol go. One sip less each day. We'd clean him up and set him back on the right path.

Deep into his drink, he started telling me again of a place he was dying to visit. Aurora Heights, where forsaken and rejected shifters were given a second chance. I think he would forget that he's already shared tales of this frozen utopia in what sounded like a pocket dimension to the far north.

"If this place is your dream, then you should go," I said quietly. Maybe someday I would get a more sober shifter to tell me if Aurora Heights even existed, and where to find it.

"I couldn't leave you behind, man."

But he should. If there was even a small chance the Hungering Darkness had its claws in my soul, he should've already started running.

"Maybe we could go together someday," he suggested.

"Perhaps," I agreed. I thought of Cress again, wondering if she was safe in her dorm by now. If the too-close stars in Earth's sky were kind, I would see her again under less hostile circumstances. I was far too eager to see where we stood when that day came.

2O

BEN

I SPENT most of the afternoon on a couch in our coven's room in the clubhouse, my arm around Cress as she hugged tightly to my side. It was like the fae girl's death had set her back to that grieving place after her seer friend died. I did my best to comfort her, but in reality, I was usually the one to break things, not help the mending process afterward.

Geo had demanded he come inside too and watched us with a crease between his brows. I couldn't help a smug smile. She'd wanted me, not him. One point for Ben. Her anam cara, I reminded myself, occasionally glancing at the mark on my palm with a softer expression. She and I were meant to be, soul friends with our spirits cut just right to fit together.

I stuck around as long as I could. The deadline started to burn deeper in my chest, sending radiating waves of pain through my whole body. I had only a couple hours left before it killed me if I didn't return to Garroway with my task completed.

My phone buzzed with several annoyed messages from Bianca, demanding to know where I was. I put her off as long as possible, too. Despite the circumstances, there was a little bubble of peace around my heart as I held Cress and helped her through the news as it came to us in bits and pieces.

The fae who'd died was not a target I expected Lucas to strike, though. The university released a report in haste to explain that she'd come from the Winter Court, one of the many grandchildren of the Winter King.

I needed to talk to Seth, see if there was anything we could do for Lucas. Because this was another blood witch killing, confirmed by the university. A different spider had a hold of my brother's strings, and I would sever them if I could simply *find* Lucas. Mabon was celebrated in a huge area, but I still simmered in frustration, knowing I'd been in the same place as him.

"I'm sorry, I have to go," I whispered into Cress's ear as the sunlight started to wane through the window. She had her head on my shoulder, eyes closed but not asleep. She stirred with a low sound, her big brown eyes fixing on me. When she gave me a look like that, I was ready to do anything for her, except stay and run the risk of not meeting my deadline.

"Okay," she murmured.

"You should go home too. You don't want to miss curfew," I said. I'd read the email off her phone, pretending it applied to me too. All students were to be in their dorms by eight at night. It seemed the university wanted everyone inside by nightfall, and it'd canceled any activities and games outside of curriculum requirements for the time being.

Worse, they were implementing increased security for those coming and going from the university grounds. Cress had sighed with relief, but I took the news with a sinking heart. They were partnering with the SPDI to allow only students and authorized personnel onto campus grounds.

I may be able to trick Cress and the others into thinking I was a guardian witch with a little blood trickery, but trained supernatural police would be much harder to fool and much less likely to have a sense of humor about it. So when I left the clubhouse and turned to say goodbye to Cress, I knew this could really be the last time I saw her.

"See you tomorrow?" she asked, hope lacing her voice.

"I hope so," I murmured, opening my arms to her. I lifted her off her feet and into my waiting kiss, swallowing her startled laugh. She held on with her arms around my shoulders and her legs clinging to my waist.

I kissed her with everything in me. She didn't hold back either, matching me tongue for tongue, clinging like I was her only anchor. My cock began to harden, pressed against the covered heat of her, and I felt the shiver that went through her when she noticed and tensed for a moment. I expected her to wiggle her way free of me, bashful as she could be, but she surprised me by relaxing and leaning further into my lips.

I only put her down when someone catcalled us from the other side of the road. I gave him a stink eye until he kept walking.

A flush took over Cress's cheeks again. "God, Ben. You know how to kiss," she said.

"What can I say? I was motivated to learn for a moment like this." I brushed the hair out of her face, smiling when I saw some of the light had returned to her eyes. She'd come back from the low place she'd visited today.

I took her hand in mine, pressed the lingering red symbols in our palms together. "It might not be tomorrow, but I'll come back to you, anam cara."

"You'd better," she said. "Or I'll go find you."

Part of me trembled at the idea of her ever stepping foot in Garroway's lair. "Let's not let it get to that point," I said before stealing one last peck on her lips in farewell. I forced myself to leave before I was tempted to linger for too long.

The deadline on my chest pulsed with a few warning warbles of deeper pain, leaving soreness in my muscles. I donned my gloves and checked the pocket of my hoodie, looking over the four rose gold cupid feathers. They were still perfect and gleaming.

Out of nowhere, strong hands seized my arm and ripped the glove off my right hand. "Ben, what the fuck?" Bianca hissed.

I already had a dagger in my left hand, halfway poised to strike her. "What the fuck, yourself," I muttered, putting the weapon away and jerking my arm from her hold.

She'd snuck up on me out of nowhere. Now that we were away from the clubhouse and together, we started jogging back toward the manor.

"I thought you were smarter than this," she practically growled.

"What are you going to do when the master sees you have an anam cara mark?"

"I was hoping to convince him to try calling Lucas back to the manor and cancel his mission to kill Cress," I said. I knew I could talk the master into it. By his twisted logic, Lucas was his property, and I knew he had to be furious at someone else stealing access to Lucas's blood rune.

Bianca looked over at me in stark disbelief. "He's not going to call your brother off because she's your anam cara."

"I wasn't going to tell him that part," I admitted, snapping the glove I'd placed back onto my hand. He wouldn't see it today as I revealed what I knew about Lucas and his activities.

"And you shouldn't bind your fate to someone who's got a hit out on her," she added, glancing over at my palm. "It might be too late for that, though."

She was probably right. Our less than traditional education didn't include much about anam cara or other forms of soul mates, but I understood the anam cara bond kicked in right away, no matter what Cress or I wanted. We'd always be drawn to each other as friends and even lovers; now we just understood why. I was thrilled and terrified for what it meant for Cress to be pulled toward someone like me, though.

"I have a plan," I said. "I'm going to tell him that we have no concrete proof that she is actually the lost Darkmore heiress and that Lucas hesitated too long because of that and got himself captured by an enemy. I'll put it in his language. He's losing money having Lucas out there, drawing attention to rogue blood witch activity. We're getting unwanted exposure that he will have to work around, especially on the NSU campus, which is locking down on the free flow of visitors."

"Okay, fair," she said, tipping her head for a moment.

"You think it's going to work?"

"Fuck no. Because the next thing he'll do is assign the mission to someone with better follow-through. Someone on hand, trying to manipulate him. And when he assigns *you* to kill her, what will you do then?" Behind her glare, I saw the emotion she lashed out with: fear.

It was something we were both intimately acquainted with. An unhealthily overwhelming fear of Master Garroway and the way he always seemed to twist situations into nightmares. Because that was what an order for me to kill Cress would transform into. A living, breathing nightmare come to life. I slowed to a walk, barely able to breathe past the clog of terror in my throat.

"Let me handle the master, all right?" she asked more quietly.

I frowned over at her. "What will you tell him?"

"I can't think past this damn deadline," she muttered, rubbing right next to one of her breasts. "But I'll think of something better than your fool plan."

True to form, Bianca thought of something better than my fool plan. The master called me back into his office after accepting the proof that we'd both finished our missions as directed and ending the pressing pain of our deadlines. She spoke to him first, and then I had my turn on the comfortably upholstered chair in front of his desk.

Garroway's nostrils flared. "You smell different, little Ben."

The blood nearly froze in my veins. Could he somehow sniff out that I'd found a bubble of happiness, or even the cupid magic forming the anam cara mark on my palm?

His lip curled, and he steepled his fingers. "Some sun did you good. Bianca tells me you believe Lucas's blood rune was hijacked by someone else."

"Yes, Master. There have been two amateur blood witch murders on the NSU campus," I stated. "Neither of which you've ordered. And Lucas has been off grid for more than a month."

"Has it not occurred to you, in your desperation to see him again, that these facts could be unrelated?" he asked in his slow drawl.

I considered rather than blurt a hasty answer. "I think they're too related to be coincidences," I said carefully.

He sniffed, immediately dismissive. "Coincidences or not, the lockdown of the university poses an interesting problem. I have interests in New Salem that cannot be blocked." The wheels were turning behind his dark eyes, and they were fixed on me. I shifted uncomfortably until he came to some sort of decision. "Bianca made an excellent point earlier. You are currently of little use to me."

Gee, thanks Bianca.

"Perhaps you are the best candidate to station in the city until further notice. I will allow you into one of my properties, and you will continue a few simple ventures until the lockdowns cease."

I kept myself very still, barely daring to breathe. He was going to set me loose in New Salem? I could go see Cress more often, maybe every day.

"This is not a reward, little Benjamin," he said sternly. "You will work yourself around the clock if that's what's required. But in the meantime...I am agreeable to the idea of you hunting down your errant brother."

I began to nod. "Yes, Master. Whatever is required, I will do it."

"Anything to find him again, hmm? If he has indeed betrayed me, you know it will not end well for him," he said with quiet venom.

I felt myself pale at the implications but forced another nod. "I understand."

"Good. And if the jumped-up pink Barbie that leads the university acts against me again, you will be on hand for retaliation as well." He spoke mostly to himself, looking pleased.

I thought of his missions for Bianca and me today. A warning in the form of hurting Dr. Aurina's child and plucking a few feathers from the cupid demigoddess's wings. I hadn't realized they were the opening salvo of some personal vendetta.

21
CRESS

MONDAY EVENING WAS the earliest I could come see Dr. Voidbinder for extra training. With the curfew looming over my head, we had to move the time to seven at night rather than eight, which meant I'd barely gotten a meal scarfed down before running to the library.

He directed me to the small room where the practice weapons were kept and steered my shoulders toward a lineup of dusty silver swords. "It's time you learned some magic. Pick one," he said, acting like he hadn't just invited me to my own personal candy shop.

I picked up and inspected each one and found them all to be nearly identical. Straight-edged, plain, and more lightweight than I expected. Most were battered from practice, reminding me of old band instruments that'd been loaned out, dented, and returned a few times.

I ended up choosing one with a grip that felt right in my hand, and Dr. Voidbinder magically assigned it to me and let me store it in the tall, slim locker assigned to me on floor negative one. This was it. I was really going to learn magic!

My excitement soured to frustration quickly. If only practice was as straightforward as picking a weapon. On the first day with a real sword, I made the same motion with it until my wrist ached. "Criss-cross. Just an x," Dr. Voidbinder had said like it was no big deal.

Just an x, my ass. My first rune was a study of precision and patience. Each line had to be the exact same length, formed by a figure-eight swish of my sword's tip. The length of metal grew heavy in my hand as I made the motion over and over while saying the name of the rune, Lux, with each attempt.

Our time together was too brief. I tried again on Tuesday to no avail, and then Wednesday, channeling the pitch of my frustration into increasingly choppy strokes through the air.

"Lux. Lux. Freaking...LUX!" I shouted before tossing the sword to the ground in frustration.

The professor looked on, disapproval and concern tugging at his lips. "Young lady, it is a snappy gesture." He showed off how to do it again with his sword, creating the rune with a couple stiff motions of his wrist. The *x* lingered in the air, two clean and translucent librarian-purple lines, until he said, "Lux." The rune disappeared, the magic sucking back into the tip of his sword. It began to glow from within.

"Now you try." He stooped and put the leather hilt back into my hand.

I heaved a sigh, thankful at least that Geo wasn't here to witness this particular practice session. He'd been more distant than usual since Mabon, transitioning back to a stony, businesslike persona. I wouldn't be surprised if I walked out of the library tonight to find him turned back into his form of obsidian and quartz, if he wasn't scrolling the Internet on my phone.

It was probably my fault. Upon learning that Phaeron had taken another victim, he'd muttered, "You lied to me. He was there, and you spoke to him." I didn't deny it. A look of shock had crossed his face before the distance he imposed.

Yet I needed Geo now more than ever, and his protection may be the only thing warding Phaeron away from eating my soul next. Needing to apologize to the gargoyle weighed on my stress even now. I'd taken a glance at the search history he'd left behind...it was focused on emotions and regulation. It stung to know he was seeking out this kind of thing without asking me to help.

Distracted by my thoughts, I moved my sword in another figure eight, saying tightly, "Lux." When light erupted from it, I nearly dropped the weapon in shock. I gaped at the shining length of metal.

After three days, there it was, beautiful, *real* magic that I'd cast with my own hand.

"Mighty fine light you have there," Dr. Voidbinder said, grinning. He lifted his sword up to mine, showing how I'd lit mine brighter than his somehow. "I think that's enough for the evening. Let's get you to the powercore and home before curfew."

I nodded, blinking away the dazzled spots in my eyes. "Thank you, sir," I murmured, following him to the elevator. He scanned his badge to take us down to the level with the library's powercore.

I asked something that'd been lingering with me ever since my librarian's handbook had mentioned power levels. "What do you think my power level might be?"

Dr. Voidbinder lifted a skeptical brow. "It's a little too soon to tell. Your first few years as a witch are for learning and challenging the boundaries of what you can do with your magic," he said. "Usually, we test after that. Even modern machines run the risk of harming a new witch through the defensive and magical conduction power level tests."

All I really heard was the "usually" and turned a hopeful look his way. "No, Miss Cress. I think you need to be patient," he said.

I deflated as the elevator doors opened. At this time in the evening, we didn't see any other librarians as we went to stand before the powercore. The sight of the massive orb resting in its stone loop still lifted all the hair on my arms and neck. Its magic electrified the air, forming a soundless call to come forward and commune with it.

It'd only spoken to me one time, when it'd bonded me to the librarian witch affinity. Ever since, I'd seen it twice a week and siphoned more of its power in wordless communion. I'd gotten the sense that it wanted to give me as much magic as possible to fuel my spells. The more powerful I was, the better equipped I was to defend its library.

As I placed my hands within it, I expected more of the same, just for a force to slide me forward several inches. My arms plunged into the powercore to the elbow, covering my skin with a cold jelly-like sensation.

"Hello again, dearest and brightest soul."

Its ancient, electric presence filled my head, rendering me wordless and frozen.

"You bear my prince's mark of protection."

A little lasso of pressure surrounded the shadowy knot of magic Phaeron had left on my wrist. His boon, before going and killing again in cold blood. I tried to flinch back, shocked that the powercore acknowledged the murderous dimensional as its prince.

"I wish to commune with him. He has not visited since his release."

I shook my head stiffly. There was no telling what would happen if Phaeron got access to the raw energy of the powercore.

"Your distrust is high. I have a task for you before I allow you to commune with me again. Call to him. Ask him about the Age of Decay. See if he is truly the monster you think he is."

Electricity flowed into my body, courtesy of the powercore, far more than it'd ever given me. I trembled and pulled back, thinking its magic was going to burst out of my veins at this rate. Numbness coursed over my whole body, leaving me limp when it pushed me away. I ended up on my back, hair dangling over the first step down from its pedestal.

"Are you okay?" Dr. Voidbinder asked, helping me up slowly. My limbs felt heavy, too full of the library's coursing electricity. I felt like I could draw a thousand Lux runes, but that was my only outlet for all this magic other than losing it over time.

"Yeah, I think so," I mumbled. "Is it normal for the powercore to order you to do something?"

"Quite so," he said, giving me a curious look.

I decided to keep the task to myself. The powercore also likely knew I was too much of a coward to do as it ordered, so it kept further communion with it hanging over my head.

Sometime soon, I needed to talk to Phaeron again. The thought was a stone of dread in my stomach.

TRUE TO ITS WRITTEN WORD, *The Librarian Witch's Handbook* told me Phaeron's last recorded power level the next morning since I'd successfully cast a Lux rune.

Well, I kind of lied. His fancy-pantsy dimensional magic defied the testing methods of the time. So he's somewhere north of where a demigod starts, which is PL9.

I nearly spat a mouthful of cereal and milk over its open pages. It flapped at me in distress.

1. Gross.

2. Regretting this little vendetta yet?

"Frick! Why couldn't you just tell me he was that powerful?" I muttered, ducking my head when I felt the attention of others also eating breakfast in the cafeteria.

It replied by quickly sketching out a photorealistic version of my face on its next page, with a dunce cap on top of my head. "Captain Oblivious" was written across the hat.

I smacked it closed with a scowl. "Rude-ass book," I muttered.

After a minute, its front cover flipped open.

C'mon, Cressie-poo. You know you love me.

I glared at it harder. "Don't call me that."

It flipped another page and started aggressively spamming me with ink hearts.

"Just let me eat my breakfast in peace, and I'll forgive you," I sighed. It dutifully closed itself for me.

My bad mood persisted as I let my cats out for the day and strolled out of the dorm. Bella and Milo sensed my mood and stuck close to me, while Jin went off to cat around on her own for the day. I sighed to myself. Another day, another chance to get frozen out by Geo and look around hopefully for...

Ben stepped out of the garden path, offering forward a small bouquet of multicolored flowers. "Good morning," he said, flashing his crooked smile. It was like the clouds parted, and the sun warmed that little sad spot in my chest. I gasped and flung my arms around him.

"Aww, you missed me already?" he teased, pressing his lips to my cheek.

"Says the guy who disappeared for, like, two weeks," I said.

He handed me the flowers, and I took a happy sniff of their sweet scent. "Well, I'm gonna be around a lot more now," he said. "Walk you to class? What's first?"

I heaved a sigh. "Latin. My least favorite class."

He laced my free hand with his and let me lead the way. I didn't even glance back to see if Geo followed us. "Why'd you sign up for that?" Ben asked, wrinkling his nose.

"It's kind of a requirement. Most librarian runes are Latin-related," I grumbled.

"Oh, that sucks."

"Wish I had guardian magic sometimes," I admitted. Their magic replied to will and strength after they spoke a rune's name aloud. No making shapes with a weapon like librarians had to do. At least I wasn't a celestial witch, who had to keep complex strips of runes pre-prepared for most of their spells.

He pulled a face. "Yeah, you know, every affinity has its pros and cons. When do you get out of class for the day?"

"About two. You?"

"Yeah, close to then. What do you think about going out, just you and me? No need to bring Geometry. I'll keep you safe." His evergreen eyes glimmered with mischief.

I glanced over my shoulder, spotting Geo trailing us. It would be kind of nice to go somewhere without him always in my shadow. But the last time I'd been even partially parted from him, Phaeron had latched on to me.

I *did* need to talk to the dimensional if I ever hoped to commune with the library's powercore again. Eventually I'd run out of magic and be as useful as an ordinary woman with a sword. But I was skeptical that Ben's presence would keep me quite as safe as the gargoyle who'd already humbled Phaeron once.

"Sounds like a great time. I just don't think Geo will go for it," I said.

"Well, he's your assigned gargoyle, right? Just order him to go do something else," Ben suggested. When I hesitated on that idea, he threw up his hands. "Or give him the slip! What's the matter with a little fun? It's not like he has any emotions to be upset with you when you come back."

I raised a brow over at him. "No. I do need him. If we want more privacy later, I can ask, though."

Though frustrated, Ben didn't argue anymore, and we met up again after all my classes. He ignored the gargoyle doing some doomscrolling on my phone, standing at a polite distance away, when we met up at the library and settled at the first floor study area on a well-loved couch.

"Guess we need to use my phone," he teased, and that was the only acknowledgment he gave Geo before pulling out his device and pulling up some Myth-Flix for us to watch. I got the left earbud and he took the right one.

In the midst of us trying not to laugh too hard and interrupt people actually studying, I turned and said, "Hey, Ben. Are there theaters around that show these movies?"

"I'm sure. I'll look one up later," he promised. In the meantime, we finished the episode we were watching. So engrossed, I didn't realize he'd slowly inched his arm around my shoulders until we were cuddled closer together. I felt a little blush but settled into his side with a glance up at him.

We'd cuddled like this after the news of that fae's murder at the Mabon celebration, but that'd been a little different. Or was it? I was so aware of Ben now, getting a little shivery feeling from his fingertips brushing the skin right under my shirt's cuff. His breath smelled of mint...

His kiss had tasted like mint, too. I wondered how the smell made me want to kiss him again so much.

Ben didn't leave my side until dinnertime, only going to get to his off-campus apartment before curfew. "Same time, same place tomorrow?" he asked.

I smiled eagerly. "Sounds good."

His goodbye kiss left me with butterflies and I smiled through my dorm food meal, a big bowl of spaghetti. I pulled out my handbook and propped it up a safe distance away from the potential splash zone of red sauce. "Hey, *The Librarian Witch's Handbook*," I recited.

Its front cover lifted up. The first page simply said: *Hey.*

"Can you tell me more about anam cara?"

Are you asking me about...

It flipped the page and surrounded two big, bold words in a circle of hearts.

TRUE LOVE?

I stifled a surprised giggle. "I suppose I am!"

Okay, toots, let's see here.

Someone drew out the chair opposite mine at the little cafeteria table. I glanced up in surprise to see Geo with his own bowl, giving my handbook a confused look. "Are you talking to the blank book again?" he rumbled.

"Yes," I said. Now I was the one giving simple yes or no answers and staring. Geo rarely ate and usually didn't sit when he needed to scarf down something small.

The handbook was blank to anyone but its owner, a fact I'd learned with some surprise when I'd tried to show Geo one of its more kooky explanations to my endless stream of magic-related questions. While he twirled his fork with far more attention than the simple task required, the handbook flipped a page to give me an answer to my question about anam cara.

It displayed a sketch of the same mark on my palm. *"Anam cara" has come to define a phenomenon experienced across the greater supernatural community. Some believe one whole soul is split into two before birth and that a person will never feel complete without the person who received the other half of their whole soul. Because no supernatural power exists that can verify this, it is simply a theory. However, it's pretty widespread and accepted by those who have found their anam cara.*

An anam cara pair can establish their bond as either platonic or romantic. Either way is defined by a deep bond of friendship. Would you like me to tell you how to fix the bond in place and strengthen it?

My heart skipped along happily. I definitely felt like Ben and I were heading down the path of a romantic bond.

"I wish to speak with you about Ben," Geo said, drawing my attention out of daydreaming about the next time I'd see the man in question.

"Oh yeah?" I drew myself up, the handbook's question forgotten.

"He is your anam cara." He pointed to my hand. I'd explained what the mark was after Mabon, since he'd been curious. "I have noticed... you prefer his company."

I heard the words hanging unsaid and bit my lip. This could easily be an emotional minefield for the gargoyle who'd never experienced the nuances of relationships. It almost sounded like...well, he couldn't be jealous. I sincerely doubted it, at least.

"I have feelings for him," I said, weighing this explanation carefully. "You have to understand, that's separate from you. Just because I'm dating Ben doesn't mean I think any less of you. You keep me safe, and I appreciate that. But...there's going to be times when I will want to be alone with him. You'll have to trust him to keep me safe."

He frowned immediately. "But you are my purpose. I cannot simply entrust him with my job."

"I'm just asking you to be a bit flexible with that," I said. "I'm not in trouble if I'm with Ben." His expression shaded to distrust of that statement.

"I am a gargoyle. Stone. Rigid."

I reached across the table and poked his arm. "Not right now. You're flesh and blood, and part of that is being flexible. Bend like a reed and all that," I said, hoping he'd understand.

He looked down at his skin, where the imprints of pressure from my fingertips were rapidly fading. "I'm not sure...I am capable of what you're saying," he said slowly.

"Maybe with time," I suggested.

His face took on a neutral, stony expression. "Perhaps."

22

CRESS

B_{EN} and I took the shuttle into New Salem that weekend to visit a supernatural movie theater. A new experience for both of us, I'd learned, and I was excited to see how it was different from an ordinary trip to see the latest blockbuster.

Geo rode along in the seat behind ours, and I could tell Ben was getting frustrated with the other man's constant presence. Honestly, so was I, but I hadn't gotten through to Geo that I would be okay. Therefore, he sat behind us through a showing of a superhero movie composed of a star cast of varied supernaturals while Ben playfully fed me popcorn and chocolate-covered peanuts.

In those moments in the dark, it was almost like it was just Ben and me there. But the moment we took a walk through New Salem, I was aware again of Geo following us. Unhappily. It felt wrong, like I was teasing the gargoyle, forcing him to watch me have fun without him. But at the same time, he refused to leave even for a few hours.

"I've got a lot of...classwork to do tomorrow," Ben said apologetically at the end of our date. "I'll see you Monday night? Maybe Tuesday if it's a lot."

It would be Tuesday, I found out, spending Sunday and Monday catching up on my own work before my grades could slip from the time I spent hanging out with Ben and training with Dr. Voidbinder.

Monday evening, I picked up my silver sword and learned a slightly more advanced rune called Repello. It was...basically what it sounded like. Cast with a diagonal cut of the sword, in a motion that took it up and back toward my chest, it activated when I turned the hilt of the sword so the flat of the blade was facing outward.

"Now, young lady, be aware that this is the weak version of a rebounding spell you'll learn later," Dr. Voidbinder told me once I successfully cast it. A squared-off section of air glowed with translucent magic in front of me, prepared to cancel out the next spell aimed at it. "It will stop most magic in its tracks, but only one spell per shield. If you face an opponent that casts multiple spells at the same time." He made a popping sound and flared out his hands.

"Got it," I murmured.

"Luckily for you, you can layer up to three shields on top of each other..."

Casting Repello once was easily enough, but I didn't quite grasp how to put one shield on top of another by the time our session ended. Still, I knew two runes now. I was so proud of my progress.

I was riding that high when I put my sword away for the night and retrieved my phone. Geo hadn't wanted to use it tonight, and I was relieved when I saw what was on my screen. Ben had texted me a string of short messages, which I put together in my head. *Want to go somewhere, just you and me? No Geo?*

I shot a guilty glance over my shoulder, toward the gargoyle waiting outside the locker room. *Yeah. Where do you want to meet up?*

Thoughts of my upcoming date with Ben lasted me through the drudgery of Latin and the dry facts in Introduction to Supernatural Society, and by the time I was in Introduction to Fashion, I was in full daydream mode. It was a sunny autumn day outside. I wondered what Ben wanted to do on a nice day like this.

I snuck a glance at Geo standing in the back of the class with his arms crossed. His expression wasn't quite blank, but he certainly looked bored. I'd decided that tricking him would be for the best, but that didn't mean I didn't feel guilty as hell about it. I just didn't want him stuck so stubbornly to his duty, to the detriment of his budding emotional state. Maybe he'd thank me later for giving him the slip.

When class was over, I went to Geo and whispered, "I'm going to go to the bathroom real quick. Meet you back here?"

He nodded stiffly. "I shall wait."

I walked out at a normal pace and then booked it down the stairs, taking them two at a time. By the time he realized I wasn't coming back, I was probably way down the street and spotting Ben standing on the sidewalk with two steaming cups in hand. He fell into a jog next to me.

"This way," he said, somehow managing those cups without a spill. We took several turns down side streets on campus until slowing. "Unless he flies after us, we should be fine. Here, I got this for you. Extra sugar."

I took a deep breath of the white chocolate mocha he handed me and beamed. "Thanks! Where to now?"

"Just follow me, babe. I know the perfect place. Hope you have some walking shoes on." He glanced down at my dusty sneakers and nodded in approval.

We crossed to the fae side of campus, passing varied species of fae. They had one thing in common despite their varied looks, which were black clothes of mourning. "I thought I could show you the best part of Mabon you missed," Ben said, drawing my attention away from the dark thoughts threatening my headspace.

"Oh yeah?" I asked. He motioned forward with his chin, toward the approaching tree line. Two trees had their branches so intricately entwined that they formed a natural archway. Stepping past it was like a gateway to another world strung with the autumn rainbow.

We followed a dirt path further into the forest and my gaze fixed above us with awe. The trees here didn't simply rust. Their leaves turned into shades of ruby and gold, carnelian and bright yellow and bronze. Little creatures flew around the branches—I recognized that they were much like the diminutive people that the university some-times used to deliver letters.

"Wow," I breathed. "My friend Áine told me that New Salem used to be the Fall Court. I can totally see it here."

"This isn't even the best part," Ben laughed. We walked hand in hand deeper into the forest together. The colors grew richer, like someone had turned up the saturation filter even as the trees spaced out more and grew impossibly taller, towering over us and releasing carpets of jewel-toned leaves with each gust of wind.

Wisps of light danced around the biggest tree, set apart from the rest in a clearing heaped with leaves. I inspected it curiously, realizing I'd need about five of me to encircle its massive trunk with my arms.

"Here, hold these for a sec," Ben said, passing me his empty coffee cup and backpack. He dove headfirst in a mountain of leaves he'd vaguely shaped up, scattering them everywhere with a boyish laugh.

He stacked an even higher pile of leaves for me to jump into. They were fresh and dry, crackling perfectly under my weight. I popped my head out of the pile, watching Ben open up his backpack and start drawing out a towel and all the fixings for a little picnic.

"You came prepared," I giggled. Together, we made a mostly flat surface of leaves for the towel, and he lay out a lunch of sandwiches and other goodies.

"What can I say, I'm a good boy scout," he said with a hint of humor.

His food had gotten a little squished, but I didn't complain, instead tucking in and relaxing to the sounds of wind rustling through the massive branches of the huge tree. When we were done, I laid out with my head on the towel, more content than I'd been in a long time.

"Ben," I said, breaking the companionable silence between us. "I had a thought."

He settled next to me, close enough that I could count the sun-kissed gold flecks in his eyes. "Hmm?"

"I've told you all about my dreams. What are yours?" I asked. Not once had he mentioned his major or what he wanted to do with his life after college.

"Oh, I dream of being free—" He coughed suddenly, turning away from me and having a fit of painful-sounding coughs.

"Damn, are you all right?" I asked, catching him rubbing the corner of his mouth with a leaf before tossing it away.

He turned back to me, nodding. "Sorry, yeah. I mean, I do have dreams, but they seem so far away." He lifted his shoulder. "Still feels like I could do anything and go anywhere with half a reason to. You know what I mean?"

I considered him before smiling wide. "I think...you don't know yet. That's okay too. I thought I wasn't going to get the hang of all this magic stuff, but I know how to cast two runes now."

"I think you'd make a good librarian. I mean, you've already got the look down." He ran his fingers into my hair, dislodging a couple leaves, and let the purple strands catch the light.

"Completely unintentional."

"Still. It works. You're beautiful, babe." He continued playing with my hair, and I lidded my eyes, enjoying the brush of his fingertips over my scalp and the nape of my neck. His featherlight touches turned a brush down the curve of my cheek and neck into a shivering sensation.

Ben paused when he hit my neckline, shifting closer, closing the space between us until I could feel his heat through my shirt. My breath quickened as he resumed his gentle perusal of my body with his knuckles skimming around my arm. I shifted into him when he traced the curve and dip of my waist, and by the time he stopped to give my hip a firmer squeeze, his lips were on mine again.

He was unhurried now, exploring my mouth with the same patience. This wasn't like his fevered goodbye on Mabon, when I swore he was trying to fit all the affection of two more weeks into a few passionate moments. Something had changed in him, like he knew he could take his time and fully intended to.

I asked myself, was this handsome, mysterious man the one I wanted to be my first? I wasn't so inexperienced that I didn't recognize where this was going. Perhaps he took it slow for my benefit, as my first touch on his chest was shy, nearly unsure. A voice much like Mom's in my head reminded me that I'd just met him, and he certainly seemed like the type who could get anyone he wanted.

That wasn't why I was drawn to him, though. The answer lay on my palm, the red cupid magic seeming as permanent as a tattoo. He was my anam cara, a friend to my soul. Being apart from him had been hard already, but being with him...it just felt right.

I found the contours of his muscles through his shirt, surprised at how defined he was without a bulky hoodie on. His strong arms looped around my waist, pulling me to straddle him in one smooth motion. His hair made a golden halo around him, kiss-swollen lips drawn in a confident smile. This was exactly where he wanted me.

Until we began to slide. Squealing in surprise, I tumbled off him as the pile of leaves under us shifted with the sudden change of our weight. We landed at the base of the pile, limbs awkwardly entwined, and laughed together. "Hey, Ben?" I licked my lips, chasing away the nervous feeling in my belly until I realized it was a squirm of anticipation. "Why don't we go somewhere more private?"

23
CRESS

IT WAS late afternoon as we crossed the campus back to my dorm. "We'll go into the front," I said, knowing Geo would probably return to the garden out back to wait for my return. I was not feeling up to a confrontation with him, not when I had Ben by my side, eager at the promise of alone time.

"Lead the way," he said. I walked a little faster than normal, not that Ben was complaining. We approached my dorm from the opposite direction I usually took, going through the front with a swipe of my student ID. Unfortunately, that meant we needed to pass by the service desk, and the woman working this afternoon gave us the stink eye as we passed through the foyer and to the stairs.

That particular woman was why I didn't like going in through the front, preferring the side entrance that led directly to the stairwell. Oh well. I got Ben up to my room and locked the door behind us. I dropped my backpack next to my desk, and he did the same, taking in the little box that was my dorm again.

"It's just enough space without a roommate." Though the blank side was a constant reminder of the time when Lanie's stuff filled it, my things were slowly creeping into the void she'd left behind. The posters of my favorite classic rock bands covered the far wall now, along with an analog clock to keep me on track.

But I didn't care what time it was. Not when Ben looked at me with such singular intent, only a few feet of electrified air between us. We met somewhere in between, tumbling onto my bed until we began right where we'd left off, with my knees around his hips. I jolted when his warm fingers tunneled under the hem of my shirt, spreading along the bare skin at the small of my back.

"Cress, you're sure?" he murmured between kisses.

There he was, making sure he respected my boundaries. He pulled back from my lips, resting our foreheads together as his gaze searched my face.

"Yes," I said breathlessly.

He smiled, broad and pleased. "Just know, I think this will strengthen our anam cara bond and bring us closer to a romantic bond," he said.

I considered and began to nod to that. I wanted to follow the magic, which sang with happiness any time Ben was around. We already had a romantic bond forming, and the magic would just affirm that. "But what about protection?" I asked.

He lifted my hips with his as he pulled out his wallet, withdrawing something before flicking it to the side. He had a condom tweezed between two fingers. "Being prepared is sexy," he said with a smirk before moving his index finger to reveal he actually had two condoms in hand.

It was a little too late to be bashful, but I still felt a hint of embarrassment as I said, "Before we do anything else, you should know, um. This is my first time."

He set the condoms aside and hooked his thumb through the back loop of my jeans, sneaking a squeeze in as he lowered my core to press against him. "Don't worry, babe. It's natural," he murmured. He guided me through a bold grind against his groin, right against the bulge in his jeans.

I felt an answering jolt of wet heat between my thighs, rolling my hips into his erection as it grew underneath me. He trailed kisses over my jaw and neckline, and I moaned, a tender "oh." Questing hands drew my shirt up and over my head, his lips tracing back and forth on their way to my breasts. He paused to greet each one with a kiss and a teasing graze of his teeth that made my whole body hum.

I reached for the hem of his shirt, and he caught my hands. "Not yet," his lust-roughed voice whispered in my ear. With a sigh, I nodded. It was all I could do to keep my weight balanced on my palms while he played my body like a fine instrument.

He undid the button of my jeans, pushing the zipper aside and slipping his hand between my thighs. I practically trembled on a rush of excitement. This was really happening; I was going to lose my virginity to my anam cara, someone I saw myself staying with through college and even beyond.

His gentle touch spread my folds and his callused thumb found the button of nerves and desire at the apex. "Ah, fuck. You're already so wet for me, babe." My hands grabbed his shoulders as I felt him sink one, then two fingers into my eager channel.

I concentrated on doing what felt right, circling my hips and riding the wave of pleasure tinged with a fleeting twist of pain as he flexed his fingers and stretched those intimate muscles. Pressure built at the base of my spine, urging me to ride his digits. He felt deeper in my channel as his gaze fell to my lips. The pad of his finger brushed an intimate patch of skin that turned my legs to jelly.

"Ben," I moaned, on the edge of a cliff only his expert touch could push me over. He was watching my expressions like I was the hottest thing alive but pulled away before I found that release.

"Take the rest off," he ordered.

I sat up and pushed my panties and jeans off my hips with shaky hands. His smoldering gaze seared every inch of skin as I exposed it. He knew how to make me feel attractive rather than experiencing even a moment of doubt being this vulnerable with him.

Once I was naked, I reached for his shirt again, and this time, he obliged by holding his arms out. I gasped in surprise, taking in a broad, circular tattoo over his right side. The thing was at least six inches in diameter, covering a sizable portion of his ribs. "What does all this mean?" I asked, my gaze taking in the spiky, foreign-looking runes lining the inside of the circle, with one large rune standing out in red at its center. A few uneven lines stretched from the edge of the circle, crossing his broad chest.

"Tell you after. C'mere." He made a grabby motion and helped me into the bed and onto my back. He shucked his jeans and boxers in a quick motion, his erection bobbing free. As he reached for one of his condoms, I stroked the length of him.

He was velvet wrapped in steel, throbbing with desire. My fingers barely circled him. He laced his grip through mine, encouraging me to hold him firmer. "That's right, just like that." He let me take a few moments to admire the size and strength of him, milking out a bead of slick arousal as I slid my hold up and down his cock.

He checked my expression one more time. I smiled back, flushed with anticipation, and soon he was rolling the condom on and nudging me to lie back. He rested over me, and our lips met, tongues dueling as I felt his crown pressing to my entrance. He kissed me all the more intensely, swallowing my moan of pained pleasure as my pussy stretched to take his cock to the root. "Good?" he paused to ask, and I nodded eagerly, pulling him back to me.

My discomfort was quickly erased as he took my body to new heights. I rocked my hips into the pace of his thrusts. It *was* natural, like I was made for him, and I sank into the sensations of the moment. Already primed for him, I quickly found my first release as he shook the aging bedframe until it creaked in complaint.

"Damn, you're beautiful," he whispered, watching me ride that high. He continued a stream of praise between open-mouthed kisses and I hung on every word, holding them within like they were precious and fragile.

When we parted for air, my mouth drifted to his neck, kissing and nipping the taut skin. I wanted him to find the same completion, the same level of pleasure from me as he delivered each time our bodies rocked together. His moans were my reward as he panted and gripped my hips harder, holding me steady for the pounding of his thrusts. Our skin slapped together in time with the constant chorus of moans I breathed.

My fingernails sank into his shoulders as I felt pressure building again, swiftly detonating in a second, bigger peak on a rush of liquid heat. He followed me over that edge with a hoarse shout, finishing with a few slower thrusts before he came to a panting stop.

As we held each other afterward, I felt a tingling on my palm. I'd noticed this morning that the cupid magic that'd formed my anam cara mark was starting to fade, making the mark watery around the edges like a juice stain. Now, to my astonished eyes, it firmed up around the edges and deepened to a rich maroon.

Ben scratched at his skin before lifting his hand too, tipping it to show me his mark was now librarian witch purple. "Huh. I didn't know it'd do that," he murmured.

"You didn't?" A bit of nerves tickled my insides, threatening to tear down my afterglow.

He sucked on the inside of his cheek as he considered his purple mark. "As far as I know, it's cosmetic magic. It came from a cupid, after all." It seemed like he was trying to laugh it off, but I was relieved nonetheless. "I bet it could be removed if you didn't want it."

I shook my head. "I wouldn't want to take it off." It was like a memento of our time together, something I could show off to show that I had a romantic bond with my anam cara. Intimate, but subtle. A mark only fellow supernaturals would fully understand.

"Me neither," he said, accompanied by another kiss, which led to roaming hands and...it was a good thing he came prepared with two condoms.

Night had fallen by the time I saw Ben out of the dorm. I didn't really want him to go, but I also didn't want to be caught with a guy in my dorm room after curfew. He promised I'd see him tomorrow, and I was going to hold him to that.

"I know it is not my business." Phaeron's voice rose from behind me. "But all the same, he is the one cupid's arrow led you to? Really?"

I whirled around with a startled gasp. Sitting casually on the bench right outside my dorm was the dimensional man. He had Bella cradled like a baby in the crook of his arm, and the sight of his claws resting on her tender belly was like a bucket of ice water over my good vibes.

"Phaeron," I said carefully, edging toward him.

"Yes?" He quirked a dark eyebrow. I realized Bella was making air biscuits, purring thunderously as he rubbed her. I released a tense breath.

He jerked his chin in the direction Ben disappeared down. "He is a blood witch on the wrong path. His soul is tainted with dark magic."

"Right," I said dubiously.

"Don't stop," Bella squeaked.

He turned a smile down to her. "Mrraw," he replied, jiggling his hand between her front legs as she slow blinked at him. Aw man, why'd he have to be a cat lover? He'd turned Bella into a content puddle.

I cleared my throat. "Could you put my familiar down?"

"Oh, this sweet girl is yours? All the better," he said offhandedly, but he didn't put her back on the ground. "Come sit with me a moment. There are matters we must discuss."

The powercore's demand came to the forefront of my mind, and I bit my lip. There wasn't a clearer chance than this. "I'm supposed to ask you a question," I said. "Something about decay?"

He slanted a look sideways, his topaz eyes seeming to blaze. "She is quite meddlesome, isn't she?" His tail twitched.

"She?" I echoed, confused.

"Many facts about the object you know as a powercore are secrets closely guarded by my people. When you last communed with her, she sent a bolt of pure power through you, to me, with a short message to come find you." He lifted his right arm, which appeared to be completely healed. I hadn't realized the powercore could send anything *through* me to him, let alone the kind of power to heal broken bones. "So...here I am."

I wet my suddenly dry lips. He seemed irritated to be here, summoned and forced to interact with me because of the powercore.

"Y-you could just go. You came, I asked, and—"

"No." His expression softened as he placed Bella on the ground and patted the bench next to him. "It appears I am required to give you a history lesson. She wanted me to tell you about the Age of Decay for whatever good it may do us both."

See if he is truly the monster you think he is, it had said. She? Could an orb of pure power have a gender?

"She wanted you to come commune with her in person," I murmured. I sat next to him, close enough to touch. His gaze flashed toward the bare inches between us, clear awareness in his expression.

Then he sighed, tilting his head back and folding his hands in his lap. "Do you know something I never grew accustomed to in your world? The stars are so much closer. You can count every spark in your constellations. My world, Soiluire, had few stars. None so close to us as the sun, especially. On any given day, the light of our closest star would send red-tinged light over only half of our cities and townships."

I startled again when a furry shape jumped into my lap. It was just Milo, apparently jealous of Bella getting attention. He bunted my chest as Phaeron chuckled at my expense. "Two familiars. Good potential, bright soul," he said.

My hand paused halfway down Milo's back as I slanted a glance at the dimensional. "The powercore called me something like that," I said.

"I know. It is literal." His topaz eyes slanted back in my direction, admiring for a moment. "As I was saying, I came from a place of darkness. The only major source of light was a flare of sudden light across the sky one night that fell from the heavens. It was...an egg of sorts, and even when the goddess hatched from it, her vessel remained and glowed like a pure white sun. We worshiped her immediately, this being that emerged fully formed. The goddess of light, Myuna. Any touched by her grace glowed with her radiance. She turned our shadow magic from black to white, a phenomenon that makes it look like fire. We emerged from the darkness to surround her anointed Torchbearers.

"Our civilization was rebuilt around her vessel. Great temples, high powers. The three tribes of my people came together and crowned a king and queen." He finally turned back to me, a bittersweet look on his face. "My parents. They ruled for an entire age before deciding to have children. My royal mother birthed twins. First my brother, Endaeron, and myself a few minutes after."

He extended a hand, two wisps of shadow taking form on his palm. One was extra broad with a pair of bat wings and horns that stuck outward. I recognized Phaeron in the second shadow, which was shorter and leaner next to his twin, without the wings. His brother had to have been huge to be even taller and broader that the already massive Phaeron.

"Myuna chose him from the cradle to carry her blessing. I cannot summon white shadow to show you, but her magic's presence bleached his skin stark white, and when he summoned his shadows for the first time, they glowed from within with her radiance."

"What about you?" I asked, my brow knitting.

"I bear the blessing of the land itself. I am shadowborn, a guardian of the spaces untouched by the sun. Don't be alarmed," he cautioned before shadows wrapped around his hand and extended his fingertips into massive, sharp talons. I watched them with a surge of fear anyway, imagining what damage they could do to myself or my familiars.

When he stopped flexing his hand, the talons retracted, and the little shadows he'd summoned warped and were now facing each other. I recognized the silhouette of the same ram-horned wolf creature that my librarian's handbook had shown me, and his brother's true form was like a mirror to it but with forward-facing horns and more bulk. "Technically, Endaeron was also shadowborn, but Myuna turned him into...something else. They called him lightborn, and as crown prince, he was celebrated and loved."

I frowned, not sure I liked his tone or where this story was going. "We had a very deeply rooted problem," he murmured, closing his hand on the shadows. "I was many centuries into my existence when Myuna revealed her true face. She was no benevolent goddess at all, but a monstrous creature who'd bided her time and ingratiated herself in our culture, spreading her influence until the right moment."

"Oh shit," I muttered.

He inclined his head. "To say the least. The Age of Decay tore down our society within a day. Myuna's Torchbearers died instantly, their souls enslaved and forced to bring a steady stream of my people to Myuna for her to feed upon. She glutted herself on the souls of millions." Phaeron's gaze was years in the past, dulled by the grief of what he described.

"The white shadows of Myuna turned instantly from a blessing to the worst of curses. My brother's corruption was the direst of all, as he was afflicted by the same hunger for souls as the goddess who chose him as a babe. He transformed into a monster and became known as... well."

When he hesitated, I blurted out what I thought he was going to say. "The Hungering Darkness?" I asked in a small voice.

"Don't say its name! You don't want its attention," he hissed, going bolt upright.

I sucked in a fearful gasp as a chill wind blew over us. Phaeron got to his feet, shadowy claws overlaying both his hands as he crouched protectively in front of me. "Cress. Go inside," he ordered. When I simply stared at him, fear having me by the throat, he roared over his shoulder. "Now!"

"*Cress?*" a soft voice, merely a thread of sound, hissed from the darkness. "*At last...*"

That certainly motivated me. I stumbled over my own two feet in my haste to book it to my dorm. My shaking hands made swiping my student ID a challenge, but when I got the door open, in bolted three furry shapes ahead of me as Phaeron bellowed, "Coward! Show yourself!"

With a flimsy glass door between me and trouble, I turned back. There was...nothing outside. Just a wave of shadow magic that eclipsed the light of the closest streetlamp. A little sting swiped over my shin. It was Jin, who hissed when I looked down at her.

"Sorry, sorry," I said, remembering myself. Phaeron could handle himself, but I rushed up to my dorm to take shelter behind a solid wall of cinderblock.

All three cats pressed to my legs as I lay out on my bed. I could feel Bella and Milo's terror like my own, but Jin's presence was a shock. Her scratches may just have saved our lives. As we waited there, I heard nothing, no way of knowing whether a battle occurred right outside the dorm. I should've gone to bed, but I just lay there, sweating, waiting for any sign that the Hungering Darkness wasn't outside, lying in wait to consume my soul.

Eventually, I met Jin's eyes. She was curled up by my hip, but she raised her head when she realized she had my attention. "It wasn't him, was it?" I whispered.

The cat simply stared for a moment. Lanie had trusted her familiar immediately to explore the campus and chose when she wanted to come and go from our dorm room. A little-known fact about that night: Jin had been there. But I'd never asked, assuming this whole time that Phaeron was the murderer.

Finally, Jin meowed, and Milo stirred. "She says no," he translated.

"This whole time," I murmured in a broken whisper. "It...it wasn't him. But then...who was it?"

"She wants to remind you that Lanie left you answers," Milo squeaked.

24
CRESS

Dearest Cress, began the hardest read of my life.

Lanie's pages and pages of frantically typed notes filled my computer screen at last. I'd let her email get buried under the mundane traffic of a college student's life, but no longer.

I'm sorry I left your life so abruptly. I knew you would try to stop me if I'd tried to warn you. We may not have known each other long, but you were a good friend to me, and I appreciated getting to know you.

"Ah, fuck. I can't do this," I said tearfully, closing my laptop and holding my face in between my hands. A small cat jumped into my lap, and at first, I thought it was Bella, come to comfort me. I stroked her back and glanced down in surprise, because Jin's fur was longer and softer than I expected.

She couldn't talk to me like my two familiars, but when she pawed at my laptop, her message was still clear. I couldn't keep pushing off reading the message...and disrespecting her deceased witch because of my own pain.

"You're right," I sighed, and she settled into a tight, not-purring ball in my lap as I opened the computer and started reading again.

I know you're not going to read this right away. But the pathways of fate have shown me you do eventually, sometime in early October. Jin is there to offer what comfort she can, and you've just had a scare.

I nodded along, my lips twisting wryly at just how correct she was.

It is very difficult to scry events that happen after one's death, but for the first time, I must brag on my Graygazer heritage. I've opened up small windows into the future to give you tidbits of what is to be. Be careful what you do with it all, because scrying this way is usually pretty inaccurate.

First, I don't know who it was that killed me. For years, I had nightmares of a man painted with blood witch runes but with claws of white fire for hands. I knew he was my destiny.

Pausing, I read that line again. White fire for hands... It sounded a lot like the white shadow Phaeron was just talking about. If I was right about his brother, she *was* killed by the Hungering Darkness.

But the Hungering Darkness *wasn't* Phaeron. He wasn't wearing any sort of runes that night, nor did he need to.

I wondered what else he'd told me that I hadn't believed, my gaze falling to the maroon-tinted anam cara mark in my palm. I minimized Lanie's note for a minute, pulling up the document where I kept my class notes instead and searching for auras. We'd covered them in both my introductory classes, and I'd pasted images from the slideshows to have a reference for aura colors I could return to.

I zoomed in on the image that had all seven witch affinities side by side. Librarian purple, verdant green, celestial yellow...

Guardian witches were oddballs, with auras that were either a soil brown or a neon green accompanied by the shapes of spiked geodes. I'd seen spikes and that same shade in Ben's aura countless times. Yet the mark in my palm was in the range of crimson to maroon that was associated with blood witches.

A sour feeling stirred in my belly as I compared my mark to the chart, double and triple checking to be sure. *Shit. Things are not as they seem at all.*

I didn't fully understand how this could've happened...but one thing was for sure. Ben had lied to me somewhere along the line. I could still feel the ghost of his touch on my skin and hear his praising whispers, but the pleasure had turned to ice. He'd concealed what he was, but his soul couldn't lie. Not to the anam cara mark and not to Phaeron, who'd mentioned that his soul was tainted with dark magic.

I took a shaky breath, muttering some of my handbook's more colorful euphemisms for "shit" as I returned to Lanie's letter.

As far as I can scry, the monster that killed me is a parasite of sorts, jumping from host to host and bringing out the worst in them. It is fed entirely by souls and absorbs their power. Considering it has no body of its own, it can hide for ages, slowly breaking down the willpower of its host.

I think you know by now that dimensional monsters are really scary and alien. I may be biased, but this is the scariest one. That's why you have to kill it, Cress. For good. But you can't do it alone. Only you can bring together a team capable of defeating this creature.

I read the paragraph again, frustration needling under my skin. It was asking too much to think she'd give me a convenient list of everyone needed for this team, but who could kill the monster that even Morgana Voidbinder, a demigoddess, had failed to destroy?

By the way, you have to know that Geo woke up only to help you. He has no emotions to understand it is the pull of a true mate bond between you two that constitutes his "duty."

"What!" I yelped.

I know it's hard to believe, but he needs you to show him the way. Then he'll understand and maybe even embrace who he is.

I sat back, clutching my head. The cupid's feather *had* heated in his presence, though. Perhaps if I'd offered it to Geo rather than Ben, I wouldn't be simmering with a knife of betrayal buried so deeply in my back. If Geo was anything, he was brutally *honest*. And he'd been right about Ben all along. I needed to do better for my gargoyle guardian, then perhaps we could say the words "true mate bond" out loud.

That was the end of Lanie's most world-shaking revelations for me. She shared other, smaller facts about the people, friends and otherwise, that I spent the most time with. Things to say to Wren to get her to think rather than react. A research path for Roe so she could find out what "fae trickery" Grant was involved in, which made me feel all kinds of uncomfortable for just assuming he was usually high off his mind.

She encouraged me to tell the truth of what I'd seen and experienced since before her death to Roe and anyone else I trusted. At the end, she signed off with love and a blessing to adopt Jin. And a PS: *You will have to hurt Ben to help him.*

I closed my laptop with the finality of another goodbye and rested my forehead on its cool lid. It was still the middle of the night, and instead of giving me the kind of concrete answers to go forth and conquer, it felt like Lanie had dumped an unmanageable end goal on me.

Bring together a team capable of helping me destroy an unkillable creature.

Take down said creature, the Hungering Darkness, a dimensional parasite currently latched in secret to someone else.

Pass my classes. That was kind of important too.

If Ben was in class tomorrow, somehow, I needed to not tip off that I knew he was lying about...maybe a lot of things. Because as I sat there thinking, I connected a few circumstances too neat to be mere coincidences.

I strongly suspected that the man who'd appeared right after Lanie's death with a strong curiosity for me...

A guy who I hadn't kept tabs on for hours at the Mabon cele-bration...

Someone who'd still be within a couple blocks of my dorm when I'd said "the Hungering Darkness" aloud...

A blood witch in disguise, hiding who knew what else.

Ben had to be the true host of the dimensional monster who'd killed my friend. He was someone I had to hurt to help, because I wasn't letting the Hungering Darkness nibble away at my anam cara, even if he was a liar with a lot to answer for.

SINCE I HADN'T SLEPT, I felt like absolute trash when my phone's alarm went off. Jin stirred in my lap with a low chirp before putting one of her front legs over her ears. That was about my mood, too.

I shuffled through the morning motions before exiting the dorm out of my usual door. I quickly spotted Geo in the garden, since the bulk of his gargoyle form's wings was unmistakable. He'd frozen the clothes he'd been wearing yesterday into solid stone over his figure. My heart sank somewhere in the vicinity of my knees when he turned stiffly to look at me, his expression coldly blank.

Pausing mid-step, I gulped a swallow. Lanie's words about a true mate bond flowed through my mind. I'd truly made him miserable, making him watch Ben and I together, none of us knowing he had a different kind of supernatural draw to me. It was easy to see in retrospect, and now my fuckup was staring me in the face.

"Hi, Geo," I said tentatively.

"Greetings," he ground out.

I figured it was best to address the elephant in this garden. "You're in your stone form again." I braced myself for his reply as his stone lips dipped toward a frown.

"You left me in the cold. This was more comfortable." Between the gritting of his stone voice, I recognized a steely thread of anger. He lifted his heavy arm and pointed at my chest. "I searched for hours for you. Just to learn you were off with Ben."

My shoulders drew in. "Look, Geo, I'm sorry."

"Then I find the dimensional murderer here this evening. Yelling into the night," he continued as if I hadn't spoken.

"Was he okay?" I asked, wondering how long after I took shelter that this happened.

"I chased him away. Neither of us felt like another fight." Stone scraped as he tilted his head at me. "You ask after his wellbeing while ignoring mine."

I put my palms up. "That's not it at all."

He stood straight again, withdrawing his accusing finger. "It is fine. You are still my duty. Killing Phaeron is still my purpose. And then I can go back to the library, where I belong."

"Geo, no, I—"

"To Latin?" He turned away, starting to head that way.

I watched him turn his back on me with a sinking sensation in my chest. Damn, this was bad, maybe irreparable. That would be what I deserved, stuck with the liar I'd chosen rather than the loyal man I'd upset.

"Geo, please listen. I didn't want to hurt your feelings. I just wanted to go out for an afternoon without an escort," I said to his back as we started down the sidewalk.

"What feelings?" he said woodenly. "I have none. They are nothing but trouble."

I winced, feeling his words like a physical blow. "And I've discovered some things that you should know. I think we've been mistaken about who killed my friend this whole time."

He stopped abruptly, and I nearly ran straight into his wings. Whirling faster than I thought was possible for his stone form, he glared hard enough that I took a step back. "Is he so charming that he can disarm you so easily?" he demanded. "Have you been playing with not one, but two distrustful men behind my back?"

"No, I just...I actually listened to him last night. We were wrong. Phaeron and the Hungering You-Know-What are two different people." I spoke rapidly in the face of his rage.

He stared, considering. "The Hungering—"

"No, don't say its name!" I burst out.

"—Darkness."

I tensed with a rush of terror, remembering all too well that little voice from the shadows that'd appeared nearly instantly when I said its name.

Geo's expression softened a fraction. "He will not attack you in my presence. You are safe. That is what you said before, yes? That I help you feel safe."

I touched my chest, where my heart raced with a burst of adrenaline. "Y-yeah. And that hasn't changed. I just made a dumb mistake."

He released a dry huff and resumed the trek to my first class. Well, forgiveness wouldn't be easily earned, but he still stopped and waited as I took a pit stop at the campus coffee shop. The line was long today, but I absolutely needed a caffeine fix.

The person at the back of the line turned when the door slammed closed behind me, and I sucked in a gasp. It was like looking at a ghost come back to life. I'd seen that face dozens of times, with its slightly crooked smile and a hint of chub stubbornly clinging to the apples of his cheeks. Lucas. A younger, slightly shorter version of Ben here doing something as mundane as ordering a coffee.

"Excuse me," I said, tapping him on the shoulder. "You look so much like someone I know. Are you related to Ben?"

"Oh!" He lit up immediately. "Yeah, that's my big bro! Have you seen him lately?"

I tilted my head, wondering if he knew Ben had been looking for him for ages with a reaction like that. "He's in one of my classes," I said, extending a hand. "I'm Cress."

He shook my hand quite firmly. Ouch. "Lucas," he said. "I've been looking for...for him for a while."

I chuckled, rubbing at my palm. "No kidding?"

"Yeah, family stuff, you know? Things aren't so great back at home. His affinity turned out to be blood, and he didn't take it well. Our family expects us to be guardians." He shrugged, putting his hands casually in his pockets. "He just ran off one day."

"Well, I can get you in contact with him, no problem," I said, taking out my phone. I snapped a quick picture of him, to his half-formed protest, and texted it to Ben.

"Missing something?" I sent with the picture.

He responded immediately. "O shit brt."

"Y-yeah," Lucas was saying, scratching behind his head. "He been doing okay? How do you know him?" My phone buzzed several times as he spoke.

"We have a class together and...I think maybe we're going steady." My smile was sad, though, considering the gulf of secrets I'd just discovered. I didn't trouble Lucas with any of that, though, especially as I started to really consider his presence and obvious lies. He wasn't nearly as slick as Ben.

He was, like, sixteen at most. What family sent a kid who should still be in high school onto a college campus? Especially one now on lockdown after two gruesome murders. I peered at my phone, frowning at the series of short messages.

I pieced it together in my mind, reading it in a panicky tone with how much Ben repeated my name. "Cress, don't go anywhere with him. Stay there. Okay? Cress? Make sure you have Geo! Cress, read your messages."

My brows rose steadily as I turned my attention back to Lucas. He was beaming and saying, "Aw, he got a girlfriend! Look at how much I missed."

He was next at the counter and ordered his coffee quickly, as did I. We stood at the bar together, waiting for our drinks. "It's only been about a week or so. You haven't missed much," I said.

"Cool, cool. Maybe I could walk you to class or something?" he suggested. "I gotta know the girl that's caught my bro's eye."

"Yeah, sure," I said, only feeling a twinge of unease because of Ben's messages. Something weird was afoot, and I needed one of the brothers to explain.

We stepped outside with drinks in hand, and Geo turned to acknowledge me with the barest of nods before glaring at Lucas. "Oh shit," the young man murmured.

"Lucas, this is Geo, my guardian from Moongrove Library," I said, watching the uncertainty play over his face.

It wasn't a surprise when he laughed nervously and hitched a thumb over his shoulder. "Actually, I think I should be going. It was nice to meet you, Cress!"

"But your brother—" I said before cutting myself off. He'd already turned and was power walking his way to the corner where two streets intersected. I watched him take on a burst of speed as he hooked a left with the sidewalk.

"Good riddance," Geo muttered.

I was about to ask why the sudden hostility when a pair of hands seized my shoulders. It was Ben, who looked me over with a frantic air. "Where'd he go?" he demanded. I pointed and started to answer, but he was already taking off in hot pursuit.

I turned back to Geo instead. "What the fuck," I said under my breath.

"So, Latin?" Geo asked.

"...Fuck Latin. I want answers," I decided. I pointed at his stone wings. "How well do those actually fly?"

"They are adequate."

"Let's follow them from the air," I suggested, waiting impatiently for him to consider before offering a single, grinding nod. He scooped me into his arms, bridal style, only jostling a dribble of coffee onto the sidewalk.

I held on to the cup despite the obvious dangers of dropping or spilling it. Geo lumbered into a running start, flaring out his gigantic stone wings before lurching into the sky. He was unsteady at first, listing to one side, and I cried out, certain we were about to crash. With a few mighty pumps of his wings, we accelerated and lifted higher into the sky.

Cold wind streamed by, but pressed to Geo's solid presence, I gained more confidence that we weren't about to suddenly fall out of the sky due to his weight. Obviously, he could still fly despite being made of solid stone. I wasn't questioning it, not when we gained rapidly on the brothers. I spotted Ben's golden head first, dodging around people and obstacles with all the agility of a parkour expert.

Two blocks up was Lucas at a full sprint. He glanced over his shoulder before hooking a sharp left. I was tempted to shout directions to Ben, but he wasn't so easily shaken. Geo slowed to follow Ben, staying over buildings so we didn't throw off a noticeable shadow.

"What do you think this is about?" His voice grinded next to my ear.

"Lucas said he was looking for Ben, and Ben's been looking for Lucas for ages," I answered.

"Then this makes no sense."

"Exactly."

"I have never trusted Ben."

"Yeah, I get that. He's been hiding his blood witch aura." I glanced over my shoulder at Geo's serious expression, backlit by the blinding halo of the sun. "That's what you really meant by him having a chameleon aura."

"Indeed."

"Couldn't you have just *said* that?"

"You were not ready to listen," he rumbled.

I breathed a sigh. "You were right all along, and I'm listening now."

For a moment, Geo smiled. Just a faint tilt to his obsidian lips, but a small victory nonetheless.

I ducked my head as he banked hard, slowing further when Ben finally lost sight of Lucas and came to a stop, bending over and grabbing his knees. Distracted as I'd been talking to Geo, I hadn't noticed the younger brother disappear, but there was no sight of him even from the air.

"Shh. Let's see where he goes," Geo said in his quietest voice as we landed a few buildings back, on the side not facing Ben. A good thing, too, as the gargoyle's weight made a noticeable thud when he came to a stop. I could just imagine Ben startling and looking up, but if we couldn't see him, he couldn't see us.

Geo held up a finger for me to wait, and a couple excruciating minutes passed before he motioned for me to go to the other side of the roof. I crouched and stepped over a clutter of old junk being stored up here, taking to my hands and knees before the lip of the roof and peeking over the edge.

Ben's golden-brown head of hair was just passing underneath, heading back the way he'd come at a slow, defeated pace. I watched to see if he would turn right with the sidewalk, but he glanced left to right and crossed the street instead.

I returned to Geo and nodded. His takeoff was a lot smoother this time, with several stories of air between us and the sidewalk below. We circled around and went higher into the sky, to the point our shadow shrank. I hoped Ben would simply return to the coffee shop, but he didn't, instead taking a turn off campus grounds and down the main road leading into the city section of New Salem.

Leaving the campus was a lot easier than entering, and I knew that Ben had mentioned having an apartment in the city. "He's probably going home after all that," I said. My phone buzzed with a few messages, likely from him, but I didn't trust myself to take out my device with the possibility for the wind to snatch it and dash out its innards several stories below.

"You wanted answers. We will demand them," Geo replied.

That sounded damn good to me.

25

BEN

I'D JUST UNLOCKED the door to Garroway's private property when a *whoosh-thud* sounded behind me. I whirled around in one smooth motion with a dagger in hand, just to see Geo unfolding from a landing crouch and letting Cress down from his arms. *Shit.* I jabbed the weapon back into my sleeve before she could notice it.

"Cress? You followed me...from the *sky*?" I asked, uneasy by the tight look she spared me.

"Hey. We need to talk."

"Ah. The four words a guy dreads most," I said, sparing a nervous laugh when Geo squared up behind her, his bulky arms crossed. He flexed one of his wrists, and I heard the hiss of air.

She licked her lips, tucking a bit of her bright hair behind her ear. "I need you to come with me to Moongrove Library," she said.

I cocked a brow. "Why?"

"Well, um. I think I understand why you were gone for two weeks now. You've been feeling kind of sick, huh?" Sympathy mixed into her tone, and she held out a hand. "The librarians should be able to sort you out. Let's go now."

I glanced from her proffered hand back to her face. "Babe, you're scaring me," I said, trying to laugh it off again. "I feel fine. Why don't we catch a movie or something since you're here? You can even bring Geocentric in if he promises not to break anything."

"Look, Ben. Try not to freak out, okay? But I think you have a dimensional monster tagging along in your soul right now, and we need to get it out," she said. Even Geo turned a confused look her way.

I put my hands up. "I have no idea what the fuck you're talking about."

"There is no harm in getting tested," Geo rumbled.

"I'm not sick," I protested. "You two are coming at me right now with some shit. I'm not going to the library."

Geo cracked his stony knuckles and smiled. Fucking smiled. He was going to force me to go along with this mess and would enjoy every moment of it.

"This is…this isn't how I thought this conversation would go." Cress heaved a sigh, rubbing her forehead. "Something really weird is happening with you—and your brother, too. He didn't say much to me that actually made sense with how he was acting."

That's because he was only in the coffee shop to kill her, I thought, still quivering with nerves at the thought of how close a call she had. "I don't really know what he's doing, either," I admitted. If he had a new master, then his first mission assigned by Garroway shouldn't matter to him anymore. "I'm on your side, all right?" As much as I could be, at least.

"I know," she said faintly before coming to some sort of decision internally. She lifted her shoulders and took a deep, steadying breath. "But I also know you're a blood witch. You've been lying about that and probably a lot of other things, too." She tipped her hand, flashing the blood-witch-maroon mark on her palm.

A queasy feeling settled in my belly, and my veins chilled with ice water. I should've known I would get caught, but this was so much sooner than expected. "You're right," I said, and each word emerged from my throat like razor blades. I winced at the sudden taste of blood in my mouth. I was dangerously close to admitting too much about myself. "But…that doesn't change the fact that I'm on your side."

At last, with the truth revealed, I started trying to word the impossible. My warning that she needed to leave, forgotten in my own greed for more time with her. I'd acted like Lucas would never find her, like she would be mine forever...like I could escape Garroway's iron-clad grip on my blood.

As if I'd summoned him, my blood rune began to heat. "Oh no. No," I murmured in horror. Crimson light erupted from under my shirt, and Cress gaped as I bent double from the sudden searing agony of Garroway's singular attention.

"*Benjamin!*" he snarled in my head. Somewhere in his manor, he had his black dagger raised and his eyes closed. My own eyes blazed with red light as he hijacked my senses. "*I have watched you lead these two to my property. Do you think I didn't install security? 'I am on your side,' hmm? She is your brother's mark to kill.*"

"*Master, please.*"

"*No, little Benjamin. You haven't been doing your job.*" A jab of pain lanced my head, like he pressed his finger a little too firmly into my temple.

"Ben?" Cress asked fearfully, but I was blinded and reeling from the sudden assault on my nerve endings.

"*I believe you have been...incredibly distracted.*" I felt my hand uncurl from the heated rune on my chest, held stiffly in front of my watering gaze. Garroway laughed, the sound echoing in my head. "*As I suspected. Return to the manor.*"

He manipulated my body like the puppet master he was until I was standing stiffly upright with two of my hidden daggers now unsheathed and deadly in my fists. My vision swam back into focus as Garroway started relinquishing his hold on me. Geo had pushed Cress behind him, and she looked over his shoulder in horror, her slim hands wrapped around his muscled arm to try holding him back.

"*Return to the manor,*" Garroway repeated, his voice now holding the echo of an order I could not defy. "*Do not let anything stop you. Between fight or flight, you will fight first.*"

"*Yes, Master,*" I had to answer, though every cell in my body screamed defiance.

His presence left, as did the sudden knife of pain he'd jammed into my ribcage. But even with the lightshow dimmed, the danger was far from over. Geo had his arm lifted, and light winked off the needle-sharp tip of a quartz spike aimed straight at my heart.

I threw myself to the ground as he fired it. With a *thump*, it sank to the root in the solid wood door behind me. "That was rude, Geology," I snarked before cursing when I realized he had a second one primed and ready to go in his other arm.

"Put down your weapons at once," he demanded.

"No can do," I replied. My fingers would literally not uncurl, except my thumb and pointer to seize the little vial of Garroway's blood I flicked out of the ring on my right hand. I shattered it, coating my fingers in vampire blood, and deftly painted the runes for speed, strength, and regeneration up my arm as the gargoyle took aim at me.

"Geo, don't!" Cress screamed. "He's not himself. We can still save him!"

He shot the second spike at me without hesitation. Honestly, I didn't blame him. But with a vampire's preternatural speed, I flipped out of the way and landed in a crouch. Aggression pulsed under my skin, Garroway's command urging me to leap out and try to damage the gargoyle's obsidian skin. I'd probably just break good steel in the attempt.

Cress jumped out from behind Geo's aggressive stance, and I had a new target. I judged whether I had enough control to pull off what I was thinking of and leapt out at her. She gasped in surprise as I held the edge of a blade to her throat, my hand shaking with the effort to hold back from following up with any number of other attacks.

She looked at me like I was the worst kind of monster, her wide brown eyes filled to the brim with fear and betrayal.

"Forget about me," I shouted. "Go! Far from here. Not just to campus!"

Geo lunged at me, and I peeled away from her just in time to avoid the grasp of his stone hands. I pulled back with effort, taking off at a run before my compelled body could launch another attack at either of them. My primary directive was to return to the manor, so I did, running at an impossibly fast pace until the speed rune on my arm dried and flecked off into blood-red dust. Those never lasted long enough.

I tried to stop and catch my breath, but Garroway had tied his web too tightly around me for any hint of rest. I climbed one of the high walls that'd been lifted on this side of campus with sheer strength, bypassing a need to go through campus security with obvious blood witch runes on my skin. At least for the climb, I'd managed to sneak my daggers back into their sheathes.

As I took back streets to avoid most students on campus, it really sank in. I was compelled to run straight toward my funeral. Garroway had glimpsed the anam cara mark through my eyes. *As I suspected.* His smug words played on repeat in my head. How long had he been on to me?

All I knew was that it was over. Ruined. Even if I survived Garroway's punishment, there was no way Cress would ever trust me again. Cress knew I was a blood witch and, now that I'd held a dagger to her throat, probably figured out I was an assassin too. She would regret the anam cara mark on her palm, just like how I kicked myself for wearing such an obvious sign of affection for her for Garroway to find.

Hopefully she took my words to heart and got the fuck out of town.

I finished my marathon of a run to the manor's pocket dimension and nearly collapsed right outside the front steps. Two men caught me, Seth and one of the other senior blood witches. "I'm sorry, son," Seth murmured.

Panting hard, I turned to see my mentor's face twisted in hard sympathy. Yet he followed orders with the other witch. They marched me inside on my jelly-weak limbs and took an immediate turn for the room Garroway kept connected to his private rooms.

His torture chamber, a box of tiny red tiles that were painfully textured on bare knees. No matter how much we scrubbed and bleached it, it always smelled faintly of dried blood.

I was thrown to the ground, forced to kneel in front of Garroway seated in the only chair in the room. He wore a black satin night robe and a disgusted expression as he looked down his nose at me. After dismissing the other two witches with a nod, he lifted the night-black dagger and activated my blood rune, leaving me on the ground before him like a limp marionette.

Seth closed the door behind him and plunged us into near darkness, except for the dim red light Garroway preferred to work under in this room.

"How eagerly I have waited for this day," he drawled. His voice was deeper in here, every edge of his slow cadence magnified with sharp edges as I quivered in helpless fear. Under the red lighting, he was a demon with blood-red skin and half the planes of his face in shadow.

What he said sank in as he drank in the moment. My brow twitched the barest bit from confusion. Eagerness was not something I associated with Garroway. He'd lived long enough that I doubted he even felt the joy of being eager for anything.

"Going on sixteen years, in fact." He set the black dagger down, a minor relief. There wouldn't be any more pain through my blood rune for a while if he was settling in for a lecture. "Are you familiar with the butterfly effect?"

With my mouth sealed and my body frozen at his feet, I merely stared at him.

"A small action having a greater aftereffect, of course." Garroway answered his own question without missing a beat. "I have made millions just by being there to take advantage of whatever aftereffect was started by my clients' requests. Let me tell you a story, little Benjamin."

Dread pooled in my stomach. I hated Garroway's lectures and stories, because ultimately, there was some analogy that looped back to our current situation and a punishment to come along with it.

When I was fifteen, I was caught stealing medical supplies. The infirmary was available to everyone except during a particular part of our training, when Garroway carved the blood rune into our skin. It was the most painful thing in existence, and when he'd given me mine, I'd sworn for days that he'd killed me as I came in and out of sober consciousness as the blood rune's magic seared its way into every pore of my body.

For Lucas, that'd been when he was eleven. When Garroway was done with him, I'd snuck into his room with painkillers, antiseptic, and ointment to save him some of that agony.

After I was caught, Garroway sat me down in this room, just like this. He'd described in detail how a blood rune could take root incorrectly if it healed too early. A similar case came about in the early 1900s, when a blood witch managed to drag herself out of bed and treat her wound with a healing potion. The rune bonded incorrectly to her body, resulting in constant pain no matter what she did until she committed suicide to make it stop.

He'd described her death in vivid detail before taking a mallet to my hand for stealing and had me stand outside the door as he "reapplied" the rune to Lucas. I wasn't allowed to heal myself for three days, and Lucas took a whole week from there to recover; the initial application of the rune should've taken him four days.

"I once was acquainted with a celestial witch by the name of Marie Evenstar," Garroway began, sitting back like we were sitting before a fire, sharing stories. "She was rather powerful, but of course, most witches of her affinity are. She had a business reading star charts for supernatural children. With unerring accuracy, she could tell a parent what was in store for their child. I imagine there were a few embellishments. Not everyone is destined for greatness under the stars.

"Marie came to me with a tale of woe. You see, misfortune had struck her in a series of three acts. The stars had not warned her that her business partner, Eris Darkmore, would meet an untimely end along with the rest of her family as part of an electrical failure in their house."

Seth must've burnt the house to the ground to hide any evidence of the truth. A sour feeling began to squirm in my belly. Why would he bring up the Darkmore job again?

"She was not, in fact, all that skilled at celestial magic, as it turns out. But her best friend Eris was and could channel great amounts of celestial energy into and through Marie, who had a power level of five, but only in that skill. Without Eris, she was useless with star charts. Her business tanked, and she started taking on debts she couldn't pay.

"Then her husband passed away in a car wreck. Marie was inconsolable as she sat on my couch, explaining how desperately she needed money. She'd lost everything at that point. Her husband, her best friend, and soon her business as well. She begged me to loan her a sum every bank balked at and promised to sell the business, her home, and most of her possessions to afford paying me back. Bankruptcy was out of the question for a woman who'd married into such a storied family as the Evenstars. She still had appearances to maintain, she explained."

He tilted his head, a smile playing at his lips. His fangs flashed red in the low lighting, and I realized he actually was looking eager to tell this story. I didn't like the way he looked at me at all, like I was about to deliver him the most delicious feast.

"You see, Marie was desperate to move forward on a good foot as a single mother," Garroway continued. "For she had two young boys at home, Benjamin and Lucas."

My lungs spasmed with a gasp I wasn't able to utter. He was talking about my fucking *mother* right now, more details than he'd ever spared. I didn't know her name, her affinity, or anything past the incredible sum of five million Garroway had paid her to take my brother and me off her hands.

"She'd said you both had such promise in your futures. Tearfully, she even admitted that one of you had a star chart linked with the sweet girl who'd perished in that fire, little Luna Darkmore."

Cress. He was talking about Cress. Holy shit! Hot needles seized my shoulders as I tried to move, to scream, to react at all.

"She just wanted enough money to get by. And do you know what I gave her?" He took up the dagger at last and gestured, loosening my jaw so I could answer him.

"Five million dollars," I said through a mouthful of dry sandpaper.

"No. I gave her nothing at all, in fact. But in the dark of night, I sent a team to her door, and *they* gave her a bullet to the brain and made it look like a suicide." His eyes flashed with satisfaction as I moaned quietly, just a small echo of the emotions rending my heart in two.

He'd made me hate her, the nameless, faceless woman who'd abandoned me. What kind of monster sold her sons to a sadist like Garroway? Not my actual mother, it turned out. She'd made the incredibly unwise mistake of trusting him, though. And he'd murdered her for it.

I could barely breathe as he gave me time to really feel her loss and the crushing guilt that threatened to choke me. I didn't cry, though. I couldn't. Garroway had already had his fill of them from my childhood and training. Every bit of pain, physical and emotional, had taken their toll until I couldn't release another tear. My sobs were completely dry as I mourned the mother I didn't remember.

But something else crystalized in me as Garroway breathed in, savoring the medley of emotional pain I was feeling. I hope it soured the taste. There wasn't a witch under Garroway's command that didn't hate him, but the level of animosity I felt reached blood-boiling levels as he enjoyed the fruits of ruin he'd sown in my family.

Eventually, my vampire master continued his little story. "The butterfly effect in motion. Eris Darkmore dies, and I end up taking Marie Evenstar's precious sons as my own. And so far, you have paid me back with about what I've invested in you...next to nothing." He scowled at me as he toyed with his black dagger, flipping it through his fingers. "But your pain has been extra delicious, little Benjamin. You've taken more than your share for your brother. Would you like to know how he repaid you?"

"No," I said flatly. I just wanted it to stop, even as I knew he would twist the knife as hard as possible.

He raised the dagger, making a come hither gesture with his other hand. The door leading to the rest of manor opened, and backlit by the sudden glare of light was a familiar face, not a hair out of place. "Lucas," I croaked.

"Hey, big bro." He flashed me an apologetic look like he was begging me to understand what a sucker punch it was to see him, whole and hale, after he'd given me the run around for over a month.

"Lucas here has done an outstanding job at his first mission." Garroway gave him a brief golf clap. I stared at my brother, wondering what the hell this mission was since Cress was still alive and untouched. "When he felt no draw to the Darkmore girl, all I had to do was wait. You snuck out of the manor and went to her all by yourself, little Benjamin. And what do you know...Marie's star charts were right." He pointed the tip of his blade at my right hand. "You even took the bait to steal an extra cupid feather to test your connection to her."

Of course that had been bait. Garroway was about five steps ahead of me on whatever demented chessboard we were playing on.

"And now we come to a special time in your life," he said, gesturing Lucas into the room. The darkness closed over us once more. "I do not permit my witches to have anything so pedestrian as a soul mate or anam cara."

He gestured for me to stand, and my body did, pulled up like a puppet with its strings tugged. His last statement was beyond ominous, and cold sweat beaded my back as I realized exactly what my punishment would be. "Master, please. I promise I won't see her again. We can put this behind us," I begged.

The vampire bared his fangs and patted me on the cheek. "When will you learn, little Benjamin? You are mine, body and soul alike. Therefore, this is not a punishment, only destiny. *I* am your destiny. Lift your shirt."

Sensation returned to my fingertips. He wanted me to bare my blood rune with my own hand, ready for the forthcoming mission.

"She's innocent, Master. She doesn't deserve this," I said instead.

"Lift your shirt," he repeated tonelessly while lifting a brow. Even that minute expression told me he wasn't all that amused.

"Just do as the master says," Lucas whispered.

My nostrils flared as I resisted the impulse to turn and glare at him. I knew he didn't want to see me punished worse, but he could at least have the dignity not to pile on with Garroway.

The vampire got tired of my resistance, though, and compelled me to bare my blood rune to him. The moment the tip of the black dagger dimpled the skin over the edge of the rune, I went unnaturally still from the touch of its dark magic. The rune prickled with a feeling like a thousand tiny beestings and glowed from within with crimson light.

"Your next mission is to carry out the assassination of Luna Darkmore, also known as Cressida Rollins, by any means," Garroway intoned. The point of his dagger dug into my flesh, and I cried out. My pain was much more than physical as he damned me with one flick of the weapon. "I give you until Samhain to make a ghost of her."

The weapon left an inch-long red line under my skin, extending out from the wound. My new deadline, active until I did as he ordered. "And as an added incentive to carry out your task, I invoke Agonia." He traced the jagged red marking in the center of my rune, making it burn all the brighter.

I staggered away from him, covering the rune with both hands as it heated and circulated a sudden pinch of pain across my whole body. It wasn't the full agony spell, not like the one that'd knocked me unconscious recently, but I knew this punishment well. It wasn't going to go away until my mission was complete. I would carry constant pain with me, no matter what. The further my thoughts and actions strayed from the mission at hand, the worse it would be.

"I hate you," I hissed, nearly blinded by the sudden hot, needling feeling as it settled in my spine and radiated outward. I could barely keep myself upright, staggering into the wall where I stayed propped up with a fist. "Every waking hour of the day, every breath I take as I rest, I despise you."

"Ben, stop. Please," Lucas said in a begging tone.

It was too late for that. I clamped my teeth through a wave of vertigo as I stared down the vampire who assessed me with a cold stare. "If given even a fraction of a chance, I will cleave the head from your shoulders," I gritted out. "I will shove your body outside and dance in your fucking ashes, Garroway."

"Is that so?" the vampire asked.

"Yes—"

I was on the ground in a split second, gasping for air. The rush of agony from his kick to the center of my blood rune nearly threw me straight into the arms of unconsciousness, but I couldn't be that lucky.

He seized the front of my shirt, pulling me upright until we were nearly nose to nose. There was nothing human in his eyes as his stale breath washed over my face. "You and every other blood witch I own," he practically purred. "But there are no chances like that here, little Benjamin. Now run off and plan how you will kill your anam cara before you provoke me to tear your throat out instead."

He released me, and I fell limply to the ground. Everything hurt, pounding to the wild pulse in my chest. Light rushed over me as the door opened, but I remained down, making a low sound in my throat like a wounded animal.

Someone tentatively touched my shoulder. "Let's get you back to your room," Lucas said.

"Don't touch me," I muttered, shrugging off his hand.

I scraped myself off the ground without his help, staggering from the red-tilted room. "You know he made me do it, right?" Lucas asked in a small voice, trailing after me.

"Did he make you kill those two other people, too?" I asked after coming to a stop braced against the back of a sofa. It would be a long walk to the stairs when I couldn't walk straight.

"What two people?" He sounded bewildered.

"Never mind," I said curtly. "It doesn't matter."

I slogged all the way up the stairs and to my room, refusing to even look at him. Logically, he was just fulfilling a mission by leaving me in the dark for a whole month...but he could've at least hinted that he was okay. There were ways around almost every directive from Garroway's mouth to lessen the pain they caused.

Except times like now, when he'd turned my blood rune against me. I was exhausted already from exertion and now the bone-deep agony that clawed me with every step. When Lucas opened the door to my room, I had nothing left in me to argue. I thumped onto my bed fully clothed and tried to lie as still as possible.

My foot lifted, and I felt Lucas start picking at my shoelaces. "Go away," I muttered into my comforter.

"Please let me help you," he said in a small voice. "I'm really sorry, Ben. I hate that you're in pain right now."

I didn't respond. I couldn't find the words right now. Lucas tugged off my shoes and set aside the wallet and phone that were in my pockets.

As the silence stretched between us, I caught the sound of thumbs on a screen and the familiar buzz of my phone. "What are you doing?" I asked no louder than a mumble.

"Setting up an opportunity for you. A chick named Roe is asking if you want to go to a party. She says that Cress will be there."

The icy feeling of dread was soon replaced by even more needling viciousness as I resisted my mission. "I'll help you, big bro. We'll put this past us," Lucas said, a thread of hope in his voice. "We'll kill Cress together."

His words caused my rune to let up on the pain, and for a moment, the absence of it felt like the headiest relief.

I hope she's running away right now.

And then the Agonia spell returned with all the force of an avalanche, and I finally sank into oblivion.

26

CRESS

By late afternoon, I stood in the middle of my dorm room. Roe straddled my desk chair, while Willow sat cross-legged on the floor and Áine was on the spare bed, keeping Milo spellbound by pulling out single cat treats from her pocket dimension and had him looking around in awe.

Geo, in his human form, leaned against the door with his arms crossed. He was reluctant to leave me and deeply unhappy to transform back into the form that gave him unwanted feeling. It still gave me hope that he'd come to this little meeting of the minds as I came clean to my friends.

About everything.

How I'd freed Phaeron from Moongrove Library and how it'd been him who I'd seen over Lanie's body that awful night. I shared how I'd been studying for weeks to learn magic two years ahead of schedule, with the express purpose of killing the dimensional I was sure had murdered my friend.

They listened with sympathetic expressions, knowing I wanted to share everything before the questions came. So then came Ben...and the mystery he turned out to be. I set out the pieces of his puzzle for them and how I suspected he was the one possessed by the Hungering You-Know-What this whole time.

Roe's fingers turned white around my chair. "So you're telling me Ben lied to us and held a dagger to your throat?" she demanded.

"Yes, but—"

"That bastard!" she exclaimed.

"He's not really himself, though. I've seen the real Ben and...he's sweet and thoughtful." I showed them the anam cara mark on my palm again. "He just needs to meet an experienced librarian who can yank the Hungering You-Know-What out of him."

"Let's just call it the Hunger," Áine suggested.

"Are we just going to ignore the thing with his brother?" Willow asked in her wisp of a voice. "Because that's too weird."

"He had a blood witch aura too, but it was much weaker," Geo supplied.

Roe's tanned skin reddened further. "Nothing to it, then. They're both liars."

I nodded and cleared my throat awkwardly. "I'm sorry for keeping all of this from you. I didn't want to get expelled from NSU...this place is just incredible. But the situation has gotten so far beyond me."

"Aww, girl. C'mere." Roe got up and bundled me into a bear hug, which Willow and Áine joined after a moment. "You're not going to handle any of this alone anymore. We gotta stick up for each other."

I practically cried then and there; her words were so welcome. It felt like a weight off my shoulders at last that my friends finally knew everything and could help me figure out what to do from here.

"And it just so happens that I have an idea," Roe said. She sat down and started fiddling with her phone. "You want to catch Ben and haul him off to Moongrove Library, right? Well, there's a party this weekend at the marina for a merfolk holiday. There's an attendance limit, of course, but curfew is going to be loosened to let the mer celebrate. It's the perfect opportunity. We can set a trap for him there."

"What kind of trap?" Geo asked warily.

"Well, if we're not getting the SPDI involved, it'll have to be a relatively simple one," she said thoughtfully. "I'll text him about the party and say that Cress will be there and see what he says. He could see right through it and say no, or he can pretend that nothing happened today and go so he can party with his girlfriend. Then we nab him."

"And how do you suggest we...'nab' him?" Geo asked with air quotes.

Roe smiled and rubbed her hands. "Well, my mama taught me a ton of runes before I came here. I can make shackles for him from rock and soil. Blood witches rely a lot on their hands, so that will neutralize him."

"I can summon vines to help immobilize the rest of him. And if anyone gets hurt, I know some healing magic," Áine volunteered.

Willow bit her lip. "My magic isn't really strong, but I can always help be a lookout or something," she murmured.

"And..." I sighed as I looked down at Phaeron's mark on my left wrist. "I will call Phaeron this evening so we can get his help too. It sounded like he's been dealing with the Hunger for a long time and wants it dead even more than we do."

Geo's mouth thinned with displeasure. "I would prefer that we did not involve the dimensional."

"I know. But you'll be there too." I smiled his way. "And you will keep us safe just in case something goes wrong."

He considered for a few long moments. "I will agree if you learn two specific runes first and that you will not talk to the dimensional anymore without me present."

I needed to convince Dr. Voidbinder to be on call to take the Hungering Darkness from Ben in the first place, so I started to nod in agreement. "So, we're doing this?" Roe asked.

"We're doing this," I confirmed.

She started sending off a couple texts. The air was tense in the room as we waited for Ben to reply. To my surprise, it was nearly instant. "He says he'll be there," Roe said.

GEO

I made sure my demands were difficult to meet. The two runes I had Cress practice in the mere days we had were Luminare and Inemos, both power-level-three spells she had little chance of mastering. Dr.

Voidbinder had been hesitant to even start her on them, but then again, he was already wary of her request for him to be at the library this coming Saturday.

He was a good man, though. He agreed both to teach her and to be here, just in case.

And Cress succeeded at the Luminare spell within a night. My brows rose, impressed when she raised her sword to the sky and shouted the rune name before erupting into light. It poured clear and bright from her sword but with a purple glare where the magic flashed from her skin in its less pure form. She blinded me with a three-second blaze of brightness.

By Friday night, Inemos was still far from her control. The symbol was complicated to make with the tip of a sword; plus, it required precise timing as it charged within the sword before being shot from the tip. This one, I absolutely hoped she could get. Inemos was a stasis spell that could lock down a dimensional.

Should Phaeron turn on her—and I strongly suspected he would— Inemos would be the difference between her quick death and his when I finally had the excuse to bludgeon him to death. For all her talk about how she thought she was wrong about him...I still thought he was too dangerous to live.

She didn't get the Inemos rune correct and seemed in low spirits as we walked back to her dorm. It was evening, technically past her curfew, but my presence kept anyone from questioning her. Even in my flesh form, it seemed the authorities wandering the street recognized me as one of the library's gargoyles.

"Does this mean you won't come help us tomorrow?" Cress asked me finally. She had her hands in her hoodie's pocket. The silver sword she'd "borrowed" from the library swayed under the material with every step. I'd distracted Dr. Voidbinder while she slipped it from the locker room and let my guilt rest by telling myself she was going to return it very soon.

"Hmm?"

"I didn't figure out the rune," she said.

It was after a long, thoughtful pause that I said, "No."

She glanced up at me, a little crease between her brows. "Huh?"

"I will not try to stop you," I clarified. I disliked how my chest felt lighter when her expression became a beaming smile. I cared about her happiness too deeply in this form. The logical side of me thought I was taking liberties with her safety by allowing this plan to go through.

However, there was one thing that tipped my judgment further. As we stopped in the shadows of the garden outside her dorm, she placed her fingers on Phaeron's mark and tried calling his name. She tried three times. He didn't show up from the darkness.

She'd tried again and again, but it seemed he, too, had lied to her. Or he would not show his face with me by her side. Either way, the effect was the same. He would not be at the party, friend or foe. I could handle Ben all on my own if it came down to it.

Her shoulders lowered and she sighed. "We still have a solid plan," she said.

"He would be an unpredictable wildcard anyway," I said, putting a hand on her shoulder in an attempt to comfort her. "We shall capture Ben and put an end to this whole affair tomorrow."

Unexpectedly, she put her arms around my middle. "I'm not ready for you to go," she said into my shirt. My arms hovered awkwardly until I finally settled them around her. My first hug. It was...nice.

"Who says I am going anywhere?" I asked, puzzled.

She looked up at me, our faces inches away since I had learned to lean down to speak with her. Her wide eyes flicked to my lips for a moment before she nibbled on hers. "You did," she replied quietly. "You said once you fulfilled your purpose here, you'd return to the library."

I nearly had the kneejerk reaction to remind her that killing Phaeron was my purpose, but that wasn't the truth. *She* was still my duty, and nothing about our current situation felt finished. "I also said I would not take this form again. Yet here we are. It pleases you, so I have returned to it."

"I appreciate it," she said. "Does this mean...you've forgiven me?"

I tilted my head as I thought back to the conversation she was referencing. I'd been furious, angrier than I'd ever felt, and said many things that I now realized she'd kept a memory of. She thought I was going to abandon her while Phaeron still walked free and that I carried a grudge for her rash actions that I'd already forgiven after seeing her obvious remorse.

"I…" I hesitated. Saying I bore no grudge seemed so cold. "I am not angry. I just want you to be safe. That is all I have ever wanted."

"Yeah?" she asked quietly. "That's all you want from me?" Her gaze searched my face for something, though I could not fathom what.

"Is there something more you desire?" I murmured.

She started to smile, and I recognized that look, the same one she always had when she was about to give me a new experience. "I'll show you, okay?"

"All right."

She lifted to the tips of her feet and laced her hand behind the back of my neck, pressing our mouths together. Like with the hug, I didn't respond for a moment, too stunned that this was happening. I knew I was not charming like Ben or Phaeron, but here she was, kissing *me*. I trembled from a foreign rush of emotions as I finally returned her affection before she pulled away a moment later.

"Good night, Geo," she said, backing away slowly.

"Sweet dreams," I murmured, watching until she returned to her dorm. Usually, this was the point where I returned to my gargoyle form to go dormant for the night, but my stone heart was pulsing at double its usual speed, so I sat on a bench instead to catch my breath.

With my lips still tingling from the touch of hers, I'd never felt so alive.

27
BEN

"The party's at the marina," Lucas reminded me as my numb fingers fumbled to fasten one of my daggers under my left sleeve. He rushed to help me. Evening had fallen already, and I was sluggish on purpose.

I hadn't surrendered to the sweet abyss of painlessness that plotting to kill Cress brought me. Garroway's trick was wearing away at my self-control, though, because every day that passed made it more tempting to stab something to make the awful screaming of my nerves stop. I knew it was by design.

The vampire undoubtedly waited with his version of eagerness for me to fulfill his sick mission. He'd harvest my pain like the finest vintage of wine and continue to do so. The loss of an anam cara came with a permanent yearning for someone who was no longer there, after all.

"Look at me," my brother commanded. His hands on my shoulders set off a stinging sensation, and I blew out a hiss of pain. I forced myself to meet his gaze. "You have to do this."

I glanced away, muttering, "No, I don't."

"Ben, you *have* to do this," he repeated. "You're going to die if you don't!"

"You don't understand. I'm already dead," I sighed. I was only agreeing to go to this party to deliver one last, dire demand that Cress leave. Once she was gone, there was no way I could end her life, and the deadline would end mine instead by Samhain.

"Do you love this chick? Really love her?" he asked, raising a dubious brow. "Nothing's more important than staying alive. There will be other women."

Mutely, I went back to strapping on my weapons and checking my ring. A new vial of Garroway's blood was primed and ready to go, just in case. "Do you remember talking to Seth about principles?" I asked finally, determining I was as ready to go as I could get.

Lucas shrugged. "Yeah."

"There are some things you just don't do," I prompted.

His lips pursed, and for a moment, he sneered. He'd never scoffed at wisdom from Seth before, our mentor more like his idol. "That's stuffy and out of touch when your life's on the line," he said. "Let's go."

He led the way as I limped after him. The touch of fresh air and the night-kissed wind on my skin outside was a fresh torture as it ghosted over my raw nerve endings. Still, I went, and Lucas sighed impatiently as he had to slow walk so he didn't outpace me too much.

"Are you allowed to help me?" I asked. Ordinarily, I wouldn't ask, but I really wanted him to turn around and go back into the manor tonight.

"Yes. The master gave his permission." He flashed a thumbs-up over his shoulder.

We traveled the back streets of Salem before I caught my breath enough to ask, "What was your real first mission? Last I remember, it was to kill Cress and make a stop at Moongrove Library for something."

"It was just to hide from you," Lucas said with a shrug.

"So, what was up with the library thing?" I asked. "Did you go there too, or was that another misdirection?"

He turned to glare. "I told you my mission, all right?"

I put my palms up. "Sorry." I didn't know what'd gotten into him. He seemed so impatient to get to this party. That wasn't like Lucas. My brother still hadn't drawn the blood of a real victim, compelled by the blood rune on his body to put his deadly skills to use for Garroway.

We disguised ourselves by mingling with a big inbound group of partygoers. I saw picnic baskets and blankets for those who couldn't stand being in freezing cold water, while the merfolk just wore big, excited smiles along with jeweled nets and shiny shells in their hair. We followed them to the marina. Lucas hummed a happy tune under his breath while I gathered the tatters of my self-control for what needed to be done.

The party stretched from the marina on back to the grassy shoreline, which teemed with bodies bouncing and swaying to the bass rumbling from several speakers bigger than I was. Lucas bounced his head to the beat while I glanced around, wondering how the hell I'd find Cress in this crush of people.

He grabbed my elbow and pointed. There was a better lit area past the main party, where a series of picnic tables held a small group not interested in dancing. Cress sat right below a streetlamp, the distinctive purple of her hair standing out like a beacon.

My mouth ran as dry as a desert breeze. *Kill her. End it.* My thoughts grabbed on to the relief of imagining fulfilling my mission here and now rather than suffering the prolonged agony of the death that awaited me if I didn't.

I headed her way. My palms itched to grab my daggers. I could surprise her with a strike to the heart. Quick, painless, done.

No. No, I'm not doing that. I won't hurt her, I vowed. I staggered like I was drunk. Fuck, I didn't know how I would endure more than a minute in her presence.

Cress stood and turned to me, a smile already shaping her lips. She was lovely in a dark lipstick, with dramatic makeup giving her eyes the kind of seductive flare that made my heart pump. Soon I was only feet away from her, and my mind filled with dozens of ways to take her out nearly instantly.

"Hi, Ben," she said, holding both of her hands out. She caught both of mine, as I couldn't help myself even now. It felt like I closed my hands around glass shards as Garroway's Agonia spell made sure I would never enjoy her presence again. My sight swam alongside the vicious jabs of pain.

Something closed around my wrists. When I blinked, I realized Roe had rushed over and clamped onto me.

"What the—" I started to struggle, trying to jerk away from her strong hold.

She uttered a rune, Figura, and the earth under my feet rippled and sank a few inches, rapidly feeding her a stream of soil and rocks that became unbreakable shackles that pinned my wrists together. It was done, and I was bound within a few seconds.

"That's for threatening Cress," Roe said tightly. "And this is for lying to us." She cocked back a fist and smashed it into my jaw.

As I stumbled back, the night erupted with a flare of eerie white fire.

PHAERON

I emerged from another blackout somewhere on the NSU campus, hearing the infernal thumping of what modern supernaturals considered "music."

I approached with an uncomfortable sensation dribbling down my spine. The last time a big gathering had occurred here, the Hungering Darkness had struck with all the deadly agility of a venomous snake.

Gnawing pain sank its teeth into my gut. How long had I been wandering, out of my mind? I would need to find a meal soon.

"Come, brother. I will let you get a taste."

I froze to the spot, taking a wary look around for any hint of white shadow. "Show yourself," I said.

"We don't have to fight. You feel it, don't you? The same hunger that I do."

"We are not alike," I said stiffly. My shadows uncurled around my hands, forming knife-like talons.

Its laughter was thready. *"Not yet, but soon. Come join me. The witch with the bright soul is here."*

I rushed into motion, my senses screaming. There was a flare of dimensional magic ahead, past the heart of this party. "You will not consume her soul," I demanded, cold with fear that it was anywhere near her.

"Such beautiful purple hair. So soft. I could reach out and touch it right now if I wanted."

"Leave her alone, damn you." The music playing was so deep it was disorienting to my sensitive hearing. It was suddenly like I was slogging through air ten times as dense as I fought to keep my wits about me and find Cress.

The monster who'd once been my brother was close enough to threaten her, and instead of the clear-headed adrenaline that should've flooded me at the thought of him taking another victim, I was growing confused. Lost.

The people here partying started to scream and run away from my destination. It felt like it was growing farther away the more I labored.

"So, you will not eat her with me tonight?" That blasted voice was still in my ears. *"What a pity. Come back when Myuna has a stronger hold on you."*

I sank to my knees, clutching my face as its willpower clashed with my own, recognizing now the clawing blankness that threatened to send me into another blackout. It'd been its voice in my head all this time, triggering the episodes so I wouldn't be able to interfere with it.

Dread left me breathless. How had it gained such a power over me?

One of the last things I saw before I turned into a curl of shadow was Cress only a few yards away. Blood streaked down one of her cheeks, and her soul blazed a bright halo around her, brilliant and beautiful in its intensity. Our gazes met, and I just barely registered her scream, "Phaeron! Help!"

28

CRESS

BEN STAGGERED BACK from Roe's punch, falling like she'd hit him much harder. I glared at her. Striking him was definitely not part of the plan.

"How dare you hit my brother," Lucas said. Well, the words came from his mouth, but they were soft and hissed. The young man's head jerked to the side, screwing up with pain and twitching like it'd gotten stuck that way. My eyes rounded to the size of saucers as white fire leapt out of his palms, quickly overlaying his arms and forming long, pointed weapons in place of his fingers.

Not white fire. White *shadow*.

"Oh shit," I yelped, reaching behind me frantically for the sheathed sword I'd rested on the picnic table. I snatched it up and drew the silver weapon out, casting Lux before holding the brightly lit metal up to Lucas's face.

He stumbled away with a sound like boiling water in a kettle, shielding his head. His body jerked the next moment, blood spraying as the pointed tip of a quartz spike emerged from his chest. "Hmm," he uttered.

He inspected it for a moment while Ben screamed hoarsely, "Stop! That's my brother!"

Lucas wrapped a white clawed hand around the foot of bloodied mineral sticking out of him and pushed it back out. With the leisure of someone who knew he was in little danger, he drew a rune in his blood over the wound.

The first person started to scream and point, which scattered most of the group sitting at the picnic tables. They ran off into the night while Roe stood there, her mouth a shocked "o." She slammed her foot down into the grass and muttered a rune's name, causing the ground to shake in a circle around her. It buckled and cracked, which was her signal to Áine. The fae lifted her head from behind a table to circle her hands, and a gnarled pack of whip-like vines burst from the churned earth, aimed straight for Lucas's ankles.

He leapt to the side, so I saw Geo charging forward in his gargoyle form, a club of pure quartz held above his head. He brought it down, and Lucas evaded with the lightning-quick movements I'd seen Ben using after painting himself with runes.

Ben himself stumbled forward as the gargoyle and his brother squared up. "I said stop! Don't hurt him," he said on a gasp.

Geo, who'd been about to swing again, paused as Ben threw himself in between them.

Lucas didn't pull the strike of his talons. They raked over his brother's back instead, and Ben jerked, his expression going slack with shock. He tumbled to the ground.

When Lucas brought his bloodied claws to his lips and licked one clean, I realized he wasn't in control at all. The Hungering Darkness sighed as he tasted Ben's blood. "Such a tease," he breathed before launching at Geo.

I exchanged a glance with Roe, who was trembling. We both were, actually. "Is that the thing you thought was in Ben? The Hungering Darkness?" she whispered.

His head whipped our way. He already had one of his clawed hands deep in Geo's chest, dealing him a grievous wound. "You're in luck, Morgana. It seems they want to be eaten first," he purred, withdrawing his talons and leaping at us.

"Uh. Uh. Figura!" Roe shouted in a rush, making a lifting motion and drawing up a compacted ball of soil out of the ground about twice the size of my head. She grabbed it and threw it to explode in Lucas's face. Dirt flew everywhere, and he stumbled, snarling.

I cast Repello as he came for us again, only momentarily distracted by Roe's magic. For once, I was glad for the endless drills Dr. Voidbinder had put me through. On pure muscle memory, I took a ready stance as Lucas rushed at me. His white talons descended on my shield.

For a moment, the magic held him back, and I took a chance to jab my sword into his shoulder. The shield shattered a moment later, his swipe slowed but still grazing my face. Pain exploded across my cheek, and I flinched back.

Roe grabbed his forearm when he tried to follow through by impaling me on his other hand's talons. She hissed in pain, smoke sizzling from her skin, but she still pulled him into a punch she reinforced with stray rocks over her hand like an improvised knuckle weapon. The Hungering Darkness staggered backward from the force, his head whipped to the side.

I cast another Repello shield and held my breath as I quickly repeated the gesture, successfully layering a second one over the first. That might last me a second longer, because it seemed we'd barely harmed the creature. He leapt for Roe, and I pushed her out of the way, letting my shields absorb the impact that could've killed my friend.

"Baby witch magic," he hissed, smashing his way through my magic. "Have any more tricks?"

"I do, actually!" Roe exclaimed. She'd cast another guardian rune and had two sharply pointed rocks floating above her. With a gesture, she sent them smacking into his wounded shoulder and face.

Motion caught my eye to the left, toward the roadside. A mass of partygoers were fleeing the scene, but closer to us was Phaeron, skidding to a stop and clawing at his face. His eyes were replaced by two pits of white fire, but still, I think our gazes met. "Phaeron!" I screamed. "Help!"

His shoulders heaved, and the mass of his body disappeared into the shadows. Out of habit, my right hand flew to my left wrist, the sword hanging to the side as I touched his mark of protection. "Phaeron, come back!" I called desperately.

He took shape again from the shadows, on his hands and knees. After shaking his head viciously, he leapt into motion.

"Uh, Cress," Roe shouted, pulling me back as the Hungering Darkness approached again with his talons raised.

I dragged myself out of Roe's hold and whipped my sword over my head, using the only other rune I knew. "Luminare," I whispered, and light exploded from my sword and skin like a ground-level firework.

The dimensional monster took shelter behind a picnic table. I blinked the spots from my eyes and saw Phaeron just standing there, his otherworldly features slack with admiration and a kind of awe. *Of me.* He looked at me like I was the sexiest woman alive. His eyes, blessedly, were back to their shined topaz state, reflecting sparkles of my light, and dark shadows swarmed up his arms as soon as the spell faded.

Phaeron turned, and the moment was broken with his sneer. He pointed a claw where the Hungering Darkness hid. "Cowardly wretch, hiding in the body of a boy. Face me!"

"Gladly," the thing within Lucas hissed, leaping out at him. Phaeron caught him by the elbows and threw him further away from the dregs of the stampeding party, into the darkness of the space between the marina and the next building.

Phaeron was soon running straight at me. He plucked the hilt of the sword right from my hand with an incline of his head. "Thank you, bright soul," he said.

"Wait...I needed that!" I shouted after him. It was still glowing with my Lux spell, but he didn't seem to mind.

Another shadow passed overhead. Geo landed hard, silvery liquid leaking from his chest wound. He and Phaeron exchanged a glance and a nod before rushing the Hungering Darkness at the same time.

With no weapon, I ran away from the fight, picking my way back to where Ben had fallen. He lay face down in the grass with Áine bent over his back. Green magic flowed between the hands she hovered inches from his gashes. "I ain't touching your blood, so stop asking," she was snapping as I skidded to a stop on his other side.

"Cress," he moaned. He tilted his chin to fix me with one bleary eye. "Please. Healing runes."

"What do I have to do?" I asked. Unlike Áine, I was willing to do anything to get him to survive this.

With a shaking fingertip, he drew a rune in his own blood on his forearm. Two lines with a third bisecting them. "Like that," he croaked.

"Eugh, why?" Áine asked as I began to make the mark around his open wounds with his blood. It was nasty work, but it made a noticeable difference when combined with her efforts.

"It's working. It's part of his magic," I said. The gashes crossing down his back started to knit closed before our eyes. It was a bloody affair to watch the bits of muscle and veins combine themselves again, and had I had any sort of meal before this, I would've thrown it back up on the spot.

Ben worked his jaw. "My brother attacked me," he whispered.

"That wasn't your brother. He's possessed by...what I thought was in you," I admitted. "Look, I'll explain later. Can you walk?" I offered a hand up before realizing he was still shackled by Roe's first spell.

He glanced down at where I was looking. "Don't take them off," he murmured. "Just...leave me."

"What? No," I said immediately.

"No way are you getting left behind after I spent so much magic healing you," Áine protested. She and I helped heft him to his feet as a cloud of darkness rolled over where we stood. Phaeron's gray figure jumped in front of us. Gashes dripping purple blood covered his arms, and four jagged lines nearly cleaved his tail in two where it was most slender.

He brandished my sword in front of him. It was still glowing, and everywhere its light touched him, his shadows receded. Its edge was coated in blood.

"Know why this way is superior, brother?" asked the monster puppetting Lucas's body as his white shadows cut through the gloom of whatever spell Phaeron had cast. His clothing was cut to ribbons, but the skin underneath was flawless. "This body heals nearly instantly. Yours does not."

A whistling sound pierced the night, courtesy of a rock the size of my fist hurtling through the air and smacking the Hungering Darkness in the shoulder, staggering him. "Hah! Take that!" Roe called.

Phaeron surged into motion, holding the sword up to Lucas's face in a mirror to what I'd done earlier. His shadowy claws sank into the space behind the young man as he cringed away. Phaeron tugged like a fisherman with a prize catch on the line.

For a moment, I could see the true creature of white fire as its head emerged. Phaeron had him by one forward-facing horn. I watched with my mouth popped open. Just like the drawings of him and Phaeron's other form, he was much like a horned wolf, and when he opened his mouth to howl and thrash, white teeth bristled from his jaw.

He went berserk, squirming in Phaeron's hold and making Lucas's arms swing. Fuchsia blood spilled in twin arcs as he gouged two swipes into Phaeron's chest before he was forced to let it go. "This isn't over," he hissed before compressing into a curl of white shadow and disappearing.

The dimensional man took a knee, planting his fist in the dirt. I cautiously went to his side, gasping when I saw how much blood he was losing. A stream of it stained the grass. "Áine!" I called.

She bounded over and reeled with both hands over her mouth. "Mother Tree!" she practically squeaked before going to work with her green healing magic.

"Phaeron...what happened to Geo?" I asked. I had my head on a swivel and counted my two friends, Ben, and him. The marina was deserted otherwise, blankets, food, and other knickknacks discarded in the group's haste to leave. Willow had left with them as we'd agreed on beforehand, only acting as a lookout since she wasn't sure of her magic yet.

He met my gaze, his pupils shrunk to tiny slits while his expression was tight with pain. "The gargoyle lost too much of his enchanted oil. He's frozen until he can turn human," he answered.

"He's alive?" I breathed.

Phaeron nodded tightly. "You still need him. I made sure his injuries weren't fatal."

A relieved smile crossed my face. "Thank you. I...I don't know what I'd do without him."

He stared at me in his probing, intense way for several long moments. "Do you see now that I am not a monster, bright soul?" he asked.

My throat clicked in a dry swallow. It was hard to think when he looked at me like that. "Y-yes," I murmured.

Those topaz eyes flicked down to where Áine was finishing up with staunching his bleeding wounds. "I shall live, faeling. Thank you for your help," he said with a bow of his head. "I owe you a debt of gratitude."

"I accept your admission of debt," Áine answered gravely. It sounded like a fae formality. She helped him to his feet, and he immediately turned and towered over Ben, who'd collapsed back into the grass.

Gently, Phaeron lifted him under his back and knees and walked to a picnic table that'd survived the battle. He laid Ben down on top of it, then peeled back the hem of his shirt to reveal Ben's tattoo. Phaeron made a little *tsk* noise. "This is some of the cruelest magic I've seen," he murmured.

I joined them on Phaeron's other side, noticing that the skin around the tattoo was puckered and pink, with reddish veins spreading from it. The last time I'd seen it, only the big rune in the center was red, but now every line pulsed crimson and glowed faintly. "Do you see this?" He pointed toward the center rune. "That is Agonia. Something...or some*one* has triggered it. He is in a lot of pain right now."

"Who did this to you?" I looked up at Ben, who lay motionlessly with his shackled hands resting to the side. He was breathing, but his skin was pale with blood loss and the effects of the Agonia rune.

His only response was a weak couple of coughs. More blood dribbled from the corner of his mouth.

"Is there anything we can do for him?" Roe asked. She was behind me, looking over my shoulder.

Phaeron tapped his chin. As he deliberated, I noticed Áine had bounded off into the gloom. I recognized her distinctively bouncy stride as she returned alongside Geo in his human form. He was looking remarkably shiny with new silver gouges in his chest and limbs. He shambled toward us, powered on sheer willpower alone.

The dimensional man glanced that way as well, a thoughtful frown on his face, before he said, "There is something that can be done, yes. It will be extraordinarily painful."

"Do it," Ben mumbled.

Phaeron crooked his fingers, and shadows descended over them. He pulled them back until only his index was coated in a hooked talon. That wicked point was pressed to the edge of the circular rune. "Three... two..." There was no one. He raked his claw across the diameter of the rune in one fast swipe.

Ben nearly flopped off the table before Roe and I caught him. "Son of a *bitch!*" he shouted hoarsely.

"Don't heal it. Let it scar," Phaeron said. He pressed what was left of Ben's shirt to the wound he'd made.

Ben released a relieved sigh after a few moments, going completely limp. "No more Agonia. That feels...so damn good," he murmured. "Did you...am I free?"

"You may speak freely. But without the tool used to carve this rune into you, nothing can stop this." He pointed to a single red line among the ones fading back to black. It was like the others that streaked across Ben's chest, aiming for his heart, but it was only a couple inches long.

Ben lifted his head and then let it thump back down with a groan. "Ah, shit, the deadline's still active. What about hurting..." He stopped and spoke the next word on a whisper, like he was testing if he could speak it. "...Garroway?"

"Who's that?" Roe demanded.

"Just the vampire who had my mother murdered and magically enslaved my brother and me," he muttered. "I really can talk about this with you all. That's incredible." He sounded like he was going to pass out at any moment, though.

I recoiled in shock. "Did you just say...enslaved?" I asked.

"Yeah." He struggled to open his eyes and flashed a hint of his crooked smile. "I have so much to tell you, babe. But I promise you're going to know everything. No more lies."

After this bloody night, I wasn't sure if I could handle the truth. *Enslaved.* What the actual fuck.

"To answer your question, I believe you will be able to resist direct orders from this Garroway individual," Phaeron said. "But attempting to attack him may cause the damaged Agonia rune to try and finish you."

"I'll take it...for now," Ben sighed. He mumbled something about stopping a deadline next as his eyelids flagged downward.

Phaeron sighed as well. "The authorities are here."

I looked behind us. The first arrival was a winged woman who landed next to a toppled picnic table. Dr. Aurina was bundled up for a cold evening, her expression pinched with fury as she took in the damage and the remnants of the abandoned party. The force of her emotions was so strong I could feel the ominous press of them against my skin. Her two mates who could also fly landed close by and flanked her protectively.

Now that I was paying attention, I picked up the sound of approaching sirens. Better late than never, it would seem.

The cupid demigoddess's angry gaze swept over the lot of us. Phaeron and Geo, hurt but still standing. Ben, prone on the table with his wrists bound. Roe, Áine, and I...mostly unharmed but definitely what seemed like a random gaggle of NSU freshmen.

"Well," Dr. Aurina said, hands curling to fists at her sides. "Which one of you is going to explain what happened?"

SHADOW SLAYER

MOONGROVE ACADEMY: WICKED SPELLS BOOK 2

Shadow Slayer

CONTENT OVERVIEW

This is a paranormal RH romance, meaning that the main female character does not need to choose between love interests. There are graphic sex scenes (some including more than one partner) between consenting adults. *Shadow Slayer* is book two of a trilogy with a cliffhanger ending.

Please be aware that this book continues to show depictions of grief because of the death of a friend. Also contained within are fight sequences that include death, gore, and magical violence. This trilogy is classified as dark academia because the main antagonists have magic that affects the souls of others.

This trilogy does not include a pregnancy for the FMC or MM content.

If you find anything in the contents of this book that should be added to this page, please let me know at ellahendricksauthor@ gmail.com.

1

CRESS

Though we returned to Northern Supernatural University in police vehicles, I was fairly sure my friends and I weren't under arrest. At least, not yet.

The Cress of yesterday would be worried about expulsion. Ever since I'd released an old and powerful dimensional from Moongrove Library, I'd constantly looked over my shoulder, expecting someone to realize my mistake and send me home for it.

Not too long ago, I'd thought leaving NSU was the worst thing the authorities could do to me. I'd only just discovered I was a witch and viewed the secret world of the supernatural as something straight out of my wildest imaginations come to life. The campus was like a melting pot, with mer, fae, vampires, shifters, and more all living in harmony without a need to hide their true natures. A place where I belonged, too.

But my recent encounter with the Hungering Darkness had ripped the fog from my eyes. Getting expelled was my worst fear? What a joke compared to the real possibility of my friends getting hurt. Downright laughable when Ben had just admitted to being magically enslaved to a vampire.

I was slumped in the padded, maroon-colored cushions of the couch I'd been shown to with Roe and Áine in the administration building's waiting room. My two friends and I had a few scratches and bruises between us but nothing compared to the beating Ben, Geo, and Phaeron had taken in the fight we'd barely survived.

Roe and Áine were leaning heavily into each other, dozing. Roe was an Ashbough, a storied guardian witch family, with the gym rat physique to match the physical requirements of magic that manipulated stone and made the user stronger and tougher. We'd done our best to fight side by side, but we knew maybe ten spells between us. "Baby witch magic," the Hungering Darkness had scoffed of our combined efforts.

Áine's healing magic had worked miracles when our efforts came short. She was a faun, a fae woman with warm brown skin and auburn-colored curls, plus a deer-like lower half that gave her a poofy little tail and a bouncy hoofed stride. Usually, she wove freshly picked flowers into her mane of beautiful hair, but after this evening, only a handful of bruised petals remained.

I should've tried to rest right alongside them. The lamps in the waiting room were off, and the overhead lights were dimmed to their lowest setting. A solitary owl hooted in the dark of night. I wondered if it was a true animal roosting on the building or a shifter giving in to their animal nature.

My thoughts simply wouldn't quiet, whether I was temporarily distracted by owls or just trying to pick out the murmur of voices down the hall. Dr. Melinda Aurina, the University President, was keeping us here until she had the full story of what'd happened and why. Too bad the moment she'd seen Phaeron, she'd slammed him with crimson magic and rendered him instantly unconscious. The dimensional man was powerful—scarily so—but his weakened, bleeding self was no match for a cupid demigoddess at full strength.

Unfortunately for her, I think he was the only one who truly knew the whole story of what was going on. I had a gross, uncertain feeling brewing in my stomach. Had they believed us when we swore he wasn't the Hungering Darkness, as Dr. Aurina had immediately thought? She'd attacked him so quickly that she had to know exactly what he looked like and where he'd been for the last two hundred years.

I hoped he was all right. I'd despised the man, thinking he'd murdered my friend and roommate, Lanie, just to find out it hadn't been him this whole time. *Just like he'd tried to tell me.*

Just like how saying the Hungering Darkness's title aloud drew its attention, my thoughts of Phaeron seemed to summon him. The distant *ding* of an elevator preceded the clank of chains and gruff male voices. I locked gazes with him across the room, shocked at how dull his usually vibrant yellow eyes were when shadowed with deep hollows.

Heavy manacles restrained his hands together, and a second set caught the length of his tail between his cuffed ankles. He hobbled awkwardly without his tail lending him his usual extraordinary grace. A pair of campus police prodded him along toward the University President's office.

I hopped to my feet, startling my two friends awake. "This is completely unnecessary," I snapped.

"Peace, bright soul," Phaeron slurred.

"This is a good man you've chained up. He fought to protect me and my friends," I insisted to the leftmost police officer, a burly man whose aura had the fluid movements of a shifter. My tired eyes only caught a glimpse of his magic before losing focus.

The other officer, a green-skinned fae with leafy fronds growing from his arms and down his scalp like hair, gestured sharply. "Come along, then. Dr. Aurina wanted to speak with..." He consulted his phone and read off our names.

"It's pronounced 'Anya,'" grumped Áine, who bounded to my side within moments. Roe was still rubbing her eyes as she followed suit.

"Standard procedure," the shifter cop murmured to me behind his hand. "Don't you know how strong this guy is?"

All too well. I took in Phaeron again. He'd gotten a change of clothes that weren't stained with his purplish blood and shredded to bits from the Hungering Darkness's talons. His eyelids drooped, and he seemed truly out of it. "You think he poses a threat right now?" I countered.

"You never know with dimensionals."

The greater supernatural community would call this man backward or even racist for a statement like that. Dimensionals were people from another world, whose unique features were easily confused with the human idea of what demons looked like. And Phaeron was their prince, the man with enough magic to lead his people away from their dying, corrupted world.

His face was striking but attractive nonetheless. Sharp cheekbones, ashen-gray skin, and the pair of curling ram horns that cupped his pointed ears. His hair was a sleek and shiny black and held back by a fresh hair tie. When he smiled, he had vampire-like fangs, and when he wasn't so lethargic, his slit-pupiled gaze, colored as bright as cut topaz, seemed to see right through me.

He was the dimensional I'd freed from Moongrove Library. A devil with a deep, smooth voice that could instantly flutter my insides. But not a monster. He didn't deserve the criminal treatment he was subjected to as the cops practically hauled him to Dr. Aurina's office.

Roe put a hand on my shoulder. "It's not worth the fight. Let's just go," she sighed.

I muttered under my breath as I followed a pace behind them. Dr. Aurina's office wasn't far, and enough chairs had been dragged in across from her desk to accommodate for a large gathering. She liked blond wood and warm colors, especially the rich red of the upholstery and rugs.

The woman herself sat in a raised chair like a throne behind her desk, with her mates arranged to either side of her. I counted, thinking one was missing. Perhaps tending to the group's little daughter, who was also—thankfully—not here.

Dr. Aurina was easily the most beautiful woman who'd ever graced my eyes. Even wearing a simple woolen gown and a pinch between her brows, she had some cupid mystique about her that airbrushed over any flaws she might have. Her chair had special slits cut in the sides to account for her rose gold wings. Each feather glinted like molten metal even in low light. Her delicate fingers played with a lock of pink hair as the four of us sat across from her desk.

She nodded curtly to the two campus police. "I can handle it from here," she said. They left without a word of complaint.

I'd slipped into the seat next to Phaeron, noticing my friends' discomfort with him, even with the state he was in. "The gargoyle and the blood witch should be joining us soon," said one of Aurina's mates after consulting his phone.

"The blood witch?" Roe echoed in shock. "Ben?"

"He nearly bled out," I said at the same time. Was he really going to be pushed into a meeting like this in the condition I'd last seen him in?

I'd also thought I'd have time to get my head straight before seeing him again, considering the massive gulf of secrets and lies I'd recently discovered between us. He had a lot of explaining to do, and I was not in the right mind to hear it all yet.

"As did the gargoyle, in his own way," Aurina herself answered. "They've been patched up in the student medical center for now. Once we hear the full story, they can go rest."

"I can tell you everything," Phaeron said with effort.

The demigoddess raised her brows. "Will you do so if I reverse my spell on you?"

"Yes."

Magic sparkled on the palm she lifted and aimed toward him. A cloud of sparkling pink mist blew from her skin and swirled around Phaeron's head, seeping into his nostrils until he'd breathed it all in. The links of the chains binding him clacked as he shifted and jerked.

Clarity returned to his expression, and he bared his teeth with a vicious, otherworldly growl. "These restraints won't hold me for long," he warned. I put a hand to my belly, trying to hide the relief I felt at hearing the smooth, seductive lilt return to his voice now that it wasn't gritty with forced exhaustion.

"Fulfill our agreement first," Aurina replied.

He muttered what sounded distinctly like a couple curses in an alien language that rolled off his tongue. Then he turned his head, inspecting first Áine, then Roe, and finally me.

"All of you are well?" he asked.

"As good as we can be," I answered.

The office door swung behind us, and in stumbled Ben, escorted by the same pair of campus police. At some point, the makeshift manacles Roe had created for him out of rock and clay had been replaced by real, metal ones. His golden-brown fall of hair was damp, and his skin pink, like he'd received a rough scrubbing of any blood runes.

At least he had some color. Last I'd seen him, he'd been covered in his own blood and deathly pale as his magic struggled to close several long gashes that split open his back. My lips fluttered into an uncertain smile as the butterflies in my belly grew leaden wings.

There was no hint of the easy charm Ben had used to his benefit through our short acquaintance. He snarled and cursed at the policemen, jerking his shoulders from their grip when they practically shoved him into the room. Yet he froze the moment he spotted me.

We stared at each other for what could've been two seconds, but it felt like an eternity. Did I ever really know this man? Despite the fact that our palms had matching anam cara marks, it felt like I was only just meeting the real Ben. I set my lips, trying to hide the pain that thought brought me.

"Cress—" he began to say, his expression falling. I would dare say he looked devastated, and I hadn't given voice to the betrayed thoughts crowding my head.

"Move," grunted one last person, pushing Ben further into the room. The promised gargoyle, Geo, walked stiffly behind him. He was in his human form, with several wounds up his arms and the exposed skin at the hollow of his throat. They glinted solid silver against his ebony skin, sealed with the enchanted oil that circulated his body like blood.

The tension hanging in the room could be cut with a knife from the moment Geo spotted Phaeron.

"Cress, kindly vacate the seat next to the dimensional." He spoke in a flat tone I'd once confused for robotic. Geo didn't have the best grasp on his emotions, considering he usually didn't have them in his true form of quartz and obsidian.

"No one's in danger here," Phaeron replied, though the way he stifled another growl made me wonder how true that was. They may have fought together earlier this evening, but I figured it was a temporary truce.

Slowly, I eased from my seat. Phaeron shot me an incredulous look. "Ben should sit here," I said, gesturing to it and avoiding looking at any of them. I dragged a different chair over to wedge myself between Roe and Áine. The faun nodded in approval, while Roe squared her shoulders and shifted to shield me from Ben's gaze.

Geo remained on his feet, standing in the space behind his two seated and restrained adversaries. He'd never liked Ben, sensing something was off about him from the moment he'd appeared in one of my classes, and had a longer, more complicated history with Phaeron.

"Well, now that we're all here, I would like to hear from you first." Aurina gestured with an elegant hand. "Ben, is it?"

"Who's asking?" he replied flippantly.

Her fingers balled into fists, and the force of her anger was like a physical blow, making me feel about an inch tall. All of us leaned away from her, even her mates and Phaeron. The only one who watched impassively was Geo, who settled his lips into an unimpressed line.

"Be careful, assassin. I need little reason to harm you sevenfold for the pain you brought my daughter," she said through clenched teeth.

2

BEN

Accusing gazes skewered me from all directions. I swallowed with effort, my throat drier than the nearest fire fae. Even though a blood witch could heal the most devastating injuries with the power of a rune, as I already had this evening, my body couldn't go forever.

There were two furious cupid women in front of me, swimming in and out of focus. In my current state, I knew the next thing I said might be my last unless I could convince her of the truth.

"That..." I struggled to breathe under the pinning power of her anger. "That was my associate. She...she tried to make it a light cut."

"Light!" Aurina screeched.

One of her mates reached out, stroking her arm and murmuring in her ear. Her emotions drew back from their chokehold around my neck, and I filled my lungs gratefully.

Closing my eyes, I probed at the ruined blood rune tattooed on my side with my fingertips. It was tender to the touch, with a swollen ridge cutting it in half. I tried to say what I could, aware that the rune at full strength would boil my blood for daring to say a breath of Garroway's secrets.

"I was sent to NSU's Mabon celebration to collect a few cupid feathers with their magic intact. My associate, as I said, was tasked with, and I quote, making your daughter 'bleed.' When we're given an order from…" My fingers curled over the rune, which pulsed a painful warning. "…from the master, we have to obey."

"What master?" Roe asked.

"His name is Garroway. At least, that is the name he's used lately," Aurina replied for me. "I'm sorry, young man. It is not your fault he sank to new lows recently."

I cracked my eyes open to see her flashing me a brief pitying gaze. "This is the first opportunity I've gotten to talk to one of his witches without them immediately committing suicide."

"Not like any of us have a choice in that," I replied.

"If I don't miss my guess, you are speaking of a blood baron?" the dimensional asked.

Aurina nodded. "Indeed. We've played a song and dance for half a century, first with polite overtures and gifts from him. When I didn't climb into his coffers and allow him unfettered access to the pocket dimension that holds NSU and New Salem, then came the severed fingers and bloody knives secreted in my bedsheets. Obviously, he grows bolder still.

"Ben, you must tell me where to find him. I sense the echoes of your pain, like any of his witch assassins. His signature is unmistakable."

I knew before I even opened my mouth that I wouldn't just be able to tell her an address. The rune gave another warning pulse, and I tasted blood just from the thought of saying it, writing it down, or even leading one of the people in this room there.

"Now hold on," I hedged, also sure Aurina wouldn't take a deflection for an answer.

"What *can* you tell us?" Roe asked, a thread of concern in her tone.

The redhead's change in sympathies gave me whiplash. She was obviously protective of her friend, my anam cara, who had barely looked me in the eye since I'd walked in. My necessary lies had obviously fucked up that relationship. The moment I had to hold a dagger to Cress's throat, I knew I'd ruined one of the only good things in my life. But if our coven's mother hen was willing to hear me out, maybe not all was lost.

Before I died about two weeks from now, of course. The dark magic branded in my flesh still had a deadline ticking down for one last cruel mission Garroway had demanded of me.

"Let me show you why those witches all died," I said with effort as I stood.

I pinched the hem of my shirt and bent my elbows to expose the blood rune for everyone to see. A spiky, circular tattoo that covered most of my right side. The inside of the circle was one giant red glyph. An ugly, ragged slash bisected it now, still weeping, courtesy of the dimensional who nodded next to me and averted his eyes politely.

"This is my blood rune, carved into my skin by...Gar...the master himself." I huffed from the pulse of pain from it, but this time, Aurina, Roe, Cress, and the fae girl all gasped when red striations appeared around it as a visual cue to how much it hurt. I collapsed back into the chair from my wobbly legs. "All of his witches have one. If we speak of our missions or the master's secrets, the Agonia rune in the center activates and gives us a quick, terrible death."

"I didn't know," Aurina said quietly. Her beautiful face softened, dipping into a thoughtful frown.

"I've hunted a few blood barons in my day," the dimensional pitched in. "The runes are created by a shard of a dimensional weapon that was already illegal on Soiluire."

Cress spoke up, leaning past Roe's shoulder to address the cupid woman sitting across from us. "There are lines that branch from the rune too."

"Deadlines," I said. I pinched my eyes closed again. The room was spinning. If I taunted my damaged rune much more, it just might kill me anyway.

"Perhaps you can question the young man at a different time," the dimensional said in a cool tone. "And offer him something in return for the pain he suffers to give you information."

There was a long pause from the cupid demigoddess. "Well, let's hear your story, then, Phaeron. Or should I say—"

"Don't," he interrupted sharply. "His name was Endaeron. You may refer to him thusly."

Someone tugged at my shirt. I cracked my eyes open to see it was the faun, Áine, with a weak aura of green light haloing her earthen-toned fingers.

"Thanks," I mumbled, letting her touch the rune. Gentle warmth replaced the hot needle sensation prickling out from my skin. She was careful not to touch or heal the scratch that'd deactivated the deadly Agonia tattoo in the center of the rune.

"Don't mention it," she replied, but it seemed my story had softened her some. I just had to hope Cress felt similarly, as this wasn't the right time to pour my heart out to her about the true damage Garroway had done to my family.

"I have already told Cress part of this story, but it bears repeating so you all understand," Phaeron was saying in the meantime.

I was momentarily distracted from my brother and Cress as Phaeron described Soiluire and the mysterious goddess of light that'd shown up one day, Myuna, who'd turned out to be a parasite, transforming anyone she'd gifted magic to into monstrosities.

Phaeron's brother, Endaeron, had been closest to her and thus became the worst of the creatures when she showed her true face. He became the Hungering Darkness, a cursed being that eternally hungered for souls.

"The three tribes of my people combined their powers to come here. We sealed the way behind us, thinking we would be free of Myuna," Phaeron sighed. "Unfortunately, my brother had come along with us, hiding dormant in another's soul. Without a body of his own, he picks one victim to slowly corrupt and uses *them* to kill and consume other victims' souls. He is hard to detect and nearly impossible to stop.

"I recruited humankind to help, as the seal we created between our worlds was not as complete as we'd hoped. I personally taught the first librarian witch how to use dimensional magic, and together, we founded Moongrove Library, the first prison for unnatural beings and items too dangerous for mortals."

He turned slowly, glaring up at the gargoyle standing over the two of us like we were some kind of war prize. "We chased my brother from victim to victim. I'd vowed to end my brother's tortured existence, and in the process of learning from me and ascending to demigoddesshood, Morgana Voidbinder became my partner and mate. We hunted Endaeron together."

"Again, I am not her," Geo said in his usual monotone.

"Trust me, I am well aware," Phaeron rumbled. "Morgana died two hundred years ago when we nearly had my brother in a containment room. We were *so close* to ensuring he was contained when he unexpectedly murdered the woman whose body he was occupying and lashed out at Morgana. Her last act was to seal the room—with both Endaeron and me inside. Presumably, she succumbed to her wounds minutes later. Had she waited a moment more, I would've been able to leave the room and get her treatment, but she didn't give me the chance.

"I just want to speak with her one last time, gargoyle. To ask her why," he said. "Two hundred years may have passed, but I've been in stasis for that time. Her death was a blink of time for me."

"That's rough," I muttered.

"You will not be speaking with her. She does not exist anymore," Geo replied.

"Her soul is clearly—"

"Phaeron, that doesn't explain recent events," Aurina interrupted.

He heaved a sigh and turned back to her. "Of course. Someone unsealed the containment room, and my brother latched on to him immediately. The boy I fought earlier."

"My brother," I said, swallowing painfully. "The master sent him to Moongrove Library. All he told me was it was 'a stop there for something.'"

"Was he the youngest assassin in the blood baron's coven?" Phaeron asked me.

"Yeah. There are some other kids, but Lucas is the youngest who'd taken the blood witch affinity," I confirmed.

"But why unseal the room in the first place?" Cress breathed.

"Many reasons, I am sure," Phaeron answered. "But first, to escalate with you." He nodded toward Aurina. "All of the victims have been taken on the NSU campus. I do not know this man, but I know blood barons always have multiple irons in the fire. Until my brother takes over the boy's soul completely, he is leashed by the blood rune Lucas carries. He will fulfill any order the blood baron makes."

Aurina's flawless skin paled considerably.

"I'm not okay with any of this," Roe burst in. "We have to do something."

"Kill this vampire," Cress said in agreement.

"Get the monster out of my brother," I said.

"And throw him back in stasis, where he belongs," Phaeron finished with a nod. "Which means we are all on the same side. It is time we worked together, and there is one easy first step." He rattled his chains as he held his arms out toward Aurina.

"Seconded." I smirked at the cupid demigoddess as I mimicked his stance.

Her nostrils flared before she turned her face away. "There is one more piece of this puzzle to uncover before I decide what to do with you two," she said. "Tell me your story, Cressida."

"Me?" she asked, brows lifting.

"Were you not the witness that reported a dimensional standing over your roommate after her untimely death?"

Cress sucked in a breath, a pained gasp to have that memory unearthed.

"Yeah, that was me," she admitted.

"How did that get us here?" Aurina pressed. She steepled her fingers, inspecting the other two ladies in the room with her. "How did your friends get pulled into this situation?"

Phaeron reluctantly put his arms down, turning his attention toward her as well. I blew out a breath, knowing this was going to be hard to hear.

"Well," Cress hedged. She took several deep breaths. "You're right. The night of Lanie's murder, I saw Phaeron standing over her. I immediately assumed he'd killed her."

"Her distress activated this unit," Geo rumbled.

"And the university announced it was a blood witch's killing. I didn't understand it, but one of my professors told me to keep Phaeron's identity quiet to prevent widespread panic. He agreed to teach me librarian witch magic early," Cress continued. "I picked up a silver sword and started learning how to defend myself, and Geo became my bodyguard. But I have a confession."

She bit her lip, eyeing the cupid demigoddess and the unsmiling males on either side of her. "I released Phaeron from the bottom floor of the library. All this time, I thought the...I thought his brother's actions were my fault. I didn't tell anyone this because I thought I'd be expelled."

"Endaeron was long gone when you helped me shake off the disori-entation spell keeping me in the library," Phaeron said, his expression softening. "You truly blamed yourself?"

She gave him a shy smile, a hint of color brightening her cheeks. "I did. Which was why I was so determined to handle you."

"You can handle me any time you like, bright soul," he practically purred.

I couldn't help a sudden and acute flash of jealousy. She was really going to let him flirt with her right in front of me? Geo cleared his throat, a sound like two stones grinding together. With a flinch, Cress shifted with embarrassment.

"So, anyway, I kept it a secret, and around that time, Ben showed up. He was interested in me nearly immediately, and we found out we were anam cara, destined to be the closest of friends or maybe even lovers. In the meantime, another person died, and the university blamed a blood witch again."

"I thought it was Lucas being sloppy," I admitted.

"And I thought it was Phaeron because he'd been there at the Mabon celebration. Sorry, Geo," she said. His usual stony expression was twisted in displeasure. "I spoke to Phaeron while Geo was, uh, otherwise occupied. He warned me to leave the celebration early, and I did.

"I still hadn't told anyone about Phaeron, but he took me aside one evening after Ben left my dorm to tell me of Soiluire and his brother. I said the monster's name, and it came out of nowhere to attack me, which is how I then knew the...the Hunger, it wasn't Phaeron," she said, drawing a hand down her cheeks. "Lanie was an augury witch, and I finally read her last message to me. In it, she said she'd seen her murderer was a blood witch, so I started connecting the wrong dots. The university obviously thought a blood witch was involved—"

Aurina shook her head, muttering, "It was just a cover story. A lie."

"—Well, I realized a blood witch was involved then. And only one had come around at the same time of Lanie's death, pretending to be a different kind of witch, and been in the same place as each time the Hunger had appeared. I thought, if it wasn't Phaeron, it had to be Ben. I finally told my friends everything, and together, we set a trap for Ben, but instead of him being the monster, it'd been his brother all along."

"Hey, next time, you could just ask first," I said, trying to make a joke despite the tense atmosphere. No one laughed.

"And now we're here," Roe said.

"Indeed," Aurina said. She considered a few sheets of paper on her desk for a prolonged moment. "I'm glad to have had you all in the same room. It is, of course, disappointing that you did not come forward with your story earlier, Cressida, but in the scheme of things, it wouldn't have been all that useful without the other angles." She gestured to Phaeron and me.

"What will you be telling the campus?" Áine asked. "A bunch of mer saw the fight break out."

The cupid demigoddess pressed her lips together tighter. "To go to class on Monday, of course. We will continue to say that we have it under control."

I shifted uneasily but didn't point out that she obviously didn't have this situation contained. No one else seemed willing to challenge her obvious lie either, leading to an awkward pause until she nodded and gestured. "Ladies, you may go. You as well, Geo. I imagine you want to see your charge safely to her bed."

"Indeed," Geo said, taking a stiff step backward.

"He couldn't defend anyone from a fly right now," Phaeron remarked. "I will see Cress and her friends returned to their lodgings."

Aurina was suddenly twirling a keychain between her fingers, having the metal clink. "Well, I wanted to talk about your future first. And your freedom."

3
PHAERON

BBEFORE SHE LEFT THE ROOM, Cress stopped beside my chair. My gaze traced the scratches on her face, left to seal themselves over. My brother had done this, marred her beauty. That was his nature, to ruin and destroy the prettiest of things. Especially if I was enamored with them.

Her shoulders were lowered with fatigue. This had been a long evening. By the time she retired to her room, the night may be over. "I just wanted to say, I'm sorry about ever thinking you were a monster." Earnestness shone in her wide brown eyes, and I cursed Aurina again for leaving me restrained.

I was so tightly bound I could not draw her hand to my lips to kiss the mark of protection I'd left amongst the bluish veins lining her wrist. "Let us put the misunderstanding behind us. Perhaps I will see you soon," I said.

She flashed a little smile. "I hope so."

With one last nod and an uncertain glance toward Aurina, she left the room. If she heard Ben softly hiss her name, she ignored it. She'd carefully avoided interacting with him. When I'd first chanced a glimpse of them together, I'd known he was concealing his true nature from her immediately, as his soul was stained with dark magic and twisted by the pain of the rune embedded in his flesh. One such as him didn't have anything to offer a bright, innocent soul such as herself, and it seemed she'd realized that.

Neither do you, I reminded myself. I strongly suspected there was more danger brewing in my own condition than I'd dare divulge to this group.

"Ben," Aurina said once we were alone with her and her mates. She cooed his name, weaving a thread of calming emotion in the single syllable. I'd felt her magic suffusing the room this whole time, feeling out everyone's emotional state with invisible tendrils.

Unlike me, Ben was unaware of her subtle manipulations, and he sighed as he struggled to focus on her rather than the door snicking closed behind us.

"Is this where you show me the secret dungeons you have under this building?" he asked. It might've been a snark, but his tone lacked any sharp edges, drooping like he did the moment Cress was gone.

She rolled her eyes. "No. You obviously need rest as well. How old are you?"

"Twenty," he said.

"Congratulations, then. In accordance with supernatural law, you are now enrolled as a student at NSU for two mandatory years of education in your magic."

"Whoopee. I better call home and tell them the good news," he mumbled.

"We will find accommodations for you that are safe and reinforced. I do not put it past Garroway to send some of his assassins for you if he realizes you are out of his control."

"Oh, guaranteed."

"Do you think he may still be able to send you orders and compel you to fulfill them?" she asked.

He hesitated. "Maybe."

"If I may," I interjected. Aurina's lips pressed together again, but she nodded. "I have an idea that may suit all our needs. You may remember how I just told you about teaching the first librarian witches and building the foundation of what became Moongrove Library."

"Mmhmm," she hummed suspiciously.

"It is time I claimed my position there as an instructor."

"I never said I trusted you with my students," she said.

I flashed my fangs and lifted my bound wrists. "It is clear you do not trust me at all. However, you have little choice."

My shadows had been probing at the manacle around my tail; the metal was inscribed with runes of containment. Most supernaturals would have their magic completely bound by such a thing, but my power was too much to restrain so easily. I picked it open and felt my shadowborn abilities flood back in like they'd never been locked away. In an instant, I'd transformed into a curl of smoke and back, holding the cuffs that'd been on my ankles and wrists dangling from one clawed finger.

The shadows themselves surged around me, overlaying my form until my hands were tipped with wicked-sharp talons. I let the shadowborn transformation go further than it had in a long time. Darkness enveloped my head, rendering me momentarily blind as thick shadows formed a wolf-like maw lined with jagged teeth and a canine skull protected by the circular shape of my horns.

"I have a few demands following my poor treatment this evening." My voice was an unearthly, reverberating snarl. "You will relinquish my rightful territory to me, Prince Phaeron Sudair of the dimensional travelers."

"Holy shit," Ben breathed. He was on the floor, inching away from me.

Aurina's mates were on their feet, reaching for weapons or magic as I sat there with my hands laced on my lap. She lifted her hand with a whisper of calming magic all around. "There's no need to fight," she trilled. "Of course you can go to the library. It's just...this is mid-year, and the students all have instructors... Perhaps you could be an assistant?" Her laugh was edged with nerves. "I could make you an assistant instructor? You would still have access to the library."

"I also require an instructor's lodging. One with enough room to comfortably house both myself and Ben." I pointed a single talon in the young man's direction. "I alone can see if his soul is tainted with more of the blood baron's black magic. Besides, his brother is currently victimized by what's left of my own kin. It would only be fair for me to look after him, yes?"

"N-no, I could make due somewhere else—" Ben was starting to say.

"Done," Aurina interrupted. "Consider all of that done."

I let my jagged shadows go, reclining casually in the chair and smiling just enough to show the edges of my fangs. "I knew we could come to an agreement."

She reached across the desk, offering me a key. "For Ben's cuffs," she said.

I took it and gave him a hand up before freeing him from the restraints. He tottered as if dizzy, and I steadied him with a hand on his shoulder. He flinched, a hint of fear in his hazy green eyes.

"Just step outside for a moment while I take care of a few last details," I murmured, and he nearly tripped over himself to go.

I turned my full attention to Aurina, who was also standing now, just a desk between us. I was suddenly hyperaware of every inch of wood as her subtle magic drifted around me with another shift in emotional direction.

"Perhaps I can offer you a better deal, Prince Sudair," she purred. "You are clearly quite powerful. What if I told you my mating circle is always open for one such as you?"

It was hard to ignore the luster of her candy-pink locks, or the gorgeous lips she pursed at a coy slant. Every breath, I took in more of her lusty magic. "I will be in the library, awaiting my accommodations," I said, forcing my coldest tone. "Do not make Ben and me wait."

"Must you go so soon?" she asked. Brazen in front of her mates, but the same magic she tried to influence me with was drawing their attention too. They might all have her the moment I left.

I turned into a curl of smoke, thinking sobering thoughts as I drifted from the room and located Ben. He'd found a chair and promptly dropped unconscious the moment no one's eyes were on him. He seemed more hurt than he'd let on, so I didn't wake him, instead enveloping him in my shadows and carrying him on an incorporeal wind toward Moongrove Library.

It saved me the embarrassment of explaining why I was leaving Aurina's presence fully aroused and eager to catch a glimpse of a different beauty instead. Now that Cress knew she could trust me, I wanted to explore the draw between us, preferably with my tongue over every inch of her delicate skin. I could practically hear her breath quickening and feel her pulse ticking beneath my lips.

When Aurina had made lust circle the room, my first thought hadn't been for the curvy demigoddess. I wanted my fist wrapped around purple hair rather than pink. My fantasies had emptied Aurina's room in an instant, replacing her with Cress screaming my name while I pinned her to the desk and claimed her wet heat.

It'd been far too long since a woman had spread her thighs for me. My mouth watered for a taste of Cress. What would a little nibble of her sex—of her soul—taste like, other than the purest nectar? As sweet and bright as it was, it had to be delicious...

I let out a metaphorical gasp, realizing I was on the edge of the abyss that'd wash away my consciousness. I'd suffered from these blackouts far too much, especially around my brother, who seemed to know how to trigger them.

It was Myuna's corruption coming to root within me. Even as I lusted for Cress, I realized I didn't just want her body. I wanted *just a taste* of that beautiful soul that blazed around her and kept drawing me back like a moth to flame.

I'd watched dozens of my people succumb to a taste for souls, afflicted by the barest drop of corruption in our hurry to flee from Soiluire. One taste was never a "just," but the gateway to an addiction that could only be ended by the thrust of a sword.

In a panic, I slipped into the library that'd been my prison for two centuries, finding it just as modernized and alien as when I'd first escaped with Cress's help.

This time, however, a woman's voice reached out to whisper in my mind, *"My prince, have you returned at last?"*

"Braza. What a relief it is to hear you," I replied in kind.

"Do you mean that? Because last I heard, I was 'quite meddlesome,'" she teased.

I recognized the words I'd spoken in ire when Braza had forced me to seek out Cress and explain the Age of Decay to her. It'd been the best decision, in retrospect, but her offhanded comment also told me she was more aware of the world outside her library than I thought.

"Well, you are, but some meddling is for the greater good."

"Who's the boy you're carrying?" she asked.

"My self-appointed new charge. Do you have somewhere he can rest?"

She directed me to floor negative three, where there were small rooms for a librarian's occasional overnight stay. Ben was still asleep when I removed my magic and we emerged from the shadows. I placed him on the bed and turned back into a wisp of darkness, locking the door before flowing out of the miniscule gap on the bottom of the threshold.

"I'll keep an eye on him for you. Come visit me," Braza invited.

With her help, I found the stairs again and flowed down them until I located the floor where the mortals kept her nowadays, some thirty stories down. She was the powercore, after all, the beating heart of Moongrove Library. She siphoned from the ley line I'd identified centuries ago, creating a reservoir that was then tapped by the witches to keep order within the many levels of the library.

I took form again at the stairs, bowing to Braza. "May I approach?" I asked.

"Please. How I've longed to see you again."

I ascended, seeing the reflection of my shadowborn self in its dome of magic, its canine leer making it look like I prowled with lethal intent toward the jelly-like orb. I stopped short. The powercore showed me the truth, much as I didn't want to see it. My shadows lapped off my silhouette like flowing fur, pitch-black all over, save for the blaze of corrupted white taking over the yellow of my eyes.

"Come in. It's still you," Braza whispered.

I stopped staring at myself and strode for the orb, taking a larger step up to where I knew there was a hidden ledge. Loose dimensional magic enveloped me and ran over my skin like a static-filled blanket. I absorbed none of it as I entered the hollow secret nook within the core.

A female dimensional stood there waiting for me. She was not flesh and blood like I was, but constructed of the same purple-black magic of the powercore's dome over us. Braza had the forward-facing horns and bat-like wings of my mother's tribe and the same youthful features she'd died with, having not physically aged a second in the last two centuries.

Static prickled the back of my neck as we embraced. Her body, such as it was, squished in my hold. "I've missed you, my prince. It's been torture knowing you were in stasis with Endaeron's remains."

"You knew, and yet you told no one?" I pulled away as if stung.

Her face fell. "I was well aware that to release you meant we released him as well."

"Of course."

I tamped down my resentment, eyeing her space. Braza could become a part of the powercore at will, but she was aware of every inch of the library and unable to rest. She had this stone platform with a bed and a couch formed of magic taking up most of the space, plus a chest where she kept who knew what.

It didn't seem like the kind of existence I'd be able to endure, but Braza had preferred this to the uncertainty of death when her soul had been torn nearly in two. My brother was responsible, of course. She'd surrendered herself to power the library eternally as its custodian, maintaining everything as a stationary sentinel.

"How are you? Truly?" I asked.

She smiled and reached for me. I let her cool, electric touch drift down my cheek and the spiral of my horn, like she wanted to memorize every feature. I held my hands out and cupped her daintier clawed hands, letting her draw on my warmth.

"Lonely but well. The library has changed in your absence. Most of the mortal witches don't realize they can stop and chat at any time, and our kind have forgotten I exist."

"I will strive to change that," I promised.

"The new ones only know your name from a history book. We are not united anymore," she sighed.

"Do we need to be?" I asked gently. "If we have found our place here, I say that is better. The old ways brought us Myuna and her endless hunger for souls."

She lifted a shoulder. "I believe we all need a light to follow. Especially those who are shadowborn."

"Has anyone birthed a shadowborn since we came to Earth?" I asked, tilting my head curiously.

"Yes! It passes on in the family lines now. They're not nearly as powerful as the shadowborn from Soiluire, but the darkness is different here. Not as oppressive."

"It is," I agreed. Earth was far too bright, but beggars couldn't be choosers. "I have come to you with a heavy heart, Braza. I cannot be the returning prince you're hoping for. It seems that during our forced stasis together, my brother somehow infected me with his corruption."

"I see this," she said, leaning in to inspect my eyes. "I will give you raw power to resist. You cannot give in to the cravings to taste anyone's soul, else you are lost."

"Is there any hope for a cure?" I murmured.

She shook her head slowly, and my heart sank. "So, my days truly are numbered," I said, numb.

"I wouldn't say that! Those of our kind with similar afflictions have gone on to live fulfilling mortal lives with regular infusions of power. I am, after all, giving them parts of my extra-large soul." She squeezed my hands with a little laugh. "Don't go thinking you need to do anything drastic. Just stay in the library for now. Look, I saved something for you…"

She released me, and I rubbed my chilled fingers as I watched her unlatch the chest on the platform and rummage through it. What she handed to me were the perfect gift to lift my flagging spirits. Twin swords, perfectly maintained. Their sheaths were black, with ornate silver-colored filigree up the sides to match the oiled hilts. I drew one, admiring the pristine dimensional language etched into the metal.

The blades were edged in silver, a metal that wasn't native to Soiluire. It was deadly to me and anything else that originated from my home planet. They were the perfect unnatural-killing weapons, and I itched to plunge them both into my brother's husk to finally end the cycle of suffering he caused.

With Braza's help, I'd never follow in his footsteps and become a soul-craving monster.

I could court Cress without being constantly distracted by her bright soul. In time, I could trust myself to leave a mating mark on her without also consuming some of that light-filled aura she carried.

I resheathed the weapon and turned back to Braza. "Thank you. By the way, you are looking at Moongrove Library's newest assistant professor. I won't be far."

4
CRESS

After Lanie's passing, I'd asked to stay in my dorm room alone to give my familiars and me a peaceful haven. I'd never expected to have Geo out cold, sleeping off his injuries in the stripped bed while my three closest friends stuck around to offer moral support the next morning.

We ended up studying together. I sat cross-legged in my bed, cramming for midterms with an iced coffee in one hand, the other buried in Bella's fur. My tabby girl had tucked herself into a ball in my lap, purring idly. Milo, my other familiar, had stretched out next to Geo's sleeping form, acting like the stoic man's nurse again.

"I'm so going to fail," I bemoaned. After everything I'd been through lately, I'd completely forgotten to study for some of the most important tests of this semester.

"With that attitude," Áine commented. She had her hoofed legs stretched out on the floor between the beds, alternating between chirping to Jin in a fae language and doing her own studying. Jin seemed to like her, or maybe she was just coming back from losing Lanie. I had my friend's permission to make her my third familiar, but the small black cat wanted little to do with me.

Roe was at the desk closest to my bed, the two of us occasionally comparing notes over the class we had in common, Introduction to Witchcraft. While I was a true beginner, she'd already learned some of the details covered in the class from the special witch-exclusive private school she'd attended. She passed me some of the benefits as a patient tutor.

Meanwhile, my third friend, soft-spoken Willow Frost, sat at my usual desk. "Look at the bright side. At least you've learned some librarian witch magic ahead of schedule," she said. The brunette was always pointing this out, as her grasp on her oceanic witch magic was shaky at best. She'd wanted to help us fight the Hungering Darkness but had seen the wisdom of sitting it out until her control improved.

Bella pawed at my arm, looking up at me earnestly. She sent friendly warmth over our bond of witch and familiar. "Don't panic. You can do this," she squeaked. Where others heard her high-pitched meows, I understood her directly.

"You're right, ladies. It'll be okay," I said, meaning to return to my studies with those words.

That was when someone decided to knock on the door. Assuming it was one of the other witches rooming on this floor, I called, "It's not locked!"

The hinges creaked, and Ben poked his head in the room. I could practically feel the air shift as we all turned to look at him, cats included. "Oh, hi...everyone," he said, sounding like he'd rather just close the door and slink away.

I flushed hot and cold at the same time. "What do you want?" I asked.

"Shouldn't you be resting?" Roe added a breath later.

"I'm fine, mother hen," he said to her with a tight smile. "Look, Cress, can we talk?"

I could practically feel the disapproval rolling off the other ladies in the room with me. If Geo were awake rather than unmoving as a stone in his healing sleep, he'd probably toss Ben out himself.

But this was my decision, and I was unlikely to get another opportunity to get him on his own and answers out of his mouth. I gently nudged Bella off my lap and made to stand.

"Do you want me to come with you?" Roe asked in an undertone.

"We're just going to go out to the garden," I said, hitching my thumb over my shoulder.

"I'd feel much better about this if the *known assassin* would swear to me that he means you no harm," Áine interjected.

Ben's fingers dug into the cheap wood of the door where he held it open. "I swear I won't hurt her or let anyone else do so," he said.

"On your blood, honor, and true name?" she pressed.

"If I had anything sharp on my person—which I don't—I would pierce my thumb and swear it right now." He sounded honest enough.

I wanted to trust him and believe he'd come here without any bad intentions. "I'll be okay, Áine. He knows I'll never speak to him again if he dares to lie to me one more time," I said for everyone's benefit and to draw a flinch from him at my steely tone.

Her keen gaze inspected him for a moment before she nodded, and I left my friends to their studying as I joined Ben in the hall. I was aware of Bella following on my heels, a silent observer to how I gestured Ben toward the stairwell.

"I know I'm probably the last person you want to see right now." He stuck his hands in his pockets as we wound down the flights of stairs.

I didn't reply. It would be rude to agree, but I just didn't know what either of us could say to fix the chasm that'd opened up between us from the moment he'd held a knife to my throat.

"There are just a few things I need to tell you, and they can't wait," he continued in an urgent hush. "I'll be out of your life soon enough."

What was that supposed to mean? I slanted him a dubious look as we emerged into the afternoon sunshine. It was a calm autumn day, with a scattering of fluffy clouds flowing across the sky, accompanied by a gentle breeze that lifted a few locks of my purple hair sideways. Ben went straight to a bench within the small garden and sat with a groan. I settled on the bench's edge next to him, glancing up at my dorm window, where Roe's face was in the middle of disappearing from view.

"This isn't going to be easy for me to tell you, but I think you need to know," he said, drawing my attention back to him. He had a hand pressed to his right side, like he'd already aggravated the disc of dark magic that caused him so much pain.

"What is it?" I asked quietly.

"A politician...a man named..." He sucked in a sharp breath. "I guess I can't share his name."

"Can you call him by a nickname? Something like Bob?" I suggested.

His lips quirked into his usual sideways smirk. "Bob sought the master's services back when you were a baby. Your parents...your real mother, was in his way politically."

"You know who my parents are?" I asked, sitting up a little straighter when he nodded. Some of my old friends had wondered if I'd ever sought out my "real" parents, not realizing I didn't care much past their names and the big question: why had they surrendered me?

I'd been raised by a good woman I considered my mother now, but that didn't prevent me from wondering about a few basic things I'd been too young to understand. Why hadn't I been wanted? Why had my—presumably witchy—parents let me get raised away from the supernatural world?

"Bob had them...ugh." He suddenly bent over with a pained wheeze. I muffled a gasp of surprise, reaching for him.

"Is this hurting you that badly? You don't have to tell me—"

"I do," he interrupted. "There isn't enough time." He pulled a paper towel from his pocket and dabbed at his nose as he straightened. It came away soaked in crimson.

I reached out and put my hand over his, feeling the heat rising from his side. That couldn't be pleasant, yet he was trying to endure it for my sake. The fact that it was active and harming him meant he was telling the truth, which meant my birth parents were...murdered, perhaps, at a politician's whims. It was the only thing that made sense, even if he couldn't say it aloud.

Ben's callused fingers entwined with mine, and he pulled me away from the overheated rune. I felt a jolt of awareness. Our anam cara marks had brushed, reminding me of the bond we shared. Two halves of a soul, destined to find and complete one another. I'd been drawn to Ben since the moment I'd met him, which made the twisted net of lies between us all the more painful.

I tugged my hand away from his. It didn't feel right to be holding hands like we used to, like nothing had changed. "You couldn't tell me anything before, could you?" I asked.

"Not without my blood rune ending my life," he murmured. "I'm sorry I kept so much from you. In the time I have left, I swear I'll make it up to you."

"What do you mean, the time you have left?" I asked. It seemed he was feeling some kind of time limit, as he'd mentioned it a few times now.

He sighed and ran a hand through his overlong hair. "My former master is an emotional vampire. He seems to enjoy feeding on fear and pain the most." He lifted the hem of his shirt again, pointing out a few lines rising from his blood rune. "Each of these is a deadline, a magical time limit for every mission I've been sent on. The black ones are successfully completed."

Ben's fingertip stopped right below a deadline that was as crimson as the center of his rune, stretching a couple inches long. "Only the master can declare a mission a success and stop an active deadline. Else it will reach the witch's heart and kill them."

I felt a chill creeping up my arms. "That's an active deadline, isn't it?" I breathed.

"It is. And there's no way he would ever stop it from killing me now that I have a taste of freedom," he muttered. "I have until Samhain."

"Ben—what?" I spluttered. There was no way he'd just calmly told me he was going to die in a couple weeks after also dropping the bomb about my birth parents. It felt like the world shifted a few inches on its axis, everything slanting in a new light. "What was the mission? If you complete it, won't the deadline stop on its own?"

He shook his head, pressing the paper towel back to his nose. "Never mind that. He has the tool to stop it."

"Well, we've got to get it from him!" I was ready to push from the bench and get started when he slanted me an incredulous look.

"In a couple weeks?"

"Where is it?"

Jaw clenched, he shook his head again.

With a sinking heart, I leaned back. Of course Ben couldn't say. His vampire "master" would keep his powerful magical tool out of easy reach, probably in the secret home Ben couldn't talk about.

"I don't think I can tell you much more today," he rasped.

I flashed a tentative smile. "Okay. You want to come inside and study with us? Midterms are about to destroy me."

His trepidation was unmistakable as he physically recoiled from the idea.

"It won't happen immediately, but you'll earn everyone's trust back faster if you don't hide from them," I said more gently.

"Maybe when Geo won't wake up and immediately try to make shish kabob of me. What about your trust, though?" His green gaze searched my face.

I found it easier to meet his eyes after this conversation. It was progress in the right direction, to see his pain and know he was a victim too. The evil vampire he kept referring to as his former master hadn't taken control of his mouth and lied for him, but it was obvious Ben had had to balance what he *could* say with what he felt for me as his anam cara.

"That will take time," I said honestly. While I empathized with him, I wasn't sure how close I could let him come to my heart anymore.

His gaze fell as he nodded with some reluctance.

"However, I want to make sure you have much more of it than just a couple weeks. Does Phaeron know?"

Ben paled some. "Why are you bringing him up?"

"Maybe a second scar over your blood rune will loosen the restrictions on you more," I suggested.

"You're probably right." His lips quirked. "I'll have to show you my new place sometime. Tall, dark, and terrifying has decided that he's going to look after me, so we're roommates."

Tall, dark, and terrifying? Well, if that was his new nickname for Phaeron, he wasn't quite wrong. "Then you'll have no problem telling him you need another scratch," I said.

"Maybe. I think you underestimate how painful his *scratches* are. But if it'll help me speak freely, I'll do it." He nodded, setting his jaw. I could feel the brush of heat from his blood rune from where I sat and flashed him a concerned look.

"I'd better go lie down." He lurched to his feet as he spoke, and I jumped up too, afraid he'd topple over from any stiff wind.

Ben reached for me, and I let him take my hand again. Those callused fingertips brushed against mine, and I felt a now familiar flutter lower in my belly. His little smile was less guarded, not like the mean smirk he wore like armor. This was the young man I'd fallen for, the Ben I'd daydreamed about, the one I'd taken to bed without hesitation.

Without the layers of pain and cruelty that'd formed the past he could still barely speak of, I recognized him, and I still liked the truth of him. If only he hadn't had to hide it under so much dishonesty and misdirection.

"Ben," I breathed.

He pressed a kiss to my forehead. I closed my eyes for a moment, flushing warm from the gentle brush of his lips. "See you soon, Cress."

5
CRESS

THE COZY STUDY group in my room kept going until late in the evening. My gargoyle guardian stirred in the afternoon, inhaling suddenly and cracking his joints like the quick snap of rocks tapping each other.

He startled the rest of us, but not Milo, who purred happily after Geo curled his stiff fingers and pet my cat's white belly. The ghost of a smile touched Geo's stoic features.

"How are you feeling, Geo?" I asked.

His quicksilver eyes tracked to my face. He still had the slow, uncanny movements that meant his gargoyle body was still in the process of healing from its trauma.

"I will make a full recovery," he replied. After a lengthy pause, he added, "I will be mended enough to return to my duty of protecting you tomorrow."

"Take your time," I encouraged. "You were banged up pretty bad."

A small crease appeared between his brows. "That does not mean I should laze in bed. I failed to kill that monster, and as soon as I am physically able, I will be seeking a means to improve."

"You and me both," I said. My three friends all nodded in agreement as well.

When Monday dawned, Geo was waiting in the garden in his gargoyle form, his stony arms crossed. His clothes had frozen to his form, taking on the same color of obsidian stone, with silvery veins lightly interspersed. A grand pair of carved bat wings was furled tightly to his back, and his chiseled expression was, shockingly, twisted with annoyance.

Ben was there next to him, leaning against his side as if the gargoyle were a real statue. The blood witch's smirk was mischievous. "Good morning, Cress," he said cheerfully.

"Good morning," I replied, gaze darting between them. "Are you bothering Geo?"

"We just had a chat, man to man. Well, man to stone," Ben said.

"He told me he is in need of my protection as well. I informed him of my primary directive, yet he has not left." Geo's voice in his gargoyle form was like the grinding of stone, deep and slow and a little abrasive.

I was worried to see him wearing his rocky form again, as he seemed to lose what little progress we'd made with him understanding and expressing his emotions each time he transformed. My biggest concern was that he would take his gargoyle form permanently and forsake the budding life he was forming for himself in the name of duty.

The problem was, *I* was his duty. I was his soul mate, according to Lanie's last letter, the duty that'd forced him from his rest and back into the real world. If he truly wished to embrace his duty, he had to figure out how to be a man instead of a statue.

I could see why he was confused. To a gargoyle, duty was protection. I was the safest witch with him never taking a break unless he was physically incapable of fulfilling the job. Which made things awkward for me with Ben right next to him to remind me that I had, essentially, two soul mates.

"Well, let's go, then," I said. I hoisted my backpack higher on my shoulders and set off for my classes. Ben walked by my side, with Geo just a few paces behind.

In the supernatural world, it wasn't unheard of for someone to have more than one partner. I was raised fully human, where the idea was more taboo, so it felt like a conversation and an unwelcome choice looming over my shoulder. I was feeling some contentment to return to normal with both of them here with me; I didn't want to ruin it by picking Geo's companionship over Ben's, as I would right now if forced to make a decision.

"So," Ben said, cutting into the silence that'd fallen between the three of us. "How do you feel about those midterms now?"

I breathed an uncertain chuckle. "It's just a couple of tests. How hard could they be?"

"Aw, don't jinx yourself there." He tisked. "Dr. Aurina wanted me to enroll as a student. If a registrar can find me, they can put me in real classes. Until then, I'm just going to Introduction to Witchcraft with you and hanging out with Geo or Phaeron."

I glanced over my shoulder at the gargoyle. Geo's expression had eased to a handsome carved mask with no emotion present. "Why?" I asked, raising a brow at Ben.

"Earlier"—he made a vague gesture—"I learned how to fight anything, be it supernatural or unnatural. A blood witch can take advantage of nearly every situation and fight almost any being. But there are a few things we were taught to avoid at all costs."

He ticked off what he listed on his fingers. "Gargoyles, for one. No blood, just solid rock. For another, dimensionals with shadow magic. They *do* have blood, but if you don't get the jump on them, they turn incorporeal, and then your average blood witch is unlikely to survive what comes next."

I barely missed a beat this time, rather than puzzling over why he was mentioning fighting either man. "*Oh*. Others, uh, like you..." I said, stumbling over mentioning assassins when we were in the midst of heavy foot traffic in the heart of the NSU campus.

"Would be heavily discouraged by either of their presences," Ben finished for me. "More Geo than Phaeron, but only because he keeps his tall, dark, and terrifying act under wraps in public."

I smothered a little laugh. By the time we reached my first class of the day, Latin, Geo was transforming back to his fully human form. It was nearly seamless and gave him an opportunity to follow me into the classroom. I held out my phone to him but kept a grip of the other side when he moved to take it. "I know it's unusual, but would you mind staying behind to protect Ben?" I asked.

His scowl was quick to arrive. "My only duty is to you, not him."

I brushed my fingertips down Geo's arm. "I know. And it seems he likes to bother you," I said, slanting Ben a disapproving look when the blood witch began to grin. "It would, ah, make me happier to know that you would step in if any danger comes for him. And the least he can do in return is stop trying to get a rise out of you."

"That would be a requirement," Geo rumbled.

"I can promise I'll try?" Ben asked.

"Then I would *try* to protect you too," the gargoyle said.

Seeing that that was the best I'd get out of both of them today, I let Geo take the phone and unlock it with a twitch of his thumb. He went to sit on a nearby bench to get lost in one of his many Internet rabbit holes while I went to my Latin class to sweat through my first midterm.

Latin was one of my most difficult classes. I just didn't seem to get it, and my other friends didn't have to take this class to help with the practical aspects of casting their magic. Most of the people taking the midterm with me today were fellow librarians or celestial witches, who had the only affinity more complicated than librarian magic.

By the time I was finished, I wasn't sure if I'd done well or not. Usually, I chalked that feeling up to an inevitable failure, but I'd already learned a smattering of Latin words along the path to practicing librarian witch magic. Maybe my extra studies did me in good stead.

Ben and Geo went with me to Introduction to Witchcraft, but this time, they both came into the classroom with me. Geo stood in the back of the room to wait. I sat toward the end of our coven's row, with Ben leaning casually against the wall with his legs in a figure four. Seated in front of me today was the other oceanic witch in our coven, Heath Storm, a welcome change from the perfectly groomed blonde who usually claimed that spot. He nodded and murmured a good luck.

Wren Starsurge, said blonde, was up front today, putting a set of pens in just the right order on her desk in anticipation of today's midterm. I imagined she sat away from me, Willow, and Roe to avoid the distraction of coming up with some catty remark.

Most of my classes were having written tests in one long marathon, and this class was no exception. Heath seemed well-rested, and the back of Wren's head showed she'd had enough time to style it in soft waves.

I was sure I looked like a mess next to them. There were shadows under my eyes from my late-night cram session yesterday evening. I'd combed my hair and tied it back into a ponytail but otherwise ventured out of the dorm wearing no makeup and the last clean top at the back of my closet, the sky-blue turtleneck sweater Mom had insisted I take to NSU but I'd formerly sworn I'd never get caught dead in.

As I fiddled with its fraying cuff, I remembered that conversation as if it'd happened years ago. I'd tossed it on without a moment's thought this morning, more preoccupied with midterms, men, and monsters. And not necessarily in that order.

I fished out a single pen and set it down, breathing out a tense sigh. If I could push myself to learn my magic two years ahead of schedule, I could pass a few tests. I exchanged thumbs-up with Willow and pretended to fist bump Roe a couple seats up from me, then the whole room quieted as elderly Dr. Heartwood cleared her throat.

"Good morning, students. This test was designed to take you this whole class period to complete. Best of luck." She passed out thick packets whose contents looked like they were on their twelfth pass through the copier.

No one who knew me in high school would recognize the spirit that possessed me as I focused on this second test with everything I had. I'd always been a B student at best, knowing the limits of achievement that were required of me and coming in just a bit above average.

There'd never seemed to be much of a point, not when I spent my spare time working as a cashier at the fast-food place up the street. The only place I thought I'd go, at least in the short term, was to a full-time position there upon graduation. There was a purpose to the work, which was to take money home to support Mom and my younger sister, Carly.

My NSU coursework had purpose to me now, and for the first time, I wanted to be an A student. Key word: *wanted*. After the stress of cramming for this test and the others upcoming, I wouldn't get caught slacking on my studies again.

Which meant in the space between this test and the next, I needed to go see Dr. Voidbinder, if he was available. He'd agreed to wait in the library last Saturday, should I need a master librarian's assistance, and I'd left him hanging. I needed to apologize, explain, and ask to step up our training schedule even more.

If I wanted to truly tackle the joint problems of the Hungering Darkness and Ben's deadline, I needed to be a better witch yesterday. The practice of stretching out a curriculum and job path over the course of four years' worth of classes just wasn't going to cut it.

I turned in my midterm a little early and stood next to Geo to watch the muted video he played from my phone. It was one of those satisfying videos where an experienced soap maker cut finished bars of soap to reveal pretty patterns and details within. He made the occasional soft, impressed sound.

"What?" Geo whispered, realizing I'd stopped watching and was smiling up at him instead.

I lifted onto the tips of my toes to kiss his cheek, only confusing him more. "I'll be right back, okay?"

"Okay." He turned back to the screen and touched the spot where my lips had been. I smiled to myself as I slipped out of the classroom.

Hopefully, Dr. Voidbinder wasn't administering a test of his own, as I had a sliver of free time. My next class, Drawing for Fashion, didn't have a midterm, so I was going straight to Moongrove Library after this conversation to see what basic test of librarian knowledge I could ace in Library Science 101.

The door to Dr. Voidbinder's office was closed, but I heard muffled voices within. I lifted my knuckles, then hesitated. He was a director of sorts at Moongrove Library, as well as one of the professors who taught advanced librarian students who wanted to dedicate their life's work to their magical calling. Surely he didn't want me barging in on his meeting.

During my moment of indecision, someone else opened the door, and I took a step back in surprise when it was a tall dimensional on the other side of the threshold. "I thought I sensed you," Phaeron said, beckoning for me to step inside the room.

Dr. Voidbinder was seated behind his desk. I'd rarely seen the portly man red-faced and uncomfortable, but he was now. "Hello, Miss Cress. Speak of the devil, really. We were just discussing your training," he said.

"You were?" I asked in surprise. I eased myself in the second chair across from his desk, as Phaeron had already sat in the one closest to the door. It wasn't quite big enough for his tail, which draped over the armrest between us. I noticed the snap and flick of it, like the dimensional man was hiding some irritation under the polite smile he fixed on Dr. Voidbinder.

"I will be assuming your evening training," Phaeron said. "In fact, with the piddling position the library has placed me in, I might as well take you aside during your librarian classes as well."

"Well, I'm only taking the one..."

Phaeron lifted a brow. "One?" he echoed in a low voice. Oh yeah, he was pissed.

Dr. Voidbinder cleared his throat nervously. "As I was telling you, Prince Sudair, most of our students aren't interested in becoming trained librarians after their time at NSU. Miss Cress, for example, is in the fashion design major."

Phaeron's yellow gaze followed the line of my body up and down, seeming unimpressed. "Did you design those garments you're wearing?"

I shifted, nearly as embarrassed as when the library's powercore had called my interest in fashion a "youthful endeavor." Then a flash of anger replaced it, and I set my teeth. "I've made plenty of clothes for my family when money was tight." And when wasn't it? Before I'd gotten a part-time job, sometimes ends just didn't quite meet. "While there's no need to be so judgmental, you should know that I was planning on changing my major at the end of this semester to take more magic-focused classes."

He dipped his chin in acknowledgment. "My apologies. The end of the semester is in how long?"

"Two months, plus a break for Christmas," I answered.

A fine line appeared between his dark brows. "Yule," Dr. Voidbinder supplied.

"Ah. Alas, we do not have the luxury of time."

"Can you promise you won't endanger her unnecessarily?" my professor asked. "Dr. Aurina won't keep you employed long if you involve any student further in your mission to capture your brother."

Employed? I turned to Phaeron for some answer.

There was a grim set to his lips. "I won't be the one to draw her into danger. However, Endaeron will return for her, and she must be prepared for the next encounter."

"All right. You can tell Aurina that yourself," Dr. Voidbinder replied.

"I will, from afar. If she uses her magic on me again, I doubt she'll enjoy the results." Phaeron scowled, tail lashing. He finally seemed to notice me waiting impatiently for them to stop talking about me while I was sitting right there with them. "After you left, I convinced Aurina to give me a job at the library and quarters for Ben and myself. I will begin earning the common currency shortly as an assistant professor."

"Dollars?" I ventured.

A flicker of shock passed over his expression. "Finally, something that hasn't changed in two centuries," he said dryly. "It turns out I'm an assistant to the basic librarian witch classes, and the course work is inexcusably slow. I will have you and your peers training on the sword shortly."

Dr. Voidbinder cleared his throat for attention. "Just a reminder, Prince Sudair, assistants still have to adhere to existing curriculums."

"I'm sure the proper curriculums exists in later classes," Phaeron said dismissively.

"If you don't, you run the risk of losing this job," he warned.

Phaeron bared his fangs in a dangerous smile, shadows flickering to life around his curved horns. "Let's see someone try to remove me from the library, then."

He got to his feet, signaling the end to the conversation, and offered me a hand up. I suppressed a swallow, but not because I saw him as tall, dark, and terrifying from that glimpse of what he could do.

It felt validating to know he had a poor reaction to perfect, airbrushed Dr. Aurina. Most men would salivate over a chance to see her again and let her magic wrap around them, but not Phaeron. As he looked down at me, his expression shifted, and he quirked his lips when he folded them back over his fangs.

I didn't like the idea of him and Aurina alone together in a room at all. Did that make me jealous? I had no claim on this man, just the stirring of warmth in my belly when he looked at me that way.

I took his hand up, following him out of the room. He rested the barest touch of his claws on the small of my back, standing closer than a professor probably should. A soft chuckle escaped his lips.

"What is it?" I asked.

"Geo looks like he wants to murder me," he remarked, motioning down the hall. "And Ben isn't sure if he'd help or run."

I looked up, startled to see the two men waiting for me at the juncture where the hall branched off to the elevators and the stairwell. Geo had frozen in place where he leaned against the wall, my phone forgotten in his broad palm as he leveled what could be labeled a death stare at my hip, where Phaeron had coyly slipped his hand. Ben was clearly noticing it as well, a line drawing between his brows.

Oh, hell no. I jerked away from him. "I'm not part of your male posturing," I muttered.

Only one of the library's silver swords could cut through the tension that threaded between the three of them in close proximity. Ben's charm hid behind a leery mask as he eyed the other two men, Geo could've pulverized my phone with one squeeze of his hand, and Phaeron smiled and relaxed against the stairwell railing in a self-assured way that said he thought he could win if this strained meeting boiled over into full conflict.

"I'm going to the library," I said, hitching a thumb over my shoulder.

"That's where I was headed as well," Phaeron said smoothly.

"Where you go, I go," Geo rumbled.

Ben shook his head slowly. "I guess we're all book enthusiasts here, because I'm coming too."

Books. Right. I was hyperaware of the reason these men had met at this junction, leering at each other like competition.

They all wanted a piece of me.

6

GEO

CRESS HAD TAUGHT me that emotions didn't always have to be acted on. All people on the face of this planet would be criminals if they succumbed to every whim when they had one.

However, if I was accused of criminal behavior by finally getting two particularly untrustworthy individuals out of her life, I would just say I was doing my duty.

I hadn't forgotten how Phaeron had attacked me in the dark of night after I'd refused to allow him to speak to my honored witch, whose soul powered the stone heart which gave me life.

I also recalled vividly the moment Ben had drawn twin daggers concealed on his person and held the edge of one to Cress's throat.

They wanted to cozy up to her now? Well, they would have to get through me first. She was my duty; her protection my number one goal. My human skin tingled with the urge to turn back to unfeeling stone, better to fight them with.

The only thing that stopped me as we walked together to Moongrove Library was that I had a task of my own to complete. I wanted it to be done with utmost secrecy, so I spoke no word of it until Cress was comfortably seated in her classroom and focusing on the paper before her. I was in my customary position at the back of the room, such a fixture now that the other witches either greeted me with casual hellos or ignored me completely.

Phaeron had disappeared into a curl of smoke, going who knew where within the bounds of the library, while Ben apparently went off to nap in one of the overnight stay rooms. Now was my chance to query around the library for what I sought.

I started with the man who taught Cress's class, Lars Eriksson. He was a guest professor from another library in Sweden, but perhaps he could help me all the same. I didn't break the silence of the room, instead sliding him Cress's phone with my request typed in a quickly created note.

Where is the gargoyle keeper in Moongrove Library? I am seeking tempering.

Eriksson blinked up at me owlishly from where he sat on a stool at the front of the room. "I'm not sure what that is," he whispered.

Another emotion pressed up against my headspace. Frustration, I identified. A close companion of late.

He stood and stepped partway out of the classroom, flagging down a different adult librarian witch to watch the class, before he motioned for me to join him outside. "You see, new gargoyles haven't been created in some time," he continued at a normal volume. "You are one of the last."

"A status I am aware of," I replied.

"So, anything like a person dedicated to the upkeep of gargoyles would be assigned elsewhere. What is tempering?"

This man had presented himself as a master librarian to the students, yet here he was, asking me a basic question. Either he was as much a useless flirt as he seemed, or knowledge of the upkeep of gargoyles had disappeared with the practice of making my kind.

"Magic tempering," I gritted. "My defensive capabilities are not where they need to be, so I need a gargoyle keeper or equivalent to strengthen my stone."

His eyebrows drifted to his hairline. "Aren't you an obsidian gargoyle? I thought you were already created to be above and beyond a common granite model."

"My current abilities are not sufficient," I answered firmly. The multiple gashes I'd had to heal in my flesh form were testament. If I'd been able to drag myself to the library while damaged, he wouldn't be looking at me like I was malfunctioning.

It was still common enough knowledge that I had a special soul within me. Morgana Voidbinder was her name, a librarian witch demigoddess who'd unfortunately been Phaeron's last mate as well as the woman to imprison him in stasis for two centuries. To honor her memory, I'd been fashioned to be unique, made of obsidian rather than granite, with quartz accents. I was the Quartz Gargoyle, one of a kind.

That didn't make me resistant enough to fight the likes of Phaeron or the Hungering Darkness. I could not successfully fulfill my duty to Cress if either were able to disable me with their shadowy talons.

"I will talk to the head librarian. Perhaps he can get you the help you need," he finally said. Frustration tumbled through me again, sure he was talking about Dr. Voidbinder. I could've just spoken with him when Cress had and chased off Phaeron before he'd had a chance to put his claws around her hip like he was staking some kind of claim.

"Very well. I need this done as quickly as possible. I appreciate your haste and discretion in the matter," I rumbled.

"Yes, good," he sputtered, caught off guard.

We returned to our posts in the classroom, and I waited with a neutral expression for Cress to finish her test. When she did, she turned to the side and met my gaze. "We need to talk," she whispered.

Were I a human with good sense, I'd dread those words. Instead, I simply nodded in agreement and waited with the patience of stone for her to turn in her test and gather up her things, stuffing them back into the backpack she swung onto her shoulders.

She didn't take me far, scoping out the other classrooms on this floor until she found an empty one in the corner. She closed the door behind us and settled onto the stool up front while I stood, as I was most comfortable doing.

"Hey, so, we had an awkward moment back there," she said.

Awkward: an uncomfortable or embarrassed feeling accompanied by a sense of not knowing what to do next.

Oh. I knew exactly what she was talking about. Awkward for her, perhaps, but I'd known exactly what I should've done in that situation.

"I am not sure why you allow either Ben or Phaeron so close to you," I commented, crossing my arms.

She blew out a sigh and let down her hair from its loose tail, combing her fingers through the violet mass in agitation. "There's something I'm coming to terms with still," she said.

I waited for her to elaborate, and for a moment, she seemed to pause, like she expected me to ask what it was on the tip of her tongue. But I was patient with her, as always.

"It seems, in the supernatural world, there's a way to have more than one perfect match. I feel a draw to Ben because we are anam cara, soul friends. A cupid's feather gave us these markings." She held out a palm to me, showing a maroon-colored symbol.

My breath caught. Something hot simmered in my core, like my stone heart beginning to overheat. "He is no friend to you. I saw him attack you. I witnessed him lie," I gritted out.

"You're right, and I'm not about to offer him easy forgiveness. But there's more to the situation than we know," she said, putting both palms up and lowering her voice to a tone intended to soothe.

"And how do you know that is not another one of his lies?" I asked heatedly, furious that she would entertain any more heartbreak with him.

"I mean, I've seen his blood rune. Haven't you? Someone cruel tattooed him with a rune to cause him pain and control him. I think he deserves more of a chance than he's gotten."

Wetness gathered in the corner of her eyes. I reached out, carefully wiping away a droplet before it could form a trail down her face. I cupped her cheek, forcing her to meet my gaze. "You truly care for this... boy," I said with distaste.

"I do. I can't help it any more than you can help how protective you feel over me."

"That is hardly equivalent," I rumbled. My hand moved to the soft hair hanging partway over her face. I ran its silk over my fingers before tucking it behind her ear.

"Geo," she breathed. "It *is* the same thing. You're confusing your budding feelings for your duty."

"That's not possible. Duty is infallible," I said.

"And feelings are everything but that."

She stood and placed her hands just under the line of my collarbone. I stilled as she brushed a path of sensation down my skin. It didn't matter that I was wearing the cloth barrier of a shirt; I felt every-thing as keenly as if she stroked me directly. I tingled now just as I had all over in the wake of her unexpected kiss earlier.

"What do you feel right now, Geo?" she asked, the light in her brown eyes intense.

You, I wanted to answer. But she was asking about within, where her touch had turned my emotions into a tangled bundle of sparking nerves.

"I am unsure," I answered.

"Protective?"

"Yes."

"Anything else?" She pressed closer to me.

I rumbled wordlessly. There wasn't any way for me to describe what welled up within me and drew trembles through my body. I decided to show her with a gentle tug on her hair, pulling her head back so I could claim her lips.

Her hot breath mingled with mine in a soft gasp. Yes, this was right. Her smaller body fit perfectly into the line of mine when I looped my arm around her hips, tugging her against me. I'd never felt such a way before. My stone form would be incapable of feeling pleasure, let alone the softness of a woman pressed against me.

What did I truly feel? I'd been made for protection, her protection, but it was obvious she was my perfect match. She was…"Mine," I practi-cally growled when we came up for breath. "You are *mine.* And I was made to be yours."

Her kiss-swollen lips parted with something akin to surprise. "That is how I feel," I said earnestly. I had never lied to her, and I wouldn't be starting now.

"Geo—"

She began to speak in that tone that I knew would only upset me. I caught the words with a finger over her mouth. "No. Not right now. I know you're going to say you feel for Ben too. Maybe even Phaeron. But right now, it is only you and me."

"Okay. You know what, that's perfectly fine. This conversation is so much better."

I wanted to point out that we'd hardly conversed when she drew her pink tongue across the pad of my finger.

Right, she wasn't speaking literally. I liked where this conversation was going as well when she drew the digit into her mouth and slanted her eyes in a way that had my enchanted oil pooling lower in my belly on a rush of heat. My cock stirred.

In a century of service to the library, I'd heard plenty of jokes about how my kind must always be hard. But in my two hundred years of existence, I'd seen little use for my member. Its needs got directly in the way of my appointed duties. With it now pointing straight at the duty I'd come back to life for, I finally understood the humor.

Until she curled her fingers around its shape through my pants. She looked down between us, her smile eager. How she made me feel was anything but funny, and I came to full, pulsing life from the touch of her hand.

Of course, that was when the door to this classroom opened. "There you are, Cress—" the most unwelcome man interrupted as we both froze. She ducked backward to take my finger from her mouth, her cheeks stained brightly.

At least I had my back to Phaeron to disguise the wrath that crossed my face and stiffened my shoulders.

"I'll give you two a moment," he said, quickly shutting the door again.

I cupped Cress's face with both hands, asking seriously, "Are you certain I cannot kill him?"

7
CRESS

"BEN IS awake after his ordeal and wants to speak with you," Phaeron told me once Geo calmed down a fraction. I felt like I was on the back foot. What ordeal? He read my expression and immediately explained. "He mentioned your idea of scarring more of his blood rune, and we took the opportunity to do it."

"Oh, did it work?" I asked. I cringed at the amount of pain it'd had to be to knock Ben unconscious.

"We're about to find out together." His tail lashed behind him as he turned, beckoning for Geo and me to follow.

Geo took his customary position a few paces behind us, and Phaeron walked just slightly ahead of me, slanting a look in my direction.

"Don't say it," I said tightly, recognizing the same expression he'd had when he'd witnessed me walking Ben out of my dorm one evening. One that spoke the words silently: *really, him?*

"It's not my place to voice an opinion," he said. His usually smooth cadence was stiff with a reaction he was trying to hide.

I couldn't help a bit of whiplash. My lips were still tender from the way Geo had kissed me, like he'd bottled up every ounce of his passion to unleash it all at once. I was a little wet between the thighs at how incredible it'd been to finally break through to him that we might be something more.

Yet I had the sinking feeling I'd made some kind of mistake. Where were my relationships truly going? Though I hadn't quite forgiven Ben, I'd still slept with him before learning who he really was…something I'd just considered doing with Geo too, had we not been interrupted. Thank goodness we were before I could make a mistake that put everyone off.

We needed to have a conversation—Ben, Geo, Phaeron, and I—once I figured out what I wanted, and I'd better do that fast, before I might be forced to choose only one of them.

Geo was strong and steady, a comforting presence that was sometimes too protective. I worried he'd try to chase Ben away or come to blows with Phaeron. As much time and effort he put into keeping me safe, I had to admit that he was possessive, and our moment alone was only likely to make him more so.

And here Phaeron was, obviously hiding his own hurt feelings.

I'm new to this. I've barely held a relationship with one man before, I wanted to tell him.

The fact the three of them were all interested at the same time was the kind of new, uncharted waters that had me worried I'd pilot all of our budding relationships into a capsizing storm. The last thing I wanted to do was lead anyone on.

The tension was thick in the air as Phaeron guided us to floor negative three and to a hallway lined with small rooms. Within one was a shirtless Ben, who had a towel pressed to his side. My gaze traced the lean muscles of his torso, snagging on the series of dark lines that crossed from his blood rune toward his heart. One of the deadlines was dangerously close to it, but it was a fading black, like a real tattoo that'd been on his skin for years.

"Hey, all of you," he muttered. "Did you really have to bring Geology?"

"Geo," the gargoyle corrected in an irritated rumble.

"Yeah, that's what I said."

"No, you keep using these ridiculous nicknames. I tire of your impertinence," Geo said through gritted teeth. His earlier frustration hadn't cooled much.

"Gentlemen," I put in before a smirking Ben could make this worse, "we can't all be in the same room if you're constantly at each other's throats."

Ben worked his jaw, saying a clipped apology to Geo, who crossed his arms at his post by the door. He lifted the towel from his blood rune, letting us get a good look at what Phaeron had done.

I'd thought a second cut across it lengthwise would be ideal, but the dimensional man had taken it a step further. The outer ring of the rune, which was made of spikey, unreadable characters, was now ruined by several smaller incisions that cut through each one. "Garroway's blood runes attach to the nerves," Ben explained. "So, it's safe to say this hurt like fuck, but I think I'm really free this time."

"It's a shame it can't be removed from you completely," Phaeron said.

Ben traced the one crimson deadline still branching from the ruined circle; it was noticeably longer than the last time he'd shown it to me. "I'm going to put what time I have left to good use," he murmured. "Cress, do you still have your phone?"

Geo wordlessly withdrew it from his pocket and handed it to me. I checked the screen, eyebrow raising when I read a message already on the screen. I dismissed it with a flick of my thumb and made a mental note to ask Geo about it later. "You don't have yours?"

Ben shook his head. "Bugged. I ditched it."

I turned to Phaeron. "The first thing you're doing with your money is buying a phone so I can reach at least one of you."

He pointed to one of his wrists. "You can always reach me, bright soul."

I held my forehead. That wasn't what I meant, but I bet Phaeron was just as tech illiterate as Geo had been before he realized how entertaining the Internet could be. If anyone needed their own device, it was the gargoyle.

"Anyway, I was hoping you'd record what I have to say. There's no telling whether Garroway can feel that he's lost control of me completely or if he's positioned an assassin right outside to kill me before I can talk to Dr. Aurina," Ben said.

"Has she been demanding information?" I asked.

Phaeron answered for him. "She has requested to see him again, yes. Keep in mind that she is still one of our allies. If this blood baron operates how I suspect, her emotional magic could disable all of his assassins by overloading their senses with pain and fear. Plus, she has the power to give us more fighters than us three." His hand gesture encompassed himself, Geo, and Ben.

"And me," I protested.

"I'll be damned if you get anywhere *near* Garroway," Ben said viciously.

"Or close to the assassin that carries my brother," Phaeron added.

I glanced toward Geo for some backup, but he had cracked a smile. "Finally, something we all agree on," he rumbled.

Wow. While I liked the moment of harmony, it was unfair they were probably right. A smart Cress would sit out a fight in the heart of a nest of trained assassins, plus whatever this Garroway vampire could do. Lump in the Hungering Darkness, and that was a battle meant for professionals.

"When were we starting training again?" I asked Phaeron.

His pupils narrowed to suspicious, cat-like slits. "This evening."

I started fiddling with my phone, pulling up the camera and getting Ben in frame. This wasn't his most flattering moment, and the camera seemed to fixate on his extra-pale skin and the shadows forming under his eyes. "All right. Let's start the recording, then," I suggested.

He nodded, and I hit the little red button. His green gaze lifted to meet mine, and he seemed to be talking to me alone. "I'll start from the beginning, even though I only just learned the extent of what Garroway did to my brother and me a few days ago," he began.

He told me the story of his mother, Marie Evenstar, a woman pushed toward financial ruin after losing her business partner and husband in two separate tragedies. She'd come to Garroway for a significant loan, which Ben theorized to be in the realm of five million dollars, as that number had been thrown at him several times over the years.

Instead of loaning her the money, Garroway had sent his assassins for her in the dead of night. He'd had Ben and Lucas stolen after framing their deaths so no authorities would come looking for them. I suppressed a gasp and looked toward the ceiling, trying not to cry. If Ben was starting this way, I had the feeling the rest of his story would be so much worse.

"Yeah. I don't know the stories of the other assassins, but Garroway is a creature of opportunity. His network of blood witches likely started as a bunch of orphans and unwanted kids with witch families. He forces all of us to take the blood affinity, but as you may have noticed, my parents were celestial witches, and I've gotten the feeling I've never been a particularly *skilled* blood witch. Just well trained."

He sighed, drawing a hand through his hair. Despite his freedom from the restrictions of the blood rune, the pain from his wounds seemed to be slowing him down all the same.

"We could do multiple takes," I suggested. Despite myself, I just wanted to hold him and soothe away some of his hurt.

He shook his head slowly. "No, I can do this. I want there to be a record of everything I know."

Ben explained the experience of growing up under Garroway's control to me and the camera. I snuck a glance at the other two men, who were listening just as intently as me. A muscle ticked in Phaeron's jaw, and his clawed fingers flexed. He looked ready to plunge into the past and save Ben and his little brother from the bloody, grueling training regiments they were forced into as boys.

Next to him, Geo still had his arms folded, but he'd resumed a patient, stony mask that showed no reaction to Ben's words. I was still glad he was here listening.

It sounded like Garroway took advantage of a blood witch's ability to heal to an obscene degree. He shattered bones for punishments or activated the Agonia rune on a whim to sear one of his witches from the inside out. Haunted shadows crossed over Ben's eyes as he described Garroway's favorite game, which was asking another witch what their peer's punishment should be.

"If it was bloodier and more gruesome than what he had in mind, he would make that their punishment. But if it wasn't as bad as he wanted to hear, he'd suggest things like making them eat their own pinky toes or whipping them until their backs resembled raw meat. 'Why does it matter? It all grows back anyway.'" He took on a slow, flat cadence as he mimicked his former vampire master.

"Disgusting," I muttered.

"Yeah...let's see how far we can push this. The clients that I can remember Garroway working with..." He started listing names. His breath hitched after the first few, and he clutched his side with the towel while continuing the litany in a rasping voice until it seemed he couldn't take it anymore. "It seems the blood rune still has some fail-safes to keep me quiet. That list isn't everyone, but it's a good start to unraveling the network of clients and informants.

"I want to talk about one man in particular, Blaize Starsurge. He's a politician appointed to the Crown Coven, the ruling body of witchkind." I had a sinking feeling from how he looked up into my eyes with a sympathetic little twist of his lips. "As I understand it, his closest competitor for his spot in the coven was a woman named Eris Darkmore, a fellow celestial witch who had the edge on him in every poll."

I forced a swallow, my throat suddenly dry. "Any relation to Wren?" I asked.

"Her father. I sincerely doubt he's told her any of this," he said. "Because to win his seat, he went to Garroway and paid to have his best assassin set up a murder of the whole Darkmore family. As I've told you, the only wiggle room we have to any of Garroway's orders is his wording. He instructed this assassin to 'take care of' the Darkmore family, so he did.

"What said assassin told me was that he hid the murder of Eris, her husband, and her sister by setting up an electrical fire in the house. But Eris had a daughter, a newborn, and he couldn't bring himself to kill her too. So, he took care of her by surrendering her to the local hospital, thinking she'd never reappear."

"Which hospital?" I asked from numb lips.

"Probably the one you were adopted from. Because recently, Starsurge reappeared in Garroway's manor all pissed off because, in his paranoia, a witch orphan had appeared, and he'd gotten an augury reading that she was *the* Luna Darkmore, sole heir remaining to claim the Darkmore hereditary power. He was so sure that was you, Cress, that he paid someone to sabotage your affinity test so you wouldn't pick the celestial affinity."

"Oh, shit," I said quietly. I swayed on my feet, my mind flashing back months in the past. The machine had seemed to malfunction, flashing the celestial symbol for a split second before lighting the one for a librarian witch instead. I'd second-guessed the decision, wondering if I should get tested again. But in the end, I'd decided that being a librarian fit my nature better.

Strong arms caught me before I could fall. Phaeron's topaz eyes glittered as he inspected me anew. "That explains it," he murmured.

"Explains what? That my parents—my whole birth family—were murdered?" I asked, voice gaining strength as the reality sank in. "That Wren's fucking *father* paid to have it happen? No wonder she was filming me when I was getting affinity tested! Her father put her up to it to make sure I picked the wrong thing."

"Peace, Cress. I mean the power lurking within you." Phaeron stroked my arm in soothing circles.

"My so-called bright soul?" I demanded.

He smiled slowly. "Indeed. I have noticed you've picked up and excelled at two of the basic librarian spells that utilize light, Lux and Luminaire. You may have bound yourself to the 'wrong' affinity for your bloodline, but it will lead you to being a bright spot in a dark world." The slow brush of his broad palm was starting to calm me down, just for my heart to leap as his gaze shaded with white. *"Beautiful,"* he hissed.

His hand tightened around my arm, and he licked his fangs. He drew me closer, inhaling in the space over my crown with a low growl. "Uh, Phaeron," I said uncertainly.

I'd seen white fire in his eyes before, right before he'd started to claw at his face and disappear into a column of smoke. I slapped the mark of protection he'd left on my wrist and repeated his name, my fingers trembling all the while.

Phaeron jerked with his mouth open and shook his head. In a blink, he seemed back to himself.

Geo shifted closer, eyeing the dimensional man with suspicion, while Ben was saying, "I suppose now I better try to tell you where Garroway's manor is."

"Hmm, yes. That would be Aurina's first question." Phaeron sounded distracted. He stepped away from me, rubbing his forehead.

"It's..." Ben froze with his mouth open. "It's..."

He bent at the waist with a groan. "Another thing you still can't share?" I closed the distance between us and ended the recording when he nodded. Tossing my phone aside, I eased onto the bed next to Ben.

Meanwhile, Phaeron said something to Geo, and the two of them descended into the hushed tones of an argument.

Ben and I watched them. At some point, he slipped his hand into mine, and I gave our twined fingers a squeeze. "They'll be all right for a moment," I said.

"Yeah. It's...probably fine," he agreed. It felt like he'd caught my gaze in his, and after hearing his story, I couldn't keep pushing him away.

This man had gone through so much suffering and yet came out on the other end sane and still looking after the well-being of his brother and me. Garroway's evil had taken both of our families, yet somehow, it'd brought us together. I yearned to have Ben alone when he was recovered from his wounds, away from Phaeron and Geo and their drama.

My gaze dipped to Ben's lopsided smile. I pressed a little kiss to the slant of his lips. "I forgive you for a few lies to hide all this," I whispered in his ear before squealing when he banded an arm around my middle and hugged me to his side. I returned the gesture, careful of touching his wounded side.

"No more lies, babe. I promise," he said fiercely.

He cupped my cheek, drawing me into a longer, sweeter brush of our mouths. I got lost in it until I realized Geo and Phaeron's argument had lapsed to silence. Reluctantly lifting my head, I noticed Geo was leaving the room. Phaeron hadn't moved but began to blur at the edges, turning into wisps of black shadow. "When you're ready to train, Cress, find me by the library's powercore."

"Great, bye," Ben muttered and tugged me into another kiss. He didn't have much in him past a good make-out session and ended up falling asleep holding me to his chest. I lay there for a while, just thinking. I was feeling a little too hollow to rest with him, not after everything he'd told us. I ended up seeking out Phaeron after a few hours for the promised training.

8

PHAERON

I SPENT hours meditating at the base of Braza's power, communing with her to wash away the hunger still gnawing deep in my gut. I'd lost myself in less than an instant as I'd admired Cress's beautiful soul, full of the light of her celestial witch heritage.

As I'd looked into the depths of her light, my brother's voice had crept out to whisper in my ear. *"Just one bite wouldn't hurt her. Let yourself go."*

He was the trigger to my blackouts, but there was no way he was in the library. Braza had no sense that he'd passed anywhere near her territory. We were linked some other way, my monster of an undead brother and I, and the speed in which he'd tapped the kernel of corruption in me and compelled it to take control shook me to my core.

Then she'd called me back to myself. That could only mean one thing. Mix it up in the soup of jealousy that boiled within me at the glimpse of her intimacy with the other two men, and I had an explanation for my behavior that I couldn't ignore. My fixation on her soul was no accident. She was my True Light, and I, her Shadow.

To my people, those with the shadowborn blessing were considered powerful but incomplete. As beings born to protect others by being the biggest, baddest thing lurking in the night, we always sought the light for balance. A beacon in the darkness to return to, to defend, cherish, and pleasure. Only a mate can call a shadowborn back from the urges of their bestial side, as she effectively had twice.

On the heels of this revelation, I caught the sound of her footsteps before she cleared her throat and murmured my name for attention. I opened my eyes and stood, keeping my tail wound around my legs to show I meant no harm in the way of my people.

There she stood, haloed in the radiance of her own soul. She had no idea how beautiful she was with warm golden energy always washing her skin to my sight alone. How could I ever question my draw to her?

"Well, here I am. Ready to train," she said, stopping several yards away.

I could pinpoint several signs of stress and anxiety just from her expression and posture. *If I confess the truth to her now, she'll push me away.* But I still wanted to comfort her a lot more than I wanted to put a sword in her hand. Training could wait one more day.

She scuffed her foot. "Could I ask you a question?"

"Always."

"Isn't white fire a sign of corruption from your planet?"

I stilled. There was no hiding that I'd flashed my darkest secret in a moment of weakness earlier. "You saw it in my eyes."

She nodded and shifted back a step, angling herself so she could bolt if she needed to.

"I do not fully understand it," I said slowly. "But I am resisting a seed of hunger I must've picked up while locked in stasis with my brother." Her expression shuttered, and I breathed a sigh. "This isn't an either-or situation yet. I have the possibility of corruption if my willpower is weaker than my hunger for the taste of something I've never tried to consume."

She wet her lips. "So, you aren't corrupted."

"No. Not in the way that is a menace like my brother. I didn't bow to Myuna at the height of her strength, and I don't intend to bend to the temptation of her evil now." Slowly, I unwound my tail and approached her cautiously. "Some souls are more tempting than others. For the longest time, I've wondered why yours was so appealing."

She stiffened. "Its brightness?"

"Sure. If you could see the average librarian's soul, you would know it's full of the darkness of Soiluire. That's what I truly taught the first librarian witches—how to use the magical energy of dimensionals. What comes naturally to me." I manipulated a coil of shadows to dance around my arm. "Moongrove Library is built from the bottom up with the essence of my people. With our shadows. And yet, here you stand, one of us."

I held up a palm full of darkness toward her, and the tendrils of smoke naturally curled away from the light coming off her soul. She watched the effect with her mouth dropping into a surprised O.

"I'm a mistake," she murmured. "I don't belong here."

"No. You are needed, like the night sky needs its stars." I closed my fist, absorbing my shadows back into my skin. "There are more comfortable places to have this conversation. Besides, you are unprepared to begin practicing with me."

She scoffed. "What do you mean? I have my practice sword right here." She patted the battered hilt at her side.

"Yet where are your familiars? And your handbook? If you were assigned one," I pointed out.

"They're cats, Phaeron. They don't fight. And I do have one, but it's...special."

I shook my head. "Come, let us retrieve them all, and we can talk along the way. Can't believe what they're not teaching young librarians."

"Sure, I guess," she said with her brow drawn in confusion.

When we were in the elevator heading back to the surface level, she turned to me with an expectant look. "So, I shouldn't be worried if I see your eyes flash a different color?"

I considered how to answer without giving her a falsehood. "You seem to ground me, bright soul. Perhaps to the point where I should have you close when I next fight my brother." She could call me back again if he tried to send me away at a crucial moment.

She seemed hopeful, like I would invite her along to the dangerous battle that would follow when Ben finally admitted the location of Garroway's hiding place. It was likely Endaeron would be there, too. Before I'd consider that, though, she would need to relearn almost everything she'd already been taught about her magic. A daunting task.

"If I come along, my friends will want to as well," she said.

"The two young women who were there when Endaeron revealed himself?"

Cress had a genuine smile as she nodded. I'd barely glanced at their souls, but I'd been struck by how young and inexperienced they'd been to even consider fighting a monster of my brother's caliber.

"Then they will train alongside you," I said. She perked up further. That sunny expression would be my undoing, and she had no idea I'd do most anything to see it more often. "Where is Geo, by the way?" He would be the only one, I thought, who'd immediately try to thwart this idea.

"He's in stone form right now, waiting for Ben to wake up. He thinks I'm training with you in the library. I had to beg him not to follow me so he could pick another fight with you," she said.

"Good," I muttered. Finally, some uninterrupted time alone with her.

"Do you want to meet my friends tomorrow? We'd better start right away," she asked.

"Sure."

She pointed out a large building called the Witch Clubhouse once we entered the witchy side of the NSU campus. The women she trusted most were half of her coven.

"What of the other witches in your coven?" I asked.

"One's just a bitch." She affected a shrug but gritted her teeth hard. "Her father was the one Ben was talking about..."

I eyed her soul again, letting it dazzle my sight. I didn't doubt that the celestial affinity ran heavily through her family line. "Have you felt any of your hereditary power come in yet?"

"Uh, no. We covered the possibility of it happening in one of my classes, but I haven't had any dreams or anything."

"I know of a way to encourage the process," I told her.

"Oh?"

I nodded. "On Samhain, the night when the barrier between worlds is the thinnest."

Cress stopped abruptly, looking up at me with her lips parted. The overbearing sun was setting, and at that moment, like everything around us, she cast no shadow. My instincts told me *I* was her Shadow and that I could earn her attention with a few flexes of my otherworldly power. "I can help you commune with the souls of the dead on that day only."

"Really?" she burst out. "Like, any soul?"

"Within reason."

Cress bit her lower lip. "What is 'within reason' for something like that?"

I waved my hand vaguely. "On Soiluire, such a thing wasn't possible at all. I've only done it a couple of times with the recently deceased. It was an excellent way to give my old friends some closure."

"Yeah." Her eyes moistened, and she cast her gaze away in a quick jerk. She started walking again. "You're thinking of drawing my potential birth mother back and seeing if that makes me start to inherit my family line's excess magic?"

I caught her wrist gently, tugging her back. "Cress, listen. I could see about calling back a different person, if you wanted."

Her shoulders hitched, and she sniffed. "Y-yeah. I'd...I would really love to see Lanie again."

I took a moment to brush back her hair and gently wipe her cheeks dry. That she didn't flinch away from my touch emboldened me to pull her into a quick hug. She clutched the front of my shirt and closed her eyes with a ragged sigh.

I remembered Lanie. More specifically, closing her eyes for the final time after my brother murdered her. *What do you mean, she's dead?* Cress had cried, catching me leaning over her friend. The echo of her sudden anguish resonated within me now. I had to give her the chance to say goodbye properly on Samhain.

"It has been a trying day," I said gently when we parted. "Let's begin your training tomorrow. I don't want you distracted with all the emotions of today rolling around in your mind."

"All right. But at least tell me why you need my cats to come along too," she said.

At some point, we began moving again, and I explained as we approached her dorm. "They are magically bound to you as your familiars. During day-to-day activities in the library, they are your scouts for danger. Most dimensional creatures don't recognize small animals like cats as threats to attack, and their souls are so tiny that they are not in danger of being noticed by corrupted unnaturals. In a fight, you can borrow an ounce of feline grace and their superior senses. The more you practice, the longer that moment lasts."

"Oh, I had no idea. I've been treating them like pets I can talk to," she said.

"It's a shame you weren't told, because most witches seem to see their familiars that way in this day and age. The fact that you have two cats is good. You'll have different bonds with each, but you can explore that over time."

"Three, maybe." She paused to get us into the building and took me up a few flights of stairs before letting me into her room. The perfumes of several women lingered in the air, as well as the earthier scent of Geo's enchanted oil. He must've laid across the other bed, as there were two in this cramped space.

Her brown tabby cat jumped atop the bed with a friendly chirp, tail straight up. I smiled and scooped her into a purring snuggle.

"That's Bella," Cress said. She had her chubby black and white cat in her arms and put him on the comforter next. "And this is Milo. Somewhere in here is...ah! That's Jin." A small, pure-black cat joined the other two and accepted a couple pets from Cress before edging away from her.

While I was distracted by her cats, she tapped on the screen of a device I'd learned to be a laptop. Technology had run laps around me during my forced stasis, but I had bigger problems than trying to learn how to use it.

"No emails. That's good." She closed the laptop and lifted the book resting next to it.

I put Bella down and took it, sensing the power within the handbook immediately. "Ah, an original. You said you bought such a venerated handbook?" I asked, inspecting it.

It was definitely from the first batch of books made by Morgana, animated by a minor dimensional creature called a wispfly. I gave the wispfly within this one a jolt of power and watched its front and back cover crack open and close on their own.

"What's happening?" she asked, staring as it tentatively flapped, hovering midair.

"Hooooo boy," the wispfly said, flying the book into a curlicue. It had a squeaky voice, like a toy, emanating from the pages. "No one's trusted me with a lil' pip of magic like that in decades!"

"Why is *The Librarian Witch's Handbook* talking and flying around?" Cress asked in an insistent whisper.

"Cressie-poo!" it exclaimed. "I can flap my pages like you flap your fleshy lips! Isn't that great?"

"I told you not to call me that," she said, her cheeks starting to heat.

"C'mon! We're friends, right?" It perched its spine on her shoulder like an odd bird.

I stroked my chin, watching it go with a grin. "You didn't tell me you claimed a malfunctioning handbook."

"I'll show you malfunctioning, you—wait, Cress, who is that?" the book asked.

"Phaeron."

"Eek!" It clapped itself shut and fell off her shoulder, causing her to fumble to catch it.

"How did you not see this?" she asked. She and I were both laughing at this point.

"I'm a nearsighted handbook. All those years of humans squinting close to my pages does a number on the magical sight, you know?"

"Sure," she chuckled.

"Are you still..." It dropped its voice to a dramatic whisper. "*Trying to kill him?*"

"Noooo. He's a friend now," she said quickly, flashing me an apologetic look.

I touched her arm with a little smile before taking the book from her. "Okay, good, because he's like—oh, hello, big, strong man hand."

I held its flapping pages up to my face. "Be quiet," I ordered.

"Hah, it's funny, because you're definitely the strongest dimensional to ever hold me and all, but I don't have an on-off switch like an electronic, you see—"

Shadows gathered around my head, lengthening all of my teeth into ebon fangs as I spoke with a deeper intonation. "*Stop* talking."

It quieted at last with a little squeak.

I passed it back to Cress. "We could get you another book, if you desired. It's a simple process to break the bond between witch and handbook," I offered.

She shook her head, holding it to her chest. "I love my snarky book, actually."

"I was on sale," it whispered.

"Well, this is unusual. Handbooks are supposed to wait in silence until they're needed, but fully empowered ones fly and can speak their knowledge aloud." I didn't think even I could convince this one to shut up for long. Not without adding a sturdy clasp over its pages, which was another option.

She shrugged before yawning hugely. "Ah. Let me send a message to the library so Geo returns to you," I said, reaching out to Braza's energy to do so. "Once he's in place, I'll leave you to rest."

She didn't argue, only sitting at the foot of her bed and placing her book aside. I sat next to her, tempted by the scant space between us, but let her be the one to reach out and brush her palm against mine. Our fingers twined, and I traced the shape of her blunt little thumbnail as I waited to hear the telltale thump of a gargoyle landing somewhere close.

I forced myself to be content if this was all I could have of Cress right now. We'd come a long way to get to this moment, even if I only wanted more from her. I imagined her resting her head against my solid shoulder and her not flinching if I were to put my arm around her waist and draw her closer.

I could be patient. When she was ready, I'd be here for her.

9
BEN

PHAERON RETURNED to the library by evening to help me return to the modest faculty house where we now lived. Neither of us had left much of a footprint here to make it "home." I'd been saved with the clothes on my back and a nearly empty wallet, while it seemed the other man had little to his name.

The house had a basic set of furniture in each room, else we wouldn't have any. We both settled in the living room. The threadbare couch creaked when I dropped my weight into it, and I made a similar sound from the way my side's throbbing doubled. I was used to pain, but it was exhausting to carry it for a day and know it would be worse tomorrow.

Luckily, NSU staff got to eat for free from the campus dining halls, so we had a couple takeout boxes laid out on the battered coffee table between us. I barely knew the guy, but Phaeron seemed quieter than usual this evening, and his gaze was distant. As he leaned back in the armchair set at an angle to our couch, his tail drew restless patterns across the rug.

I shrugged to myself and began eating while it was still hot. One didn't wait when it was dinnertime in the manor. The strongest assassins would edge the rest of us out and eat the best parts of each meal.

I'd made a habit of getting to mealtime early to have a chance at some protein and only ever shared with Lucas and Bianca.

Until she'd really come into her magic, Bianca had joined my brother and me in dreaming of freedom and quiet nights like this one, without the cutthroat atmosphere encouraged by our vampire master. I slowed my chewing as my shoulders dropped.

I'd left both of them behind with Garroway. Even now, my brother and the woman I saw as my sister were still in the manor and under his complete control while I slurped free food. I *had* to share the manor's location, but even the thought of it replaced the taste in my mouth with that of copper pennies.

My body was telling me not to push it any further. Tomorrow, then. I'd try every tomorrow until the deadline stopped my heart. Not just my own life was on the line here.

"Hey, dude," I said.

Phaeron cracked his eyes open, raising a brow in my direction. It was not quite the reaction I was hoping for, but he'd proven himself harder to pester than Geo.

"What happens when we see my brother next?" I asked, setting aside my empty box. I knew I couldn't have this conversation over food unless I wanted it to taste like ash on my tongue.

He seemed to see through me immediately, answering the core of my concerns. "He is still alive right now. Endaeron is not interested in inhabiting the bodies of his victims unless their soul is intact and aware."

I cringed. It reminded me of when Garroway took complete control, which he'd done to me a time or two. It'd felt like a second person inhabiting my mind, pushing me aside to take command of my body and its movements. I imagined the same happening to Lucas, but with him aware and screaming on the inside, banging his fists against the walls of his mind as they closed around him like a cage.

"Our best course of action is to capture Lucas and bring him to Moongrove Library. It'd be safest to remove my brother there and throw him into a stasis room."

"I'd say great, except he kind of cut you and Geometry to ribbons a few days ago," I commented.

He nodded slowly, looking as worried as I felt. "With access to a blood witch's healing, he was able to outlast us both. The good news is that he will want to prolong his time with Lucas because he knows we will avoid causing fatal harm to him. It is something he'd do, shield himself with the body of a boy to gain an advantage."

My hands balled into fists. I wanted that monster out of my brother by any means before the Hungering Darkness could leave any lasting scars on his psyche. There were some things worse than physical pain, things that couldn't be healed away with the application of a rune. "I'd do anything to have him out of Lucas."

"I know. I will do everything in my power to separate them. Just a word of warning...my brother is not a living, reasoning creature anymore. He has clever instincts and a bottomless pit of hunger to tend to. When threatened, he's been known to abandon his host. A sudden explosive exit from his host's soul is fatal."

"So, you're saying..." My stomach soured, and I shook my head. "Thank you for the warning, but I have to get my brother back. There has to be a way."

Phaeron's tail had stopped its restless coiling, lying flat on the ground while he leaned forward to pick up his own dinner. I caught the pitying look on his face before he glanced away.

Maybe it was naïve, like I was an ostrich with my head buried deep in the sand. The odds of Lucas's safe return were obviously long, but I couldn't just give up and accept that he was lost forever. I would not bow to the inevitability of his death, not when he'd never had a moment of freedom in his entire life.

"The manor is...is..." I started to say. "...not in..."

I pretended the *thunk* noise that sounded nearby was the reason I stopped talking, but the pain in my side was nearly debilitating. Damn Garroway for making sure I couldn't breathe a word of his most important secret.

Phaeron shot to his feet first. "What was that?" he asked in a low growl.

He started to walk toward the front door while I was still in the process of standing while clutching my side. "Wait—"

But he was already opening the door. He stiffened in surprise before turning into a cloud of darkness. A crossbow bolt sailed through him, disturbing the shadows in its wake before it struck the far wall with a similar noise to the first. I cursed as Phaeron took physical form and charged outside.

Our front door had a piece of paper attached by a still-quivering bolt. I tore it free to read what was written on it. "The next one won't miss. –B"

"Still a bitch, I see," I muttered. Bianca's signature weapon was a crossbow, and it chilled my bones to know Garroway had sent one of his best for me first.

If I were Bianca, I would have taken that shot from as far back as possible while wearing runes of accuracy and speed. She'd be ready to take off running should she miss, despite the ridiculous flex she'd left on the door.

Was Phaeron faster than her? No matter what the answer to that was, I was clearly standing in the open with one of Garroway's assassins nearby. I turned to go back into the house.

"Do you know this person?" Phaeron's smooth voice sounded behind me.

Startled, I whipped back to see him standing over Bianca, who was bound in coils of shadow magic. Her muffled voice shouted around a ball of darkness stuffed in her mouth, and her reddening face had an expression promising painful death.

"Yeah, actually," I answered. "Think you could give her some blood rune surgery?"

In response, he extended his shadowy claws to their full, pointed length. Her eyelids lifted to show the whites of her eyes.

I couldn't help a little smirk. "By the way, Bianca. You missed."

"Fuck you, Ben," Bianca muttered on our way to Dr. Aurina's office the next day. She'd passed out when Phaeron's claws cut through the magic of her blood rune and had woken on our couch in a spitting fury the next morning.

It'd been nice to see her, too.

"Do all the women of this age curse so much?" Phaeron asked from her other side. He had her hands bound behind her with a coil of shadow since she'd said good morning with two kitchen knives and a whole litany of foul language.

"Fuck you too," she answered.

"No, thank you," he replied politely.

She rolled her eyes hard.

"Are you ready to listen yet?" I asked, doing the same at the exchange.

"You do know I'm still on deadline, right?"

"I am as well."

"Great. So we're both going to die," she muttered.

I'd done my best not to dwell on it, but she was right. Our only hope was if we could share where Garroway's manor was and infiltrate it with a team of professionals to get his black knife. The fact that I now had Bianca, willing or not, to talk to was enough to lift my spirits. One of us would muster the strength to tell Dr. Aurina where the manor was. Unless...

"How much time did Garroway give you?" I asked.

She lifted her chin. "Until Samhain, the same deadline he said he gave you. But he was sure I wouldn't need that much time."

I hid my relief with a crooked smile. She and I had the same amount of time left. "Uh huh. Yet you tried one of your most overdone tricks."

"I was trying to warn you," she muttered. "And how was I supposed to know this fucker would run me down despite my speed runes?" She tilted her head toward Phaeron.

"Sounds like poor planning to me," I needled.

The look Bianca swung on me could make milk curdle. She'd get over it soon, though, once the reality of her situation really sank in. At least, I hoped so, since she was a prized assassin who was treated relatively well by Garroway's standards. Unlike me, she'd seen the upside of working for him—preferential assignments and praise. But she'd still been a dog at his beck and call, sicced at his command and forced to heel at his whims. Surely she'd still prefer her freedom and turn to our side.

"For all your appreciation, maybe I'll knife you in the back for fun," she said with faux sweetness.

Phaeron cleared his throat. "I was under the impression you two were friends?"

"We are," she and I said at the same time.

"Just checking," he said with a chuckle.

We were soon in the administration building, speaking to a wide-eyed secretary who looked at Phaeron like he was the menace of our trio instead of my stabby friend. Most people would be forced to wait for the attention of the University President, but not us. We were soon in Aurina's office again, speaking with the demigoddess alone this time.

"A second assassin," she remarked from the moment we sat down. "Not nearly as saturated with pain as you, Ben, but she still stinks of Garroway's influence."

I glanced toward Bianca, expecting her to tell off the cupid too. Instead, the color had drained out of her face as Aurina inspected her more closely.

"I take it Cress has sent you Ben's story from yesterday?" Phaeron asked, briefly drawing her attention.

There was some unspoken tension between the two of them. His sharp face was set in a guarded expression of dislike, while Aurina avoided looking at him directly even with him speaking. *Interesting.*

"Yes, she emailed it, and I've reviewed it several times. While I empathize with the horrors that have been committed against you, Ben, I need facts. I need to know where he is hunkered down," she said, her gaze cutting to me. "Preferably before the Samhain Ball."

"The manor?" Bianca asked. "It's—" She cupped her hand over her mouth, coming away with blood coating her fingers. Aurina reached over to offer her a tissue box.

"Yeah, I was worried that'd happen. I can't say it, either." I frowned, knowing we desperately needed to get around this.

"Try one more time," Aurina ordered. Her aura lit up with her pink magic, inspecting me closely as I attempted to disclose the location again and came to a stuttering stop after a couple words.

Her brows lifted, and she pursed her lips.

"We cannot push them too hard. If this is the rune's doing, it's clear it'll kill them before they can say anything," Phaeron said.

"We are running out of time," she replied.

I considered her for a moment. "What does some ball have anything to do with finding Garroway?"

"Every major event this year has had an attack of some kind. The

Samhain Ball is nearly as universally loved as the Mabon feast. Yet I had to cancel the ball. What better way to show that we've ended the threat than reinstating it and allowing students out past curfew again?" She gave a wide, magnanimous gesture but hadn't quite hidden a quaver in her words.

I narrowed my eyes. I wondered how long she could stay at the helm of NSU if students kept getting endangered on her watch. Her job could easily be in the balance along with everything else.

"Before we go any further, I have a question for you, girl," she said abruptly.

"My name is Bianca," my friend gritted.

"Bianca, you wouldn't happen to know who harmed my daughter at the Mabon celebration, would you?" Aurina leaned forward, her fingers steepled as she focused intently. If there was a flare of magic, I didn't see it, but Phaeron loosed a soft growl beside me.

"Yeah, that was me," she answered. Carefree, like sharing what the weather was outside.

I jumped to my feet with a shout when Aurina slammed her palm down and Bianca's chair toppled over as the latter woman jerked backward. "I thought I recognized you," the demigoddess snarled.

Phaeron's shadowy claws extended. "Stop this. I thought we already discussed how it was a light cut."

I ducked to help Bianca right herself and her chair despite her restraints. "Why'd you tell the truth?" I muttered.

"She cast some spell on me," she replied just as low.

"...and that she did it as Garroway's slave," Phaeron was saying.

"All the same, she will be the one to disclose the manor's location. I will assist." Her cool gaze fell on Bianca again, who lifted her chin a notch in defiance. "I will take your pain away. Where is it?"

Working her jaw, she took her time saying anything at all. The Bianca I knew would say something flippant like, "At the corner of Third and go fuck yourself."

Instead, she said, "Sorry about your daughter. I didn't want to do it. Principles, you know?" Following that, she gave a whole address for the abandoned house in Salem that hid the pocket dimension where Garroway had his manor.

Then she passed out.

10

CRESS

I DID my best on my second round of midterms before showing up at the Witch Clubhouse midday with a coffee in one hand and the other firmly clamped around the pages of my handbook. It wiggled in protest the whole journey from the café to here, but I appreciated the moment of quiet.

It was obvious why no one had given it the magic to talk and fly. I'd had to hand it to Geo to take it out of the classroom when it'd whispered in a pin-silent room, *"Psst! The answer to three is A."*

It would be a wonder if I passed that test. Regardless, I set it free in my coven's room in the clubhouse, and it shook itself in disgruntlement before flapping to a corner of the room to sulk. I held the door a moment longer to let my cats slip in before securing a seat at the couch before anyone else came in. I was a little early, for once, and took a moment to catch my breath.

Unless I was sleeping, lately, it seemed I was never alone. Geo was keeping watch at the front of the clubhouse today—in theory, to tell Phaeron where to go—so I had some time just to sprawl and pet my familiars. Jin had come along with us, tentatively sitting on the opposite arm of the couch, just out of reach. We were making progress...I think.

Just like I'm making progress in my relationships with more than one man? I asked myself. My mother had taught me not to lead anyone on, that love was meant to be kept between two people. She wasn't a supernatural, though. She'd also stopped believing in true love a long time ago, saying soul mates were firmly the realm of fiction.

But I had *two*. I'd woken Geo from pure stone when I'd first been in trouble, and my connection to Ben was undeniable. Ben was the man I hoped walked through the door first. I yearned to see him again, but it was more than that. I wanted his hands on me, his sweet whispers in my ear, and his hard body between my thighs.

Yet when I closed my eyes to visualize it, it was the texture of Geo's palm that I practically felt skimming up my thigh. He'd hesitate at the apex of my legs before skimming his thumb up my wet seam. I imagined he'd want to explore my sex fully.

I leaned my head back. In this fantasy I built, the ghost of warm breath skimmed the shell of my ear, and goosebumps rolled over my skin. The smooth, seductive voice behind me was Phaeron's, though. My hand tensed on my knee as he just breathed, "bright soul," as clearly as if he were in the room with me.

My eyes shot open and darted around, heart leaping like he'd caught me. I was more flushed than mortified at the idea. But he wasn't there, just the lingering sense that I *wanted* him here with me.

Make that three men, because despite everything, Phaeron and I had some kind of draw, too. He'd been a perfect gentleman last night, holding my hand as the sun set. I really appreciated it, because I'd been at my emotional limit, and I think he was well aware of it. He knew when to push. My belly tingled with the idea of him trying again soon.

I could curse my traitorous thoughts, though. I'd originally been thinking of Ben, yet my mind lumped in Geo and Phaeron immediately. I wanted Ben most, though, and it wasn't just the lust talking. Just to see that he was okay and to hold him again following his confession yesterday. He needed to see that I accepted him despite the lies that'd first brought us together and that I trusted him to give our relationship a second chance.

The deadline ticking down to Samhain stood in the way, though. My words were air if we couldn't save him from his former master's cruel send-off.

If my friends were true, they would feel the same way. I'd sent Ben's confession video to Dr. Aurina first, but soon it was in the hands of my trusted coven mates, who drifted in one by one and filled this space with color as we awaited the men. Roe had blasted my phone with rapid-fire texts, all in capital letters.

She arrived first for once, seeing me and exclaiming, "Training is my middle name. We should be fighting as a coven anyway!"

"I doubt the dimensional can teach me anything more about my magic," Áine said in her shadow.

"It'd still help if we knew everything you could do," Roe said. She was dressed in her workout gear, clearly expecting to go straight to the library for the group sessions Phaeron had alluded to yesterday.

The faun shrugged, her gaze falling on my sulking handbook. "Is that book flying?"

Uh oh.

The handbook twitched, flapping over to hover too close to her face. "Hi! Who are you? Wait, you're the faun, right? Áine?" it asked rapid-fire.

"Last time I checked," she replied.

"Coolio. I'm *The Librarian Witch's Handbook.* I've taught Cressie-poo everything she knows!"

I tried to cover my embarrassed blush. "Cressie-poo?" she echoed with a wicked look my way.

"Noooo, don't call me that," I complained. I explained how it had the magic to fly around as Willow arrived and was quickly enamored with the talking book. She chased it around the room for a few minutes, giggling all the while.

We were soon settled and restless, though, chatting idly about midterms and magic while Bella visited with each of us for scratches and Milo napped in my lap. I was beginning to think the men weren't coming after all when Jin lifted her head and cocked one ear like a tiny radar.

Geo's voice preceded him. He held the door as Phaeron slid in sideways, supporting an unfamiliar woman around the waist. Roe hopped to her feet first, helping support her from the other side and guide her to slump upright on the other side of the couch. Her head leaned against the backrest, spilling dark hair around her pale face.

Ben closed the door after them, his expression set in a displeased line.

"What happened?" I asked.

"Aurina." Phaeron's reply was a low snarl.

When I set Milo aside and was on my feet, I realized all three of the men who'd been on my mind turned to me at the same time. I went to Ben for a quick kiss but didn't miss how Geo uttered a sound somewhere between a growl and the rumble of a distant rock fall.

"She didn't hurt you, did she?" I asked, searching the lidded eyes and little smile Ben flashed just for me.

He shook his head. "Just Bianca. She extracted the address of Garroway's manor from her."

My next breath caught in my throat. I turned toward the unfamiliar woman, torn between elation and concern, with more questions piling up behind my lips with each moment that passed. Bianca's gray gaze met mine, and her pale lips quirked in the cocky manner I always associated with Ben.

I suddenly recognized her from Mabon, but she'd been dressed much differently, with her dark hair braided and crowned with turning oak leaves. For a moment, she'd seemed to be there with Ben when I arrived, and I'd been struck by a pang of jealousy that he'd been chatting with the slim, stunning woman who'd exuded self-confidence.

"It's nice to finally meet Ben's crush," she croaked. She was significantly paler now, her olive-toned skin white with the trauma she'd undoubtedly gone through if she was another of Garroway's assassins and forced to say something Ben hadn't been able to past shredding pain.

"Uh, yeah," I said, hesitant. Who was she to Ben? He was obviously concerned for her.

"So, we know where the manor is now," Roe put in. "What's the plan?"

"We all may as well be sitting for this." Phaeron reached out and curled a tendril of shadow around the edge of a chair, pulling it over so he could lounge in it. Geo remained standing behind him, arms crossed, while Ben and I settled on the couch with him between Bianca and me.

He put an arm around me, and I sank into his side with a sigh.

Bianca lidded her eyes, draping her arms around her middle and making no moves toward him.

When we were settled, Phaeron spoke. "Everyone in this room has a reason to go on this raid to Garroway's manor, which is not scheduled yet. We left Aurina's office quickly after she stabilized Bianca and ensured that she'd wake following the trauma of sharing such a protected fact as Garroway's address. Certain details were not decided, but Aurina will allow anyone I can muster and vouch for to come, while she will be summoning a force of professionals and accompanying us personally to assist.

"Blood barons thrive on corruption, however, so Aurina will keep her moves secret until it's time to go. We can trust very few people outside of this room, so what we discuss must remain a secret." He met everyone's gaze in turn, and I had tingles. It was like he'd erased the secretive, shadowy Phaeron and come forward with the prince and leader of the dimensional people. I appreciated the change more than I could say.

"That being said, I don't think we all *should* go," he said. His topaz eyes landed on Willow, whose shoulders slumped. "Perhaps some introductions are due."

Roe jumped in to facilitate that, and Bianca sat up with a groan to pay attention and say, "Bianca Cross, blood witch," when her turn came.

Phaeron asked a few questions of the other women. He seemed most impressed with Roe, I think, who was undoubtedly the best fighter of the freshmen present. When it was Willow's turn, he inspected her again. I recognized the way she reacted and sympathized. His gaze was particularly intense sometimes; I think that's when he was looking into my soul.

"Do you have trouble with your magic?" he asked her.

"Um, yes. No spells have worked quite right for me," she mumbled.

"Curious. The magic in your soul is quite strong, but the two sides are at odds with each other."

"Sides...?" she echoed.

"Storms and winds versus scales and song. Were you aware that you're half mer?" Though he asked it casually, he had a knowing look as she gasped and clapped both hands over her mouth.

"No way!" She turned to Roe, joy flashing over her face. "You were right. I'm not broken!"

Roe reached over to hug her fiercely. "I told you something else had to be up, girly."

"That's great news! If you end up growing a tail, I'd love to make you some new clothes," I said, already looking forward to it. I admired the mer for their natural beauty and grace, both in and out of the water. There were a few in my fashion design classes, unmistakable with the patterns of scales on parts of their bodies and the iridescence of their skin.

All traits Willow didn't have. I wondered if she'd pick them up if and when she unlocked this secret side to her.

"Do you think I might?" she asked, glancing over at Phaeron.

"I suspect so. But we can discuss it later, yes? Right now, you don't have control over both sides of yourself," he said. She nodded in acceptance, as this had been why she'd sat out our first fight with the Hungering Darkness. Raiding Garroway's manor would be so much more dangerous. "However, I don't see why you couldn't join us to train your magic. You *all* need it."

Phaeron's plan was pretty direct. We had two former assassins now, who could teach us how to fight Garroway's trained blood witches. If we could prove ourselves capable, he would take us on the raid, but we only had a week to do it. Everyone agreed, even Willow, whose face was set with new determination, and Bianca, who'd regained some of her color.

We were finalizing when we'd be training every evening when the door opened and in fell Wren Starsurge, her lips locked with another of our coven mates, Heath Storm. *I knew it*, I wanted to crow. Those two had totally been into each other from the moment she got over not matching to the same coven as her best friend.

The air turned icy, as I wasn't the only one glaring daggers at her from the moment she and Heath sprang apart. She looked around and huffed, adjusting her top and bra with a dignified lift of her nose. "I guess this room's occupied today," she said and dragged Heath away.

"Damn. I was looking forward to telling her the truth," Ben muttered.

"Time and place," I said. I wanted to see her knocked off her pedestal with the truth of her father's dealings, but like all revenges, it had to be delivered at the right moment.

PHAERON TOOK us to the heart of the library, floor negative twenty-six, where a padded space awaited. Weapons straight out of a medieval armory were racked along the wall, which made the bright red modern first aid kits stand out where they were posted at regular intervals.

With Bianca resting out of the way, Ben was busy for the whole time we were here, sharing tips about fighting blood witches and sparring with anyone interested in trying their luck. I resolved to talk to him later, distracted by Phaeron, who spent most of his time that evening teaching me directly.

Geo remained apart from everything, watching with his arms crossed. I had a sense of his disapproval when Phaeron stepped behind me, helping teach me better form with my silver sword in hand. But I quickly forgot about the gargoyle when Phaeron's hands drifted to my hips.

"You shift your weight like this," he said close to my ear.

I was all too aware of him, goosebumps rising on my arms when he leaned in further to whisper, "Just like that, bright soul." And in that moment, I was no longer preparing to sword fight an invisible foe, but instead about to shift back to rub against him.

No, bad Cress, I chastised. "Got it," I said aloud. I had just as much to prove as Roe or Áine. If I wanted to help Ben and go on this raid, I needed to get my mind focused on what mattered.

It was just, his fingers seemed to tighten like he wanted to pull me against him before he continued critiquing my form. Soon, we reached the end of my limited training, including the few spells I knew. He ended our training session with a neutral hum, and I turned to see his gaze intent on me, eyes narrowed to slits.

"What is it?" I asked.

His lips lifted into a confident smile, flashing his fangs. "I'm just thinking, we can work with this. Let's try one more thing." He slid a little closer to me, and my gaze slipped to his mouth. All he'd have to do was lean a little closer to my level...

"Call over one of your familiars," he murmured.

I gave myself a mental slap and turned, spotting Bella first. She, Jin, and Milo were across the training room, taking turns playing with my flying handbook. Jin was currently perched on its spine as it labored to stay in the air, so it seemed the little black cat had won the game already. When I called her name, Bella came running and leapt into my waiting arms.

"Hi, sweet girl." I giggled as she purred and headbutted my chest.

Phaeron walked me through checking the connection that linked us as witch and familiar. My bonds with both Bella and Milo were strong enough to work with, but apparently, they could be even stronger.

"Familiars are more than pets. They're lifelong companions, here to help with whatever you need. This will tire her out, but if she's okay with it, let's try to have you borrow some feline senses from Bella," he said. I asked her if she was okay with it, which she squeaked an affirmative to. "Focus on your connection with her," Phaeron continued.

I closed my eyes and did so. Other than being able to understand her meows as her witch, I could feel her simple emotional state, which was a deep contentment to be in my arms. *Aww.* I loved this silly little cat. She purred a little harder in response as she felt that back from me.

"Now, the tricky part. You have to communicate to her that you need to borrow from her. When you're more experienced with it, it's as easy as reaching out over your connection in a split second and taking some of her grace or her senses, but right now, you should simply ask for what she can give and know what it feels like."

I clenched my eyelids and tried it, wordlessly asking Bella over the familiar bond for her senses. I understood why it seemed Phaeron couldn't explain it fully. It just happened. My face tingled, and I was suddenly overwhelmed with the scent of sweat and metal in the air. I wanted to clap my hands over my ears, but that would mean dropping Bella, who was frozen in a state of concentration.

It only lasted for three seconds at most, leaving as abruptly as it arrived, but in those moments, I had the same senses of smell and hearing as Bella. My nostrils were still full of the closest smell other than mine—Phaeron's. His shadows carried a particular signature scent that I'd caught here and there, like clean earth and night air. It left me with the impression that I'd just gone on a walk outside in the dark.

"That was amazing," I said, glancing down at my cat, who yawned hugely. "But...I don't understand how that was possible at all."

He smiled and shrugged. "Familiars are a little magic, which is how they bond with witches in the first place. I doubt you borrowed all of her senses or really wanted to. With practice, you'll be able to do this more for longer and be able to specify between her sense of smell, or her grace, or her reaction speed."

"We'll definitely be practicing," I promised. I could already see where this could come in clutch in a fight.

He rubbed her ears, dropping his voice to a gentle coo. "Just not too much. This little girl needs to rest first." She leaned into his touch with a smug kitty smile.

My connection with her was stronger than ever, so I sensed first-hand that she approved of Phaeron quite a bit. I smiled up at him with an echo of the same feeling, and it took him a moment to notice. His sweet talking of Bella faded, but that more tender side of him remained. He tucked a few strands of hair behind my ear and cupped my face.

His gaze dipped to my lips, tracing the path of my tongue as I wet them in anticipation. When his thumb tipped my chin up and he slid closer, my heart leapt, and I rose to my toes—

"Dimensional." Geo's voice startled us apart. "The witches need to leave now to make it to their dorms before they stop serving dinner." His stoic features curled at the corners as Phaeron lashed his tail with a poorly concealed growl.

I had no doubt this was supposed to be payback for interrupting Geo and me in the classroom yesterday, but *damn*, couldn't a gal get a kiss around here?

11

CRESS

FRUSTRATED, I invited Ben to walk back to my dorm with me, ignoring whether or not Geo followed. Phaeron had stayed behind to get Bianca set up in one of the overnight stay rooms in the library, the safest place for her to sleep off her trauma, while my friends walked ahead of us, giggling at some story Willow was telling. I sensed my cats frolicking in the grass, keeping up with the group.

"I have a question," I said while they were giving us some privacy.

He'd fitted his hands in his pockets and raised a brow at my tone, which had come out more tense than I'd meant. "Uh oh. What'd I do this time?" he asked.

"Who's Bianca to you?"

I knew Ben could be an effortless liar, so this was the first real test for our trust. He seemed honest when he met my gaze and said, "She's another witch who grew up in the same situation Lucas and I did. She's more of a sister than anything—you haven't seen her real personality yet, but she's more likely to stab me than ever want to kiss me. She's not your competition, babe."

I couldn't hide how my shoulders lowered with relief. "Okay, I just wanted to be sure," I said.

"You're cute when you're a little jealous." He winked, and color rose to my cheeks. "Honestly, no one could be your competition. I should be jealous instead, with how much attention you're getting from Geo and Phaeron."

If there was a sign hovering over my head right now, it would be flashing *hypocrite* in big neon letters. "About that..."

Ben saved me from putting my foot in my mouth with a casual shrug. "When you come into your family's power, no supernatural will be surprised that you have three men."

"*If* I do," I replied. There was still no guarantee that I was secretly a Darkmore and the sole inheritor of the family line's hereditary power. Anxiety prickled its way up my spine at the thought.

In class, we'd discussed how magic was inherited from our ancestors, but it was magical theory. Like science had its theory of relativity, witches had a theory of inheritance, and it would remain a theory, as the only beings that knew exactly how it worked were the deceased. As far as we understood it, when a witch passed on, they left a piece of themselves behind to protect and support their children and their children's children. Witches across the ages reported dreams of the past, ghost stories, and tales of impossible feats, especially when their lives were in danger.

If I were, in fact, Luna Darkmore, miraculously saved while the rest of my birth family was murdered, the concentration of power in the whole Darkmore line would fall to me. The problem was, I didn't know what I'd inherit, because I was a librarian witch, while the rest of the family line were celestial witches. If I were to borrow lingering magic from, say, my grandmother, would I be able to cast spells outside of my affinity? Or would I simply be haunted by all the ghosts down my family line? There was no way of knowing until it happened.

I swallowed past the sudden dryness in my mouth. "Phaeron was going to help me figure this out on Samhain, but I'm nervous. It might not turn out to be a net positive. Instead of being a stronger supernatural, I might just turn into an overwhelmed one."

"You're letting doubt take over too much," he said. He held out his hand, and I took it, lacing my fingers with his. "See what happens when it happens."

I squeezed his fingers. "Yeah. And you're going to be there too. Maybe inheriting from your own true family line," I said.

"I sure hope so. If we're waiting a week to attack Garroway, it's going to be my only chance." He placed his free hand over his side. "Can I tell you a secret?"

There was a serious shift to his tone, which struck me as unlike him. "Of course," I answered.

"My extended family, the Evenstars, probably think Lucas and I are dead. Garroway made them sound like callous rich people, but it's not like I can trust anything he's said. I just wonder if they looked for us or if they bought the entire setup." He looked into the distance, where we were coming up on my friends' dorm. Troubled shadows played in his green eyes as we passed under a streetlamp.

"You wonder if they'd care," I said quietly.

He nodded slowly. "If they knew what'd happened, would I have a family, or just a group of strangers who pity me?"

"There's only one way to know."

"Yeah, that's true. But if they met me right now, I'd just be a penniless beggar—I don't have anything to offer but my story and my name. I want to meet them when I've made something of myself, you know? If this deadline doesn't kill me first."

He released my hand when my friends stopped before their dorm, waiting for us to catch up. Ben's vulnerability retreated behind the mask of his smirk. "Well, here we are, huh?" he said. "It's too bad I'm not a real student. Guess they'll let me starve while you all eat."

Áine rolled her eyes. "We'll bring you something, drama king."

"Actually," I ventured. "I'm feeling pretty beat. I'll take care of Ben back at my dorm."

As I was hugging Willow goodbye first, Áine and Roe exchanged a knowing look. "Bye, girlie. See you tomorrow," Roe said, crushing me in her arms next.

"Have fun," Áine said in a laughing tone, twinkling her fingers.

Ben and I turned away when Roe called, "Hey, Geo, come get a bite with us!"

I glanced over my shoulder, knowing exactly how this would go. Geo wouldn't leave his duty. But the gargoyle was frowning over at Ben and me. He eventually dipped his chin in a reluctant nod and followed the young women up the steps to their dorm.

"I'll be damned," I muttered.

"He's probably hoping I get assassinated on the way there," Ben whispered back.

"That's definitely *not* it. We had a talk earlier," I said.

Well, it didn't seem Geo quite *accepted* anything at the end of that chat except that his duty was something more than passionless servitude, but it seemed he understood that he and I didn't always need to be sharing the same space.

He smirked. "I'm not going to complain."

Of course he wouldn't. As soon as we were half a block down the street, he warned me before drawing a concealed dagger and twirling it in between his fingers with practiced ease. Ben was busy scanning the shadows, his stance more guarded now that we didn't have a gargoyle ready to come to our defense, but he kept stealing glances at me, too.

I admired him in the same way. This was a side of Ben I'd barely gotten to see—the trained assassin alert to any potential threats. He probably still had runes under his long sleeves from our time in the library. While I'd been occupied with Phaeron, Ben had been demonstrating what each rune did and how to counter them.

Luckily for us, he didn't need to give me a firsthand demonstration of him using those runes in a real situation this evening. I took him in the back way and let him into my room before doubling back to grab dinner for us both.

That was the first time I realized I'd left my handbook in the library, as I usually spent my meals quizzing it for random knowledge, but I shrugged it off. It was probably off bothering Bianca or Phaeron with its endless chatter. My cats had followed us without issue and were getting their daily scratches from the cafeteria manager, who looked the other way when I loaded up my to-go box a little too much.

When I let myself back into my room, Ben was lounging on my bed, arms behind his head. He slanted a coy look at me when I stopped dead in the threshold. He'd tossed aside his shirt, leaving his leanly muscled chest on display. I was glad to see his color was back.

I hesitated for an extended moment before closing the door behind me, knowing where this would lead. It was a choice I made as I turned the lock and set dinner aside. My heart picked up speed in my chest as I turned and read the hints of uncertainty that lingered on his face.

Mere hours after the first time we were intimate, things went right to hell. I still chose to climb into bed with him again despite a nagging sense that there was no guarantee that any pleasure we shared wouldn't be followed by more peril.

He was still on a time limit, after all. At some point, he'd bandaged over his blood rune, leaving only the active deadline to peek out from under the white linen. I was glad to see it, considering how I'd been afraid I'd hurt him by brushing over his wounds by accident.

I kissed him first, grabbing a handful of his longish hair and pouring all my frustrations of the last couple days into the slant of our mouths. It felt like true forgiveness to give myself to him again and feel his arms tighten around me. For all I'd had budding thoughts of intimacy with Geo and Phaeron, it was Ben I chose to be with tonight.

His tongue pressed against the seam of my lips, and I opened to him, letting our tongues duel and twine. He was already working the button off my pants. Callused fingers brushed the line of my hip and down to cup my ass, pushing my panties down in the process. I lifted and kicked the clothes off, sighing into his mouth as cool air caressed my needy sex.

He'd woken something in me the last time we'd been alone in this room, and I was only just realizing it. The moment my anam cara mark turned blood-witch maroon, I should've known I would crave him again. I straddled his waist, breaking our lip-lock and rolling my hips against him. His hard length pressed back, trapped within the meager barrier of his jeans.

"Hey, babe," he said, husky with arousal. "Why don't you have a seat up here?" He tapped one of his cheeks.

I flushed at the suggestion. He wanted to put my pleasure first. Even still, I was hesitant to spread my legs right above his face until I saw the glimmer of eagerness in his eyes as he took in the sight of me.

"You're so sexy, babe," he murmured. He guided my hips down and angled them just right above his face. My belly quivered, nerves and anticipation clashing for the moment it took for him to move. He ran his tongue up the seam of my pussy before delving deeper with a groan I felt through the tender petals of my sex.

I didn't know what to expect; he was still my first lover, and this was the only time I'd let another use their mouth to bring me pleasure. I followed his lead for the grind and roll of my hips, sighing with a growing smile as his lips and tongue stoked the pressure in my core. His hands kneaded my ass and held me steady when he laved my clit in a sudden shock of bliss.

He tugged at the hem of my shirt, and I pulled it over my head before releasing my breasts from the confines of their bra. Our anam cara marks brushed when he took my hand and placed it over one of the nipples pearling from his darkening gaze. We moaned together from the brief shock of pleasure and *rightness* that came from those little magical symbols.

It took me a moment to realize he wanted to watch me play with myself. I fondled my tits, flicking the tips, and watched him smile by the lines around his eyes before he closed them to savor the moment. He licked and sucked on me like he couldn't get enough of my taste.

When he transferred his lips to my clit and sucked, I came apart with a sudden cry. I wondered if I drowned him for a moment when he lay back before noticing how smug he looked with my slick shining on his lips.

"I have a bit of bad news," he murmured. "I don't have any condoms."

Panting, I rested a hand on my chest. I didn't want to hear about *bad news* when I was naked with him. But he'd presented a problem I had the solution to.

"Well..." I leaned over him, only saved from falling when he caught my hips. My legs were akin to jelly, leaving me to fumble at the end of my reach to open the first drawer of the bedside table next to us and withdraw a condom package to toss to him.

He walked it between his fingers before squinting at it. "The student center has a whole bowl full of them," I explained as confidently as I could.

I'd gone out of my way to find them and make sure they were on hand after forgiving him. Just in case he'd share my bed again. I cleared my throat and added, "Someone told me recently that it's sexy to be prepared."

He shifted to sit up with a wince. "Damn straight."

We shared a look, silent understanding passing between us. First, we worked together to free him of what remained of his clothes. He fumbled the condom package when I went for his balls, giving them a testing roll in my palm while claiming his lips. His mouth held traces of its usual mint, mixed with lingering, sweet musk. It hit me suddenly. To have this strong, confident man at my mercy felt *good*. It was satisfying to know I was his world, his full focus.

He was *mine*, as fate intended.

Then he grabbed a fistful of my hair, sending a shock of pleasure through my scalp. "Get on your hands and knees for me," he whispered into my ear.

I gave his balls a parting squeeze that had his cock twitching before swinging around and getting comfortable in the suggested position. His roughened fingertips ran up my waist and back down to grasp my hips as he shifted his weight behind me.

I expected to feel the head of his cock at my lower lips, but instead the heat of his shaft pressed along the length of my slit. There was a subtle shift of the condom's plastic, the smallest of possible barriers between us. He rubbed against me, holding my hips to keep me from angling them.

My lips parted as he pressed...no, grinded against me harder. With a glance over my shoulder, I caught the playful smile on his face.

"You want this, babe?" he purred.

I moaned in reply. My body language clearly said, *take me*. I could barely think with how much I wanted him inside me properly.

A sound of denial escaped my lips when he pulled away instead. "Let me hear you," he said.

Tease, I wanted to accuse. I found my voice to reply, "I want you."

"Tell me what you want me to do to you."

"Come back," I whimpered.

He hadn't gone far, but watched me with the kind of anticipation that required a response. A deeper flush took over my face, but I was aflame with need, far past any kind of modesty. I exclaimed, "I want your fat cock in my—oh!" In one swift motion, he'd pulled my hips into him, pushing his cock deep. This angle made him feel thicker than ever.

Something told me he'd had mercy on me this time. He was definitely the type to draw out the moment, but I felt how he pulsed within me—he wanted this just as badly.

"That better?" he asked as he withdrew, forcing the air for my reply right out of my lungs with the next drive of his hips.

I let out a breathy laugh. "Ben!" And by that, I meant, *you know it is, you tease.*

He was grinning as we rocked the bed. "Yeees?"

"Don't stop."

He had my toes curling and my hands feeling out a more stable place to hold than two fists in the blankets. I grasped the edge of the bed to push back against him as we found a rhythm together. I kept stealing glances at him, enamored by the play of pleasure on his expression, an echo to mine.

He listened well sometimes—he didn't stop, not until I came again and so did he with a jerk of his shaft within me. I breathed out with relief as we curled up together in the afterglow, cuddled up until our breath settled, trading little kisses and soft words. I enjoyed gazing into his unguarded eyes and counting the little flecks of gold within the evergreen while he traced his fingertips over my skin.

It was a relief to have him back, and in these moments, I would've done nearly anything to have his deadline miraculously pause. Especially when he peeked into the drawer I'd left half open.

"Did you take the whole fucking bowl?" he asked with a laugh.

"I wanted to be *really* prepared," I said.

I'd taken a couple handfuls, enough to fill the small space. It was a private wish of mine he'd uncovered—I wanted him here until we used them all up, and then some.

He took one and turned to kiss the tip of my nose. "Well, you're *really* sexy."

12

GEO

 before disappearing into the night with Ben.

As much as I wanted to understand emotion, I found I had a basic misunderstanding of *her* feelings. What else could explain why she'd slipped off with Ben, of all people, instead of with me?

It got under my stone skin, needling within my tender flesh. I was made for her, and she was mine, as she had just convinced me. What need did she have for another man? I'd had the feeling she was trying to ease me into the idea earlier, but I couldn't help but feel... inadequate.

While I'd watched Cress and her friends train that afternoon, an unfamiliar librarian witch had slipped into the room briefly to pass me the note now crumpled in my hand. I turned to Roe, the young woman who'd invited me to dinner. I'd pretended to accept for Cress's sake, but my flesh form did not have hunger pangs tonight.

"Will you send a message to Cress for me later?" I asked her.

She hung back to talk while the other two headed inside, likely drawn to the promise of dinner. "As long as it's not a hurtful one," she said, raising a brow. I liked Roe. She reminded me most of myself— solid, strong, and loyal.

"No, never," I rumbled. I showed her the note, which had details for a place and time tomorrow to begin my tempering. It would start earlier than she usually woke. "I must leave her side for a time to temper my body."

"What does that mean?" she asked, her tone lowering as she read the message.

"It is a process I thought the library had lost. Our foes have magic my stone body is not impervious to, so I am going to strengthen myself. The process takes time. I do not wish for Cress to worry, so now seems like the right time to leave," I said.

"Well, big guy." Roe tilted her lips aside. *Skeptical,* I told myself after a moment of studying the expression. "It'd be for the best if you told her yourself."

"I do not wish to...interrupt her," I muttered.

She propped a fist on her hip, really looking me in the eye. "Fair point. Tell you what, I'll share what you've told me, but only if you promise to explain to her later why you chose *right now* to leave with that heartbroken expression on your face. Okay?"

"Heartbroken," I repeated without emotion.

"You might think it's subtle, but this time, it's not. Just don't be a dick to my friend because she chose to go home with a different guy, that's all I'm saying. She's going to be upset when you're not there tomorrow morning."

My first thought was, *Perhaps she should be.* But it wasn't my duty to be cruel to Cress. "That is why I am leaving the message with you, since I don't have a phone," I said on a sigh.

"All right." She sounded reluctant. "You want to talk about her before you go?"

"I do not have the words. Nor the emotions."

"Consider it an open invitation, then. Cress isn't the only one who can help you work through what you're feeling, and it seems like you need someone else," she replied.

Her offer stirred some appreciation in my stone heart. I dipped my chin in acknowledgment, knowing she was likely right. If I was confusing my duty and my affection for Cress, then I had to be making other mistakes. Pushing her away. This evening's events reminded me of the time she'd tricked me just to have time away from me. The memory stung nearly as badly as when I'd first realized what'd happened.

"I appreciate your assistance in this matter." I stepped away from her and transformed back into my gargoyle form. She waved in farewell, and on a delay, I returned the gesture and flared my wings.

I flew back to Moongrove Library in a fraction of the time it took to walk to the girls' dorm. Without Cress or her friends, I had no need to shift back once I arrived. The librarians were used to a few still-active gargoyles coming and going from their missions.

I arrived for my tempering appointment several hours early. The master librarian they found for the task had chosen the same level where the others were training earlier but bade me wait in a second room. It was more enclosed and had fewer weapons available to use, ideal for close-quarters combat or the focused assault of magic I'd need to strengthen my stone.

Satisfied with the choice of location, I exhaled a soft gust from my stony lungs and let myself rest like a true statue.

Now that I'd experienced sleep in my flesh form, I knew there were a few key differences between the sleep the people around me needed versus the motionless stone of a gargoyle.

I preferred what I knew, because I was still somewhat aware of the occasional voice nearby or the thumping of footsteps on the stairs. Sleep reminded me too much of stasis, where I'd been akin to a real statue for far too long. Unaware. A shade of existence close to death.

So it was an unpleasant surprise to be rapped on the forehead by a set of gray knuckles. My resting gaze focused in an instant on my least favorite being, Phaeron, who'd crept into the room without detection. I rumbled deep in my stone throat, straightening from my slouch.

I had the sense that it was early morning, hours still before my tempering appointment. "What do *you* want?" I demanded.

"You're early," he commented.

Were I more flexible in this form, I would have narrowed my eyes at him. "Explain."

"You're here for tempering, yes? A process the librarians of this time have forgotten."

"But you have not," I said. That was logical.

I hated it. The emotion heated my stone heart, where the soul of my honored witch animated me. A heart Phaeron had already tried to rip from my chest once.

He nodded. "When you started seeking tempering, they asked if I would help you. It makes sense that you want it. You were built with the best enchantments and advancements of your time." In a blink, he vanished into curls of smoke. I whipped toward the sound of his voice behind me. "Your reaction times are fine. It's your defenses that are lacking when faced with a creature such as my brother."

"Or you," I gritted out.

"Or me," he echoed more mildly. "So, as unlikely as it seems, I'm here to help you."

A dubious silence hung between us. I inspected him for signs of untruth: fidgeting, looking away, even a desire to fill the air. His tail had its usual casual sway, and he had an expectant air as the seconds rolled by.

"What do you want?" I said.

"You've already asked me that," he pointed out.

"In exchange for your help."

"Oh, I think you know the answer to that." His yellow gaze dipped to my chest.

"I told you. I'm not her!" My raised shout echoed back around us in the small space.

Phaeron's brows rose. "I know. And I must apologize—for earlier. I was not in my right mind." If he thought I was going to accept and forgive, he'd be waiting far into his immortal lifetime. But he wasn't done talking. "Samhain approaches. On that day, I just want to call her spirit out of its...your heart for a talk."

"You wish for an explanation. I remember."

"I did. But the more time that passes, the less I desire to vent my grievances with a long-deceased woman. Morgana made her choice, and now I must make mine. All I want to do is say goodbye to her." He cleared his throat, stepping forward slowly with his hand outstretched. "Let us make peace, gargoyle. If we are to have the same woman, we must find some common ground."

Instead of staring at his hand, I took a few moments to transform into my form of flesh and bone so my emotions wouldn't be so muted and dissonant. I took my time opening my eyes.

My feelings pushed and pulled in at least three directions, becoming a tangled skein that I picked at as quickly as I could. I recognized the rage first. Anger was easy to come by, alongside its cousins, frustration and unwelcome surprise.

I realized it was his comment about Cress that displeased me most. His apology, even his offer to help me with my tempering, were all wrapped around the idea that we needed to get along better because we had to share her. When I finally looked at him again, he still had his hand out, waiting with a knowing glimmer in his otherworldly eyes.

I would find no one else who could make my stone resistant to the Hungering Darkness's claws. If he did not help me, I would be unable to protect Cress when it returned for her soul. And it *would* return.

"For you to speak with Morgana...it would not damage me?" I asked, shocked to be even considering this.

"Your heart would stop beating while she is outside of it. It'd be a lot like stasis. Asleep without the soul, your same self when it's returned as your heart."

Odd, shivery bumps crawled up my skin. *Stasis*. Cold, unaware. Unfeeling. I didn't want to return, not when I could spend my time with Cress.

"You have my word that I will return the soul quickly," he said.

"Then...I accept." Finally, I shook his hand.

He grew and flexed shadowy talons over his free hand's fingers. "Let's begin. Do you know your power level?"

"It's a six, all in defensive ability," I replied, assuming my stone form again.

Power levels were determined by three measures: offensive capability, resistance to magic, and the level of magic one could hold at one time. Gargoyles of my time had a standard power level of four, which was concentrated in defense and magical resistance. I'd been tempered far more as a special gargoyle to honor my witch and set me apart as one who carried the soul of a former demigoddess.

It didn't prepare me for the pain of being tempered anew, though. The process was one of exposure, and by the time I started to withstand power-level-seven spells from Phaeron's shadowy magic, I was sheened from my oil leaking from hundreds of tiny cuts...and forced into the nothingness of stasis to rest and recover for the next round.

TIME LOST MEANING after that first session. I'd wake, allow Phaeron to damage me further, return to stasis, and repeat. My stone didn't part like butter for his talons anymore, which meant when I faced the Hungering Darkness again, it would not be able to stop me so easily.

At some point, I shook off the clinging fingers of unwelcome sleep to see that Roe was standing across from me, inspecting the oil that stained my obsidian body like splashes of silver paint.

"Who did this to you, big guy?" she asked. My rigid lips curved at the corners to hear her tone, like she'd take on the aggressor herself.

"It's what I asked for," I replied in a low rumble. She only calmed herself once I explained I was improving myself one spell at a time. She hadn't realized what the strengthening process looked like in reality.

"So, you're done with this tempering thing and ready to say sorry to Cress for making her worry?"

I stared at her, unblinking. "I am not yet ready to leave this room."

"Dr. Aurina wants the raid to happen in two days. You're out of time," she replied.

Two days could mean one more tempering session and hours to recover before facing the true threat.

"Besides, there's someone I want you to meet. He's here now, waiting for you," she added.

"Oh?"

"You'll have to come with me. I promise it'll be worth it. He'll help you with what you're going through."

I was...nervous, perhaps, to see Cress again after leaving her so abruptly. A part of me knew I didn't have the tools to have that conversation. Perhaps this mysterious visitor did.

"Who is it?" I asked.

"Someone you used to know." She smiled mischievously. "C'mon, Geo. Come out of that rock form and live a little. Have a conversation with an old friend."

I sent her out of the room and cleaned off the worst of the oil before becoming human as she requested. If this were to be a quick chat, perhaps I could continue preparing my stone to withstand the Hungering Darkness's magic afterward. Before we even took the elevator to the surface level and I spotted him, I had an idea of what, if not who, this old friend was.

Another gargoyle. And once I saw him, he seemed familiar, even if he was in human form and looking older than I remembered. "It really is you, Geo!" He waved a pale arm.

"Marl?" I guessed. He had the same features as the common granite gargoyle I remembered, though I'd never seen his lips stretched into such a big smile.

"In the flesh." He laughed and slapped his thigh. I suppose it was funny, since we both were in our flesh forms.

Roe beamed. "I'll let you two catch up! I've got a class to get to."

"Thanks again, young lady," Marl said as she bustled by him. He turned back to me and let me have a few moments to inspect him.

Granite gargoyles were not blessed with a human form that looked fully human. Some retained the ugly, exaggerated features found in gothic architecture, or others, like Marl, simply were too gray to over-look. His pale skin held undertones of rocky marbling, and his short-cropped hair was the color of wet stone. He had a more pronounced gut under his casual clothes, and wrinkles were slowly invading the spaces around his eyes and mouth.

"Last I heard, you were a decoration in the University President's office," Marl said quietly. "It's been a while, Geo."

"What..." I hesitated. It would be rude to ask what happened to him, and something told me he was in tune with himself enough to be offended.

He inclined his head toward the library's exit. "Let's take a walk, shall we? It looks like you have a lot of questions."

"Sure." But I didn't ask, unsure of this new, jollier Marl.

He picked the path, and we walked at an aimless pace. When I didn't speak, he filled the space between us. "My daughter is a senior here. When Roe learned she was half-gargoyle, she reached out to tell me a little bit about you. We're rare now, you know. Most gargoyles who've served a long time go into stasis and never return."

"Duty compelled me to awaken," I replied. "You have a daughter?" What I meant to ask was, *It's possible for a half-gargoyle child to exist?*

"Sure do." His gray eyes twinkled, and he pulled out his phone to show me a couple pictures of him making silly faces at the camera beside a young woman doing the same. "Took after her old man, too. She's a guardian witch about to graduate with a degree in Criminology. I've worked with the SPDI for about thirty years now."

"I have heard the acronym before but don't know what that is," I admitted.

"That's because it's a mouthful. It stands for Supernatural Police Department and Investigations. The only time I need to shift anymore is when a criminal gets it in their head that they can use their magic to escape the long arm of the law."

"And that is common?"

"Eh. Once a month, maybe."

Hmm, no wonder he was aging. Stone didn't wrinkle and shrivel up like humans do at the end of their life cycle. He would eventually expire if he continued to remain out of his gargoyle form.

"I...don't understand. Why wouldn't you spend more time as a gargoyle?" I asked.

"Well, duty had me waking up from stasis too a few decades ago," he said. He veered toward the coffee shop Cress liked. "First, let's get a sip. My treat."

"My body does not require—"

"Trust me, it does," he interrupted. "Once you start eating and drinking regularly, you'll feel so much better."

I eyed him skeptically. I felt fine, if a little sore from my recent tempering.

"I can give you all the tips I've learned from my transition. Once you realize how good it feels to be alive, you'll never want to return to stone unless you absolutely have to," he promised. His words echoed common gargoyle knowledge. Many of those who caught a fancy for their flesh form and the pleasures it provided veered away from their duties to the library.

Transition was an interesting word, implying that he'd moved from one lifestyle to another. Marl was no longer the gargoyle I knew. It was his happiness, and the way it radiated from him, that had me open to hearing more about *transitioning*.

He placed a complicated coffee order, and we settled at a small table with the steaming cups between us. "Tell me of your life," I invited.

Marl nodded and began speaking of the moment he woke from a long period of stasis. He'd felt a new duty pulsing in his stone heart, which had led him to serve a verdant witch. It sounded quite familiar thus far.

"There was no danger to her, though, other than herself," he shared. A fond smile was aimed toward his coffee cup before he picked it up to take a cautious sip. "The clumsiest woman I've ever met. My first emotion was confusion at being called to the side of a woman after she tripped over a curb.

"Of course, out of an abundance of caution, I stayed with her for a time to be sure she wasn't threatened by something unseen. I ended up carrying cupcakes and other orders to her clients since she was always afraid she'd fumble and drop them. She's a baker—an artist with icing, really—and she'd tempt me into my flesh form so I could sample her treats."

Marl patted his belly with a laugh. "I grew a taste for them. Once all the dust cleared from my lungs, I enjoyed them even more. I carried emotions like joy and love with certain flavors, and that was how I eventually realized I loved my clumsy baker and wanted to make a life with her. Everything about her made me *feel*, and that was better than years and years of being alone. On my own, I'd chosen to sleep, to leave the world. Now, the idea makes my skin crawl."

"I would rather not go back to stasis, either," I said.

"You must've found your own woman, then. Do your instincts call her your duty?"

I pictured Cress with a wistful twist of my lips. "Yes."

"It sounds to me that you've found your mate, too. Congratulations," he said warmly.

My expression didn't shift from stony concern, and his expression fell after a few seconds. I felt I could confide in Marl, though. If anyone would understand my deepest concerns, it would be a fellow gargoyle who'd been through this before. "I am not her only male, and no matter what I do, she clearly prefers the company of other men."

"Hmm, I want to hear more, but let's try something first." He gestured for me to pick up my coffee cup. "Take a smell of it."

I did as he bid, taking in the aroma of rich, warm coffee blended with milk.

"You may not realize it, but you're building a memory right now. It's normal to pair memories with tastes or smells. Have you had coffee before?"

"Only sips," I replied. "Cress...my duty, she enjoys coffee that tastes very sweet."

I tasted the blend he'd ordered, which was not nearly as sweetened. With more of the flavor of the coffee apparent, I didn't mind it or the heat that traced its way down my throat as I swallowed.

"Coffee is great post-shift. I have a particular drink I always get after having to take my stone form that reminds me of leisurely Saturday morning wakeups and my family." He inhaled the vapor above his coffee with a sigh. "It grounds me and reminds me of what's most important in life. I suggest you find something that does the same for you."

I took another sip and closed my eyes. I was at my most relaxed right now; no wonder this shop was so popular.

"You're human now, Geo. You're alive. Do you feel alive?"

I took in a deep breath and let my eyelids lift more slowly. My emotional state was stable. No, content. For the first time in a long while, I felt fully in control and ready to take on the problems that followed a messy, living existence. Even like learning to coexist with the men who intended to share Cress with me. "Yes."

13
CRESS

My days felt hollow without Geo's presence. It was almost funny how much I noticed one person's absence with how often I was surrounded by others.

The spirit of motivation had taken hold of me, and I didn't struggle within its claws. I did my best in my classes, staying at or above a passing grade in them all. However, it was a relief to get my ass out of a seat at the end of the afternoon to head back to Moongrove Library and pick up my sword. Its grip and weight were becoming as natural to me as an extension of my own arm.

Without Geo, I saw a lot more of Phaeron and Ben. They didn't walk me to every class, but early morning and late evening trips across campus were usually colored by Ben's humor or Phaeron's wit. They'd both taken places in my friend group, too. Well, Ben more tiptoed back into the spot he'd already made for himself, while Phaeron was cautiously accepted as a mentor figure.

Bianca, too, fit easily in the group, despite her origins. She just seemed to keep some of her thoughts firmly sealed behind her lips, especially when Ben wasn't around. Once she was recovered, she'd started helping him train the rest of us for what we'd potentially see in Garroway's manor.

It was Phaeron I had to thank for most of my bruises. On Monday,

Wednesday, and Friday, I trained with him twice a day thanks to his assistant professor job, which meant he now co-taught my Library Science 101 class. He'd "abandoned pretext," as he called it, and used Mr. Eriksson's obvious fear of him to steal me away from the classroom for private tutoring sessions.

Though white fire occasionally flickered in his gaze like embers trying to set something ablaze, he was strictly professional during these times. Too often, he had me flat on my back and a sword to my neck. It wasn't fair—he had two of them!

"No one will hold back against you in a real combat situation, bright soul."

Speaking of unfair, though, as a librarian witch, I had a huge disadvantage against a blood witch in a fight. The first time I trained with Ben, he'd swept my sword aside with one dagger, stepped into my guard, and held the other blade to my throat. *Without* any blood-drawn runes for strength or speed.

"There's no such thing as a fair fight, babe."

Five days did not make me an expert duelist, but I learned several new spells and every blood witch trick Ben or Bianca could drill into my skull. Phaeron had called the level one through three spells I was learning "foundational" and wouldn't test my magic further with more advanced techniques until I was ready. The librarians I saw working in Moongrove Library every day had to at least have a grasp on power-level-four magic, the spells of which were geared toward controlling and commanding the dangerous forces contained in the lower levels.

In what little free time I had, I experimented with my familiars. Bella was better at lending me feline senses, while Milo, despite being my chubbiest cat, always preferred to give me enhanced reflexes. Jin watched but remained a little apart.

When I got exasperated one time too many at my flying, babbling handbook, Phaeron borrowed it for an evening and returned it with a thick leather clasp over the pages. "This way, it can talk when you permit it," he'd said.

He also gave me a modified belt made for fully trained librarians, to which I could attach a book and my sword's scabbard on either hip. I'd been so thankful and posed in the mirror with the belt on and loaded, feeling official.

The one thing we didn't notice was any sign of Garroway himself. After we'd freed Bianca from his control, I wondered if he wanted to keep the rest of his assassins away from us, just in case. I didn't want to consider the other possibility, that he'd packed up his people and things and moved his operation now that it was compromised.

Ben had less than a week left of his deadline. He spent most of his evenings in my dorm room, where other activities gave me too many peeks at the red line creeping ever closer to his heart like an insidious blood infection. We had to get the magical weapon that'd made this from Garroway, no matter what.

It was Thursday evening when a tiny winged person delivered news of Dr. Aurina's plans in a sealed envelope addressed to Phaeron. "We're going this Sunday, midday," he told us, then took another glance around the room. "Some of us will, at least, be joining volunteers from the campus security team and Dr. Aurina's private contacts, along with the cupid herself."

Willow and I exchanged a glance. She started to wilt, knowing he had to be talking about her staying behind when he referenced "some of us" going. Her grasp on her magic was shaky at best. The bubbles of water she worked with would either inflate into too-big domes and explode in her face or fall to the ground like she had no magic at all. I went to put a comforting arm around her.

Roe, Bianca, and Áine were the only obvious choices to attend alongside the friends Phaeron had found on short notice. I'd met them all briefly over dinner last night. Mostly a couple of dimensionals old enough to remember Soiluire, who'd been keen to discover their prince returned from his wrongful imprisonment. There were more dimensionals who *hadn't* wanted anything to do with our fight, however, too afraid of the Hungering Darkness to pick up their weapons and fight. And then there was David.

David, unlike everyone else, had greeted Phaeron with an effusive hug that nearly dragged the big gray man off his feet. "I got the job!" he'd exclaimed. "Campus security."

I'd peered at his aura and nodded to myself. Shifters were still the hardest supernaturals for me to identify at a glance if they didn't wear features of their animal sides openly, but their auras didn't lie.

"Congratulations, friend." Phaeron had slapped him on the back. I'd learned that David was a bear shifter and apparently the first friend Phaeron had made upon waking up in the modern day.

With all the allies we'd come up with, I was more than aware that a stony one was missing. We couldn't stall for time, not with Ben and Bianca both on a deadly deadline due to expire on Samhain. I just couldn't help but feel that it was my fault that Geo was spending so much time away from us.

When presented with the choice, again, I'd picked Ben and our immediate physical connection over the deeper, slower, forming emotional bond that linked Geo and me. I hoped he was all right, whatever he was doing. Roe had shared that he was undergoing tempering to strengthen the resistance of his stone to magic. While I recognized it as important, I wanted to see him again.

The group agreed to have one last training session Friday evening so we could recuperate and recharge our magic before the big event. I intended to ask Phaeron if he still needed me to come along to ground him. As hard as I'd worked, I didn't have a lifetime of grueling training and an affinity for magic meant to fight other people, like the majority of the witches we'd face in Garroway's manor. Yet I still wanted to go and support Ben.

I entered our training room in the library, waving a hello to Roe already doing some warmup stretches, and stopping dead as I saw who else was already here. Geo was standing against the wall like he'd never left. My heart leapt to my throat.

"Geo," I said in surprise.

There was something different about him. Maybe it was his smile and the way it carried an air of confidence that had his silvery eyes twinkling. He closed the distance between us in two long strides and had me securely in his arms the next moment. Nearly a week's worth of tension fell from my shoulders in one whoosh of breath. Though I tilted my head up for a kiss, he cupped the back of my neck to draw me further into his hold.

My protector was back. I held him just as securely, murmuring into his shirt, "I missed you."

"My absence was necessary." He cleared his throat. "I mean...I'm sorry for my abrupt disappearance. I needed some time to improve myself."

"I heard about it from Roe." I turned and realized that she was no longer in the room with us. In fact, neither was anyone else except for my cats and handbook, which was hovering in a corner at a safe distance from cat paws. Roe was outside the room, chatting with Ben and Phaeron's less distinct voices and proving why she needed an award for being the best friend a gal could ask for.

"Did she tell you about the process?" he asked. I shook my head no. As he described it, my eyes widened. It sounded a lot like torture, but he'd promised that was how tempering worked.

"You didn't have to go through all that. Or make such a big promise to Phaeron," I protested.

He touched a fingertip to my lips. "I did. I had to, for you," he said. My breath caught as his fingers brushed my cheek. "Truth is, I needed time to think and be away as much as I needed to temper my body." It was clear what he'd been thinking about, too, which made me hyper-aware of each touch.

He cupped my face and gazed down at me with a sparkle of adoration. "I needed to realize what you mean to me and how I can show you." He read my face, memorizing it, before lowering himself to finally meet my lips in a slow, tender kiss. I basked in the way his hold made me feel so safe and shielded from the rest of the world.

My heart could've busted right from my chest. "Don't leave me like that again. Without saying goodbye," I murmured.

"Never," he promised. "But perhaps...I would be willing to share your time more."

Who was this man, and what had he done with Geo? I smiled hopefully, thinking maybe we could begin setting more healthy boundaries not just between us, but also between the other two men who rivaled him for my time.

"We will have to discuss that very soon." I knew now wasn't the time when the others began filtering into the room and Phaeron approached us, his gaze lifted over my shoulder at Geo. *Uh oh.*

They exchanged nods of acknowledgment, and Phaeron said, "Welcome back. Shall we start training?"

"I have a quick question for you," I said to the dimensional, trying to step to the side to have a more private conversation with him. I leaned in close and whispered, "Do you still need me to come along to help you fight?"

"What?" Ben exclaimed, having not moved far enough away to miss the question. He whipped back toward us. "I thought we agreed that she was staying behind." This drew Geo's attention, whose expression showed he hadn't changed his mind, either.

Phaeron's keen eyes darted. He was thinking quickly, which gave me hope. "The agreement was that the young ladies who proved they could handle themselves could go. Cress has."

Fear bleached Ben's face. "Bullshit. You saw how that...that *thing* in my brother wanted to eat her. She's the last person who should be going." He stepped forward, catching my hand between his. "Cress, please. You know you should be sitting this one out."

"She won't be fighting unless she has to," Phaeron interjected. His tail lashed, betraying some inner turmoil, and he avoided my gaze when I turned a look of betrayal his way. "She will be with Geo and me, acting as bait."

Ben's eyes bugged wide. "Bait! Fuck that."

"Bait?" I asked more calmly. He'd mentioned that he'd needed me there to ground him, not that I would be a draw for the Hungering Darkness. But if it meant I could join them and help Ben, I would. I could take care of myself.

"If Endaeron is there, he will sense Cress, Morgana's soul within Geo, and me in one place. I don't know of any better trap than that. You do want us to capture your brother alive, yes? This may be our only chance." Phaeron's tone was as hard and cold as stone.

The three men had the kind of stare-off that made me worry they'd spark an actual fire.

"I consent to this. I've learned from the best, and I'll run if things become too dangerous," I said first. Phaeron tipped his hand my way as if that concluded the matter.

Ben was about to argue when Geo responded, "I will only tolerate this because I've been tempered and prepared for the fight ahead. We will lure out the biggest danger to Cress's safety and dispatch it."

"Fine," Ben sighed. He ran a hand through his honeyed hair, leaving it in a tousle. "We'll be a happy unit, because I'm coming too."

"Fantastic. I'm glad we could all agree on something...for the second time ever." Phaeron's lip quirked with humor.

14

BEN

WE GATHERED EARLY Sunday morning in a building on the outskirts of campus, the office and training grounds of NSU's campus police. The bulk of the group going were professionals with affinities or powers that matched up well against blood witches. I was exceptionally nervous around all these guardian witches and shifters and the scattering of cupids.

Dr. Aurina was here, meeting with Phaeron and the head of security, and her mates and a couple of her friends were coming along. I understood the strategy—we might have an easier time if Garroway's enslaved coven were crippled by an overload of pain and fear, magnified from the magic of multiple cupids.

I had a sour feeling in my stomach, regardless. My deadline was up in a few short days, and the pain from the magic was a constant pulse reminding me of what would happen if this raid failed. Garroway was too clever not to be prepared for us.

I'd put my limited affairs in order, just in case. I'd enjoyed my taste of freedom to the highest—I had the opportunity to make friends, to have Cress in my arms again, and even mailed off a message to one of my estranged Evenstar aunts with a carefully worded explanation of where Lucas and I had gone and what had really happened to our mother. Bianca had helped me track down what was left of my family online, and I'd picked this aunt in particular because her smile on various social media posts seemed kind.

But as I faced down my own mortality in the wait we had to endure before the raid started, I knew it wasn't enough. I was not ready to check out. I'd do nearly anything to stay, to keep this nice little life I'd started to form for myself.

I wanted so much more.

My gaze traveled the length of the room we all waited in. Cress stood against the wall with Geo, his dark arm wrapped around her hips. She giggled at something he said and leaned her head against his shoulder. I loved that laugh...actually, I simply loved that woman, enough to share her, which I never thought I'd be willing to do for anyone.

I hadn't told her how I felt, not wanting to cause her more pain if I didn't live past this evening. Instead, I'd tried to show it through every tender kiss, each stolen glance and brush of our fingertips. I'd followed her back to her dorm night after night, and she hadn't hesitated to let me in so I could show my love skin to skin with her. In that, I'd indulged in the selfish urge to keep her to myself and out of anyone else's bed.

Cress came to see me before long, greeting me with a brief kiss. "Hey. How are you holding up?"

"Just fine." I may have promised not to lie, but it sure felt like one. "It's not too late to go back to your dorm."

Her lips pressed into the stubborn line I was familiar with. "No, Ben. I'm coming along to help you. And Lucas."

My palms were a little sweaty at the reminder. I'd face down my demons with a smile on my face, but to think Cress would be there too... used as *bait*, no less.

She placed a hand on my chest, right above my heart. "This is everything I've been training for. Don't try to leave me behind." She batted her lashes up at me.

"Okay. Right," I relented. If only her charms worked on the people we'd be facing as well as they did on me. At least she'd be well guarded, whether she wanted to be or not.

Phaeron gathered us around soon after to tell us the plan. "Given that our two main targets are going to cower inside away from the sunlight, we will be heading into the manor and going straight to the vampire Garroway's quarters," he said. He spoke to a team made up of the people he'd personally recruited—myself, Bianca, Roe, Áine, Cress, Geo, David the bear shifter, and a group of four grim-faced dimensionals.

Phaeron unfolded a map, a photocopy of the sketch Bianca and I had made, and explained that we'd be going in last, through the back entrance. Aurina and her cupid companions would enter first to cripple with their emotional magic, and then the campus police would engage anyone still standing while handcuffing and removing any blood witches they could. I was glad to hear that we might have a chance to save some of the men and women enslaved to Garroway's will.

I put an arm around Cress, holding her protectively. If all went well, she would see very little of the place I'd spent most of my life. I could have Lucas back by this evening, and we'd be freed of Garroway forever by dragging him into the unforgiving sun.

I just hoped I wasn't dreaming while the bulletproof vests and weapons began being passed around.

WHEN IT WAS GO TIME, we loaded into unmarked vans and came screeching to a sudden stop in front of the dilapidated lot in human Salem, where Garroway hid the pocket dimension to his grand manor. The sun was high in the sky as Bianca cut her palm and opened the doorway to the pocket dimension wide for the rest of us to pass through.

We piled out of the van, waiting tensely on the cracked sidewalk. No one lived on this stretch of road, but that didn't mean a mixed group of armed supernaturals wouldn't bring immediate alarm if we were spotted. Despite the autumn chill, sweat dripped down my back as I imagined everything that could go wrong in the minutes that passed.

Phaeron crouched a foot ahead of me, his voice hushed as he turned to the crimson-skinned dimensional woman next to him, who hid her face from the sun with a lift of one of her wings. "I sense a disturbance. He's here," he said.

"We'll follow your lead, my prince," she replied. "Let's get him contained swiftly."

He nodded and looked past me, sharing a meaningful glance with Cress, who was toward the middle of our group. I made a note to ask what that was about if I had the chance.

There could only be one "he" they were referring to, and I struggled to calm my racing heart. I'd soon be face to face with the monster who thought he could use my brother for a puppet. This time would be different, I vowed.

A whistle went up, the signal to enter the pocket dimension. I twirled one of my blades between my fingers and kept one eye on Cress as we approached the rip in reality Bianca had opened.

The manor's roof was smoking, with fire flickering along the upper levels. I stumbled over my own feet, staring.

"Uh, I don't remember this being part of the plan," Roe commented.

"It was," Phaeron said. "A backup if Aurina thought her magic wouldn't be enough. We're now on a time limit—let's move."

"Shouldn't we have known about this?" Áine grumbled, her deer-like ears folded back.

"This is a little unexpected for me as well. But we must adapt," the dimensional answered calmly.

Out on the lawn, guardian witches and familiar faces were locked in deadly dances of blades, stones, and the occasional gunfire. Most of Garroway's assassins preferred edged weapons that required an up close and personal touch, all the better to steal someone else's blood and magic, but we were prepared for projectiles as well.

We skirted the edge of the battlefield. Cress summoned her magical barriers, layering one atop the other, while Roe formed a solid shield of rock from stone pulled from the ground and carried it along. She'd slam it into the ground to give us a wall to take cover behind, if we needed it. Filling the gap between them was Geo in his gargoyle form. His shiny stone body didn't even flinch when a bullet ricocheted off him.

Winged shapes circled over the manor, fanning the flames. I didn't see any distinct rose gold wings, but it had to be Aurina and her mates smoking out the place. We reached the rear door and slipped inside. An assassin jumped out at Phaeron, dagger whipping toward his neck with enhanced speed.

He flinched and turned his body into smoky shadows, which were disturbed by the path of the weapon. It was the winged dimensional woman who reacted first, blasting the assassin's side with a super-heated gust of air from her palm. If I thought I was sweating before, between her magic and the crackling flames overhead, I'd soon soak through my shirt under the bulletproof vest I'd borrowed.

The assassin hit the wall hard, his head clunking against it with an audible *thump*. He sagged, unconscious, and Roe clamped handcuffs of solidified dirt and rock around his wrists.

"Calling in. One neutralized," whispered David into a radio while we moved on cautiously.

At any given time, Garroway had anywhere from five to fifteen of his blood witches on hand. If he were expecting this attack, that number could triple, as he had reserves of men and women tucked in places the rest of us didn't know about. I often suspected he had more than one manor, run by someone he trusted and staffed with a separate coven of witches that never interacted with us here in Salem.

My fears about how many assassins he'd brought was confirmed when we entered the main foyer. Garroway was always a stickler for the angles of the furniture here and the presentation of the valuables he put on display. I couldn't help a grin at how one couch was upended and a handful of artisanal lamps were shattered on the floor alongside the big shards of what'd once been an immaculately polished glass tabletop.

Some of Garroway's assassins pushed the furniture away, making room for the two people who circled amidst a drizzle of embers catching in the ceiling high above. One of the combatants limped, a shiny wing askew as she tracked the familiar form of Garroway. Both wore clothing meant for combat, but hers was already stained with blood, while he seemed cool and in control even now.

We didn't have to say anything—this *definitely* was not part of the plan. Instead of beaming her magic out to cripple Garroway's coven, here she was trying to take on the master who'd taught most of us how to fight the painful way. I doubted the curvy, beautiful cupid could overwhelm a vampire who fed off of emotion, which threw out her magical advantage.

"Shame it had to end like this, Melinda," he said. He spared our group a brief glance before snapping his fingers, causing any nearby assassins to turn on us in a whirl of steel and crimson magic.

"No," she gritted out, flaring her wings behind the onrushing assassins. I staggered from the force of emotion that rolled from her.

Fear dug familiar talons in my gut. The emotion seized me, cold and unrelenting. I'd only ever been afraid of one man this deeply, the red-eyed vampire who drank up every nuance of fear and pain from his witches like they were the finest vintage. He was doing that now, even, while his trained men and women stumbled for a crucial few seconds.

The others rushed forward to meet the assassins while I whipped my head to dislodge the clinging cupid magic. I wasn't really afraid to the extent Aurina made me feel. No longer did I have to fear for my life or cower in front of Garroway, knowing that pain was coming and I was helpless to stop it.

My gaze flashed over the makeshift battlefield, which had quickly descended into chaos. I spotted Áine sweeping the legs out from under one blood witch while Roe knocked him out with a punch reinforced with stone. Geo had locked his hands around the wrists of a different assassin and held the struggling woman steady as Cress quickly ruined her blood rune with a swipe of her sword.

Garroway whipped a glowing dagger through the air, narrowly missing Aurina's sculpted cheekbones. She was significantly slower than him, and it reaffirmed for me that she was outclassed. She had a sword in hand and a gun at her hip, but she would not be fast enough to hit him with either.

However, he was fighting with only a shard of darkness, the weapon I needed to end my deadline. I tightened my hold on my weapons and stepped forward, ready to come to her defense, when one of his loyal assassins intercepted me.

Flipping a dagger between his fingers like he'd taught me years ago was Seth, his weathered face set in a professional mask. With his salt-and-pepper hair and premature wrinkles, he was the eldest blood witch under Garroway's control. He stood there as calm as ever, even as something in the roof cracked and gave way, releasing a shower of stinging soot and drawing more than one person to cough around us.

"Hello again, Benjamin." Even as he spoke, he slid fluidly into a ready stance. I did the same, mirroring him.

"Step aside now. I don't want to hurt you," I said.

"Nor do I want to hurt you. But it's rather inevitable, don't you think?"

"Bare your blood rune. I can save you from this life." I gestured around me to where the foyer was filling with smoke. We wouldn't be able to stay much longer.

He chuckled and did as I asked, showing the crimson rune along the right of his ribcage. A thicket of old deadlines created braided patterns along his chest from it, and at least three of them were red and active. I still lunged without hesitation, blade aimed to cut through his rune, and he caught my wrist with the edge centimeters from his skin.

"It's too late for that," he whispered. His hold on my wrist tightened, and he twisted, forcing me to release the weapon. "Listen to me, Ben. The master has engaged dark forces beyond our understanding."

Blood began to run from his nose and the corner of his lip. "Seth, no," I said, horrified. "Let me—"

"Shh. I've made my decision," he said gently. I could feel the heat from his blood rune from here as it spread through the rest of his body and became a furnace. He'd die a slow, painful death for betraying the master. While he struggled to speak, I leaned in to take in every word so his choice wouldn't be for nothing. "He converses with...what used to be Lucas. He's turned the black dagger on himself. He wants to contain the darkness next..."

Seth coughed blood. His eyes were glassy with fever and an unnatural shimmer of heat lifted from his head, beyond the point of no return. "He has...teleport charm...leave..." he wheezed.

"Thank you," I said.

Heat pricked the corners of my eyes. This man was the closest thing I had to a father, and even now, he was looking out for Lucas and me. His sacrifice meant more than he knew, and all I could do was put my gratitude into those two words before he drew a second dagger, pivoted, and threw both of his weapons.

Seth collapsed, gone in a split second. He'd chosen to go in the only way faster than betrayal of secrets—a direct attack aimed at Garroway. One of his daggers sank to the hilt in the vampire's back, the other opening a nasty gash in his thigh. He turned his blood-hued gaze our way, his lip curling when he realized what'd happened.

"He always was a sentimental fool," he drawled.

My shock and sorrow stoked to an instant inferno, just as hot as the flames that threatened to come down on our heads. "We have some unfinished business, *Garroway*," I said.

I didn't stoop to pick up the weapon I'd dropped, instead switching the other to my dominant hand. I extended my fingertips, pulling at the blood pooling down his pants leg to do what blood witches did best: steal the best attributes and magic of other supernaturals.

I painted runes in his blood up my arm, borrowing his innate vampire agility, strength, and enhanced senses. "Oh, yes, what was it again? You wanted to drag my body outside and dance in my ashes," he mocked.

I lunged, my steel a silvery blur that opened a cut on his arm. He'd stepped back, giving Aurina an opening to thrust her weapon at him. His vampiric blood sprayed when it made an appearance through his shoulder, mere inches from his heart.

Garroway looked down at the wound with an amused tilt to his lips. *Fuck.* I knew that look. He was still several moves ahead of all of us, with something else up his sleeve. That was the only reason he'd be smiling while his manor burned down around him.

"Too bad you won't get the chance," he said, confirming my suspicions as he lifted himself off the sword and disappeared with his enhanced speed.

With the runes I'd painted in his blood, I was able to track where he'd gone, retreating away from the worst of the fighting. He lifted his hand in a signal.

Another person landed before him from a leap from the second story balcony. Lucas unfolded to his full height, eyes full of white fire and a glowing charm dangling from his fist by a dainty chain.

"Hey, big bro," hissed the Hungering Darkness.

15

CRESS

"HE'S GOT A TELEPORT CHARM!"

Ben's shout drew my attention. I'd been in the process of helping move unconscious blood witches away from the worst of the fighting. Our forces had met up in this foyer, and multiple campus police officials were trying to get us all to leave before the manor collapsed with everyone inside.

There was Ben, standing across from his brother, who stood protectively in front of the man that had to be Garroway. My gaze darted around, looking for Phaeron. I'd held my own, just like I'd been trained, but I knew why I was really invited to this raid. When I finally spotted the dimensional, he'd collapsed to his knees and was clawing at his face, leaving rivulets of fuchsia blood to run down his cheeks like tears. White fire started eating into the shadows that lined his hands.

I touched the mark he'd left upon my wrist, the sign of his protection. Stepping back into a darkened corner, I called out Phaeron's name. His head jerked in my direction, but it wasn't quite like the last time. Ivory flames had already claimed his gaze, which roved over me with obvious hunger.

Quaking with a sudden surge of fear, I jabbed my fingertips into the mark harder. "Phaeron, snap out of it!" I shouted. He paced toward me, licking his lips and the points of his fangs.

"Aren't you hungry, though?" whispered the hissing voice of the Hungering Darkness. Despite being several yards away, I heard it clearly, like it was breathing in my ear. Lucas was looking my way as well, turning his back to Ben.

A huge mistake. Ben moved impossibly fast, leaping onto his back and grappling for something he was holding while thrusting a dagger into his shoulder. "Get out of my brother, you body-snatching freak!" he shouted. With a stumble and snarl, the Hungering Darkness's attention fixed on the young man trying to throw him off balance.

Phaeron shook his head rapidly and paused mid-step, taking a shuddering gasp. He lifted his chin and watched the white flames dancing along his arm rapidly shade back toward their natural color.

"Thank you, bright soul," he said before summoning his full magic. The harsh shadows around us shuddered from the pulse of power that I felt in a wave of goosebumps head to toe.

I'd seen sketches of the shadowborn form Phaeron could take, covered in flickering black shadows that danced like layers of fur in the wind, but this was the first time I saw it in the flesh. Darkness enveloped him head to toe, with features emerging from a ball of shadow that covered his head. First, pointed ears, then a muzzle packed with razor-sharp teeth. He remained upright and looked like a pseudo werewolf with his burning topaz eyes. Shadows covered the length of his ornate swords last, lending them a deadly new edge and several inches of extra reach.

Pivoting, he lifted his weapons horizontally and charged back into the fray, leaping over our friends' heads with one mighty bound and an unearthly, eardrum-shattering sound that could've been a shadowborn's howl. I made to follow, but a mountain of muscle shouldered into my way. Giant, claw-tipped mitts caught my elbows. It was David, showing some of his bear features in the thick of battle.

"We have to get out of here!" he shouted.

"Not yet," I said and coughed. Thick smoke was rolling through the air, suggesting the manor was truly burning. Most of the campus police, and even some of my own team, were already evacuating. I'd barely noticed, but the manor had to be close to full collapse.

I sidestepped David despite the danger, lifting my sword. He growled and grabbed my shoulder, holding me in place. "You can't go back there," he said, his grip impossible to shake off. I accepted this reluctantly, watching the rest of the fighting from a safe distance.

Garroway and Lucas were the only enemies I saw still standing, separated by my allies. Aurina and Bianca were both attempting to strike Garroway, who had barely slowed down despite several bleeding wounds. It was possible his vampiric healing had already sealed over the worst of the damage.

Phaeron had leapt straight for the Hungering Darkness, which relied on Lucas's reflexes to avoid the sweep of shadow-lined swords. It was not fighting well with Ben and Geo also focusing their attention on it. Only one of its arms was coated in white shadow, while the other clutched something to its chest defensively.

For once, I thought we could win—if only we had more time. Sunlight rushed in over the stairs as part of the roof collapsed with a dramatic *crack* and the whoosh of flames finding new, dry carpeting to burn.

The Hungering Darkness attempted to swipe at Geo, just to send up sparks and a distinctive screech like metal shrieking together. Geo flashed his quartz teeth and said something too low for me to understand before launching a spike of stone from his palm.

Instead of hitting Lucas, Geo had aimed for and impaled Garroway through the shoulder. The vampire was mid-taunt toward Aurina as the cupid was mid-swing for another strike that he easily dodged. Turned out, he wasn't expecting the foot-long projectile. He dropped a shard of black stone, releasing a furious snarl.

Ben shouted and scrambled for it, as did Bianca. She caught it first, before Garroway's boot came down upon her wrist. It rolled out of her palm.

Ben grabbed it before the vampire could and touched it to his blood rune. A flash of red and black magic blew his protective vest to the side. It looked like spikes emerged from under Ben's skin, erupting out like shrapnel.

Ben's movements, so fluid and fast with the blood he'd obviously borrowed from Garroway, had slowed and taken on a clumsy edge as he stumbled toward Bianca. She met him halfway, clawing at her clothes to expose her blood rune. He touched it with the weapon and flinched away from the same sharp burst of magic from her rune just in time.

Garroway nailed Ben's jaw with an uppercut, and Ben's eyes rolled upward with the force before he collapsed. The black shard went flying. Peeling away from the fighting, the vampire ducked around Aurina's wing to run after his weapon.

With an irritated hiss, the Hungering Darkness stabbed at Phaeron and took advantage of his flinch, flowing into a wisp of white shadow that formed up again next to Garroway. The bloodied vampire had the shard, and Lucas rested a hand on his shoulder, the other holding a glowing trinket aloft.

David uttered a curse as tendrils of magic swirled around both men before they were gone. His big bear mitt finally released my shoulder.

"What was that?" I asked. Everyone else suddenly cursed a blue streak, even delicate Aurina, who fluffed out her undamaged wing with a sneer up at the burning ceiling. She was the first to turn and run toward the exit.

"They teleported away," David told me before he ran too, probably assuming I was a step behind him. I would've been, but both Bianca and Ben were limping and clutching their sides. They needed help.

That moment of hesitation cost me, and a fiery avalanche came down from the second floor, right over my head. My lips parted to scream when I saw it coming, but a dark blur knocked me out of the way.

Phaeron and I went tumbling, coming to a stop a few feet from the open door, the kiss of cool wind on my uncomfortably hot skin.

"That was a close one," he said. His voice was husky and deeper as a shadowborn, though the magic was receding from the touch of sunlight coming through the threshold.

He'd landed above me, his legs tangled with mine. The shadows dissipated around him, revealing the tracks of scratches down his cheeks and deeper claw marks across his chest.

"That makes us even today, then," I said. A fierce light gleamed in his topaz eyes.

"We are always even, bright soul," he said in a low purr. My heart leapt in surprise when he took a moment to kiss me before standing. With his grip on my hips, he easily placed me back on my feet so I could dash to safety with the memory of his pointed fangs running ever so delicately over my bottom lip.

"Why—" A fit of coughing interrupted me, like the clean air was too much for my abused lungs. Phaeron slowed to match my stumbling pace as we rejoined the dregs of the group escaping to human Salem and safety.

"Because I could see the questions in your eyes, and I'm afraid I don't have any answers," he replied.

My eyes narrowed at the reminder. I did want an explanation from him, but if he truly didn't understand what'd just passed between him and his brother, I at least had a guess. The Hungering Darkness had somehow compelled him and suggested he take a bite of my soul. This was far more serious than I thought. He'd definitely been downplaying the meaning behind the occasional flicker of white in his eyes.

He was quiet when we got back into the van, closing his eyes and holding still when Áine came over to mend his scratches. I moved seats to sit next to Ben, who was one of the last to arrive. I dug into the open kit of supplies on the van floor and started wiping some of the soot off his face with a towel.

"Did it work?" I dared to ask.

"You look. I don't know what I'll do...if it didn't..." He puffed with the effort of speaking, exhibiting all the signs of deep pain like when we'd originally damaged his blood rune. Slowly, he shifted the ragged edges of his shirt to expose it, and I pulled it further to the side to trace his deadline with my gaze.

It'd gone dark, as black as a fresh tattoo. He'd stopped the deadline. He'd live! I told him as much but added with a frown, "You're still hurt." The whole rune was puffy and enflamed, puckering around the scars that marred it to make an ugly, misshapen mass on his skin.

He wet his lips and chuckled. "It hurts more to take out something lodged in you. I'm free from him, Cress." He laced his hand with mine, moving it away from his side to rest over my thigh instead. "But it's not over."

The weight in his words warned me. He sniffed and let me guide his head onto my shoulder; I cupped his cheek and held him while a few tears slipped silently down his cheeks. "He's gone," he whispered.

"I know," I murmured. "But we'll find him again. They've only gotten away from us temporarily."

His brows scrunched before he sighed. "I more mean...you never met him, but..." In hushed tones, he told me a bit about Seth, the father figure who'd just sacrificed his life to warn Ben of Garroway's plans. We could look at what he'd said to Ben at another time, though. I held him until the van stopped and everyone else piled out.

We walked hand in hand to the campus security building to surrender our borrowed equipment and receive any healing we might need and a lecture out the door not to breathe a word of what'd happened to those uninvolved.

"No worries," Ben had answered with a hint of his usual smirk. As soon as we stepped out of earshot, he turned to me. "I'll be passed out in my room until Samhain anyway. Want to join me?"

16

CRESS

ROE CALLED a coven meeting the next afternoon, after all our classes. Six of the seven of us arrived pretty promptly, sprawling around our little room in the Witch's Clubhouse. It felt odd to see Wren, Heath, and Grant again, knowing how much had happened without them present as part of our coven.

The topic of the day was going to be the email we'd all received this morning. It was the talk of the campus, after all. I'd passed whispered conversations several times today, mostly fellow students sharing what they knew about blood barons.

I still had the email up on my phone, knowing it wasn't the triumphant message Aurina wanted to share, with a bolded title like: **ATTN: Curfew Extended**.

Northern Supernatural University
Office of the President

Dear NSU Family,

As Samhain approaches, many of us are looking forward to celebrating the lives of our ancestors. It is with regret that I must inform you that the school-wide curfew will continue until the end of the semester. This means our annual Samhain Ball will remain canceled for the safety of everyone gathered on our campus. Students are encouraged to practice their rituals and traditions indoors.

The reason for our caution has been properly identified. A blood baron vampire going by the name Garroway has decided to target our campus and student population. Below is an artist's rendition of Garroway and one of his closest associates. Do not attempt to engage them; these men are very dangerous. Contact the campus police immediately in the case of a sighting.

If you are a blood witch, you will be receiving a separate email with further instructions.

You may notice an increased presence of campus police, who are here for your safety and protection. Thank you for your understanding and patience as we work to bring these men to justice.

Sincerely,

Dr. Melinda Aurina

Attached were artist renditions of both Garroway and Lucas. They had a precise, police-sketch air about them, accurate and colorized. It might've been the first time Garroway's likeness was shared with a large audience. As a vampire, no photo or mirror would show him, and given his line of work, I doubted he had anything but the utmost anonymity until this morning.

Ben sat next to me on the couch, his arm slung casually around my shoulders and fingers playing with the ends of my hair. He'd gone quiet the moment he spotted his brother's likeness right next to Garroway's. "I guess this was overdue," he'd muttered.

They looked so alike, especially when one was just a drawing, that I worried he'd be mistaken for his brother and reported constantly. I considered scrounging my pennies to buy him a hat or encouraging him to wear a disposable mask to hide his nose and mouth.

Roe was always the last to arrive to coven meetings, and this time, I wondered if that was intentional to bring out the worst in Wren. She was inspecting her perfectly manicured nails with a bored air, flashing an irritated look over her curled fingers when my redheaded friend burst into the room with a boisterous hello.

"Some of us have things to do, Ashbough," Wren muttered.

Roe's expression fell, her brows kitting. "The door's right there," she said, jerking a thumb over her shoulder.

The blonde's nostrils flared. "Excuse me?"

"You're free to leave. I know exactly the witch I want to replace you with, even," Roe answered, looming over Wren with her arms crossed. "I think the university made a mistake, pairing you with the rest of us."

I had a sinking feeling in my chest that this was about to be a messy confrontation. On the way here, I'd asked Ben to keep from mentioning Blaize Starsurge and his alleged role in my life. Without me talking to my mother on Samhain to confirm it, there was still a possibility that there was a different orphan out there who was Luna Darkmore, victimized by Wren's father instead. But I hadn't asked the same of the mother hen of our coven, who was just as likely to get in Wren's face.

"Roe," I said uncertainly.

"Now hold on, you two." Heath sat forward, putting his shoulder between the women. "There's no need for this. Wren's just frustrated that we haven't had a coven meeting in a while, especially with Samhain so close. Right, sweetheart?"

Wren grumbled under her breath. I repeated Roe's name, catching a moment of her attention. When she saw me shaking my head rapidly, she mouthed the word "why?"

"She shouldn't hear about it in a confrontation," I answered aloud. "She doesn't know." As bitchy as she could be, I sincerely doubted she knew the details of her father's illicit dealings. And throwing all of it in her face was the worst way to go about a difficult conversation. Besides, if we judged her for the sins of her parent, what would I need to answer for if I did turn out to be the last Darkmore?

"Are you two talking about me? You better tell me now," Wren snapped.

Ah, shit. I'd walked right into this.

"Could you let go of each other's throats for a minute so we can talk about Samhain?" asked the last person I expected to speak up. I wasn't the only one turning to stare at Grant. Usually, he sat in a corner at meetings like this, staring into space and only answering when asked a question directly. I'd assumed he was usually high, but Lanie's final letter to me had described his condition as "fae trickery."

"I want to know what you're talking about first," Wren demanded.

Grant rolled his eyes. Glaring around at all of us, he seemed to lack any air of a prim fae. "By the Mother Tree, this must be the most annoying coven they could've put me in," he grumbled.

"Are...are you feeling all right?" Roe asked him.

"I'm fine. Let's talk about Samhain," he prompted.

After an uneasy silence from everyone, Roe cleared her throat. Heath held Wren's hand, glaring over at us while she had her mouth twisted with displeasure. Willow was watching everything with wide eyes, her lips moving silently as she repeated something to herself. Next to me, Ben's teeth were practically grinding with how hard he'd set his jaw to remain quiet. I nudged him and smiled, grateful he'd kept himself out of the argument.

"Samhain. Do we want to do anything as a coven? I was thinking perhaps a nature walk or a Dumb Supper. We could have it here, even," Roe said, throwing her arms wide in the narrow space of our clubhouse room. "I've already made an ancestors altar in my dorm. If you don't have one and would like help making one, I wouldn't mind giving some advice or coming over to help set it up."

"Okay, I'll ask it first. What's a Dumb Supper?" Ben said after noticing my puzzlement.

Roe was happy to explain at least, tapping into the same enthusiasm she'd shown for drawing us all together for Mabon. "Dumb" was another word for silent, in this case a silent dinner held with an extra, empty place setting for the dead with an offering of a bit of the food and drink from the meal. After the dinner was finished, the plate and cup were traditionally left outdoors as an offering for the deceased.

"I'm down. My roommate is going to be annoyed that I'm putting it forward, but my place has a big table and more room than in here," Ben said. "You all bring the food. We'll host."

I lifted a brow in his direction. He hadn't once invited me over to see where he was living with Phaeron, but now he wanted to host our whole coven?

"Sounds like fun," Willow ventured quietly.

Wren breathed a heavy sigh. "Why did some vampire have to ruin our chances to have a Samhain Ball? I had my dress picked out and everything."

Roe spoke over her. "I believe we should set up for Lanie to be the guest of honor. I remember a lot of her favorite foods and things. Would your roommate mind if I came by early to set up?" she asked Ben.

He shrugged. "Yeah, sure."

My throat tightened up. I was so grateful that we'd be doing this ritual to honor the friend who'd given her life for the rest of us. "I'd like to come early, too," I said with a little cough.

"There, that's settled." Roe then turned a baring of her teeth on Wren. "You can go now. Sorry for wasting your time."

For once, the blonde didn't have a catty remark. She seemed more confused than anything as she eased herself to her feet and motioned for Heath to stay. "Could we have a quick chat?" she asked, pointing one of her long nails toward the door.

With a nod, Roe followed her into the hall. The exchange was brief enough that I barely had time to worry before Roe returned and told Heath that Wren was waiting for him. When they were both gone, my redheaded friend blew out a tense breath and leaned against the wall. "Don't worry. I just told her to ask her father about Garroway," she told me. "We'll see if she does."

"I doubt he's going to tell her the truth," I scoffed.

"She'll believe it when SPDI comes knocking. Dr. Aurina wouldn't just keep the list of Garroway's known associates to herself, and Ben named him first," she pointed out.

"You overestimate the police's efficiency." Again, Grant startled us. He was usually the first one out the door, scrubbing away some of the boredom from his face.

An awkward pause hung in the air. Grant wasn't involved in the eventful couple weeks the rest of us had had. He didn't even know what list Roe was referring to.

"Hey, Grant. Where are you from?" Willow asked.

"Just outside of Lowell. Why?" he asked.

She loosed a nervous laugh. "Isn't it super rude for a non-fae to swear to the Mother Tree?"

I raised a brow and glanced back at Grant curiously. Was that true? The only other person I'd heard swear to the Mother Tree was Áine, but if it were forbidden, a verdant witch from a storied line like Grant would know that.

He glanced at his hands and chuckled. "Knew I should've kept my mouth shut. If I show you my secret, it will not leave the lips of those in this room. Understand?"

"Sure," Roe said easily, her eyes narrowed on him.

Willow and I also agreed, but Grant didn't do anything but stare at Ben until he also said yes.

"Thank you for agreeing to my terms. I believe it would benefit us all if you knew a little something about me." He flexed his fingers as he spoke, his voice taking on a soft, lyrical quality that was entirely not human. A transformation rippled over him, and in a few heartbeats, it was a completely different person sitting there and flexing four iridescent wings that wouldn't look out of place in miniature on a dragonfly's back.

Roe sucked in a breath. "Changeling."

Ben stood, dagger in hand. "What did you do with Grant?" he demanded.

The fae now straddling a chair in Grant's place waved a hand dismissively. His skin tone reminded me of the polished pinewood table my mother kept pristine back home, a light brown with striations reminiscent of wood grain. "Off at the Norwood estate with his girlfriend, I presume. His family hid him away in Maine after he struck a deal with me."

"You've been Grant this whole time?" Roe asked. "To think I was worried about you!"

His smile over at her was indulgent. "I rather enjoyed having a beautiful woman's concern. But fear not. I am not broken, just terribly bored with being forced into this coven."

Her face reddened. "Flattery's not going to get you anywhere, changeling. Time for you to go."

"I could leave." He folded his arms around the back of his chair, tilting his head. A braid fell over his shoulder, revealing how his evergreen hair shaded to orange about halfway down. His mischievous, sharp-angled features and unusual amber-brown eyes were quite fae, as was his nonchalance in the face of Roe's anger and Ben's threatening stance. "But you would have a tougher time removing Grant Norwood from your coven than you would, say, Wren, considering you've agreed that my secret does not leave this room. So why don't you hear me out instead? And perhaps put that dagger away?" He glanced Ben's way. "I get that you could gut me about five different ways in as many seconds. I'm a talker, not a fighter."

"I think we should let him speak," I suggested, tugging on the hem of Ben's shirt until he reluctantly sat and rested the weapon across his lap instead.

Roe crossed her arms. "I'll give you five minutes," she muttered.

"Five minutes? Guess I'll speak quickly," he said with playful cheer. "I borrowed a librarian's likeness the other day and saw some of your training sessions in Moongrove Library. You're elbow-deep in something my sponsor would be keen to learn about."

"Who is your sponsor?" Willow asked quietly.

"The less you know, the—"

"Probably the Autumn Queen," Roe interrupted.

"See, you're smart. I knew I liked you. But I don't work for her specifically," he continued on without missing a beat. "I want in on your intelligence. There is a list of Garroway's known associates? There was a confrontation with him and this mysterious young man who looks so much like Ben?"

Ben scowled. "Careful. I could just throw this dagger at you."

"How unfortunate for me! But more so for you. If you share what you know with me, I wouldn't mind putting my skills to use for whatever you need."

"Absolutely no—"

"Ben, wait," I said quickly.

"What's the catch?" Roe asked skeptically.

"Could you help us find Garroway and Lucas again?" I asked, pointing toward Ben. "His brother?"

"I'm sure I *could*," the changeling answered. "Your information in exchange for finding two dangerous criminals. Those would be my terms. Alternatively, we can stop these formalities and be friends instead. I'd do a lot to stop having asinine conversations as Grant."

I opened my mouth but closed it again with a look of warning from Roe. "We'll have an answer for you soon," she said.

"Before our silent meal, I would hope?" He got to his feet, approaching her. Tall and slim, he could look into Roe's eyes without trouble, but I figured if there was a fight, she could knock him out with one good uppercut.

"Sure," she replied.

He flashed his teeth in a smile as he sized himself down to be human Grant again, leaning up to say close to her ear, "Great. I'll bring the potatoes." He sauntered out of the room, leaving her a little pink around the edges.

She finally selected a chair and sat heavily. "All right, I'll let Áine explain how bad that was."

"Mother Tree!" the faun squeaked once we found her as a group and took her to a relatively private location. That ended up being my room, where there was just enough room for the five of us. "You want to hear about the Autumn Court? Why?"

As it turned out, the changeling spy had gotten us to agree to a proper fae bargain. None of us could tell her the true intentions behind the question since she hadn't been in the room when the fake Grant had revealed himself.

"Just a sudden interest in history," Ben grumbled.

"*You* want to know about fae history?" Áine snorted. "I find that hard to believe."

"I could explain the court instead," my handbook said from its position hanging on the ceiling, pages swaying back and forth like a pendulum. "I'm, like, the authority on everything."

"No, no. All right, history lesson," Áine sighed. "The Autumn Court is rather new, in fae years. There are fae courts all over the place, and most are tiny and weak, but the biggest, strongest ones name themselves after concepts like, well, *Fall*. I've told you that NSU and New Salem took over the pocket dimension that used to be the Fall Court, right?

"I skipped telling you the bloody history of this place. Fall was at war with my home court, Spring, for hundreds of years. The red-haired bitch that leads their court was stealing away fae from everywhere between Salem and the Spring Court, which is located in Florida. By using her captives as sacrifices, she empowered the Fall Court to grow close to the massive pocket dimension it is today."

"For the record, this happened way before any of us were born," Roe put in.

"Yeah. Moongrove Library wasn't even here yet," Áine agreed with a nod. "This was entirely a fae versus fae conflict. Every pocket dimension created by a group of fae and dubbed a court is kept stable by a tree nurtured by the life force of every fae that swears allegiance to the court's ruler. It's the court's Mother Tree. It grows bigger and stronger with the number of fae, which in turn makes the pocket dimension larger and the ruler's magical power level higher.

"What most outsiders don't realize is that the Mother Tree also determines how many fae can be present at one time. There comes a time when the fae cannot have any more children and the Tree does not grow any further. The pocket dimension is complete at that point. The Fall Queen's way around that was not our modern solution—inviting other races to use their own magics to make expansion possible—but instead to force all of her captives to swear allegiance to the Fall Court before slitting their throats with iron at the base of Fall's Mother Tree."

Willow and I both gasped. "Oh, how horrible," she murmured.

"I know," Áine said, frowning. "This caused the Fall Court to grow and grow, supplying the Fall fae with the ability to continue reproducing past the natural numbers a court should reach. We... I mean, the Spring Court only won the war and stopped the sacrifices by doing the unthinkable. A Spring changeling infiltrated their court and burned their original Mother Tree, by then an ugly abomination left to grow with no pruning.

"Big swaths of the pocket dimension collapsed. Thousands of fae simply...ceased to exist." She gave a delicate shudder. "It's the downside of living in a pocket dimension, you know? Fae bend reality to stay apart from humans, but the magic is vulnerable if the Mother Tree is. Because of this, the Fall Court abandoned their remaining land and fled. Many more fell because Spring Court soldiers were waiting for them. Unfortunately for us, several still survived, including the Fall Queen, who rebranded herself the *Autumn* Queen and hid her people away in a new dimension we've never found. Witches took over the remnants of the Fall Court's lands and, over time, rebuilt it to the massive pocket dimension we're in right now.

"Before you go feeling sorry for them, Autumn Court fae have proven to be just as awful as they were when they were trying to eradicate my court. Kidnappings, sacrifices, and trickery abound. They seek to take this pocket dimension back because the new Mother Tree here is nearly as powerful as the one they originally lost. They're banned from returning, as the Autumn Queen has eternally schemed about conquering both NSU and New Salem like it's still the old ages. She wants to have a massive sacrifice session to make a new mega Fall Court. She might reach demigoddess status if allowed to connect to a Mother Tree that powerful."

"Clearly, she can never come here," Roe said, a little louder than conversation volume. She looked between the rest of us meaningfully.

"How is she kept from simply walking in?" I asked. Obviously, her spy hadn't been stopped.

Áine waved vaguely. "Fae magic. Any Autumn Court fae over a certain power level and anyone related by blood to the Autumn Queen are not permitted to cross the barrier unless expressly invited by the fae the new Mother Tree has bonded with."

I exchanged a glance with Ben. His expression was drawn, but he met my eyes and shook his head. "We'll find another way," he said under his breath. I nodded in agreement. Any more deals with an Autumn fae sounded remarkably dangerous.

17

BEN

"Couldn't you have invited our little friends earlier?" Phaeron asked while we watched Roe transform the front room's plain table into a proper Dumb Supper display. Lanie's cat, Jin, sat in the place of honor for the moment, accepting scratches behind her ears. "For a dinner where we can speak to each other, perhaps?" His tail whisked with some annoyance, but his gaze followed Cress as she went back and forth from the kitchen to retrieve plates and silverware.

"Maybe if they have enough fun, they'll come back," I suggested. I'd known damn well if I'd brought Cress around, he'd try to steal her away for a visit to the master bedroom. When I had a deadline marking the days in a burning path across my chest, I wasn't willing to share. But now that Garroway's unnatural magic was fading to a series of scars, I'd finally felt comfortable enough to invite her here.

He replied with a noncommittal hum. "Entertainment is the last thing on my mind," he said. I hoped he was focusing on the magic he'd have to do this evening to help us commune with the lost.

"Same, honestly. By the way, if Grant shows up, will you take an extra hard peek at his soul?" I asked. He raised a brow in my direction. "You know, just in case?"

"He's a verdant witch with no dark magic tainting his soul," he replied.

I opened my mouth to ask if he was sure about that when the words got stuck in my throat. I coughed into my fist instead. The limitations of the fae agreement I'd stumbled into chafed my nerves. The restrictions reminded me too much of Garroway's influence.

"Hmm. I'll take another look," he said.

Roe passed us on her way to the kitchen with food safety gloves on. "Thanks again for buying all of this on short notice," she said to Phaeron, who put on a charming smile and inclined his head.

The man had gotten a paycheck early due to his "unusual circumstances." The first thing he'd done with the money was buy the best versions of all the ingredients Roe had listed to make two dishes for everyone, a stir fry and beef bulgogi. When Roe had arrived, she'd sliced the meat and prepared the marinade, which had been resting in our fridge for a while now.

I'd made about a dozen recommendations for the rest of his paycheck, which he said he was going to save. Something told me he'd spend the rest of it on Cress if given the chance.

Cress had followed the redhead into the kitchen, quickly becoming a sous chef for everything Roe needed. That left Phaeron and me to welcome everyone that came to the door. The first arrival was little surprise, Áine bouncing into the room with a big plastic container with several layers of sweets in parchment paper.

"They're renewal cakes. My family makes them around this time every year," she explained. I reached over when she popped the top, mouth watering. Each little cake was decorated like tiny succulent gardens, some with fine vines and itty-bitty flowers for pops of color. The faun batted my hand away. "They're *very* sweet."

I smacked my lips. "Fine. I'll wait, just because you asked so nicely."

"The last thing you need right now is a ton of sugar," she said with a roll of her eyes.

Our next arrival was Geo, just starting to transform from gargoyle to man, with a plastic bag in hand. "I got them," he said.

"Is that Geo?" Roe called. "I need those sesame seeds!"

One benefit of not having wings, I guess, is that I didn't get picked to go to New Salem and retrieve the ingredient Phaeron had forgotten. When he went around the corner, he received excited praise from both women for how quick he'd been. I was a little jealous, but I didn't have much time for that as I greeted everyone who followed and got caught in the flow of casual conversation. The sun was high in the sky and we were observing Samhain in the light of day, just as NSU wanted.

"Don't keep us waiting for Wren. She's not coming," Heath said when he arrived.

I tried for an innocent tone as I closed the door behind him. "Trouble at home?"

He set his expression. "She's trying to get transferred to another coven again. I don't really blame her." I shrugged to myself. Roe wanted Bianca to join our coven, but I personally thought we should be removing "Grant" first, not Wren.

And speak of the fae, he came along too, holding a plate covered in tinfoil. "Potatoes, as promised," he said, far too cheerful about his tubers.

"Welcome, Grant," I said, then muttered under my breath, "If that's your real name."

He chuckled. "It's not. And this distrust is really rich, considering who you were."

I bared my teeth in a less than friendly smile. "You know much about that?"

"I've been asking around. By the way, the registrars are concerned that you haven't been by to specify your major and pick up your schedule, so I helped you out."

"You didn't," I practically growled.

"I didn't impersonate you. Who do you take me for?" he put a hand to his chest in offense. "I just told them to reach out to Cress. She's the one who can always find you."

"Thanks," I said with gritted teeth. I stepped aside for him to come in, missing the old, glaze-eyed Grant.

We'd decided that Roe would put this fae back in his place today. We weren't going to feed him information, not when it would get back to the Autumn Queen and endanger us all. But there wasn't much else we could do to chase him off, for now.

He went into the kitchen while the rest of us mingled for a while. Heath and Willow chatted about a couple classes they shared as new oceanic witches. Bianca and Áine were laughing and gossiping together. With Phaeron and Geo in a corner, putting their heads together about something—probably our upcoming visit to the local graveyard, defying every new rule NSU and Dr. Aurina wanted in place —I snuck a peek at the altar Roe had set up at the head of the table.

It was a simple display, with candles and autumn leaves propping up several images of a young woman.

"I wish I'd gotten a chance to meet you," I murmured. My gaze snagged on a picture of her with Cress, the two of them smiling in front of their dorm room full of unpacked boxes.

When Garroway first received information about Cress from Blaize Starsurge, it'd come with several candid photos of her. The only one where she'd been smiling was when she was alongside Lanie, the girl with the dark bob and a penchant for brightly colored clothes in each image here.

I felt...guilty. She must've been a great friend, judging by how much work Cress and Roe had put into honoring her memory. And it had been my brother who ruined that.

No. The Hungering Darkness had, and it was still at large. Still puppeting my little brother and plotting with Garroway. Now that the manor was gone, where were they?

"I think I'm being stupid, Lanie," I said under my breath, turning on my heel to go find Grant. The kitchen was a little too empty, with Cress alone chopping vegetables.

She turned, sniffling and red-eyed from fresh onions. "Have you seen Grant or Roe?" I asked.

She pointed down the hall. "They're having that chat," she said. That's what I figured, so I hoped I wasn't too late.

Roe was the one we'd chosen to turn Grant down since she under-stood the fae situation the best. The Autumn Queen somehow using us to return to power was obviously awful, but so was my brother's soul succumbing fully to the Hungering Darkness's evil. Every day, we crept closer to the moment it corrupted him or got bored with him and killed him. We needed help... *Lucas* needed help.

We could handle the fae situation another time. But when I found the two standing before the closed door to the master bedroom, they were in the midst of shaking hands.

"I knew you'd see reason," Grant was saying.

"Wait...what?" I looked between the two of them. Grant had his teeth bared in a victorious smile, while Roe's expression was vaguely irritated.

"Meet our new friend," she said, gesturing to him.

The wind whooshed right out of my sails. "You made a deal with him?" But *I* was about to make a deal with him in secret, and she was supposed to turn him down.

"For you, my services are now free." Grant smiled a little wider. "I just ask that you share your juiciest gossip, of course. Right after this meal, I'm off to tail your monsters."

He left Roe and me alone for a moment, and I turned to her for some kind of explanation. "I know," she muttered, refusing to meet my eye. "You're going to find this hard to believe, but I trust him. He swore on his true name that he's working against the Autumn Queen."

That was a pretty big deal, as far as I knew. Fae guarded their full names like treasure. It was a sign of trust and truth to tell someone else their name or to swear on it. "What's the catch?" I asked.

Her lips pressed into little white lines and she shook her head. "I'll share that when I'm good and ready. All you need to know is that I want us to give Grant a chance to be our friend. For all intents and purposes, he's a verdant witch in our coven who can get us any information we might dream of."

I narrowed my eyes, and she lifted her chin stubbornly. Well, she was entitled to her secrets. "I just hope the price wasn't too high," I said and left it at that.

We went our separate ways until supper was cooked, and we all served ourselves before sitting down. Roe rang a bell to signify the start of the ritual, and from then on, it was silence.

It was interesting to see who was comfortable here. Willow, Grant, and Geo seemed the least bothered, which didn't surprise me too much. Cress kept glancing at the head of the table, where a bit of everything had been served to the empty chair. Her gaze fell back to her plate more slowly each time, as if disappointed Lanie's spirit hadn't taken that seat.

The scrape of cutlery punctuated the meal, which Roe eventually concluded with a second ring of the bell. She exhaled loudly. "Okay, everyone, that's it," she said. Her usual lively voice seemed too loud for a moment, until the table broke into conversation again around her.

"That was good," Cress said, mostly to herself.

Áine passed around her little decorated cakes, which were just as sweet as promised. I admired mine for about half a second before biting it in half, tilting the second part up to save the slow ooze of caramel. "Wow. I'm going to need about ten of these," I said.

"Or the recipe," Cress added.

"That's a secret." The faun puffed her chest with pride. "I'll make them more if you guys want."

There was a circle of yeses around the table. By the time the sun was beginning to set, Áine bounced back to her dorm with an empty container. The rest of our friends trickled out until Cress was convincing Roe that she could handle helping us with the rest of the cleanup. "You've already done so much," she said, patting the redhead's hand. "The ritual was really nice. It was like Lanie was here with us."

"It was, huh." Roe smiled sadly. "Well, if you're sure..."

"See you tomorrow," Cress said, practically pushing her out the front door. They parted ways with a hug. Once the door was shut, she turned back to the three of us who remained.

Phaeron glanced toward the kitchen. "We may as well actually clean up. I need it to be full dark to sneak you off campus with my magic," he said.

She nodded and headed that way. "Tell me how this works again?"

We worked as a team on the simple task: Phaeron at the sink, Cress drying, and me putting various things away. Geo retrieved from the table and back, a thin excuse to let him pace with a troubled expression.

"The veil between the living and dead here on Earth is truly at its thinnest tonight," Phaeron began. "My magic can call to the souls of the recently deceased by asking for them by name. But you should be aware that it is always a *request*, and the dead sometimes do not answer, especially if they're comfortably resting in the next life."

Cress worried her bottom lip between her teeth. "So, there's a chance my maybe birth mother won't answer your call?"

"Indeed. However, if she does not answer, you could sacrifice some of your blood, and we can try again. In theory, I could boost your call to the other world, and if you two are truly related, she will answer. She may be angry to be summoned more forcefully, but it's practically a guarantee she will appear."

His yellow eyes flashed toward me. "The same goes for your mother, Ben."

I swallowed thickly and nodded, momentarily robbed for words. When Phaeron had shared what he was doing for Cress, I'd wanted in as well, if only to apologize to my late mother for believing some of Garroway's many lies for too long.

"Let's go," I said.

Luckily, NSU faculty housing was on the side of campus that wasn't *really* the campus, so we didn't have to climb any of the high walls that'd been erected to separate NSU from the rest of New Salem during the lockdown. They'd been lifted to make checkpoints to screen those coming and going. There was a checkpoint for the faculty and staff, but it was in the opposite direction of where we were heading.

As soon as the sun set, Phaeron shrouded us with his darkness magic, and the four of us walked to a cemetery a few miles away. Discreetly dressed campus police patrolled the outside edges, looking to either stop any trouble or enforce the curfew for any who attempted to follow certain Samhain rituals after dark.

Under the cover of magic, we slipped past a couple of policemen and continued walking. The cemetery was massive, as many supernaturals wanted to be laid to rest with their kin. This also meant the police presence couldn't cover every square inch of the space.

Phaeron led us to a section with headstones worn by time but freshly scrubbed clean for Samhain. "This is the place," he breathed. "Cress, Geo, go keep watch. Ben, you're first."

Geo and Cress conferred for a moment before going to stand far enough away to give us some privacy. She moved under the shadow of a spindly tree, while his gargoyle form's obsidian stone disappeared into the night except for the hulking outline of his bulky wings.

I turned to the dimensional, swallowing my nerves. "I just need to know her name," he said.

"Marie Evenstar. How long will I have with her?" I asked.

"Half an hour, maybe. It entirely depends on factors beyond our control." He gestured for me to stand back.

I watched from a safe distance as he wove a ball of shadows between his hands and stretched it out into a paper-thin rectangle. He spoke in a foreign tongue, rolling smooth words into a chant. When I started to tune out and let his voice become background noise, he abruptly said my mother's name and reached toward the shadowy shape.

The rectangle glittered like starlight, and he resumed his spell casting. He said her name three more times until there was no hint of shadow in front of him. As gently radiant as the moon, the original rectangle had become a gateway of sorts, and through it stepped a transparent woman with her silhouette outlined in gentle white.

"Is this her?" I asked quietly. The magic faltered for a moment as Phaeron grunted an affirmative. He had his head bowed, lips still moving.

The ghostly woman scrubbed her eyes and looked around in confusion. She was shorter than me, pleasantly rounded around the edges with some extra weight under a modest sweater and dark pants. Her blonde hair was piled up atop her head in a messy bun. I wondered if this was what she'd looked like when she'd passed away.

I could just *ask*, but my tongue felt paralyzed in my mouth. *How many people would give anything for a moment like this? And here you are, struck dumb,* I chastised myself.

"Um, hello," I said, drawing the ghost's attention. "I'm Ben... Benjamin. Your son."

She stepped closer, tilting her chin up to look at me. I held my breath. Being told about this woman all my life was one thing, but I didn't really know how she'd react seeing me as an adult. I definitely wasn't expecting her to lunge forward and to be embraced by the feeling of icy pins and needles. The sensation moved to the back of my neck, and I bent down just as she wanted.

"Ben!" Her teary, white-lined eyes met mine. "My not-so-little boy! Look at how you've grown. Why, it was just yesterday, you were..."

She released me just as suddenly, her brow crinkling. "You were just a baby. What happened? How...?" Looking down at herself, she inspected her arms and then felt the back of her head. Understanding dawned. "I...I was murdered, wasn't I?"

"Yes," I murmured.

Her shoulders shook with sobs. I reached out and held her as best I could, joining her after a few moments. There was a time where I thought I'd cried my last tear, unable or unwilling to give Garroway another drop of weakness from all the pain he'd inflicted. This was much like reopening an old wound, revisiting the horrors that monster had imposed on my family.

I got myself back together first, however, saying, "We don't have much time."

She wiped her cheeks with her sleeve. "Of course. It's so nice to see you, Ben. Where is Lucas?" she glanced around like she expected him to surprise her from behind the nearest bush.

"Uh. That's a long story," I said. "Did you know a vampire named Garroway?"

"Vampire? More like snake," she muttered.

That was definitely a yes, then. "Did you try to get a loan from him?"

Marie seemed to deflate with the question. "Well...yes. Your father's family left me out to dry because they thought I sabotaged his car for some insurance money. I loved him, Ben. His death was a terrible tragedy that followed the passing of my best friend, Eris Darkmore. She and I were business partners, but without Eris or Liam, your father, I was down a creek without a paddle, so to speak. The debts were piling up, and the bank would've kept your inheritance if I declared bankruptcy, so I sought other options and ended up getting in contact with Garroway."

"He heard you out, then refused to lend you anything, right?" I sighed.

Her lips twisted, and she shook her head. "No, much worse. He offered me millions to buy you and Lucas. Way more than I was asking for as a loan. It was disgusting, and I told him as much and left."

My free hand balled into a fist, the other still resting close to Marie's back. "Then he killed you," I sighed, "and took us anyway."

"What happened next?" she asked with some hesitation.

Aware of Phaeron starting to sweat a few yards away, I kept the recap of my life brief. Marie's anger was understated, her nostrils flared and face reddened by the time I was finished sharing what'd happened with Lucas and why he wasn't here. "I'm glad you're free, I'll say that much. You said you reached out to one of your aunts, though? Which one?"

"Jordan Evenstar. She seemed the most approachable," I said, not mentioning how I'd seen her image. We could be here for days if I needed to explain social media to her.

"Jordan's a good choice. She was still a kid when I passed, but she had a fine head on her shoulders. If she is still an honorable woman, she will be able to give you your inheritance. Now that I know that you're alive and of age, though, I'm going to share some of my power with you. This may hurt," she said.

We'd been so busy theorizing over Cress's ancestral magic that I hadn't considered what'd happen when I inherited mine. "I wasn't very strong in my magic, but my channeling skills were exceptional," she told me. "As a blood witch, you'll have use for it when you take other peoples' magic from their blood. After this, I will try to wake Liam in the next life and have him give you a piece of the Evenstar legacy as well."

"Thanks, Mom," I said, letting her take my hands in hers. Her outline was starting to fade, and I had the feeling our time together was coming to a close. "I'm going to use anything you give me to save Lucas. I'll do everything I can. I promise."

The tingling sensation over my palm faded. Looking down, I spotted a twinkling spark of celestial-yellow magic absorb into my skin. Despite the warning, it didn't hurt for a moment, just felt like another living person had curled their hand around mine.

"What was the inheritance?" I asked like an afterthought. She was fading faster, and I wasn't ready for her voice to become a memory.

"A fine tool," she replied. For a moment, I swear I felt her hand tighten on mine. "Goodbye for now. I will see you in your dreams, and you will know me from my memories. That is the beauty of ancestral magic."

My throat tightened. I didn't want dreams or memories. I wanted her here with me.

"And I have no doubt, Ben, that you will save your brother and bring him here next Samhain. You've grown into a strong young man... I'm so proud of you."

With that, she was gone. Phaeron breathed in a little harder, his eyes opening into two yellow beacons in the dark. I still grasped air, reaching for her like she'd still be there, before turning my face away. I had a new goal now, at least—to bring Lucas here, alive and whole, next year. That way, she'd remain proud of me.

18

PHAERON

"IF THERE'S TIME, there's one more person I'd like to speak to after Cress has her turn," Ben told me before slinking into the shadows to trade places with her.

I released a weary sigh. The process was so much more taxing for bringing back souls that'd been gone for longer than a year. Either that, or I simply didn't remember how difficult it was to use my magic this way.

While witches and most other supernatural creatures relied on reading each other's auras, my kind had always been more attuned to souls. I imagine any confident and powerful dimensional could call to souls like this. Delicious, sweet souls...

With a groan, I shook my head, clearing the stray thought. I called both Geo and Cress back to me. His obsidian expression showed understated dread, and she eyed me with her lower lip between her teeth. My fangs ached to be the one to nibble on that full lip next.

"Geo, you're next. Do I have your permission to speak with Morgana briefly?" I asked.

"You do."

Cress began to turn away. I caught her wrist with my tail while extending a tendril of darkness toward Geo. It took a few moments for it to push past the boundary of his stone skin and wrap around the crystalized heart beating in his chest. Geo simply froze where he stood, all signs of life leaving his quartz eyes.

I released Cress's arm when she tugged herself free. "I want you to hear this conversation, bright soul."

Her brow crinkled. "But...why? Wasn't she your wife?" she asked.

And that reaction was exactly why I'd asked. I worried that when she looked at me, she saw someone still mourning his losses. I wanted to break down another barrier between us. "I think you need to be here," was all I said.

"Well, all right," she mumbled.

I tugged on the tendril of shadow, which had wrapped around Morgana's soul. It flowed free from its cage of crystal and stone, taking shape just like any other soul with white-lined limbs and a transparent form. Unlike Marie Evenstar, though, Morgana was tethered back to Geo by several thick chains made of spell runes wrapped around her. If I severed them, she'd be free to cross to the afterlife, but otherwise, when I released her, she'd go right back to animating Geo.

When Morgana took full form, I struggled with my next breath. She looked just as I remembered her from that fateful day in Moongrove Library. Raven-dark hair back in a strict braid, face free of any cosmetics but still boasting full, kissable lips and a fan of naturally dark lashes around soft brown eyes. She wore what used to be considered a man's clothes, with a tucked-in tunic and tight pants hugging her shapely hips from which hung a librarian's handbook and a sheathed sword.

Even as a ghost, she exuded palpable power. "Hello, my love," she said with a knowing curve to her mouth. "You have freed yourself."

I dipped my chin a fraction. "I was released."

Cress, who'd looked ready to inch away at Morgana's greeting, glanced between the two of us at my chilly tone.

"You must have questions," the ghost said, going nearly as toneless as Geo in gargoyle form.

"That is why I've tried so urgently to speak with you. I lost two hundred years of my life because of your actions, Morgana. I woke to a world changed, with many believing *I* was what Endaeron had become. You abandoned me when you could've saved me." I stepped closer, leaning towards her spectral face. "Why?"

She held her ground, unflinching like she'd been in life. "I did what I had to," she said in a low tone. "I had no time to share that both you and Endaeron were in the stasis room. I painted instructions in my own blood to those who found my body, saying that the room was never to be opened again."

I released a bitter laugh. "Mortals forget a lot in two centuries."

"I thought you were lost." She spoke more gently. "Endaeron left a wound in your back. Do you remember?"

I tried to recall that fight, but the details were like sand, running right between my fingers. Unexplained gaps in my memories and awareness were no longer strange. I'd figured out they were the work of Endaeron but not how they connected us together, giving him some level of control over me. "No, I don't remember that," I answered.

She sighed, her shoulders falling. "After dealing me a mortal blow, he struck you from behind and sank his teeth either into your back or right above your skin. I've never heard you make such a hideous noise. While I can't see souls like you can..." She cast her gaze away from me. "I knew he must've taken a bite out of yours."

"What?" I breathed out.

"I knew that there was no coming back if he'd damaged your soul, so like I said...I did what I had to. I sealed you in with your brother so you could not transform into a monster too. There was no way I was going to allow any taint into your legacy." She reached out and clasped my hand between hers.

I looked down at her spectral hands leaving cold tingles over my skin. "That explains it all. *Everything*." I looked over my shoulder at my soul, which seemed fine. Someone else would need to study it for any faults. Morgana had saved me from becoming a second Hungering Darkness, but she may have just bought me time. Damage of this sort always allowed Myuna's corruption in.

And my brother, who'd consumed a part of my life force, had power over me because of it. He finally had what he always wanted—a way to drag me down to corruption and depravity with him. There was no way to undo it. We were irrevocably connected.

"You didn't betray me," I said through numb lips.

"In a way, I did, and I see why you would think it. You were the great love of my life, Phaeron. I didn't mean to hurt you."

I leaned back when she reached up for my face. Her huge revelation didn't change how I felt or the fact that she was merely a spirit now. "I know," I murmured. "But that life is over. You chose to become a gargoyle?"

She nodded in understanding and folded her hands over her middle. "I did." Turning, she admired Geo's frozen form. "Brave, loyal, and protective. Isn't he special?"

"He is," Cress agreed under her breath, catching both of our attentions.

"Who is this, Phaeron?" Morgana asked.

Cress smiled at me uncertainly but looked like she'd rather be anywhere else. Here came the moment I'd been practicing. The grandest gesture I could give her. "A bright soul, a beacon in the night. Cressida Rollins, the woman fate sent to free me." I caught her hand and encouraged her to step closer, face to face with the ghost. "Morgana, I wanted to introduce you before you went back to your rest."

"Your next True Light?" Morgana asked.

I smiled warmly down at the purple-haired woman. "If she will have me."

Cress's sudden blush hid within the blue tones of the deep night with a waning moon overhead. "I...this is unexpected. It's nice to meet you," she said, offering her hand to the ghost to shake, then dropping it after they attempted to make physical contact. "Especially after I've heard so much about you."

"Hopefully none of the more boring events." Morgana laughed. "Phaeron, give me a moment with her, hmm? Go cover your pointy ears over there." She gestured to a patch of darkness.

I narrowed my eyes, but I'd gotten my closure with Morgana. I gave the two of them a moment and let myself brood on the problem of my soul in the meantime.

CRESS

The last thing I expected this night was to meet *the* Morgana Void-binder, demigoddess and first librarian witch. The soul that gave Geo life was a completely different person than him. Despite the sadness that's shown over her expression when Phaeron treated her with chilly distance, she seemed to come from the gargoyle's heart content and well-rested.

"Is that your handbook?" she asked, pointing to the book I kept on my belt. I had the clasp securely locked to keep it from babbling and flapping around, especially while we were sneaking out here. When I nodded, she asked to see it.

"It's a little special," I warned. Keeping a firm hand on its spine, I unclasped it and held it to my face. "Shhhhhhh."

"Quiet, got it," it said just as loud as always.

"You'll have to hold it steady," Morgana said. She laid her transparent hands on the book's cover, closing her eyes in concentration.

Could souls do magic like this? I watched avidly, seeing her faded purple aura ebb and flow around the book like the flow of the tide. Its pages flickered, and it whispered in my grasp, "That tickles."

"There, I hope that takes. I tried to give it more of what I know," she said, releasing the book.

It immediately started flapping laps around our heads in apparent distress. "So. Much. Knowledge!"

She chuckled. "I don't intend to come out of my gargoyle's body again. I lived my life, and it feels...odd, to say the least, to be myself again. So, while we have this moment, let's talk about Phaeron."

My amusement with the book's antics faded to nerves. "Oh, yeah? What about him?"

He'd looked at me with such longing. *If she will have me.* It was a surprise, but not an unwelcome one.

I might not know what a True Light was, but the context was pretty obvious. I really was fated to three men, and Phaeron was the one I'd tiptoed around the most. This woman was part of the reason—I'd thought he'd need some time to come to terms with her passing.

But the other part, well... Ben had called it. Phaeron was tall, dark, and sometimes scary. What Morgana had revealed about his soul was the most terrifying thing about him, though.

"You are his only hope of surviving what his brother has done to him without succumbing to Myuna's corruption. I don't know the extent of your relationship, other than it seems quite new." Morgana reached out for me, and I flinched at the cold touch of her spectral hand. I turned over the wrist she'd brushed, revealing Phaeron's mark of protection. "Just know that he needs you more than he will ever admit to. You'll have to contend with his princely pride and certain old-fashioned notions of who protects whom in the relationship."

"Can I save him? From what his brother did?" I asked, tracing the outline of the mark. Phaeron stirred from where he stood, glancing back at us. I put my palm up to signal that I wasn't calling to him, and he seemed to nod.

"I don't know, but you should consider it your duty to try. To remind him that he's in control and still the same noble gentleman he's always been." Her determined gaze met mine. "And should he fall, it is then your duty to do what you have to. Can you promise me that you will?"

"I can. I will try, at least," I said.

"Good. Now…" She gestured for me to lean forward and began to whisper in my ear. Cheeks heating, I nodded along, trying to memorize all the naughty secrets she shared about Phaeron. We said our goodbyes when she was done, and I pressed on the mark again, fascinated that I didn't need to do anything else to get his attention.

I walked a few paces away to give them a chance to say goodbye without me there as a third wheel. It wasn't long before he released her from her magic and her form dissolved, melting back into Geo.

I crept back to his side, tempted to run my hand up his tail. Morgana had mentioned that it was sensitive and tended to wrap around things he liked, but I wasn't sure if he'd want an intimate touch right now. He turned his attention toward me, inscrutable in the dark.

"Are you all right?" I murmured.

"I'm not sure how to answer that question, bright soul," he sighed.

So, *no*.

He leaned down, and I caught a better glimpse of his expression. His otherworldly features were colored with longing, his topaz eyes fixed on my lips. Yet when we were nearly touching foreheads, my breath caught in my chest, he paused with the sharp tip of one claw tilting my chin up.

The self-control was masterful. His desire was obvious, yet let me be the one to cup his face, drawing him into a kiss. A proper one, not stolen in a moment of danger. I gasped when he nipped my bottom lip, and he used it as an invitation to deepen the meeting of our mouths. He kissed like a man starved, ravenous for the taste of me. His fingers tunneled into my hair, pulling just right to make my knees weaken.

I was panting for breath when Geo came awake with a sudden scrape of rock. He startled me off Phaeron, whose pupils narrowed to irritated slits as the gargoyle caught on to what he'd woken to, and turned away with a huff.

"We don't have all night," he said. His voice was as rough as when he'd first awoken, like his vocal cords had something grinding within them. He went to stand guard at his original post.

Phaeron began to chuckle, which turned to full-fledged laughter that he muffled behind a hand. "I swear, we're going to have to share you together at this rate," he snorted.

With him adjusting the bulge in his pants, I had a feeling what kind of *sharing* he was suggesting and nibbled on my bottom lip. I wasn't entirely opposed to the idea.

He turned away from me with a low groan, starting to weave up a coil of shadow magic. "Unfortunately, he's right. You have two souls to visit with. Shall we call Lanie first?"

That effectively dropped a bucket of cold water on my arousal, and I swallowed thickly. "Yeah, her first," I agreed.

I whistled quietly into the gloom, signaling to Jin, who emerged like a shadow and brushed against my ankle. She'd followed us at her own speed from Phaeron and Ben's home. Cats had an uncanny way to notice things that people didn't, so I hadn't been surprised when Jin told my familiars that she wanted to come say goodbye to Lanie too.

We watched him create a doorway with his magic, which turned into a gently glowing portal to the afterlife when he called Lanie's name. She emerged, a petite figure with a dark bob and a navy blue hooded jacket.

"I thought this might happen," she said. Like she'd predicted my reaction too, she opened her arms before I was in motion, and I hugged...cold, static-filled air.

"Lanie. It's really you," I said.

"It is. Thank you for the meal, by the way. I heard everything you all were saying about me. On the other side of the world, my family remembered me too. I've never felt so loved." Her smile crinkled the skin around her eyes, just as kind as I remembered. "If you've called to ask for more advice, I'm afraid I gave you everything I know."

I sniffed, shaking my head. "No, I just wanted to talk to you again. To say thank you for everything you've done. Jin's here, too." I gestured to the black cat who'd moved forward, her silky fur glossy in her former witch's ghostly light.

"Goodness, you're welcome. I would do it again if I had to." Lanie knelt and reached out for Jin, who mewed quietly when she tapped her forehead through the ghost's hand. "Have you accepted Cress as your new witch?"

Jin mrrowed something back.

"It would be okay if you did. I know she will take great care of you. Hasn't she already? I just want you to be happy, Jin, no matter what you choose for yourself. I love you," Lanie said to the cat gently.

With a snort, the cat stood, saying one last thing to Lanie before going back to sitting by my feet. The ghost stood, addressing me again. "I've been resting since...the moment things ended. The next life isn't so bad. You'll see it for yourself one day."

"One day," I echoed. "There's so much I want to tell you. I haven't avenged you yet, but I'm well on the way."

"Answer a question for me first. Are you on the road to happiness?"

"Well...yes, I think so."

I realized that was all she needed to hear. She retreated back a step, toward the doorway where she'd come from. "Then I am content to rest. I am happy for you, Cress, and glad you're not wasting the chance I gave you. It's time you let me go."

A single stinging tear made its way down my cheek. Of course she wanted to sleep, like she'd earned. I couldn't just bring her back to listen to all my problems and deliver keen advice. "You're right, I'm sorry. I just wanted to make sure you knew how much I appreciate what you did."

She nodded. "I know. Of course I know. I saw greatness in your future, by the side of three men who adore you. Just consider it this way —I'm keeping your spot in the afterlife warm for when you're old and weary. Don't come any sooner than that, okay?"

"Okay," I said, fighting the emotions that wanted me to start bawling. I'd gotten more than most, a chance to say a proper goodbye.

"Bye for now. Share my love with Roe and the rest. Oh! And don't forget you have my mother's number if you ever need real help," she said. She soon faded, and the doorway closed.

Phaeron's chanting ceased. For a moment, his eyelids lifted halfway, fatigue weighing his bearing. "I can see that was hard, bright soul," he murmured. "Would you like a break, or shall I start trying to call your mother?"

"Maybe birth mother," I corrected. "I...I should be okay." He really needed to call Eris Darkmore before I lost my nerve or let my doubts sink in. How would a spirit know I was her daughter or not anyway?

With a grounding sigh, Phaeron began his chant again and made a new doorway. This one remained dark, no matter how much he spoke to it. He stopped and crooked his finger at me, which turned into a talon of shadowy darkness. "She does not answer my call. Let's see if your blood will help."

I offered my non-dominant hand and flinched as his claw turned toward my skin. "How much of that are you going to need?" I asked.

He pricked the pad of my middle finger, squeezing a few drops on the ground around the darkened portal. "About that much. Repeat after me so you are the one calling to her," he said.

Presumably, he translated his dimensional language into Latin, as I recognized some of the words to the spell now. If this worked, it would be the most telltale sign that I really was related to this woman. I'd repeated the spell three times before the doorway started to twinkle with magic.

"She's coming," he said with a low hiss. "Keep your distance." That was easy to do when he was holding my hips, taking up the chant in his old home's language when the portal seemed to tremble with the incoming arrival.

Eris didn't so much emerge as explode through the barrier between worlds with a scattering of golden rays and a roar of power about her. "Who dares disturb my slumber?" she full-lung shouted.

I winced. The campus police were definitely going to come running at such a loud disturbance. "I do!" I practically felt timid under the steely stare of this ghost. My mother, summoned by my blood and call.

She smoothed the sides of her dress, an elegant black evening gown with a low shimmer from her ghostly outline. "Well, what do you want?" she prompted.

I cleared my throat, standing a little straighter. I didn't want to make an even worse impression on my birth mother. Gently pulling Phaeron's hands off me, I stepped forward to get a better look at her. She'd apparently died right before attending a function of some sort, as she wore a full face of makeup that gave her honey-colored eyes a sultry angle. Her hair, the same shade of dark brown as mine without the dye, was styled into a full head of ringlets draped carefully around her shoulders.

A soft voice squeaked somewhere around my feet, but I paid it little mind.

"You're my mother," was about all I said before Ben's shouts tipped me off to a disturbance. I reached for my sword, drawing it and casting Lux to make it glow in one practiced movement.

Phaeron's attention shifted, his chanting fading alongside the image of my mother and the otherworldly portal behind her. He stumbled, panting with fatigue.

Leaping over Ben was a white figure, but not a ghost. The Hungering Darkness howled as it swung its foot-long talons down to strike at my chest. I caught those talons with the edge of my sword, sending blood everywhere when it cut into its hand. The monster flinched away from me.

"Such a delicious feast of souls you've called tonight. Did you do that for me?" It tilted its head.

"Oh, fuck," I whispered.

Lucas's features were swallowed up by white shadow, replaced by a wolf's maw lined with jagged canines and topped by two forward-facing horns. It traced a healing rune in his blood over its split hand before looking over my shoulder.

"I *told* you," that soft voice said. I glanced down in disbelief for a split second at Jin arching her back and hissing. Otherwise occupied, I hadn't felt the familiar bond slide into place between us, but Jin had taken Lanie's blessing to heart.

Behind me, I heard Phaeron drop to the ground, his unsheathed swords clattering away from him. *Fuck!* I imagined him clawing at his face but couldn't take my gaze away from his brother.

I reached out to the one trick I had up my sleeve, Jin, asking to borrow from her. I needed her reflexes, but that wasn't what filled me a split second later. My hand clenched around the sword, and I jabbed and slashed at the Hungering Darkness, taking it by surprise with a sudden burst of ferocity courtesy of the witch's cat it had wronged. I slashed its shirt and dug the point of my blade in its side while side-stepping a couple swipes of its claws, feeling invincible for the few seconds my connection with Jin was active.

The moment it faded, I moved my sword in a new pattern and shifted to a defensive posture, casting Refracto with the spell word under my breath. Phaeron himself had taught me that only baby witches shouted their spells like Roe and I had done in our last fight with the Hungering Darkness. The shield Refracto produced would stay in place while I had my sword held at the right angle.

A silver blur flashed in the dark and caught the Hungering Darkness with a jerk and howl. "Hey, ugly!" Ben shouted.

"I'll deal with you in a minute," the monster said. Its next strike caught my shield, but unlike its weaker cousin spell, Repello, this barrier pushed back hard, throwing its arm wide and taking its balance with it.

I felt the impact through my sword, vibrating through my arm, but managed to keep it upright. I just had to bide my time, and my three men would help me fight him on more equal grounds.

"New tricks, little witch? How qua—"

A quartz spike grazed his forehead, exposing bone as it also blew off the shadowy mask over its puppet's face. I couldn't help a shocked shout at the grotesque sight. Had Geo aimed a little to the right, he would've ended Lucas's life right there.

While he stumbled backward, I risked letting down my shield and turning to Phaeron. The tendons stood out on his neck as he resisted the white fire starting to claim the shadows over his arm. I touched my fingertips to his mark of protection, calling his name. Clarity returned to his expression, which dropped to horror as my body jerked.

I looked down at the points of three white talons emerging from my torso. It didn't hurt until he ripped them back out the way they came.

19
GEO

CRESS HIT THE GROUND, her body rolling with her momentum. There was no movement for a moment, like we all held our breath. My gaze flashed from her to the Hungering Darkness, who started to grin in apparent victory and...I saw red.

Even within my gargoyle form, my stone heated with my mounting fury. That creature had hurt Cress, and for that, it would pay with its very existence. Any quartz I still had in my body was rerouted to form a club that I removed from my palm and the hollow pocket within my arm.

"Stand back," I barked at Ben, who stood in my way. His brother's face turned my way, half of it stained with blood and gore from my initial strike. The monster within him put up its fists. Sidestepping the heavy swing of my weapon, he hammered my chest with punches.

I didn't feel them at all. No matter how augmented with shadows, no matter how quickly it healed the fractures it had to be giving its host's finger bones, I was beyond any kind of pain. I'd drag its sorry shred of a soul back to Moongrove Library myself and stand guard over its stasis room for eternity.

First, I'd tenderize its chosen body until it couldn't continue to regenerate from every blow. My next swing caught its shoulder, knocking it to the ground. It barely rolled away from the overhand strike of my club.

"She's not dead yet, Morgana. If you act quickly, you might still save her," it taunted as it stood. Extending its blood-soaked talons, it lunged at me.

There was a pulse from within my chest, my recently stirred patron's soul speaking with me. "I am not Morgana, I am Geo, animated and given new life from her death." I caught its talons with my club, which began to crack from the pressure of being between us. "Killing you would bring her soul great pleasure, however."

"Hah! That's impossible," it said, baring crimson-stained teeth in a rictus grin. "You cannot kill that which has no body."

Ben attacked it from behind again, this time reaching around and burying a dagger to the hilt in its lung. "Shut the fuck up," he said. He hooked an arm around its neck and arched its spine while I jabbed its solar plexus, shattering my weapon in the process. "Quick, bind his wrists!"

I had no more quartz to form manacles, so I grabbed it with my stone hands instead. The Hungering Darkness caught its breath and snarled, struggling between the two of us. "If you value your brother's life, you would let me go," it hissed once it caught its breath.

Ben froze, paling. It was the opening it needed to slam its skull into his chin and knock him off its back. Thrashing out of my hold, it reduced to a white wisp before either of us could grab it again.

Ben picked up the dagger that'd dropped when the Hungering Darkness went incorporeal and slammed it into the ground point-first with a vicious curse. I busied myself picking up the pieces of my quartz, absorbing them back into my body, and looking around for Cress. The only sign of her was a patch of bloodied grass where she'd fallen.

"Phaeron said he was taking her to Moongrove Library," Ben explained.

I touched my fingertips to my forehead, snarling like an animal. "There's a perfectly good medical center where you were seen—"

"He said he was taking her to the powercore. Do you know where that is?" he interrupted.

"Yes."

"Let's go, Geo."

Were I in my human form, I might marvel over how this may be the first time I'd seen Ben fully serious. Maybe I would later, when I had Cress back in my arms. I didn't want to consider what would happen if Phaeron made the wrong judgment call and took her to bleed out on an unforgiving stone floor.

Ben startled more than me when the glare of flashlights approached. One focused directly on his face. "NSU campus police! Freeze!" a man shouted.

"Wow, they are truly worthless," Ben muttered.

Definitely. We could call the dead and fight a dimensional monster without them finding us. Now that all the danger had passed, of course they arrived.

"Geo? A lift? Any time now."

I didn't feel it, but Ben had grabbed one of my stone wings and rattled it. I shook him off and folded my arms around him. When I'd flown Cress, it'd been intimate to have her pressed flush against me, but that same sensation was uncomfortable for both of us as I surged into the air with Ben in tow.

"I didn't realize you could fly so well," Ben commented once I got up to speed, taking him on a relatively smooth ride straight toward Moon-grove Library.

"Guess I'm full of surprises," I rumbled.

"No more of those tonight. Cress had better be all right, or I'll burn the library down."

Another thing we agreed on. I took on speed to get us there as quickly as possible.

CRESS

The darkness moved in to sweep me away on feather-soft wings. I hung there, suspended and wondering if I'd slid into the afterlife to rest despite my promise to Lanie. It was my fault; I'd broken one of the first rules of combat. *Never turn your back to an enemy.*

Phaeron would be so disappointed in me. We'd drilled the basics over and over until I could slip into basic combat stances and recite his rules in my sleep.

The first thing I became aware of was his voice, panicked. "Braza!"

I cracked my eyes open, boneless and woozy. A familiar ceiling swam into focus as I thought, *That's not my name.* The purple glow of the library's powercore washed over everything except for the ethereal white glow of the ghost suddenly standing beside my head.

"Look at me, Luna," Eris commanded. I tilted my head toward her shiny heels, recognizing that could've been my name in another life. "You cannot die. Do you understand me?"

A laugh bubbled in my throat, along with a stream of blood that escaped the side of my lips. I was definitely dying to be hallucinating my mother's ghost. Gentle hands started to lift me.

"Stay with me, bright soul. Just a little more," Phaeron soothed. He supported me against his strong chest, my limp body swaying in his hold with each step we took upward toward the luminescent powercore.

Then he leapt straight into it. The tingles from touching its surface were all over my body, probing my injury, surging into the gaps. Needles of pain erupted over each inch of my skin, and I knew no more.

I knew the passing of time by the voices that came and went.

Phaeron was always there, as was a woman's voice that seemed like one I should know. Ben and Geo were around, too, but never too close. Strangely, my birth mother's presence also seemed steady. They blended to a blur, no words distinct amongst a melody of fear, pain, and anger.

I came to full awareness with the gentle pressure of a cool washcloth passing over my hot forehead. "She's not ready for that kind of power." Phaeron's smooth tone was soft, like he was cautious of waking me.

"It is her birthright. She will be receiving it soon anyway," my mother answered.

"She took the librarian affinity. Have you considered what will happen to her if you blast her with the might of your celestial magic?"

"She can handle it!"

"No, Eris, she cannot," said a third presence, the one that felt familiar. "She is still an inexperienced witch with her chosen affinity. Her soul blazes with the potential of the Darkmore line, but she will be unable to express any celestial magic from her body. The two magics are incompatible."

"Well, what do you suggest?" Eris demanded. "The Darkmore line stretches back centuries, and she is the sole recipient of the whole bloodline's pure celestial hereditary magic. Why was she ever permitted to take the librarian affinity in the first place?"

"It was her choice," the other woman replied.

"Can you not take it back?"

"It would bring her soul needless trauma. She would never be the same. Affinities are considered lifelong choices for a reason."

"She's awake," Phaeron said. He helped me sit upright, propping up my back with what felt like several pillows. I peeled my eyelids open slowly to a blurry world, my other senses slow to return.

I'd been moved into a bed of some sort. Everything was shaded with purple and black, and when I tipped my head up, I realized the dome of the powercore shimmered overhead. We were *inside* it, which I hadn't known was possible.

Phaeron pressed the cool lip of a glass into my lips, feeding me slow sips of water. "How are you feeling?" he murmured.

"Confused," I replied, coughing from a scratchy throat. He gave me more water, raising a brow slightly at my answer.

I peeled back an amethyst-toned sheet, revealing the clothes I'd been attacked in sporting three new rips. The skin underneath was puckered with new, pink scars.

"You are fortunate, brightest of souls. Phaeron got you here just in time."

I turned my head to pinpoint the speaker. There was a couch a few feet away on this stone platform, and on it sat the ghost of my mother and a dimensional woman formed of the same purple and black magic as the powercore.

I shifted my attention back to Phaeron, my expression begging for some kind of explanation. He sighed and helped me sit back, his fingertips drawing some of the hair out of my face. I recognized the feeling on my skin. How long had he been here? The ghost of his touch lingered in my memory. His roughened fingertips had cupped my face what must've been dozens of times, his concerned tones registering in my mind where his words did not.

He was also still dressed in the same clothes as he'd been wearing on Samhain, and purplish shadows lingered in the hollows of his eyes. It looked like he hadn't left my side. "Braza healed you from the inside out with a surge of magic. You were punctured in some vital places and bleeding internally—had I taken you anywhere else, the outcome would've been much different," he said.

"Who?" I asked weakly.

"Me, dear girl," the other dimensional said in that too-familiar voice. "The powercore of Moongrove Library."

My mind flooded with dozens of questions. Well, Phaeron had referred to the powercore as a person, as a *she*, before but hadn't elaborated. "I didn't realize you were a person," I mumbled.

She laughed to herself. "*Was* a person. I'm only a bit more alive than your mother here. I'll let Phaeron explain the whole story some other time. We have other news."

Phaeron cleared his throat, shaking his head slightly.

"I'm glad you're okay, Luna," Eris said. "Now we can talk about your magic."

"I think that can wait," Phaeron put in pointedly.

She threw her hands up in frustration. "First you strand me here, and now you won't let me fulfill my purpose."

"Again, I apologize for the timing. I will attempt to reopen a portal back to the afterlife for you as soon as—"

"Oh no, it is far too late for that. Not after everything I've learned," Eris burst in, waving a delicate wrist. "My daughter obviously needs my guidance. More than I could've given her with a brief visit on Samhain night. I think I'll stay."

"Great, now we're haunted," he said under his breath.

I squeezed his hand, finding it nestled in the covers over my hip, and laced our fingers together, hoping to ground him at least a little like how he was keeping me steady in this surreal situation. "Let's start over, shall we?" I suggested. "Hello, uh, Mother. I'm Cressida Rollins, your daughter."

"Hello...Cressida." She made a face like she'd had to swallow something bitter with the name. "Let me tell you a little about myself. I am Eris Darkmore, formerly a celestial witch of renown and a contender for the fourth seat of the Crown Coven. By day, I was a professor in the Mystic Collegium, where witches and other supernaturals of all kinds go to study magic for their masters and doctorate degrees. In my spare time, I helped my best friend run a successful business reading star charts for newborns."

It felt a little like she was reading a resume to me, but I understood. This was awkward. What did a ghostly mother say to her grown child who'd never really known her? "Did you have any hobbies?" I ventured.

Finally, her ruby red lips lifted into a subdued smile. "I enjoyed making art."

I seized that, learning that she was something of a painter in her free time, which she had very little of. Phaeron excused himself to let us talk, and Braza left by transferring herself into the sphere of magic that surrounded my mother and me.

I got the impression that my birth mother was something of a career workaholic with a long list of accomplishments. The Mystic Collegium was a blip in my mind, a place that existed but one I had never aspired to go to before. Eris not only had a doctorate in celestial witchery, she'd out-competed hundreds to become a professor there. No wonder she'd told me about that first. She'd been highly proud of it.

I told her about my life. How I'd been adopted by a kind nurse who'd been Mom in her place, and a little about Carly, as close as a sister. I felt a twist of sadness—I hadn't spoken with either of them in ages. I'd need to fix that. Once I was finished, I asked, "Are you aware of how it all ended?"

Eris frowned. "I remember being taken by surprise in my own home by a blood witch. And flames."

I took a deep breath. "That was an assassin. Blaize Starsurge paid to have all of us killed that night." I wasn't expecting the surge of power from her ghost. Her aura blinded me with rays of light, leaving me to blink rapidly to clear away the spots in my vision.

"That lowlife snake in the grass." She bared her teeth in a disgusted sneer.

"That's not all," I sighed. I shared the rest, that he'd prompted Garroway to send another assassin after me when he became aware that I'd survived the tragedy. As I recapped, I noticed Braza taking form against the edge of the platform, waiting with her hands folded over her middle.

"Hate to interrupt," Braza interjected. "But I've had my librarians do a bit of research, and I think I know how you should proceed with the transfer of hereditary power."

Eris jumped to her feet. "Tell me! My daughter has a man to smite."

The powercore leaned away from the force of her shout. "Ah, indeed. It's not quite as effective as her inheriting her family line's magic directly," she said in a tone of warning.

When she held out her hand, my handbook came flying over, its spine landing in her palm. It strained against the clasp over its pages, making, "Mmf!" noises as it struggled to put in its two cents.

"I suggest you augment her librarian witch's handbook. It is bound to serve her for life." Braza stroked down its spine to make it relax in her hold. "With suitable channeling ability, she will be able to tap into the magic you and the rest of your ancestors have left for her."

Eris looked skeptical. "Do you know your power level yet?" she asked me.

I shook my head. I was too new of a witch for anyone to put me through the tests to see what my power level was out of fear of hurting me.

"I think it sounds like a good idea, if it's possible," I said.

"It should be. The book is connected to you by magic, thus a viable object to turn into an artifact. There's one downside, though. This basically restarts the Darkmore bloodline," Braza said. Eris's expression twisted with distaste. "It cannot be undone, and any children of yours will have nothing to inherit until you pass the book along. You also won't have any dreams made from memories of your ancestors."

I turned to my mother, hoping she'd understand. "It's better than the alternative. This way, I can actually use what you give me."

"If that's your wish," she sighed. "Before I start the process—and lose the energy to be semi-corporeal to you—about Blaize Starsurge. You said you have an idea of how to ruin him?"

I wet my lips to keep from grinning. She cackled as I outlined what I was thinking, giving pointers along the way. Since she understood the system better than me, she explained and adjusted a few parts to a more realistic course. With her help, Crown Starsurge would be on trial by December break.

20
CRESS

The Librarian Witch's Handbook flew in drunken zigzags just above my head. Granted, I wasn't doing much better. My mother's ghost had disappeared for now, all the power she'd gone on about condensed into the brilliant star of magic she'd shoved into my book.

After exiting Braza's glowing chamber with her assistance, I'd nearly acquainted myself with the ground at the bottom step of the powercore's pedestal. It was a good thing Geo stood there, waiting in his human form. He lunged and caught me in the nick of time.

"Cress," he said with a long sigh and pulled me to his strong chest. He rested his chin atop my crown, rocking gently with me in his arms. "I was so worried."

"Sorry."

"Don't be. You're okay now?" He didn't move to look for himself.

For someone recovering from at least three punctures through the chest, I felt remarkably well, actually. "Just a little weak."

He shook his head. "You've been unconscious for three days after losing a great deal of blood. It's amazing you're on your feet at all."

"Wow," I said before reality really set in. "My friends! And classes."

Geo cleared his throat, withdrawing my phone from his pocket. "Ben and I have made sure they know what's going on." At this point, the device was basically his, but I was grateful he'd kept everyone from panicking. "The college also tried to contact you."

An icy feeling doused its way down my spine. "What do you mean?"

"Mmm. Don't worry about it right now," he said, handing over my phone. He also offered a bundle of fabric he'd been holding in his other hand. One of my shirts.

I pulled off the ruined one before he had a chance to turn around. His quicksilver eyes widened. Though I was hardly at my best right now, I still lifted my chest as I practically felt his gaze trace a path over my cleavage. It was like my new scars were invisible for as little attention he paid them.

"You can touch if you want." I crooked a finger to invite him closer. Any new wobbliness in my knees could be attributed to the desire that twisted his expression. He didn't hesitate to cup my chest with his broad palms, exploring the silkiness of my bra and the soft squish of my breasts with an experimental squeeze.

I didn't know when it happened, but Geo was all man, no sign of his cool stone façade now. He freed a boob from its confines to roll in his hand, thumb circling the hardening nub and giving it an experimental pull. I stumbled forward into him from the sudden shock of pleasure, and he caught me for a second time.

"Perhaps we can continue this another time," he said, eyeing me with concern.

"Soon," I replied, meaning it.

With that agreed upon, he helped me into the clean shirt. The next thing I knew, he'd swept me up bridal style and was carrying me to the elevators despite my laughing protests.

He took me straight to one of the overnight rooms, where Ben, Phaeron, and Grant were chatting. The conversation died abruptly as their heads turned my way.

Ben stood, rushing over. "Cress!" He kissed me with relief, helping steady me after Geo finally put me down.

"Hey, Ben. Sorry for giving you a scare," I said, though I leaned past him to the changeling sitting in full view of all three of the men as his actual fae self. Now that was weird.

Grant waved enthusiastically. "Glad you're not dead."

"What's going on?" I asked, wary.

"I decided to reveal myself to your men. They're under the same agreement about my identity that you are," Grant said.

"I figured out that he was a changeling," Phaeron put in. "He hid it well."

"Yeah, that too. Now I get to tell the big guy the juiciest details." The changeling pointed to Phaeron. "He's basically your leader, you know."

"So, what are these 'juicy' details?" I asked with air quotes. I let Ben guide me to a chair and closed my eyes for a few moments to ward off a dizzy spell.

When I opened them again, I realized the men were staring at each other. "Fine, I'll tell her," Ben said, rolling his eyes. "Spy extraordinaire here thinks he's found evidence of Garroway. Meaning, he hasn't found the vampire, just linked a number of sudden kidnappings back to him."

"He's stealing more witch kids?" I asked, feeling sick at the idea of anyone else being put through the same childhood that Ben had to endure.

"No," Grant put in. "Adult witches. The fae courts and other supernatural cities are all on high alert because his people haven't struck in the same place twice. Any abductions caught on camera end with the abductees being taken away by teleport charm. And those are *very* pricy."

My hands curled into fists. "So he's building an army."

"I was just saying, Garroway carves the blood runes into his witches at age eleven. There has to be a reason for that," Ben said. He flipped a pen between his fingers with some agitation.

"Is this the moment I make it worse by telling you it's not just blood witches he's stealing?" Grant put in. "Assuming they can handle the blood rune, he's taking any witch with an affinity good in a fight. Mostly blood witches, but also guardians and a few witches who've already made a name for themselves with their weapons, like a trio of librarians and an augury witch known for being undefeated in the dueling circuits of the Night Court."

Anxiety made me want to scratch my skin all over. "But there's no sign of Garroway himself?"

"Not a single one. Don't you worry, though. I'm on the job." Grant winked. "By the way, you're in huge trouble with the college for breaking curfew and summoning spirits. Maybe you should use all this information to sweeten the pot with Dr. Aurina when she inevitably calls you in to yell at you."

That really wasn't helping my headspace right now. Geo and Phaeron shot him looks of censure. "Well, there goes my chance to ask her for a favor," I sighed.

"Oh, what might a freshman librarian witch want from the University President?" By the glimmer in the fae's orange eyes, I'd intrigued him.

"Don't worry about it yet." I got to my feet slowly. "I'm going to go shower. We won't get anything done by sitting around talking anyway."

IF I THOUGHT I was walking to my dorm room without all three of my men coming along, I was quite mistaken. Phaeron held my hand and also used his tail to help my balance if I ever faltered, while Ben lingered at my other side, and Geo walked behind us protectively. With them all supporting me, it was easy to think of them as "my men," even if the claim felt a little premature.

When we arrived at my dorm and I patted my pockets for my key, it was Ben who handed it over. "I fed your cats," he said.

"Thanks." I felt some tension between them, though. Glances were exchanged as I moved toward my destination. I'd only ever had them up here one at a time, after all. "Hey, guys. I appreciate you walking me this far, but I need some alone time." And honestly, I needed to figure a few things out on my own.

"I'll be here," Geo replied.

Ben shrugged, fitting his hands in his pockets. "Guess I'll keep trying to convince Phaeron to spend his money on some cool stuff." The dimensional rolled his eyes. I had the feeling this was an ongoing conversation. "See you for dinner?"

I confirmed it and took the stairs up to my dorm room slowly, breathing a sigh of relief when I was safely inside and greeting my familiars. Milo and Bella crowded the end of my bed, while Jin sat in a cat loaf in the center of the mattress on the far end of the dorm.

"I heard you were so brave," Milo said.

"And strong!" Bella pitched in.

"And a monster attacked you from behind." The boy cat sounded indignant.

"That's about right," I confirmed, giving them rubs at the same time before I went over and scooped up Jin.

She made a soft "hey now" in protest but settled in my lap when I sat cross-legged on my bed and put her there. I realized that was just her voice, a demure hush compared to Bella's squeak or Milo's purr.

"What you should also know is that Jin helped me a lot and let me borrow from her when I needed it most," I said.

She started to purr a bit. "It was nothing."

"What's wrong with the book?" Bella asked. While both of my other familiars seemed impressed for a moment, their attention had bounced up toward the ceiling, where my handbook was flying drunken zigzags in uncharacteristic silence.

I shrugged. "I'll check in with it in a minute." Until then, I had some messages to read. Dozens had been sent from my phone on my behalf, and I could tell from the texting style that the ones as short and to the point as possible were from Geo, while the ones sent in bursts of individual thoughts were Ben.

They'd comforted my friends individually, letting them know I was okay and spending some time in the library. Roe and Áine had the longest message logs to read, as they wanted to know why they weren't invited to participate and help guard. They'd been told the truth—we'd thought the Hungering Darkness was far away, like Garroway. How wrong we'd been.

"If I'd known it was possible, I'd want to say my final goodbyes to Lanie too." My heart hurt to read that from Roe. Phaeron had wanted to keep the group small, predicting that everyone would have a spirit they'd want to chat with, but I still owed Roe an apology.

There was also a new group chat, started by Roe. "Hey everyone, two things: 1—We need a coven name. We've been putting this off too long. And 2—The Ashbough family always hosts a giant Thanksgiving celebration, and I wanted to invite you all to come. We're going to be in the Crystal Court, which is in Tennessee. Portal service available!"

Ben had made it clear that he was texting from my phone and said he'd go if I went. Presumably, he'd also saved the numbers of Grant, Wren, and Heath, as their names appeared with their messages over the course of the chat.

I read the resulting argument over our coven name with a relieved smile, glad I wasn't a part of it. From silly to serious to far too edgy, none of the names put forward had much agreement. We had to come up with something that didn't overlap with the name of another registered coven as well, which added to the complication. Roe had to shelve the discussion and asked for us to think on it.

When I saw who was, and who wasn't, going to this Thanksgiving get together, I tapped the message bubble and sent, "This is Cress now. Are ordinary people allowed?" My adopted mother and sister knew about supernaturals because of me. I'd love to see them again over the week-long break coming up, and if they could meet my friends too, all the better.

I'd questioned whether or not witches celebrated Thanksgiving, especially after experiencing Mabon. The week off was built into the college schedule no matter what, and it seemed Roe couldn't resist any event that brought us together.

Jin's ear tilted back lazily as my phone buzzed with several incoming messages. Roe responded in the chat but also messaged me directly asking if I was all right. While I was halfway through a reply, both an apology and an explanation of why I wanted to take my human family to her Thanksgiving get-together, Wren's name and part of a message flashed across the top of the screen.

My thumbs halted. That was a direct text, not one to the group chat. I backed out of my current text to see what she wanted.

It was the first message between us. "I have something important to ask you. Can you take a call right now?" she'd texted.

My heart flipped within my chest at the question. I never expected Wren of all people would want to talk to me over the phone, but when I texted back a yes, my device started ringing nearly immediately.

"Hi, Wren," I answered.

"Hey." Her sigh breezed over the receiver. I heard her muffled voice whispering to someone else, and then the steadier blowing of wind before she must've cupped her hand over her phone outside. "Okay, I'm alone."

"What did you want to ask?" Though it sounded like her claws were sheathed right now, that could change in a heartbeat.

"Um, yeah. How to even start... I feel like I'm missing something and maybe you know what it is."

Oh, she had no idea how big of a "something" she was missing. I petted Jin idly and waited for her to get her words straight.

"I know we're not on, like, the best of terms. But it sounded like Roe was going to tell me something the last time our coven met, and you stopped her. She then told me to ask my father about the vampire who got the Samhain Ball canceled..." She drifted off uncertainly.

"Well, did you?" I asked.

"Yeah. He, like, freaked out and asked how I knew the guy's name and if he'd reached out to me. He didn't know there was an email sent out with his name and picture, and when I told him, he seemed embarrassed and ended the call real quick," she explained, sounding uneasy. "It was really weird. But he's been weird in general lately. Remember our affinity test?"

"Yeah. Of course."

"He wanted me to film you getting tested. Like, just you."

I distinctly remembered that. It'd been really uncomfortable to turn around to see a stranger with her phone camera pointed straight at me.

"I can tell you why," I said carefully. While I was glad I was getting the chance to tell her myself, I wished she were here in front of me so I could see her expression.

"Please. I think he's the reason we were placed in the same coven. He's asked a few times about my coven but seems rather interested in you, and that makes, like, no sense. He doesn't know you."

"Okay, hear me out." I spoke a little slower than usual, afraid I was going to lose her once the shock of this revelation wore off. "About twenty years ago, he was running for an open position on the Crown Coven. His closest rival for it was a woman named Eris Darkmore."

"Oh, stars. He's told me this story so many times," she burst in. "She was a shoo-in for the job; all the polls said so. But she died when her house burned down a few weeks before the election. My father won and dedicated part of his victory speech and his first year ruling on the Crown Coven to her, blah blah blah."

I gripped my phone hard enough to hear the case's plastic flex in protest. That fucking bastard, to offer my birth mother such tokens after having her murdered. "Okay, so you know about all that," I said, working my jaw to loosen it. "Do you know what a blood baron does?"

"I think everyone knows by now," she huffed.

"Well, consider this. Your dad acted weird when you asked about Garroway because not only is he incredibly dangerous, but he knows just how dangerous. He's hired Garroway before."

Silence buzzed along the line, punctuated only by her breathing. "I find that really hard to believe. He's not a dirty politician," she said finally.

I bit my lip hard to contain a laugh. "What the rest of us know is from one of Garroway's former assassins. Not only has your father worked with Garroway before, he paid big bucks to have Eris Darkmore and her family murdered. You said it yourself; he didn't have a chance at the Crown Coven with her as his rival."

"No, that couldn't—"

I didn't let her interrupt me for long, wanting to get it all in before she hung up on me. "And we know this because your father went back to Garroway a few months ago with pictures of *me*, Wren. Eris had a baby girl who everyone thought perished in the fire, but she survived and was adopted by a human family. He wanted a loose end tied before the Darkmore hereditary power was passed on and the memories of the murder—"

"What the f—"

"—And I can confirm it to you. I'm that survivor."

I thought she hung up, but her hitched breathing registered after a few moments. "You're lying," she accused in a watery tone. "My father would *never* do that. Where's your proof?"

"It's here with me." My gaze lingered on the book flying a little more steadily along my ceiling.

"Aren't you worried I'll go tell him everything you've just said?"

Of course I was. But more importantly, I wanted to be the one to plant the seed of doubt within her. Perhaps mistakenly, I assumed the coincidences would line up in my favor and she'd see the truth. "Go ahead. Let him know just how fucked he is," I replied, calling her bluff. "See for yourself how he responds."

"Maybe I will!" *Click.*

I glanced at the screen and the call disconnected message with a smile. The first piece of the plan I'd concocted with my birth mother was now in place.

21
GEO

CRESS'S COLOR was returning by dinnertime. I forced myself to consume a full meal, despite not being hungry. As Marl had told me, it took time after shifting out of gargoyle form for all the human functions to return, like hunger and the full vibrancy of emotion.

I sat by Cress's side with my full plates. We'd gotten a booth in one of the dining halls with Ben and Phaeron across from us. I'd noticed we all greeted her a little differently. While I was satisfied with the warmth of a drawn-out embrace, Ben gave her a quick hug and a kiss on the lips, while Phaeron folded his tail around her hips and rested a chaste brush of his lips over her forehead. I wondered which one she preferred and made a mental note to ask.

"Okay, we have to talk about something," Cress said once we were settled. "How come none of you mentioned the fact that we have a disciplinary hearing to attend this weekend?"

"Verrrr-eee rude," the book flapping just above her shoulder put in. It looked like it was struggling to stay aloft.

Ben smirked, and Phaeron crooked a finger, catching the book with a lasso of shadows to drag it over and inspect it.

"Well, let's put it this way," Ben said. "I'm not a student, Geo's an agent of the library duty-bound to hunt the Hunger no matter what time it is, and Phaeron does whatever he wants. We're going to whip up a different story to sell Aurina and her people. You weren't there. You were just out of town or skipping or something."

"I'm going to go alone to the hearing," Phaeron said, sounding distracted. "Aurina is unlikely to challenge my word."

"That means I missed nearly a whole week of class," she protested.

"Well, you know you have an A in at least one class, bright soul," Phaeron responded in his effortless purr. A touch of pink dusted Cress's cheeks.

"You're helping me catch up with the rest," she said, waving her fork in his direction. "And by that, I mean my fashion classes."

His smile widened to show some fang. "Does that mean I get to model for you? Might I suggest—"

"Okay, we're not doing this right now," Ben interjected.

"I wanted to hear what his suggestion was," Cress said.

"C'mon, you know what he was going to say."

"You're making it weird, Ben."

Phaeron calmed his grin with another bite of his dinner. Once he swallowed, he said, "I was just going to say I look best in dark colors."

Ben rolled his eyes. "Sure you were."

I turned to Cress and said earnestly, "I will wear anything you make proudly, regardless of color."

"Thank you, Geo. That's sweet of you to say." Her smile and the brush of her hand on mine left me feeling warm. I felt a bit of my appetite return.

It wasn't long before Phaeron released his hold on the book, which fluttered slowly to Cress and perched its spine on her shoulder. "Its handling the influx of power and knowledge it was given well, all things considered," he said. "The wispfly within the book is still adjusting."

"I'm plenty well-adjusted," it replied before tumbling shut and landing in Cress's lap.

She picked it up with both palms. After a few moments, she gave it a little shake. "Uh, book?" No reply. She looked up at Phaeron. "Are you sure the wispfly didn't just die?"

"Cressie," the book whispered. "Come closer. I have some final words." She lifted it up to her ear.

"It's fine. Just dramatic," Phaeron sighed.

"Wispflies don't die. They just fade away. And should I fade, I want you to know…" It rattled off a string of Latin at twice the volume, causing her to jump. "That celestial witch spell summons light! You're good at that!"

"Okay, I think I need a break from you," she said, closing the clasp over its pages and tucking it against the wall. "Maybe if it's quiet and still for a few days, it'll figure itself out."

"Mmf! Cwess!" Despite the volume it tried to speak at, it could barely flex its pages and was greatly muffled.

"Well, mostly quiet," she added.

We ate the rest of our dinner in relative peace, conversation turning to the coming Thanksgiving break. Cress intended to invite her human family to go to the Ashbough family's event since they already knew about the supernatural.

"I will go if you do," I said, echoing what the other men had to say about it.

Her safety was of utmost importance, after all. And…I looked forward to accompanying her to something more relaxed like a big feast for friends and family. For a moment, I imagined her on my arm in a couple weeks, seeing the Crystal Court's namesake together. It sounded like we'd be going to a lesser known, subterranean fae court. I could pull out my understanding of minerals, something in every gargoyle's baseline knowledge. Since I'd lost some of my quartz by this point, I could also take the opportunity to look for more with the fae's blessing.

Once the meal was over, we lingered to chat a little longer. I don't think I was the only one feeling a flutter of anticipation when Cress was finally ready to leave. Her brown gaze took the three of us in before she walked slowly for the exit.

Would she invite one of us to accompany her into her dorm this time? Her promise earlier lingered in my ears, the breathy "soon" she'd uttered.

Yet I couldn't forget how she'd been tangled up in Phaeron's arms Samhain night or how often she'd dragged an eager Ben through the dorm's back door with her. She had two more men to take her pick from, both more experienced and charming than me.

She turned toward them as we stepped into the evening air.

"Thanks for dinner, gentlemen. I think Geo can see me home from here."

The unearthly light behind Phaeron's yellow eyes flared brighter for a moment. "Very well. See you for class tomorrow," he said and winked.

"Actually, same," Ben said. "It'll be Friday."

"Not a student, huh," she teased.

He laughed. "I am for exactly one class!"

They waved a quick goodbye, going the opposite direction. Cress drew the zipper of her jacket up with a shiver and shifted closer to me. It felt like a hint, so I put my arm around her waist, and she slid into my side. "Oh, Geo. You're warm this evening," she said.

Think charming. Don't just comment on the weather, I told myself.

I was feeling more human than ever, actually, with her soft curves nestled against me like she belonged there. It wasn't so difficult to think of something more clever than usual to say. "Enough to warm your bed as well?"

She covered a surprised giggle with her hand. Well, I thought it was clever, at least. "Is that where you want to be?" she asked. Her full lips pursed as she considered me. The light from a passing streetlamp lent her gaze a playful glint. "Is that what you feel, Geo?"

"What I feel hasn't changed," I rumbled. "I feel that you are mine and that I haven't had a chance to show that I was made for you."

She was quiet for a while, until her dorm was close. "Haven't you?" she finally asked. I took her to the door, and she unlocked it, extending a hand to me in clear invitation. I curled my fingers around hers.

Giddiness bubbled in my chest as she led *me* up to her room. Not Ben, not Phaeron, but her guardian gargoyle. Yet when the door closed behind us, a bundle of nerves knotted lower in my belly. Her body was a temple and a mystery to me. How would I please her best so she wouldn't regret her invitation?

I'd seen snippets of sex online. It was inevitable, really, with how much regular people loved the act. At first, my adventures down the pocket dimension that was the Internet led to me turning off and browsing away from such things, too distanced from the rest of the world to see why watching two people get intimate was desirable.

Lately, though, I'd avoided it out of respect for Cress. Her naked body was the first one I wanted to see, the only one I wanted to be aroused by. But it left me in a pit of inexperience, and now I could kick myself for not at least learning the basics.

She sat at the foot of her bed and patted the space next to it. "Relax. We don't have to do anything you're not ready for," she said.

I sat as she indicated, not sure how to reply to that. I felt ready...but also conflicted with other emotions I still had little grasp of. I worked through listing them in my head, finding that they were all negative ones: doubt, indecision, and fear of disappointing her.

Her palm traced a path down my chest. "I don't suppose they program gargoyles with anatomy lessons."

"No." I cleared my throat, correcting myself. "I mean, unfortunately not."

"How about this? We'll go slow. You'll tell me if you get overwhelmed, okay?" she offered. With her fingers slowly tracing patterns lower on my abdomen, I would've agreed to anything she said.

"Yes."

She breathed a little laugh. "All right, Geo."

I sucked in a breath at the sensation of her fingertips slipping under the hem of my shirt and stroking over my skin directly. Each touch was faintly electric. I didn't want her to stop—I only needed more, so I was the one to lift the fabric off and toss it to the side.

"I still wish I could thank your sculptor," she said, tracing the lines of my muscles with her hands. I lifted my shoulders, proud of my physique simply because she liked it so much.

Her thumbs rubbed over the tight buds on my chest. My moan came out throaty, and my manhood twitched, hardening in my pants for her and the sensual sway of her body as she lifted herself and sat astride my hips.

"Cress." I practically moaned her name too, begging her for more.

"Touch me," she said, guiding my hands to her body. I obeyed eagerly, shifting my hold from her waist down to her hips. She took off her shirt for me and unclasped her bra, setting both aside and letting me look my fill.

I was never more aware of how large my hands were compared to her body or how fragile she seemed with skin like silky satin. My fingers followed the trails my eyes had set, worshiping her delicate body from the planes of her belly to the weight of her breasts, which were enough to fill my palms. I rolled them like I'd wanted to earlier, plucking at her nipples again and smiling when that drew a breathy sound from her. Anything she liked, I would do a hundred times more, given the chance.

She cupped my nape, drawing me into a slow kiss to match the pace of my roaming hands. I mapped every inch of her exposed skin and listened to the hitch of her breath when I found the most sensitive places, committing each to memory. The kissable curve of her neck, the curve of her shoulder, those breasts that weighed soft and full without the support of clothes or my hands.

My hands inevitably found the top of her jeans last, and I hesitated for a moment. There was more of her to view and explore, and I wanted to experience all of her. I tunneled my hands under the layer of fabric, giving her ass a squeeze. A shudder went through her form.

With a roll of her hips, she rubbed the heat of her core over my cock, which strained against the fabric of my pants, begging to be released. The starburst of sensation spread like an explosion, and again I understood why my fellow gargoyles would abandon their duty for this.

Time and again, I'd judged my peers for setting aside their services and the reason for their creation to pursue women. But I was the one who'd been mistaken, who'd jumped to conclusions too soon, and denied myself for too long. As I held Cress against me for more, to *feel* more, I recognized this as the point where I transitioned.

I was no longer a statue in the service of Moongrove Library. I was a man, here to serve my woman.

My fingers trembled as I undid the button on her jeans, and she helped me get them off of her, discarding the slip of her panties as well. "C'mon up here," she said, lifting off of me and moving further up her bed.

Sitting upright, she spread her legs, and it was all I could do to keep myself in my pants as she beckoned for me to look at the folds of her sex. "Couple pointers," she said, taking my wrist and guiding my hand between her thighs. "This is the clit. Most men can't find it, but I bet gargoyles can." With a wink, she pressed my thumb to a nub of flesh at the apex of her folds.

I rubbed it, getting an electric thrill to see the pleasure that flushed her. "Doesn't seem so hard to find," I rumbled.

She smiled at that and guided me by touch through the rest of her slick sex, which opened like the petals of a glistening flower. I pressed one of my fingers into her channel and watched her legs draw up. "Ooh," she breathed.

Fitting a second one in with the first, I felt the strong muscles within her stretch around the digits...and I knew what she needed from me and why she was already reaching out to take it, freeing my cock at last and shoving my pants away.

"Lie back for me," she ordered. I kicked my clothes the rest of the way off and did so, propping up my back on her pillows while she went rummaging in her bedside table.

"Condom. Very important." She showed me the package and how to apply one.

Properly protected, I throbbed in the open air for her, my breath coming short at the sight of her beautiful bare form. She straddled my waist, too far up, so that I nestled in the cradle of her ass while she rested her weight atop me and let me draw her in for another, fiercer meeting of our mouths.

"Geo," she whispered between kisses. "Are you sure?"

Pulling away, her gaze searched mine while I cupped her neck, thumb grazing her cheek. Had there been a more stunning sight than her with kiss-swollen lips, her lidded eyes full of intimate promise? "I'm sure. I was made to be yours," I said.

"I love when you say things like that." She kissed my neck and jaw, rolling her hips again to tease my throbbing length. Just as my grip tightened with a thread of impatience, she guided herself back and took my cock in hand.

I bit my bottom lip as she lowered herself inch by inch. To be sheathed within her was bliss. She took it slow for my sake, bracing on my chest. Each bounce of her body had her breasts jiggling, a feast for my eyes alone. Her full lips parted, panting and moaning as she took her pleasure from me.

We fit together perfectly, just as I knew we would, and the rest came from the fleshy instincts I hardly knew I had. With a grasp on her hips, I met her halfway, rewarded by the delight that flashed over her face.

"That's right. Take me," she invited. I hardly needed encouragement when her expression was flush with pleasure.

I rolled us, still inside her, rocking the creaking joints of her tired bedframe. For once, I just felt. I just *was*. Her moans and cries, the way she curled her legs around me, inviting me deeper, it was my purpose fulfilled. I shuddered with bliss as she came, soaking in the smell and the feel of her, the flush of her skin.

She was *mine*. But more importantly, I was *hers*. My stone heart beat for her alone, a realization I had after I came and nearly collapsed atop her. I shifted onto my side, holding her to me with both arms.

"I feel like I adore you," I said. And that, truly, was an understatement.

"Sure that's not the sex talking?" she whispered.

I shook my head, stroking her silky purple hair. The shift in the bedrock of my emotional state was something I could self-analyze at a later time, but I knew it was permanent. My duty was answered only in her pleasure.

"Do you have another condom?" I asked.

"Mmm. Plenty." She rested with her eyes closed. "Aren't you tired, though?"

In answer, I pressed my erection, still rock hard, against her thigh. "Some of the rumors about gargoyles are true."

22

CRESS

I SPENT the following weekend with my books, missing work, and laptop spread out over Ben and Phaeron's table, nearly despairing at how much there was to do. Keeping me out of trouble with the university was a double-edged sword: though I wouldn't have a blemish on my educational record for breaking curfew, I wouldn't get any forgiveness or extra time for the work I'd missed.

I wasn't alone for any of it, at least. Phaeron was around early Saturday to help with Latin, but he disappeared for the rest of the weekend after that. Presumably, he attended the disciplinary hearing for us, but he didn't return. Geo and Ben helped where they could, the latter going so far as to forge my handwriting and finish some assignments for me.

Roe and Willow visited separately to help as well. "Any luck on mastering your mer magic?" I asked Willow while we puzzled over some of the Introduction to Witchcraft work together.

My shy friend scrubbed at her cheeks, as if she could rub away a sudden blush. "One of my professors looked into it. He thinks I need to visit one of the mer kingdoms because that side of me is dormant right now. Maybe if I was around the people and their energy, it'd help."

I took her in for a moment before asking, "Did he offer to take you himself?"

"No, but one of his assistants did."

"Is he cute?" I laughed.

"Cress!" she protested.

I tilted my head and gave her a look until she sighed and nodded. "I guess you could call him that. He's going to take me on a day trip to Neptris—a mer city in the Atlantic Ocean—sometime soon. I really hope it works." She traced the wood grain on the table with a sigh. "I'm tired of sitting out all the dangerous things you and the others are doing because I can't control my magic."

"It's really overrated, trust me. You get behind on your work," I tried to joke, gesturing to the piles of books on the table. She gave me a skeptical look. "Danger or not, I hope you get in touch with your mer side soon."

Maybe it would help her self-confidence, which was always low when the rest of us were able to use our magic without trouble. I'd seen Willow's troubles. She was still the Goldilocks of oceanic witches, either summoning too much or too little of her water-based magic for a given task. Having access to this mysterious other half of her abilities could be the balance she needed to get it just right.

She left to enjoy her weekend, and Roe came by Sunday afternoon with a bag full of snacks and soda to share around. "I looked into petitioning the Crown Coven for you," she said with little preamble, having a seat at the table across from Ben. Both of us perked up.

"Can a coven of baby witches do it?" I asked.

She wrinkled her freckled nose. "Yeah, but we need endorsements from two established covens in good standing with enough clout to get our case heard. It'd be easier to take it to the supernatural court system."

"Crown Starsurge is rich enough to rub elbows with a blood baron," Ben put in. "He'd just hire a bunch of lawyers to legally fight us on his behalf."

As Eris had explained, there were two different systems I could use to go after Blaize Starsurge. The courts were for supernaturals of all kinds, while the Crown Coven only involved itself in witch affairs. It was particularly ballsy to petition the Crown Coven to air a grievance against one of its members, but it was also my only chance to stay out of a prolonged court battle I didn't have the money to fight.

"That's true. My mother and her coven can be one of our endorsements, but we need another," she said. "And, you know, an ironclad presentation with proof of Cress's claims."

I sighed, glancing upward. My handbook was still acting erratically, but it'd let me sift through the newest knowledge left within it this morning. Its pages had literally quivered with the power forced into them, making it difficult to read for long. "Still working on that. All the memories my ancestors wanted to pass down are in the book, but I'm not sure how to share them."

"You have time," Roe sighed. "It takes up to a year for the Crown Coven to decide whether or not to hear a case. It really depends on who you have behind the petition, though."

The Crown Coven was a lot like a combination of the Senate and the Supreme Court, able to pick and choose who they spent their time listening to. Appointment to one of the seats was for life, and they alone made new witch laws for the whole continent of North America. There were six more covens like it across the world. It showed me how limited the witch population truly was for a handful of covens to be able to run the show that way.

And, also, how powerful and corrupt Blaize Starsurge had to be. Despite my bluster at Wren and the limited guidance I'd received so far from Eris, I was still just a mouse taunting a venomous snake.

"We do have an ace up our sleeves, though." Roe raised a brow. "As long as you've made sure that's true?"

Well, no. I still had Hana Graygazer's business card somewhere on my desk. I wanted calling Lanie's mother to be the very last step of our plan, which was foolishness Roe wanted to address head-on.

The seventh seat on the Crown Coven was currently filled by the venerated Kwan Graygazer, according to a well-hidden website. His short biography confirmed that he was from the famed family of augury witches.

"Cress," Roe grumbled. "Didn't Lanie even tell you to contact her mom if you needed help?"

"Uh, yeah." Shame warmed my cheeks. "Sorry again."

She waved my apology away, as she'd been doing from the moment I was healthy enough to text her. She wasn't hung up on not being able to talk to Lanie directly, especially after hearing how brief the conversation was and how much our friend wanted her rest.

The sticking point was that I hadn't brought her along to watch my back. I could only promise to be better in that regard. I'd never had such a loyal friend and needed to do better by her.

"Call her soon, okay? Maybe she can convince her coven to be our second endorsement. Imagine if she could just pick up the phone and have the ear of Crown Graygazer," she reasoned.

"You're right, that would be amazing. I will call her, promise," I said.

"One more thing for now—you're aware that if you go this route, Crown Starsurge will know exactly why you're appearing ahead of time? Petitions are read out, and a majority vote within the coven is what decides whether or not they're heard," Roe said.

I bit my lip. "Yeah. My birth mother mentioned that too." I wished Eris were here to lend some advice. After passing the Darkmore hereditary magic into my handbook, she'd vanished and hadn't reappeared yet. "I have to have a damn good case."

"*We* do have a damn good case," Roe said. "You're not doing this alone—the whole coven will be behind you, one way or another. If we have to bring Bianca instead of Wren, we totally will."

I smiled at last. "Thanks, Roe. I'm thankful this is a whole-coven affair. Maybe we'll even decide on a name soon."

"Well, yeah! We can't submit a petition without an official coven name. I'll text everyone about it again."

She shot off a group message, and we sat there chatting and laughing as this kicked off a second argument over the group chat about what the name should be. She showed me where to access a database online where we could type in prospective names and see if they were taken or not. Many otherwise good names were, and she didn't want to add a numeral to the name we decided on. What a headache.

THE BUSINESS CARD had a couple dented edges and was buried under a few assignments I'd felt were important enough to keep. "Graygazer

Augury Services" stood out in big, black letters, along with a phone number and email address. I flipped it back and forth, working up my nerve.

"Just do it," Jin sighed from my lap. "They're nice people."

At first, I'd put off the call because it was dinnertime, but I couldn't be sure where Lanie's mother was right now. The Graygazers were known to move around, using their power of future sight to slightly alter the path of fate, saving lives simply by being in the right place at the right time. Lanie had believed strongly in this calling because it was her parents' lifestyle.

"You're right. I should get a hold of myself," I said.

"Yes, you should," the little black cat agreed without sympathy.

Well, maybe Hana wouldn't pick up. I dialed the number listed on the card and put the phone to my ear, counting the rings.

But it barely rang. "Hello, Cress," a woman answered.

"Err, hello, Missus Graygazer. Have I reached you at a good time?"

"I've been waiting for you to call for some time now," she said. I felt my cheeks heat, but she sounded kindly over the speaker. "Do you seek advice about your future?"

"Yes. And help in the present. I have so much to tell you." I recognized I echoed what I'd said to her daughter's spirit and cleared my throat. "How much time do you have?"

"I have time. Tell me everything."

I watched the light of evening shade to full night as I ended up doing just that. Jin left my lap to sleep on the spare bed in my dorm, while Milo and Bella came and went for pets and to take turns in my lap when I wasn't pacing the length of the room.

Hana listened quietly, occasionally confirming that she was still on the line. The faint sound of typing signaled that she was taking notes as I spoke. When I was done, she said, "You should have called sooner. This is no simple gaze into the gray, but a convoluted puzzle with multiple dangerous angles."

"Sorry, ma'am."

"Don't apologize, I'm happy to help."

"Would you be able to convince your coven to endorse our petition?" I asked, holding my breath while she considered.

"Hmm. I will discuss the possibility with my coven mates and Madigan."

My lips pursed to ask who that was when she answered in the next breath. "Your friend Roe's mother. I'm positive this will lead to my husband and me attending her Thanksgiving celebration, so I will see you there with a list of possible futures."

"That sounds amazing," I burst out.

"Let's discuss your immediate future, though. You've been entrusted with the Darkmore hereditary magic in a way that makes your librarian book a powerful enchanted item. With enough practice, you will be able to cast basic celestial witch spells. This means you will need to find a mentor who will be willing to teach you how to use the magic. I suggest you get a hold of a woman named Jordan Evenstar, who, as we speak, is trying to verify whether a letter she received in the mail is truly from a nephew she thought was dead."

"I think Ben gave her my number," I said.

"He must've. I see her reaching out after Thanksgiving and acting quite skeptical when you answer the phone. You will need to convince her to come meet Ben in person. What else... The monster that attacked you has returned to its master. They've burrowed far under cover." Her voice took on a dreamlike quality as she spoke. "The best thing you can do right now is train and improve yourself, because the next confrontation with it will decide the fate of its host's life."

I grimaced, imagining the panic Ben would have when he heard that news. We hadn't even come close to freeing Lucas of the Hungering Darkness up until now. "What about Garroway carving a blood rune on himself?"

Ben had finally shared what his mentor and father figure had died to tell him. "That is quite concerning, to think anyone would willingly take that monster into their body," Hana answered. She sounded like she was coming back to herself. "However, my magic encounters a fog any time he is involved in one of your futures."

"Is it because he's a vampire?" I asked.

"That could be part of it. More likely, he is wearing some sort of enchantment to be untraceable."

I put a finger over the receiver. "Shit. Fuck."

"However, when you've done this as long as I have, this kind of fog on your timelines suggests whether a decision leads you into danger. I will have more for you soon," she promised. "Is there anything else you'd like help with right now?"

"Can I ask for someone else? My friend Willow just learned that she's half-mer, and she's trying to access that side of her magic."

"I will speak with her when I see you all for Thanksgiving. Anything else for you?" she prompted.

"Got it," I said, running my hand through my hair as I mentally crossed off concerns too small to ask her about. "Do you know when I'll see Phaeron again? He's been missing almost all weekend." I was starting to miss him, even if I had spent most of my time with my other two men. I just didn't quite feel complete without the third around.

She answered after a couple minutes of silence. "Monday if you find where he hides in Moongrove Library. Wednesday if you wait for him to come to you after he resolves what troubles him."

"Is there something wrong?" I asked, instantly worried.

"I will let him explain," she answered with a chuckle. If she was laughing about it, I figured it wasn't so serious and relaxed.

"Okay, last question. Will my birth mother's spirit be returning?"

"Oh, a good one," she murmured. She was quiet as she read the future again. "Yes. If you spill your own blood and call to her ghost, it will come to you for a short time. She is much diminished but still present on the mortal plane out of sheer stubbornness. I see her being an excellent ally and source of knowledge when you need her most."

I breathed a sigh of relief. "Thank you. I feel so much better."

"Find your peace, but don't be complacent. I will see you soon," she said.

We said our goodbyes, and I glanced at the time with a sigh. I'd need a lot of coffee to get through tomorrow's classes.

23
CRESS

"Braza?" I said in a quiet corner of the library's lobby, hoping to get the powercore's attention the next morning.

I wasn't willing to wait until Wednesday to see Phaeron again, and if he was hiding in the library for some reason, there was one being that would be able to tell me where—the powercore herself. I was usually marked present for my class in the library, regardless of whether or not Mr. Eriksson saw me that day, so I took my chances on not appearing for one more session.

A feeling like static had the little hairs on the back of my neck lifting. *"Good morning, brightest of souls,"* Braza answered promptly.

"Good morning. Do you know where Phaeron is?" I asked quietly, hoping none of the people studying a few tables overheard me whispering to myself.

"Floor negative fourteen."

"Thanks." That was nearly painless. I headed for the elevators.

"I'll tell you which containment room he's entered if you chat with me," she said. She followed that up by teaching me how to talk to her silently...since she could skim the most dominant thoughts in my head. A side effect of holding on to some of her power to fuel my librarian witch spells.

"Is there something wrong?" I asked her.

"Oh, no, I'm just horribly bored. Phaeron won't talk to me right now, and nothing's happening in the library out of the ordinary," she sighed.

Well, that did sound boring. As I took my elevator trip down to floor negative fourteen, she told me a little about her existence. There was no such thing as sleep for a powercore, but she preferred her constant vigilance over the certainty of death she'd been left with long ago.

I tried to lighten her mood with a quick story, picking up pretty quickly that she wanted someone to gossip with. I stepped off the elevator and leaned against the wall until the conversation was finished.

"Okay, chat later? He's in the room at the very end of the left wing," she eventually told me.

"Sure. Thanks again," I thought to her. Her static-filled presence faded as I walked down the left hallway, which had only a few doorways on either side, signifying the rooms here were quite large. The last door was shut, and no one answered when I knocked.

With a shrug, I tried the knob. It was unlocked. Braza hadn't given any warnings about this room, but I still peeked inside and blinked owlishly as I received a nose full of night air.

The "room" was like a pocket dimension from the moment I closed the door behind me and shut out the hallway's artificial lighting. Springy, grass-like plants cushioned my feet as I stepped further inside and took my handbook off my belt. *"The Librarian Witch's Handbook, scan for any hostile entities,"* I instructed it quietly.

"Aye aye, captain!" it answered at full volume, fluttering off into the underbrush.

Logic dictated that no door in Moongrove Library was left unlocked if there was something hostile inside, but I just wanted to be sure, considering the size of the space I'd entered. I didn't feel like there were any walls here, just an open stretch of forest with the sound of rushing water somewhere close. The sky was a beautiful spread of stars, with a slivered crescent moon lending dim light that my eyes eventually adjusted to.

I didn't recognize any of the trees, with their sharp, irregularly shaped leaves and deep ruby hue. Everything around me was one shade off from black, severely desaturated from normal.

I took a few steps forward, calling, "Phaeron?"

"Over here," he answered. I shifted toward the sound of his voice, finding a trail through the underbrush. The sound of water became a louder rush by the time I spotted him sitting on the rocky edge of a cliff hanging above a slow, small waterfall of violet water.

He turned to look at me, his eyes twin lamps, but didn't move to stand. "Stay right there," he said. "Did Braza tell you where to find me?"

My feet stilled, and I paused, uncertain. There was a certain husky quality to his voice, but I couldn't make out his expression from here. "She did. I haven't seen you in a few days… Why are you hiding out here?"

"It beats several alternatives," he said in a near growl.

"What's wrong, Phaeron?"

"Nothing. You should go."

I took a step closer. He definitely growled at me this time. "I'm finding that hard to believe," I said.

His hand passed over his eyes, muting their light as he released a tense sigh. "Fine, but I did warn you. I am not in full control of myself."

"Is it the soul hunger again?" I asked, feeling a flutter of nerves in my belly. Usually, that was accompanied by the presence of his monstrous brother.

"Partially. Aurina used her magic on me again. I could kill her for it," he snarled, snapping his tail. "She asked me to join her mating circle."

A surge of anger hit me too, but also an intensifying of my nerves. "What do you mean, she used her magic on you again?" I asked. It was clear her request had pissed him off.

He stood, stalking over until his features were bathed in pale starlight. His face was taut with desire, and his otherworldly eyes practically blazed with feverish intensity. "She filled the air with lust," he answered. "And I made it clear that I would rather drag you to her office and fuck you right in front of her than be forced to become her mate. I've been here ever since, waiting for my desire to cool, and *it hasn't*, not even by a fraction."

"That's not her asking. That's coercion," I said, pissed for him. Yet my face was flaming. He nodded and edged closer, leaning toward me. My gaze snagged on the rather impressive bulge in his pants. "Do you want some help with that?" I offered, reaching for him.

He moved away at the last moment with a frustrated snarl. "No.

There's...there's more." He balled his clawed hands into fists. "I've fantasized about you joining me here, wet and eager. I could take you against a tree or out on the grass where it's softest. A hundred times, in a hundred different ways. I could have you naked and screaming for me in minutes."

My knees went weak. *Yes, please!*

"But I also lust to sink my teeth into your pretty soul just as much. I could bite your neck and leave my mating mark or simply tear into your soul. Would it be as sweet as you are?" He gave his head a vicious shake.

"Hey, Cressie!" exclaimed my book as it flapped over to us. "There you are. Everything's clear—"

With an irritated swipe of Phaeron's hand, a coil of shadow snapped the handbook shut and secured its clasp. It thumped to the ground and rocked indignantly.

"You need to go," he growled at me. His familiar, otherworldly power pulsed in the air around us, hanging there like humidity.

I worked my jaw, struck nearly speechless. After all that, he wanted me to leave? I don't know who that would hurt more. While he was so worked up and trying to warn me, I couldn't find an ounce of fear.

"I can't just leave you like this," I said. He narrowed his eyes, tail undulating behind him. "If you weren't in control, you wouldn't have the words to tell me all that. You'd have just acted."

"Don't tempt me, bright soul." He slid a little closer, but I didn't back away.

"I don't think you will hurt me," I answered. We were nearly nose to nose. Heat rolled from his body in waves, and he breathed shallowly, staring at the full curve of my lips. And there was the truth of his intentions, his eyes on what he wanted, not what he was afraid he would damage.

"Cress," he said roughly. It had the sound of a final warning.

The man just needed a little relief, and I knew the way to give him some without his fangs anywhere near my soul. My coy smile was my only answer, and it frayed the last threads of his self-control. His mouth met mine with bruising intensity, our tongues and teeth clashing. My eyes widened, recognizing he'd snapped the powerful leash that kept both his lust and power in check. Tendrils of shadow took form around us, trailing off him like smoky fur and wrapping around my curves.

He lifted me effortlessly by the hips, lips still locked with mine. Roughened bark met my back, and he pinned me there with his erection grinding against my core. He tugged my hair and smoothed a hand up my waist, his claws hooking over the band of my jeans. It took me a few feverish moments to realize he'd lifted and supported my hips with the solid muscle of his tail, and the flexible tip was wrapped around one of my thighs, keeping that leg spread.

When we parted for breath, he trailed sharp-edged kisses down my neck, hesitating at the curve of skin where he'd tugged my shirt aside, exposing my shoulder. "I won't mark you today. Not like this," he murmured. I moaned from a firm thrust of his hips. "But one day, you will carry my mating mark. You'll beg for it."

"I will," I agreed breathlessly. I could already tell that I'd beg him to take me in all ways with the same fierce, animal desire that he wore openly on his expression.

But for right now, I pushed his shoulders. It was like trying to move a wall. "Second thoughts, bright soul?" He began to disentangle us, unable to hide the disappointment the thought gave him.

Even in the grasp of a lust spell, he had the control to stop. I would compliment him on it—later. The moment he stepped back, he gave me an opening to drop to my knees and pull open his pants. I felt his reaction in the squeeze on my thigh from his tail and watched a desire-filled grin erase his doubts.

"Naughty witch," he practically purred.

I freed his cock, pleasantly surprised as it bobbed free. I didn't know what to expect, but he was shaped and proportioned like a human man. With how dark it was around us, I felt him for any surprises, and he throbbed in my palm. His shaft was designed for pleasure, with a few extra nodules that seemed well-placed to rub a partner intimately. I wanted to feel it for myself.

I cupped his balls and licked a trail down his length, trying to contain my eager smile so I could fold my lips over my teeth. The pressure of his tail was shifting up my thigh, and I only noticed it when it snaked around my waist, the tip hooking into my waistband.

Magic leaked from Phaeron's fingertips, hard to detect until I felt his shadows like tiny fingers plucking at the button of my jeans. I had the crown of his shaft between my lips when one last nudge had my jeans coming undone and unzipped. He tugged with his tail, exposing my bare ass to the night air.

My gaze flashed up to his face as I took the rest of him into my mouth. I wasn't the only naughty one here, it seemed, as his tail felt a lot like a third hand as it brushed over my skin and through the lips of my slick pussy. He threaded his fingers through my hair, guiding my head while he rolled his hips at a slow pace to start.

I loved the look of relief in his expression, all of his attention and focus on me. The thin tip of his tail searched for and flicked my clit, sending a starburst of pleasure through me. I jolted in his hold, fingers digging into his thighs.

"Spread your legs more," he ordered. He had me tilt my hips back, and I did so with a thrill of anticipation as his tail stroked and teased.

Was he going to fuck me with that tail? I sure hoped so as I wiggled my hips, shivering from the cool breeze touching my wet lips. It nudged my pussy, and his grip on the back of my head tightened. He'd looped the thinnest part of his tail around itself, creating a knobby ride that he thrust into me like a cock. The drive of his hips matched its pace.

For a moment, I wondered how exactly I'd gotten into this situation. I'd come to the university a blushing virgin, and within a few months, I'd become an anam cara for a blood witch, awakened the emotions within a gargoyle, and was now getting tail fucked by this demonic man who'd never worn his emotions so openly on his expression as now.

His desire was no longer buried under decades of poise and princely dignity. I was proud to help him strip it away to the honest, raw core of who he was. He looked at me like the wolf his shadowborn form resembled, hungry and passionate.

It was a shame I could only give him my mouth until he figured himself out, because I wanted to feel him in the hundred different ways he promised he'd fantasized about. It was the truth that had my pussy growing slicker for his tail. I'd become far too aware of the pleasure my three men could give, that we could share.

"Cress," he breathed raggedly. I shuddered in echo to the naked pleasure he spoke into my name. With one last throb, he came, flooding my mouth with the taste of him.

I'd barely swallowed all his come when he took a knee, still pumping his tail into me. Cupping my cheek, he kissed me without shame for the taste of him that remained on my tongue. The pad of his thumb circled my clit, pressing, demanding I find completion too.

He was soon swallowing my moan as I came apart, slowing the frenzy of his kiss and helping me down from that sharp peak with a slower, more gentle touch. I didn't miss that he gathered my slick with a touch down my folds and licked it from his thumb with an expression I could only label as both vicious and victorious.

I lay a little limp on his shoulder, panting. "Better?" I asked.

"Much." His voice was back to its smooth warmth, and the feverish intensity in his eyes was fading. I knew all he needed was a good release. There was no talk of souls or biting or tearing, just his reverent touch over my cheek, combing through my hair. He held me against him as we both caught our breath. "Thank you, bright soul. I think I can return to polite society now. What time is it?"

I fumbled with the jeans tangled around my knees until I withdrew my phone. "About lunch time." I'd completely missed the time block for Library Science 101, but I'd had a hell of a lot more fun here in… "What is the room, by the way?"

Phaeron sighed, casually using tendrils of shadow to fix his clothes back on and offering a hand up once I'd done the same. "My sanctuary. I was a little surprised it was still here, to be frank." He guided me back to the ridge where I'd originally found him, the two of us sitting with our legs dangling over the trickle of the small waterfall. He put a casual arm around my waist as I leaned against him. "It's mostly an illusion."

I blinked away the afterimages of my phone's screen. We could see a valley of dark plant life stretching far into the distance, with the spires of buildings even further. "I made it with my magic and memories. This was one of my favorite places to stop and think back in Soiluire. Of course, there was more life back then. The call of animals, the slow creep of mushrooms, and the turn of seasons," he continued, glancing toward the sky. "I gave it Earth's stars as well."

"It's beautiful." But so was this moment, with the continuing glimpse of him so relaxed and open.

"I agree."

"You must miss it."

The back of a claw traced up my waist as he considered. "Sometimes, I do. But there's no going back, so there's also little sense in yearning for the impossible." He turned a fanged grin my way. "Besides, I've never had a complaint about Earth's women."

PHAERON and I went separate ways until that evening, when I showed up in our usual spot in workout gear and my sword. Neither of us mentioned the moonlit tryst, yet things had changed between us all the same. Thus began the game Morgana had warned me about.

"He'll drive you mad with little touches and whispers in your ear. He'll pretend he has no idea what he's doing to you, but he knows and is waiting for you to snap and tear his clothes off."

I saw Phaeron nightly for training from then on as the days counted down to Thanksgiving break and the moment I'd need to explain my relationships to Mom and Carly. There was no hiding it now, not with my time divided between my three men.

Mornings and midday were for Ben, grabbing coffee and flirting before and between classes. Late afternoons went to Phaeron, who continued to drill me on sword skills, magic, and, with a *tisk* after hearing me butcher some Latin homework, proper pronunciation of various Latin words. He snuck little touches in between sessions, sweet kisses on my neck and nibbles on the shell of my ear. Inevitably, I took his teasing and unleashed the results on Geo, who turned out to be rather insatiable since he hadn't shifted back to gargoyle form during this time. He slept in my bed instead.

Things were oddly peaceful, a portent of a storm to come. I felt it looming as I worked with Roe to fill out a template petition to the Crown Coven, leaving it saved on my computer for now. All we needed was a coven name and for me to get more than a few meager sparks of light from the celestial power locked inside my handbook.

For once, I was confident. I was becoming strong and capable. It was only a matter of time before Blaize Starsurge paid dearly for what he'd done to my family.

24

BEN

"I don't need a familiar," I said one sunny afternoon as Cress tugged me along by the hand. I was hopeless to resist, even if she was taking me toward a familiar fair to meet up with the rest of our coven.

"Nonsense. Every witch needs a companion," she said.

"But *you're* my companion."

She wiggled her brow at me over her shoulder. "Yeah. But not that kind of companion. My familiars feel more like built-in best friends. They never judge me."

"They're literally cats. That's what they do," I pointed out.

"Okay, Jin judges a bit."

"See?"

"That just means a cat probably isn't for you. But there's a company bringing in potential familiars of all kinds. There's going to be something for you, promise," she said. And from her excitement, I figured she was looking forward to meeting them, despite her three familiars trailing us at their own paces.

We slowed as we spotted a series of multicolored tents set up around one of the university's fields, this one crisscrossed by sidewalks and featuring a few fountains. "There's Roe," I said, pointing out the distinctive redhead a moment before she noticed us and waved.

When the fair had rolled in, we'd learned that Cress and Wren were the only witches in our coven who'd already bonded with familiars. My babe had her cats, while apparently, the queen bee had a finicky hawk that preferred to keep to itself. Heath was texting for her in the group chat now, and we were told not to expect either of them to come with us today.

Her loss. Roe, Willow, and a bored-looking Grant were already there waiting. "Why are you here?" I asked him as Cress let me go to greet her friends.

Grant shrugged. "I have to keep up appearances."

"What appearance?" Bianca found us in that moment, smirking his way.

"Some discretion would be lovely," he answered dryly.

At this point, I'd lost track of who he'd revealed his changeling form to. It seemed like everyone who regularly came in contact with our coven except for Áine—for obvious reasons—plus Heath and Wren since they'd become so standoffish.

"Aren't you cold?" I asked Bianca. She was dressed in a tank that left much of her trim midriff exposed and the tiniest of shorts. All the better to show off the new piercing on her belly button, which was a silver stud until it healed naturally.

"Haven't you gotten the memo?" she countered. "I do what I want now."

"And this is different from normal, how?"

She punched my shoulder, drawing a laugh from me. She was too easy to bait sometimes.

Roe cleared her throat. "Now that we are gathered here today, let's decide on a coven name." She showed her phone screen around, which displayed the official registry of witch covens.

I tapped my forehead. "Using the familiar fair to rope us into this again. Smart."

She rolled her eyes at me. "Thanks, Ben. If we can't agree on something, I'll stop being stubborn about adding a number to our coven name. We could just be NSU Coven Number Fifty-seven if it means it's done. There's always a way to submit a coven name change later, or we're allowed to shuffle around at the end of the year if anyone wants to do that."

Cress pulled out her phone and brought up the same website Roe was on. "Okay, I'm ready," she said.

"Witchy Ways?" Bianca ventured.

"We already looked up that one," Roe said, but she typed it in anyway. "Fifteen versions of that name."

Roe and Cress alternated looking up potential names and telling us how many of those were in use. "Ben is Awesome Coven?" I put in eventually.

"No," Roe answered.

"Oddly enough, there is one of those," Cress said a few moments later.

We kept trying. When no two registered covens could be named the same thing, we just had to agree on something and add a number to it. "Try A Little Wicked," Grant suggested.

Roe did and leaned back in surprise. "It's available," she said. I exchanged a glance with Cress, whose face had lit up. "Guys! There are several covens with that name, but the one without a number disbanded...four days ago."

"Better lock that in," Grant murmured.

Willow scuffed her foot. "Are we really wicked enough for a name like that, though?"

"A little bit." Cress shrugged. "I mean, doesn't the name suggest that we're just a bit that way?"

"Don't question it," Roe said, holding her phone closer to her face as she tapped its screen rapidly. "We're taking it. You guys enjoy the fair. I'll be right behind you, okay?"

The rest of us left her to submit the name application and crossed over to the tents. Most of the animals were out of their cages, the hum of conversation everywhere as college-aged witches conversed with the handlers, most of whom were fae. Certain types of fae could talk to any animal they wanted to, and it seemed they had, as we passed by a fully grown tiger lounging on its own stretch of grass like a striped king. He paid us little mind.

"What kind of familiar do you guys want?" Cress asked.

"Something fierce. Maybe that big kitty or a wolf," Bianca answered.

Willow shrugged, her head on a swivel. "I'll need an aquatic familiar, but I don't see any."

"It's not like there's a body of water around," I pointed out. "Unless you count the fountain."

The soft-spoken girl cracked a little smile. "You haven't been around many oceanic witches, have you? There's magic that can put a floating bubble of water around anything that can't breathe air. They basically swim behind their witch on land. One of my classmates has a dolphin and has a charm to shrink it down to teddy-bear size!"

"That doesn't hurt it?" Cress asked.

"Not at all." Willow clasped her hands with a little happy shrug. "It's so cute! I want one of my own."

A witch wearing a shirt with the familiar company's green logo approached us. "Hello, have you all been helped?" She faced Bianca with a trained customer service smile as the young woman tickled the tiger's massive back paws. It flicked its tail in annoyance but didn't lift a claw to bat her away yet.

The worker led us on a tour through the tents, showing off everything from lizards and snakes lazing under heated lamps, to a flock of various birds perching on specialized bars set up under one tent. I found it interesting that the fae bird keeper had managed to enforce harmony with eagles sitting next to sparrows or, in some cases, tiny birds twittering playfully as they hid in the wing fluff of their much larger cousins.

There were also a *ton* of critters that were more popular pets. Cats and dogs made up a good third of the animals we saw, and there was a sizable population of other small mammals too. At some point, we lost Grant, who snuck away after stopping to pet a couple of the dogs. Bianca stopped to ruffle a wolf's thick pelt.

The next thing I knew, Willow and I were the only ones still on the tour. I turned to say something to Cress, but she was a few yards away, talking to Phaeron, who had a hand resting on her hip and was whispering something in her ear that brought about a distinctive blush. *Sneaky fucker,* I thought. I'd been the one to clue him in about the familiar fair earlier by complaining that Cress was making me go.

"Our aquatic pets should be along shortly. They'll have to be walked here from the marina," the worker was telling Willow when I tuned back in to what she was saying.

"I'll just wait here, then," Willow answered. With a nod, the worker slipped away to help some other newcomers.

Since I wasn't all that keen to see any animals, or interrupt Cress and Phaeron's moment, I turned to my coven mate. "Sooo...how exactly do the swimming familiars get to NSU? Isn't the marina a lake?"

Willow had that amused look again. "There's an ocean gate at the bottom of the marina. It's like a standing portal that only activates if you have a magical key, but it links up to a couple locations in the Atlantic."

"Those finned folk have their own technology, huh," I said.

"It's like a whole different world." Her eyes suddenly widened at something she spotted over my shoulder. Her mouth popped open in a wowed O.

I turned to see what it was and stifled a laugh. A merman in his land form strode our way, followed by a fleet of fish and other aquatic creatures swimming in their own personal water bubbles, just as Willow had described. Two oceanic witches in damp wetsuits flanked the animals. They both carried gleaming tridents, creating a nearly invisible tide of water midair to wash their charges along faster.

It was definitely the merman she was staring at. He wore nothing but a pair of shorts, cerulean scales glimmering on his broad shoulders and sculpted cheeks. The man had abs for days; if I wasn't happily taken, I'd stare too. Instead, I turned a smirk Willow's way. "You wanna go talk to him?"

She ducked her head shyly. "Who?"

I elbowed her. "C'mon, you know who. Let's go."

Though she made a sound of protest, she followed a step behind me as I approached and waved to the merman. "Hey, man. Are these for the familiar fair?"

He skimmed over me with disinterest. "They are," he grunted. His gaze landed on Willow next, and he stood a little straighter. "We ran into some trouble along the way from Deeptide. A hungry kraken thought to get a familiar snack, but I put a stop to it."

"Oh, wow," Willow said quietly.

She startled when I nudged her forward with a hand on her shoulder. "Willow here is in the market for a familiar or two," I said.

"Is that so?" the merman asked, flashing a perfect white smile.

She bobbed her head. "Yeah."

"Well, you're in luck." He offered her his elbow like an old-fashioned gentleman, escorting her back to the fair. "We have many interesting and powerful potential familiars for a discerning oceanic witch."

I watched them go for a few moments, proud of how well that went. I drifted back to the tents with my hands in my pockets, a little lost with all my friends now spread out. Usually, I had someone around to distract my thoughts, but alone, one threaded in to take over my headspace.

Lucas would love to be here right now.

He was definitely the animal lover between the two of us. I imagined he'd be thrilled to pet a real wolf and debate the merits of the various types of familiars. Here I was, enjoying a few moments of peace while he was still out there somewhere in serious trouble. What kind of brother did that make me?

Cress was sure we'd have another chance to properly fight the Hungering Darkness and pry it from Lucas. When we did, I'd take him to three familiar fairs to make up for him missing this one.

"Are you just going to brood, or try to find a familiar?" Cress asked, startling me from my thoughts.

"I wasn't brooding," I protested. "I'm just...overwhelmed. Where do I start?"

Phaeron had followed her like a shadow, the two of them flanking me now. "Have you tried over there?" he asked, pointing to the tent overflowing with tiny furry bodies. I shrugged and headed that way, standing a good foot away from the animals.

A cotton-white blur jumped on me anyway, clinging to my shirt. It was an albino mouse, tiny and cute with beady red eyes. I scooped it into my palm and smiled awkwardly to the fae woman watching. This section had a number of rodent-adjacent creatures. I'd have been offended if I didn't realize they were having the equivalent of a mini party, playing within assembled plastic gyms of pipes both big and small and chasing each other. It looked like a good time for a small creature.

"How, exactly, do I know I've found a familiar?" I asked the fae just so she'd stop waiting for me to do something other than pet down the mouse's silky fur with just my index finger.

"You'll feel a kind of draw to an animal you're compatible with. They choose you as much as you choose them. If an animal speaks to you in a way you understand, you know you've been adopted," she answered happily.

I held the mouse closer to my ear, only hearing squeaks. I placed it back on the table, just for it to jump and cling to my shirt again. "Okay, okay. You could sit on me for a minute?" I asked it like it understood, lifting it to sit on my shoulder. To my surprise, it stayed.

Cress watched this with a giggle. "Try a ferret, Ben. I think one would be perfect for you." She knelt down and offered her hands to the opening of one of the tubes big enough for the energetic things, coming back up with a wiggly ferret.

"What's that supposed to mean?" I asked in a teasing tone, taking it from her and looking into its face. "Do I seem like a mischievous, masked thief to you?"

It had a darker stripe across its eyes, like a bandit mask. When I asked the question, though, it tilted its head thoughtfully and sniffed my arm more closely. "Kind of," it said, clear as day.

In shock, I dropped the poor thing. "Hey!" it protested in a small, boyish voice. He scampered his way up my jeans and back into my hands.

Cress leaned in, smiling wide. "Did it talk to you?"

"It...he, I think. He did," I answered. I didn't feel all that different, but the ferret must've picked me, because I was vaguely aware of him laughing at me even if he showed no signs of it, simply sitting stretched between my palms.

"Nice to meetcha," he said. "I'm Flit. Are you fun?"

"Am I fun?" I echoed to Cress with a little smirk.

"Sometimes," she giggled.

"C'mon, I'm trying to impress a ferret here."

"Very," she amended. "*Very* fun."

That seemed to satisfy Flit. Before we could leave, the fae woman started to talk about an adoption fee and produced pamphlets and a starter kit for caring for him. Cress and I both turned to Phaeron, who lifted a brow. "What?"

"You got money, Big P?" I asked.

"Oh." He rolled his eyes, taking a wallet out of his back pocket. "How much is it?"

I cringed when she named the sum, but he didn't flinch.

"And the mouse?" the fae asked.

"Yes, the mouse too," he sighed before I could say anything. It was looking right at him from my shoulder with a piteous expression. It only added twenty bucks to the total, at least.

"Well, they made off like real bandits with that one," I murmured as we rejoined our coven mates, most of whom had a new companion.

"Good one!" Flit exclaimed. I think I liked the little guy already.

Bianca had her arms crossed. "Really, a mouse?" she asked.

I looked around her in an exaggerated fashion. "Where's yours?" I asked in the same judgy tone.

"Not here, I guess," she sighed.

"Well, I have a ferret now, actually. His name's Flit," I said, letting her take him off my hands for the moment. She scratched between his ears and nearly fumbled him when he went boneless.

Cress was kneeling before the dog that sat obediently by Roe's side. "Yeah, he's a retired police dog. They said the gray on his muzzle should fade pretty fast along with his aches and pains since he'll live as long as I do," the redhead was saying.

I took a closer look at the dog, recognizing his markings as a purebred. He was a unit of a Belgian Malinois with tan fur and a darker muzzle, alert despite a few signs of old age. "Going to chase down bad guys together?" I asked.

She grinned. "Sure are. Right, Tank?" The dog woofed in agreement.

That was a good match, I thought. I would be about a thousand percent not surprised if she got a job with SPDI enforcing supernatural law once she graduated.

I turned to Willow, who held a bubble of water with a squid-like creature within. "Well, did you get it?" I asked.

"Yeah, this is my familiar now. She's a cuttlefish," she told me. I leaned forward and squinted, and the animal within the bubble shifted colors to be harder to see. Just as shy as her witch, apparently.

"Cool, but that's not what I meant," I said. "Did you get his number?"

The question was a magnet, drawing the attention of the other three women. "Whose number?" Bianca followed up with.

"Who was it?" Roe asked.

Willow's shoulders lifted, a red tinge spreading across her cheeks. "Uh, yeah, I got his number."

Grinning, I stole a high five before our friends converged on her for details. I took that moment to coax the mouse from my shoulder. "Hey, you. Sure you want to come with me?" I asked it. It bobbed its whole body like a nod. "You want to be my familiar too or something?" It made a sound like it was sucking on its teeth, regarding me with little red eyes. After a few moments to consider the question, it bobbed another yes.

"All right. Welcome to the crew." I chuckled, setting it back on my shoulder. With our new menagerie and name, it felt like we were finally becoming a proper coven.

25
CRESS

I FIDGETED with my sleeves a few days later as I waited on a sidewalk in human Salem for an old sedan to roll down the road. We were around the place where Mom and Carly had to drop me off so I could pass into NSU without them.

The rules about ordinary people visiting the university were loosened slightly around vacations. Witches having human family members was not unheard of, and they were permitted to use portal services like the couple of companies that'd set up on campus to send students home the fast way for their vacation.

I bubbled with an overflowing mix of nerves and excitement. So much had happened since Carly and I had dyed our hair different bright colors and had a tearful goodbye last summer. Mom had taken a rare extended break from work to come for the whole vacation week, too. They expected to see a lot of me...

But that also meant they'd be meeting all three of my guys. Since one of them was always around, I'd asked Ben to be there with me as we waited. He was the most approachable of the three when it came to meeting a supernatural.

I had a *lot* to explain because I'd saved the serious topics to talk to them about in person. I was seriously hoping my three men could play it cool until I had an opportunity to sit down and chat with Mom and Carly.

"Relax, babe," Ben said, for once the less fidgety of the two of us as I jittered in place with my thoughts.

"You try explaining to your regular human family about supernaturals taking multiple mates," I muttered.

"Oh." He grinned, tapping the side of his chin. "Want me to do it?"

"Noooo. I don't want anyone to, frankly."

"They're going to notice that Geo, Big P, and I follow you around like lost dogs," he pointed out.

I sighed and nodded. They definitely were, and Carly would be the one to ask, loudly, if I had three boyfriends. "What happened to 'tall, dark, and terrifying'?" I put up air quotes. Now that I thought about it, he hadn't called Geo anything but his regular name in a while too.

He shrugged. "Too big a mouthful."

Seemed more like he was maturing and trying to get along to me. I was really proud of his progress, and some of my fondness must've leaked onto my expression, as he smiled back and said, "What? It is."

"You're a good man, Ben Evenstar," I said.

He put a hand to his chest, smacking his lips in mock offense. Any sassy response was lost when someone leaned on a car horn for two honks. My heart jolted, and I leaned past him to see Mom's old junker rolling to a stop a couple feet away.

Mom cut the engine, and Carly half-fell out of the passenger's side, rushing over with a big grin and her arms open. The corners of my eyes pricked as we hugged for a few prolonged moments. She was petite and fair, just like Mom, and the electric blue dye she'd put in her hair was faded to a greenish shade with exposed blonde roots.

"How'd you get yours to stay so nice?" she asked, fluffing my still-purple locks.

"Magic," I whispered behind my hand. Verdant witches sold potions that changed hair colors, and I was waiting to give her a couple as a gift later.

Mom came over for her hug next, a briefer embrace. "Hi, baby," she said. "Let me get a look at you."

As a nurse and the woman who raised me, she had the uncanny ability to sense if anything was amiss. She could practically tell me when a cold was coming on when the symptoms were barely showing themselves. "Hmm, you're practically glowing. Who is this young man with you?"

"Mom, Carly, this is Ben, my boyfriend," I said. He'd stepped back to wait but came over for a round of handshakes with his usual charming smile.

Carly pointed to his back while he chatted with Mom briefly. She flashed two thumbs-up, a rare double approval, and I mirrored the gesture. We giggled together.

"Well, we'd better get ourselves to NSU. How will this work, exactly?" Mom asked.

We piled into the car, with Ben and me sitting in the back. I offered her a plastic sign to hang off her mirror, with the university's "normal" name, Northern State University, spelled down its side. "Just keep driving down this road. This will activate the entrance to the pocket dimension, and the scenery will change in a blink."

The engine gave a labored start, but Mom still got a feeble *vroom* from the old car after we rolled into motion. She had the same look of excited anticipation I remember first entering NSU with. It was like going into one of the story worlds I loved to read about, and I'd gotten my love of books from Mom.

I heard more than saw my family's wonder as we passed onto the roadway that led in two directions. Left for the NSU campus, and right for New Salem. The sky had shifted from overcast to bright and sunny in a blink, and the roadside plants had a vibrancy that came entirely from it being late fall in the former Fall Court.

I guided Mom around campus, parking in a lot on the outskirts of campus. We wouldn't see much of NSU, as the company of celestial witches creating the portals today were set up not far from here to catch most of the non-supernatural visitors before they wandered far. Ben helped carry some of the luggage my family had brought for their extended stay, leaving Mom and Carly with rolling bags and the chance to look their fill at our surroundings.

"Just try not to stare. I know it's hard," I told my sister.

The Ashboughs had bought us tickets with the biggest portal company, which had a large crowd amassed for their turns. I could practically feel Carly's giddiness as we slid around the side of the gathering, looking for my coven and friends.

"Is that a mermaid?" she whispered, inclining her head toward a woman standing with a tower of bags, greenish scales glimmering on her cheeks and her black hair giving off an emerald sheen in the sunlight.

"Yeah, in her land form," I said just as quietly. "There are several mer in the Fashion Design program. They're gorgeous, especially in the water."

The question made me think of Willow, who'd been disappointed following her trip to one of the underwater mer cities. She was as human as ever, with no sign of her latent mer side emerging. The professor she'd been conferring with about the problem suspected her magic would rise to the occasion if she were ever in serious trouble, but none of us were keen to push her into danger to give it a try.

"Over here!" Roe's shout and wave drew us to her. She'd watched our things while Ben and I had gone to get my family, the two of us only having a bag each. I'd brought my laptop too, for entertainment and to check on the status of my petition, which was still open for sponsoring covens and minor changes before it was sent off.

Roe was happy to lead introductions, sharing names and affinities of those coming. Áine waved shyly as the immediate center of my sister's attention. Not everyone had taken up Roe's offer to feast with her family and spend their break in the Crystal Court, but Willow and, to my surprise, Bianca had decided to come along.

Our newly expanded group of familiars were tagging along too. Bella and Milo chirped hellos to my family from where they snuggled up to Tank, Roe's retired police dog, who was already looking a little more spry. Ben's shoulder mouse had found him again, climbing up to its usual spot and observing the world from its safe perch.

Geo stood at the back of the group, offering a stoic nod when introduced. He'd been in human form long enough that his eyes had darkened from an uncanny silver-white into a gray that was warm and looked more natural against his dark complexion.

The least human-seeming of us was the last to arrive in a wisp of smoke, taking form next to the gargoyle with a single bag of his own. "Glad I'm not too late," Phaeron said.

"Whoa," Carly breathed.

In the middle of introductions, he came over to kiss Mom's fingertips. "A pleasure," he said smoothly. His gaze flashed to me, and I knew this was the moment my secret came out. "Your daughter is a delight."

Mom turned toward me, a thoughtful frown tugging at her lips. "She...certainly is."

Roe observed the interaction and said, "Something you should be aware of, Mama Rollins, is that supernatural families can be rather nontraditional. Powerful men or women usually take multiple mates. My mother's a legend, and as such, she has three men she calls husband. You're about to meet them when we reach the Crystal Court."

This effectively distracted her from what Phaeron had said. I gave silent thanks yet again for a friend like Roe. "That does sound unusual, I must admit," Mom said.

"It's pretty normal if you grow up with it." Roe smiled and shrugged. "Just means there's a lot more family around for big gatherings like Thanksgiving!"

We moved up in line, and I fell in step with Roe, pushing some of our luggage along with us. "I didn't realize you had three dads," I said in an aside.

"Well, surprise." She clapped me on the shoulder. "Seven younger siblings, too! My mama only retired for a little bit to have all of us. Now she's back in action."

Wow, that was a *huge* family. No wonder she was always trying to draw the coven together for rituals and meet-ups.

"To save you from another big surprise, one of my dads is a prince of the Crystal Court. My family owns about a third of the caves, which is why my mama always hosts big groups there. You'll have your own hotel room for yourself or...well, you know." She lifted both shoulders in an exaggerated shrug.

"No way—why didn't you mention that before?" I asked with a disbelieving laugh.

"I'm not the one who's a big deal here, so it's not like I'm going to brag about what my family owns," she said. "All I can do is point at my mama and remind people that I'm related to her."

I nodded in understanding. There were times I'd done the same with my adopted mother, proud of the lives she'd impacted and even saved in her line of work.

We weren't waiting too much longer before Roe's name was announced as having the next portal up. I went ahead, eager to see how this worked. If Eris were here right now, she'd be reminding me that I could've done this magic myself someday, but thankfully, she was resting instead of making subtle jabs at my choice to be a librarian witch. That gave me a chance to see the process in peace.

A pair of celestial witches were working with a loop of metal engraved with flowing runes around its edges. A third man moved heavy brackets along its side as they calculated together the exact place we were heading from details on a printed piece of paper. It took fifteen minutes before they were satisfied. They touched the tip of their magical staves into the sides of the metal loop. Sparkles of buttery yellow, like sunlight, flowed from the staves. They circled midair at ever-increasing speeds, expanding and stretching until the loop contained a sheet of magic with the thickness and consistency of a soap bubble.

"Let's go home," Roe said. She went through with a bounce to her step, making the portal wobble as she disappeared inside of it.

The celestial witches gestured me on impatiently, so I swallowed my nerves at trying this unfamiliar magic and stepped through with my luggage. It was like taking a long blink, except when I emerged in the Crystal Court, there was a dizzying whiplash from the change of scenery and abrupt yank of appearing in a completely different place.

I held my head with a groan. Roe pulled my elbow gently to clear the area for the next person arriving. "Don't worry, the feeling passes fast. I can't wait for you to see everything," she said.

I cracked my eyes open as the rest of our friends and family piled through. The wall behind us was one of the exits to the court's pocket dimension, according to Roe. It looked like a blank granite surface, no sign of a doorway or anything else to walk through.

The Crystal Court was nothing like I was expecting. When I'd heard "subterranean," I'd imagined low ceilings, tight corridors, and the distant *plink* of water falling from eternally growing stalactites. Instead, the nearest ceiling was ten feet up in this entranceway, and it transitioned smoothly to a cavern with a dome of earth overhead three stories high. A generous seam in the rock let in fresh air and light, which hit clusters of spiky crystals lining the walls that gleamed in every shade of blue I could imagine.

"Each section of the Crystal Court is big enough for a village," Roe told me. "There are paths between the formations and signs to guide you. You're actually staying here...over there." She pointed to a structure leaning against one of the cavern's walls. The windows suggested it was three floors high, with a roof that could brush the ceiling. It looked a lot like a hotel, if one could build with gleaming crystal blocks rather than bricks. In fact, most of the buildings along the way were also made of different shades of gleaming stone, like they'd grown there over the long weathering of centuries.

"It's so beautiful," I said, turning to her in awe. "You grew up here?"

Her smile was wistful. "Part of the time. We also have a house topside, with enough of a backyard for us to run around. My family took over the red cavern for our house and the business—there's no exit out that way, and it's mostly twisty, sharp corridors. It's a great place to stow and protect valuables."

Geo caught up with us and tugged the bag out of my hands. "Let me carry that for you," he said.

"Thanks." I lifted my chin so we could share a quick kiss.

"Do you think I could take some of the crystals here?" he asked.

Roe eyed a particularly large and jagged shard that'd grown partway over the path we took toward the hotel. "I'll ask my fae dad, but I don't see why not. They sell shards at the tourist shop." She grinned and cupped a hand over her mouth, whispering in my ear, "You should take one of your guys to the singing caverns. Folks come from all over to see them."

I nodded, already thinking of who I wanted to ask. I hoped the hotel had a map to point the way and a list of everything there was to do like any other hotel I'd stayed at. In the meantime, I fell back to chat with my family, who seemed both impressed and overwhelmed by everything at once.

The hotel had a short staircase out front, but the fae had roughed the top texture of the crystal bricks so shoes wouldn't slide around. Its entranceway was built for giants, spanning eight feet tall. An intricately carved statue of a fae man propped one of the crystal doors open, which I was thankful for since they seemed heavy.

The fae of this court had imported wood and other materials from somewhere, as the main foyer was far more familiar, with wood floors and a marble countertop. A pair of women stood below a chandelier dripping with teardrop-shaped pearlescent crystals. "There they are, just as you said!" the larger of the two exclaimed before sweeping up Roe in a huge hug.

"Hey, mama," Roe said.

My eyes widened. Roe's mom was practically a giantess, well over six feet tall, with obvious muscle in the flex of her arms. She wore clothes that molded closely to the lines of her body, with a big circular pendent of multicolored crystal hanging from her neck. Her wavy orange hair was slicked back in a puffy tail, bouncing behind her. Roe was her smaller, less fit double, which was crazy when I knew how much my friend dedicated her time and effort to physical fitness.

"And you brought your college friends," she was saying with a big smile. "I can't wait to meet you all! For now, get yourselves checked in. Your rooms here are free of charge."

She waited at the end of the line with Roe as we assembled a line to do as she said. I glanced past the two to make eye contact with the woman who'd been speaking with Roe's mom, waving shyly to Hana Graygazer as she stood a few yards apart from this gathering. Her gaze was faraway, and when I checked her aura, it pulsed with the gray-tinged magic that suggested she was glancing into the future.

After I received my room key, it was my turn to meet Madigan, who introduced herself and asked permission a moment before she squished me in a hug. "Roe's told me so much about you," she laughed.

"Good things, I hope," I squeaked, taking a deep breath when she released me.

"Of course." She rested a hand on my shoulder. "I'm sorry to hear what happened with your family. Hana and I were just discussing the circumstances of your petition."

I was quite aware of my adopted family behind me, listening. "Would you be willing to sponsor it?" I asked.

"My dear." She sounded indulgent. "Sponsor it? First, we're going to get you a date before the Crown Coven as soon as possible. Then, my coven and I will be there with you all. I'll wear my old armor, as long as it fits." She patted her flat stomach.

"Really?" Roe's eyes glimmered as she looked up at her mom. "You're going to pull Mad Ash out of retirement?"

"You know it, kiddo. Don't worry, Cress. Stick around here long enough, and you'll hear all kinds of stories about me in my prime." She didn't sound like she was bragging, either. I glanced toward Roe in curiosity, who just mouthed "later."

I stepped aside for Madigan to meet Willow, nearly bumping into Carly. "Hey," she said, lowering her voice. "Um, did you know the guy with the white dreads is totally into you?"

I hazarded a glance toward Geo, who was still carrying my bag for me. He smiled warmly from where he was still waiting in line.

Could my sister be a *little* less perceptive? I leaned in and whispered back, "Yeah...I can explain. Later. In private."

There was intrigue in the curve of her lips. "Okay. It better be soon," she said.

26

CRESS

Carly took the news well. I mean, she kind of shrieked, but at least she helped me talk to Mom when the three of us eventually ended up in her hotel room together. Each suite was twice the size of my dorm, with full room service, so we sprawled out on the couch and loveseat with snacks. More friends and family of the Ashboughs were expected later to fill the whole hotel, but we were amongst the first arrivals and situated on the ground floor.

"So, uh, that's not all of my news," I said once Mom got some of her color back.

She held up a hand. "Wait. You just want to skip over the fact you just told me you're dating three men?"

Uh, yeah, I definitely did. "It's not, like, as unusual as—"

"Cressida Ann," she interrupted sternly. I sat a little straighter. "*What* have you gotten yourself into since we dropped you off at NSU?"

Carly leaned in, hands under her chin. She was definitely ready for the gossip and romance side of things.

I breathed a sigh. "We're going to be here a while. I actually have a ton to tell you, but maybe it'll explain why I haven't been calling home as much as I should."

We ran out of snacks by the time I was done. I told them nearly everything, filling in their understanding of events from the details I'd told them here and there over the phone but editing the edges around events like me almost dying on Samhain night. The whole tale showed how I was connected and drawn to my three men, which delighted Carly, but Mom had a troubled frown while I mentioned Eris, Garroway, and the petition I was about to put in to appear before the Crown Coven.

"I never expected any of this when I adopted you." Mom said finally. "Forget about the men for a second. To think you're from a secret, powerful witch family and confirmed it by summoning a *ghost*. If you are truly going forward with this petition, then I want to be there to support you. Tell me the when and where, and I will speak to the authorities about the circumstances in which you came into my care as a baby."

"Okay," I said quietly. If she could come with me to appear before the Crown Coven, I'd love to have her there for support. "Thanks, Mom. I know it's a lot." I hesitated but knew I needed to bring up one more thing rather than blindside her with it. "Witch families and their bloodlines are a big deal. So much so that when I first enrolled and was tested for my magic, the NSU officials wanted me to take a new last name to start my bloodline. I was a nobody to them as Cressida Rollins."

Realization crossed Mom's face, but I continued before she could take it the wrong way. "I would have more respect in the supernatural community if I took the Darkmore name, but I want to honor where I came from and everything you've done for me. I was thinking of being Cressida Rollins Darkmore."

She dipped her chin in a short nod. "What about 'Luna'?"

"That's not what my mom named me," I said, getting a little misty when she did. Mom wasn't much of a hugger, not like my college friends, but when she reached out and squeezed my hand, I knew she approved.

"Whatever works best for you, baby," she said. "Never say no to opportunity."

My lips curved at the familiar advice. "You're right, Mom. I won't."

"Now, you'd better reintroduce me properly to your...boyfriends," she added. "Especially the demon."

"Dimensional," I rushed to correct. "He's from another planet, not Hell." Even though his descriptions of what became of Soiluire definitely qualified his old world for hellish status.

I stood and checked my phone for the time. "I'm sure you'll get the chance to talk to him at dinner. Looks like we have some time." Madigan had wanted to see us at seven for a meal downstairs.

I left to take some quiet time in my room, tending to my familiars for as little as they needed it. They'd found food and water downstairs, plus plenty of scratches from the fae staff. I put some of my stuff away and rested on the couch, surfing the Internet and reading my messages with Bella napping on my lap.

There were a few emails waiting for me. Two covens had signed on to sponsor my petition, and the online portal asked whether I wanted to submit it yet. Madigan had sent me a message over the system, telling me not to. I assumed her coven was Mad Ash Coven, but the second one was a mystery, Inevitable Defeat Coven.

As I read all my emails, another popped up. "Guardian Alliance 3 Coven has signed your petition as a sponsor."

"Whoa," I said under my breath, containing an excited wiggle so I didn't wake Bella. Roe's mom must've been pulling some strings at that very moment.

I put my phone away rather than refresh a hole in the screen hoping to see more sponsors. I'd snagged a map of the Crystal Court and a few pamphlets downstairs and leafed through them instead. There was plenty to do down here if one liked hiking and pretty vistas, enough to fill nearly a week's stay with the Ashbough family's hospitality.

I must've dozed off, because the next thing I knew, I opened my eyes to a knock on the door. The angle of light through the windows had changed to reflect coming evening. I fell off the couch in a clumsy moment, and Bella went launching off me with her fur all puffed out.

"Cress?" There was a note of concern in Phaeron's muffled voice on the other side of the door.

"Coming!" I called. I checked the time and muttered "shit" when I saw how close to seven it was. Instead of going to the door, I rushed to the en suite bathroom and checked my reflection. My makeup was all smudged on one side, and I could do with a change of clothes.

I rifled through the chest of drawers at the foot of the bed as Phaeron knocked again. "Is everything all right?" he asked.

"Yeah, just...just come in," I said, taking a moment to catch my breath after I found where I stowed my shirts. With that invitation, he turned into shadows and curled under the door, solidifying in a moment wearing a comfortable gray sweater and pants. "Have I seen you wearing this before?" I gestured to his whole ensemble.

He glanced down. "Probably not? But I assure you, I look better without them," he replied.

Oh, he was still playing this game, I see. Two could do that. "I agree. Clothes should be optional." I ditched my current shirt and felt a shift in the air. Phaeron only touched me with his gaze, burning brighter as he took in my exposed skin and little lacy bra.

"Take off much more, and we'll miss dinner." There was an edge of a growl in his tone.

"Oh, I don't intend to do that. Madigan wants to see us all, so we'll be there," I said, putting on my next shirt and heading into the bathroom to do something about my makeup.

I saw him join me in the mirror as I cleaned off what I was wearing and started putting on a simpler look so we wouldn't be late. "You're lovely without all that," he said. He tested the steadiness of my arm as he traced his claws up my sides, pressing featherlight kisses up the side of my neck.

"A lady never goes to an event without makeup." I answered, struggling to give my lids appropriately small wings. I nearly dropped the brush when he nipped me with those fangs of his. Okay, no wings. I tried to have even eyeliner instead.

"You *just* said you don't want to miss dinner," he pointed out while his lips traveled to my ear for more kisses.

I paused to take in the sight of him in the mirror, the dark and deadly prince, his fingers moving slowly over my hips and sides. Even if he was just teasing, his attention was fully on me, eyes dipped to watch my reactions to him. As much as I wanted more from him, I didn't mind the anticipation that had my thighs pressing together more firmly.

"I did. You know what I think?" I drew out the moment by applying mascara.

"I'd be thrilled to know," he said in my ear, his warm breath drawing a shiver down my spine.

Turning in his hold, I reached up to kiss him. "You'll be my date to dinner," I said.

I knew he'd find a way to tease me throughout the meal, but that meant he'd be coming back here with me afterward. If he wanted *me* to rip *his* clothes off, he'd have his wish.

I felt more than heard his soft laughter. "Very well, bright soul. I'll get you safely there and back. If you're ready?"

"I just need my lipstick—"

He interrupted with another kiss. "No lipstick. I'd rather not wear it later."

I had a shiver of anticipation, but I was the one that eased away, reluctant to break the simple contact between us. *Tonight*, I promised myself. It would be better for all the soft touches and gentle kisses, the whispers in my ear when no one else was looking. "So, is this the night you finally seduce me, or are we still just playing?" I asked, closing the lipstick tube and putting it aside.

He stilled, pulling his hands away from me. "Bright soul." The sigh in his tone was telling.

That'd been the wrong question to ask right before we'd have to go be social. The sinking feeling in my chest was my feelings taking a tumble to the ground, slipping through my fingers from putting myself out there so boldly to this man.

He stood there with his lips parted, gaze darting. "I...It was not my intention to..." Breathing another sigh, he shook his head. "No, that is a lie. I've wanted more of you from the moment you rescued me from Aurina's magic."

Some of the tension in my spine relaxed. I had a feeling I knew where this confession was going, with the obvious *but* hanging at the end of his statement.

"But I am still not sure I can trust my desire when it comes to you. I've been testing myself." He brushed the back of his fingertips across my cheek, his expression a mix of yearning and the deepest frustration. "Hoping that, with some familiarity of desire for you, the foulness of my lingering hunger will fade."

"And it hasn't," I said.

"No. If I am to claim you as my mate, then I must be in full control." His touch fell away from my face, fingers curling to fists.

I nibbled on my bottom lip. "Have you considered that it doesn't have to be that serious?"

His eyebrows creased. "Ah, but I am not human, Cress. I think and reason much like you do, but get me naked, and the instincts come out to play."

I nodded, as I'd definitely seen the animal in him before, the wolfish shadowborn side he usually kept under firm control. He slid closer, mere inches between us as he bent down and placed his lips on the smooth curve of my shoulder. I felt the pressure of his fangs through my shirt.

"I would mark you here. As you are not a dimensional, I would take care of making it a mating bite."

I tilted my head, breathing shallowly. "What makes that special?"

His warm breath washed over the curve of my neck. He nuzzled my sensitive skin, like those instincts were coming to bear as he imagined it. "A mating bite is not just a mark. Not like this." The tip of a claw circled the mark of protection he'd left on my wrist. "It's an exchange of essence. A near-instant swap of a tiny piece of our souls to bind us closer together. You may see now why it is too risky?"

"I know you won't hurt me," I said.

He hugged me around the hips, and I rested my palms on his solid chest. A stream of velvety, unknown syllables slipped from his lips as he pressed our foreheads together. I closed my eyes, enjoying the tender moment for what it was—as far as we could go, for now.

"What did you say?" I murmured.

He stirred with a slow breath, replacing the warmth of his touch with a fleeting kiss. "Roughly translated: my heart grows more enamored with you hourly, True Light, and I am helpless to resist."

I drew in to reply, dangerously close to using the L word in return. *Love.* I'd been flirting with the concept, sure that my affections could not be cut into three even pieces for each of my men. But...I'd never been so sure I loved princely Phaeron, just like I loved loyal Geo and playful Ben. It just seemed too soon to say it and risk him withdrawing from me more.

A harsh rap of knuckles on the door interrupted me. While I startled, Phaeron breathed a low growl. "Cress?" called Ben from the other side.

"It's time for dinner," Geo added a moment later.

"We almost missed it after all." Phaeron offered his arm. "Don't forget, *I'm* your date tonight."

I took his arm, not missing the glances exchanged between all three men when I emerged from the room on Phaeron's arm. Ben shrugged first, but Geo's lips tightened in reaction. No one said much until we arrived and took what seats remained open at a banquet table in a large conference room. Rich red and gold wallpaper and several hanging fixtures of multicolored crystal made for a warm, cozy atmosphere.

Madigan sat at the head of the table, with three unfamiliar men alongside her. Geo ended up seated next to the fae to her left, while I sat between Phaeron and Roe further down, across from Ben. "That's my fae dad. And those are my witch dads," Roe told me. The men in question turned their attention toward us as she did introductions.

The fae, Prince Orthus of the Crystal Court, was immediately eye-catching, with granite-colored skin that held a faint sheen and growths of jagged crystals that forced him to tailor his shirt to be sleeveless. They poked out a few inches around the side of his shoulders and trailed down his arms to form sharp, exaggerated elbows and hooked stone claws. Despite how inhuman it made him, they were pretty and polished, a pure emerald green like his eyes. He had the sharp elfin features typical of a fae and short-cropped hair a shade darker than his crystals.

Madigan's witch husbands, Aaron and Ajax, were twins and nearly indistinguishable except for their clothing choices. Aaron wore an eclectic, colorful ensemble, while Ajax preferred a suit. But their features were similar—short brown hair, neatly trimmed beards, and easygoing smiles. They were also guardians, with strong auras to match built, muscled physiques.

More of the Ashbough family were here, seated further down the table. Of Roe's massive roster of siblings, the four eldest were sitting politely as we awaited dinner, while the three younger kids were under the tablecloth, emitting the occasional giggle. As soup, salad, and drinks were served, Madigan glanced down. "Josie, please," she said.

A fluffy black and white border collie went trotting around the table, tongue lolling cheerfully. With a few authority-filled barks, she herded the kids back to their places, even helping the smallest climb back into his seat.

"What a beautiful dog," Mom said.

"Josie's been an Ashbough longer than anyone else in this room," Madigan shared. "She was my grandmother's familiar and helped keep me in line, too, when I was smaller." The dog had also disappeared on the other side of the table, except when her nose popped back up to accept a few table scraps.

Dinner was pleasant, the food a far step up from what I'd been getting in the dorms. Madigan made a point to ask all of Roe's friends about themselves, but the person she chatted with most was Mom, connecting over a show they'd both watched recently.

Geo and Orthus talked at length about rocks and crystals, using scientific names. Under the cover of conversation, Ben circled his fork toward Aaron and Ajax. "Which one's your dad?" he asked Roe quietly.

"All three of them," she answered.

"You know what I mean."

She exaggerated a shrug. "I dunno what else to tell you. I have three dads."

"You've never been, like, curious?" he asked.

"Ben," I said, raising an eyebrow his way. I wasn't exactly sure if it was different in supernatural families, but I thought pushing for an answer was a little rude.

"We get this question all the time," said Aaron, picking up on the conversation. "Our official tally is Orthus with three, me with five, and Ajax with one."

Ajax pulled an annoyed face. "That is *not* true."

"Hey, it could be," Aaron replied, grinning. His brother punched his arm. "Okay, it's not. Truth is, we don't test it. If you want to live in harmony in a family like ours, things like this can't be a contest."

"Even though those two are the most competitive men I know, it's still good advice," Orthus added. His voice had a ring of fae power, soft but deep. He was looking directly at me, so I nodded. I'd already seen how difficult it was to bring together my own three men, and there were still lingering tensions.

One day, I wanted a family that looked like theirs. Maybe with less kids, though. Just the thought of more than one made my belly suck in. No, I just wanted the tender looks like the ones Madigan's husbands gave her despite them being married and together for quite some time. An easygoing, tight unit.

I knew my men and I could have this, too. It would take time and hard work, but I wanted this to be a glimpse of our future.

27
CRESS

Thanksgiving was a communal event in the Crystal Court. My Thursday began when sunlight started to peek through the cracks in the cave's ceiling, helping a small army of people, both fae and witch, prepare a massive feast.

The cavern where we were staying, named the Sapphire Cove for its blue crystals, was too small to host what felt like the entire Crystal Court, the Ashbough family, and friends and other visitors. We spent time carrying over food and setting up tables two caverns over to the Diamond Square. Ringed in crystals formations both clear and cloudy white, it was a space kept for a few shops and restaurants, with an empty field ready for blankets, picnic tables, and fryers.

Mom had insisted we help, as the least we could do for our hosts. We weren't the only ones, by far. The cooking took up the kitchens of three restaurants in Diamond Square, and I saw friends and hotel neighbors alike helping prep and cook. It'd felt right, like we'd come together to assemble a community for this one meal. As Mom said, it was "the spirit of Thanksgiving."

Between tasks, I looked for Hana. She'd been exceptionally elusive during the last few days, though I'd caught glimpses of her in serious discussion with Madigan or sharing hushed whispers with other older, trained witches. I had the sinking feeling something was happening, or *about* to happen, and it wasn't being shared with me or my friends.

When I finally caught sight of her, she was sitting at a picnic table, drinking from a steaming mug across from Madigan herself. The matriarch of the Ashbough family was rarely still or quiet, always meeting with someone or doing something. But right now, she was quietly rubbing the ring of her mug, turning to face me a moment after Hana did.

"Ah, Cress!" The redhead looked happy to see me. "Have a seat."

In a moment straight out of an old film, Hana gestured to the space beside her and said, "We've been expecting you."

"Oh, you have?" I released a nervous chuckle and slid onto the bench where she'd indicated. It seemed they'd decided the time for secrecy was over the moment I did.

"The future is set," Hana replied as serious as ever. "Every route from this moment ends in the clouds that shroud your blood baron enemy from my sight."

I sucked in a breath. "When? I mean...when does he appear again?"

"We're going straight into the unknown, young woman," Madigan said for her.

Hana's softer voice behind hers reminded me keenly of another time, seated at a merfolk restaurant with Roe and Lanie. My friends took so much after their mothers. "Your upcoming petition to the Crown Court is where the timelines grow shrouded. Sometimes, you disappear in that fog. But there are no other options except to go forward," Hana said. "You should have several allied covens sponsoring your petition by now. It's going to be heard."

"I haven't submitted it yet," I said, turning to Madigan.

The redheaded woman dipped her chin. "Hana has suggested we keep it open until you make friends with some celestial witch."

"Jordan Evenstar?" I guessed.

"Yeah, her. You'll set the date, and we'll all be there."

"We will go prepared for combat. You should do the same," Hana added.

I nodded slowly. Ever since word had returned that Garroway was raising a new army of unwilling witches, I'd known the only way this ended was more bloodshed. But I hadn't expected it to be focused around the time of my audience with the Crown Coven.

"We'll be ready," I said. If Hana thought there was no other choice, then I believed her.

"I don't believe anyone is truly ready for the future, even a Graygazer," Hana replied.

Madigan slapped the table with a hearty laugh. "But we have a head start on destiny, and I give thanks to the goddess for that. A feast awaits, ladies! Let's not get dragged down by what will be." She was up and off with her mug the next moment, calling after one of her younger kids, who was creeping behind a crystalline fae who carried a still-steaming pie.

My gaze fell to the roughened wood grain of the table. I thought it was wise to be a little "dragged down" by what Hana had said. "Will we be able to save Lucas, Ben's brother?" I asked her.

"There is a chance. But he is caught up in the section of the future I have not been able to gaze into," she replied with a vague circling of her hand.

Well, that was frustrating. Ben, in particular, was taking this more peaceful time hard, knowing his brother wasn't nearly as safe or happy.

She contemplated the dregs in her mug with a sigh. "Things are falling into place, and that's all you really need to know right now. Let's go enjoy Thanksgiving." It was obvious she didn't want to dwell here, so I did not push her.

Nodding, I stood and went back to meal prep, so deep in thought that I appreciated the repetitive tasks of peeling and slicing and a near-endless parade of pots and pans to scrub and rinse to be used again.

Dinner was ready before I knew it, and by the time I emerged from the kitchen, I'd decided not to share what I'd learned with my friends and men today. Instead, I looked around as I joined a parade of chefs, bearing a jumbo bowl of stuffing to the longest table, set up with a cheery cloth covered in cartoon turkeys and cornucopias.

The fae had brought out a kind of projector and fastened a matte sheet of crystal much bigger than any wide-screen television to one of the walls. It looked like they'd used their magic to warp the naturally growing geodes to clutch it on all four corners. As I passed by, there was a zone I walked through where I could clearly hear the football game that was being projected on the screen.

Ben was seated up front, a bowl of popcorn between him and Geo. He threw up his hands. "Did you *see* that?" he exclaimed.

"I fail to notice anything particularly significant," Geo answered.

Ben gesticulated wildly as he explained whatever foul the referees hadn't flagged. I smiled to myself, glad to see them trying to spend some time together.

"Would you keep it down?" a pregnant fae called to him. I blinked rapidly as I continued walking and the sports commentators faded out of my ears. From another angle, the screen was playing an animated kids' movie, and I stepped into a zone where I could hear the sound effects, but also Ben's excitement over his football game.

"Sorry!" he called back.

A cluster of kids, under the watchful eye of Madigan's border collie familiar, were gathered around. Actually, an assortment of familiars were here, including Bella, who was slow blinking up at a young girl who snuggled her in both arms, and Ben's ferret, Flit, who was stretched to his maximum length and sleeping with his head poking out of a blanket fort.

Heads turned all around as the food was set up, and by the time everything was in place and straining the table, a line was forming. "Chefs, helpers, and kids first," Madigan's fae husband, Orthus, was saying, opening a space at the front of the line for us.

I wasn't sure who the man who carved the turkeys and hams was, but judging by his crystal-encrusted shoulders and the simple diadem he wore, he could've easily been the Crystal King, Orthus's father. If so, he made no fanfare of himself, other than making sure we all got our protein. I was glad he wasn't as ostentatious and grand as I assumed most fae rulers were.

When I had a plate piled high from the feast, I looked around at the picnic tables like it was a high school cafeteria, unsure of where to sit. Some folks filtered around me until someone closed their fingers around my hip with familiar pressure.

"Hi, Phaeron," I said without turning around.

"Hello. I believe our friends claimed that table," he said, pointing with his tail. We both headed that way, soon joined by Roe, Mom, and Carly.

"I wish I was a supernatural," Carly told me as she sat down. She had taken the hair potion I'd given her a couple days ago, so now she twirled a lock of candy-blue hair between her fingers with a wistful sigh.

"I know," I said with sympathy. It was hard not to want that when surrounded by the merriment of fae and whimsy of casual magic usage. No one here had to hide what they were.

Phaeron eyed her with a soft hum. I glanced his way, and he met my gaze, shaking his head briefly. Pure human, then, just like Mom.

"You can come back here any time you like, though. Open invitation," Roe said.

Mom caught the glowing look in Carly's face and added, "But if you want to live here, you'll wait until *after* you graduate college, young lady."

I started quizzing Carly on the colleges she'd applied for to distract her as Willow, Ben, and Geo eventually came by with their own portions of the feast. "How's your game going?" I asked Ben with a playful smile.

"Fuuu—effing awful," he amended quickly with a glance toward Mom.

"He is quite displeased that his team is losing," Geo reported.

"*Our* team, Geo. You're in this with me."

"I thought you wanted to watch the other side of the screen after this," the gargoyle said.

"Well, yeah. I'd rather watch animated ogres than whatever the heck our team is doing," Ben grumbled.

"I was thinking we could go for a walk after dinner," I said. I could've gotten whiplash from how fast Ben agreed to do that instead. "All of us could go, maybe? We still haven't seen the singing caverns."

Carly pulled back from her initial interest for the idea, leaving my three men the ones nodding. I'd hoped the singing caverns would be less crowded right after everyone stuffed themselves. I definitely needed some time to digest first after eating everything I'd taken, plus a slice of still-warm pumpkin pie. For a while, I lingered with my table, chatting, but followed the lead of others who wandered from table to table, talking and hanging out. I felt I'd made a few new friends here, especially amongst the Crystal Court fae, who were mostly quite friendly.

It'd be hard to return to NSU this weekend, but I'd enjoy the time we still had here. When my belly was more settled, I gathered up my men and followed the signs out of the Diamond Square, leaving behind the waves of sound from multiple voices speaking at the same time. Geo breathed a soft sound of relief.

The corridors between major caves here were wide enough to be a two-lane street, though there were no cars here. "So, the singing caverns are supposed to be like a maze," I said.

"And the walls, like, ring when you touch them or something?" Ben asked.

"The formations you'll see are a different kind of mineral than those in the other caves," Geo said. "They're grown from exposure to fae magic and resonate when exposed to sunlight. The people here make their weapons and armor from them."

I glanced his way curiously. Orthus had agreed to give him some new crystals, I knew, to replace much of the quartz he used in his gargoyle form. "Armor? Wouldn't armor made of crystals just shatter?"

He smiled back at me. "That's why they're grown from magic. They crack from excessive force rather than dent, which a Crystal Court fae, guardian witch, or gargoyle could fix. I'm fortunate. Prince Orthus gave me a tempered shield of it for free. Usually, it's incredibly expensive."

And the fae here had a whole cavern full of it, wow. My awe only grew when we turned down the proper path toward the singing caverns and I started to hear their namesake. We passed a building labeled the gift shop and emerged into a narrow cave with several small slits in the ceiling to let in patches of light.

The crystals here were definitely different, lining a maintained path that went up, down, and around this space and led to a hole in the farthest wall that looked like a tunnel. Instead of growing in giant, jagged shapes, the fae-grown minerals were like clusters of slim stalagmites, reaching up to hip height.

I started forward eagerly, inspecting the first couple formations. They were opalescent under direct sunlight, emitting a sound similar to the ringing that followed when someone rubbed the rim of a glass half full of water. I tapped one formation, delighted when it made a reso-nant *piiiing* and sparkling dust seemed to ripple within it.

"Different crystal sizes and colors make different sounds," Geo said, escorting me up the path to another patch of sunlight. It seemed these minerals came in all shades of the rainbow, too, some obviously growing back after being harvested at around the halfway point of their maximum height.

"How do you know all this?" I asked. He'd found a slim, silvery formation that made a higher-pitched *biiiiing* when tapped. "Wait, that's a dumb question. You're made of rock sometimes."

He flashed his teeth with a grin, which sparkled even amongst all the beauty around us. I paused, captivated by the easygoing display. Geo had come so far, and I think it was all the time he'd spent in human form. "One might say I have a passion for such things," he said.

"It's in the name," Ben joked. He'd roamed ahead of us, poking formations that were currently in shade. No sound came from them.

We kept climbing in relative silence, coming across the occasional diminutive fae lingering amongst the patches of sunlight. The first one I spotted went very still, like he was trying to become one with the formations. Others were spider-like, with many spiky legs, watching us with eight sparkling eyes as we passed by. They must live here, I thought, not wanting to disturb them.

I stopped to admire a disc of crystal that'd been fused of many different colored minerals and placed in the path about halfway in. It glittered half in sunlight, rippling from within around my shoes with each step. I walked into Geo's arms and relaxed there as we overlooked much of this cave and its singing geodes.

I met Geo's eyes, a bit like crystals themselves, and leaned up to kiss him. He pulled me closer, sure to give the native fae critters a show as he squeezed my ass. I'd forgotten about the other two until I picked up the smooth murmur of Phaeron's voice. I opened my eyes, spotting him nudge Ben.

"I'll keep watch," the dimensional said a little louder. I felt the heat of his gaze as much as Ben's clever hands brushing up my belly and his kisses on my neck. Both men had me sandwiched between them and the growing hardness of their arousals.

My hands fisted in the fabric of Geo's shirt. We were doing this...

now? Here? There were still fae around, the shy kind, and the chance we'd get caught by others seeking a post-Thanksgiving walk.

Ben palmed my breasts, making me reconsider complaining. Our hotel rooms were a several-mile walk from here—talk about a mood killer.

"Did you guys plan this?" I asked when Geo and I parted for a breath.

Ben tweaked my nipples, his laugh husky. "Who plans things?"

"I just wanted my beautiful woman in this pretty place," Geo said. He loosened the button on my jeans, sliding the zipper down.

Ben opened the clasp of my bra through my shirt and then tunneled his hands underneath the hem, his callused fingertips teasing my skin. "And so do I. So we might as well share. Right, Geo?"

Geo's answering grunt was less enthusiastic, but he still helped push down my jeans, my panties following shortly after. I couldn't complain, not with him caressing my thighs and helping keep me upright as having both of them touch and tease had me feeling weak in the knees.

"All right, but…" My gaze sought the blaze of Phaeron's other-worldly gaze. He watched me moan and arch into Geo's touch as his thick fingers explored up my leg to gather some of the slick from my pussy lips. The dimensional's jaw was so tight he might've grinded off the tips of his fangs.

If I thought this was the moment he'd let go of his control and join us, I was mistaken. Cool disappointment made goosebumps up my arms when he turned away to focus on his post and keep watch for anyone coming while he cupped his obvious arousal.

Ben and Geo more than filled the space between us, though, chasing away any chill I felt. Ben edged around my shoulder, kissing me deeply and swallowing my sharper cry when Geo finished sampling my slick from his fingers and delved between my thighs to collect more with his lips and tongue.

I was panting and out of breath, grinding on Geo's face, when Ben lifted his head to ask, "Hey, Geo, you bring any protection?"

Geo's muffled response sounded a bit like "no." He held my knees open to him, eating me out like a man starved. I trembled and held fast to Ben to keep me upright.

With an eager grin, Ben flashed a condom at me, plucked from his back pocket. "I know exactly how we'll share you, babe," he said.

"Oh?" I asked with a breathy whine. Geo had me on the edge of oblivion already, and that was where he stopped, leaving me slick and needy. If they hadn't told me this was unplanned, I wouldn't have believed it. Ben guided me down onto my hands and knees and hurriedly freed his cock.

The face of the crystal disc below us was pleasantly warm, rippling with pearlescent patterns around my body. I reached for Geo, helping him withdraw his own arousal from where it strained the front of his pants. As the pressure in my belly slowly eased, I glanced over my shoulder at Ben.

I didn't need to ask when I saw him getting onto his knees too and rolling the condom over his length. They'd take me between them, like how this surreal event had started, with Geo's mouth on mine. I beckoned the gargoyle closer and licked my swollen lips, dipping my gaze to his throbbing cock with obvious intent. His fingers threaded through my hair, guiding my head down to lap at the bead of precome welling up for me.

I gripped the base of his shaft, sinking him into my mouth until my jaw ached. He held me there while Ben grasped and positioned my hips, his length teasing through the cleft of my body. "You're ours, babe," he said before sinking home within me.

Usually, I responded to him saying, "You're mine, babe," with a simple, "Yours." But I simply moaned and swayed with his claim. They took it easier on me than usual, my body rocking from their rhythm. The slow roll of Geo's hips gave me momentum back into Ben's thrusts and vice versa.

They shared me beautifully, I thought through a haze of bliss. Like they were meant to. They'd put aside their differences for the moment, for this. And I had no complaints but one. Phaeron stroked himself as he stole glances at us yet made no move to join in. I wanted him too...to share in this moment.

It was obvious he wouldn't, though, so I kept my attention on the two who'd made me the center of theirs. Geo's stoic features were slack, and he tightened his fist in my hair while he chased the pleasure of my mouth. Ben's usual teasing was absent until I heard him ask Geo in the same tone he reserved in the bedroom with me, "Know what she really loves?"

"Many things," Geo rumbled back.

"This might be a new one," he replied. I shivered with anticipation as he spread my legs further, his thumb coming down to tease the rosette hiding between the globes of my ass. I came like a sudden detonation, as I had the first time he'd tried it a week ago, shocking the hell out of both of us.

Geo's eyes widened. His thick flesh absorbed my sudden cries, and he throbbed on my tongue. His laugh was deep, and his grin eager. "That'll help us share her more." I think he finished just from that thought, filling my mouth with liquid heat.

I liked the sound of it, too, fantasizing about doing this again, pinned between their solid bodies. The moment Geo withdrew, Ben quickened his pace to follow after us, and I saw stars by the time he came with a harsh breath and ground his hips into mine.

"That was amazing," I said. Now that I was full of both food and pleasure, though, I figured they'd need to carry me back to my room. I stood unsteadily with them, the three of us helping each other fix our clothes.

"Of course, because you were here." Ben threaded an arm around my hips, guiding me back the way we'd come. Once we were done, Phaeron had disappeared into a curl of smoke—avoiding temptation, or just avoiding us, I thought. But he was a fleeting thought as Ben and I kissed, and he said, "I fucking love you, babe."

I released a surprised laugh. The blurted admission was so like him. "I love you, too." After a moment, I turned my smile toward Geo. "Both of you."

The gargoyle seemed startled, his eyebrows raising. He mumbled something about duty as he took his place walking just a few paces behind us. "C'mon, you can say it too," Ben encouraged.

Geo cleared his throat. "I...I love you as well," he said. "And it's still not the sex talking."

Well, the sex had certainly opened up some talking, as the two of them bantered all the way down the slope until we had to tiptoe past the remnants of the Thanksgiving party back to our hotel.

28

CRESS

THE NEXT DAY, I was packing to leave when my phone started ringing. An unfamiliar number flashed on the face of the screen and my belly twisted with nerves as I swiped and put the device to my ear. "Hello?"

"Ah, hello there. Do you know a man named Benjamin Evenstar? He left me this number to call," a woman replied.

My heartbeat became a staccato pulse. "You must be Jordan. We've got a lot to talk about."

BEN'S AUNT teleported herself to the Crystal Court within an hour, after I convinced her that she'd received a legitimate letter from her long-lost nephew and then put my phone into the hand of said man. He and I awaited Jordan's arrival at the same cave wall where we'd first come in, and he tried to mute his twitchy energy by shoving his hands in his pockets.

I had my arms around him, feeling how he shook with nerves as the air thrummed with the movement of magic. It became visible in golden tendrils, forming a circle through which Jordan stepped through, holding a staff that glimmered with gold plating. She was tall and elegant in a gown with a slit up the side that showed a glimpse of her thigh.

I expected her to be wearing obvious signs of wealth, but she had no jewelry on, not even a wedding ring. Her brunette hair was down in simple waves around her shoulders. She placed the staff on the ground and said, "Ben? Is that you?"

"Hi, Aunt Jordan," he replied with a stiff wave.

I let him go so he could approach with his hand extended, but she went for a full hug. "Oh, goddess. It's been ages. I was still a kid when you were born," she said, releasing him except to hold his shoulders to take him in. "Liam let me hold you when you were a baby, and we all nearly regretted it. I remember you were the last baby I held, even."

"It's okay, Aunt Jordan." He repeated her name like he barely believed this was happening. "My friends will tell you I act like I was dropped on my head a few times."

"Hmm, I doubt that." Her smile started to fade. "That was the last time I saw you. I see that you have a blood witch aura. Everything you wrote—it was true?"

"Unfortunately," he sighed.

"In that case, there's something for you here. I just need to find— well, her." Jordan brushed past him. We both turned to see her hugging Madigan as the redheaded woman approached with Hana by her side.

"Jordan! A certain augur saw you coming," Madigan exclaimed. "You'll be wanting access to the vault, right?"

Ben and I exchanged a glance. "Does it feel like everyone knows everyone in the witch community?" I asked.

"I think Madigan does, at least," he replied.

"This way, then!" The redhead in question was saying.

I'd learned that the Ashbough family home was at the very end of the Crystal Court, a few miles' walk from here. They'd claimed a back wall of sorts for their business, a line of caves terraformed with only one entrance and exit. Madigan's business, the one Roe didn't particularly want to inherit, guarded those caves, which were filled with other witches' valuables. Ashbough Protective Services also offered escorts for valuables and bodyguards for events, and I'd heard they had a hundred percent success rate in keeping both important items and people safe.

Jordan claimed Ben's arm, keeping him talking about his life and preferences on the way to the vault. When he introduced me as his anam cara, her eyes shone with unshed tears. "Oh, you're Eris's girl, aren't you?" she asked. "Marie read the star charts and was sure you two were destined."

"She was right," I said, a little surprised she remembered that detail.

"Eris was practically another sister, with how often Marie would bring her around. Marie convinced her to take it easier so she could have you," she told me. "I'm glad you survived, too. It just breaks my heart to know how much love you two were born into but barely got to know."

"Us as well," Madigan said, glancing over her shoulder. "But we're going to fix what we can. Has she told you about the petition?"

She dropped her voice and told Jordan of the petition I'd written to appear before the Crown Coven. We stepped into the narrow cavern that held the Ashbough's vault, this one lined with jagged red and orange crystals and a ceiling that sloped lower after we passed their sizable house.

The door to the vault was obvious, a disc of polished fae crystal with no obvious handle. It rolled to the side at Madigan's touch. "That's as far as you two go until you have something to store in here," she told Ben and me.

Madigan, Jordan, and Hana continued chatting in quiet voices, the latter sharing something when she was just out of earshot. I sighed and turned to Ben, squeezing his hand. "How are you feeling?" I asked.

He turned a conflicted look my way. "I mean, she seems nice. Just, it's weird to have someone who remembers all these things about me and the family I never got to meet. I think...Lucas would've loved to be here. I wish he was." He pressed his lips together until they were a tight, white line.

"He'll meet her too. We're going to save him, Ben," I said. "Then we'll get to catch him up on everything he's missed."

"I hope you're right. I just don't want my aunt to think I'm a shitty person because I'm here while he's not," he muttered.

I put my arms around him, and he rested his head on my shoulder. "You're not. You're doing what you can so the next time we see Lucas is the last time there's a monster within him. We haven't been able to free him when fighting as a team, so you know you can't just…go off on your own and try to do something."

"I know that you're right. It just doesn't stop my guilt, though," he sighed.

I didn't think anything would until he had Lucas safe and healed. I simply held him until approaching footsteps suggested that Jordan had found what she wanted from the vault already. She carried a long leather-bound case, which she set before Ben. "What's this?" he asked.

"Your inheritance," she answered. He sucked in a sharp breath. "Your father's staff. I know about ten relatives who're chomping at the bit to have it, but no one's been able to unlock the box."

She knelt and gestured to the clasps, which were overlaid with glowing blue runes. "We should've known you and Lucas were still alive. If you are truly Liam's son, you should be able to open the box without effort."

Ben swallowed audibly before bending down to give it a try. Madigan and Hana inched forward, looking over Jordan's shoulder. There was a click of metal unlatching and the sound of glass shattering as the runes popped off the box without trouble. He lifted the latch with shaking fingers, washing the room in silvery light as an ornate staff was uncovered, lying in a custom velvet mold.

"Wow," Jordan breathed. "Just like I remember it. Its name is Evening Guidance, Ben, one of a set of five that have been in the family for generations. Now it's yours."

Ben picked it up carefully, setting it upright. A few delicate chains clinked as they met gravity for the first time in nearly two decades, linked to dozens of slim pieces of paper etched with celestial witch runes. They hung down from the centerpiece of the staff, which was a silver-plated crescent moon wrapped in the tails of several falling stars. It was how their magic worked—each represented a spell pre-prepared and stored on the staff, awaiting use. Jordan's staff only had three, by comparison.

He turned and offered it to me. "You'll find more use for this than I will," he said.

Even though I took it, I immediately opened my mouth to protest. There was no way I'd accept Evening Guidance from him, not when it was such a valuable link to his family. I didn't voice those thoughts yet when its solid weight filled my palms and I found the smooth grooves where I was supposed to hold it properly.

It was heavier than I expected, wobbling awkwardly as I manipulated it. I figured, by its height and balance, it was made for a man. Yet it pulsed with power that felt familiar, reminding me strongly of Eris when we'd first summoned her ghost and the taste of power that was locked deep in my handbook.

"It's beautiful," I said, inspecting the intricate pattern of silver stars and falling trails painted into the dark varnish of the wood. I simply *knew* it was an expensive tool, not truly meant for Ben or me to have. Yet I passed it back to him, and he set it reverently back into its case.

"It is," he agreed. "Thank you, Aunt Jordan, for giving it to me. I imagine there are family members that just wanted to break into the case and steal it."

"Plenty of them. But it belongs to you by right," she said with a nod.

There was a pause where aunt and nephew simply looked at one another for a while. "Do...you want to stick around for a while? There's something I was hoping you could do for us," Ben finally asked.

"Anything you need," Jordan answered.

SHE MEANT IT, as evidenced by her presence in NSU after we said our goodbyes to the Crystal Court, Madigan, and Hana. I hugged Mom and Carly long and hard, feeling the pain of parting from them again as keenly as our original goodbye when I went off to college. They *all* promised that I'd see them again by the time my petition was heard by the Crown Coven.

I'd finally sent it off with an incredible sixty-three covens sponsoring it. The Ashbough, Graygazer, and Evenstar families had gathered friends and allies and backed me with the kind of force that *had* to be heard by our governing council of witches. So it would be, December nineteenth, a day before the Crown Council rested for the holidays and New Year.

That gave me three good weeks to finish up my first college

semester with decent grades, rehearse what I'd say in front of the Crown Coven, and continue advancing my magic. Training with Phaeron fell to the wayside with Jordan around, as she'd taken an extended leave from her job and moved into an apartment in New Salem. Ben's big ask was getting her to teach me how to use my family line's celestial magic, which she'd agreed to.

I spent my evenings with her in the combat practice room, splitting my attention between her and Eris's spirit. Unfortunately, I was the only one who could see Eris, and she had...opinions.

If I had a dollar for every time she said, "She's teaching you wrong," I'd have...some money. I eventually convinced her to watch and add on what she could. It had to be frustrating to be a ghost in the first place, unable to touch or guide past the sound of her voice.

With my chatty handbook in hand, I was able to start casting basic spells, summoning both hot sunlight and cool, soothing moonlight. The phases of the moon started meaning something to me, as did the positions of various constellations. It was progress.

It'd be enough to show the Crown Council that I had celestial witches in my family line, and that's what was most important.

The biggest breakthrough of all happened at random when my phone rang early in the morning. I'd answered in a disheveled mess, reaching over Ben's snoring form and pawing for my device. "Hello?" I'd said groggily without checking the screen.

"Good morning," Wren's voice answered. I shot upright so quickly that both Ben and Geo startled awake. "So, our coven is named A Little Wicked now?"

"That's right."

"I like it," she said quietly. "I read your petition." Such things were public documents, if you knew where to look online.

I gestured to Ben that everything was okay and that he could put the knife away. "Yeah?" I asked with a twist of nerves.

"Yeah. I'm going to be there, as will Heath. Don't go replacing us." Her tone was perfectly neutral, and with the subtle crackle of shaky reception, I had no clue as to what she was feeling.

"Okay, um. We're having a meeting this Saturday to go over everything one more time."

"Perfect. I'll bring a gift." She bid me a quick goodbye and hung up.

I eyed the phone, grumbling when I saw that it was still four-something in the morning. "Well, that was weird," I muttered.

The "gift" wasn't, though. She'd rooted through her father's office over the holiday and taken pictures, which she supplied me copies of, all while acting like she was about to attend a funeral, black dress and red-rimmed eyes and all.

"He wouldn't tell me the truth. He's ruined so many lives," she'd muttered. She wouldn't meet anyone's eye during her brief stay at the coven meeting, slinking away once she confirmed the time and place.

Only once she was gone did I review the folder of printed pictures. It was correspondence—messages she'd pulled up on a computer from an odd-looking browser or aged paper she'd unfolded from crumbling envelopes.

I could count on my fingers the number of people I knew who I thought might turn on their own father. But after reading the contents of the secret messages...

I'd sell out Blaize Starsurge, too.

29
BEN

Aunt Jordan opened her pocketbook for the hearing, buying Cress and me traditional sets of clothes to wear. They were...akin to armor, and I felt like I was suiting up the morning of December nineteenth, sliding my hands into fingerless leather gloves. The rest of what I was supposed to wear was leather too, and I'd broken it in from its too stiff state so that it hugged my body perfectly.

She'd also bought me a bandolier that I slid over my shoulder, with needle-sharp knives lining it all the way down. "It's like you want me to fight someone," I'd commented when first presented with it.

"You can never be too prepared. Besides, you look the part of a strong blood witch now," she'd answered, patting me on the shoulder.

Phaeron had bought himself black leather armor at about the same time and wore most of it while we walked toward the campus and our agreed-upon meeting spot before we'd take a portal to Cerris City, Washington DC, a huge pocket dimension metropolis where the Crown Coven held its audiences. We'd only be spending a day there if all went well.

Unlike me, Phaeron had modified his armor, etching runes along the seams one at a time with his claws. He'd fastened his two swords to his hips and carried a helmet dangling from his fingers, alongside a bag full of supplies. He hadn't been convinced that this would be a one-afternoon visit.

One of the buildings that taught celestial witch classes had a teleportation loop, the stone circle they used to create portals to nearly anywhere. Most of our group was already there, waiting. Aunt Jordan wore a formal robe stitched with subtle patterns of falling stars, like the ones etching Evening Guidance, which rested in the case I was carrying.

Next to her, Cress was bouncing the waves she'd styled into her purple hair and adjusting her own robe. I'd seen what Aunt Jordan had intended with the ensemble immediately—it was a shorter robe with wide slits up to her hips, showing the dark pants Cress wore underneath. She'd buckled her belt over the robe, carrying her sheathed sword and handbook on either hip. It was a hybrid of styles, not quite librarian and not quite celestial, but showing both sides of her at a glance. Her three familiars lay together in the grass, napping in the sunshine.

Standing as a protective shadow was Geo in his gargoyle form, holding a new shield made of tempered fae crystal. It was bigger than his torso and sang gently in the sunlight as I came forward to steal a kiss from Cress. "You look stunning today," I said.

She hugged my side, avoiding the bandolier. "Thanks. What's all this?"

"Aunt Jordan wanted me to wear it," I said a little quieter.

"Hmm." Cress's eyes narrowed suspiciously.

I slid to the side to give Phaeron a moment with her, inspecting the rest of our friends and coven mates for a moment. Grant and Heath wore suits, while Wren was in a black robe with dark makeup and a staff in hand. Willow had dressed up some, and Bianca played with a knife, wearing a similar set of leather to me but with her trusty crossbow hanging at her side. Roe was late, as usual, as was Áine.

Grant jerked his chin away from the group and took me aside. "Well, spy extraordinaire," I said in a low voice. "You want to tell me what's going on?"

"I mean, your eyes work," he answered with his usual mocking edge. "But I have figured out a little after you asked me to look into it. Crown Starsurge is still in your blood baron's pockets. The Graygazer witches have been spreading around a heavy-handed rumor that there will be coordinated trouble between them to interrupt your coven's audience before anything too damning can be revealed."

I went a little cold to have it confirmed. We *would* be fighting today. "That doesn't sound safe for Cress. We could reschedule—"

"The augurs are also suggesting that we *have* to do this today. As you can see, it's being taken quite seriously," Grant interrupted, circling his hand to encompass us all.

"Do you fight?" I asked. I cracked my knuckles. Having another chance to kill Garroway, or even punch the asshole politician whose actions had gotten my mother killed, quickly overrode my hesitations.

"Not even a little," he answered with a laugh. "I'll leave that to you and her." He turned his head toward where Roe approached with Áine bouncing after her. The redheaded witch wore casual street clothes, which surprised me, while the faun had a flowing dress that almost hid the fact that she had vines wrapped around her arms that disappeared under the cuffs of her sleeves, which glowed with their own magic.

"Waiting for me? Never fear," Roe announced. "Is this everyone?"

Cress lifted her head. She was pressed to Phaeron's side now, touching the runes he'd put on his armor. "Oh, my mom and sister should be here any moment. They've got an escort walking them here now," she said.

"Are you sure they should be accompanying us, bright soul?" Phaeron asked.

"Mom wanted to provide testimony. It'll help our case," she said.

He frowned and dipped to whisper in her ear. I could tell when they started to argue from here, but her family arrived before he could convince her it was a bad idea. We moved as a group into the celestial witch building, walked into the back by a secretary who showed us to the teleportation loop. Aunt Jordan got to work setting up the portal to Cerris City, ushering the rest of us through until she was the last one in.

I shook off the sense of disorientation as we emerged on a concrete block already full of people. "So lovely to see you all again," Madigan said first, lifting the glimmering visor of her helmet.

She wore a variegated suit of red-shaded crystal, a hybrid of fae style and knight of old, which was instantly recognizable. She wasn't attending this meeting as a concerned mom, but instead as Mad Ash, leader of the guardian witches who'd never failed to protect an important item or person. Her armor came with a matching geode-formed hammer, big enough that she could sling it over her shoulders.

Most of these men and women were guardian witches, wearing variations of crystal and stone. It looked like Madigan had brought as much of Ashbough Protective Services here as possible, but interspersed were a few witches with augury gray auras, including Hana Graygazer herself, accompanied by a man who had to be her husband.

One man took off his emerald-green crystal helm, and I realized he was actually a fae, Prince Orthus. With a startle, I double-checked the auras and armor of the people around us. A good third were Crystal Court fae, some of which had grown armor out of their naturally embedded crystals. I smiled to myself. They were kind folks, going against many of the common trickster stereotypes fae carried around.

"Hey, kiddo. I have your gift right here," Orthus said to Roe. A large pendant hung from the fist of his crystal gauntlet, similar to the one that Madigan wore casually. It gleamed like an orange sun in the light. Roe came over and placed it around her neck, holding up the glimmering pendant with a big grin.

I watched in fascination as he explained how it worked in a low voice, leading her through a spell that ended with her pressing on the center of the circular crystal, pushing it to her chest. It flashed, and crystal grew outward from it rapidly, flooding over her body to form a suit of tangerine-and-yellow-colored armor that broke at the joints to give her range of motion. She flexed her hands into fists, which were exaggerated with an extra-thick layer of crystal.

"Thanks, Dad," she said.

They clasped forearms like warriors of old. "That's my girl," Orthus replied proudly.

Someone tapped me on the shoulder as we got moving shortly after that, surrounded by guardian witches and armored fae. "Bet you I get first blood today," Bianca said, falling into step with me.

"Sure." I rolled my eyes at her. "If we're going to fight today, I know you'll be right in the middle of it."

"If?" she echoed with a laugh. "You mean, *when*. Bet I get more kills than you, too."

"Well, that's a guarantee. You've got more practice," I said.

I was distracted by the sights. We walked a slowly narrowing path overlooking a bustling city of supernaturals. We'd been teleported to the highest point of the city, where the Crown Coven's grand complex was set as the only structure on a tall hill. I was just glad we hadn't had to climb the steps. Bleached white and softened by the passage of thousands of pairs of feet, they lead all the way up to the front entranceway of the building we approached.

The complex was palatial, built like it housed giants rather than seven important politicians and their staff. Its pointed roof transitioned into a dome ringed with seven flagpoles, each flying the colors and symbols of each witch affinity.

One side, I knew, was for a grand library of knowledge, though Cerris City made it redundant with its own separate library to house dimensional secrets, like NSU had. The other side was for residences. Wren may have been raised here, in the lap of luxury. She lagged behind us, the slowest and most reluctant member of our group.

We filed into the front hall, joining clusters of other witches waiting for their audiences. They eyed our group nervously, not that I could blame them when we were the ones armed and ready for a conflict.

"Look at this fancy-ass place," Bianca muttered.

We were encouraged to sit by the staff, though few did. I stood braced against the wall a few feet away from where Cress paced, muttering her rehearsed lines under her breath. It *was* a fancy-ass place, not that I had time to admire the glitter of the gem-encrusted walls or how grand the chandeliers were. We'd arrived right on time—Cress's audience before the Crown Council would happen at any moment.

An orderly in a fine suit caught Cress's attention, and she nodded along to what he was saying until one rule gave her pause. "It's tradition, miss," he said apologetically. "Only witches can come into the audience chamber unless it's absolutely necessary."

"What if they're providing testimony?" she asked.

"If you identify them, we'll get them in front of a computer so they can do so over a conference call," he replied.

She pointed out Phaeron, Geo, and her mother to him, and he bustled away. With a sigh, she turned to me. "So, we're only allowed one other coven in the chamber with us. I picked Madigan's, but everyone else has to wait out here."

"Kind of bullshit," I agreed, pointing out one of many screens just above eye level to her, which lined the walls. They showed the current audience that was before the Crown Coven, with signs describing how to tune in on a cell phone or computer. "They can watch us, at least."

"I guess." She bit her lip, sliding closer to me. I held her, recognizing the nerves playing over her expression.

"You're going to do great, babe. You're a hundred percent in the right," I reassured her.

She rested against my chest with a sigh and nod, the two of us waiting until a grinding scrape and groan filled the air. Everyone looked to the two twelve-foot-tall stone doors coming unsealed just enough to let the last group of witches filter out. Someone tapped on a microphone. "Up next, the Crown Coven will hear A Little Wicked Coven, accompanied by Mad Ash Coven."

"Let's do this," Cress murmured, standing straight and adjusting her robe before walking straight-backed toward the audience chamber. Her mother caught her hand, giving it a squeeze on her way by, and she exchanged a nervous smile with Carly.

She stood in the center of our coven, with Roe and me following in a step behind her. My breath caught for a moment at how fancy the Crown Coven's audience chamber really was, designed to display the might of all seven affinities.

To the left of the long path leading to the raised dais where the Crown Coven sat, a glimmering lake of blue water churned with waves that lapped the far wall. Intricate statues and carvings lifted from the water, forming elegant ripples through the air. The right held a field of flowers and medicinal herbs permanently stuck at peak maturity, surrounded by formations of rock and crystal.

The domed roof above us could open to the night sky, but right now, it had several flying books circling high over our heads. They were enchanted tomes of magical law, as I understood it. To complete the set of affinities, a set of tarot cards glimmered at the stone base of the dais where we stopped, ready to spring up into the hand of a talented augur. And resting on an ornate loop was the cup and dagger ready for the blood oath every Crown Coven member had to make before they ascended the steps to sit in state above their petitioners.

A man, also wearing a fine suit, stood to the side with a microphone and a tablet in hand as we arranged ourselves on the platform right underneath the stare of the seven most powerful witches in North America. Madigan's coven formed a protective half-circle behind us.

We'd been allowed to keep our weapons only because of the other tradition in this room. Seven witches stood to the side of each politician, dressed in the ceremonial garb of their affinities. In the old days, when it was first formed, the Crown Coven had been required to have one witch of each affinity. Times had changed, and rules were loosened; since they were elected into power, it had inevitably balanced toward celestial witches since it was seen as the strongest affinity. This way, they were at least guarded by one of each.

The suited man cleared his throat. "Let us get this underway. Appearing before the honored witches of the Crown Coven today are the witches of A Little Wicked Coven, accompanied by Mad Ash Coven, one of their sponsors. Their petition involves the circumstances around the untimely death of Eris Darkmore."

He went on to introduce each of us one by one; then he named the seven politicians eyeing us with an assortment of suspicion, eagerness, or curiosity. Seated first in line was the leader of the coven, dark-haired Tempest Wildsong, an oceanic witch wearing an elegant seafoam-colored dress that complimented her honey-toned complexion. "This shall be interesting. Won't it, Crown Starsurge?" she asked with a sharp smile.

"There's no need to assume him guilty so soon, dear," said the elderly verdant witch in seat two, Sophia Greenridge.

The third in line, celestial witch Zander Shadowsoul, crossed his arms and smirked over at Blaize, whose face was reddened as he looked down at us. He'd skipped his gaze right over Cress, his head tilted toward Wren. "Sundrop, why are you here?" he asked.

She tapped a perfectly manicured nail against the wood of her staff. "I want the truth, Father."

A bead of sweat trailed down his temple. "You should get out of here. Now."

She lifted her chin stubbornly, shaking her head.

"Can't say I've ever seen my own kin here behind a petition about me. Rotten luck," said the man in seat five, the only blood witch, Daire Grimsbane. He was a tough-looking Black man with a similar bandolier to mine looped around his shoulders.

"If I wanted your opinion, Crown Grimsbane, I'd ask," Blaize muttered.

"We're all equals here," pointed out the youngest appointee to the Crown Coven, celestial witch Einar Nightwalker. She wilted when both men turned to glare at her.

Silence followed when Kwan Graygazer was announced last, as the man in the seventh seat. He was an older member of the Graygazer family, his features wizened and thoughtful behind the thick rim of his glasses. He shuffled the cards of a tarot deck back and forth in his hands until they were nothing but a glowing blur.

Cress stepped forward when the announcer beckoned, taking the microphone. She drew breath to speak, to begin the speech she'd rehearsed so diligently.

Blaize stood. "Before you begin, there's one thing I want to say."

"Sit down, you bottom dweller," Madigan shouted.

"I should have you evicted for poor manners," he replied with a sneer. "However, whatever you've come here to say won't matter." He lifted the staff he'd had rested against his high seat, casting a quick spell and flicking a superheated missile of magic toward the sealed stone doors of the audience chamber. As they crumpled, I caught the sound of screaming and stamping feet from the other side.

GEO

The moment the doors sealed behind Cress and her witch friends, Hana Graygazer went and snatched the microphone from the coordinator outside the audience chamber. "Listen to me, everyone," she said, her voice raised to a boom as she leaned into the device. "You are in great danger. You need to leave *now*. Escape the pocket dimension if you can!"

"We could use your help, friend," Orthus said to me. I cast him a bewildered look, but he was already pushing confused and panicking witches out the front door. I followed his lead, using my shield as he did to make a wall no one could say no to.

"What's happening? I have to testify for my daughter!" Cress's mother shouted. She was one of the few that weren't being herded outside. Phaeron had her by the shoulder instead, with his tail looping around Carly before she could complain. They disappeared into a curl of smoke together.

I turned to Orthus, brow drawn low. "Explain," I said.

"I'm sorry for keeping you in the dark," the fae prince replied. "One always takes the word of a Graygazer, and Hana was insistent we be here to stop what comes next."

"Which is?" I demanded. My stone heart raced faster, and I thought of Cress, sealed in a room with all of those unknown people and the man she wanted to embarrass and expose live on camera.

"Even Hana wasn't quite sure. She sensed a danger so vast only the best were meant to face off against it," he said. "We'll talk later. These civilians need to be cleared out as soon as possible."

He, his fae, and the guardian witches who hadn't made it into the audience chamber worked as one unit ushering people outside. I followed their lead, clumsily reassuring strangers where I could but inevitably shoving them toward the doors with questions still on their lips.

The last stragglers and most stubborn were still here when the air shimmered. I turned, recognizing the feeling of dimensional magic, but it was white shadow that unfurled and slammed talons through the nearest person. Blood sprayed everywhere, and the Hungering Darkness's wolfish maw formed, opened in rapture as it sucked up and consumed the soul of its victim.

"We have company!" I shouted.

Magic swirled behind us, more and more people equipped for combat appearing. They'd teleported between us and the sealed audience chamber doors, inciting screaming panic amongst the last civilians still in this space as weapons were drawn and magic started to fly. I didn't waste time in forming my crystal club, swinging it at the grinning face of the Hungering Darkness and knocking some of its shadows aside.

It raised its talons to catch my weapon, smiling at me with a pale face so similar to Ben's yet so different, seeming waxy and slack. There was little glimmer of Lucas's humanity within the monstrous enjoyment the Hungering Darkness was taking in this moment. No hesitation, either, as it threw off my weapon and followed through with its claws aimed at my gut.

"Hello to you too, Morgana," it hissed.

My new shield sang a higher note as I caught its strike. "You've made a grave error," I said, determined to crush it once and for all.

Bang! The stone doors leading into the audience chamber shuddered and started to crumble in a fall of rubble and thick dust. The Hungering Darkness grinned viciously as its shadowy white maw reformed over Lucas's face. "No, *you* have, by being here," it replied with a cackle, disappearing in a curl of smoke.

Garroway's army was still teleporting in, but one of the witches aimed a trident at the collapsing doors and blew away the dust with a harsh gust. Witches of all kinds rushed the audience chamber in eerie, robotic silence, leaving the rest of us to give chase.

Ahead of us, the protective semi-circle of Mad Ash's coven turned, weapons brandished. They formed a solid wall of crystal, shields raised, as the first onslaught of mixed magic hit.

"What is the meaning of this?" a man dressed as a blood witch demanded, starting to stand from his high seat amongst the Crown Coven.

The Hungering Darkness took form again behind him, sinking its talons in his chest before anyone could react. "Destiny," it hissed.

I spread my wings, taking flight to get up there faster. A balding celestial witch, who I recognized as Blaize Starsurge, turned his staff toward me, throwing a blistering hot wave of magic in my direction as I arrowed toward the dimensional creature now fighting one of the other witches up on the dais.

My flinch was enough time for it to kill the guard and tear into the woman who'd extended her own trident toward the lake of water within this chamber. The tongues of water she'd been weaving into heated whips fell when she died next.

"Father, what are you doing?" Wren's scream echoed off the ceiling.

"Come up here, sundrop. You'll be safe," he replied in a begging tone.

I circled in for a landing on the dais, but a blur of shadow was quicker in taking form and tackling the Hungering Darkness away from a screaming man crawling away from the bodies of his peers. Phaeron grabbed his brother, rolling both of them off the dais. I checked my momentum and landed next to them instead, club raised.

"I have this. Protect Cress!" Phaeron shouted. His black talons were wrapped around the space over Lucas's shoulder, trying to tug the Hungering Darkness free of him. I grunted and turned, seeing her with her handbook floating just over her shoulder, sword clutched in both hands as she dueled with another librarian witch with dead-looking eyes.

Most of Garroway's army had that blank look to them, no spark of intelligence or free thought on their faces. I swung my club over her head and bashed the skull of Cress's opponent, who crumpled.

"Thanks," she said, taking a moment to cast a shielding spell in front of her.

I stepped in front of her with my physical shield raised and slammed my weapon at the next dead-eyed witch that came forward. It seemed like they were endless, the sheer amount of them creating chaos in the audience chamber, but they were weaker than the assassins we fought in Garroway's manor.

With my height, I could pick out the trained assassins from the crowd and the vampire that lurked amongst them, shredding through all but the toughest crystal with enchanted blades of his own. Most of these people Garroway had brought were bodies—distractions from the few big threats hidden amongst them.

"There's an emergency exit behind the dais," Blaize was saying behind me, still begging his daughter to join him. I picked up on the possibility of escape and started trying to map ways around the crush of bodies crowding us in on all sides. I had to get Cress out of here by any means possible.

Garroway looked up, flicking blood from his weapons. He was the only person here with enough space to think, standing over the dead body of one of our allies. With a lurch of my stone heart, I recognized the suited young man he'd cut down. Heath. Wren hadn't noticed yet, judging by the argument still ongoing between her and her father.

It happened so fast. Garroway took a running leap, boosting his back leg off the shoulder of one of his enslaved witches. I watched his trajectory, tightening my hand on my weapon and reflexively raising my shield, should he come for Cress. Instead, he landed on the dais and had his dagger through Blaize's forehead in one smooth thrust of his arm.

"No one escapes today," he said in a slow cadence, smiling viciously as he retrieved his weapon from the man's skull. "And you've outlived your usefulness, Crown Starsurge."

30
PHAERON

THE HUNGERING DARKNESS thrashed within Lucas, evading the pull of my claws. I could barely feel the life force of the boy it latched on to—a sign I recognized grimly.

"Dance with me, brother," it said, grinning. "One last fight before we bend the knee eternally." It shoved me off and sprang to its feet, drawing twin swords and gesturing for me to do the same.

I didn't pay its words much mind, knowing it'd long passed into the abyss of insanity from its eternal soul hunger. I unsheathed my swords and muttered the trigger word for the spell I'd etched into my armor. It hugged me a little closer and hardened, ready to deflect its claws until the spell failed.

"We need more space, though," it mused, turning to leap onto a lace-like fixture of metal suspended over the lake of water. With bodies starting to float in it, it'd gone from a placid blue to a gore-streaked red. I jumped onto the fixture, bracing as it shook beneath both of our weights.

It hadn't lashed out at my mind yet, leaving us both in peak condition to duel. My shadows coalesced to cover me head to toe, and I released a wailing roar as I assumed my shadowborn form. Our weapons were black and white blurs as we twisted, turned, and struck at full, vicious power.

Endaeron, in his prime, had been the superior duelist, the stronger, more beloved prince. I saw a glimpse of him again as he got past my guard and the edge of one blade swiped the side of my armor. The spell held, but I'd have a bruise from the force of the strike. The fixture wobbled below us.

"What?" it hissed.

"Borrowed an idea from you," I said before cutting the nearly invisible metal thread that kept this platform over the water. We both teleported to a different piece of metal a few yards away, a fountain with a rigid U shape. I gained the high ground, cutting bloody lines across its torso.

"You never could think of your own tricks, could you, Phaeron?" It taunted, smashing both blades into mine and shoving. I turned into smoke before I hit the water, reappearing behind it. But it'd already twisted around, shoving the point of one blade into my belly. I felt my armor strain to keep it from piercing straight through me.

"One of us is still alive," I pointed out, turning into smoke yet again and reappearing with precarious balance on another part of the fountains. I lifted one blade, channeling shadowy magic through it and chopping it toward where the Hungering Darkness still stood. It became a wisp too, and the sharp blade of shadow I'd sent toward it broke the fountain instead, sending a pressurized jet from its newly blunted head.

"But we will both serve. It is Myuna's will," it answered next to me. Our swords locked again, sending up sparks.

"Why mention that harlot?" I snarled, sweeping its feet out from under it. It went down hard, breathing an *oof* as its borrowed body bent around the pipe we stood on and went sliding into the water. I reached out with several tendrils of shadow, catching its swords and flexing them viciously with my magic. I managed to snap one before it came surging out of the water, talons first.

This time, it parted my leather armor like butter, sending fuchsia blood flying as it scored deep furrows across my chest. "She rules all. And she has always wanted a full set," it hissed, leaning in. "To be served by me *and* you."

"Never," I snarled back through the surge of pain.

That was when it reached out and sank mental claws into my head.

Corruption blossomed in the black flames over my body as I fell to my knees, wobbling on the thin metal below me.

"*Cress!*" I called desperately, feeling darkness closing in.

"Get away from him!" A shrill voice pierced my awareness, accompanied by a jet of water. I blinked dark spots from my vision, gasping when I spotted Willow at the edge of the water, balancing two globes in her palms.

Her eyes glowed an icy blue, and power pulsed from her. Her *soul* grew, both sides finally intertwining into a harmonious whole. Blood wept from her cheeks like tears as pinkish scales burst from her skin.

"Monster! You killed my friend!" she screamed, turning her palms toward the Hungering Darkness.

The water churned out of control around it, reaching out with ice-lined arms. I helped him down with a kick to the shoulder, and he landed with a splash, enveloped instantly and pulled to the bottom of the lake. Around Willow, other witches started clawing at their necks, eyes bulging. Water and blood leaked from their lips and noses until they fell, spasming and struggling.

I clutched at my throat, struggling for air. "Willow," I rasped, feeling my lungs bubble with the liquid filling them. I reached for her, choking as her soul pulsed again and coral-pink fins and scales rippled down her arms and tipped her fingers in delicate claws.

She was losing control of her magic as it grew and changed with her shift toward a mer form, and there wasn't a damn thing I could do about it. My shadows faded, and my swords splashed into the water below me. I pitched forward with a desperate gasp, trying to get even a sip of air as the wrong kind of darkness closed in on my awareness.

A flash of red came behind Willow in my blurring sight, and I drew a desperate breath as the water in my lungs vanished. "Sorry, kid. Couldn't have you killing our friends," Madigan murmured down to a crumpled Willow.

I lost precious seconds recovering, struggling to catch a breath and get my shadows to obey in retrieving my swords from the bottom of the lake. A soaked Hungering Darkness erupted from the water before I was ready, claws extended toward me.

CRESS

Wren was screaming behind me, crying over her father's body. It'd tumbled over the edge of the dais while the rest of us fought. Even though it was Blaize Starsurge, I still couldn't imagine her pain.

The remaining Crown Coven witches and their protectors were caught in a desperate fight with Garroway and a couple of his assassins as they picked off the important officials one by one. Some of his enslaved army had blocked the emergency exit, or so I thought when Einar Nightwalker rushed that way and didn't return after releasing a high-pitched shriek.

"This isn't how it was supposed to go," said Eris hollowly, though I was the only one who heard her. Men and women fought *through* her transparent form. I'd summoned her ghost to witness this moment of triumph, just to show her a charnel house as our forces clashed with Garroway's.

I was in a position of relative safety, behind the defensive line of Mad Ash Coven and between Ben and Geo. I borrowed from Bella's senses, the cat hunkered down in a sheltered nook with my other two familiars. We'd practiced, so I heard the rasp of weapons over armor and through flesh at an unpleasantly magnified rate, but also the taunting between Phaeron and the Hungering Darkness.

Phaeron seemed to be losing, especially once Willow started acting strangely. I backed away from her as the men and women around her, both friend and foe, started to choke as her magic surged. That was how I tripped over the case lying forgotten where Ben had placed it.

I bent and freed Evening Guidance from its box, my pulse rocketing in my throat. "I need a spell," I shouted at my mother's ghost. "Something that will burn a dimensional monster!" While I'd take anything, I was hoping for some miracle, something that would save us all.

It was a desperate request, especially since I'd had to set my bloodied sword down to take up the staff in both hands. But I couldn't do anything for Phaeron at the back of this group and crush of people. I'd noticed that celestial witch spells were designed to be long-range, however, unlike the close and personal nature of magic cast from a sword.

"There is one," she said, reading the spell tags dangling from the staff and nodding. She followed as Geo and Ben covered me and Willow collapsed, knocked unconscious. The combatants around us got back to their feet.

"Repeat after me," Eris said, positioning herself on the other side of the staff and laying her static-filled hands over mine.

She shifted her weight, and I mimicked her, lining up the tip of the staff toward the shaky sculpture where Phaeron barely kept his balance. Latin flowed from her mouth, and I repeated it, feeling the wood warm in my hands. It felt like it was sucking on my palms, the feeling transferring up my arm and to the book that'd come in for a landing on my left shoulder.

My ancestral magic flowed down that arm and into the weapon like a coursing golden river. The star pattern on the wood lit up. It vibrated in my hold as the spell I'd activated waited to be released. "Steady, girl!" Eris exclaimed. "Aim and fire!"

I did. When the Hungering Darkness emerged like a razor-lined fish, talons extended to rend Phaeron in half, I shouted the trigger word and sent a laser of concentrated light streaming right at it.

Its head turned, golden light reflecting in its eyes before the spell slammed into it, knocking it backward with an otherworldly howl. My jaw dropped as the Hungering Darkness went visibly tumbling out of Lucas's body as it hit the far wall and slid downward. The monster fled the intensity of light from my spell.

"Lucas!" Ben called, dropping his weapons and diving into the lake without hesitation.

Phaeron launched himself from his perch, shadowy claws extended. The Hungering Darkness was just clipped by his reaching talons, turning into white smoke as it wound over our heads and surged toward the dais. I turned my head, watching it slam into Garroway's body. The vampire jerked his head to the side, frozen for a moment above Kwan Graygazer lying prone on the ground. The elderly man scooted away, crab walking backward to a safer spot.

"Trying to control my magic, Garroway?" the Hungering Darkness hissed from the vampire's lips, clawing at his side to expose a red-rimmed blood rune etched there on his skin. It was unlike Ben's, three rings thick and lined with spiky runes. He'd nearly covered the whole right side of his body with intricate spell patterns. "Don't you know it's *my* magic that makes this possible?"

It grew talons of white shadow over Garroway's hand, and they jerked back and forth for control of the body. Unlike with Lucas, Garroway had some struggle left in him, but that was before the points of those claws raked across the face of the rune. Garroway's body went slack with a sibilant sigh.

"Bright soul, this is nothing good. We need to leave at once." Phaeron appeared in a curl of smoke next to me, his otherworldly eyes feverish with pain. The front of his armor was stained with his fuchsia blood.

"Let us end this farce, shall we?" the Hungering Darkness was saying, drawing the black knife-like shard from its pocket and crushing it in a shadow-lined fist. The sudden collapse of dozens of bodies had me startling. Like puppets with their strings cut, every single member of Garroway's unwilling army and his trained assassins fell.

"They're dead," announced one of the guardian witches, looking as shocked as I felt.

The Hungering Darkness raised its arms, chanting in another language. Phaeron wavered on his feet, his gray skin paling to a sickly shade. "Run. All of you, run!" he shouted.

My mother's ghost looped her arms around me. For a moment, it was like she was tugged toward the chanting dimensional monster. "You can't see it, can you?" she asked. "The souls...everyone who's died..."

The bodies were twitching briefly before going still. It must be using souls for some kind of awful spell.

"This way's faster," came the hoarse voice of Kwan Graygazer as he limped his way down the stairs from the high seats, supporting a blood-soaked Daire Grimsbane, who had healing runes hastily painted across his chest. They led the rest of us behind the curve of the dais, where the emergency exit was clearly marked with a closed metal door and keypad, along with the fallen bodies of several people.

He keyed in a number on the pad, and the grate-like door swung open. Madigan and Orthus took places on either side of the opening, shoving people through. I watched as the elderly man shuffled to a box set right inside the exit tunnel and opened it, pressing on a giant red button. The air in the room shifted suddenly, like an increase of pressure along my spine.

Ben was amongst the guardians protecting our escape, dripping water with his brother slung over one shoulder. He was joined by a fae in cracked armor, who carried Willow, and others who helped our wounded and unconscious to safety. Geo was toward the back of this group, meeting my gaze grimly. He supported Wren, who stumbled along with a deeply stunned expression, and a battered Áine clip-clopped a few steps behind him.

"Phaeron?" I said, lingering when the dimensional stopped mid-step toward safety, a tremor passing through his body. He turned and took a step back the way we'd come. I tugged on his arm, trying to stop him. "What are you doing? We can't stick around."

"It's too late for me, bright soul," he said softly, his expression shifting to obedient blankness. "Leave me behind. Save yourself."

He shook me off his arm with a frown. His eyes flared with aggressively bright white shadow, which persisted even when I pressed on his mark of protection and called his name. It only seemed to annoy him, as he cast one last inscrutable glance over his shoulder.

A gauntlet of red crystal closed around my shoulder, pulling me back. Madigan pushed me into the tunnel as I cried out, reaching for Phaeron anyway, who marched his way back into the death-filled audience chamber.

The whole structure shook, showering dust over us. A voice, great and terrible, rose from nearby. It seemed incomprehensible at first, speaking in dozens of languages before finally settling on English.

"Endaeron? It has been so long." It was feminine but vast, with the kind of power that made it feel like my head was being crushed just by hearing it.

"Myuna," I breathed in horror. The soul-consuming deity that'd destroyed Soiluire, *here*. Tears stung the corners of my eyes as I imagined the same level of depravity seizing Earth. But first, she'd taken Phaeron, and there was nothing I could do about it.

It's too late for me, bright soul.

"What is this place you've summoned me to?" the goddess asked.

BRIGHT SOUL
MOONGROVE ACADEMY: WICKED SPELLS BOOK 3

Bright Soul

CONTENT OVERVIEW

This is a paranormal RH romance, meaning that the main female character does not need to choose between love interests. There are graphic sex scenes (some including more than one partner) between consenting adults. *Bright Soul* is book three of a trilogy that ends with a guaranteed HEA!

Please be aware that this book continues to show depictions of grief because of the death of a friend. Also contained within are fight sequences that include death, gore, and magical violence. This trilogy is classified as dark academia because the main antagonists have magic that affects the souls of others.

This trilogy does not include a pregnancy for the FMC or MM content.

If you find anything in the contents of this book that should be added to this page, please let me know at ellahendricksauthor@ gmail.com.

1

CRESS

My heart was still a thrumming pulse in my ears when we emerged onto a dirty backstreet. Flies buzzed around what smelled like days-old garbage left to fester in a weak winter sun. The chill, stale air nipped my cheeks.

There was a silent neighborhood beyond where we paused to regroup as the last of the pack of survivors emerged into the light. Those who'd lived through the fight we'd fled from were in various states of injury. We'd walked for what had felt like hours through an underground tunnel lit only with red bulbs, giving us the bare minimum to see by. Worse, there'd been no cell service while we made the trek to safety, so I had no idea if Mom and my sister, Carly, were okay.

Healers like my friend Áine wove between the ranks of guardian witches, Crystal Court fae, and my coven, mending the worst of our wounds. They'd been too busy stabilizing those most hurt throughout our trip through the tunnel to fix the minor scrapes and bruises we all had, and by the time Áine's bouncy hoofed stride came my way, she had mere sparks and curls of green magic left on her earthen-toned fingertips.

"I'll be okay," I told her, though I wasn't sure that was entirely true.

I barely saw her concerned frown, too busy watching my phone's screen as I restarted it, hoping it would find a connection.

Physically, I was fine. I should count myself lucky, because the vampire Garroway had interrupted my coven's petition to the Crown Coven with a small army of assassins and enslaved witches, and yet here I was, alive. Terrified, but alive.

My phone buzzed in my hand. Several messages and missed calls flashed across the screen, all from Mom.

"My mom's safe. She found a hospital and is pitching in there," I told Áine with a trickle of relief, cut short when I saw Mom was also asking if I'd seen Carly. My thumbs moved as I spoke, asking Mom for a name or location of this hospital.

A few of us needed more medical attention than could be applied on the fly, like Ben's brother, Lucas, whose unconscious body Geo carried in his gargoyle form. Both of my boyfriends were distracted from me, speaking in low tones and inspecting Lucas. I understood the worry Ben wore openly. Our healers had revived almost everyone who'd passed out, but Lucas remained limp and wan in Geo's arms.

Áine shifted on her cloven hooves. "I, uh, have to tell you some bad news," she said quietly.

My belly soured. I didn't think I could handle anything else going wrong after watching so many people die to summon a truly evil being, the soul-hungry goddess Myuna.

It's too late for me, bright soul.

God, I was going to be sick. I'd done my best to put it out of mind, but a world-ending creature had just arrived on Earth behind us. And she had Phaeron.

"I'm pretty sure someone closed the pocket dimension," Áine continued. The faun paused to wait for my inevitable questions.

"What do you mean, closed?" I asked.

"There's pressure in the air above us. Maybe you feel it a little bit? Well…it's really oppressive for me. It's my fae magic." Her deerlike ears pinned back, and she winced, as if she noticed it so much more by talking about it.

Pocket dimensions were rooted in fae magic and a complicated concept I still didn't fully understand. An individual fae could create a space that existed just for them, like an extension of the natural world.

Together, a large enough group of fae could declare a leader and invest their powers into a Mother Tree, which would anchor the space and make it into a pocket dimension that could further be augmented by the magic of other supernaturals. These places existed completely out of a normal human's awareness.

We were in Cerris City, a supernatural metropolis parallel to Washington, D.C., and I had felt a change in air pressure sometime after Myuna's arrival but thought little of it. Now that Áine mentioned it, I closed my eyes and lifted my chin, letting the crush of voices around me fade to background noise.

There was an oppressive force in the air, like humidity. I wouldn't want to go for a run right now, as my whole body felt extra heavy. "I do feel it," I concluded. "What does this mean for us, though?"

"The Protector of the Mother Tree has sealed off any entrances and exits to the pocket dimension. We're trapped," she said grimly.

"Shit," I muttered.

My heart doubled its beating. With trembling fingers, I checked my phone again and tapped the address Mom had sent me. One of my supernatural-exclusive apps popped up with a map and a blue line connecting my phone's current location with the hospital as a destination. It was several blocks away.

I looked around and spotted Madigan Ashbough, my friend Roe's mother, huddled up with a small group, undoubtedly discussing what to do next. Madigan was also known professionally as Mad Ash, a storied guardian witch who headed up a company that protected important artifacts and people. She'd led the survivors to safety and was the best choice for the leader of our mixed group while Phaeron was gone.

Áine moved on to offer what was left of her magic elsewhere when I went to approach Madigan, phone in hand. With her Crystal fae husband, Orthus, next to her, I assumed she already knew we were trapped. They turned to look at me, along with the rest of their group.

Madigan's suit of armor, made of red crystals from Orthus's court, gleamed and sang a soft note of harmony in the sunlight from portions of facets that weren't blemished by drying blood. She'd removed the helmet that made her look like an old-fashioned knight, having balanced it on the handle of her geode-formed warhammer that she had resting head down. Waves of orange hair stuck to her neck from where they'd escaped her low ponytail.

I felt a crackle of fire within me for the muscle-bound woman and Hana Graygazer, who stood unmarred by combat on Madigan's other side. She was an augur, capable of seeing the future. And judging by how she and her husband, also in this meeting of the minds, hadn't fled with us but still met us here...

"You knew this would happen," I accused.

"I did," Hana replied. She laced her fingers before her, the image of poise. She'd tied her pin-straight black hair back from her face in a practical style and wore worn traveling clothes, having changed out of the formal wear I'd last seen her in. She and her husband were some of the few around us with duffle bags at their feet.

That short, blunt answer didn't satisfy me. "All those people died because we showed up to petition the Crown Coven today!" I jabbed a finger back toward the tunnel we'd just used to flee, my voice rising with every word. "Why didn't you warn us? Why didn't you stop this?"

"Watch your tone with her," Madigan said flatly.

My whole body tensed. I had yet to give her a piece of my mind for tearing me away from Phaeron earlier. Which was foolish, I told myself, trying to get my emotions back under control. If she had left me, I might be a soulless husk right now. But I had no idea of what'd happened to the princely dimensional after we fled. Was he alive? Was he between Myuna's teeth or worse right now?

Hana shifted to put herself between Madigan and me. "It's all right. Let her be angry. Cress, I apologize for withholding information from you."

My lips quirked to the side. I had a distinct feeling there was a "but" following on the heels of this apology and about to ruin its sincerity.

"But I gazed hard into the gray for any other way and didn't find one. Look around. What do you see?" Hana asked and barely gave me a chance to do as she instructed before she continued. "I'll tell you what I see: standing around us is the team that will defeat Myuna the White. She was destined to be summoned to our planet. If not today, in Cerris City, where she can be contained...on Earth itself, where nothing would stop her from glutting herself on billions of souls."

The moisture left my mouth at the thought. "But—"

"It had to happen," Hana stated, steel behind every word. "At this time, in this place, with these people. I give you my word. Do you know what happens when a Graygazer denies their fate?" She gestured between herself, her husband, and the older gentleman sitting on a curb nearby, Kwan Graygazer. He was one of two members of the Crown Coven to survive.

I cringed, moisture stinging the corners of my eyes. "Don't say that," I croaked. "The last time you said that to me..."

It was burned in my memory like a brand, along with the follow-up. *Someone else dies instead. Often horrifically.* Lanie, her daughter and my friend, had just sacrificed herself to prevent the Hungering Darkness from killing and eating the soul of a different witch. It was the curse of a talented augur—knowing when, where, and how they would die.

Hana's dark gaze softened. "I know. And if it makes a difference, it hurt to lead us all on this path, knowing what you would have to witness and endure. Now, you came over here to suggest where we go next, right?"

I'd nearly forgotten I had my unlocked phone in hand, the map route waiting to be shared. "Yeah," I said, clearing my throat and blinking rapidly. I offered the device to Hana, who passed it to Madigan. Orthus leaned over to look at the screen too. "My mom found the nearest hospital, and it's not all that far from where we are."

"The streets will be safe for now," Hana shared.

That seemed to make Madigan's decision easier. She exchanged a glance with Orthus before declaring, "A sound position for us to rest properly and plan our next steps. Let's move."

I stayed by Hana's side as Madigan picked up her helmet and hammer and began circulating to share the news that we were heading out. The group moved slowly toward a main street, our leader up front, consulting my phone and its map. I was so used to having my device disappear to be used by others that it didn't bother me.

Madigan's guardian witches and Crystal fae spread out to surround the perimeter of our group with fighters. Ben and Geo, still carrying Lucas, were pushed toward the center along with most of the members of my coven and all our assorted familiars. Roe supported Willow, who wasn't the steadiest on her feet.

Bella, my brown tabby cat familiar, jumped into my arms with a chirp for attention. Milo and Jin remained with the rest of our animal companions, pressed close to the bigger, stronger ones of the group. I snuggled Bella to my chest, finding some reassurance in her soft fur and faint purr. "You're safe with us," I murmured to her.

"It's going to be okay," she echoed in her squeak of a voice. As one of my bonded familiars, I alone could hear her meows as words.

I could hear Roe also trying to encourage and comfort Wren. The blonde had just watched her father and boyfriend die senselessly. She muffled sobs into a handkerchief and wobbled uncharacteristically in her heels as she shuffled along with the group.

I itched to go be with them rather than toward the back of the group with Hana. But I had a burning question for the augur who'd pushed us toward this situation that'd put the tears in Wren's eyes and the grief in all of us for what we'd already lost.

"What about Phaeron?" I asked. Hana glanced up at me, her expression unreadable. "Did Myuna eat his soul? Did she corrupt him? Is…is he alive?"

"He's alive, just suppressed by her presence," she answered, measuring each word carefully. "His fate branches in several directions, and the most likely outcome is yet unclear to me. I am thankful, though."

"Oh?" I asked faintly.

"You will have an opportunity to affect which fate he meets. Because of your influence, I have hope we will avoid the future where Myuna twists him into one of her monsters," she stated. The thought made my insides feel like they were trying to wrap into a knot, drawing out a pain in my gut.

Hana was as serious as ever and I felt the weight of her words keenly. "But if she succeeds and he becomes corrupted, we're doomed. Each and every one of us."

2

PHAERON

THE GODDESS MYUNA the White did not chew her food. It'd always unsettled me deep down that she didn't have teeth. But once, I'd been naïve enough to think that, as a higher being, she had no need to eat.

She slurped down all that was placed before her in offering now, her face a thin veneer over a bottomless hole. Her mouth stretched grotesquely around the whole bodies of human beings, and she uttered the occasional rumble of dissatisfaction.

I was forced to watch. While she was aware I was tethered to her, all she wanted to do was eat and eat. Endaeron fed her, dragging over the soulless corpses left behind in the Crown Coven's audience chamber. The metallic smell of blood was heavy in the still air, and only the grunting and cursing of Endaeron's newest vessel, a vampire named Garroway, broke the silence between Myuna's gulps and quaffs.

When I refused to help bring her the bodies littered around the chamber, she'd pointed a clawed finger, and I stood where she indicated, waiting with dread in my heart for her feasting to cease. My body was turned toward hers, standing with rigid obedience to await her next order. Purple-tinged blood still dripped down my leather armor, courtesy of the burning wounds left behind in my fight with Endaeron in his last vessel, the boy Lucas. I let the pain ground me, its sting reminding me of who I was.

There was a small hole in my soul and a pinprick of corruption left behind within it. It formed the strand of control by which she could command me. My logical mind was shut under a layer of her magical influence, and even now, I pushed and probed at the barrier between Myuna's control and my free will.

Once she realized there were no souls left here for her to eat except for mine and Garroway's tainted one, my life was forfeit, or worse. I had to find a way to defy the control her mere presence gave her.

"Useless fuck," muttered Garroway as he dragged another corpse past me. Though most of my body was locked in place, I could still move my head to see that he struggled with the bulk of a fallen Crystal fae, whose body was encased in a suit of armor with solid stone plates. Myuna would still consume it in one giant swallow.

I knew he was trying to insult me, but I ignored him. There was little intensity left in Garroway's voice, and I had to preserve what fight I could muster for Myuna. He carried what was left of my brother, the Hungering Darkness, within him and thus was more hopelessly enslaved to her will than I was.

Myuna sat upon the lip of the raised dais where the Crown Coven once reigned, their throne-like seats pushed around haphazardly to make way for her bulk. She was over twice my height, with bone-white skin that glowed dimly even now. Her visage still appeared to be that of one of my people, with forward-facing horns, leathery wings, slitted eyes, and a tapered tail that swung midair like a pendulum. We had once revered her as a goddess of light, not realizing the dark hunger lingering inside her until it was too late.

She'd appeared on my home planet of Soiluire within an egg-like comet, emerging a savior and a beacon for my people, who, at that time, lived in near-complete darkness. For centuries, she built her base of worshipers, biding her time until the moment was right, or her cravings for souls grew too great.

Our society had collapsed when she turned on us. Those that'd served her most faithfully as her torchbearers were killed and enslaved first, forced to bring her millions to consume. Her glutting was the beginning of our Age of Decay and eventual exodus from Soiluire.

I'd slain her monsters and endured a trip through the Void to lead the dregs of my people here, to Earth. We'd tolerated the prejudices of humans, who'd thought our features resembled the hellish demons of their worst imaginings, all to get away from Myuna. My people became known as dimensional travelers by escaping to a new world. We'd sealed the way behind us, intending to close the door back to Soiluire permanently.

I simmered with a low boil of fury. There was no end to my rage with Endaeron for undoing all our sacrifices and leading her here, but I kept my emotions contained and my breathing slow and deep. I knew I could not act in anger if I wanted to escape this room and return to Cress. I also knew I could not kill Myuna alone.

"That is everything, my lady," Garroway said in the two-toned voice that meant the Hungering Darkness was currently in control of their shared body. White shadow flickered around the vampire's form like flames, slowly enveloping his body and hiding his human features.

Myuna worked the stretched-out material that should have been her jaw. It'd come unhinged and spread wide enough to allow her to feast unimpeded. What should've been flesh and bone quickly flowed back into place. Then she...melted. I watched in horror as her entire body ran like candle wax, puddling down the carved stones of the dais.

The mass of white substance quivered before drawing into a ball. It was like witnessing a master sculptor manipulate Myuna's body as it formed four tubes and an oval for a head before etching in details. Wrists, knees, fingers, and nails formed, and the oval sprouted a nose, hair, and two almond-shaped eyes that glowed a little brighter than the rest of her.

Myuna had transformed into a human. Worse, I recognized her new face. She had assumed an all-white visage of the fallen leader of the Crown Coven, Tempest Wildsong. Instead of having flowing raven-dark locks and a dress of soft green, though, Myuna was a pale imitation in pure white, save for the toothless black hole behind her lips as she spoke.

"Is this what mortal females look like on this world?"

Her voice held power; it shook me to my very center. She spoke every possible language layered on top of one another. For her to utter anything wrapped her first exhalation and last in a blanket of incomprehensible nonsense. To listen too closely would inspire madness in most.

"Yes, my lady," Garroway responded with Endaeron's breathless awe of her.

She dipped her chin. The dots of her pupils pointed my way, even under a filmy sheen of white magic. "What small, soft people. I yet hunger for more of them. But first there's you, Phaeron et Sudair. We have unfinished business."

The language I heard my name in was my native tongue, separating my title rather than treating it like a surname as humans did. "Because of you..." she began before trailing off. Her attention snagged on a book that flew past her head.

A whole flock of books flapped above us. The audience chamber had representations of magic from all seven affinities available to witches, and these books of law were enchanted to fly with librarian witch magic and a tiny creature from Soiluire called a wispfly. For a moment, Myuna was like a fascinated cat, watching them circle the room unaware of the fight and subsequent summoning of an otherworldly goddess.

She snatched one out of the air when it flew too close. It was not malfunctioning like Cress's handbook, so it settled and reported its title with one last flick of its front and back cover. It was *The Rule of Supernatural Law* and was halfway through listing its copyright information before she sucked it into her mouth and swallowed.

"Hmm, dry," she commented. A glowing tongue emerged from her mouth to lick a slimy trail over her lips. "But that wispfly... I need more like it."

"The books will come to you if you state their title, my lady," simpered Garroway. The lack of the two-toned quality to his voice and his brief smirk told me the suggestion was all the vampire.

Myuna was tall enough to glimpse a few titles. Those books came to her hand and quickly disappeared into her maw. As she did this, I noticed a metal device mounted out of reach that seemed to be pointing our way. A red light flashed beside a dome of black glass. I gazed at the unfamiliar technology with hope for a moment. Was it a weapon? Perhaps something that nullified magic?

The sounds of rattling paper ceased, and Myuna cleared her throat. I turned away from that blinking light with a sigh. If it were something useful, then it would've been utilized in the fight that'd killed most of the Crown Coven and their protectors earlier.

"As I was saying." The goddess wove light into threads between her fingers. Watching her brought back hazy memories of seeing her do the same thing when she was bored at functions or needed to keep her hands busy. "I spent too much time sitting in place on Soiluire, feeling the advancements and indulgences of the mortals on planets innumerable. Their peoples growing plump for harvesting...but I could not reach them."

She crushed the braid of light when her fingers fisted on the dais, cracking the stone underneath. "Because of *you*, Phaeron. You and the other souls that fled the death you were due."

I drew breath to reply and felt the force of her will. She didn't want to hear my voice.

"You meddled in forces outside your control. I am entropy, the death of civilizations, the reaper of worlds." She leaned forward, her finger pointed accusingly. The hairs on the back of my neck lifted from a shift in air pressure. Here it was...the moment she consumed me for saving what I could of my people.

"I came short on power when you disappeared alongside thousands of souls. I have been stranded, sitting alone on a rotting world. I ate my half-formed interstellar vessel waiting. I endured the pain of eating my own power, pleading with my fellow gods to take me away in my darkest season. Their silence was damning. And yet, I am saved."

She turned her head toward Garroway and whispered, "You shall be rewarded beyond measure."

I slanted a glare his way, my lip curling in disgust. He would enjoy that reward for half a second before I made his death as painful as possible.

Myuna made a come-hither gesture, and my legs jerked forward at her unspoken command. Light sputtered against her palms before she managed to make them both glow. She had an old trick that she used on me, where she lifted and suspended me in a bubble of light she formed between her hands, making it seem like I floated before her looming, all-powerful presence. Pain twinged in my chest as the muscles shifted from the lack of gravity.

My forehead was level with her mouth, which leaked the carrion smell of her last meal. "Any last words, Phaeron?" Her words boomed, her presence all-consuming.

She returned my voice to me, and I wasted little of my limited time left. "You are a foul, narcissistic shade. To tell me of *your* suffering, as if you have no concept of the damage you have wrought... I wish you had agonized further, for you deserve so much worse. You would be doing innumerable worlds a favor by feasting upon the last of yourself and leaving the rest of us in peace—"

Myuna made a pinching motion, suffocating the last of my words before I could utter them. She seemed to roll her eyes while I coughed off the choking sensation. "I should have known better," she remarked.

She unsheathed one of my swords between three of her fingers, drawing it out to inspect it. They'd been sheathed in a hurry, so the weapon was dirty. Of course, she had to lick her way up the side, cleaning off the dimensional language etched into it. I began to sweat as the moments passed. If she was going to consume me, she would've gone ahead and done it. Her intentions had to be far more sinister.

"Hmm, half of Soiluire, half of this planet. You must value this weapon very much," she stated. "It is fortunate you have two. One for each of my most loyal servants."

She slid my weapon out of sight, toward Garroway. I stared at her in defiance, unable to do more when caught in the trap of her light and will. So it would be death by a thousand cuts, starting with losing one of my last physical links to my home planet.

Myuna wove magic between her fingers just like she'd made threads formed of light. She wrapped me in a potent spell that sank into my mind. This, I could still fight with a jerk of my head. I closed my eyes tight against her intrusion and pushed her presence away.

A slimy, warm sensation coated my wounds. While I struggled against her mentally, she'd licked the blood from my chest. A shrill tone of panic and disgust rose in my ears before she delved further into my thoughts and memories, ripping through them with little care.

"So bitter," she whispered, no more than another voice in my head. I saw what she did as it played over the back of my eyelids in vivid detail.

She watched me wake in Moongrove Library, disoriented and slow.

I tried to push her away again, but her talons had hooked in deep. She combed through the faces of the humans I'd grown fond of and the knowledge of who they were. We pushed and pulled our way closer to my memories of Cress, and I heard her utter an "ahh" when she finally won this contest of wills and beheld my bright soul in all her glory.

Cress was unique amongst librarian witches, with a soul that haloed her in a glow. She dazzled me constantly with the power of her presence. I twisted to jerk the memories of her out of Myuna's sight, yet she quickly learned she was looking at my True Light. It was my duty to protect and cherish Cress, to make her my mate.

The goddess viewed her from all the angles she could wring from me. She saw the surprised and uncertain Cress who first freed me from Moongrove Library. The heartbroken Cress who'd caught me standing over her friend's body. Tired Cress, angry Cress, silly Cress...coy Cress, her lips around my cock as I rode the feverish lust induced by a manipulative cupid.

I shoved Myuna back again, feeling further violated by the way she lingered on that memory. She obliged by switching to rest on a moment before a mirror, my fangs pressed to Cress's neck. So close to claiming her as my mate...yet the awful hunger born of the goddess had been there, urging me to consume some of her radiant soul instead and taste its sweetness.

Myuna laughed, releasing her hold on my mind. "You have grown weak, Phaeron. Leaving your mate without your protection or even your mark."

My eyes opened. Little had changed around us, except that I was drenched in sweat under my armor. I was sure to develop an infection in all the wounds she'd licked, as my chest smelled of her foulness.

Myuna set me down from the bubble of light. The only reason I didn't collapse was her control, which steered me to stand back in my original spot.

"Endaeron," she breathed, a toothless grin spanning the empty void of her mouth. "Go forth from this place and bring me a purple-haired human named Cressida Rollins Darkmore. Her life and soul are mine to take."

Garroway bowed, but under his breath, he muttered, "Her *again*?"

3
BEN

We weren't the only group that'd come to this hospital upon being stranded in Cerris City. The waiting room for emergencies was overflowing when we arrived, alive with energy in a city that'd seemed dead on the outside. Luckily—if you could count anything that'd happened to us lately as "lucky"—Lucas had jumped to the top of the list of priorities for the medical staff.

I sat in a quiet room with him on the third floor. My brother was hooked to several machines, so pale and still in the heaps of white sheets he'd been buried in. They'd just allowed me in the room after a doctor had cast a hurried set of spells and then rushed off to the next patient.

An equally harried nurse had told me not to touch anything, then left me with Lucas. I'd withstood the silence afterward for only a few minutes before jittering in place, all my excess energy and worries spilling over. I could barely look at the state the Hungering Darkness had left my brother's body in, but I had to. The sight had to be permanent in my mind. This was the evil we faced...the evil I hadn't protected him from.

I sat alone for a while, until there was a tentative knock on the door, followed by Cress peeking inside. I gestured for her to come in, sweeping her into a hug and a quick, delicate kiss. It was a relief to have her here, to touch anam cara marks with her and feel the spark of wholeness between us. She wore a couple butterfly bandages over the cuts on her face and had the bulk of wrapped wounds peeking through her torn sleeves.

"My mom told me where they put Lucas. Is he...?" She bit her lip, looking over at the bed.

"The doctor called it a magic-induced coma," I answered quietly, weighed down by worry. "There's not enough healing magic to go around for everyone right now, so they... He's on life support."

"Oh, Ben, I'm sorry." She gave me a squeeze around my middle, still standing in the circle of my arms.

I tried to give one of my usual carefree shrugs. "Hey, it could be worse, right? The Hunger could've gobbled him up...or..." I wracked my brain for how this moment could be worse. Having my brother alive but unresponsive and sickly was somehow more severe than if he'd simply died.

There was no guarantee he'd wake up or if he'd be the same person after carrying the Hungering Darkness within him for months. The brother I knew may be long gone.

I choked on the burning sensation of tears. Out of long habit, they lingered at the corners of my vision, half formed. Cress gathered me closer all the same, holding the back of my neck. She smelled of antiseptic and the musky staleness of the tunnel we'd come through. But she was okay and had scrubbed the blood from her clothes and skin... something I still needed to do. We stayed that way for a few long minutes. I was glad to have her with me, warm and whole.

"He'll be safe here, for now," she eventually said.

"Is there such a thing as 'safe' anymore?" I asked with a sigh. "Did you hear that we're stuck in this city?"

"Yeah." She shared what Áine and Hana Graygazer had told her, drawing a muttered string of curses from me.

"But there's some good news," Cress added with a hesitant lift of her lips. "Hana says we're not going to be kept in the dark anymore. We're invited to meet with the leadership of Ashbough Protective Services, plus the Graygazers and the surviving members of the Crown Coven, tomorrow to decide what to do next. The rest of the day is for us to rest and recover."

My gaze veered back toward Lucas. I didn't know how much of either task I would be doing. As a blood witch, I'd already healed all the cuts and bruises I'd sustained in the earlier fight. My body was ready for another round, even if my heart and soul remained wounded and in denial.

"And your aunt is waiting to talk to you, too," she shared.

She released me so I could open the door out into the hall, and standing there patiently were two people. I should've expected as much. Aunt Jordan had yet to see my little brother, and Geo was never too far from Cress if he could help it.

Jordan had escaped any serious harm. She still wore a beautiful formal robe stitched with falling stars, but dust clung stubbornly to it and the limp brown hair around her head. She had a soft face made for kindly smiles and sympathy, which I could barely stand to see on her expression when our eyes met briefly.

"You want to see Lucas," I said, stepping to the side so she could enter the room.

She pushed off the wall and went straight to me for a big hug. I froze, surprised. "Tell me you're all right first," she said.

My aunt released me just to look me over critically, and I wondered if this was what it felt like to have a mom…someone who would fuss because they liked you whole and healthy, even if it was a little embarrassing.

"As good as can be expected." I felt stiff and awkward. Before we'd met about a month ago, I'd never been fussed over. There had been no mother figures amongst Garroway's coven of assassins, only blood and pain.

She nodded and gestured over her shoulder. "I made sure to take your staff with us. Unfortunately, the case was left behind…but such a thing can be replaced."

Propped against the wall were two celestial witch staves. The first was made of golden wood and embellishments, with a single piece of paper hanging from a bar that crossed under a small, molded sun resting at the top of it. That paper was a prepared spell, waiting in reserve. Since high-level celestial magic was a long and grueling process, it was typical for spells to be ritually created and then stored on paper slips on a staff.

"My" staff was the impressive creation next to it. Its name was Evening Guidance, and it'd been my father's before his untimely death. The wood was coated with black varnish and painted with silver trails of stars to match the centerpiece of a silver-plated crescent moon wrapped in the tails of several falling stars. Dozens of prepared spells were still attached to it.

The last time it'd been used was in Cress's hands, firing a ray of pure power at Lucas to separate him from the Hungering Darkness. Neither of us was a celestial witch, but somehow, she'd called upon the power to use it anyway. I saw Evening Guidance as her weapon now, even if it were sized and balanced for a man's use.

Her magical book's spine was perched on it, front and back cover flickering like a strange butterfly. As I ushered my aunt into my brother's room, I heard it utter, "Hey Cressie-poo, were you worried about me too?" It sounded a lot like a squeaky toy, and Cress loved it to death even though it was a flying, talking, know-it-all nuisance.

"Of course I was, *The Librarian Witch's Handbook*," she cooed.

Oh, and she had to address it by its full name, else it pouted. "Annoying" was part of its charm.

Their voices were muffled as I closed the door behind us, letting my aunt meet Lucas for the first time. She took his hand and prayed to the witch goddess while I stood back to give her some privacy. Something told me his condition was not for the divine to heal.

His soul needed Phaeron's help, the one thing we didn't have.

EVENING CAME SWIFTLY, and I'd been dragged from Lucas's bedside to join my coven and friends in one of the only rooms left unused on the fourth and final floor of the hospital. It had two curtained beds, and we drew straws for who would pile into them versus sleep on the cold floor tonight.

It was like a strange slumber party, all of us huddled under blankets, watching the evening news from a tiny television mounted in the wall, and eating our rationed share of hospital food. Geo, who'd returned to his human form finally, helped me bracket Cress between us in the back of the group. I played halfheartedly with my familiar, Flit, who was full of ferret energy despite everything.

The supernatural news stations were dominated by grainy footage taken of a glowing white figure sitting on the Crown Coven's dais as if it were a throne. News anchors warned viewers multiple times before playing a few carefully curated shots of Myuna interacting with the two men still alive with her.

Though the news jumped around to avoid showing the reality of the situation, Myuna's mouth and chin were streaked with blood, standing out in shades of gray and black from the grayscale recording.

"She's eating the bodies left behind," Cress murmured, the first to acknowledge the gruesome truth.

"And Garroway's feeding her," commented Bianca.

The olive-skinned woman was the only other person in this room that didn't bear any injuries. She and I were perhaps the only two blood witches to escape Garroway's coven and live to tell the tale. We would always bear the runes he'd carved into our skin and the scars from his relentless training. That made us trauma siblings, even if she was about as friendly as a lit fuse most days.

As much as I wanted Garroway to suffer for everything he'd done to us, I hoped Myuna didn't kill him. I'd vowed to finish him myself and intended to keep that promise.

Cress's voice drew me out of my dark thoughts. "But not Phaeron." She sounded like she was clinging to hope.

The news only showed the dark gray figure of the dimensional prince standing there, watching. He appeared to be standing in the same place in every shot.

The talking heads on every station reported that it was Myuna, quoting a red-skinned dimensional woman who'd come forward earlier to set the record straight for the greater supernatural community. She'd shared who Myuna was and why she was there. And once that footage was exhausted, talk turned to that of survivors and missing family members who hadn't had the means to escape the pocket dimension in time.

It looked bleak for them...for us. Cerris City would not come off lockdown for anyone when a world-eating goddess could escape behind them.

"I bet you someone is streaming the uncut footage." The husky-voiced suggestion came from Wren, who sat on one of the beds. Though she'd stopped crying, she looked and sounded exhausted, wearing her grief with her spine curled in.

Several of us spoke up at once. Wren ignored it all, typing away on her phone screen.

"We need to have some eyes on the inside. Why not a camera?" suggested our resident changeling in disguise. We only knew him as Grant Norwood, the verdant witch he appeared to be at the moment. Since Áine was also in this room, he kept his true form hidden. As they were from enemy courts, she was bound to be the last to know we had a changeling in our midst, and I didn't want to be around for her wrath if she ever learned the truth.

I glanced over at him, wondering if we could send him to spy on Myuna. It would be more accurate than the news or a recording presumably being streamed online.

An awful buzzing noise came from Wren's phone, startling most of us. She grimaced and turned it down with a few rapid clicks on the side of her device. "This hacker is saying that when Myuna spoke for the first time, all the audio got messed up. But this is what's happening right now," she said.

Her phone was passed from hand to hand, quickly ending up with Cress. "They're just…doing nothing?" she asked. Myuna hadn't moved from the dais, and Phaeron was a motionless statue below her.

The device stopped in Roe's hands last. She angled its screen away from Willow, who had recently received magical healing for a concussion. Our coven's leader was the only one here willing to scroll as far back in time as the stream would go, making a sound of disgust as the black and white shadows played over her face. "Okay, gross," Roe muttered. "So she eats everyone…then she starts talking to Phaeron… Oh, this might be something."

We gathered into a tight knot behind Roe as she played the video at three times its normal speed. Myuna made a come-hither gesture, and Phaeron responded. She worked magic over him and blinded the camera with beams of light…

"Fuck," Cress spat in frustration. "What'd she do to him?"

When the light cleared, Phaeron was assuming the same spot where he'd apparently been standing since this moment. Myuna turned to Garroway and said something, then Roe paused the video. "He's taking one of Phaeron's swords and leaving," she said.

"We have to go get Phaeron," Cress said.

"Not yet," Geo rumbled. "He has to leave the goddess's side first. And something tells me she won't allow him to do that unless he is fully under her control."

"We'll figure out how to nab him, promise," Roe put in.

Everyone voiced their agreement in their own ways. Willow, Áine, and Wren gave weary nods. Grant, Bianca, and I cracked our knuckles, signaling a readiness to fight. I raised a brow at Grant since he'd said more than once that his pretty changeling ass was no good in combat. He offered a brilliant smile and a shrug in reply.

Roe, Geo, and Cress exchanged glances, determination in their faces.

"In the meantime, I'm declaring Yule to be on pause. I bought a gift for each and every one of you, and you'll get them when we escape this pocket dimension," Roe continued.

"If you haven't noticed, they're not unsealing the pocket dimension for anyone to 'escape,'" Grant said with air quotes.

"Not until Myuna is dead," Cress spoke up. "And Hana Graygazer believes the right group has been trapped in here with her to make that happen."

"Who...*us*?" Wren asked, glancing around. A bit of that rich girl judgment returned to her gaze and tone. "Most of us can barely cast five spells."

"Two of us are trained assassins with many kills to their names," Bianca retorted. A claim she could make about herself, especially in hunting unnaturals, but less about me. I had the "trained" part down, but Garroway had barely sent me on any missions.

Wren turned a glare her way. "You're not even in this coven."

I knew that look on Bianca's face, ready and excited for a fight. I murmured her name, practically begging for her to glance my way and not start this conflict. Not now.

She said without pause, "I will be tomorrow."

Several emotions passed over Wren's face before she settled on betrayal. She tilted that look toward Roe. "Heath's body isn't even cold yet," she said, going breathy with emotion. "I mean, before some monster everyone calls a goddess ate what's left of him. He. can't be replaced like that." She snapped her fingers.

"Wren, you have to understand—" Roe began to say.

"I'm not having this conversation around everyone," the other woman said abruptly. She stood and snatched up her phone, putting it in her pocket and sailing out the door. If she was trying to outrun the first sob before we all heard it...I could pretend it hadn't happened before she was out of earshot.

Roe heaved a tired sigh before following after her. After a few moments of hesitation, Cress followed, motioning for Geo and me to stay behind.

4

CRESS

The next morning, Bianca was sworn in as the seventh member of A Little Wicked Coven with the rest of us bearing witness over a cold breakfast. Wren hadn't had it in her to argue when Roe and I had presented Biana's strengths as a talented assassin who knew one of our main enemies, the vampire Garroway, with more familiarity than even Ben.

That didn't mean she liked it. Not that I ever got the feeling she ever particularly *liked* any of us, anyway. She stared off into the middle distance in the hospital's cramped cafeteria and ate her ration of food without relish. If someone had told me I'd feel this much sympathy for Wren even a week ago, I'd have cackled like it was a bad joke. Yet here we were.

The meeting Hana had invited me to started right after breakfast, in a conference room on the hospital's first floor. I attended with Ben, Geo, Roe, and Bianca and wondered why we were invited at all when I saw the faces that ringed the other half of the long table. Madigan and Orthus represented Ashbough Protective Services. Hana sat with the remnants of the Crown Coven, Kwan Graygazer and Daire Grimsbane. A few fae and verdant witch doctors, all carrying a tired, fearful gleam in their eyes, were here too as hospital leadership.

And sitting in one of the only unoccupied seats was a ghost only I could see, of my deceased birth mother, Eris Darkmore. Ever since Phaeron had called her spirit back on Samhain to talk to me, she'd remained on the mortal plane to haunt me on and off under the guise of helping.

She could be helpful, but it was awkward at the same time. We barely knew each other. She was endlessly judgmental about my decision to become a librarian witch, and I was sure there was an unpleasant day ahead when she popped in while I was having private time with my boyfriends. Just the thought gave me a full-body cringe.

"We're gathered today to discuss what to do next," Madigan said. She'd claimed the head of the table, fingers steepled as the room quieted down and faces turned her way. "The goddess that destroyed Soiluire is now here, locked inside the Cerris City pocket dimension with us. The majority of the city's population received the emergency alert about the lockdown and fled, including many medical professionals. Thank you for staying to support and heal the sick and injured." She nodded toward the doctors present.

I smiled their way briefly. I hadn't realized the crew keeping the hospital running had had to make the conscious decision to stay. No wonder they'd thrown scrubs at my mom so readily when she'd volunteered to help.

"Unfortunately, there are civilians still stranded here, and many of them are kids or young families. We have to act fast to bring them to safety and gather supplies," Madigan continued.

Hana interjected, "Myuna will not sit idle for long. She has one loyal servant right now, but that will change as time passes. As a goddess, she is used to being served by a legion."

Bianca raised her fingers as Hana spoke. Madigan gestured for her to speak. "The 'loyal servant' you mentioned is the vampire Garroway, who won't be able to take anyone to her while it's daylight outside," she said, punching into her palm. "We should hunt him when the sun sets, to cripple her further."

"She will then turn her attention to Phaeron to break his will early. This is a future we do not want," Hana replied.

"Early?" I echoed in a pained whisper.

"Right now, she wants him aware and in pain. Last night, she sent Garroway out to hunt you," Hana said, her gaze flashing to me. My ghostly mother gasped in surprise. "We might have one more night where he tries again. One thing is for certain...Myuna will remain in place and expect her every desire to come to her. That makes her predictable and thus something we can outwit and kill."

"So, she can be killed?" asked Crown Grimsbane. He was a tough-looking Black man and the only blood witch in the Crown Coven. He still wore a bandolier lined with daggers but had replaced whatever expensive clothing he had been wearing for a plain t-shirt and jeans. It was probably the miraculous healing powers of his affinity that'd ensured his survival of yesterday's attack.

"She can be," Hana confirmed.

"Hell, why don't we go do that now? We've been patched up. We know where she is and who her allies are. All of us versus the three of them," he commented.

Hana drew breath to reply, but it was Crown Graygazer who spoke up next. "We would lose and feed ourselves to Myuna. And afterward, there would be no one to stop her from taking over the pocket dimension until it has to be collapsed."

I wasn't the only one paling at the implication of collapsing Cerris City. I'd only heard of it being done once, when the Fall Court's Mother Tree was burned, but a collapsed pocket dimension simply ceased to exist, as did any living things within it at the time.

If that meant Myuna died, great. Except I wanted to live...as did the hundreds, perhaps thousands, of other supernaturals still trapped here with us.

The elder Graygazer continued talking while we reeled from this revelation, "There are a few paths to victory we can take...but they must be selected with care. Hana and I will guide us in the right direction."

I nodded to myself. Hana had gotten us into this mess with the idea that we were the right ones to fix it.

Geo cleared his throat, drawing attention even though it wasn't the sound of clashing rocks like it would be in his gargoyle form. "I have a suggestion," he stated, voice still flat with how recently he'd been in his stone form.

"Let's hear it," Madigan said with some of her usual enthusiasm.

"As you've said, once she gets her bearings, one of Myuna's first goals will be to recruit allies. Is there a library here?" He looked around, asking the room at large.

"Cerris City Library, yes," one of the doctors confirmed.

"We need to secure it before she realizes it exists. Most of the unnatural creatures and artifacts stored by librarian witches can trace their corrupted origins back to Myuna," Geo said.

"That's true. She could gain a lot of dangerous servants, depending on what's in the library," I pitched in.

"Civilians can shelter in the lower levels," Geo rumbled. "And I will activate the library's gargoyle units to defend them."

Madigan dropped her voice to whisper with Orthus for a brief conversation. "We can split our people into three groups. One to rescue survivors; one to secure food, water, and other supplies; and one to head to Cerris City Library," she said finally.

"Let's talk locations," Orthus added. Like the crystals that originated from his home court, his voice was resonant with power, soft but deep. His crystal armor blended in seamlessly with his granite-colored skin and the sharp emerald crystals that grew from his shoulders and formed points at his elbows and fingertips. "It would become an extra challenge to hold both the hospital and the library should they be too far from each other."

A few of us dug out our phones to look at the digital map of the city. The hospital was at the corner of a block, occupying a lot of space considering its conjoined parking garage. Unfortunately, the library was two miles away and a close landmark to the Crown Coven's complex and Myuna's new seat of power.

We noted a supermarket between the library and the hospital, and the planning began from there. Several vehicles had been abandoned in the hospital's garage, and it was Bianca who suggested some grand theft auto to speed up the process of gathering supplies and people. Roe, who'd been quietly absorbing the information around her, made a disapproving hum.

"A Little Wicked Coven will go to Cerris City Library. Cress and Geo can help us convince anyone remaining there to work with us," Roe said.

A flash of protectiveness passed over Madigan's expression. "I will send a few friends to help you," she said.

Roe shook her head. "We can do this, Mom. More of our people should be securing food and survivors before things get really dangerous."

Though hesitant, Madigan agreed and began divvying up those healthy enough to undertake these tasks. While she was occupied, Eris turned her ghostly head toward me. "Just don't go out after dark. If that vampire is hunting you, he had better not realize you're in the library," she said.

"Right," I whispered.

If Myuna wanted me, she must know I meant something to Phaeron. Maybe that's what she'd done to him when her light magic had blinded the camera. Read his mind...or made him admit things against his will. If she aimed to break him, consuming friends and family in front of him would be an evil first step.

As I tuned out of the meeting, my worries for him flooded back in. He'd been wounded when we were separated. We'd checked the hacker's stream this morning to see that he and Myuna had still not moved overnight. I doubted she'd let him care for his wounds properly.

His absence was a loss for this meeting. I had no doubt he would know what to do to take Myuna down quicker than our plan to gather survivors and entrench ourselves. Maybe we'd even put him at the head of the table, as the only ally who'd fought Myuna and her creatures before.

I knew we had to protect ourselves first before helping others, but I wanted to do more for him than this. And, on that note, for Carly. I swiped over to my texts and tapped her name, worried when I saw she still hadn't read any of the messages I'd sent her. Hopefully she'd just lost her phone fleeing with the crowd and had either been pulled out of the pocket dimension by another supernatural or was hunkered down somewhere safe.

A message from Mom popped up on my screen—her telling me to come find her after the meeting was over. It wasn't much longer before we were done, and Roe set off with Geo to get our group together. Mom told me she was working on the second floor.

I waited for her at the nurses' station and texted her back, waiting a good few minutes before she emerged from one of the occupied rooms red-faced and fuming. Mom, angry? She was a nurse with nerves of steel, but her usual kindly air was frazzled.

"Did something happen?" I blurted.

Her blue eyes flashed before she took a deep breath and put on a smile for me. "I'm just finding Crystal fae to be more difficult patients than I'm used to," she told me in a low voice.

I glanced over my shoulder to make sure we were alone. Even ghostly Eris was faded out for the time being, and the other nurses were hustling to keep the hospital functioning.

"I'm sure they can be as stubborn as rocks. Fae take on some of the qualities of their court, after all," I answered.

"As amazing as it is to live in a world where fae exist, you're probably wondering why I wanted to see you. I want you to sit down with one of the doctors for a few minutes."

I agreed warily since she said the doctor was already waiting to see me next in a room being cleaned and prepped for the next patient. Mom made herself scarce, then the steel-haired verdant witch doctor started asking the general questions I would answer for an annual physical.

Then she inquired if I was sexually active, and it all clicked into place. My ultra-perceptive Mom had made sure I was leaving with my friends for Cerris City Library with a new prescription of birth control pills in my pocket. Sure, it was a little embarrassing, but I couldn't wait to tell Geo and Ben.

5
GEO

THE TRIP to the library was short, aided by two cars borrowed from the hospital's parking garage. Getting them started was Bianca's job, something she did with practiced ease. Cress and her coven packed themselves into the small vehicles, while the larger ones and especially the trucks went to the guardians and Crystal fae for the task of gathering supplies and people.

If I wasn't escorting the two cars making the brief trip to the Cerris City Library, I would've flown right past it. It was a building made of chrome and glass, modernized with a flat roof and sharp angles. I'd gotten my hopes up for nothing. There were no gargoyles here, waiting in stasis for when they would be needed most.

It seemed the building was made very recently, without the spacious eaves where a gargoyle could perch. I flew overtop it, frowning to myself and recognizing why modernization had moved away from my kind.

The creation of gargoyles was outlawed some time ago due to a moral argument, something I had experienced personally. Ritually placing a witch's soul inside of a stone heart to animate a gargoyle made the resulting construct a new person with its own life to live, if they came to realize it.

Once most of us took our human forms of flesh and blood, we were loath to return, inevitably abandoning the duty we'd been created to perform. It was unfortunate I was seeing the downsides of this, with a lack of protectors to call upon when this library needed it most.

What a hypocrite my disappointment made me. I felt muffled and numb in my stone form now. I'd been out of it long enough that it felt like I was suffocating the complexity of my emotions. If I stayed this way too long, it would all fade until only cold reasoning was left, and what a shame that would be.

I was no longer comforted by unfeeling duty. My heart belonged to the purple-haired witch exiting one of the cars two stories below where I flew. When I'd awoken from self-imposed stasis, my duty had simply been *her*.

Her wants, needs, goals, dreams. My stone heart resonated for Cress, and she was mine. My purpose, my future. The reason I craved the warmth and illogicality of emotion within me once more.

I completed one last, wider pass overhead to check for threats before coming in for a landing on the sidewalk nearby. At the last second, I checked my momentum to set down my obsidian body without cratering the cement underfoot. I only remained a gargoyle for the authority it gave me...if the librarians within this space would give me jurisdiction as its new protector.

"Door's open," Roe said, holding back what looked to be a solid pane of glass for everyone else to pass through.

"The defenses here are insufficient," I ground out. "How are we to hold control of a house of glass?"

Cress was the one who answered. "Easy. Everything of value is down below."

"I don't like the idea of enemies three layers above our heads," I replied.

She went ahead of me into the library's inside foyer, head bent over her handbook. It replied in a squeaky, "You got it, toots! Look for hostiles quietly!"

"*Quietly*," she hissed back.

"Yup!" It flapped off to fly around the first floor. I stood next to Cress and watched it go with a low, rumbling chuckle.

In my stone form, I towered over her, taller in stature than any human man and much broader even with my wings folded as tight as they would go to my back. I carried a new addition, too, a shield made of tempered crystal. It was a gift from Prince Orthus and as large as my torso. It'd already come in handy in our last fight, and Cress liked it, finding how it rang from the touch of sunlight and glittered like an opal delightful. If I appreciated its function and she enjoyed its form, then it was perfect in my eyes.

I likened it to myself, as I had been sculpted and given new life for her. She enjoyed my form and functions quite a bit in private. My longing was a meager ember compared to normal, yet I yearned to touch her, to take her hand. I flexed my digits as much as they would bend, frustrated with how it felt I was working with an oven mitt rather than graceful fingers to twine with hers.

Later, I thought. In my own head, I was as taciturn as ever.

Would I have Cress to myself soon? *Yes.*

Would Ben join us? *Probably yes.*

Did I care? *Hmm.*

No. He could assist in clearing away her troubles for an evening. And if the dimensional returned... When he returned, Phaeron could join us. His absence was grinding through her thoughts, creating the shadows that danced in her eyes. If he was that important to her, then it was time for my pride to take a step back so I could fulfill my duty as her man.

"...Geo? Are you even listening?" Cress's voice cut through my thoughts. I refocused my quartz-formed eyes, realizing I'd stalled in place, gazing down at her absentmindedly. And apparently, she'd been trying to talk to me all the while, as her lip was quirked with annoyance and she'd crossed her arms.

"My apologies," I said. *I was merely daydreaming of you.*

"I was saying we should head down a level and see if there are any librarian witches still at work here."

"A sound plan," I answered. The library's inside was familiar, though the stacks were sparser than I was used to.

"Wait," whispered Áine. She'd declared herself the eighth member of the coven and tagged along with us, along with Jordan Evenstar, as Ben had not been able to dissuade her. A good thing, too, with their abilities.

Áine pointed to the left, where the handbook had stopped and bobbed in place ten feet above the ground. It was analyzing something.

A vine as thick as one of my stone fingers sprang from Áine's wrist, unspooling at her will as curls of green mist rose from her palms. Someone yelped behind one of the stacks when Áine made a circular motion with her hand and tugged backward. The plant returned to her, towing along a young teen by a loop of vine curled around his ankle. He clawed at the ground in futility. When I checked his aura, sure enough, he bore a weak but fluid halo of shifter magic.

He also hissed when Áine released him from the vine. "You are not a librarian," I stated.

"Obviously," the kid muttered, standing and dusting himself off. His gaze flickered between us, and he ran a hand through unruly russet-brown hair a shade darker than his skin. "If you guys are looking for a place to stay, keep going. The library's closed."

"We are looking for the librarian witches," I stated.

He shrugged sharply. "And they don't want to see anybody."

"We're here to help," Cress put in hastily. She patted the sword fastened to her hip. "I'm a librarian too."

His eyes widened. "That might be different. Wait here," he said. Without waiting for a reply, he moved behind the nearest stack and shifted. His clothes hit the ground with a rustle before he dashed away on the four padded feet of a brown tabby cat.

Cress watched him go, smiling broadly. "Aww, look how cute he is." She stooped to pick up one of her familiars, Milo, who purred in her hold. The other two had listened to her instruct her handbook and disappeared into the first floor to search for dangers.

"Not that I know many shifters, babe," said Ben. "But I think they'd object to being called cute."

Her expression barely dimmed. "I thought shifters were only able to turn into bigger animals?" she asked.

Roe was the one to pitch in while everyone else waited in various states of nervous idleness. "There are shifters of pretty much every animal you can imagine. They just keep to their own clans for the most part."

There was a loud snap. Several of us glanced over at Wren, who was chewing gum with a few aggressive pops in her mouth. "Two bucks says the kid ditched us," she said.

"Let's give him a little benefit of the doubt. The librarians will trust him more than us," Cress said.

Wren released a little "hmph."

A few minutes later, the cat shifter returned, leading a woman toward us who didn't look much older than Cress and her friends. "Oh, wow. A real gargoyle," she said, stopping short when she spotted me. "No wonder Steven was in such a fuss!"

The cat's ears pinned back, and he growled before going back around the stack to shift back. I heard the rustling of clothes before he emerged wearing what he'd shifted out of. "There's a gargoyle and a librarian, and they wanted to talk to you," he said.

"Hi, I'm Aurora," she said, waving to me shyly.

"Greetings. I am Geo."

"Nice to meet you, Geo. Is that short for anything?"

"No."

Ben muffled a snicker behind his hand. The librarian shifted on her feet, still looking uncertain as she took in our group. "Well, okay then. If you're trying to find shelter, I'm afraid we've closed the library. There are dangerous, unstable creatures down below that are trying to escape their containment rooms. It's not safe."

"We are here to offer assistance and partnership," I said.

"And Ashbough Protective Services is only a couple miles away to shelter and protect any civilians you might have," Roe added, gesturing toward the shifter boy.

She glanced at him. "Oh, Steven? He's practically our mascot. We, err…" She leaned in, lowering her voice. "Most of the staff abandoned Cerris City right before the lockdown. If you're really here to help, jump in and do it. Those of us who stayed can barely keep up with what's going on down below."

"We definitely want to help," Cress said.

"We'll do so as a group, though. As a fair warning, you should know that many of us are new to our magic," Roe added.

The other librarian nodded, waving the concern away hastily. "Let's be on our way. The powercore is going to need contact with you first"—

she nodded to Cress—"and then it will communicate where you're most needed."

Cress nodded, determination creasing her face. "Let's go."

6

CRESS

THE POWERCORE WAS on level sixteen of thirty. I eyed the buttons on the elevator's wall as I descended in relative silence alongside Aurora and Geo, my handbook now fluttering just off my shoulder. Since Geo refused to leave his gargoyle form, we would exceed the weight limit with all of us in here, so the others would follow along shortly.

Moongrove Library had had fifty floors, with many levels specialized for the containment of specific kinds of creatures, unnaturals, and artifacts. I'd met dozens of librarians who'd worked there, often seeing more than one person working every day on the more labor-intensive floors. To think Cerris City Library only had three librarians left. Even with its smaller size, it would become unmanageable quickly.

Geo's suggestion that we come here immediately was rock solid... pun not intended. He was my protective shadow as we followed Aurora through a foyer that looked like it could be any modern office's reception area and passed a waiting area with a cluster of plush chairs.

"What's your home library?" Aurora asked.

"Moongrove," I answered.

"Ah, I went to college at NSU too. The powercore here is different, and so is the process of drawing from it," she said.

I quirked a curious brow. "How so?"

"Moongrove's powercore felt a lot like talking to a person, especially when I touched it. It felt ancient and mysterious. There's no mystery here. The powercore in this library is a computer," she said, gesturing us into the next room.

"Can a computer be a powercore?" I asked mostly to myself.

My handbook rustled its pages. "Yeah, almost every powercore across North America is powered by artificial intelligence. You've been spoiled by one that thinks like you do," it said.

"It was weird at first, but I've gotten used to it. It monitors the library just as well as Moongrove's powercore," Aurora said.

I bit my lip. She was so close to the truth. Moongrove Library's powercore *was* a person, once, named Braza. After her death, her soul had become the beating heart of the library. She'd formed into a large, immobile sphere that rested on a ley line, siphoning raw magic from the earth to create a reservoir her librarians could tap. Through her awareness of the fifty underground floors of her domain, Braza guided her librarians to maintain order.

I'd only learned this much about her because of Phaeron, who'd known her in life. She'd healed me of some devastating injuries and sheltered me within her dome. I was disappointed I was about to let go of the magic she'd given me so I could attune with a computer-controlled powercore instead. It just wouldn't be the same.

The powercore chamber came to light slowly as I approached the sphere at its center. It reminded me of an LED with its faint but growing light, marked a pure and crisp white. Like with Braza, the massive powercore rested in the cradle of a stone loop.

"The other change is that you can climb inside of it. There's a seat and a terminal within to enter your information," Aurora explained.

"That does seem weird," I said. I took a couple steps up to the powercore before I touched its jellylike surface. It wasn't as dense as Braza, and I pushed my hand through to the pocket of air within it.

"Just step forward!" Aurora encouraged. She and Geo waited a few paces away. He'd crossed his arms, gazing up at me with a vague frown. With his stone form, even a small downturn of his lips was as intense as if he were about to rush over and snatch me away from danger.

I braced myself and took the suggested step. The powercore blinded me for a moment, but the sole of my foot found a solid surface on the other side. Blinking away dazzled streaks from my eyes, I inspected the computer terminal and seat that took up much of the space inside. I sat and put my fingertips on the keyboard extending out from under the monitor.

There was a jolt of static over my skin. "Beginning startup procedure," a robotic voice said from the terminal.

The hair rose along my arms. There was some kind of magic analyzing me, and it felt reminiscent of the same magic Braza wielded. My handbook giggled. "That tickles!" it squeaked.

After a minute of this, the sensation faded and the machine said, "Scan complete. Welcome, librarian witch. What would you like to do?"

The monitor flashed with a menu list of options. I used the arrow keys on the keyboard to highlight option three, which was to attune to this powercore, and hit enter.

"My sensors detect lingering magic from the powercore in Moongrove Library. Enter identifying information to begin the transfer process."

The screen went dark before loading in what looked like a job application. I started typing in my name and date of birth with a sigh, hoping I wouldn't leave my friends waiting for too long. There was a spinning wheel in the corner of the screen that kept distracting me as text flashed next to it. "Connecting to Moongrove Library..."

I was halfway through the application when the connection went through and the screen froze. I muttered a curse and tapped the keys with more force than necessary, past annoyed with this cumbersome system.

A voice entered my head, sudden and loud. *"Brightest of souls! Why are you trying to switch libraries?"*

"Braza?" I whispered.

"What has happened? Did I not grant you sufficient power for your audience with the Crown Coven?" she demanded.

I had questions for her, too. Like how she'd managed to bring her presence across so many miles to shout in my head. I could feel her lingering in the air with me, a presence of power and static.

"It comes with the job of needing others to do what I physically cannot,"

she answered. She could also skim the thoughts off the top of my head, which meant there were no secrets I could keep from her.

Instead of using my words, now that I knew she was in my thoughts, I projected my most recent memories to her. The interrupted audience, the fight and deaths, Myuna's summoning. All the while, her magic thickened further in the air.

"Uhhh, Cressie-poo, maybe we should get out of this thing," my handbook said nervously, flapping circles around my head.

The small space filled with the humidity of a mounting storm, and I teared up as it reminded me of Phaeron. I could close my eyes, and it would be him next to me, his magic on a short leash. But I knew that was a lie. Braza had a zip of electricity to her that he did not. It felt like potential I could reach out and take to wield as well as I could.

"Step out of the powercore," she instructed.

I scrambled from the seat and took a leap out of the white power-core. The room shuddered as my feet landed. "W-what's happening?" Aurora asked. She clutched the front of her chest and gasped as the tremors under our feet grew.

Geo grabbed me with one arm and her with the other, shading us with his heavy wings. I was pressed between his shield and the outside world, my eyes twice their size as the computerized powercore went dim. Aurora screamed and reached out for it as its jellylike surface shrank and fell into the hole underneath its stone dais.

"The powercore!" she shrieked.

"Wait!" I shouted. Something else was flowing up from the hole, its soft form expanding once it'd cleared the stone and emitting a piercing purple-black glow.

I had no idea how, but it was Braza, and her presence expanded out rapidly through the room and likely the library as a whole. *"Emergency protocol initiated: temporary placement of an ancient powercore. Reinforcing all existing spells..."* Braza projected this outward, and Aurora's mouth fell open.

Geo released us both as the shaking beneath our feet stopped. A door slammed, and in ran Ben, followed closely by Roe and the rest of our friends and coven. "Hey," Aurora tried to shout, but she was breath-less. "Only librarians and gargoyles this close to the powercore."

I whispered Braza's name, awe keeping my face slackened. Her magic flowed from her in waves, like a beating heart.

"It is quite all right. I have welcomed this young coven in my halls before. As I used to see you daily, small shimmer. Fret not, I have secured the creatures attempting to escape. Come attune with me so we can hold this library against..." Braza faltered for a moment. *"Hold this library for as long as we can with the few resources that remain here."*

"I didn't know you could switch places with another powercore like this," I said. And my thoughts added, *"Aren't you afraid Myuna will come for you?"*

"In my prince's absence, you need me more than ever. We shall fight. Together," she answered. No one else seemed to hear her reassurance or feel the way her power curled around me like an embrace.

"Together," I murmured aloud in agreement.

"You will see how literal that is soon. For now, I must meet with the three librarians who remain here, and you need to claim a place to rest. Might I suggest the rooms on floor negative two?" She hummed, adding as an afterthought, *"The living spaces set aside on floor negative one bear signs of occupation. I don't think they have grounds to complain if you borrow their things. Clothes, especially."*

I looked down at myself and the wrinkled and torn formal robe and pants combination I was still wearing. She was definitely telling me to change into something else.

As I turned to go, motioning to my friends to come along, a woman who looked like she could be Steven's grandmother stalked into the chamber. She had a similar brown skin tone and the first touches of gray through her dark hair. The cat shifter peered around her ankles as if he were a familiar taking shelter behind his witch.

She wore a sweater and jeans but carried an ornate silver sword in one hand and had a book flapping just over her shoulder obediently. Her brows drew in a surprised scowl. "Is it true? An ancient powercore just arrived?"

"That is correct," Braza answered for us.

The older librarian's voice broke as she said, "Thank the goddess. We were bound to be overrun without some kind of help."

"Do I smell a round of firings once this is all over, boss?" asked the last librarian as he sauntered in. He could've been Lars Eriksson's American twin, with sideswept blond hair and a leanly muscled build. His sword was sheathed at his side and his stance cocky. A low whistle escaped him as he eyed Braza's glow.

The boss in question smacked her lips. "You're not coming any closer to my job, Jonah, if that's what you're really asking."

Roe cleared her throat, stepping forward with her hand extended. "Sorry to interrupt, ma'am. Since you're in charge, I wanted to let you know who we are and why we're here."

"Yes, I was wondering what you all were doing this close to the powercore," she commented, shaking Roe's hand. "Leona Whiteside, head librarian."

We gathered for a group introduction, and even Braza presented herself formally. Leona seemed like a strict woman who didn't take much shit yet had seen too much of it lately. She still was visibly relieved that our group included another librarian and a gargoyle. She offered us rooms, same as Braza had, and accepted a partnership with Ashbough Protective Services through Roe.

"If the monster eating corpses on the nightly news is the reason our dimensional aberrations are suddenly gaining the power to wake from stasis, we will need any defenders you can spare. Preferably people who won't hesitate to slay anything that tries to escape," she said.

I only hesitated for a few moments before telling her that monster was Myuna, the goddess of said aberrations. Jonah paled beside her, while Leona's eyes flashed with defiance. They exchanged a glance before Leona said, "Then we must initiate a new protocol. Please, put me in contact with your leader. I believe we must do something quite desperate."

She told us not to worry about it for now and practically chased us out of the room so we could claim places to rest for the evening. I, at least, would not be leaving the library once it was after dark, knowing a vampire was hunting me in Myuna's name.

Braza reached out to me, whispering the idea that'd come to Leona. *"She was not willing to tell you that the only way to keep Myuna from summoning the servants and magic waiting for her in this library is to destroy it all first."*

I swallowed thickly, thinking that we locked the monsters away because they were dangerous, unknowable, or both. And the books and tools of occult use were kept here for careful study, considering they could never be replaced. To set all of that alight represented a huge loss of knowledge.

"I know, brightest of souls. But we must mitigate the threats we can."

I trembled as I thought of how unprepared my friends were to fight the creatures that even a fully staffed library had preferred to keep in containment rooms. I couldn't lose any of them, especially not after having to leave Phaeron with Myuna and an uncertain fate.

7
PHAERON

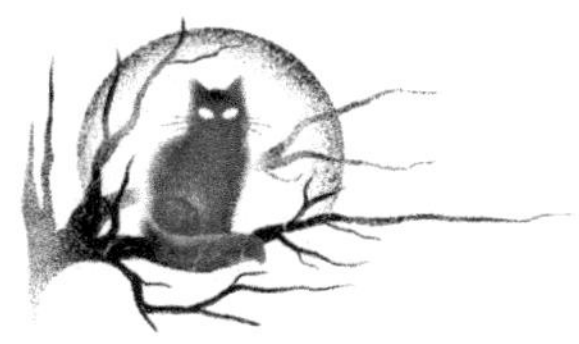

THE ACHE of my injuries prevented me from focusing on counting the heartbeats thrumming within me. Time passed with the madness of the Void. Hours felt like minutes; moments felt like days. The goddess must have taken the chill of it with her for time to dilate in such a confounding way.

There was a Void between dimensions, an endless blackness. The closest thing humans had come to understanding the Void as a concept was through their study of the celestial bodies. It was similar to space, but *things* still existed out in space, hanging there suspended with vast distances between them. As much as the Void held the illusion of nothingness, it also retained an echo of all that touched it. It was a chamber where voices and experiences remained, slowly twisting into nightmarish form.

I'd had a few brushes with the Void before, even though I was not of the Vrassorm tribe, the Void-touched. I'd had a friend once who was, and he was excellent at making the darkness answer to his whims. The same friend had helped me guide our people through the Void to Earth. It'd felt like walking through an endless tunnel, the atmosphere cold, cold, *cold*.

My skin prickled, and I shuddered. I'd lost enough blood to miss it, some of it dried in the creases of my shredded armor. Myuna had not licked me again, but her carrion smell lingered to sting my nostrils. I hadn't left this spot in...days?

No, that's not right. I blinked away the fog starting to creep over my eyes. Garroway had yet to return, so it had not even been a day yet. He was bound to the day-night cycle as a vampire, so I could judge time passing by his arrivals and departures.

I knew for a fact that Myuna would eventually rest as well. Until then, she occupied herself with consuming the rest of the enchanted books in the chamber. It would've been easier for her if she stood and snatched them, but she was as lazy as I remembered. Either she read their titles aloud and they came to her hand obediently to meet their end, or she lassoed them out of the air with the strands of pure light she'd woven into rope.

This was fun for her. Her occasional laugh threatened to split my head in half, the *ha ha* layered with so many other voices. It felt like the souls she'd consumed screaming out while she had her gaping maw open to laugh.

Or a small amount of Void doing what it did best, echoing. Its chill lingered in the atmosphere, its many lurid eyes watching Myuna with me. She was too busy trying to call down the final two books from the rafters to notice.

I couldn't close my eyes for longer than a blink, not when Myuna had forbidden me to sleep or rest. Time's passing increasingly felt like torture, with me trapped in a silent, alert body with no reprieve.

So, I embraced the Void, just a little. Letting it giggle for me when she grew frustrated. Her lassos broke several human fixtures, casting us into full darkness, even knocking off the object I'd hoped was a weapon secretly pointed at her. It fell to the bloodied ground and shattered with the crunch of smashed glass and fragile metal.

With no artificial light in the chamber, it was obvious when the sun rose. Garroway returned, dragging two unconscious people behind him. "My lady," he said in the Hungering Darkness's two-toned voice. "I was not able to find the purple-haired witch. But I brought you a meal..."

Myuna's lasso flashed out and closed around the torsos of the two victims Garroway placed before her. Her magic faded, allowing her to hold up the man and woman in either hand as if they were dolls.

"...for us to share," Garroway finished in a whisper since it was already too late. Myuna consumed their souls with all the fanfare of taking a deep breath, then swallowed the bodies together in one ravenous gulp.

"You have forgotten my appetite if you believe that was a meal for me," she tutted, dabbing at the corners of her mouth with her sleeve.

"Yes, my lady."

"Forget the girl for now. Bring me *more souls.*"

Garroway bared his teeth. I doubt the blood baron had made an expression of chagrin like this in decades. "I will remind you that this vessel cannot go out in the daylight, my lady."

She gazed down at him as if he were a bug to crush. "Worthless. I will make more servants since none of the ones I sense want to answer my call." Then she turned that look on me, instructing me to walk myself out of the audience chamber to wait five paces from the door for her summons.

My feet moved for me, pivoting me away before she could read the realization on my face. There was a library in the city...and Myuna could sense the denizens within it. It was only a matter of time before she corrupted a small force and tried to raid the building for access to her captured unnatural creatures. It'd be ruinous for this world if she went there personally to slurp down the powercore's accumulated energy. If she grew powerful enough, she might be able to muscle through the closed doors to leave Cerris City.

I'd figured out at some point overnight that the pocket dimension had been sealed shut. The change in air pressure was noticeable once Myuna was no longer bearing down on me. That meant the supply of unwilling servants was the small pool of people who didn't, or couldn't, escape from Cerris City in time.

A group of people that might not include Cress and her friends. Perhaps they had escaped not just the audience chamber, but Myuna's grasp completely. I hoped that was the case. The last thing I wanted was for Cress to see me become one of the goddess's servants, but it was only a matter of time. Myuna could already command my body. She'd make it as slow and torturous as possible, but she would inevitably seize control of my soul as well. A fate that loomed over me with great, ever-present dread.

Thankfully, five paces from the audience chamber took me to a battered bench I turned upright. My legs became one constant ache once I sat and finally took the pressure off my feet. I wanted to stray farther and find a restroom to clean my wounds and scrub away Myuna's stench, but I couldn't defy her order to wait five paces from the door.

I massaged feeling back into my muscles and reminded myself that I was still nearly whole. *Cress will still recognize you. She will still want you.*

I clenched my hand around one knee. *I will return to her,* I vowed. No matter what tortures Myuna inflicted upon me, I had a mate to claim and protect. It was up to me to find a way out of this situation before it was too late.

The Void's madness struck again while I was lost in my own thoughts. It felt like a blink's worth of time before Garroway stood before me, arms crossed. "I was sent to retrieve you," he said without the two-toned voice that indicated Endaeron was in charge.

I stood, wincing and reaching for the wounds that crossed my chest. They were weeping a hint of fresh blood. I spoke with effort, "Before we go back in there, I need to clean my—"

"Quiet," Garroway practically purred. My teeth clacked together so quickly I tasted the cut on my lower lip before I felt it. "Ah, it seems she's given me the end of your leash."

If I could correct him, I would. It was my brother, the one who'd swallowed a piece of my soul, who had originally had a finger's hold on my consciousness. With the Hungering Darkness inside of him, Garroway had it too, and I was too weakened to fight back.

He took a more confident stance; this was familiar territory for him, having his orders obeyed unquestioningly. I tamped my anger down with a deep breath. *He's a blood baron. He's used to mute glares and the futile struggles of those he controls,* I reminded myself. When I met his gaze, I wore my calmest expression.

He eyed me for a few moments, his face also a practiced mask. There was no telling if my reaction was also expected or if he was even a little unsettled. "I'll take you to a public bathroom in exchange for an honest conversation," he said.

I waited with patient blankness.

With a soft huff of breath, he added, "You may speak."

"I find these terms acceptable," I said.

He motioned for me to follow. There was a men's restroom just down the hall. Unlike the waiting room, which looked as if a hurricane had ripped through it, the restroom was mostly untouched. I could've used a shower, but this public space was better than nothing. I bent over one of the sinks and got to work with soap and lukewarm water, soon ringing the drain with my fuchsia blood.

My skin was purpled and puckered around the wounds as I scraped them clean with cheap paper towels. The paper ripped when I scrubbed the remains of my leather chest piece too, desperate to be rid of Myuna's dried saliva.

Endaeron had made the furrows across my armor and chest with his claws, ruining the new chest piece I'd painstakingly etched with runes next to the seams. Once it smelled of soap rather than carrion, I inspected the damage with a tisk.

"What did you wish to discuss?" I asked while I continued to clean myself. Not because I wanted to hear Garroway's voice, but if I kept him talking, it was less likely the Hungering Darkness would rouse.

Garroway had changed into a new set of clothes since the last time I'd seen him. He undid his belt to tug the line of his pants down on one side and removed his shirt, revealing a gigantic blood rune. Its magic was dormant and black, forming three spiky rings of runes that encompassed most of his right side from hip to armpit. Four healed and scarred slashes crossed the rings in jagged lines.

"I was wondering if there was any salvaging this, to regain control of myself," he said.

I pictured the moment of his possession by the Hungering Darkness. Endaeron had made those scars to prevent this blood rune from... I leaned in, reading the intent of the many runes Garroway had tattooed onto his skin.

He'd wanted to make his body a cage. The intricate spell bore marks of suppression and containment. If Endaeron had not destroyed it immediately, Garroway would have gained all the power of the Hungering Darkness with no foreseeable downsides.

It was unthinkable. And now he sought my help, as if I'd allow him such unchecked power.

"It is not possible," I stated.

Such a flat answer displeased Garroway. He bared his fangs and said, "The truth, dimensional. Tell me what you know about how to fix these runes."

Pain hooked behind my eyes the moment I thought to defy his order. I knew a great deal of things I wasn't willing to share, but I told him enough to soothe the pounding headache setting in. "There is a pinprick of hope for you. Your kind has always used dimensional magic to make these blood runes," I commented. "From a single weapon shattered into several pieces."

"Yes. And your fool brother destroyed the part I possessed," he stated through gritted teeth.

I tipped my head. "If you were to get a second piece..."

"There is nothing else that will fix the magic of these runes?" he demanded.

Again, the pain dug into my skull. I hissed with all the banked hostility within me. He was poking a predator through the bars of its cage, and I was just about ready to snap off his finger for it.

I answered in a low voice. "The weapon you were using to make the runes was unique. Endaeron was the one who forged and shaped the original great sword. It was made less for carving intricate displays of runes like this"—I gestured to his body—"and more for branding the flesh of any he faced in battle. It marked body and soul alike for his control."

"Ingenious," Garroway breathed.

I was about to call it *cruel* and share that I'd convinced Endaeron to shatter it, but the remains of my goodwill shriveled up. The few pieces of the sword that'd come to Earth with us had ended up filtered into the hands of the blood barons. They used them to mark the skin of their victims, witches like Ben, who bore the Agonia rune embedded into him permanently.

I knew his type. I'd slain a couple vampires like him in my time searching for the pieces of the sword, trying to destroy Endaeron's legacy before it endangered too many lives.

Unfortunately, I'd learned the hard way that destroying those shards also killed those who were being directly controlled by the man or woman who'd branded them with it. The mass casualties that'd followed when Endaeron had crushed Garroway's piece a mere day ago were additional stains on Garroway's already black soul.

"This is Myuna's work, marking souls, permanently branding others for control." He traced one of the runes marked in his own flesh.

Hatred flared within me at the reverence in his tone. "Myuna had little to do with it," I said, but he wasn't listening anymore.

"She is the most powerful being I've met in my long life," he continued. "A true *goddess*, not like the imaginary figurehead witches pray to. And she has chosen me as her right hand. Since it's not feasible to repair this rune, as you've said, I think I will accept what she's given me." A slow, cruel smile shaped his lips.

The Void's chill seeped into my voice. "That only means she will eat you last. You are a servant now, truly disposable to Myuna. She will slurp you up without a second thought, just like those two poor witches you brought before her," I sneered. I finished scrubbing my wounds clean and threw away a bloodied wad of paper towels.

He jabbed at my inflamed skin with a finger. "Don't take that tone with me, dimensional."

I snarled as his control dug in yet again, this time swiping my claws at him. He reared back with vampiric reflexes. "You wanted honesty. Here it is: you are a fool to think you're anything but a pawn," I snapped, switching to full venom since he forbade cold judgment.

"Wait. Pause." He held his hand palm up, and I froze.

I probed at his control, finding it as solid as Myuna's.

His voice became a velvet drawl. "We don't have to be enemies. Don't you want to see your purple-haired girl again?"

My whole body tensed further, recognizing the threat.

"Now, I'm going to let you go, and we can discuss what we can do for one another."

The moment he released his hold on my body, I grabbed him by the throat and shoved him through the bathroom mirror. Glass shards fell to the ground in a clanging rain around him. His eyes bulged, and skin reddened, face going slack with fear as shadows erupted from my body, closing around my head to form a wolflike visage protected by curled horns.

Yes, much better. I hated Garroway's presence less when he wasn't wearing that look of smug superiority. I caught his wrists with tendrils of shadow, pinning his arms down to his sides and his legs together with them.

"Let's get one thing straight, *blood baron,*" I growled, baring ebon fangs at him. My voice deepened with shadowborn power. "I do not tolerate petty tyrants. You will not dare speak of my mate if you want to leave this bathroom intact."

"Is that so?" asked the Hungering Darkness, disembodied from the choking grip I had Garroway in.

"Fuck," I said under my breath. There went the opportunity I had to make good on my promise and be rid of Garroway forever.

"Release my vessel, Phaeron. That's a good brother. Now, let's return. You obviously can't be trusted away from Lady Myuna's gaze."

I jerked away from him and didn't move to the door until he ordered me to walk. We marched our way back to the audience chamber and the waiting goddess. Garroway spoke behind me in a two-toned voice, "Our lady will be quite interested in the interaction we just had. How do you think she'll react to such an assault on her favored servant?"

"Her only servant," I muttered.

"We'll fix that. You'll join us very soon."

I stopped in my spot before Myuna, who had her chin propped on her fist. Her white-filmed eyes were dull with boredom. She would rest soon, which would delay Endaeron from sharing anything with her.

"...I can't wait to have you back, brother," Endaeron whispered. I glanced over my shoulder, but it was just a trick. Only madness from the Void lingering around us.

A fine shiver worked its way up my spine.

My breath came shorter. I was trapped...an animal in a cage of wills, stuck between a goddess and my brother, a victim she had corrupted beyond saving.

No help was coming. How could it? No one could stand against Myuna, even as weakened as she was.

Everyone left in this pocket dimension would end up dead or worse. And I stared into the maw of *worse* as the white figure on the dais yawned impossibly wide and closed her eyes.

She rested for a minute, or perhaps an hour, or it could have been an eternity. But her eyelids popped open again suddenly at a distur-bance underground. Something had shifted beneath our feet, but it emerged as a beacon to my magical senses, glowing with pure power.

Braza.

My hopeful smile came and went quickly. *Braza, here?* The power-core's energy was a buffet in front of Myuna's single-minded hunger. "That soul's power...it is familiar," she commented, turning her gaze my way.

She beckoned me forth, lifting me in an orb of her energy so I floated before her. "Tell me what you know," she ordered.

Talons of pain sank into my skull when I tried to keep my silence.

"Don't make this so difficult on yourself. I know the feel of souls... but it has been so long..." She tapped a finger to her lips. "Hmm. She feels like the girl you were going to adopt. But I ordered her dead. Endaeron, why is she alive?"

My eyes widened, but shock turned to pure wrath. Many deaths in my family could be traced back to Myuna, but here she gloated over one that was still a ragged wound within me.

"I'm not sure I know who you're talking about, my lady," he replied.

Her lips spanned a toothless grin. "Perhaps Phaeron is ready to enlighten us."

The pressure was mounting, making it feel like my horns were about to implode and crush my skull. "Her name is Braza," I muttered.

"More," she demanded.

"I *did* adopt her." I stared at her in defiance. My hatred was an unsheathed blade before her, ready to cut.

Her expression shifted. Something like worry tugged at her brows before they creased with growing wrath. "*More,*" she hissed.

"And then my brother murdered her. She was one of his first victims on Earth. We thought we were safe from you and your creatures, your madness, your endless hunger for our life force," I spat, picking up fervor as I spoke. If she would just silence me before she probed for the relevant information. "But we had no such luck. He cleaved her soul nearly in two in his frenzy before I killed his vessel. We gave them both the best funeral we could, but—"

Myuna made a silencing gesture. "Yes, yes, yammer more about how terrible I am." She rolled her eyes. "If she is dead, why is she here? And why does her soul feel so *powerful* and *juicy*?"

Slowly, she unspooled the truth from me about libraries and power sources. Her eyes glittered with interest as we discussed the possibility of there being a Cerris City Library and what "delights" might be locked within it.

8

CRESS

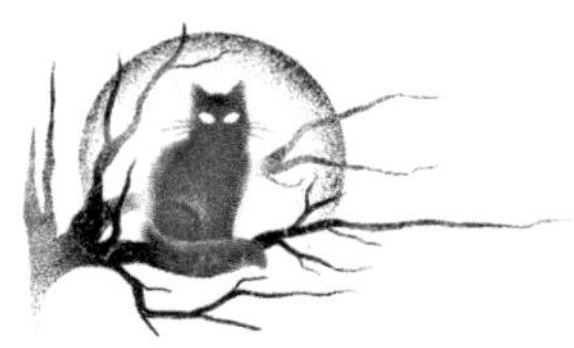

THE FIRST THING I did was shower and change into a clean, fluffy robe left behind in the room I'd claimed. With my damp hair still piled on my head with a towel, I took up my phone and flopped onto the bed. The room was little more than a rectangle of space with all the essentials lined up—a small kitchen area, a bed and closet, and finally a bathroom, with utilitarian decorations that were probably uniform across all the temporary living spaces on the second floor of this library.

I paid my surroundings little heed as I waited for a website to load. When it did, I muffled a curse in the off-white duvet I lay on and jabbed the refresh button like that would change the fact that the hacker's feed of the Crown Coven's audience chamber was disconnected.

I scrolled past a couple paragraphs the hacker had written, gaze snagging on a moving GIF. Myuna was swinging a startlingly bright rope that blinded the camera before the viewpoint went dark. Had she known the supernatural community was watching her? I took a breath to calm my racing heart before reading the text above the GIF.

In it, the hacker explained there were no other working camera feeds in the audience chamber. He also linked a petition, which I tapped.

Thousands of digital signatures already graced the plea to open up Cerris City again for long enough to evacuate everyone left behind. It read like the powerful men and women debating collapsing the pocket dimension were nearing a decision and that it looked bleak for us.

"It is an unnecessary cruelty that they should die with the dimensional monster we've seen on the news," I read out loud, my dread rising. "Please save these innocent people before it's too late."

Hana had mentioned the possibility that Myuna would be winked out of existence this way if we failed. A future she'd seen that didn't need to happen if we killed Myuna. But someone had to reach out to the supernatural community on this side of the pocket dimension to mention that we were going to try fighting her and needed more time to regroup. Had Madigan or Hana already done that?

Was the greater supernatural community just going to collapse Cerris City anyway?

As cynical as it was, the hundreds of lives stuck here were a small sacrifice compared to Myuna escaping and consuming the whole world instead. With a ragged sigh, I closed my eyes.

Everyone I held dear was here. If the pocket dimension was destroyed now, the mother who'd adopted me and the sister I was raised with would be gone. I saw Carly in my mind's eye and wondered where she'd fled to. She still hadn't answered her phone or any texts I'd sent. I hoped she was all right.

There was also my coven to consider. All of them were my friends... maybe even prickly Wren. She had come here to stand behind me in the audience chamber and confronted her father's misdeeds head-on. I found myself hoping that she would be all right too, after the loved ones she'd lost and all the emotions that'd rocked her rich-girl world.

My mind strayed back to my men, though. With the softness of bedsheets under me, it was inevitable I thought of the three guys I wanted here with me.

First Phaeron, the one who kept me at arm's length despite acknowledging something between us. I felt the ghost of his touch skimming goosebumps up my arms. He liked to lean down and whisper in his deep, smooth voice over the shell of my ear. Though he didn't trust himself and his instincts not to harm me, he'd still teased and tasted and given me glimpses of the animal that lurked underneath his princely veneer.

I only hoped those moments weren't all I was left with. I missed him with a fierceness that made needling pains in my chest. If he were here, I'd slip this robe off my skin ever so slowly and watch the heat light in his otherworldly yellow eyes. Maybe he'd touch, maybe he wouldn't. He'd seen it all before, even had the self-control to watch as Ben and Geo took me right in front of him without joining in.

Hell, both Ben and Geo were a shout away, and here I was fantasizing without them. But with Geo in gargoyle form for so long and Ben burdened by his brother's condition, would either of them want me right now? I moved to sit at the foot of the bed, robe gaping around my body with how the tie had come loose.

Well...I wasn't going to be much of a seductress like this. I went to the bathroom mirror to dry my hair and lamented my plain face. I hadn't packed anything, least of all makeup, and I wasn't about to go take some half-used cosmetics from one of the librarians who'd abandoned the pocket dimension.

I supposed my men were getting serious, plain-faced Cress for a while. My face didn't rest in a friendly expression, but I poked color into my cheeks and forced my lips to turn upward in my reflection.

"It's not all bad. They've seen this before," I said for my own benefit. We'd gotten past the stage where all they saw of me was the primped, polished Cress rather than the rumpled, morning-after Cress. Ben usually enjoyed tousling my purple hair further, mirth a shine in his eyes.

We should be sharing this room, not going to different parts of the library. I secured my robe firmly and peered out into the hall, looking left and right to be sure it was quiet. On bare feet, I padded to the door I thought Ben had claimed and knocked.

He answered as I was raising my knuckles to knock a second time. He'd been scowling, but his expression brightened the moment he saw me standing there. "Hey, babe. Come tell Geo to eat," he invited, stepping aside.

Puzzled, I came inside and spotted Geo in his human form. His tall body was folded awkwardly over the squat table in the kitchen area, a plate of smoked meat and crackers set out next to a steaming mug before him. His eyes gleamed with quicksilver irises, a sign that he'd just recently changed back from gargoyle form.

"You need to eat," I parroted.

On cue, Geo coughed up a puff of dust. We'd learned that eating and drinking gave his human side a kick start, drawing back the man I loved from the shell of stone he could encase himself in.

"As you insist." His voice was deep and guttural, yet his generous lips curled into a smile before he drank from his mug.

They'd made coffee, the smell of it lingering. I searched for creamer before committing to a mug of it, knowing I couldn't stomach it black but wanting the kick of energy all the same. Ben came behind me while I poured and stirred, his hands warm pressure around my hips. I placed everything on the counter and leaned back, tilting my head toward his.

The same longing I'd been feeling reflected back at me. I knew Ben well enough to gauge the slant of his clever mouth. "We were going to come find you," he said. His fingertips skimmed up my waist, finding the soft tie of fabric holding my robe together.

"Well, I found you first. What is my reward?" I snared his fingers with mine, drawing them away from freeing me of my clothes so soon.

"Us, of course," Geo answered. Straight to the point, as always, while Ben punctuated it with a kiss on the curve of my neck.

I shivered, the chill in the air only a contrast to the heat of him. I should've told him about the online petition, one representation of the executioner's axe looming over us regardless of whether we had a chance to confront the evil in Cerris City. Maybe I should have mentioned the destroyed camera that'd once offered us a glimpse at Myuna and Phaeron.

But what would we do about any of that now? I twisted in Ben's hold, taking him in again now that we were face to face. His worries were shadows in the hollows of his face. The last thing he needed was more to shoulder.

"I'll take that reward. Let's forget what's outside this room, at least for tonight," I said, tracing my fingers up his freshly shaven jaw.

He leaned into my touch. "That's the best idea I've heard in a long while," he said.

My hand drifted to the soft strands of his honey-brown hair, drawing him down to meet my lips. He opened up, kissing with the intent to forget. He tasted of coffee with a hint of his usual breath mints. Effortlessly, he lifted and spun me around, my lower back hitting a hard surface.

I opened my eyes, meeting Geo's gaze, which was darkening with lust. My head was next to his plate. Ben smiled against my mouth, holding up a strip of cloth...the tie to my robe, which pooled around me to reveal my naked form. I hadn't bothered with underwear.

Ben released me suddenly, skimming his touch up my curves. His calloused fingertips rubbed the chilled pucker of my nipples. "Hey, babe, lean back. I need to eat too," he said with a hint of his usual smirk.

"What if I'm hungry as well?" I asked playfully.

Geo eased his meal aside and helped guide me so my back was fully on the table. He stood and left my line of sight while Ben cupped my thighs and eased my legs around his shoulders. A little sound of pleasure left us both when he ran his tongue up the seam of my slit and kissed the bud at its apex. I moaned from the electric thrill that jumped through me.

I heard Geo return to his seat and the scrape as he repositioned it. He set something ceramic down close to my ear. "I will feed you anything you desire," he rumbled.

He pressed the pad of his fingertip to my lips, and I opened, surprised by the taste of sweet coffee. I licked his finger clean and sucked on the digit. The swirl of my tongue hinted that I expected him to "feed" me something else.

In response, Geo next placed a circle of smoked meat in my mouth, and I chewed carefully, experimenting with this while Ben coaxed his way between my lower lips with shorter licks. He'd picked up on the mood and slowed down from his usual eager feasting to prolong the moment.

I swallowed, accepting a cracker next. Though a little stale, this food packed more flavor than the last meal I remembered...my breakfast in the hospital. My belly rumbled, suddenly ravenous. I tightened my thighs around Ben, grinding against his face for more. His eyes were slanted with amusement as well as the lust that grew sharper when I closed my lips around Geo's finger again for a small taste of coffee.

I was glad they'd brewed some, even though we were taking in the caffeine later than we should. I'd come in here feeling drained and stressed, but my heart zipped with new energy as they teased out my pleasure. They just so happened to meet two needs at once, though any hunger I felt faded when Ben closed his lips around my clit.

I came and bit Geo's finger; he moaned deeply. He breathed without trouble now, no sign of stone dust or the apathy of his other form. The eager way he watched the pleasure break across my expression and how I threaded my fingers through Ben's hair told me that Geo was fully with us, completely a man.

As I lay there recovering from my pleasure high, they motioned between themselves, negotiating how they'd share me next.

"If we're doing food-themed tonight," I said, my voice husky. "Then I had better be sandwiched between you as soon as possible."

"You heard the lady." Chuckling, Ben flipped Geo a condom. We'd discussed the birth control I'd started taking in a private moment, but they still had to use protection until the pill took effect. I was just glad Ben had taken a few condoms in his wallet.

Geo caught my chin between his thumb and forefinger, stealing a kiss. "He got to taste you. I want you next," he practically growled.

I felt a brief pang of worry that he was letting his old reluctance to share me rise to the surface until his fingers skimmed down my lower belly, cupping and rubbing my slippery womanhood. His thick digits spread me, and I moaned as he curled them, shooting a bolt of pleasure through my core.

"Fine by me," Ben said.

I nodded in breathless agreement and slipped off the table, the fabric of my robe making it a fast trip to land on my jellylike legs. Ben caught me and helped pass me to Geo. Soon, I was lip-locked with the gargoyle, pressed firmly to his clothed front.

Geo had to release me to get the shirt off his body. I took that moment to help him, shortening the time between acts so I wouldn't need to think. After freeing his erection from the confines of his pants, I stole the condom from his fingers and slipped it onto his heavy shaft in one loving stroke.

I'd been shared by these two men enough to prefer having them at the same time rather than needing to choose between them for an evening. Sometimes I wondered what it would be like to add a third man, especially one with a tail and shadows solid enough to feel like stroking fingers. But I shook off thoughts of Phaeron, knowing longing would sour the night if I let it into my heart.

We didn't make it to the bed. Geo was strong enough to lift me without trouble halfway there, and I anchored myself with my legs around his solid thighs, arms braced on his shoulders. I tugged his white locs and shivered with anticipation as Ben stepped up behind me, squeezing my waist while Geo had my ass cupped in his broad palms.

Ben's teasing touch ran up and down my back, his mouth on my neck from behind. He brushed my slit and teased his thumb between my cheeks, using my own slick to prepare my ass for a bigger insertion. My breath came in slow, eager pants against Geo's mouth. Ben leaned down, lips brushing my ear. "Is this when I make a sandwich pun?" he whispered.

"No," Geo answered shortly.

He practically pouted. "I had a clever one. Salami was involved."

I struggled not to burst out laughing. I'd missed their back-and-forth. "Actions over words, Ben," I said.

Geo grunted in agreement, lowering my hips to spear me on his manhood. He caught his lower lip between his teeth on a hiss of pleasure.

"All right, all right," Ben conceded quickly. I knew he was taking himself in hand, waiting for me to sink halfway on the gargoyle's cock before he made his move. He pressed me more firmly between the heat of their chests and helped angle himself into my ass.

Mouth hanging half open, I moaned loudly at how full I felt between them. I tried to shift in Geo's hold, but he dug his fingers into my skin to hold me still, as immovable as stone. By unspoken agreement, they moved like two pistons; where Ben pressed, Geo withdrew, and back again.

I held on to Geo's back. His skin was slick, already sheened with sweat. I would marvel later at how quickly he bounced back from his stone form. Maybe it was just the food, as his kisses still tasted faintly of his scrounged meal, but I wanted to think it was me. Us. That this act was the true switch to flip for him.

I was glad to have him back...to have both of them still here with me. I cried their names out until I came and jumbled them up together. Once we cleaned up and lay out together, with me still blissfully between them, they had a good-natured debate over who I called out to when I'd said something akin to "Beneo."

9
CRESS

LEONA WHITESIDE MET WITH MADIGAN, Jordan, and Hana early the next morning, before most of us woke up. I learned about it when they emerged from a room on floor negative one and the door slammed behind them, startling me into looking up. I was rummaging through the break room with Ben for anything edible, my laughter from a story he was telling fading as I spotted the group of women walking by.

The four of them exchanged a meaningful glance. Each time a secretive look was shared with Hana, the tension along my spine notched a little tighter. I wondered what future she was guiding us toward now.

"Good morning," I said.

"Before you ask…yes, we know about the online petition. The other governing covens and councils around the world are debating our fate as we speak," Hana said.

I bared my teeth in a cringe. That was the opposite of comforting to hear from her.

"Well, damn, not such a good morning after all," Ben muttered.

Madigan brushed a hand through her hair. Unbound orange curls tangled around her head, mussed like she'd been tugging on them in frustration. "I'm going to trust Hana, as I always have, and say it will be handled. I have new instructions for you and the rest of your coven in the meantime." She gestured broadly toward Leona. "I am entrusting you all and your training to the head librarian."

Leona's mouth was set grimly. "I don't know much about other affinities...but there's little you can't learn by doing. We start purging the containment rooms today."

I swallowed down a surge of nerves and looked over at Madigan. "That sounds dangerous. Are you sending any more of Ashbough Protective Services to help?" I asked.

Madigan nodded. "Of course. We're supporting the library with an equal share of people and supplies."

"Aunt Jordan, you're going to be here with us?" Ben asked, earning a warm smile and a confirmation from her. She twirled her staff with its single stored spell, brandishing it with a flourish.

"And we'll all be helping...even Willow?" I added.

The last time Willow had used her magic had been in the Crown Coven's audience chamber. Her control had gone haywire, and many of the people who'd been around her had clutched their necks and gasped for air like they were drowning on land. It'd only been Madigan's timely intervention in knocking Willow unconscious that'd saved those people.

"I've seen a lot of spells in my day," Madigan answered slowly. "I believe what I saw was her performing mer magic."

"Yes, for the first time," Hana confirmed.

Madigan nodded, unsurprised. "It looked like an explosion of magic that'd been under pressure for a long time. It's difficult to be half witch and half a different kind of supernatural, but it's not something to be feared. If we gather any mer survivors, we will seek a mentor for her amongst them. But until then...keep her with you. It'll be better for her if she's with her coven, doing what she can without pushing her magic that far again."

The seer nodded in echo to her. If Hana wasn't offering a warning of impending danger, I would gladly have my friend here helping us.

"Additionally, I offer you a suggestion," Hana said. "Grant and Wren will need more space in the coming days. Do with that as you will."

"And don't let any interpersonal drama come between you and your duties to this library," Leona added with the air of a final word.

When Ben and I murmured in agreement, they moved on, speaking quietly amongst themselves. I turned to my man, whispering, "Grant should go spy on what Myuna is doing."

ON OUR WAY TO Grant's door, we gathered up Roe, who had donned workout gear from somewhere and was about to try to find a place to exercise.

Her familiar, a stout Belgian Malinois named Tank, panted eagerly by her side. He seemed disappointed when we distracted his witch. All of our familiars had to be getting bored. We'd set aside a room for them to take over, ensuring they were safely tucked away from danger for now.

Roe had paled at the thought of sending Grant out as our spy but didn't air any protests, only coming along and standing behind Ben and me as we knocked on his door.

Grant answered after a few minutes, looking disheveled. "It's too early for such long faces," he said, standing aside so we could come in. The moment he closed and locked the door, his real form spilled out.

The true Grant, if that was even his name, had light brown skin reminiscent of pinewood, with wood grain striations up his arms that continued at the bare vee of flesh at his collarbones before disappearing under his shirt. What marked him as a changeling were the four pretty, faceted dragonfly wings folded down on his back.

And part of what proved that he was a fae of the dangerous Autumn Court was his hair, evergreen at the roots and tarnishing to orange halfway down, and the amber-brown eyes he turned our way, alight with intrigue. He had a handsome, angular face and pointed ears that poked a bit out of his bedhead.

"I'm guessing you all want something," he said, sounding curious. He tried to call Tank over, but the dog gave him a look of distrust and refused to budge from Roe's side.

"Myuna destroyed the camera we were using to watch what she was doing," I said. "I know it would be dangerous, but I was wondering if you would be able to spy on her."

His green eyebrows rose to his hairline. "Yeah, I suppose I could..."

He drew out the moment, and I waited, expecting the "but" that came after that statement. Maybe he wanted something in return, even after striking a deal with Roe to use his talents to help us in exchange for information and our discretion.

"I just have to wait until she has a few minions. Then I can slip in no problem. Think I'd make a good monster?" He swiped his hand through the air as if it were tipped with claws. Instead of growling, he rolled his tongue to purr and grinned over at Roe.

She was looking a little pink around the edges. "Not *that* kind of monster," she protested. "Are you sure? This seems really unsafe."

Grant's expression morphed into an easygoing smile. "It's my job, Roe. I'd much rather use my talents to try instead of standing behind you and hiding from whatever violence is on the horizon. Don't you worry about me. I'm going to gather up the finest tea that's ever been brewed and share it all with you."

Roe sighed. "Fine, but be careful."

"You know I will," he answered. "It's my ass on the line too."

The tension between them seemed to break when she rolled her eyes.

"Right, so, Wren next?" Ben asked, sharing a quick look with me. He was moments away from a smug, knowing smirk, and I tamped down the urge to return that look back to him.

"What about her?" Roe asked.

"She probably isn't back yet," Grant put in.

"What do you mean?" she demanded. "Don't tell me she left the library...without us?"

That spark of interest was back in his gaze as he covered his lips with a finger. "Shh, it's a secret."

"It's probably fine," I put in when Roe placed her hands on her head, her eyes bugging wide as she started to freak out.

"The Hunger is out there unchecked, but sure, leave the library at night," she said, breathy with panic. Tank whined and nudged her. My heart beat faster in my chest, imagining Wren being wrenched away into darkness. Hana would warn us, right, rather than let us worry over discovering her body out in the streets?

"I think she was trying to prevent this." Grant circled a hand her way.

"I'm going up to look for her. You guys coming with?" Roe asked. She gave herself a shake and strode for the door without waiting. Ben and I scrambled after her while Grant locked the door behind us.

The stairs were closer, so Roe charged up them. She cleared the door to the ground-level floor first, and I found her standing a few feet away from it and motioning for us to be quiet. I heard the faint sound of a woman trying to cry and talk at the same time, making distinctive sobs of distress.

I didn't realize it was Wren at first. We crept closer when there was quiet for a few moments, before the sounds of crying intensified. "You don't understand, Mom!" she burst out. "Listen to yourself."

Another pause. "He murdered an *entire family* for that job! What do you mean? You *knew* about it?" She gasped. I felt a twist of dread and fury, realizing they were discussing my family. The death of my birth parents so her father could be voted into his spot on the Crown Coven with my mother out of the way.

Roe made a sound low in her throat and strode forward with purpose. I wished we could've eavesdropped a little more, as the raw expression on Wren's tearstained face morphed into wide-eyed surprise at seeing us before she schooled her expression as best she could. She had a pair of earbuds in and held the edge of her phone close to her face.

Wren and I met gazes, and something passed over hers with the welling of new tears. "I don't want to talk about it anymore," she said, sounding defeated. "Just...please tell the emergency council that we're going to make a stand against Myuna. They might still listen to you. We just need more—"

She winced, her tears spilling to make new tracks over her face. She wiped them away, then pulled out her earbuds and put them into their case. "She hung up," she muttered.

My heart tugged, seeing her curled in on herself like this. "Do you want a hug?" I asked. The offer felt wholly inadequate when she was hurting deep enough to show it.

She nodded wordlessly, and Roe intercepted her to pull her into a tight embrace first. "I'm glad you're okay. We heard you went out after dark without us," she sighed.

Wren pointed, and for the first time, I noticed she'd been sitting on a crate that looked like it didn't belong in a library. There were a few more piled nearby, and her staff was propped up against them, its sunny centerpiece glowing faintly. There was a swirl of magic in a matching yellow underneath the crates, buoying them up by several inches.

Once Roe released her, Wren and I hugged briefly. It was a little awkward, but it was a start. "Yeah, I couldn't sleep, so I decided to be helpful," she said, sniffing and lifting her shoulders back, speaking more confidently. "I did some adjusting on my magic and got us everything silver I could lift from a weapons emporium."

"That's a lot of silver," Ben commented.

Wren shrugged. "Whatever the coven doesn't need, I'm sure Ashbough Protective Services can take. I left a credit card for the owner to charge if they get a chance to return, though I'm not sure it will matter…"

She drifted off with a sigh before turning abruptly toward Roe and Ben and asking, "Could I speak with Cress alone for a few minutes?"

Roe's lashes fluttered. "Yeah, sure. Let's go get the coven to look at what you brought. C'mon, Ben."

Wren deflated again once they were gone and walked over to retrieve her staff. The crates landed on the ground with a jarring clatter. "You used celestial witch magic a few days ago," she said, inspecting the length of fine wood in her hands.

"I did. It was a stored spell on Evening Guidance. I'm not sure how…" I began to explain, drifting off when she held up a hand.

When she turned to look my way, her eyes were red rimmed with grief and a new wave of tears. "I want you to know that I don't regret defending you. My family wronged yours… My parents did the unthinkable. I…I'm not part of it anymore."

"Wren, it's okay, I promise. I don't blame you for anything," I murmured.

"Good, because I…" She breathed out raggedly. "I'm not a Starsurge anymore."

All the air left my lungs, a reply drying up on my tongue. Did that mean what I thought it did? "The rest of your family…" I couldn't even complete the vile thought.

"D-Disowned me," she said in a miserable whisper. "The only thing

I can keep are the clothes I came here wearing and my staff. And I don't know if I even want the staff."

What vile people, I thought. I channeled my inner Roe for what to say next, knowing her family would take Wren in if the other woman so much as suggested it.

"Wren, I'm sorry your birth givers were..." I searched for a respectful enough way to say this without hurting her further. "That they made the decisions that led us here. Family is also what you make of it. You still have the coven. We'll support you through this if, uh, if you will let us."

She gave me a hesitant lift of her lips. "I'll try to be a better friend." After a scuff of her foot, she changed the subject quickly. "And to start, I want to experiment with your magic."

I tilted my head, my gaze searching the air above us for my handbook. It held my excess magic, the whole celestial might of my family line. "Experiment how?" I asked.

"I've never met anyone with access to two affinities. Do you have anyone to teach you how to use celestial witch magic?"

Well, there was my birth mother's ghost, but she wasn't here for this discussion. Her comings and goings were pretty unreliable, but she'd wanted to be around to help mentor me. And Jordan, though I didn't know her well enough to ask for magical training.

"If you're offering, count me in," I said.

We agreed to meet up after dinner time this evening, or whenever we called it quits for the day on purging the library. Then, we waited in companionable silence. She schooled her face to hide the worst of her grief, and I decided not to mention anything to our friends about what we'd discussed. When they arrived, they were occupied with awe as crates were pried open and weapons were laid out on the floor, all made with silver.

There were a few guns and cases of silver bullets. We set those aside for now, going for the weapons associated with our affinities. Our leaders would know who could make the best use of the limited supply of guns and ammunition.

I eagerly traded out my old training sword for a newly made one with a longer cross guard. My decision was fairly easy, so I stood back to watch what everyone else took. Ben secreted away a couple daggers, while Roe tested the weight behind a length of metal with sharp bits extending from the ball at the end—a flanged mace, she called it. Each test swing she took disturbed the air audibly.

Willow lifted a delicate silver trident like she'd break it, twisting it in the light to admire the patterns of fish scales etched into the long, thin pole and up to the three wicked points at the end. It appeared ceremonial, like a celestial witch staff, not meant to actually skewer something.

"Can I really take this?" she asked in her whisper of a voice.

"Absolutely," Wren answered. She didn't even glance around as she set down her sun-topped staff and picked up a smaller, less ornate one about the length of her forearm. It was crowned with a silvery-blue glass globe framed by a pair of crescent moons. Her shoulders loosened like she'd dropped a weight from them as she gave the new tool an approving nod.

Bianca was the one to share that these were made standard for teams of unnatural hunters. Creatures determined to be aberrations or unnatural were almost always twisted from dimensional magic or simply weren't from our world at all. Silver was the one weakness most of those creatures shared.

"The perfect weapons to kill them easily while they're trapped in the boxes here," she said.

Ben elbowed her, scowling. "Don't jinx us."

10

CRESS

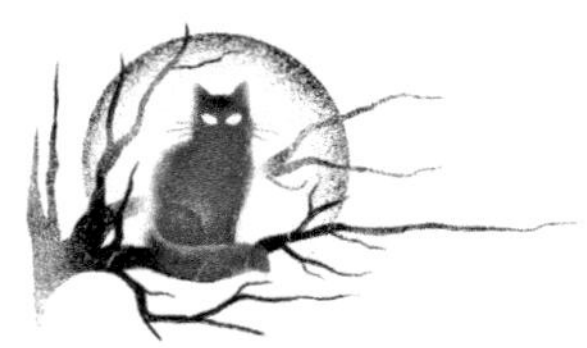

BEFORE THE PURGE WAS UNDERWAY, I joined the other librarian witches in the powercore chamber to commune with Braza. She spoke with all of us mentally as we went one by one to place our hands within her jelly-like sphere to take in her magic.

"I've already begun the extermination protocol on containment rooms with inanimate objects and the weakest creatures. Approximately a third of the occupied rooms will not need your attention."

"Where should we start, then?" Leona asked. She'd gone first to take Braza's magic and had stood there a long time, teeth gritted as she absorbed more and more while purple mist swirled around her.

"There is a mated pair of doskalo that are imprisoned in separate rooms on floor negative twenty-nine. They are attacking the runic seals with every-thing in them as we speak. Though they are not the strongest creatures in the library, they are the closest to escaping."

Next to me, Jonah muttered, "Fuck. I remember bringing those two in."

"My best estimate is that one will breach by midday. It will help its mate escape too, and then we have a serious problem," Braza said, projecting a feeling in my head. It was like I took in her urgency and concern as if it were my own.

Leona finally had enough and stepped back from the powercore, panting. Jonah motioned for Aurora to go up next. "What is a doskalo?" I asked him.

"Imagine a dog with the worst mange you've ever seen. Then picture it standing on two legs and being eight feet tall, with acidic saliva and a taste for human flesh."

"No thanks," I said under my breath.

Leona picked up where he left off. "They hunt in packs made up of a mated pair and their juvenile kids. They reproduce like crazy if left unchecked and go berserk if separated from their partner. I should've guessed the doskalos would be our first big challenge."

I went up to Braza last, still picking up on Leona whispering to Jonah and Aurora, "We'll see if the coven of kids Mad Ash left us can keep up."

Braza fed me a surge of power. *"I wish to witness the experimenting Wren tries with your magic. You two may use my chamber this evening,"* she said to me privately.

"Thank you," I thought back to her.

A feeling like the caress of cool fingers drifted across my hand. I wondered if Braza would take her full humanoid form with others in the room, but she soon traced the circular pattern that marked my left wrist. It was Phaeron's mark of protection, a bit of magic that connected us. Hope thundered through my heart as she channeled her power into it rather than me.

The last time she'd utilized this trick, I'd been too new to my magic to realize what she was doing. But now I felt the electric current and the way it flowed from me into him, a single bright line of energy extending out to him that resonated with a feeling of shock when it connected.

Phaeron's voice filled my head like Braza's did, in the alien syllables and hisses of their native language. I had an overwhelmed smile, tears pricking the corner of my eyes. His deep, smooth voice was unchanged. Even if he spoke with clipped urgency, it was still him.

"I have not yet given Cress a boon to understand the language of Soiluire. She is with us as well," Braza said to him. Her power waned, like the dimming of a light, until our connection was a filament of spider silk.

"Cress?" he breathed, as faint as a whisper from one room over. *"I had hoped you would escape."*

"Not without you," I answered in my head.

He laughed, and goosebumps erupted over my body in discomfort. It was off-tune, a scrape of sandpaper rather than the velvet I would expect. *"What manner of the Void is this? A reflection of my mate to haunt me?"*

Braza's presence nudged aside my own. *"No tricks, my prince. Ask us anything for proof."*

She pushed me from the powercore physically, through a bank of purple smoke that swirled around me and eddied around Leona's concerned figure as she approached. The connection persisted, a tense strand at the back of my thoughts.

"You must've been quite depleted," the head librarian said.

At the same time, Phaeron transitioned back to Soiluirian, and Braza replied. I couldn't focus on them and the woman in front of me at the same time, so I gave my head a stern shake. "Yeah, something like that," I said vaguely.

We went to retrieve my coven and a handful of Crystal fae who'd recently arrived alongside a nervous-looking verdant witch nurse. They were our support from Madigan and the only staff member the hospital could spare if something went wrong. The fae had armed themselves from the silver weapons we had left, and any that remained were packed up and in transit back to our allies.

We started the process of descending to the second-lowest level of the library while Leona outlined our strategy. Considering the weight of the fae's crystal armor and Geo's stone form, we would use the elevator in shifts to floor negative twenty-eight. From there, we would take the stairs to our destination.

My three cat familiars would scout things out first, along with Ben's ferret, Flit. Dimensional creatures of all kinds tended to overlook small furry companions, making them the perfect little spies.

Somewhere in the planning, Phaeron whispered my name, and I tuned out all the noise around me. He was still there, a desperate little voice over the many miles separating us. I echoed his name back, yearning for his presence and the night-air scent of his magic.

"Tell me of my name for you so I might know you from the Void," he urged.

"It's bright soul. I don't know if you picked it up from Braza or just decided to start calling me that because it's literal," I said.

"Cress... How I've desired to hear your voice again rather than the echoes of my own desires. Are you well? Wait. Do not tell me too much, for Myuna may compel it from my tongue."

"I'm fine," I said, a little puzzled. When we'd first met, he spoke like this...a touch old-fashioned. Maybe I hadn't questioned it enough when he'd picked up on modern lingo with ease.

Besides...why did it matter? He was in serious danger if Myuna was able to "compel" him to do anything. *"Has she hurt you? How do we rescue you?"*

"We are in a battle of endurance," he said. I had the impression of his weary sigh. *"I have slept not a wink since I last beheld your face. How long has it been?"*

My brow furrowed with concern. *"Three days."*

"Three days," he echoed back. *"Yet it feels like the trickle of minutes through time or a pair of eternities intertwined."*

"Are you okay?" I burst out. *"Tell me what you need. Should I sneak into the audience chamber and grab you?"*

"No!" he shouted.

I flinched, drawing Ben's attention. I affected a carefree shrug and rubbed my arms like I'd caught a sudden chill.

"Stay as far away from Myuna as the pocket dimension permits. Give me your word that you will evade her, bright soul," Phaeron continued with feverish intensity.

"I can't do that...not while she has you."

He chuffed with frustration, and I recognized the cadence of cursing in his first language before he switched back to English. *"She is a hundred times more powerful than you, even in her much-diminished state."*

Someone took a hold of my arm, and I jumped again. It was Ben, who squinted down at me. "We're going," he said, indicating where our coven was heading toward the elevator. "You good?"

"Talking to Phaeron," I whispered, tapping my forehead.

"Uh huh," he replied skeptically.

I followed with an annoyed scoff. "I think Myuna is torturing him. He doesn't sound like himself."

What he didn't know was that, without an immediate reply from me, Phaeron was repeating my name a few times in a panic. *"We're going to save you. I don't know how, but we will,"* I promised him.

"Cress," he said, but this time, he caressed my name. *"Don't. Your time should be occupied with finding an escape, not me. Do you not yet see the danger I pose to you? Myuna snatched control of me without effort. I crave to consume your soul every time I see it. I fear the desire will only grow worse with my exposure to her fell presence. You've bonded to two strong, stable men... Allow my act of love for you to be of sacrifice so you may live without fear of me losing control in the darkest corners of night."*

"Okay, Phaeron," I replied pointedly as I got into the elevator with my coven and we started to descend into the pits of the library.

"Your agreement comes too readily," he replied in a suspicious tone.

"Isn't that what you want?" Tears pricked my eyes, and anger churned in my gut. *"You should have come with us, you know. Instead, you gave up, and now you expect me to do the same. Well, I'm not! And I won't promise you something that goes against my very being. No matter how much you shout at me in my head, you're coming home with me. Hana saw that I would have a chance to save you in the future, and I will."*

For a long, terrible moment, he was silent. I worried our silk-strand connection had snapped somewhere in the middle from my raised voice.

"I did not give up." He was far angrier than me, and I immediately wanted to duck away from the sharpness of his response. *"I felt Myuna's presence create a controlling tether between her and me. If I had gone with you, she may have been able to compel me from afar. Instead of languishing here with her, I could have delivered her the souls of everyone who escaped while I stayed behind. I ask in turn, is that what you want?"*

"Of course not," I murmured. I was amongst the last to exit the elevator when it arrived on floor negative twenty-eight. Bella brushed against my ankles before disappearing into the library with Milo and Jin while we waited for the elevator to retrieve Geo and the other librarian witches.

"Sometimes I forget you are a shortsighted mortal," Phaeron scoffed. *"The passion of youth with no bracing of sense."*

I gaped, then gritted my teeth. *"Excuse me?"* I demanded.

"There is no saving me!" he roared. *"Do not court a fate worse than death trying!"*

A headache throbbed between my ears immediately. *"You know what? I really don't need this right now,"* I replied. *"We're about to face some mangy giant dog things, and I can't have you distracting me."*

"Mangy...dog..." he repeated slowly.

"Doskalos," I supplied.

"Fuck. Who is we?"

"I thought you didn't want to know what I was doing," I snarked. This was about the time I'd hang up on an argument or leave a text on read, but we were connected by magic Braza controlled, as I had no idea how to get his stirred-up presence out of my head. Not that I truly wanted to, even with our disagreement.

He scoffed. *"Fine. How many doskalos?"*

As he started probing for the strategy we were using, I realized I'd missed almost all of the plan in favor of talking to him. We were creeping down the stairs to floor negative twenty-nine, and it was a little late to ask, *wait, what are we doing?* I hated being that person at school, let alone on the edge of a seriously dangerous situation.

So, I told Phaeron everything I knew while we waited for the familiars to return. "The hallway is clear," Jin reported. The small black cat was the first to come back and accepted a single pet down her back before she stepped out of my reach. She projected a feeling of fear to match the way she hunkered down. "You can hear them on the other side of the doors. The one at the end of the hall is much louder."

I repeated her report aloud. The other librarians conferred briefly.

Meanwhile, Phaeron was giving me instructions on how to handle the doskalo pair. I wished again that he was here. *"You must fight each of them separately. If one of them sees its mate bloodied or dead, it will go berserk. The good news is they're not intelligent enough to realize you've already killed one if it does not see the body."*

Leona led the group into the hallway. The floor beneath my feet vibrated in time with a hard *thud* from the closest door to our right. A complicated array of librarian witch magic flickered with purple light over the threshold when the creature on the other side struck it again.

"Leave it. This one," Leona announced, pointing her sword toward the containment room Jin had indicated was closer to breach status. The metal of the door was dented outward and creaked ominously when hit from within by something large and desperate.

Leona signaled to us, and the Crystal fae stepped forward with Geo, who raised his shield and flared his wings to make himself a solid wall of defense.

With a complicated sweep of her sword's tip, Leona deactivated the array holding the metal together, and out tumbled a massive creature with patches of dirty brown hair and pinkish skin.

Its stench stung my nose and made my eyes water instantly. *"It stinks,"* I complained to Phaeron.

"All that matters is that you avoid being bitten," he replied, level and calm compared to the panic-fueled adrenaline pumping through my veins.

The group bristled with spells and silver weapons as the doskalo lurched to its feet. It seemed like some middle evolution of a massive dog becoming a werewolf, with arms that dragged the ground and scraped along with unevenly sharpened claws. Opening its mouth wider than any living thing should, it roared and lunged at the closest target, Geo. He clipped its jaw with his shield. Without sunlight, the crystal didn't ring, only making a dull thud as Geo leveraged it to knock the doskalo's head aside.

Behind us came an answering roar, muffled. I glanced over my shoulder. Shit, we were going to be fighting both of them very soon.

I also noted with relief that the creature might be dead before I got close enough to slash it with my sword. Geo and the fae created an effective semicircle that protected us from it, but there were only small windows for Bianca's crossbow bolts, Ben's throwing daggers, and the shards of glittering light Jordan hurled from the tip of her staff. Each brush of silver drew a whine from the creature, who started to retreat into its containment room from such a fierce onslaught.

Still, I cast Lux and inched closer. I wasn't expecting the freed doskalo to yip in pain and raise its clawed hand. It was shielding its face from the light...*my* light. The blade of my sword glowed like an incandescent shard, far brighter than any Lux I'd cast before. I nearly blinded myself looking down at it in shock.

Leona was shouting, "Make way! Chase it the rest of the way into the containment room!"

She gestured at me, my friends parting to the sides. The doskalo, bleeding from several wounds smoking from silver exposure, backed away from the blade I waved at it, snapping its jaws wildly and tripping over itself to be as far away as possible. Its acidic saliva sizzled on the ground from it frothing at the mouth, pupils contracting to invisible points. Geo moved with me, shield raised, ready to leap ahead of me if I needed support.

When the doskalo was back in its room, cowering down in a nest of sticks and rotting…I didn't want to think about what the scraps of gray skin and fur might've been, Jonah stepped around me and cast the Inemos spell perfectly. A wave of nearly invisible magic arced off his sword tip and hit the monster, freezing it into a new temporary stasis. With its muscles locked, Leona strode forward without fear and lopped its head off with a few brutal swings of her sword.

"Now the other one," she said grimly, steering me by the shoulder out of the room before I could retch at the smell and sight of the dead unnatural in its messy nest.

"Cress?" Phaeron asked tentatively.

"It's dead. I don't think it was supposed to be that easy?" I asked. Like he'd know, several miles away.

He seemed bemused. *"I shall wait for your business with both doskalos to conclude before pestering you further, however long or short a time it may be."*

The second doskalo died much like the first, leaving Ben and Bianca a little frustrated. "Put the spotlight away. I want a challenge," Bianca muttered.

I would've apologized, but when I squeezed the hilt of my sword to dispel the Lux spell, I stumbled and held my forehead through a dizzy spell. It sank in just how much of my stored librarian witch magic it'd taken to power that much light. The hallway seemed much darker without the blinding magic.

I looked down at the blade, wondering if it was special in some way. Maybe it tripled the power of any spell cast through it. Lux was a basic spell, power level one. It should've never been strong enough to strike such fear in monsters like those two doskalos.

"There are more creatures to put down," Braza reminded us when Leona started my way, a question obviously poised on her tongue.

"Let's talk about the magic later?" I suggested.

"Later," the head librarian agreed.

WHEN LATER CAME, it was after six hours of us facing down a handful of the unnaturals Braza deemed the most likely to break out of containment first. One would think those were the biggest, baddest creatures in the library, but they were just behind the oldest or weakest seals. Leona and Braza warned us of about a dozen more monsters still locked away that were deadly and unique. The kind of creatures strong enough to have titles and urban legends.

We'd handle them in the coming days. Tonight, I was the one under the microscope, and the ones doing the inspecting were Braza, Leona, Wren, and Phaeron still in my head. The head librarian had insisted on helping when I'd told her that we were experimenting with my magic.

"I've never seen a librarian with command of light like yours," she said when we were in the private sanctum of the powercore.

"I have a theory," Wren said. She'd come in carrying two staves— one was her old one, with the gold-plated sun at its top, and the other the scepter-sized one with silver crescent moons that she'd been casting with today. Without much preamble, she handed me the larger of the two.

The wood was warm and hummed beneath my fingertips. Unlike with Evening Guidance, which was sized and weighted for a man's use, this one was clearly designed for someone shorter.

"Try one thing for me. Cast Lux with my staff," she said, gesturing to it.

"Isn't it super dangerous to use one affinity's magic with another's tool?" I asked.

"Just humor me," she urged.

I looked up at the tip of the staff and shrugged to myself. The rays of the golden sun came to a point, which I used to form the midair X of the Lux spell by manipulating the staff with both hands.

The weapon erupted with light. I turned my face away, shutting my eyes tight. It felt like I'd cast a level-three spell, Luminare, which set off an explosion of light like a ground-level firework. Slowly, I peeled one eyelid up to peek at it in my periphery, seeing that the staff still pulsed with light. I'd lit the centerpiece brightest of all, and its golden halo formed a circle on the ceiling.

The remaining librarian magic stored within me rapidly depleted. I'd never felt it suction out of me quite this fast before, but the fatigue that came with being completely emptied of a powercore's magic had me squeezing the staff, fumbling with it to get it to stop glowing. The painful lurch of running dry happened first, the light fading as I struggled for my next breath past a spasm in my chest.

Wren steadied me with a hand on my shoulder, taking back the weight of the weapon while I recovered. "I think that proves it. You're not just a librarian witch... You're somehow two affinities in one. The light of a celestial affinity pushing out the shadows of your librarian affinity."

"That's not possible," Leona said.

I pointed at my handbook, which flapped down into my waiting palm from where it was circling the ceiling. "All of my Darkmore hereditary power was stored in this," I said, shaking the spine of the handbook. Its pages rattled with the motion.

"Hey!" it protested. "Careful. I'm sensitive."

"We made the handbook into an artifact, separating the celestial magic of her family line from the librarian magic stored within her. Although, Cress has always had a soul unusually suffused with light," Braza supplied.

"Bright soul, beacon in the night." Though I felt that Phaeron was still connected by a silken thread, his responses were distracted whispers once night fell.

The handbook took flight from my palm once I released my hold on it. "It's possible I'm leaking," it said slowly.

It seemed all of us asked at the same time, "Leaking?"

It flew loop-de-loops over our heads, seemingly carefree. "Hehe! You didn't think little ol' me could hold the might of an entire storied witch line, plus all the secrets of the great Morgana Voidbinder herself?"

"Uh, yeah?" I said, incredulous.

"You have entirely too much faith in me, Cressie-poo! I'm flattered!"

My cheeks tinted when Leona raised an unimpressed brow. She had a normal, obedient copy of *The Librarian Witch's Handbook* flapping behind her, unlike my malfunctioning one.

Braza hurried to pitch in, *"Perhaps it is not the worst thing that her affinities are mixing. Cress was able to cast a spell stored on Evening Guidance, if the memories she shared were correct."*

"Not just any spell," Wren muttered. "She cast Sun Surge without any preparation. Just picked up the staff, aimed, and fired."

"I had help. My... An ancestor, showing me what to do and say." I wished my ghostly mother would make a reappearance for this conversation. She'd been the one to lay her hands over mine and tell me how to unleash the power waiting to be used on the staff. That beam of concentrated light had been the miracle we'd needed at the time to turn the tide of battle.

Wren offered the sun staff back to me. "Imagine if you could do it on command, with your own knowledge and prep work. How much do you even know about celestial magic?" she asked.

"You all can make portals?" I ventured.

Her nostrils flared with a delicate snort. "That's fair. It's the most complicated and ritual-driven affinity. We have what are considered sub-affinities that we call alignments. At the beginning of each moon cycle, a trio of celestial witches link hands and align to the moon, the stars, or the sun. For the next month, they complete their rituals under the light of the celestial body they're aligned to to draw its energies. Most celestial witches inherit an alignment to one of the three options, and sometimes, like in your case, it's really obvious which one it is. Make sense so far?"

I nodded slowly, wondering where she was going with this.

"Sun Surge is the biggest, showiest spell someone with a sun alignment can cast. It's a variable power level spell, depending on stored power. The freaking laser you cast a few days ago was probably power level five or six. Judging by how your magic seems to work...you're clearly meant to be sun alignment. Maybe your mother was, too?"

Eris whispered out, "I was sun-aligned, yes." Her translucent form appeared from the shadows of the room, as perfect as ever in the dark evening gown she'd been wearing when she'd died, her brown hair styled in a fancy updo. When her gaze caught on me holding Wren's sun staff, a wide, approving grin stretched her face.

"She was," I confirmed. No one else in this room except Braza could see or hear Eris's ghost, which could be awkward if I got into a seemingly one-sided conversation.

"And Ben's mother?" Wren prompted.

I barely needed Eris to tell me she was star-aligned. Her job had been reading star charts for infants before Eris's murder, after all. I shared this information and then asked, "What's your alignment?"

Wren rubbed her thumb over a curl in the design of the scepter-sized staff she held. "Up until now, stars. But the other night, I let go of it in the dark of night, like my..." She cleared her throat and took a moment to right her train of thought. "I was never fully comfortable with the star alignment, but I was expected to excel at it with a family name like *Starsurge.* I would like a change, to experiment with the moon and her four faces. Let's try the alignment ritual with you and Ben. You're clearly the sun, and he can try the stars with his fancy staff."

"It would be highly dangerous," Leona interjected.

"Ben hasn't had an ancestor give him magic," I added, wishing the head librarian wasn't here to dissuade us. It sounded like something worth a try during this desperate time. "I only have so much access to celestial magic because I'm the sole inheritor of an entire family line."

Wren flashed a hint of a wicked smile. "There's a trick he can use to ask." Her blue eyes darted toward Leona for a moment, and she seemed to bite back on further comment. But I shared that glimmer of excitement Wren had—we would try the alignment ritual later, when we weren't under the watchful eye of an older, disapproving witch.

Maybe this would lead to the kind of power boost I could leverage to save Phaeron.

11

BEN

Cʀᴇss sʜᴏᴏᴋ me awake in the dead of night. I'd waited until my eyelids grew too heavy but eventually slipped into rest without her. She explained where she'd been and handed me a tightly knotted bag that smelled of an old-fashioned apothecary.

"Since when were you and the queen bee in cahoots?" I asked groggily once she finished talking.

Turned out, the bag *was* from an old-fashioned apothecary. Wren had slipped out of the library again without anyone's permission and left another probably worthless credit card behind to pay for the several bundles of herbs she'd lifted, along with a stockpile of verdant witch potions and tonics.

"Since the audience chamber fight, I think," she answered. "Well? Will you give it a try?"

Her suggestion was something I'd wanted to do eventually, to get in contact with my Evenstar ancestors and ask for access to my magical inheritance. I got tired of her standing over me and wringing her hands waiting for my reaction. I dragged her, giggling, overtop me, and we ended up entangled with the covers and each other.

"As long as you're in this bed with me," I said, kissing the end of her nose.

She melted into me with a tired sigh. "There's nowhere else I'd rather be."

I recognized the look she wore and bundled her close until she fell asleep, fully clothed and all. With a dismissive glance at the bag of herbs, I stuffed it under my pillow before pulling away from Cress to untie her shoes and drape the sheets over her properly. Once I turned the bedside lamp off and got comfortable, I closed my eyes and tried not to notice how strongly the herbs smelled.

It was supposed to be a soothing blend, I guess. Lavender and valerian couldn't completely cover up something foreign and spicy mixed in with them. The scent was meant to influence my dreams and open my mind to a visit from a deceased family member. My chest ached when I imagined my one memory of Marie Evenstar when I'd met her on Samhain night. My kind, doomed mother.

Cress would've liked her. In another life, they'd be close, and Cress and I would've chosen to become celestial witches. While she seemed a solid enough librarian witch, I wore the blood affinity I'd been forced to take like an ill-fitting shirt. If it were truly possible to draw forward some of the magic I was *supposed* to have, well, I'd do it even if it meant I had to accept Wren's help. I'd drag my aunt Jordan into the mix too for some more solid advice.

Despite me drifting off with my mother on my mind, I slept through what remained of the night without as much as a hint of a supernatural visit. Cress and Wren hid their disappointment quickly over breakfast, stealing glances over at Leona when she took too much of an interest in what we were discussing from her place at the head of the table.

"Today, we continue purging the lesser creatures," the head librarian announced.

Jonah, the male librarian never too far from her side, remarked, "When presented with the conundrum of one horse-sized duck or a hundred duck-sized horses, the boss chooses the big one for last."

Leona frowned over at him. "We will clear the whole library."

He nodded slowly. "If there's time."

I ate the last of my cereal without relish. We were having it dry with sides of protein bars. *Mm-mm*. The library's share of the rations didn't include anything perishable.

My appetite left me swiftly when I was reminded of what was at stake. When Myuna turned her attention to the library, anything we didn't kill would return to her side. With that in mind, we split into two groups, considering the "lesser" creatures posed less of a threat overall but there were a lot of them.

Once powered back up from a visit to the powercore, Cress shone like a prism. She was an asset in cutting down unnaturals for the rest of the time we spent in the bowels of the library. Leona pushed us harder and harder still to get our grim task completed. I felt like I barely slept a wink during this time...not the most ideal situation for a potential visit from an ancestor to fish for magic I *might* be able to combine with my existing affinity, if I was anything like Cress.

I would be the first person to say I wasn't anything like Cress, though. In the evenings, she disappeared with Leona, Wren, and soon Jordan as well to continue practicing what they were starting to call her hybrid magic, testing the bounds of what within her was librarian, celestial, or *both*. She returned late each night with an exhausted smile and the occasional superficial burn on her arms or face.

In the meantime, I put off thoughts of reclaiming my family's celestial magic for a one-sided rivalry with Bianca, who gleefully slayed monsters with the zeal of someone searching out a true challenge.

Eight days later, once all the lesser creatures were killed, we prepared for the kind of epic encounter that had Bianca salivating. We all gathered around a table where Leona had laid out articles and small artifacts depicting artist renditions of a strange aquatic creature. "When I was a young woman, this unnatural animal washed ashore just north of Myrtle Beach. It took out two SPDI combat teams before Cerris City Library was contacted to contain it. We called it the Jellywalker."

I couldn't help a poorly muffled snort.

She shot me an unimpressed look. "Laugh if you like, but I watched it tear apart two senior librarians and maim a third in the time it took to cast a stasis spell. And keep in mind, it's the lowest power level of the eleven greater creatures that remain in the library. Best case scenario...it is already dead within the dry containment room we stuffed it in.

"In the much more likely case that it is awake and biding its time like the good little ambush predator it is, you have to be aware of what it can do and how it moves." She picked up a wooden carving. "It is mostly legs. Eight feet of looming legs studded with jellyfish stingers that shred skin. It moves in quick bursts to overwhelm its prey, and its sting causes paralysis."

The carving was passed around so we all could get a good look at how bizarre the Jellywalker was. Its head was helmeted like a jellyfish, with solid plates on top that might resemble rocks if it buried itself in sand or dirt. Under the rim of its cranium, it had dozens of eyes for full sight in every direction. It supported itself on five tentacle legs and had a hidden tooth-filled seam of a mouth on the underside of its head.

"Imagine the ocean having more of these things," I said.

Willow glanced around before saying in her wisp of a voice, "The merfolk hunt unnatural creatures in the water like some of us do on land."

"So there *are* more." A few of my friends paled at my suggestion.

"Ben," Cress warned.

I cocked my usual half smile her way. "Just confirming for my night-mares, thanks."

"Anyway," Leona said pointedly. "We are running out of time. Myuna's new creatures howl outside our walls every night."

I wasn't the only one shuffling in discomfort. By some unspoken agreement, none of us had acknowledged that it seemed like unnatu-rals were calling to each other every evening above our heads. Their trills and screeches were muffled by several layers of dirt and metal, but they were still present. It was easier to pretend the sounds were from the monsters still trapped in the library...but there were only eleven of those left, and they were all far below us.

Geo had taken to standing guard over us at night, posting up in gargoyle form in the shadows of the library's ground floor. Cress visited him before bed. They'd have told me if they killed any monsters...I think.

"The Jellywalker and the rest of our targets are unlikely to be as cowed by Cress's sunshine as the lesser creatures we've faced. So, not everyone at this table will be fighting the Jellywalker. Sorry, kids, but Mad Ash would have my head if you got seriously hurt," Leona said.

She more specifically had Willow, Áine, and Wren agreeing in various states of reluctance to sit this fight out. Áine would be helping the twitchy verdant witch nurse care for any wounds, while Willow was still too unpredictable in her magic and Wren was *out* of magic except for the level-one and two celestial witch spells that didn't require storing. She needed time and rituals to store stronger spells.

Cress squeezed my hand under the table, beaming. "She wants me to fight," she murmured under the planning going back and forth between Leona, Jordan, Geo, and one of the older Crystal fae that'd been assigned to the library.

I smiled back, not having the heart to tell her that she was probably coming as a spotlight to blind the demented jellyfish. She needed to work on her channeling, because most days, she used up her storage of magic just by managing her overbright Lux spell.

If only I could share my channeling ability with her. Our mothers had had the same general problem—Eris Darkmore was all power, and Marie Evenstar had channeling for days but little oomph to back it up. Because they were of the same affinity, they could share power. All the more reason I hoped to see my father's spirit every night as my nostrils were tickled by the packet of herbs still under my pillow. My mother's ghost had given me a spark of her channeling as a gift and promised to wake Liam Evenstar in the next life so he would visit too.

So, where was he when we desperately needed him to visit me?

It took a little over an hour to devise our full strategy for the Jelly-walker. Geo would be the only one to engage it at first. Its expected tactic of jumping off the ceiling to wrap all five legs around its victim would be ineffective with all those stingers scraping solid obsidian. After that, we'd whittle it down while keeping a safe distance.

A small smile lifted Geo's face, a subtle sign of how pleased he was to protect us from this danger. "Let's go," he rumbled.

We headed down to floor negative thirty for the fight. I was in the second group down and took the short ride as an opportunity to apply my blood runes. I pricked the pad of my index finger with a blade and traced the familiar shapes in my own blood up my arm. Strength, speed, agility, stamina.

During my inspection of my gear, I flicked out the hidden vial of blood secreted within the ring I was wearing. It was a weird shade of purple...a gift from Phaeron, who'd taught me a couple new symbols where it'd be appropriate to use dimensional blood. I could use it to give myself shadow talons or paint a third eye on myself to see through unnatural magic. I was saving it for a dire emergency.

As we faced the Jellywalker's door together, waiting for Leona to unseal it, I swallowed my nerves. The fights were only going to get more difficult from here. We were lucky to be healthy and whole and have the advantage over this creature's natural weapons in the form of Geo. Even the five Crystal fae, with their armor of rock and mineral and natural geode-like growths, would be assets. Roe stood with them, her silver mace at the ready and the magical armor flowing from her necklace to encase her in a suit of polished orange crystal with reinforced fists.

Bianca and I stood to one side, prepared to shoot and stab the creature from afar. The librarian witches were another cluster, swords and books at the ready. Cress's handbook fluttered in graceful loops over her head, chattering away about the best places to get sushi that it'd recorded in Cerris City ten years ago with its last owner. She was blushing faintly, caught asking a rhetorical question that it made literal.

"Hush," Leona said sternly.

"Hushing!" It dropped its voice to a whisper and flapped closer to Cress's ear. "As I was saying, there's a place on Fourteenth Street that's to die for…"

Sighing through her nose, Leona went ahead and unsealed the door, opening it for Geo to step through. He lifted his shield high and rushed inside.

There was a screech of something scraping unfeeling stone. The fae and Roe pushed into the room next, with the rest of us following suit. I was so grateful I'd seen the Jellywalker in theory first, as it helped me make sense of the hissing, pungent creature unwrapping its limbs from Geo and scuttling backward.

The monster's five legs were fully flexible, currently bowed to drop its helmeted head several feet. Its many orange eyes darted in separate directions all at once, taking in the crowd invading its containment area. We were in an extra-large room, a twenty-foot box with a ten-foot ceiling and a dirt floor it'd been burrowed in for who knows how long.

Dust flecked off its moist skin as it used those flexible limbs to start climbing the wall.

"Heads up!" one of the fae shouted.

A silver-tipped bolt flew, and one of its eyes exploded with a splash of blue blood. I threw a few daggers while it reeled from the injury, getting them stuck in its helmet and a second eye.

One of the librarians hit it with a stasis spell at that moment, but the creature shrugged it off and scuttled further up the wall, clinging to the ceiling with its many stingers sticking it in place. It inspected us from above for a more ideal target, and that's when Cress hit it with the concentrated light of her Lux spell. The Jellywalker screeched in distress, its limbs retreating under its head that it suctioned to the ceiling to seal out the blast of illumination.

Leona unleashed a level-four spell, something I'd never seen Cress do. Living shadows curled into a ball shape at her side before answering to her will and the point of her sword tip. The ball became a giant hand, which attempted to pry the Jellywalker off its perch. In the meantime, a bolt cracked one of its protective plates, and I narrowed in on the weak spot, aiming to let fly a dagger to impale it in the brain and end this conflict.

Light suddenly flared from a new source...all of the monster's intact eyes. They turned white and refocused in one direction, its next victim. It unstuck from the ceiling and lunged at one of the fae, ripping his head off his body with a brutal twist of multiple limbs, accompanied by the crunch of stone.

Shit. It'd been so fast; there was nothing we could've done for him.

The closest person to it, Aurora, screamed. It grabbed her next, its many stingers wrapping around her body. "Help!" she cried, her hand dropping her sword and freezing half extended toward us. The Jelly-walker bundled her up in two tentacles before it scuttled out of the containment room in a desperate burst.

"Fuck!" I exclaimed.

Bianca and I ran after it the quickest with our speed runes. It seemed to glance around with intelligence before sprinting straight for the stairwell and heading upward with impossible speed by skipping the stairs and using its three undulating legs to climb straight up the walls.

Bianca flashed a grin. "Race you," she said to me.

She refreshed her speed and agility runes before charging up the stairs after it with superhuman haste. I, of course, did the exact same thing, only ducking from a warning shout from Geo. He half flew up the stairwell, landing and pushing off the handrails since his stone body was too cumbersome to maneuver back and forth for a seamless flight. The metal buckled under his weight, but he outpaced Bianca and me this way.

I worried the creature was somehow scouting for Myuna when it burst onto the first floor and paused, taking in a panoramic view of the library with a sibilant hiss. It resumed its flight upon spotting Geo cocking his arm back, preparing to skewer it with one of his signature quartz spikes.

Heedless of anything, the Jellywalker scuttled straight for a glass wall helmet-first and smashed its way through it into the streets. Bianca was starting to sing-song "Fuck fuck fuuuuuck *fuck*" since it was clear the monster was racing for the audience chamber and the soul-eating goddess awaiting its arrival with one of our librarian friends in tow. She shot a silver-tipped bolt at its retreating back.

Geo circled higher to drop on it from above, but he wasn't the humanoid form that landed on its helmeted head first. It was a block away and starting to truly outpace us when this new person grabbed the ridge over its eyes and dropped their weight toward the ground, unsettling its balance. Silver flashed, and one of its scuttling limbs came free in a gush of blue liquid, flopping like a boneless eel.

The Jellywalker squealed and shook the person free. As we gained on the monster and took aim at its back, our new ally landed on her feet and spared us a fleeting glance before sweeping her sword at the leg it tried to ensnare her with. It wrapped the limb around the edges of the weapon instead, and the woman released the handle, dodging being ensnared by the loops of its leg with impressive agility.

Bianca shot it through an already wounded eye, and the creature collapsed with one last hiss of air, deflating sideways to resemble a jellyfish in death. Geo landed on its head shortly afterward, further destroying the corpse.

"The fuck was that thing?" the woman asked in a voice like a roughened purr. She eyed the Jellywalker with disgust as she pulled her sword from its limp leg and went over to sever the two limbs still encircling Aurora.

"Identify yourself," Geo rumbled. He bent to help disentangle Aurora at the same time she did.

She was murmuring, "Monster slain and a civilian saved. You got the footage, T?" Upon seeing his stone hands, she released the back of one of the legs and let him carefully peel it from Aurora's shredded clothing and skin.

It took me longer than a blink to realize she had a small microphone taped to her ear and was angling a body camera toward the scene and Geo. "I know. I wasn't expecting survivors either," she said to the person on the other end of that mic.

Bianca got impatient and pointed her crossbow at the woman. "The gargoyle said to identify yourself, bitch," she said.

Smirking, the other woman stood and said, "I just saved your friend, and this is how you treat me?"

"You could be an unnatural in disguise," Bianca replied.

"By that logic, you could as well."

I inspected the newcomer's aura, seeing nothing unusual in the moving waves of power around her. She had subtle signs of a big cat shifter with her beast close to the surface. The fingernails she pretended to inspect were lengthened to claws through small slits in her gloves, and her naturally uptilted eyes were slitted and amber. Fur seemed to pattern the back of her neck under the messy fall of a platinum blonde ponytail.

"Ladies, please. Let's put the claws away and get Aurora back to our healers," I said, stepping between them. Bianca immediately pointed her weapon toward the ground.

Geo lifted Aurora in his arms and turned to me. "Handle this," he ordered. He fanned out his stone wings and flew toward the hospital, leaving me to deal with the two women, who eyed each other carefully.

"You must be an unnatural hunter, then," Bianca said.

The cat part of the other woman was fading. She had a feral kind of grin that still lent a feline edge to her face along with her pointed nose and strong chin. Her blue eyes lidded at a lazy-seeming angle, and she had the kind of tanned skin that suggested she often worked out in the sun.

She touched a pin high on the leather armor she wore, close to the body cam. It resembled a hissing Medusa head, with several of its hair snakes baring their fangs. "Damn straight. Soon to be a part of the highest-ranked team in Chaos Inc. The name's Grace. You're survivors, huh?"

Bianca and I exchanged a glance and introduced ourselves. "You won't be ranked anything if we don't figure out a way to leave this pocket dimension," I commented.

"Ah, well, do I have good news for you! I just got here with my teammate. Do you have a safe place for us to join you?" she asked.

"You tell us how you 'just got here,'" I said with air quotes, "and we'll take you there."

I ignored Bianca's hiss of warning. We needed all the help we could get to kill the last ten unnaturals waiting in their containment rooms, and this woman was a specialist in doing just that, with a teammate hiding somewhere.

"Lead the way, then," the shifter purred.

12

PHAERON

"*No!*" Myuna roared.

I muttered a curse as pain shredded through my already aching head. The Void laughed behind my ears. It knew I was weakened by mortal needs despite my kind's functional immortality. Myuna didn't notice my wince, and it was better that way. The moments that trickled by in her presence were more pleasant when the mistress didn't notice me.

I hissed under my breath. *No,* I told myself. *You have no mistress.*

It was hard to focus for long enough to remind myself of that fact. I'd been awake five eternities now or longer, clinging to the merest trickle of power and sanity at the back of my head. Braza couldn't feed me more than a drop of energy at a time without Myuna noticing the drip-drab of relief and coherency. Still, my body should've long given up.

Myuna and Garroway ignored the occasional unhinged laugh I uttered, in chorus with the Void or off-tune, when I was just so exhausted all I could do was chuckle at my own flaws. I was going mad one excruciating minute at a time, and surely that was the purpose of my continued existence at the goddess's side. She wanted me desperate enough to bend a knee to her. She bid me every day to submit to her will for the opportunity to finally rest.

And Cress help me, there seemed no other option than to give in.

Cress. The tones of her voice haunted me, and I was convinced it was the Void playing a trick. The version of her in my head was a distorted mirage of sound, and yet I listened anyway. She lisped in my mind in pleading tones. A human dialect, strange and blunt... I did not understand the words anymore.

"They killed the first of my children that managed to escape the pit they call a library," Myuna sighed. That's right. She'd called out in distress six seconds or hours ago, upset over something.

Garroway, who'd taken to whiling away many of the daylight hours on the dais next to her, patted her arm. He simpered something her way, and I nearly mustered the energy to sneer. How quickly he'd fallen in line and served her with devotion, even when Endaeron was not the dominant personality in his body.

Considering every supernatural he brought before her was consumed, Garroway had taken to catching animals for Myuna to experiment on. She'd twisted more than a few stray dogs into creatures resembling doskalos and created new unnaturals from other animals.

The goddess delighted in corrupting the fauna of Cerris City, as they could hunt survivors for her at the times Garroway could not. Her white skin had gained a pearly sheen from regular feedings. She was a beautiful, deadly monster again, making sure to tap my awareness so I would be forced to watch as she bloated poor grackles and seabirds into bulbous harridans and other innocent creatures into her twisted slaves.

She took to playing with her food, sucking souls one piece at a time so their screams of agony joined the Void's chorus long after they were gone. "Don't you want to look away?" she'd invited. "Just submit to me. I will do the rest."

Submit. Rest.

Had she just said that? *No, just a recollection.* Yet another voice stirring in the Void.

What she was really saying was, "...consume the group murdering my children and take the powercore for myself. We grow stronger each day."

"While time may be of the essence." Garroway pitched his tone to soothe as he rubbed her shoulder. His voice had gained the two-toned hiss of the Hungering Darkness. "You have yet to claim any other super-naturals to serve you."

"I have hungered so desperately. Surely you do not fault me for eating the candidates you've already brought me?" she asked. Their foreheads leaned toward one another, and her white-filmed eyes gave his a searching look.

"Of course not, my lady," Garroway and Endaeron purred. The vampire skimmed her cheek with his fingertips, drawing her ice-white hair back behind one ear. A daring touch, so close to her mouth pit.

I recognized what I was witnessing with a sick lurch. Affection. The worst monster to grace Soiluire had found what may be the most desperate on Earth. As Myuna slowly caressed her hand down the vampire's back, I wondered if her expression was that of lust or avarice. Did the self-proclaimed reaper of worlds have what it took to feel romantically for another? Or would she consume his soul the moment he stopped giving her what she wanted?

"Come nightfall, I will bring you new candidates, my lady. We can try until you succeed in taking their souls to serve you," he promised.

"Very good," she said, sitting straight once more. She loomed over him, glowing vibrantly in anticipation.

ONCE NIGHT ARRIVED, Garroway came and went thrice, delivering victims one at a time that Myuna held in her massive palms, hesitated over, and then consumed in a few gruesome moments. She couldn't seem to help herself.

Time whirred on, and my body grew too heavy to support. Myuna did not permit me to sit, so I collapsed, splayed before her like a dying animal. The hunger and thirst had grown nearly as unbearable as the fatigue, my needs eclipsing Braza's careful drips of energy.

"Give in," she whispered. "Submit."

My tongue felt like a flap of parchment in the desert of my mouth. "No," I rasped, tasting blood. Perishing here and now would be a kinder fate than what she intended.

"Very well... Watch," she ordered. Wavering, I lifted my head and did as she bid. She consumed a wounded animal brought to her and twisted a dozen more, releasing a new pack of her monsters into the city to hunt for her.

I dipped my chin, humiliated. The great Phaeron et Sudair could not save a housecat, let alone the innocents still trapped in this pocket dimension. The blood and gore, corruption and death... They blurred together into the Void's giggling seams.

Until she arrived, days or moments or years later.

She screamed my name with a human accent. I knew the girl struggling in Garroway's arms, and my eyes widened in recognition.

Some of the madness drained from my head, dimming the Void and muting the nonsense of time's passing. I was truly returned the moment I whispered her name, *Carly,* an ordinary human with dirty ocean-blue hair and torn clothes.

My mate's sister, here, being presented to Myuna. Panic turned my heart into a racing blur as Myuna's white-glazed eyes danced toward me and a smile curved the morass of her mouth. "You know this girl, Phaeron. I seem to recall her likeness too, from your memories."

"Leave her be." My demand was weakened by the huff of effort it took for me to stand. Shadows lengthened in the room, bending to my command.

Carly babbled, tears streaming down her face. She stared at my mouth all the while. The only thing I made out from her sobbed words was my name, repeated like a plea...

My translation spell, I realized. She had to be begging me for help and it was not being translated in a way I understood. Myuna had broken the spell I relied on so heavily, probably with the sheer force of her own mind-turning voice.

Myuna gestured for Garroway to release the girl and caught her in a weave of light. Her usual trick had Carly clawing at the boundaries of the bubble she was trapped in, still staring at me, probably wondering when I would do something to help her. The presence of Myuna's magic evaporated what few shadows I had the energy to call, rendering me useless for what was about to happen.

"What will you give me in exchange for her?" the goddess asked.

I could not give her anything.

I could not give in to her will.

But I also could not allow her to have Carly. I remembered a much more vibrant girl, who wished so desperately to be a supernatural like her adopted sister. She'd had me check and recheck her soul for any speck of magic in the hopes that proximity to the supernatural community would sprout something within her and spread flower petals toward the sun. She'd only seen the good side of magic; the Crystal Court with its friendly, honest fae folk and a tight-knit community of witches.

Her soul flickered within her now, weak and ordinary, shrinking away from the monster that had her trapped in a cage of magic. Already, Myuna eyed her like she observed every other humanoid brought to her: like a full-course meal.

"Has bringing me low not already been sufficient payment?" I growled.

In response, Myuna opened her mouth and sucked, tugging Carly's soul loose within her body. The blue-haired girl screamed and clutched her chest. "Phaeron," she begged. "*Phaeron!*"

What else did I even have to offer? My full will and body were the only things Myuna had not already taken from me. Falteringly, I offered the only other thing I could think of. "I will give you my knowledge. Several mortal lifetimes of information. Anything you would want to know about this world, here for the taking, if you would just let her go."

Carly's screams hit a feverish pitch as Myuna pulled on her soul in a nearly playful way, untethering it from her body ever so slowly.

"Please. She is still so young," I begged.

Another tug, and her soul left her body, which crumpled within the bubble of light, pristine except for the way her pupils rapidly smudged out of her unseeing eyes. Myuna cycled Carly's soul around her lips, tongue darting out to taste it.

I was seized by the inevitability of Myuna. The death of civilizations here to spread entropy, starting with Cerris City. In a couple days at most, I would be too overcome by my body's mortality, and then she'd wring control of me to help her agenda along.

Through the fog in my brain, I recognized the truth. The real reason for the methods of her torture when she so obviously wanted my subservience. She couldn't take full control of me unless I agreed or she corrupted my soul. Unlike Carly's soul, weak enough to be twisted from one lick, mine made for a challenge Myuna was obviously not willing to undertake in her current state.

I'd watched too many of the women in my life die; Carly could still be saved. And if I worded my surrender correctly…with a larger ration of luck than I deserved, so could I.

I breathed out, "Spare her, and I will slumber."

A deliberate word choice, *slumber*, the kind of blackout exhaustion she was pushing me toward. As long as I did not wake, she could reach through the tiny hole in my soul and puppet my body and powers as she willed.

It was a close second to the complete submission she desired from me.

The goddess paused with Carly's essence poised to be sucked into her pit of a mouth. "Very well," she agreed, far too readily.

She blew the soul away from her maw and manipulated it like she tied strands of light. It gained a new shape, and then it was shoved back into Carly's body, jerking her awake with a jolt. White light poured from her irises, marking her as the first human servant Myuna had successfully claimed. Back on my planet, we would call her a torch-bearer, capable of wielding the goddess's white light.

I watched her sit up and breathed out with relief. If I saw Cress again, I could tell her that I'd done everything I could to protect her family.

"There. Spared," Myuna mocked. "Rest up."

Before she could change her mind, I closed my eyes, feeling how dry and aching they were. It was the biggest gamble of my life, to go into her hands willingly, if temporarily.

Her awful, multi-layered voice whispered into the last remnants of my awareness. "We have a library to claim. Perhaps your slumber shall end…with your sweet mate in my hands."

13
BEN

"You were difficult to find," my father said.

The dream I'd been waiting for was made by a surrealist. Bursts of color surrounded us, hazy and out of focus, leaving Liam Evenstar the only solid figure around. I didn't dare look down.

He was younger than I expected, wearing a navy button-down and slacks. He'd died dressed for work, as he'd been in a wreck one ordinary afternoon when I was barely more than a toddler. A tragedy in any person's life, but doubly so when it was the event that'd forced my mom to seek out Garroway for a private loan.

The rest, as they say, was history.

I felt bad. I didn't know anything about this man except that I somewhat resembled him. Yet I needed him to acknowledge me as his heir so some of the Evenstar family magic could flow into me. Sure, it was based off of a wild hunch, but one Jordan and Wren grew more certain about every time they tested the weirdness of Cress's jumbled-up magic.

"I was starting to wonder if you were even looking," I said with an awkward little laugh.

Liam grimaced in return. It appeared I wasn't the only one who was feeling off about this meeting. "Of course I was," he replied. "I was at peace in the next life until your mother found me and told me everything you'd shared with her."

"Oh, um, sorry about that."

He gripped my shoulder. In this dream, at least, he was more solid than a ghost. "I know this is uncomfortable, but I need you to know... you deserve better than what life has dealt you. When I was alive, I wanted you and your brother to have the world. Now, all I can do is give you the power to take it instead."

That was all the preamble we had before golden light haloed his form. Raw power and knowledge flowed through him into me, and it was about as pleasant as molten lava coursing through my veins and head. But the pain faded, giving way to his memories and emotions and intentions.

Liam knew how much I needed aid and at least a cursory understanding of celestial magic. I needed to properly use the staff that was my inheritance, Evening Guidance. And I was suddenly sure that I could if it were possible to suppress or supplant my blood affinity.

Once the urgency between us faded, I opened my eyes and drew my father in for a hug. "Before you go, won't you tell me more about you?" I asked, unsure if I would see him in another dream. He deserved to go back to a peaceful slumber while I used the gift he'd just given me.

"Of course," he said. The abstract colors around us solidified. He and I sat before a campfire in his favorite park, roasting sausages and marshmallows.

I woke after hours of conversation with a huge smile on my face. That was my *dad*. His power and knowledge settled in my mind like I was always supposed to have Evenstar light just under the surface of my skin.

Cress was just starting to stir from where she was snugly pressed to my side. "Guess what, babe," I whispered excitedly. "I met my dad. I wish you could've as well."

Her answering look was bittersweet. "I wish I could've met him too," she said.

I refused to let sadness into this moment. "Sure, he's gone...but it was amazing that he could visit with me for a night."

I kissed her until she stopped frowning. We got ready together in our small shared space with growing familiarity and went up to breakfast, where we saw Geo running face-first into the one usage of the Internet he didn't understand.

He was in his stone form, coming down to greet us after a night of standing guard. Wren pointed the camera of her phone at him. "Ladies and gentlemen, our resident gargoyle has arrived. This obsidian giant has kept us protected as we continue to fight back here in Cerris City," she narrated aloud.

"Hello?" Geo gritted, still confused about what she was trying to do.

Grace and her body camera had inspired Wren. Without much useful magic to fight with, she had turned to playing in the court of public opinion. Since her ex-family had not spoken a word on our behalf, she streamed everything safe to share about what we were doing in the library and beyond. Thousands of strangers could be watching right now as we ate breakfast and planned.

We'd taken out three more of the greater unnaturals since the Jellywalker's death, but not without cost. A second one of our fae protectors had died, while a third had joined Aurora last night in the hospital for intensive care, leaving us only two fae to fight with. We'd gained one fighter in return with Grace, who'd revealed she was a mountain lion shifter, while her teammate, Tish, was her support woman.

Tish was a tiny young lady with a lavender-colored pixie cut and wide, haunted eyes. She was a hybrid of some kind, with a soul that moved like a shifter's but ears that came to small, fae-like points.

She was hard at work typing away on a laptop while taking distracted bites of dry cereal. With a click of a few keys, she had the lights flickering overhead with a dramatic buzz. According to her, this was for *ambiance* to heighten the sense of danger. The fact that she'd hacked the library's systems and could manipulate aspects of it like the cameras or electricity so easily annoyed the hell out of Leona.

An apparent tech genius, Tish had jumped in with enthusiasm and gotten Wren's stream and social media accounts set up. This not only boosted our message that there was still hope inside Cerris City, but also generated visibility for the unnatural hunting team she and Grace represented.

That was why those two were here, after all. They were chasing internal points with their organization, Chaos Inc., by killing the unnaturals here. Apparently, there were several more teams that'd chosen to enter Cerris City of their own volition through the only way still open: an ocean gate.

That the ocean gate was still operating despite the fae magic that'd shut down Cerris City was a ticking time bomb, but one we handed off to Madigan and our other senior leadership. They were the ones to decide how we would use the knowledge. If we abandoned ship now, there were still hundreds of unaccounted people out there that we'd be leaving to the monsters. But it could be used to usher out the civilians that'd already been saved.

Until a decision was made, we were all very careful not to mention the ocean gate when Wren had the stream rolling. We didn't want the mer to catch wind of it and shut it down.

I still thought the unnatural hunters were incredibly stupid to chase imaginary clout competing for a prize they might not escape the pocket dimension to see. My stay in Cerris City had made me a pessimist, sure as anything.

Tish bounced in her chair with an excited coo. "A hundred-dollar donation," she gasped, and Wren forced a big smile for the camera and thanked the generous soul.

I exchanged a glance with Cress, sure we were beyond the place where money could help, yet the stream donations were flowing in the absence of anything else from the outside world.

The only thing that might shift the landscape of the war we were in was more power...something we would experiment with tonight.

CRESS

Ben's father chose a good day to visit him, as our fights ended with Leona calling for a break in a meltdown of frustration. A corrupted dimensional had used his magic to teleport away once we'd opened his containment room, a flub Wren caught on camera. I felt for Leona, who took the embarrassment personally, as she'd overlooked this ability of his while briefing us.

It was our first true failure in a long string of successful fights, and she wasn't the only one carrying the weight of defeat. Wren shut off the stream with a quick fumble when Leona began to yell and Jonah rushed over to talk her down.

"It's been a really stressful time. We just need a rest," he said.

It gave us a chance to slip away that evening without being questioned. I met Wren, Jordan, and Ben in Braza's chamber. Jordan carried a bag to this meeting and began pulling out ritual implements while I went up to the powercore.

I reached for it, and Braza reached back, pulling me into the inner chamber of the powercore, where she stood in her dimensional form. She was made of the same purple and black material as the sphere we stood within, as the powercore was her soul and this space was where she could manifest as a shadow of herself.

I drew her into a hug and held her slightly squishy body, letting her snuggle close to my warmth. She was petite compared to Phaeron, about as tall as I was, with forward-facing horns and bat wings.

"Do you think this ritual is going to work?" I asked her.

Despite how young and soft her features were, she answered with the same air of wisdom as always. "It is a gamble and a guess, as it was to put your family's whole might into your handbook. The side effects of that decision have led to a leakage of light into your librarian affinity already. Perhaps the ritual will bolster you and Ben and somehow you will both become hybrid witches in a world that's never seen the like."

Jordan and Wren, both more experienced in this kind of ritual, thought that would happen too. "I'm just worried it will go all wrong," I admitted.

She blew out a sigh and took hold of my shoulders with a serious expression. "The worst is still possible, brightest of souls. Most who choose one path and are given an ancestral magic of another do not get to choose both because one never answers to their will. And there are books recording the celestial attunement ritual stripping potential hybrids of their non-celestial affinity. That is a trauma that can damage you down to your soul."

"I remember you mentioning that when my mother's ghost wanted to give me everything directly," I said, biting my lip on a surge of nerves.

"Unlike that situation, I believe you should still attempt the ritual. Your magic *feels* different, and your anam cara will be taking the same risk as you. If ever there was a setup for successful hybrid witches, it is this." Her hold dropped to my hands, and we both squeezed. "If you remain a librarian witch at all, I have a proposition for you."

"Oh?"

She nodded, releasing me and inclining one horn toward where I'd left my friends. "Your ritual awaits. I'll tell you later," she said.

Reassured, I stepped out of the powercore. I'd learned that Braza was lonely in her afterlife, and I meant to visit with her like that more. While we'd been talking, Jordan had drawn runes in chalk, with three large circles touching to form a triangle.

"Over here, dear," Jordan said, pointing with the nub of chalk toward the empty circle.

Wren and Ben were already sitting cross-legged in the other two. I settled in the last one and took in the markings around us. The likeness of the sun and its rays formed some of the runes around my spot, connecting to the moon phases circling Wren and the constellations around Ben. Herbs dusted an offering bowl in the center, along with an unlit candle and three of Ben's smaller throwing knives.

"You good?" Wren asked, raising a brow my way.

"Just getting some reassurance that this might work for Ben and me," I answered honestly, and she gave a little shrug of acknowledgment.

"It's going to work," Ben said without a moment of hesitation.

Jordan took a moment to confirm one more time that we wanted to do this before lighting the candle with a stray match. We let Wren speak the Latin incantation for us. We were seeking alignment outside of the new moon, when trios of celestial witches were supposed to meet and perform this ritual. To successfully align, we had to shed a few drops of blood in offering while stating the proper words.

According to Jordan, it was completely normal and even common to align when the moon wasn't new in modern times, since it was often difficult to find time for sitting in a circle under the stars with your two witchy besties with how busy our lives could get. I still had my heart in my throat when Wren went first and pricked her thumb, muttering over the bowl as the crimson drops fell. "Lunae maiestas." Majesty of the moon.

Ben was next, his confidence starting to show its cracks as he blew out an unsteady breath. He added his blood to the bowl. "Magicae stellae," he said. Magic of the stars.

They turned to me expectantly as I lifted the last clean blade and poised my hand over the bowl. My fingers were shaking. In two simple words and a few drops of blood, we'd see how this ritual would end up working for us. I drew a steading breath and poked my thumb. "Potentia solis." Power of the sun.

Power was what I'd already harnessed with the Sun Surge I'd cast from Evening Guidance. The same light I held each time I cast Lux and Luminaire. The kind of heat I felt mounting in my chest as Wren seized my hand and I fumbled for Ben's as I started to sweat.

She closed out the ritual with one last phrase. I focused on my breathing and the runes around us. The chalk turned colors...black around Wren, silver for Ben, and gold for me. A sign of success as I rode out the sensation of the worst heartburn of my life.

Ben was grinning, flexing his hands with anticipation. "You don't feel hot?" I asked.

It was Jordan's fingers that landed on my forehead first. "You have too much magic in you. Try this." She had me hold out my hand and cast a level-one celestial spell, Lumen. My palm heated and projected a gentle flashlight-level of brightness.

I gaped at it as the heat within me calmed over the duration I held the spell, which was easily canceled by shaking out my hand. "It worked," I said with a little disbelieving laugh. "Quick, teach Ben a level-one spell!"

I felt a soft probe of my awareness. *"And even better news, you are still a librarian,"* Braza told me privately while Ben learned to produce handfuls of magic that glittered like tiny star confetti and sizzled like embers.

Ben and I laughed and hugged, and I think Wren hid a little teary moment when she successfully swirled motes of moonlight around her fingertip. She covered her mouth with one hand and took up her scepter with the other, lighting it with a glow of soft silver.

"It's so easy," she whispered.

"Will you tell me your idea now?" I asked Braza.

"Very soon, brightest of souls. The hour grows late, and you must practice with one magic before I empower the other." She projected a sensation of pride. *"You are one of the strongest witches I have had the chance to witness in my time. No wonder you are fated to my prince."*

14
GEO

WHILE CRESS and Ben engaged in their ritual, I separated myself from them for our mutual sanity. If Cress wanted to explore her magic...who was I to stop her? She was fairly certain it would be fine, and Ben was more confident still.

Rather than loom over them, I went to my evening post. I was staying in stone form longer and longer by necessity, not consuming valuable rations and not sleeping when our enemies were sniffing around the library at night.

In fact, it was irresponsible for me to take human form...but I craved it. Even as I stood sentry in the shadows of the library's first floor, I ached within to transform back and hold my love through the night once I was sure she was okay.

No. I had a duty.

And *no*, that duty wasn't waiting in the same room as her ritual. It was ensuring her safety, as I was doing. She could rest easy knowing that no unnaturals had slipped into the lower floors of the library, because I was standing guard.

Someone else would have to be tasked with this if I abandoned my post. They could fall asleep while keeping watch. Everyone in our little group was in some stage of exhaustion and hurt at this point. Most of our various wounds resulted from careless mistakes no one made when we first started clearing the library.

I didn't shift my considerable stone weight side to side, but I realized after an hour that I was *bored*. I had never been bored in this form before. Could I still be considered a patient rock if boredom was leaking into me from my human side?

Had I truly changed so quickly to be considering this question during an ongoing crisis?

Hmm, yes. For better or worse, this was Cress's doing as well. I would never be an unfeeling stone construct again with duty as my only comfort. I loved my woman too much to revert to that state.

Glass crunched under someone's tread, drawing my focus. "Halt. Identify yourself," I stated without hesitation. I already had one quartz spike primed and ready to fire if I had just announced myself to a roaming unnatural.

"Geo?" answered Grant's uncertain voice. "It's me, your favorite changeling."

"You are the only changeling I know," I said.

"That you're aware of," he said with a lilt of playfulness. I decided he sounded unapologetically like Grant and tilted my crystal shield, letting it reflect what little light remained outside from a distant streetlight so he knew where I was standing. The upper floors of the library were completely dark to discourage unnatural scavengers.

"Is that supposed to be a joke?" I asked.

His outline approached, and he felt for the stack closest to me. "Depends. Did you find it funny?" Only now did I notice the hitch in his voice and how he stumbled and held his side. "Áine hasn't figured me out yet, right? She'll heal me?"

"She has more pressing matters than your secret identity," I confirmed. "What happened?"

I saw the impression of his bright teeth bared in a grimace. "Turns out it's nigh impossible to spy on someone who eats every supernatural placed in front of her. Still, I saw a glimpse of some real shit, my stony friend, and then the monsters discovered me."

"Were you followed?" I demanded.

"Please," he wheezed. "I'm not that much of an amateur. But...they might pick up on the smell of my blood. I had to land a couple blocks away to avoid the attention of Myuna's flying blobs."

"I will handle it," I stated. For a split second, I hesitated and warred with the desire to shake him down for all of his information, despite concern for his well-being. "Tell me the most pressing details of what you learned. Without jokes."

"Yes, sir." Grant didn't have his mocking tone anymore. "Straight to the point...Myuna is making monsters out of any animals that are brought to her and was consuming the souls and bodies of the people she gets her hands on until very recently. She's successfully turned three people into white-eyed zombies, that I've seen, and..." He spent a few moments catching his breath. "Phaeron has switched sides. He's started gathering people for Myuna to zombify."

A sick feeling gathered in my chest. "You are certain? You have seen this for yourself?" I confirmed. Cress would be heartbroken. She'd been so certain the powercore had allowed her a connection with him to send him support. But even the greatest men broke under the right kind of pressure eventually, and we knew it couldn't be easy to stand in a goddess's presence unaffected.

"Yeah, I did. Hard to mistake a big scary shadow dude hauling a screaming woman toward Myuna." He shuddered, which became a painful cough.

"Go seek healing. Don't go back out again. There is no point in endangering yourself," I said.

"Worried about me, huh? If you weren't made of stone, I'd daresay you were getting soft," he said with a hint of a fae's musical, teasing laugh as he left me, finding the elevator and disappearing into the depths of the library.

Little did he know how right he'd been, and how annoyed I was that he taunted me for it.

THREE DOGLIKE CREATURES followed the trail of Grant's blood scent. I heard them snuffling and fired a quartz spike through one of their elongated skulls, killing it and sending the other two yipping away in fear.

Come morning, I went to retrieve my weapon and got a good look at the body. Its eyes had glowed faintly with Myuna's white power, making its head a target even in low lighting. The corpse, though...it was simply sad. It appeared that the goddess had stretched an already emaciated street dog, trying to form it into a doskalo. Fur and skin were split over joints not built for the sudden weight and size of its transformation.

"Rest in peace," I rumbled. I would have to show the body to the rest of the group as an example of the unnaturals prowling the city streets.

When one of our remaining Crystal fae came up to swap places with me, he had his phone out. "We're getting a resupply soon. Mind staying here just in case there's trouble?"

I grinded a nod, and together we stepped outside. Cold wind and a bite of freezing rain hit us, and the fae shuddered. I scanned the drab gray of the skies, which were free of flying creatures, but a few of them lined up on the buildings around us, their glowing white eyes unblinking.

The unnatural birds were hulking, inflated in the chest with... muscle? Pus? Something of the sort. Their claws were transformed into oversized and gleaming talons.

"We are being spied on," I said quietly to my fae companion, indicating the birds. If Myuna had even a smidge of tactical capability, she would have already corrupted and sent out a legion of these birds to have her eyes on every inch of Cerris City's streets.

"Shit, yeah, they're looking right at us," he muttered back, scoffing. "Think the bounty hunters will come knock 'em down for imaginary points?"

"The endeavor may not be worth the reward," I answered.

I did not have to explain further. Usually, I didn't, but as the minutes rolled past and nothing else happened, I spoke up out of my usual turn, pitching my voice low so it might be chased away on the cold wind rather than reach the birds' awareness. "I imagine they are newly installed spying units. Their job right now will be to watch us and see what we are doing. We can resupply in peace, or we can kill them and risk a hostile response in return."

"I get it. I was just trying to make a joke, man," he said through chattering teeth.

People and their jokes, I thought with a thread of annoyance. I supposed it was asking a lot for a non-gargoyle to be as direct as I was.

A large truck rumbled down the street, its bed full of crates. A second, similarly laden vehicle followed. I noted my surprise. A lot more people piled out than were needed for a supply run. I helped heft more than a person's share of the weight and fell into step with Madigan Ashbough carrying several crates too, her arms enlarged with extra muscle from a guardian witch spell.

"Hello again, Geo," she said cheerfully enough, her voice betraying a hint of strain.

I waited until we were in the library to say, "I was not expecting our leader to deliver supplies personally."

We put the crates down and her muscles relaxed to their usual size slowly. She motioned for me to stand aside with her as the rest of the men and women took care of moving the crates deeper into the library. "That's because we've had a change of strategy."

"You are aware of Phaeron switching allegiances," I surmised.

"Yes. We've always known it would happen, but not exactly when. Our seer allies are now certain the library will be the subject of an assault with him as its head," she said with a grim set of her lips.

"How long do we have?"

As we spoke, I noted the presence of her mates, the Crystal Court's Prince Orthus and the twin guardian witches, Ajax and Aaron, identical save for their different tastes in dressing style. The blood witch Daire Grimsbane was also here, fully equipped for combat; despite being a politician, he was willing to get his hands dirty fighting with us. It also seemed he was friends with the other men now, carrying on with the twins as they worked.

Orthus placed Madigan's massive geode-formed warhammer next to her, and she smiled prettily, reaching up to kiss his cheek in thanks.

"Days," she answered me. "But it will depend on Cress and the powercore to trigger Myuna's greed. We still have some agency to prepare with traps and spells."

"I will accompany you to tell her that." A frown pulled at my stone lips, made more severe when I took a moment to transform back to human form. My concern for Cress practically pulsed out of me, along with a new emotion: anger. Phaeron was the perfect agent for Myuna to hurt Cress. Despite everything, I was halfway moved toward blaming him for this situation.

Madigan nodded. "That's a good idea," she said with a look of understanding.

We descended with the next set of supplies and emerged into a bustle of movement on floor negative one as crates were opened and the items divided and put away. Cress was there helping, red-nosed and puffy-eyed, and my heart sank to see her this way. She put down a jug of water moments before I swept her off her feet and into my arms.

"Hey, Geo." She hugged me back with a soft sigh, burying her face in my shirt.

She breathed a mild protest when I carried her away to an empty conference room so she could sit with Madigan and me. I was loath to let her go, and it seemed she felt the same, as she remained in the circle of my arms when I settled. Her hand rested casually on my knee.

"How did your ritual go?" I asked.

Cress released a little watery laugh. "Fine. It was...good. I don't feel very different, but I have to do this occasionally so I don't overheat." She raised her palm, which put off the same type of glow and warmth as a lightbulb.

I found that to be of dubious usefulness but kept the thought to myself.

"You will be luminous, my love," I murmured.

Madigan cleared her throat from where she settled across from us. Cress and I jerked apart, having been about to kiss right in front of her. "I just wanted to share a few words Hana wanted me to tell you," she said.

"About Phaeron?" Cress asked. There was a hopeful hush to her voice as her fingers knotted in her lap.

Madigan nodded. "She wants you to know that Phaeron slumbers, and if you wake him, he is yours."

My mate's brow knit. "What's that supposed to mean?"

With a sigh and a shrug, Madigan leaned back in her seat. "Kid, I'd be a wealthy woman if I got a dollar for figuring out every cryptic thing an augur has said to me. I took it to mean you can shake him out of

Myuna's control by making him aware of his surroundings. But he's coming for us soon with the rest of the goddess's forces."

Cress grew rigid in my lap and craned her head up toward me. "The rest of the greater unnaturals still need to be killed," she stated with realization.

"We have reinforcements to help us," I said.

"And Myuna has a corrupted dimensional who will teleport them away the moment their prisons are unsealed. But we will still try. It's better than them escaping unexpectedly," Madigan added.

Cress gulped audibly. "I need to go speak with the powercore about this and...other things."

15
CRESS

RAZA HAD HEARD OUR CONVERSATION, sensed my distress, and filled me with urgency to leave the private meeting with Madigan and Geo on a promise to finally tell me the idea she'd been withholding.

My face felt stiff as I took the elevator alone, assuring my companions this was something I had to do on my own. I needed to have more than two moments to myself so I could shed a few more tears and process what'd happened.

I'd known Phaeron was suffering and losing his sense of self, but it hurt so much worse to know he'd given in before I'd done much more than whisper to him encouragingly over the tenuous thread Braza was able to bridge between us. That silken strand was gone now, likely severed the moment Phaeron submitted to Myuna.

I should've done more. I *would* do more. I would "wake" him somehow, and he would be mine again, just as Hana foretold. All I had to do was figure out how to go about that.

Otherwise…he would die.

Tears continued to leak from my eyes as I exited the elevator and walked to Braza's chamber. I couldn't make them stop, not when I was on the edge of accepting that there was a future for Phaeron if we didn't successfully save him, which would be worse than death.

I loved him too much to let him become an unnatural. I would swing the sword to end him myself before he had his legacy tainted and became a monster like his brother. But only if I had to.

Braza absorbed me into the powercore and took her dimensional form within the inner chamber. Her cool, jellylike fingers brushed the tears from my face as she framed it with her hands. "Brightest of souls. I had hoped you would have a chance to practice your new celestial magic, but it seems we are out of time at last."

"Braza...he's..."

"Shh. I know," she murmured. "Come and sit with me for a moment. We have an important decision to make."

Braza had transported the stone platform and its furnishings that'd been within her at Moongrove Library. There was a bed, a couch, and an old-fashioned chest. We settled on the couch together, with her leaning against me companionably, one of her wings curled around my back and opposite shoulder.

"I would like to bestow upon you an honor that hasn't been seen since the early days of librarian witches. Before my attention was needed to contain so many rooms and monitor a busy library, I was able to elevate one librarian by merging a significant piece of myself with him or her and empower them for as long as they may live," she began.

I gaped at her. "You're picking me for this?"

"You are the only mortal I trust this deeply. But I must admit, that is partway because you are Prince Phaeron's next mate and this is a desperate measure to save him." She patted my hand to take away some of the sting of her admission. "Soul magic is heavy, Cress. If you accept the burden of Guardian of Moongrove Library, you will witness a portion of my memories. It's more intense than the aftereffects of a mating bite, or so I've been told."

"Wait, Moongrove?" I asked, overwhelmed.

"If we survive this, I will transfer back, and then the title will fit."

I bit my lip, not missing the *if* in her statement. There were no guarantees we would escape Cerris City before tragedy struck in its many possible forms.

"Memories of what kind?" I asked next.

"Nothing of my time as a powercore. You would witness my short time alive." She sighed, shifting to take hold of my hand. "Cress, before you agree to this, you have to understand that I have seen a completely different side of Phaeron. Centuries before you were even born, he had a better life, a higher place in society, and a family I witnessed him love deeply. He…" She choked on emotion for a moment and bowed her head, whispering the rest. "He was my adopted father."

I squeezed her fingers, sensing she was loosening the cork on some emotions she'd bottled up and buried deep. "I didn't know that," I murmured.

"Since my death, it has been easier for us both not to acknowledge what came before. And he has not confronted me as such…but my keeping him contained alongside his brother for so long has clearly dampened any love he used to feel for me," she said, sounding miserable.

"You were trying to protect him when you thought he might turn into a monster." I could see why she thought she owed him the most desperate measure she could reach for. "He's barely had time to process what happened to him. I'm sure he will come around to forgiving you for doing what you thought was necessary. I was just thinking he'd prefer to die than become unnatural…"

"I know. And you're right, he would," she replied.

As my hand slowly warmed hers, the other thing she said sank in. About Phaeron having a family he loved centuries ago… There was someone before Morgana. Of course there was. I wasn't sure exactly how old he was, but it made sense for there to be other women in his past. Still, I knew if we did this, it would be hard to see a happier version of him with someone of his own kind and a *family*. Dimensional kids.

Braza heard my thoughts, of course. "As an immortal culture, my people avoid talking about past mates in much depth, like humans dodge discussing religion and wages. It's considered rude. He would never tell you what you will undoubtedly see in my memories."

I breathed an uncertain sigh. "I can't let that be the reason we don't do this. I'll get over myself if it helps Phaeron. How, exactly, does this process work?"

Her nod seemed approving. "When I died, my soul was split nearly in half. It's since become two pieces…" She gestured first to the dome of the powercore above us and then to her jellylike body. "This gives me the option to empower you with one piece when you need it. I will need to leave a sigil on your person like Phaeron did with his mark of protection, except this one will create a significant tether between our souls."

"So you're saying...this has connected me to Phaeron's soul all along?" I asked, pointing to the circular rune he'd left on my wrist. I'd never quite understood how it worked.

"The tiniest thread, yes. Its only function is supposed to be a tug on his awareness when you need his attention. I've been abusing it a smidge." She gave me a brief fanged smile. "My mark will be larger and will glow when active. I suggest you put it on your back. I can try giving you something stylized, like a set of wings."

I agreed to that readily when she mimicked how large a tattoo we were talking about. It would take up the majority of my shoulder blades.

"As I create the mark on you, you will experience my memories. It will take only an hour of real time at most, but you will feel like years have passed. The truly dangerous part is that at the end, a surge of power will ring out to supernatural senses attuned to dimensional magic. We will project a buffet for Myuna to salivate over. Madigan did not tell you directly, but Hana has seen that this moment will trigger an all-out attack on the library."

"Okay, right, well..." I stammered. "We have to prepare for that fight before you and I do this. I think we should, though, when the time is right."

"I agree. I mean you no offense, but when you are forced into combat against Phaeron, you will stand no chance without me. He has had lifetimes with blades in his hands, while you have had months at most. But with us tethered, I will be able to fight him with you. I was once Phaeron's most devoted shadowborn pupil." She smiled sadly at that.

"I'm not sure your memories will turn me into a swordswoman of his caliber—"

"No, but you will be able to carry me like you have a shadowborn form of your own. I can augment your movements with dimensional speed and grace and indicate the patterns of his fighting style. My reflexes will protect you properly."

For a moment, I had a sinking suspicion that I had no idea what I was truly agreeing to. My eyes narrowed. "What can this new partnership do for you?"

"There are no sinister motives here. But I suppose you have realized...I am capable of the same kind of haunting and bodily control Endaeron is. His abilities were my inspiration to experiment with my own capabilities." She held up a clawed finger while I shifted uncomfortably. "However, I still have a home here. When half of me is not with you, it will return here. Endaeron does not have the luxury of any other vessel than the victims he possesses."

"And you said this is permanent?" I asked.

She tilted her head, undoubtedly reading all the concerns underneath that question. Things I was too polite to say aloud because she was still a friend and I didn't truly believe she was trying to trick me. "I give you my unbreakable vow as a dimensional traveler and an ancient powercore that I will not possess you against your will or do you and yours harm. I only propose a partnership for our mutual benefit."

I cleared my throat, both embarrassed and relieved that she'd cut straight through my fears. "Thank you."

WITH OUR NEW REINFORCEMENTS, we attempted to kill the rest of the greater unnatural creatures still held in the library. The blue-skinned dimensional—the teleporting, unnatural one—beat us to two of them, but we caught him by surprise the next time and killed him. The remaining monsters died before evening's fall.

There was little time to rest, though. We started setting traps on the ground floor of the library, knocking over stacks and scattering books and broken glass as part of our efforts to slow down the dozens of monsters and "zombified" supernaturals that would be coming for us the moment we triggered Myuna's greed.

According to Grant's intel, we were racing the clock more than ever. The more supernaturals Myuna turned to her side by making them white-eyed zombies, as he described them, the faster she'd be able to gather stragglers and animals to further bolster her army.

As we worked, some of my friends helped me turn over Hana's instructions.

"Perhaps he is in a deep trance. Since it's magical in nature, there has to be a trigger to snap him out of it," Áine said quietly. She and I were on book scattering duty with Wren and Willow, while Geo and Roe distributed freshly smashed glass and arranged the stacks. Roe, of course, wore her crystal armor and cracked a few smiles by getting to be the one punching the windows and walls.

Ashbough Protective Services worked around us, setting snares and other traps, hiding them under the layers of junk we set down.

All the while, there were screeches nearby as Bianca, Ben, and Grace killed the warped birds staring at us from the nearest rooftops. It made for a disconcerting background chorus, so I tried to focus on the problem at hand.

"Why can't augurs just say what they mean?" I muttered.

"Don't be such a whiner," Wren said, rolling her eyes. "At least you have a warning."

I had to agree and check myself. Hana could've just left me to my own devices with no help. It just wouldn't hurt her to be a smidge more explicit in her instructions.

"How do you think we should go about waking Phaeron from Myuna's trance?" I asked the irritable blonde.

A frown tugged at Wren's mouth. "You know, it's almost funny. Most spells or tonics we have access to are for inducing sleep, not waking someone up. Since we'd never guess what trigger phrase or spell Myuna has used..." She pondered, biting her lip. "We could lock him in a containment room until her magic runs its course."

I was already shaking my head. "If he's not placed into stasis, he'll be able to escape without much trouble."

"Well, that's an option. Her influence should fade if we manage to kill her."

Áine spoke up. "Maybe if we teamed up and beat him soundly?"

I stifled a sigh. That sounded like a great way to get several people killed, Phaeron included. But it seemed the only options we had were the not-so-good ones.

"Well, there is something else I could try," Áine said when we didn't jump immediately at her first idea. "Remember after we fought the Hunger the first time...Phaeron swore an admission of debt to me?”

My brow furrowed. That first near-deadly fight seemed like it’d happened ages ago, not months. “Did he?”

“Yeah. More specifically, it was a debt of gratitude for healing him, which is the most benign-seeming debt you can swear to a fae.” She had an impish little smile. If it weren’t for her deer legs and poofy tail, I could forget Áine was one of the fair folk. But with an expression like that...she was clearly versed in the kind of trickery that had formed legends about her kind.

“Can you call in a debt while he’s entranced?” Willow asked, her own face pursed in deep thought while we spoke.

“I can always try,” the faun answered. “If the trance is not tied with a soul debt, he should immediately respond.”

Willow seemed in, at least. “What can you ask for?”

“That’s where it’s tricky. I could hit him with the direct one we want. ‘To show your gratitude to me, wake up and say my name.’ But he could fall back under Myuna’s sway immediately afterward if he needs longer than a split second to fight her control.” Áine tapped her lips thoughtfully, standing aside while we finished scattering the last few books for this corner of the library.

“To show your gratitude to me, release yourself from Myuna’s control?” I suggested.

“It has to be something he can reasonably do on his own on the spot,” she said, shaking her head and shaking loose a few flower petals from the sad-looking blooms woven into her long curls. “Mother Tree, I don’t want to do this, but...I could hit him with one of the banes of the long-lived. Before you all ask, those are experience, memory, and wisdom.”

I was glad I wasn’t the only one looking at her in bafflement. Willow and I exchanged a glance. “Can you explain more than that?” asked our soft-spoken friend.

“All right, fine. Most people think swearing a debt of gratitude is formally promising a fae a favor. Honorable fae would never ask for something that would actively harm another when the origin of the debt is, well, a *thank you*. But when you’re immortal, like a fae, vampire, demigod, or dimensional, certain things are made more unpleasant by the passage of long stretches of time. It would not hurt Phaeron if I asked for him to recount every time and place he's ever taken a sip of water, but he would be really fucking angry with me when he was compelled to speak continuously for however long it took to do it," she explained.

"Could you actually do that?" I asked out of sheer curiosity.

She adjusted one of the flowers in her hair, causing it to bloom vibrantly again from a tiny touch of magic. "I mean, yeah. But I like him, so I think I will use the much shorter but just as baneful 'Remember yourself.' There's an old fae story about a villainous king who was defeated by those very words. He stood in place, paralyzed by years and years of things he'd forgotten all crushing his head at once. Ripe for the deposing and such. All the Crystal Court fae are going to roll their eyes, but if I have to, that's the gratitude I'd ask of Phaeron."

"Okay, that's cliché as hell, but it just might work," I said. We'd probably try some variation of all three; holding him in stasis, beating the hell out of him, and paralyzing him with memories. Though we continued to mull over possibilities as we worked, nothing else jumped out as a better solution.

Madigan wanted me to become Guardian of Moongrove Library tomorrow morning, when our enemies would be at their weakest after a full night of scavenging. More importantly, they would not have the Hungering Darkness, with Garroway's weakness to sunlight preventing him from making the trip here.

That left enough time to eat, worry a hole in the floor of the room I lived in with my men, and ignore Ben's offer to tumble into bed together until I went to retrieve Geo from his post in the shadows of the first floor. A pair of better-rested witches were already standing guard with him and helped me convince him to take the night off.

One round of sharing later, I fell into an uneasy sleep and woke blearily. Someone was going around knocking on doors.

"Sun's up! Let's go!" exclaimed a muffled voice that sounded like Orthus.

I headed down to the powercore chamber while everyone else refreshed themselves on battle stations and last-minute planning. Too nervous to eat any rations, I sipped on a bottle of water as the elevator descended. In as little as an hour, I would see Phaeron again…then we would see if he would be mine, Myuna's, or no one's.

I'd gotten fully equipped for this fight, wearing the haggard hybrid witch garb I'd since washed after wearing it new to appear before the Crown Council. I had my sword on one hip and my handbook flapping with uncharacteristic silence over my shoulder. My familiars accompanied me as well, ready to lend their small contributions to the battle ahead. When the cabin arrived on the correct floor, I picked up Wren's sun staff from where I'd leaned it against the wall. Its centerpiece and gold paint sparkled from just my touch.

It was a fairly bygone conclusion that Phaeron would appear in the powercore chamber looking for me once Myuna noticed the tether between Braza and me falling into place. Together, we would exude the kind of power the goddess wanted to devour, all light and dimensional might.

"Just like with the ritual…and putting ancestral magic in my book," I muttered to myself. "Everything that follows this is a gamble and a guess."

I marched myself into Braza's inner chamber before I could back out of our agreement. I trusted her and showed it by taking off a layer of clothing and lying down on her bed so she could start to etch magic onto the skin of my bare back.

There was a pinch of pain, then Braza saying, "If you feel drowsy, don't resist…"

Her memories came flooding in the moment I closed my eyes.

16

BRAZA

M Y MOST DISTANT memories of life begin some short time after my birth. Mercifully, not with the death of my parents, but with a hazy recollection of the patterns of whimsical creatures painted on a wall. I was in a holding house, a rare unwanted orphan who took to staring at the illustrations next to the tiny bed where I regularly tucked my legs under my chin and covered myself with my wings.

I was a miserable child. All orphans of my kind are, especially those too young to realize they were cut off from the embrace of the *animaris* of their birth parents.

But I was probably the worst example of what went wrong when separated from that essence too early. I was an animal who would bite the hands of adults who wanted to treat me kindly. My claws would extend with magic, strange, overlong, and black against the blush red of my skin. The same claws that'd saved me from sharing the fate of my parents had a parade of adults leaving the holding house with disgust, calling me "unnatural."

All that changed when a different-looking person visited. She didn't immediately try to pick me up like I was one of the brightly colored toys piled up against the far wall.

Instead, she'd sat a tail-length from my bed, with me hunched on it.

"Hello, little one," she'd said gently. I didn't reply, only inspecting her with a child's curiosity over the line of my knees.

She was from the Moihan tribe, the first one I'd ever seen, with feminine features exaggerated by a dusting of silver on her cheekbones and eyelids, around eyes that glowed crimson from within. Her glossy black hair was neatly pinned to stop just behind the thin curves of her spiraled horns.

She was dressed really nicely. The fall of red and silver fabric complimented her gray skin and stopped just short of her ankles and small, pointed shoes. Gems glittered on her fingers. That kind of finery didn't belong in this holding house, on the floor where so many adults had already stood and gone.

When I didn't reply or move, she smiled and pulled a book from the folds of her skirts. "I have a daughter your age and brought a book of her favorite stories. Perhaps you would like to hear one?" she offered.

I gave her the barest of nods and listened as she cracked open the first page and began to read to me. Her voice was its own magic, luring me to her. I watched the pictures seem to dance on the pages from where I sat on the soft textured fabric of her dress.

When the story was over and the title of the next stood out as she flipped the page, my eyes widened as I realized where I'd moved to. I froze, but she didn't do more than turn her red gaze my way.

"Did you like the story?" she asked. I nodded mutely. "Would you like me to read the next one?"

Shyly, I shook my head no. I didn't trust this pretty Moihan woman. She accepted my answer and told me her name, Keshora et Sudaira, and smiled wide in motherly amusement as I whispered mine back. "Bwaza."

"I'll visit you tomorrow, Braza."

I'd learn later that her title meant Keshora, mate of the second prince. My backwater town had never seen a noble Moihan before. They viewed the shadowy gray peoples of their tribe and the chilly blue Vrassorm with heavy suspicion.

In retrospect, I recognized I was caught under the same web of scorn with my barely restrained shadow powers. Those claws of mine, contrasted with my Iorsio heritage, were why none of the red-skinned townsfolk wanted anything else to do with me.

They were also part of the reason why Keshora returned the next day, this time with her daughter. Her kindly presence was overshadowed by Ravai, who, in that time, always wore her hair in a high tail with a bow of red fabric that matched her eyes. The immediacy of our friendship started at first sight. It was an anam cara bond all the way in another world, when two lonely girls became immediate best friends.

Ravai and I sat and played the day away while Keshora bargained with the bitter matron who ran the holding houses for orphans and the sick in town. The perfect day ended with Keshora seizing Ravai's arm and leaving in a whirlwind, with the matron muttering about "Moihan scum" once the door closed behind them.

THE DAYS in that holding house were made lengthy by my young age. It couldn't have been too long before Keshora and Ravai returned, but they'd brought someone else too. One moment, I was bored and alone, and the next, Ravai was in my room like a burst of color. She pulled me by the hand to come meet her father.

"You're coming home with us today!" she said gleefully, listing all the fun things *home* entailed as we headed into the front room of the house.

"Really?" I wasn't so sure I'd be released to go, not with all the bad names the matron had called her and her mother.

The matron's tune had apparently changed when face-to-face with a prince, though. My first impression of Phaeron et Sudair was of the shadows that moved with him as he spoke and gestured, deep in conversation with the matron. They eddied around his boots and added extra coils where his tail twined companionably with Keshora's. They stood together across a counter from the Iorsio woman.

He was offering her a stack of coins, but his fingers made a cage over them. The shadows suggested claws like mine.

I'd never seen the matron so nervous. "The people of this town have never seen her like before. It *is* unnatural for her to have a Moihan power," she was saying.

"All the more reason she should be raised by a family that understands her abilities," he replied.

Ravai ran up to him and tugged on his cloak. "Dad, Dad! Look, I got Braza!"

He picked her up with a coil of shadow, affectionately pressing foreheads with her before passing her to Keshora. I was next, weightless for a moment, until he sat me on the counter next to the money. I inspected him with shy wonder. Dark blue stain dusted his cheeks and marked runes and patterns over each section of his spiraled horns.

He was Moihan-strange, and were I a bold, outgoing child like Ravai, I'd have rubbed one of the patterns on his horns because I wondered if they were permanent. But it was his eyes that fascinated me. Slitted and yellow, they were familiar in a way the rest of him was not. I'd later learn he was half Iorsio himself, and while hybrids didn't truly exist in our world, he'd still inherited his mother's flame-inspired eyes.

Phaeron held out a palm full of shadows that curled and billowed like a small black fire. He didn't say anything, but his power called to mine, and I played with it like it was putty, squashing and stretching it. Everyone watched me, the Moihan family with understanding and the matron with fear.

"She is shadowborn," he said.

With a wiggle of his fingertips, the crude wing shape I'd made became a pair of them. They took flight around my head, and I giggled despite myself when they tugged my hair.

I missed warm wing hugs and the vague memories of a mother who would envelop me completely. Moihan didn't have wings, but still, the matron allowed my adoption and even waved with the money in her other hand as I became the fourth member of the second prince's family.

Phaeron returned to an ongoing war once we arrived at the capital. The location would become my home, but at first, it seemed far too big as we traveled through it to the palace. The capital had sprung up around the crater of Myuna the White's landing spot, curved like a crescent moon. Unlike the town they'd plucked me from, it was mixed with all three tribes co-existing and inter-mating with almost no judgment.

They placed me in a bedroom with Ravai, and we grew older and closer together. Those days were a blissful haze of dress-up and tasty food. Keshora became "Mom," and even though she couldn't give me wing hugs, she still treated me as if I were Ravai's pinkish-red double.

I knew of Phaeron only from their stories of him. The first prince—his twin, Endaeron—was even more vaguely a family member. My white-skinned cousins were adult age and served as torchbearers, so I only saw them at formal dinners and observed some uncomfortable family dynamics during those times. The king and queen merely tolerated one another and slavishly loved our goddess and the first prince's family, who were all blessed by Myuna down to their unnatural coloring.

Mom relied on Ravai and me to tolerate years of oversight, calling us *Ravita* and *Brazita* affectionately. We were the shadows that balanced Myuna's light, her less favored subjects, and even as a child, I noticed the goddess looked at Keshora specifically with something less than kind in her gaze.

THE TWIN PRINCES returned when there were two red stars above Soiluire, an auspicious sign that followed their victory. I was to meet my adopted father again when it was starting to become obvious that Ravai and I were of different tribes. She'd grown tall-ish with skinny limbs and a tail just long enough to trip over, with me a head shorter and broader than her with my wings to add to the effect. I, too, tripped over my tail in graceless moments, though.

We wore silver on our faces for the occasion and dusted up Mom's cheeks and horns for her a little too zealously. The reunion happened at a banquet for our soldiers, with Myuna and the king and queen sitting at the head of the table. In those times, Myuna did not eat, and it seemed she did not need to.

The first prince arrived at the table before Phaeron, as was tradition. He was a broad Iorsio man, his skin and hair bleached white from the goddess's touch. His mate anointed his face and horns with gold as our people cheered. He was Endaeron et Myudair, the crown prince blessed by Myuna, and the love in the room for him was palpable.

Ravai practically vibrated with her excitement as the celebration for the first prince lulled and he took his seat. We both turned in our chairs as Phaeron joined the celebration. He emerged from a whirl of shadows, casually showcasing his shadowborn powers so close to the goddess.

He and Mom touched foreheads and murmured together before she brushed dark blue powder over his high cheekbones and slid a heavy signet ring back onto his finger. The crowd loved the second prince too. They cheered for him when Mom took his hair out of its tail and twisted it to pin behind his horns. The ritual showed that he was no longer at war, and now that both princes were returned to their finery and families, the feasting could begin.

I didn't have much to say to Phaeron, ever the quieter child next to Ravai. She chattered away about our palace life and schooling for me when he asked, the buffer I needed when he was akin to a myth in my life, the man who'd intimidated my old matron into allowing me to be adopted into a Moihan family.

"I have a surprise for you all," he said, smiling with all his fangs. "Endaeron and I have bought an estate far from here to retire to. It will be a school for shadowborn...as I have noticed neither of you have been educated in your extra powers."

Mom was delighted immediately, while my heart sank like I'd done something wrong. Was I supposed to be practicing with my shadows more? They were mere wisps compared to the power he seemed to have at his fingertips. She occupied his time with questions about where, exactly, the family would be escaping to and how often they'd have to return.

"As infrequently as you prefer, my heart," he'd replied in an undertone.

Mom suggested something that had me shifting shyly late into the banquet. They were both deep into their cups, and while he fed her bits of fruit from his fingers, she leaned heavily against him and drew sigils on his horns all crookedly. Between giggles, she said, "Why don't you take the girls to our new home? I've had them to myself for years. I'll follow behind with our things."

IT WAS a great idea once we figured out the awkwardness of absence in the long carriage ride to our new home. Ravai sat on her hands and clamped her jaw so I could get to know the man who would be my father better. He was smart, athletic, and so very powerful. I ended the trip giddy to finally finish the animaris ritual with him and Mom and become their child by soul and essence.

I held a twist of fragile hope in hand for the days we waited for Mom to arrive. Phaeron had gone quiet sometime in the hours before and during a family dinner, staring into the middle distance with his food untouched. He kept rubbing at his shoulder.

I picked at my meal too, sensing something was wrong but not the scope of it. A servant burst into the room and held the door open, startling all of us. Phaeron jumped to his feet, hand on the hilt of his sword, when in stepped a familiar Moihan man. The family's head of security, who was supposed to protect the caravan of our valuables.

He placed a shrouded body on the floor and dropped to his knees. "My sudair," he said in a broken voice.

Ravai and I exchanged frightened looks. I recognized the general shape of the body and its curved horns.

"I-it happened suddenly—"

"Stop. Use some sense," Phaeron hissed. "There are children."

The head of security looked up, noticed Ravai and me for the first time, and lowered himself further. Phaeron beckoned to us, and we went to him, dinner laying forgotten on the table. His broad palm and shadowy magic covered my sight. We walked out of the room, and he closed the door behind us with his tail.

Ravai was already keening, making high sounds of mourning in her throat while her eyes shimmered with the onset of grief. I was a trembling animal next to her, my leathery wings making shivery sounds. I waited for Phaeron to tell us it wasn't the sudaira...that Mom wasn't dead.

Voice heavy, Phaeron said, "Ravita, Brazita, go back to your room. I will handle this."

Still keening, Ravai took me by the hand and tugged me away. We waited together until our room's lamp flickered with the end spurts of its oil reservoir. Phaeron let himself in. The meager light reflected the pronounced facets in his eyes.

He told us as gently as he could. Mom had died unexpectedly, her body unmarked but her skin cold and her heart stopped. There was nothing anyone could've done for her. We stayed huddled on the floor together for the rest of the night, mourning her.

The head of security continued working for Phaeron at the Royal Shadowborn School. Gossip spread amongst the staff and students about Mom's unexpected death and led me to take a peek under her eyelids before she was buried to see if the rumors were true. They were. Her pupils were gone, leaving her eyes flat circles darkened to maroon. I didn't tell Phaeron I'd seen them, but the sight haunted me for years.

Soon after the funeral, he took me aside and held out a flower with gleaming blue petals. In a world of darkness, it was one of the only pieces of flora that dared to shine as bright as our eyes. I keened low in my throat when I took the bloom, knowing it was Mom's favorite.

"I know we don't know each other well yet," Phaeron said carefully. "But your mother's love for you came through clearly in every letter she wrote to me. It is my duty to care for everything she cherished."

He'd knelt before me so I wasn't craning my head. I felt a familiar glimmer of hope as I stared into his flickering Iorsio-inspired eyes, but dread threaded through me at the possibility he was going to send me away.

"Without her, I cannot 'properly' adopt you, but I would like to be your father all the same. You and Ravai deserve to grow up together." He put his hand over the one I used to hold the flower's stem.

"I would like that," I said in a small voice. I hugged him fiercely when he scooped me up, our foreheads touching briefly in affectionate acknowledgment of one another. He was my father from then on.

Dad treated Ravai and me the same as time passed. He loved us in his own way, as the one to personally tutor us with blade and shadows alike. The other instructors thought we were child prodigies, but it was really endless drills and a ruthless regime of early wakeups and long dinner conversations about values and strategy.

As we grew into our adult bodies, Ravai and I had our petty little rivalries, but we were still the definition of inseparable. We were the star pupils of the Royal Shadowborn Academy. Other students would gather to watch our rooftop duels, the same as when Dad and Endaeron would get a wild hair and show off their skills with battles of blades and black and white shadows. Those days, my sister and I always wore shadowborn black.

I HAD a quiet dislike for the garish white shade of Myuna and her followers even before the Age of Decay. But the day it started, it became the color of death and betrayal. The teachers and students had paired off in the school's courtyard for practice duels. It was a completely mundane morning...until it wasn't.

Myuna's soul feast was marked by a palpable shift in the air. I'd felt it like a creep of dread across my scalp, stepping away from Dad mid-practice duel to gaze at the sky and then across the courtyard, where the other students were edging back from a flash of bone white.

Endaeron writhed on the ground, his claws sunk into his head and his wings tangled around him. Ravai had placed her sword aside and turned him over in a misplaced effort to help him as corrupted magic started to twist and rend his skin and bone apart.

"Ravai! Get away from him!" Dad screamed.

Even then, he'd been suspicious of Myuna, but he couldn't have predicted that she'd empower and corrupt my uncle's soul the way she had. He became the Hungering Darkness as a flash of white mist, abandoning his ruined body to jump into Ravai's. And then he hopped into several more bystanders, leaving behind soulless corpses and further spreading panic.

Dad personally killed the last student Endaeron jumped into, panting with shock and horror as the kid slumped to the ground. Not knowing the true evil Endaeron had become yet, we both thought we'd lost him and Ravai in the same breath. I saw her eyes, chilled by the pupil-less maroon circles staring across the grass at nothing.

"Her eyes...like Mom," I stammered out, giving away the secret I'd held within all that time.

"*Myuna*," Dad growled, hatred turning his face into a snarling mask.

Myuna had killed Mom. We still didn't know why, and we never would; everything happened so fast after the Age of Decay kicked off.

We received word from the growing stream of survivors fleeing to the school. Myuna had consumed countless others, first reaping the capital city and moving outward from there. Her ghostly torchbearers brought her feast to her. Murdered and twisted by her magic, just like my uncle, they were immune to common weapons yet were cut down easily by shadowborn claws.

Thanks to this, we hosted a refuge for survivors, and amongst them, the Hungering Darkness lurked unseen, biding its time. No one was untouched by loss and grief. Most faces were unmarked of colored dust and paint, wiped clean a final time after the deaths of mates and loved ones. Chief amongst them was my father, who dressed for war each day and cleared paths to the school for survivors, cutting down unnaturals with ruthless fury.

I went with him every time I could, afraid he'd get himself killed with the single-minded rage that'd consumed him. The two of us made for an unstoppable team. With my help, he returned to the Royal Shadowborn Academy every day, usually with a new group of survivors in tow.

Though I was still just a teen, I was a witness to history by my father's side. When it became obvious killing monsters would never be enough to stop Myuna's single-minded consumption of our people, he sought the insight of others.

"There must be a way to defeat her," he would say at the beginning of each meeting with the most intelligent of us left. It would kick off hours of debate and ideas.

It was Auric et Vess who came up with a mad plan that just might work. He was a Vrassorm man and an old political friend of my father's. Unfortunately, for it to work, they needed the help of a vicious rival in the Iorsio woman Mencha et Syroni. Complete with Dad, they were the most powerful survivors of the three tribes.

We could escape through the Void and deny Myuna our souls by heading to a different world far from her reach. As a Vess, Auric would bend the Void to allow them through. Dad's shadows would protect us, while Mencha's flame would light our way forward. All tribespeople with magic would follow their lead to magnify their abilities for the long journey.

"Shall we do it, my prince?" Auric asked. Everyone looked to Dad for direction now that the king, queen, first prince, and my cousins were all deceased. The second prince, who would be king if he stood still for a coronation. I stood at his right side at each meeting, trying to hide the fear from my face to look tough and capable.

Dad agreed. We gathered everyone we could and left, stepping into the nothingness between worlds. The magic of the Void marked us as we spent an unknowable amount of time walking and walking and walking without fatigue or rest. Our features and teeth smoothed out to better resemble humans', the dominant species of the world we approached. The mark of language and humanity appeared on the membrane of my wing, while the same one showed up on Dad's back and random places for everyone else.

These subtle changes were beautiful to us, but when we made first contact with humans...they were horrified by our appearances, calling us demons and fracturing the alliances within our peoples.

Most of the Iorsio tribespeople followed Mencha in becoming the monsters they decried us as. She preached that we were larger and more powerful than humans could ever dream. *Why not prove our superiority by enslaving them?* She led her followers away in disgust when Dad met and fell in love with a human woman.

Morgana was present when the Hungering Darkness started making one of my school friends act erratically. I barely remember the actual circumstances of my death, come to think of it, only bits and pieces as moments fractured into frayed strands.

The agony of having Endaeron's teeth ripping my soul into two messy pieces.

Blood spattering me when Dad killed my assailant.

His panicked face swimming in and out of my sight.

"Stay with me, Brazita," he'd begged, gathering me in his arms.

We pressed foreheads for a final time, my labored breathing and erratic heartbeat proving I was already three limbs in the grave.

I still gasped out a request and a consent to something I barely understood as my tattered soul unhooked from my body and my pupils smeared into the dull gold of my still eyes.

17
CRESS

"And that is how I became the powercore of Moongrove Library."

Braza was seated on the ground by my head as I came to and jolted upright with a twinge in my shoulders. I didn't know who I was for a minute, confused to see my teenaged dimensional face rendered in black and purple energy looking back at me.

Empathy flooded my eyes in the next moment. "My god, you weren't even my age when you died," I said.

She handed me the clothes I'd shed so she could mark my back, and I put them on, letting the fabric absorb my tears. Her life was already fading some, becoming a stream that flowed together separately from my own memories. I knew I would have a difficult time for a while reminding myself that I was *not* Braza and had never lived the life of an orphan turned almost-princess of Soiluire.

I was still Cress, an orphan turned librarian-celestial witch hybrid. I had a whole coven of good friends, all waiting for me to finish up here. Plus an adopted sister, Carly, who I was still worried about.

Braza had a best friend and sister named Ravai...Phaeron's daughter. He hadn't breathed a word of her or Keshora, but I'd *seen* how much he'd adored them. At one point, he'd doted on Braza the exact same way. Now I saw what she meant, what she feared, and why she had gone to such lengths to set me up to save him.

If we all survived this, then I would have to privately confront my feelings about seeing his former life. I was supposed to be his mate, to replace both Keshora and Morgana, but now I knew them by their accomplishments and Phaeron's love for them. It gave his slow-burn interest in me a completely different view. How did I even compare? How often did I come short in his eyes?

"I have continued to exist for several human lifetimes. It is not so bad," she answered, taking me out of my whirling thoughts.

"Stuck in one place. Never resting," I sighed, looking around at her inner chamber with new eyes. *Existing* seemed unpleasant at best.

"The last Guardian of Moongrove Library was able to take me out of the library's bounds," she said with an edge of hope to her tone.

"Then I will, too," I promised, offering her a hand up. She took it and stood, giving me a winged hug. She shrank in my hold, surrounding me in flames of black and purple shadows.

Power surged between us as the tether snapped into place. I threw my head back and screamed out a shadowborn's howl, exhilarated. The pulse of energy was unmistakable, and I felt for myself how those who could sense dimensional power would catch notice of us immediately.

We emerged from the powercore holding a sword in our dominant hand and Wren's staff in the other. The light from the tool did not damage our shadows or make them retract, as I'd seen happen with my light and Phaeron's darkness. We...*no*. I had to remind myself that I was still in charge. *I* was one coherent whole, part celestial witch, part librarian, and part shadowborn, with light and darkness swirling between my staff and sword at my will.

"Cress, tell me that's still you, kid," Madigan said. Arrayed around the chamber was a crew of her, Orthus, Geo, Áine, and most of my coven. My ghostly mother stood to the side with the cluster of my familiars, watching with a concerned expression.

"It is me," I said in a two-toned voice, mine layered with Braza's. "Plus Braza et..." I hesitated before plucking her title out of my memories. She was the second prince's adopted daughter, which made her the... "Sudairae."

"Sounds like Big P's last name," Ben commented. He had his big daggers out but a bandolier of the smaller ones for throwing at the ready over his torso.

"Title," I corrected. "Tell you about it later. It's…a lot."

Braza's shadows contracted over my skin, and through her, I sensed hundreds of monsters converging on the library. Some had two feet, an extra bad sign for us.

An alarm blared on Madigan's phone at the same time. "Incoming," she announced.

Bianca lifted her crossbow. Its loaded bolt was coated with glowing maroon. Orthus raised his hand and started manifesting sharpened crystal spikes from seemingly nowhere, and Madigan lifted her gauntleted fist to take control of them with a muttered spell. They circled over her head with slow gravity.

The fae tossed a few extra to Geo, who absorbed and reformed them with all of his quartz into a large mace to match his massive crystal shield.

"Close your eyes for a moment," Braza said in my head, using my focus and hers to comb the upper levels of the library to detect Phaeron. She knew he would enter as shadowy vapor and take the most direct route to us, solidifying in a rush to catch us off guard.

And that's exactly what he did. Her reflexes caught the strike of his sword before I even opened my eyes again. My heart threatened to stop before kicking into three times the speed. That was indeed Phaeron bearing down on me in full shadowborn form and everyone else reacting around us with shouts and fired spells.

He had one sword, the talons of his opposite hand extended into long and deadly points. It was the traditional shadowborn fighting style, to have one hand empty to weave shadows while an opponent was distracted with swordplay.

"Focus on him. Do not worry about anything else," Braza instructed. We pivoted to avoid a slice of sharpened shadows aimed to hit our back. We…I raised my left hand and blasted Phaeron with a Lux spell from the sun staff. I held the concentrated rays of sunlight out at him for a few seconds.

His talons dispelled away from the light, as did the other sneak attack he'd been manipulating from the shadows. But even as the exposed skin on his arm darkened, he didn't make a sound, not even a hiss of pain.

I struck, and he parried, the two of us engaging in a deadly dance between the fired spells and projectiles of my allies. Braza helped me find the steps to match him, her strength reinforcing my arms. Phaeron struck without an ounce of mercy. Our weapons rang with each impact, the force rattling my sword so hard it threatened to jump out of my grip.

Phaeron fought with supernatural grace to keep up with me while avoiding more than the graze of bolts and crystal spikes. My weapon skimmed his shadows and skin superficially, all made possible by the pressure we put on him at multiple angles.

Geo's obsidian form closed in from the side, shield raised. I parried another strike from Phaeron, straining as I tried to hold him steady for my gargoyle protector's charge. Suddenly, Phaeron grabbed me with tendrils of shadow, and I was hit with the vertigo of being wrenched to a different location.

For a couple precious seconds, I reeled and wavered on my feet. Thorn-studded shadows wrapped around my legs, sinking into my skin to anchor me in place. "Fuck," I muttered. A quick cast of Lux rid me of them, but the deep punctures remained, and bloody rivulets dripped down my legs.

"I will take care of it," Braza said, urging me to keep my attention on Phaeron. Her shadows flowed into the wounds, soothing and cool.

He'd taken me as far from the powercore chamber as he could carry me. The foyer of this level, with its waiting area full of chairs. I lifted one with an inexpert grab of shadows and held its legs out to keep Phaeron at bay. It caught the swing of his sword, the fabric parting like butter and the frame snapping quickly.

I flung the ruined thing at him. It clipped his shoulder, throwing off the rhythm of his footwork for a moment. Meanwhile, Braza used the telepathy of her powercore side to inform our allies of where we'd gone.

"Phaeron, stop. I don't want to hurt you," I said.

He didn't spare any acknowledgment. He seemed like an unstoppable, untiring force, while I felt the first hints of soreness and strain in my body even with Braza helping me keep up. I focused on blocking, parrying, and thrusting as darkness writhed around our feet, thrashing between his will and Braza's.

I backed into a chair and hopped up onto its cushion, spreading my wings of shadows and flapping. I put my weight behind the next strike downward. Fuchsia blood sprayed from a cut around his shoulder, quickly covered by shadows before I could determine where exactly I'd gotten him.

White shadows flicked up the side of his arm. The next thing I knew, I was landing with my ankle twisting on the unexpected arrival of stairs. I stumbled, barely catching myself on a guardrail before I could tumble down the flight we'd appeared on. Again, we hadn't gone far, but his shadowborn control was slightly stronger than Braza's. At this rate, he'd inch me up to the surface, where Myuna's monsters would help subdue me.

I lifted the staff, prepared to blast him with light. Anticipating the move, he shot out a lasso of shadow, which whipped around my left wrist and wrenched me to the side. It solidified and tightened harshly until the sun staff clattered down the stairs.

I flexed my free hand, growing shadowy talons over my fingers. Lunging at him, I moved to position myself further up the stairs than he was, taking a sharp graze on my side as he exploited the opening in my guard. Pain flared over my torso.

"*Submit,*" hissed a voice from Phaeron's mouth, unexpectedly feminine and awful.

I bared shadowy fangs and shouted with Braza, "*Never!*"

I landed a kick to the center of his chest, and he fell backward, landing at the bottom of the stairs next to the staff, his limbs briefly still and splayed like a discarded doll's. The way he stood was also disconcerting, heaving upward like a puppeteer hadn't mastered the motion of lifting with the legs first.

I used his own trick, grabbing him in my shadows and carrying him back into the foyer, where my allies were rushing past. Ben reacted quickest and turned, launching himself at Phaeron's tail. I heard the brittle snap of bone.

"*Such insolence,*" snapped what had to be Myuna, using Phaeron as her mouthpiece. He acknowledged another fighter for the first time in throwing Ben off and impaling him against a wall with an inky black spike.

I wanted to shout for him, but Braza suppressed me. "*He gave us an advantage,*" she said. Phaeron was off-balance when he turned his attention back to us and lunged.

Within a blink, he was slammed by a blur of obsidian and crystal. Geo had struck with his shield to the center of Phaeron's chest, and the momentum sent him crashing into a couple chairs and toppling in a boneless heap. This time, he recovered by turning into vapor and materializing again over my left shoulder. His shadowy claws cut through my back, forming several long lines of agony.

I screamed. Braza's voice in my head became white noise, and my hold on our tether faltered, making the shadows over my body flicker before they covered me again.

"We're not out of this yet," Braza encouraged.

My back ached, and it felt like most of my body was now slicked with hot blood. Yet I knew that she was right. Her shadows held together most of the damage I'd sustained so far. Power leaked into me from her powercore side, slowly knitting together the rips, scratches, and abrasions.

Phaeron's shadowy maw was open in a soundless snarl. He leapt at me and swung his free arm around my neck. The vertigo returned through multiple jumps, though I now knew the feel of his magic wrapping around me and how to fight it, my eyes closing at the right moments to stave off the worst of the dizziness.

We landed on stairs, carpeting, and tile, grappling for control all the while. He slammed me into the ground for most of our reappearances. At this rate, I'd be tenderized into submission, fractured and bruised too badly to fight back.

For one of our landings, we were in a containment room. I could've closed a stasis spell around him...but didn't. Myuna was controlling him somehow, and I was going to shake her out of him, even if it killed me and half of Braza.

As the pain mounted over my body, I started to realize that the death option was closer at hand than expected. I gained the upper hand during one reappearance and dug the edge of my sword into the shadows over his neck.

"Phaeron," I breathed out desperately. "It's me, Cress. Stop, Phaeron. Stop fighting me."

"Oh no, pretty thing. He's taking you straight to me," Myuna purred. Well, it was supposed to be a smooth sound, but she had a voice like a cheese grater to my senses. *"I'll only wake him up so we can see how pret-*

tily he begs before I consume you." Shadows grasped and moved us to another location, and his muscular weight pinned my hips.

Braza noted the wording as we struggled. This time, I pulled him into my shadows, still trying to drag him back toward my allies. I could practically feel the lightbulb moment she had.

"Tell me you have a good idea," I said, struggling to raise my sword to block another blow. It felt like my whole body had been pummeled—I gasped for a decent breath. Under her shadows, I had to be black and blue.

"Do you trust me?" she replied.

"Down to my soul," I answered. I'd *been* her, seen her true character. There was no doubt in me when she told me her idea, and I seized it. I let her turn my body into shadowy mist, and together we went up several levels to throw off Phaeron and Myuna.

We were close enough to the surface to hear the sounds of fighting. Dust shook from the ceiling from a surge of guardian witch power, followed by either Aaron or Ajax shouting commands.

The part of me that was tethered to the powercore marked Phaeron's position as he realized what we'd done and turned into vapor. He approached our location rapidly.

I lifted and circled my sword over my head, casting the rune for the strongest light-based spell I knew just as Phaeron appeared before me. His sword and claws bit into my body as my skin heated. I'd once likened Luminare to a ground-level firework, but that was before I tapped into my celestial side.

Light erupted from my body and weapon, which I angled under his chin. Against the glare of my magic, I witnessed Phaeron's shadows blow away completely and saw his face. He was literally asleep, but his eyelids flipped open as he took the brunt of my spell head-on. For a split second, I admired the way his irises sparkled like cut gemstones before every inch of his exposed skin torched.

Phaeron stumbled back, screaming in agony and covering his face with similarly burned and blistered hands. His sword clattered to the floor, followed by his knees as he heaved an eerily inhuman howl and rocked back and forth.

I let the tip of my weapon hit the ground, desperately hoping we were done fighting.

The sounds of battle above us faded...or maybe muted from the force of his cries. "Shit, I'm so sorry," I said. Though Braza and I still spoke together, that was wholly my own reaction.

He quieted and stole a look at me through his fingers. Those remarkable eyes I loved so much had pupils slitted like a cat's, narrowed to the thinnest of slivers.

"*Brazita?*" he asked with a hush of disbelief. She translated his foreign words through her shadows and into my ears as English. "Have I finally joined you on the other side?"

A monster released a piercing death cry above us on cue, and more dust showered from the ceiling. Phaeron's hands dropped from his burned face, and he fumbled for the hilt of his sword blindly, shaking his head with a wince. "Clearly there is no such mercy, as paradise would not have Myuna's servants."

He slid onto his feet, tail and weapon scraping the ground as he limped a step. "Phaeron, wait. You're hurt," I protested.

He huffed and struggled on. "I cannot understand your human tongue." Then, seeming to get frustrated with his body's damage, he disappeared into shadowy vapor and headed straight for the combat above us.

Braza and I both rolled our eyes with exasperation. *"That's the prince I know,"* she said before misting us up after him. She took care of telling my coven still rushing in our wake what'd happened and where to go.

In the meantime, I arrived to see our allies had been pushed back to the first-floor stairwell. The sounds and spells were like arriving in the middle of a warzone, and disoriented, it took me longer than it should've to locate Phaeron slicing the nearest unnatural in half. He released a threatening roar and threw some of his own blood toward the monsters to gather their attention.

"Shit," I muttered under my breath, lurching into motion to protect his back when he was quickly overrun. This type of fighting felt too familiar. In another life, he and Braza had fought swarms of unnaturals under all kinds of circumstances and won. The creatures threw themselves at us, sensing easy prey and meeting a swift death because of it.

What felt like minutes later, the onslaught paused, monsters freezing and then pacing away from us. Soon they were in full retreat, leaving behind a gory mess. Myuna seemed to realize she was losing servants much faster than she'd corrupted them.

Phaeron turned to me, his head tilting and expression uncertain. "We must burn the remains. Myuna can still gather energy by eating what's left behind," he said in the foreign syllables of his language, and Braza kept translating it.

I repeated his wisdom in English in a two-toned voice, drawing glances of surprise and distrust from the defenders who'd survived the onslaught. With a sigh, I released my tether with Braza, lamenting the lack of her power and support immediately. I wavered on my feet and felt my skin pull in multiple places as wounds in the process of healing reopened. "I said, we have to burn the remains." A slur crept into my voice.

Grace was the first to react. "Hate to point it out, but we're in a library," she snarked.

"Well...we made this mess. Might as well clean it up." The tired voice was clearly Aaron's by his forced cheer. His more serious twin was already kicking glass shards into a pile.

"Cress?" Phaeron eyed me top to bottom, his brow knit in confusion. He clearly still knew my name but rolled the *R* and hissed the rest, making it harder to recognize. He...hadn't realized it was me under Braza's shadows?

Maybe he was just horrifically mixed up from his whole ordeal, tortured from sleep to waking.

"And look who's back with us." Aaron, to my horror, came over to clap Phaeron on the shoulder. Phaeron winced and hissed in earnest. "Oh...damn, can I get a medic?" he called out.

Narrowing his eyes, the dimensional shook his head and gestured toward his ears. "I know. I see it now. How'd you get burned like that?" Aaron asked.

Phaeron seemed to give up and flicked out his tongue, which was now forked at the end. "He had a translation spell break," I explained for him. I inched closer, staring at his mouth in fascination. He gazed back, catlike pupils resizing.

I put on an exaggerated grin, hoping he got the message. He bared his fangs back at me and...*holy shit*, he had a mouth full of sharp teeth, reminding me of a dog's dentition. Now that I'd noticed, it was obvious that whatever the Void had done to him to make him more human had worn off, sharpening his features at unusual angles and making him that much more alien.

I remembered his many fangs from the haze of Braza's memory, but it was more real to see it in person. His expression relaxed, and he dragged himself forward a limping step, cupping my cheek and jaw. I sighed out at the familiar rasp of his calluses and even the less familiar points of his more solid, curved claws following the pads of his fingers.

He didn't speak, but he didn't have to. He was clearly somewhere between affection, admiration, and disbelief. If he could, I think he'd kiss me, then tell me off for ignoring his every warning and saving him anyway.

When the "medic," a verdant witch doctor still in his scrubs, arrived to tend to him, Phaeron cut a sideways glare before realizing why the man was interrupting our moment. He sighed out something and took my shoulder, pushing me toward the doctor.

"Wait, you first," I protested, even though I was feeling increasingly lightheaded.

He held me in front of him stubbornly. "You first," he echoed with effort.

The doctor began to heal the worst of my injuries with flashes of green and brown magic. "He will need to head to the hospital anyway," he told me in an undertone. "Actually...wow, you should as well."

I hadn't heard a doctor say "wow" before about any illness or injury I'd had. My whole body throbbed and stung with previously ignored hurts. I was going to have one hell of a full-body bruise if I didn't do as this doctor said.

I turned to Phaeron and pointed to the light outside the now-windowless library. "Hospital," I said slowly.

He frowned and shook his head, not understanding. I gestured between us, then pointed outside again.

"*Allow me to assist. She wants to take you to a hospital, my prince,*" Braza said, somehow speaking in both our languages at the same time.

Phaeron grunted. Nice to know that sound was just a universal man thing.

18

BEN

THERE WAS a lull in the patrols of unnaturals—big fucking surprise there —so several of us traipsed to the hospital. Along with their general injuries, Phaeron had patches of second- and third-degree burns, and Cress needed a blood transfusion, so they were both in a medically induced sleep as they recovered. I checked on Lucas, just to see that he was still deep in a coma.

I'd never felt so worthless than when I was waiting around for one of the trio to wake up. I'd taken a bet with Geo on who it would be first. "It'll be Cress. She's the least injured of them," I'd reasoned.

"Phaeron, so I can knock him unconscious again for harming Cress," Geo had grumbled. I'd cast him a worried glance. He and Phaeron had been getting along pretty well until this confrontation.

That conversation had been before Geo disappeared with Wren to appear on her stream. The population of supernaturals watching was swelling dramatically each time Wren went live. Tish had set up her laptop in the waiting room to monitor the chat and donations, setting it on an end table so I could listen in with the gaggle of women I'd ended up hanging out with: Bianca, Grace, and Tish.

Geo had a presence in his gargoyle form, and his big, gravelly personality was quickly becoming a fan favorite. Wren was interviewing him as they toured the area outside, showing the blockades

Ashbough Protective Services had put in. It was a little post-apocalyptic from the lingering bloodstains on the sidewalk and the way the streets were cracked and rucked up from the use of guardian witch magic.

Bianca and Grace weren't all that interested in watching, while I faded in and out of their conversation and the stream, distracted. "Why a Medusa head?" Bianca was asking about the pin the two unnatural hunters wore.

"It's not Medusa," Tish practically squeaked. Her whole expression lit up from the question. "The Furies also had snakes for hair."

"That's the name of our group within Chaos Inc.," Grace supplied.

"Because we're harbingers of *vengeance* and *death* for the wicked." Tish seemed entirely too small a lady to be a harbinger of anything. "Grace is like Alecto, an unyielding hunter of criminals."

"Unnaturals," Grace added in her rough purr, barely getting the word in edgewise.

"While I'm Tisiphone—"

"Literally her name," said her partner. Tish wrinkled her nose and gave Grace a shove, not like she could budge the more muscular shifter. "Word to the wise, don't ask Tish about Greek mythology unless you have a couple hours to spare. She was raised reciting the myths and shit."

"Weren't there three Furies?" I put in.

Tish nodded. "We're still waiting to meet our Megaera, punisher of oathbreakers."

She opened a tab beside the stream playing on her laptop. Occasionally she would go back to a random tab and type something in; she had what looked to be twenty tabs and a few programs she was multitasking between. I was rather impressed by the glimpse of how she seemed to be able to view several surveillance cameras still running in Cerris City at once.

The newest tab was for showing us her art. Most of her style was rather cutesy, but it was all about putting a modern spin on Greek myths. She'd drawn the Fury head they wore, with its snarl and spitting snakes.

We spent a few hours together until I was about to bounce my kneecap off my leg with all my restless energy. When I saw Cress's mom rush by with a medical device on wheels, I raced after her to help.

She let me shadow her, and I quickly learned the life of a nurse was *not* for me, but it gave me an outlet to distract myself. Late into her shift, one of the Crystal fae moved in front of her and stared daggers at me.

"Who's this?" he asked, jerking his chin my way.

Kathy Rollins, usually such a nice lady, scoffed and gestured for him to step aside. "Someone who's helping around here, unlike you," she said waspishly.

As the fae stared at her, the citrine-like crystals growing from his shoulders seemed to glow. "I'm keeping you safe," he protested.

"You're standing in my way," she said.

A little startled, he stepped back, and she brushed past him, saying, "C'mon, Ben, ignore him."

We helped the next patient and stepped into the hall again. There was no sign of the fae man now. "Soooo, who was that?" I asked with far more intrigue in my voice than necessary.

She rolled her eyes on cue. "Some patients set out to make your life more difficult. It just turns out that he's still doing it, but now he's ambulatory."

Maybe I'd misread something here. He'd definitely been looking at her with some interest, but she clearly wasn't returning it. "Need help with him?" I offered more seriously.

"No, sweetheart. I can handle myself."

Well, whatever. I put it out of my mind when we visited the rooms of folks I recognized. First, we saw Aurora, who showed me a gnarly row of scars that looked like tire treads on her arms and across her belly from the Jellywalker's rows of stingers. The doctors had done what they could for her, but she still froze up occasionally. She needed more time to recover from its venom and was thus bedbound.

There were more than a few guardians and fae who'd gotten seriously wounded helping out at the library too. I was glad to help them get more comfortable. They deserved that much for facing the meat grinder that was the onslaughts of unnaturals big and small.

I was starting to pat myself on the back for a job well done when we came back around to Cress and Phaeron's room. I peeked inside and gasped. I'd lost the bet—he was awake and in the process of peeling bandages off healed skin. Aware of Cress's mom behind me, I held in my "oh shit" with effort.

He'd unhooked himself from the machines without causing them to scream and settled next to Cress's bedside, still dressed in his hospital gown.

"Hey, stop that!" Kathy protested. She burst into the room and intercepted his wickedly clawed hands as they moved toward his face.

Phaeron exaggerated a grin from within the thicket of white on his face. He gestured to himself and then held up his thumb.

"I think it's okay," I said, drawing her away from him. I still reached for a dagger to cut my finger and started drawing subtle blood runes on my arm just in case there was still some Myuna in him.

His skin was shiny from ointment, but he was clearly healed as he stripped off bandages and set them in a pile next to the chair. The docs must've given him a shot of a strong verdant witch tonic...which made me hope they did the same for Cress, who slept peacefully in the bed. Phaeron casually slipped his hand into hers and started playing with the blunt crescent of her thumbnail. Bruises had bloomed all over her soft skin and aged with whatever healing regime she'd been given, leaving them a dull yellow.

"See, Mama Rollins? All good," I said awkwardly since he couldn't speak English anymore or something. He would've charmed her right out the door if he could do more than stare at us without even a hint of comprehension.

We exchanged a meaningful look, and she gave me a trusting nod, leaving me with him and my unconscious anam cara. I sighed, seeing this as my opening to ask him for help with something, but only if I could get him to understand me.

I pulled up the other chair across from him. He didn't pay much attention to me, whispering in his language to Cress before he bent to kiss the back of her hand. Yeah, there was no Myuna there anymore, thank fuck. I snagged Cress's phone off a bedside table—it was a miracle Geo hadn't already stolen it—and did some creative searching on the supernatural side of the web. I typed in something on a translation website and handed the phone to him.

His pupils retracted to slits, and he squinted at the bright screen, but a moment later, he hissed a laugh at my joke. His big thumb claw loomed over the glass, and I gestured for the phone back urgently before he poked a hole through it. Shooting me a confused look, he handed it back. I dimmed the display for him and came over to his side to show him how to type on the screen with all the swirlies and dots that popped up for the Soiluirian language's keyboard.

"See, fingertips," I said.

His forked tongue tasted the air, and he watched me without blinking. Okay, I had to get used to the dimensional weirdness or whatever, but he was starting to creep me out.

He carefully typed with one thumb, the very picture of a tech-illiterate grandpa struggling to text for the first time. Eventually he passed the phone back. The translation read, "I understand I have you to thank for breaking a few bones in my tail. So, thank you. Glad to see you haven't changed, even in a tiny glowing box."

Well, damn, that was a proper English translation; what a good website. I starred it for Cress and sat back down. "You're welcome, I guess. Only useful thing I did yesterday," I typed.

He read the message and shook his head. "You may have saved her life. And my actions sent her to this bed. I will never outlive my remorse."

"Hey, man, it's not like any of us can say anything. We thought you were a goner for sure."

"Goner?"

"Dead or worse."

He read that and grounded himself with a heavy intake of breath and a long blink before typing a response. "I have no business being alive. But Cress willed that I survive, so I have."

"You're kind of fucked up, huh?" I typed, then thought that was too rude and deleted it. Still, he caught a glimpse of the screen and breathed a humorless laugh, nodding an affirmative. I passed him this message: "Could you come with me and take a look at my brother?"

He read the question and cast a reluctant sideways glance at Cress before nodding again. My heart leapt up to the vicinity of my throat when he tucked her hand and stood after me, silent as a shadow as we left her to rest. Now that he was here, I was terrified of what he'd say when he took a peek at Lucas's soul.

Deep down, I think I already knew what the verdict would be. The

Hungering Darkness never left survivors, right? Why would Lucas be any different? Yet I led him to the correct room, and he swept up to my little brother's bedside to take a good look.

He already had the phone and angled its face away from me as he typed a message one agonizing fall of his thumb at a time. When he passed the device back to me, his free hand landed on my shoulder, giving a firm squeeze of sympathy. "A swift death would be kindest. But there's a small chance to save him if we open Garroway's chest cavity in the next few weeks."

I felt my eyes widen as I read. Well, damn, I could get behind that. The sooner the better, even. I just wondered what the blood baron had done to earn Phaeron's bloodthirsty grin.

19
PHAERON

You're kind of fucked up, huh? Ben had no idea how right he was.

He must've alerted someone that I was awake, as a sliver of too-bright light appeared at regular intervals to check in on Cress and me while I sat with her. My body was heavy with fatigue, but I refused to close my eyes for longer than a blink.

Yet I started nodding off anyway and stirred in panic at the sensation too akin to falling backward into Myuna's control. The last time I'd slept, I'd woken up mid-combat with my mate.

I'd only gleaned what'd happened from observing those around me. Ben cradling a shoulder still healing from a blood rune on our way to the hospital. The uneasy glances from everyone, even the coven of our friends, whose eyes shaded with distrust when Cress fainted and I tried to carry her the rest of the way to a proper healing. Geo had given me a murderous look and pulled her from my arms.

For a few moments, I'd held her slight, battered form clothed in the torn rags of what had once been a beautiful robe. I had harmed her. My hands, Myuna's will. It was inexcusable.

I paced the fatigue away, eventually changing from the cheery pastel-colored hospital gown I'd woken in back into the heap of scrubbed leather folded at the foot of my bed. The chest piece of my armor, with all its careful inscriptions, was hopelessly torn up, and the gloves were gone, so I remained bare from the waist up for now.

I went to splash my face in the adjoining bathroom and inched up the light switch. As soon as the bulbs buzzed to life, I hissed from the pain that flooded my head and flicked them back off. I hated losing my humanlike adaptations already. Their world was too bright, and I could not put anyone at ease if they couldn't understand me.

I had some unpleasant conversations ahead if the magic could be salvaged. It was my duty to share news about Myuna, the presence of the Void around her—blessedly not clinging to me—and worst of all, what I'd seen while under her compulsion.

Cress mumbled something, shifting in the bed. Her hand patted the bare space next to her before she shifted to sit up with a wince. My hands were there the next moment, moving pillows behind her back and holding her shoulder so she didn't twinge her bruises too much.

"Easy, bright soul," I said, then muttered a curse. She wouldn't understand me. Laboriously, I reproduced her name like a human would say it and skimmed my fingertips over her cheek.

Her hand caught mine and held my palm to her face. I imagined she saw a yellow-eyed demon in the dark of the room, as I'd covered the displays of the machine hooked to her and the light leaking from the window with casual shadow magic. Meanwhile, I saw her sleep-softened face with perfect clarity, down to the ridge of a couple purple-edged bruises across her jaw.

"Phaeron," she whispered with such hope and longing.

She shifted her weight up and used my arm to guide her hand to one of my horns, leveraging it to drag me into a kiss. I shouldn't have allowed this, not when she was wounded and her soul was so tempting, just a nibble away...

My body heated at the merest brush of our lips; it was like emerging from the cold Void onto Earth for the first time. Warmth suffused me down to my tail-tip, and the animal in me took control. I cupped the back of her neck, drawing her in deeper. I could taste the change in her magic; it was like drinking sunshine, harmless but spicy to my otherworldly senses. My fangs nibbled on her bottom lip, my forked tongue twining around her blunt one for more.

She squirmed from the sensation. It was only natural to pin her hips and pull her closer, until the tube attached to her left arm was taut. Jostling it had her gasping, the pained sound melting to a needy whimper as I trailed sharp-edged kisses down the side of her jawline and neck.

I growled. *Mine.* In my impatience to have more of her, I pulled the needle and tape off her arm.

The machine released an ear-splitting shriek. We startled apart, and I cursed myself as I took in her kiss-swollen lips and the indentations my fangs had made on the column of her throat. I'd stopped a breath away from biting right over a half-healed bruise. Was I even thinking? She needed to rest, not be subjected to my lack of control.

Light flooded the room from someone coming to check on us. Instead of it being a nurse, the heavy footfalls and the gritty sound of his transformation betrayed Geo. He pointed an accusing finger.

"Phaeron," he rumbled. There was more, something about a "streem" and "away," but the blame was clear from just the weight he put behind my name.

I smoothed my hand over Cress's hair in apology before standing and stepping away from the bed. I coiled my tail around my legs and put my hands behind my back, head angled at an accepting angle. He had all the body language of a man about to strike. I deserved it.

Geo didn't hold back. He hit me with a fist like a brick, and the force of his blow had me tasting blood from the tear of my own teeth. I slammed into the bedside table. A lamp and her phone went flying when the cheap wood splintered under my weight.

I groaned, feeling the twinge of several bruises old and new. Cress half fell out of the bed to get between us. "Geo, no!" she yelped. Instead of stopping, he nudged her out of his way with a broad obsidian palm.

That was about the time a nurse rushed into the room and shouted. Geo's wrathful expression doubled from whatever the woman was saying. Cress was breathing a sigh of relief and picking up her phone, just to tense as she turned it over to reveal several cracks on the screen. She made a distressed noise and tapped an intact section several times, producing a whirr of static and bands of color under the glass.

The combined noise and light were too much for me. I put my arms around her from behind, murmuring a promise—"I'm sorry. I'll buy you another."—before taking her into my shadows and carrying her out of the room, leaving Geo behind to argue with the nurse.

She struggled, and I had to drop her in the hallway, the two of us reforming out of dark mist. "No," she said, stabbing a finger at me sternly.

I gazed at her, desperate to retreat somewhere dark and safe. There was only one place to go, really. Gesturing between us, I said, "Braza."

Her face softened, and she nodded, not fighting when I took her into my shadows again. It was the fastest way to the library and the embrace of the powercore's crackling energy. Braza pulsed a feeling of welcome when she read my intentions, already formed within the powercore's inner chamber when I arrived and placed Cress back on her feet.

"I'm glad to see you whole once more, my prince," Braza said with her usual polite distance.

She tilted her head toward Cress and smiled warmly, replying in English to something she'd said. My mate plucked at her hospital gown and waved at me, stepping out of the powercore.

"She is going to get changed," Braza explained.

I couldn't blame her. I'd tossed aside the ill-fitting garment as soon as I could, too. "Will you take a look at my back?" I asked. If anyone could fix the rune that'd appeared on my skin in the Void, it'd be Braza. We called the Void's work the "mark of language and humanity" from the benevolent way it'd warped us, and I yearned to have it back.

"Lie down on the bed. Let me see what she did to you," Braza said with sympathy. I did as she bid and turned my head to watch her face, fearing the worst as her energy-formed eyes skimmed over the skin of my mid-back.

"She did not touch me," I murmured.

"And yet she harmed you all the same. I see the trauma in your soul, my prince."

I closed my eyes, shuttering my reaction. Braza knew my regrets all too well, but I would not think about that time and inadvertently burden her further.

After a short pause, she added, "But the mark can be repaired easily enough. I shall tell Cress when it's done."

I drew breath to tell her that it would be all right if Cress witnessed her work when the first spike of pain struck me. Braza had to forcibly transform me back, her purple-black energy shoving my nails to retract into their sockets and manipulating my teeth and bone structure. It felt like she ground and broke and healed me in stages through the process.

It took fifteen minutes at most, and by the time she finished, I was panting in a damp circle of my own sweat. I pressed my fingertips into my mouth, probing at the flat line of teeth and the points of two fangs. When I opened my eyes, I perceived the glow of her magic as dimmer. The disorderly use of light by the humans around me wouldn't be so painful.

"I added the ability for you to switch back and forth at will," Braza told me.

She told me how it worked as I sat up, head tilted. "Why?" I asked.

Instead of answering, she turned toward Cress's reappearance. Her arrival came with the damp smell of soap and flowers—she'd showered and changed into clothes a little too big for her. She'd pinned her purple hair back from her face, and there was some color on her cheeks. "I, uh, thought it was wrong to keep you from your old self," she said.

"I'm flattered you found me attractive at my most different, bright soul," I replied. For a breath, I expected her not to understand.

A subtle shiver had Cress shifting on her feet. "You're back," she whispered.

I motioned for her to sit with me and looped my arm around her, tucking her into my side. "I am," I confirmed, tracing my thumb down the curve of her shoulder.

Braza was in the process of reabsorbing into the powercore to give us some privacy when Cress asked, "Have you hugged your daughter yet?"

Both Braza and I stilled in surprise. Brows slanting lower, she pointed at the energy-formed dimensional. "Have you thanked her too? Do you realize how much she did to save you? The fact that she's *here* and that she made me Guardian of Moongrove Library was all for you."

"Picking a fight as soon as we understand each other." I shook my head and stood, holding my arms out to Braza.

I hugged her jellylike body, some of my regrets leaking to the forefront of my mind before I could hide them. In binding Braza's soul to a ley line, I'd denied her access to paradise in the next life. I still wished I'd been strong enough to let her go that day so long ago.

She squeezed me harder. She *knew*. Of course she knew. Being able to read thoughts had revealed too many of the unpleasant truths that'd swirled through my mind over time.

But Cress didn't realize all the baggage that came with the decision to save Braza while also condemning her to a half-life. All she saw was the distance and damage between us, and as they were now soul-tethered, she had firsthand knowledge of what we'd lost.

"Thank you for everything you've done. Though I wish you both had not endangered yourselves on my behalf," I said.

"Into death." Braza answered with an old oath of loyalty meant for Myuna and the royal family. *How poorly that went for us.*

I heaved an exhausted sigh and released her. I've buried too many of the women I'd loved across my long life. That Cress and Braza had both risked themselves to drag me from Myuna's talons was unbearable when I was supposed to be the noble shadowborn protector in this room, but to say that would only insult them.

"Into death," I echoed, letting it become my new vow to them instead.

20

CRESS

I ASKED what had been on my mind from the moment I woke alone with Phaeron in a dark room. "Are you safe from Myuna's control now?"

He raised a brow toward Braza, deflecting the question. "In New Salem, I was able to mitigate the hole in your soul caused by Endaeron. You were only overcome when you left the radius of my power. While I am no rival for a goddess...it's clear she has only surface-level control of you. I will be able to provide the buffer you need," she said.

Phaeron made a noncommittal "hm."

"She was able to compel me while I was in her presence. I am perhaps fortunate she did not force me into corruption," he said. He shared that refusing a direct order from Myuna had been about as painful as driving an ice pick through his skull. The goddess had gleaned information from him about the library and what a powercore was when Braza had arrived.

"Yet you were able to resist her by a fraction. That's remarkable," she said.

"It is not when she still did as she willed while I was forced to watch." He glanced toward me, a guilty look.

"Let us not split already fine hairs. You are welcome to remain here, and I will use my power to support you while we seek a more permanent solution," she said. "Why don't you go rest?"

Though purple-tinted half-moons darkened the skin under Phaeron's eyes, he refused sleep.

"You won't be taken over again, not while you're here," I said, brushing his arm in support.

He glanced toward me again, saying, "I shall retire with Cress all the same."

Braza smiled and waved farewell before absorbing her body back into the powercore. I stood on my tiptoes and looped my arms around Phaeron's neck, not missing the coy slant to his lips. "Floor negative two, please," I said.

I liked seeing him a little caught off guard. "Hmm?"

"Take me to floor negative two. I'll show you a room you can use," I clarified. We disappeared in a whirl of shadows, and I closed my eyes to keep from getting dizzy when we reemerged in the second-floor hallway, right before the elevator doors.

I laced my fingers in his, guiding him toward the original room I'd claimed before I'd moved to sharing a different one with Geo and Ben. "Maybe you'd like to relax with a shower?" I suggested.

"Implying I smell?" Though his tone was a little too flat, I could tell he was attempting to tease. I respected that he was trying for some sense of normalcy despite everything.

"Good thing you wash," I said, eyeing him askance. I'd done my best not to stare, but he was bare-chested, and I came about to pec height. He smelled more like stale hospital cleanliness than any kind of body odor, and it seemed he'd healed off the worst of his physical injuries. All that remained was the shadows in his otherworldly eyes.

"I will cleanse myself...then we shall talk," he said, slipping into the room once I showed him to the door.

I flipped the lock and patted my empty pockets. *Oh, right.* I'd dropped my ruined phone when Phaeron had stolen me from the hospital room. I imagined Geo mourning over it and stifled a giggle. Served him right for rushing in and decking Phaeron without waiting for any kind of explanation.

That phone had been the last bastion of technology between me and my three men. It'd been a fun thing to watch how Geo would change my algorithms to cat videos and "highly satisfying" type stuff, or how Ben would steal it away to leave silly or weird websites waiting for me when I needed to use the phone too.

But that left me with nothing to do after a quick trip to the laundry room to pick out a change of clothes—shadowborn black, of course—in the largest men's size that'd been left behind. Phaeron was still showering when I returned, chill mist drifting from under the door, which he'd left ajar.

I set the clothes on the inside of the threshold and raised a brow. This man was seriously taking a cold shower and singing in his own language like the deluge of icy water wasn't another form of torment. I went to remove my shoes and lie on the bed, closing my eyes while I listened to the alien syllables and soft, hissing words drifting from the shower.

It wasn't a surprise Phaeron had a nice singing voice, not when his deep, smooth timbre had the power to tighten my lower belly. I wished he would emerge from that shower wet and ready to ravish me rather than to air out the burden he was carrying.

My heart quickened when the shower shut off, as did the tune he'd carried. I heard the shuffle of fabric and the creak of the door opening, but not his footsteps as he emerged with a towel tied around his trim hips. His hair was down from its usual scraped-back tail, framing his head and tangled around the root of his horns.

Combined with a chill cast on his skin from the cold shower, for a moment, I saw the second prince of Soiluire in his prime, dressed for peace with blue contouring his high cheekbones. But it was an illusion banished in a blink. Fatigue lined his face, and he'd lost weight, evidenced in hollow cheeks and a breakdown of the perfect abs he'd once had.

"Oh, you must be hungry," I said, sitting up quickly.

"Peace, bright soul," he answered. With a flick of a tendril of shadow, he turned off the lamp behind me, leaving him backlit by the light filtering from the bathroom. He slid under the covers with a sigh, shedding the towel with his tail. "I need for little except to lie with you."

I eased myself back down and scooted closer, resting face-to-face with him. He had the uncanny way of looking right through me with those topaz eyes. They threw off twinkling sparks as he threaded his fingers through my hair, nudging my head forward to touch foreheads with me. "I have missed you far more than words could convey," he murmured.

"I should've done more to bring you back sooner," I whispered back.

He shuttered his glowing eyes for a moment, gritting his teeth. "It is I that failed you with inaction. There is something you must know."

"I doubt there's anything—"

"Your sister, Carly," he interrupted. I swallowed hard, feeling a little ill to hear him say her name with such guilt. "She was brought before Myuna."

I broke into full-body goosebumps. "She ate Carly's soul?" I could barely put the thought into words as shocked tears pricked the corners of my eyes.

He shook his head. "She recognized Carly from the memories she'd been able to extract from me. She tore the soul from Carly slowly while demanding my compliance in exchange for her. Up until that point, every supernatural brought before her was consumed, body and soul."

I was scarcely breathing as he searched for the words to explain my sister's fate. "I struck a deal with her, to sleep if she spared Carly. She'd already corrupted your sister's soul by taking a small taste of it...but still, she returned it and revived her. I'm so deeply sorry, bright soul. Your sister is a torchbearer now, an unnatural enslaved to Myuna's will."

"That's why you were asleep when you came to the library," I realized.

"Indeed." He met my gaze, resigned for my reaction.

I glanced away from that heavy expression. "Can we save her?" I asked.

"If she is captured, I can attempt to unbind her from Myuna's will. But she has still experienced death and rebirth. She will remain an unnatural with unpredictable needs and hungers, whether or not she regains control of herself."

I couldn't help but think that Carly had become a supernatural in the worst way possible. I clung to the hope that we might still be able to rescue her and any others that were similarly corrupted.

In the meantime, I drew away a lock of hair that shadowed Phaeron's face, tucking it behind the curve of his horn. My memories from Braza suggested mates maintained one another's appearance and grooming like an act of love. "Stay right there," I said.

"What are you doing?" He gazed over his shoulder when I stood and retrieved a few things from the vanity.

In reply, I ran a brush through his thin, damp hair and disentangled it from his horns. On a hunch, I abandoned combing it out and ran my fingers over his scalp. He leaned into my touch with a low moan, and I bet he'd purr if he could. Some of the tension bled out of his body.

"I don't deserve this," he said.

"I'm glad you told me about Carly. I've been worried about her, too," I said quietly, still massaging behind his horns. "You saved her from dying. It set you on the right path to be freed from Myuna's will and returned here to me. If we can save her, we will, together. And if we can't, I will carry the guilt with you for the rest of my life. For now… relax. Let yourself recover before you try to help anyone else."

I pinned his hair back with the leather tie he used. He shifted to lie on his back. "You would care for me as a mate," he said quietly.

There was a blaze in his eyes as he waited for my answer. For all the teasing touches and whispers in my ear, the nibbles and snatched kisses…the fears born of a hunger he understood but didn't fully control, this moment felt like the tipping point between us. "Of course. I love you," I replied.

I had a moment of weightlessness as he wrapped his shadows around me, lifting my hips and setting me to straddle him on the bed. "I meant to tell you for a while, but…" I said, resting my hands on his warm chest.

He raised a brow. "But what?" he asked.

But he'd been so distant. Skirting the edges of his self-control, afraid to hurt me even though his absence was the worst pain he could inflict.

But he was so different, from a different world. Far more important than I'd ever dreamed of being. To think I was supposed to be his mate and equal.

"But we haven't fucked, even when you were in the grips of a lust spell," I settled on saying. "I thought I was, um, inadequate to you in some way. Probably in many ways."

His expression twisted into a troubled frown, and on cue, he blamed himself. "It is I that is inad—"

I swallowed the rest of what he was going to say by kissing him, holding one horn to get the angle I wanted. Just like before, the meeting of our lips seemed to obliterate Phaeron and draw out the growling animal that rested just beneath his princely manner.

He flipped us and trapped me in a cage of blankets and his body, kissing like he wanted to devour me. But he jerked away, panting. "This is a bad idea," he groaned.

With each shift, I felt the hardness of him pressed against my thigh. He wanted me, and yet...it still wasn't going to happen. I gathered myself to hear him tell me no, for him to disappear in a bank of shadows and leave me with only my hand to finish what we'd started. Moisture gathered in my eyes, and I glanced away from his conflicted face. I had to stop putting so much of myself forward like this.

He caught my chin between his thumb and forefinger, turning my head back. "It will not do to have you doubting." He pulled the covers from between us, and I caught sight of his manhood for the first time. I'd sucked on him in the dark, only able to feel the shape of him, which matched the sight. His shaft had a few nubs along the length and purplish veins, with a velvety dark gray cap at the tip, matching his lips. No other surprises—he was human-shaped.

"Cress." He pressed in close to me, our foreheads touching again. "Do you trust me?"

The tenderness in his voice stole my breath. "Yes," I managed to whisper.

Shadows unfurled around him, one particularly long tendril hitting a light switch and plunging the room into darkness. Fabric shredded, and cool air hit my chest and legs, my breasts bouncing free when my borrowed clothes parted. He lifted me as if I weighed nothing and swept away the ruined material.

His magic felt as firm as his hands. In the dark, I could mistake him for having many caressing fingers touching me all over. "Tell me to stop at any time," he said close to my ear. "But I need to have control in this bed. Is that okay?"

He pinned my wrists above my head, keeping them there with a warm coil of darkness. "I can't touch you?" I asked. The bindings flexed but held when I tested them.

"Not this night." He nibbled on my earlobe, the sensation curling my toes. Everything was more intense when I couldn't see what he was doing. He'd even covered the glow his eyes put off. In many ways, he was the night pressing in around us, here to take me. *Finally.*

"I want as much of you as I can have," I told the darkness and parted my thighs for it.

"My True Light, you have called me home." He pulled back, his voice enveloping me with warmth. One clawed hand adjusted my knee and ran a palm up the tender inner flesh of my leg. "You are my beacon to return to, and how bright you have come to shine in my absence."

I squirmed some as his touch skimmed closer to my heated core. The darkness sighed with me as the firmness of his fingertips vanished. His shadows continued to play across my skin, drawing circles and little nonsense runes over every inch of me except the folds that pulsed with my quick heartbeat.

Was he wrestling with his control as I waited breathless for his return? I wondered if he'd created the absence of light to hide his struggles and protect me from having to see how thin his control truly was.

He cupped my needy pussy, and I breathed out a soft sound of relief. "In the madness of every moment I spent with Myuna," he said, stroking his way up my slit. "I clung to thoughts of you. If I would emerge from the ordeal as the man you recognized." One of his fingers slipped within me, and I moaned. I could feel the tremor that passed through him. "If you would still want me." In went a second finger, curling and coaxing within me.

"Of course I still want you," I said breathlessly.

"I worried I would not be the same within," he continued. He ran his lips along my throat and applied pressure to my clit with the pad of his thumb. My cry sounded ragged, too loud to my own ears. "That I would no longer appreciate the great power you carry within you. I feared the sight of you would no longer bring me joy. A true monster of hers would not crave the taste of your lips."

His mouth was there, his kiss first a chaste brush but deepening to a full duel of teeth and tongue. He trembled with fine control. The sensation of his kiss pulled away, and he withdrew from my pussy too.

"Phaeron?" I asked, flushing hot, then uncertain. "If this is too much, we can stop..."

"Still so sweet," he answered. I heard a wet sound and was fairly certain he was licking his fingers. "I may be a touch broken. Mere pleasure cannot mend me."

"We can still try," I said.

"Yes." Before I could worry about what he was trying to imply, he was between my thighs, nudging within me. He lifted under my back, taking away the sensation of the sheets and leaving me in a cushion of darkness. And that inky night...all of it was him. His skin, his magic, his breath upon my shoulder as he sank inside of me.

His tail twined around my locked ankles, pulling my body into the roll of his hips. He drew back, adjusted minutely, and thrust again, repeating this three times until one of the hard nubs on his shaft brushed an ultra-sensitive patch within me. Back arching, I screamed at the unexpected starburst of pleasure.

The darkness laughed, a chuckle of pure male satisfaction. I imagined his smug smile, the vicious way he tended to bare his teeth when he gave in to his shadowborn side. "Oh, Phaeron." I longed to *see* his pleasure.

He didn't reply. Now that he'd gotten the perfect angle, he slowed, sawing against that bundle of nerves. Fingertips traced my face, the curve of my jaw. This was lovemaking, sure as anything. He'd not declared his love as directly as I had, but I felt it. Every tender touch and meeting of our hips said it.

He truly was mine. But I was also his, at his mercy completely.

How well he treated me, though. I came apart in his arms, seeing stars as my eyes shut tight. He stilled, then withdrew, leaving me clenching on air with a whine of denial. Even the pressure of his tail and hands vanished.

"Come back. Please," I said. It would ruin the moment, to get off without him experiencing the same.

I could hear the rasping way he drew in breath. He wasn't far, but he was perhaps on the knifepoint of his restraint.

"You are too tempting. I cannot keep my fangs from your neck if we continue," he answered after a few moments.

I wiggled my hips to tempt him anyway, and a growl drifted from the darkness. "Take me on my hands and knees, then. No need for fangs anywhere near my neck," I reasoned.

For the space of two heartbeats, I didn't think he would come back.

But then he grasped my hips, and I had the sensation of turning over. He pressed his length between my lower lips, rubbing up and down and catching my clit against one of those amazing nubs. "I don't know how much more I'll be able to hold back," he whispered.

I arched my back. "Go ahead," I coaxed. "I want you to fuck me now."

He made a sound like a snarling animal and slammed home within me again. The driving power of his thrusts would've shoved me into the bed, but I didn't even know if we were on it anymore—the cushion of shadows underneath me had firmed up and kept me in the right position.

I had the biggest grin, exhilarated to feel him let loose. He released with a shadowborn's howl, holding my hips flush with his as he pulsed within me.

"Oh, I should've told you," I said as soon as he let me go and I fell into a boneless heap back onto the soft bedsheets. His magic was receding, and I spotted the half-lidded glow of his yellow eyes as he stretched out next to me.

He stroked his fingers through my hair, idly working free a tangle. "Is something the matter?" he asked.

"I'm on the pill now, so we should be safe, but next time, you should probably wear a condom."

He started to laugh. Deep, carefree rolls of his chest. "We're from different species. There won't be any babies," he promised.

"Says the man who was made humanlike on his way to Earth," I protested playfully. When he put it that way, I did feel silly.

His mirth drifted to quiet, and he didn't reply. Moments later, he was snoring.

21

CRESS

THERE WAS a timeless bubble around Phaeron and me. I slept a bit, then drifted in and out for a while. Eventually, I couldn't sleep any more, but I lay still for him. I enjoyed being in his arms, warm, safe, and glad he hadn't seemed to stir this whole time. He'd needed this so badly.

With the lights off and his eyes closed, the only light in the room was a bedside clock and a smoke alarm on the ceiling that flashed occasionally. I wouldn't have noticed it if this wasn't an underground room coated with eddies of shadowy mist that occasionally rolled off Phaeron's skin, swirling with his deep, slow breaths.

The unrestrained shadow magic was just one more quirk to love about him, and I was smitten. I drank in his presence even though I could barely see him—his night-air scent, the press of his muscles against my curves, and the possessive way his tail had coiled around my legs.

We'd fit so well together last night, and I was deliciously sore, sure to feel the evidence of his claim when I did eventually get up. My body's needs would be the only thing that'd drive me out of his arms before he woke. At least, I thought that until Braza's presence brushed my mind.

"Sorry to interject. I was not able to stall any longer," she said apologetically.

"Is something happening?" I asked. When I stirred, Phaeron gripped me to his chest tighter in his sleep.

"You could say that. There is another newcomer to the pocket dimension, and he has demanded to see Phaeron. Ben's memories show that he is Auric et Vess, an old friend. Do you remember him?"

"I think so," I replied. That sounded like the name of the Vrassorm man who'd had the idea to take the survivors of the Age of Decay off Soiluire for good. *"But is he still a friend?"*

"If he is not, he is an enemy of our enemy. The effect is the same."

Before I could ask how she could be so sure, someone pounded on the door. Phaeron woke with a growl and raised his voice in the direction of the insistent knocking. "Go away!"

"No can do, Big P." It was Ben. "Can I come in?"

"Braza says it's important. Apparently, Auric et Vess is here," I said.

He stared at me in shock. "Auric? Here?" He muttered something I was starting to recognize as his go-to curse in the dimensional language, but then he nuzzled into my hair, breathing in the smell of me with a sigh. We held tighter to one another for a moment before getting up.

I turned on a lamp and tidied the bed while he dressed in his old leather armor and answered the door bare-chested to let Ben in. I identified the scraps of colored fabric on the floor as the remains of my clothes and shook my head, going to don the black shirt of the set of clothes I'd gotten for Phaeron. It fit on me like a dress, the hem stopping mid-thigh. Not bad for the inevitable walk of shame across the hall.

I emerged from the bathroom and caught the end of a backslapping hug between the two men. I hung back a moment, oddly touched. Ben and Geo had seemed to be growing into close friends. Maybe this was a glimpse of a future where I was dating an inseparable trio. As long as Geo could finally accept Phaeron.

Ben turned and spotted me, making grabby hands in my direction. "Morning, babe." He had a hug for me too before tucking to my back and resting his cheek against mine. His clever hands slipped under the hem of my oversized shirt.

I felt him smile. "I see I was right. When Geo told me what happened, I kind of assumed." His thumbs brushed up and around where the band of my panties should be.

"He punched Phaeron for no reason," I said, still pissed that was Geo's first reaction to seeing him awake.

"I greatly deserved it, actually," Phaeron put in. His fingers traced his jaw, where a bruise was starting to bloom on his gray skin. "Your safety is his duty, and I have been a threat to it. I am surprised he's not here now."

His yellow gaze cut curiously to Ben, who I felt shrug. "We had a long chat about you after the powercore sent word you both were safe in the library. I think he doesn't know what he's feeling after seeing you and Cress fighting."

"Phaeron wasn't in control," I argued.

"Yeah, but we're talking about someone who's been a rock more hours than not lately. Just remember that he's not the bad guy, all right? He's just figuring himself out. That rock loves you as much as I do, babe, and that's saying something." He gave my bare hips a squeeze and planted a kiss on my cheek.

If we hadn't had an audience, I'd be tossing this shirt aside...hell, Phaeron had already seen us going at it, so modesty wasn't the best excuse either. The dimensional cleared his throat as I considered. "I expect you have a reason for disturbing our peace?" he prompted.

Oh, right. A living legend of a dimensional was here.

"Yeah, this dimensional man appeared out of nowhere while there was a fight with some of Myuna's creatures outside of the hospital. He made the unnaturals disappear with a flick of his wrist and said he wanted to speak with you, Phaeron. He also idly threatened to make our friends vanish one by one if we did not find you."

There was a knowing glimmer in Phaeron's eyes. "You barely need to say more. What color was his skin? Did he have one blind eye?"

"Blue. And...yeah. I believe one of our friends correctly summed up his appearance as 'creepy fuck.'"

Phaeron snorted a surprised laugh. "That does sound like Auric. Don't worry, he's all bark and little bite, as you humans say."

"You sound positively *ancient* right now, Big P," Ben commented.

He rolled his eyes. "When Cress is properly dressed, we shall go."

GEO

The blue-skinned dimensional held a cigar while seated on a granite wall next to a set of steps that led up to the hospital, smoking without a care in the world. I was posted several yards away across a concrete courtyard. My obsidian wings and wide stance blocked a second, smaller staircase right before the hospital doors. I stood next to Madigan's red-armored form and brandished warhammer.

Behind us ranged several more defenders, including Bianca with her crossbow and the rough-voiced shifter she'd come to spend most of her spare time with. We couldn't be sure this man wasn't another puppet of Myuna's and about to make a move to teleport us all in front of the goddess. He hadn't spoken up to dispel the notion, only demanded Phaeron and refused to move, creating this stalemate of wills.

A curl of shadows, distinctive on this sunny day, crossed the sky and took form next to me. I swung my head around, surprised to see only Cress and Ben take shape from curls of black and purple magic. When I looked back toward the unknown dimensional, Phaeron had already taken form and was speaking to him in the language of Soiluire.

"Oh, wow, he looks much cooler in person," Cress commented. "Also, hi, Geo."

"Hello," I gritted out.

It was a relief to see her whole and hale again, but that feeling was quickly pushed aside at my annoyance with her so willingly disappearing with a man who'd harmed her so badly. Magical influence or no, Phaeron was still the cause of the mostly healed wounds and bruises that'd peppered her body. I should've pummeled him further so he felt a fraction of the pain he'd inflicted on her.

She glowed, beaming like she held some sweet secret. A glint of her usual curious awe at learning something new about the supernatural community shone on her face as she watched the two dimensional men interact.

The newcomer spoke in a voice nearly as gravelly as mine. He'd leveraged himself to his feet with his tail alone, and I registered it as a natural weapon. It was a muscular coil compared to Phaeron's whip-thin version, heavier with a layer of back-facing spikes and a cluster of them at the end like a club. He rested it around his feet while he grasped forearms with Phaeron, bowing his head in a brief show of deference.

"That's Auric et Vess," Cress explained in an undertone. Even Madigan tilted her head to listen in. "He's from the Vrassorm tribe, the rarest of the three types of dimensionals. They usually have power over cold or the Void, and the stronger they are with either, the more potent the poison is that they store in their tail spikes."

"What is the Void?" Madigan asked.

"It's..." She circled her hand vaguely. "Like, it's the darkness between worlds. Less like space and more like a plane of existence that links universes together. It's what the dimensional peoples escaped through to come to Earth...and also what Myuna traveled through to get here."

"Fuck," Ben muttered.

"Agreed," I rumbled.

"Auric is a Vess. That's a title that means..." She seemed to search her memory. "Voidwhisperer. He sacrificed one of his eyes to the Void so he can better sense it and use it."

Auric glanced our way, maybe hearing his name. One eye was wholly a cloudy white. The other had a teal glow, with an unusual pupil like one black line with two darker blue scratches on either side of it. When he flicked out a forked tongue, he resembled Phaeron's unchanged form, complete with heavy claws and mouthful of sharp teeth.

His horns and build were different, though. He had one impressive backswept horn, and the other, on his blinded side, was cut short and resembled a tree trunk with a crack on the side. "Was the horn a sacrifice to the Void, too?" I asked.

She considered and answered in a voice combined with another woman's. "No, that's new within the last two centuries."

Both Ben and I flinched and pivoted her way. "Sorry. Did that startle you?" Cress asked in her usual sweet tone. "I wanted to take Braza out into the sunshine, and she just so happens to know this guy already."

I only relaxed when she further explained that Braza was the name of the powercore. She sounded like someone Cress trusted deeply. I'd found her judgment dubious in the past, but it hadn't been wrong about Ben...and it seemed it wasn't wrong about Phaeron, as conflicted as I felt about him.

When he turned and beckoned to Cress, she didn't hesitate to come forward. Madigan shifted to cover my post while Ben and I both accompanied her for protection.

Auric hissed something at Phaeron, who bared his teeth in the approximation of a smile while responding in a tone of warning.

The powercore's voice flowed into my head. Braza felt familiar, carrying the reassuring electrical presence I'd served for decades in Moongrove Library. *"Auric asked if Phaeron claims Cress in name only, and his response was to threaten to break his other horn if he's rude to any of you."*

My stone lips curled toward a smile. I'd gladly help if it was necessary.

Phaeron switched to English. "My mate, Cress Darkmore. Her anam cara, Ben Evenstar. And her protector, Geo."

"Charmed," Auric replied flatly. His single eye held a full sentence of judgment as he took in the four of us together. "As I was telling the prince, I'm here to wage war on Myuna the White. You lot are a hodgepodge in need of a Vess. I felt her arrival, as she ripped a wide hole through the Void and that has to be repaired. Plus, I later heard this one's silent screams trapped within the darkness and thought I'd be saving his sorry hide again." He tipped his good horn toward Phaeron.

He replied by resting an arm around Cress. "While I appreciate that you would rescue me, I'm pleased to inform you that my mate has already done so."

They had another verbal spar in their language. It seemed Phaeron won the quick exchange.

"I am Auric," he said toward the rest of us with a hint of reservation. He tugged the collar of a fine suit tailor-made to cover his thick barrel of a chest. Tattoos peeked from his sleeves and covered the back of his clawed hands. "Once a power and a threat, a leader of a resistance, now doomed to tiptoe around human-dimensional conflicts lest the rest of my Vrassorm brothers and sisters get crushed between prejudice and threat. I've saved this kid a time or two. Who knows, maybe I'll save you lot with what I have planned."

"I've known Auric most of my life. He is an elder of our kind,"

Phaeron supplied, and I realized he was the one Auric had called a kid. How mind-bogglingly old the Vrassorm must be to make such a claim.

"So, is joining us part of this plan?" Ben put in.

"I suppose so. On my way here, I sensed the scope of the rip where Myuna landed. If I had the proper support, I could catapult the bitch back where she came from and seal the hole behind her," he said.

Phaeron frowned. "The Void most certainly does have a lingering presence around her."

"Wait," Cress said, holding up a hand. "When my friends say you made unnaturals disappear...were you sending them into the Void?"

"That's right." He bared his fangs in a vicious smile. "They'll wander a while before its chill overtakes them, then they'll be broken down until only their voices and memories remain to haunt its nothingness forever."

"That's kind of fucked up," Ben muttered.

Cress shivered from more than just a cold breeze. "Myuna's victims don't deserve that. My sister's still out there," she said. I quickly muttered in agreement with her.

"If you intend to stay here, you will save the Void treatment for Myuna herself," Phaeron added.

For a moment, I thought Auric would step into the Void and leave with how disgustedly he looked at the four of us. "Fuckin' hell," he muttered. "Fine, you soft-hearted fools. But even the Void cannot save you if an unnatural rips out your throat."

Phaeron grinned and clapped the other dimensional on the shoulder. "I'm pleased you're here, old man," he said with affection. "I must face the judgment of this group for my own deeds, but I imagine they will offer you entry and a room if you attempt to play nice."

We turned and approached the hospital and the cluster of supernaturals guarding it. Madigan listened to Phaeron's explanation of why Auric was here, then her red helmet turned toward me. "Can we trust this as fact?" she asked.

I dipped my chin in a slow, grinding nod. "No agent of Myuna has had the presence of mind he has," I said.

"Good point," she mused. "Let's talk about your plan in more detail, Auric. I have a few augurs you should meet as well."

I cleared my throat, a sound about as pleasant as two rocks grinding together. "While you do that, I wish to have words with Phaeron."

She considered for a couple of moments. "Yeah, all right. No one's using the conference room right now."

I shook my head at Cress when she looked ready to pose a question. She'd be all right without us for a while, considering how she carried a powercore's might with her. Her gaze softened with concern as she watched Phaeron and me head into the hospital, with Ben hesitating before catching up to us.

The dimensional slowed to follow us as we took the familiar path from the lobby to the conference room that'd become somewhat of a war room. Tourist maps of Cerris City peppered the walls, each covered with different notations. One was stuck with red pins each time there'd been a sighting of unnaturals. Another marked battles and skirmishes, while a third noted suburban areas we'd tried to evacuate already.

Phaeron paused in front of these maps, his tail flicking against the carpet in agitation. He read over them for a few moments before crossing the room to have a seat at the head of the conference table. "I suspect this conversation has been due a while," he commented.

I transformed back into my human form while he and Ben got comfortable. Feelings both positive and negative flooded in, as well as the phantom sensations of hunger and thirst. I'd need to satisfy both if I intended to spend more than an hour as a human.

"Yes. We should talk about how you've put Cress in danger," I said. My voice just didn't hit the same kind of dangerous rumble in this form, but I glared across the room at him as another way to express my displeasure.

Before I sat, I fiddled with the light switch, dimming the room and earning a grateful glance from the dimensional. I went to sit across from Ben, the three of us completing a seated triangle.

"I would not willingly harm her. I am fated to her, same as you both," Phaeron answered.

"I am aware," I gritted. I'd already expressed my frustrations about this to Ben last night, once I'd calmed down in the aftermath of finding him disconnecting Cress from the machine monitoring her vitals. "All three of us are fated to the same woman, and yet we could not be more different."

Phaeron's eyes glimmered like gemstones as he took in Ben and me. "A relationship with one man and one woman can be needlessly complicated, let alone adding in two more partners. Yet it is easy to love Cress, yes?"

"Yes," Ben and I answered at the same time.

"That's the fate part of it," Ben added.

I scoffed lightly. "Fate," I echoed. "It pales in comparison to being made for her and only her."

Ben rolled his eyes. "All right, if you want to measure dicks about this, then my soul is the other half of hers. We share a deep bond."

We both glanced toward Phaeron. "She is my True Light, the only woman capable of quelling the rages of my shadowborn side," he said. "Were she one of my kind, she'd also be a perfect biological match capable of carrying my life force and thus my child."

"So, we're all specially bonded to her," Ben said more to me, with a gesture toward Phaeron.

"But that creates the other side to being her mate. We must find a balance where we can support her while not hating one another for her shared affections," Phaeron said. "I have shared a mate before. It was not always easy."

"You have?" Ben asked.

He nodded. "With my brother. She was the first mate either of us had, before we fully developed our magic and abilities. I'm glad of the experience, as it taught me that a heart like hers or Cress's should be trusted to expand to love her mates equally. It is better for all of us not to expect her to cut herself in portions and jealously look over to see if we all received an equal piece of her."

My hands softened from the fists I had resting on the table. Somehow, he'd taken what I was feeling and phrased it just right.

"I have only seen you both as my competition," I admitted quietly. They were unpredictable and changeable, unlike myself. But that wasn't a fair summation either when Cress had already improved me just by being her.

"That is quite clear," Phaeron said. "Do you remember what I said when I offered to temper your stone form?"

I thought backward. My memory used to be crystal clear when I never took human form. But since I'd been spending more time as flesh and blood, I was starting to forget the edges of things I'd experienced. Having a human's memory was disconcerting sometimes. "You helped me to make peace between us."

He nodded. "I wished to establish some common ground for Cress's sake. I still hope to build up a foundation like that with you both. As long as we can be friends, we can focus on her despite our differences. What do you say?"

Ben's answer was quick. "I'm in." He was already in, though. I was the one who found this difficult. My gargoyle side still saw the world in binary, so there was no "I will try" like I'd promised before.

I was the one who needed to change here. With a gargoyle's brevity, I answered, "Yes."

22

CRESS

For the next few hours, I toured the hospital, quietly showing Braza around. She was fascinated by the modernity of the facility, even though much of the beauty of the place was stripped. File cabinets and couches cluttered the first floor, turning it into a maze, and most of the windows were blacked out.

I introduced her in a one-sided way to the people I knew, speaking with her in my mind so I didn't startle anyone with a two-layered voice. I was happy to run into Mom, who was pushing a cart in the hall on floor four.

"Have they given you any time off?" It seemed like she was always running around when I had time to visit the hospital.

She shrugged. "You know what they say. Time waits for no one. I'm choosing to invest it making what difference I can."

"Have I told you lately that you're my hero, Mom?" I asked earnestly.

She ruffled my hair and moved toward the nurse's station. "I'm not that impressive, baby. The doctors around here... I'd give my left arm for the kind of healing magic they wield."

"Now you're starting to sound like..." I coughed, choking on the name. "...like Carly."

Mom's eyes flicked my way over her mask, concern creasing her brow. She'd always been able to read the shifts in my mood like her own kind of magic. I'd as good as told her there was something wrong.

"*Well, you had best confide in her,*" Braza commented.

"Can I tell you something?" I asked more quietly.

Mom took a fifteen-minute break and drew me into an unoccupied room, where I spilled everything I knew. Phaeron's admission was enough to scare her, and Braza's supplemental knowledge seemed to make it worse. "Torchbearers were ghostly servants during the height of Myuna's power. It sounds like she's not strong enough to enslave souls like that anymore, so if we can capture Carly, Phaeron can try to remove her from Myuna's control."

"What are the chances of us finding her alive?" With her mask set aside, her face looked aged a decade, deep lines marking her nose and cheeks. Tears sheened her eyes, but she kept them contained by pure force of will. "I shouldn't think that way...but I know the men and women protecting the hospital are treating anyone touched by Myuna as a lost cause. We have the morgue filling up with these so-called torchbearers."

I felt my skin go cold all over. "Like, how many people?"

"It's grim business. I'm not sure you really want those details," she answered.

"An estimate, maybe?"

She considered me hard, and her will caved to what she saw in my face. "Dozens. The wounded guardians talk about how the corrupted animals and supernaturals all throw themselves heedlessly into fights. There are a lot of bodies left behind," she told me in a hush.

"We're lucky the hospital has a good relationship with the closest funeral home. At the moment, any body we can salvage is being stored...just in case we come out of this situation. There will be loved ones who will want a say in what happens to those remains." It was clear that was all she wanted to say on the matter. That was fine, as I was reeling.

"*If dozens of torchbearers have already died in this area, Myuna must be corrupting them left and right. It sounds like she's using them as if they're disposable,*" I said to Braza.

Of course, I also skipped ahead to the worst possible scenario: my sister being amongst those thrown at us. I rubbed my clammy palms against my pants. Somehow, we had to save her from that fate, even if it meant snatching her out from under Myuna's watch.

"She will be pressing each new servant to bring her more and more people to consume or turn," Braza replied.

"We have to do something."

"Mom, I have to go," I said aloud, rising to give her a hug farewell. "Thanks for telling me all of this. I will find Carly, I promise."

A thread of eagerness spun from Braza, crackling with the restless energy of lifetimes stuck in one spot. *"Well, we are unstoppable together. Shall we go now?"*

I liked the sound of that quite a bit. *"Shouldn't we tell someone that we're leaving? And Phaeron..."* The only reason we'd felt safe to let him leave the aura of her powercore side was because I was carrying the other half of her with me.

She tugged on my powers, guiding me through the process of turning into shadowy mist. I may have startled Mom, passing her as a sudden breeze, but hopefully I didn't leave behind an impression of my exhilarated laughter. We reached the first-floor conference room in record time and reformed in a seat. I felt the weight of eyes on me during the dizzy spell that followed.

Looking around, I blanched as I took in the meeting we'd dropped into. Phaeron and Auric had pulled the maps off the conference room wall and were conferring over them, while Madigan and Hana had obviously paused mid-explanation to stare at my sudden entrance.

Hana broke the silence first. "Hello, Cress and Braza. We were about to talk about the ocean gate."

"Braza?" Auric echoed in disbelief.

She greeted him in Soiluirian through my lips, further baffling the old Vrassorm man.

"I didn't mean to barge in," I added sheepishly. "I just wanted to let someone know I'm going out to find my sister."

Phaeron's lips pressed into a fine line of disapproval.

"*And* I wanted to point out that A Little Wicked Coven has no job now that the library is cleared internally. Myuna is moving to take over the supernatural population. I know I can speak for my friends when I say that we can't sit idle." I flexed my hand, overlaid with purple-black claws.

Madigan propped her chin on a gauntleted fist. She'd placed her helmet aside for this meeting and shot a bemused glance toward Hana. "Well, you called it. What do I owe you?" she sighed.

"Let's call it good if you say yes. This way, you can assign them a few protectors," the augur said.

"What of protecting the library?" There was a dangerous edge to Phaeron's question.

Braza barely had to warn me. Fury blazed in his otherworldly eyes as I aired her suggestion. "You can hold it on your own with the power-core's support."

He switched languages seamlessly, the hisses and rolls of Soiluirian made crisp by his anger. "And when darkness falls and Endaeron comes for you both, I am to...what, sit idle?"

"Unless Myuna herself shows her face, you will be safe from her control this way," Braza answered in the same language.

It felt like I was double-teaming him as I added in English, "This also protects you from whatever hold the Hunger has on you."

His tail gave an agitated snap. *"He will change the subject to buy time to think of a way around our logic,"* Braza said privately.

After taking a deep breath, he said, "Let us speak of the ocean gate." Well, she'd called that. "It is surrounded by unnatural sightings and skirmishes. It's a guarantee Myuna has figured out something valuable is in the lake, but she will not know what an ocean gate is unless one of her creatures gets the opportunity to use it."

"That's only a matter of time," Hana said. "Especially with the number of unnatural hunters coming and going."

Auric loosed a displeased growl. "Those kids are pretending at being heroes."

"I know it seems that way, but they're working for the greater good out there. We simply don't have the people to rescue everyone." Madigan drummed her fingertips on the table, weighing our options with a pensive expression. "If there was a way to communicate with all of the people still trapped in their homes, we could gather them up for one big push."

"We could use Wren's stream?" I suggested.

She tilted her head back and forth with a hum. "My understanding is her audience is all supernaturals on the outside, watching for our fall with bated breath."

"Not necessarily. She's really tried to show there's hope on this side of the pocket dimension. I bet you there have been several people who've come to the hospital for protection after seeing it on her stream," I argued.

She seemed to consider it and nodded to herself. "For better or for worse. Who knows how many supernaturals were dragged in front of Myuna because they were trying to get to us?" she pointed out. "And broadcasting our plans would only make that problem more severe. Not to mention someone locking the ocean gate from the outside if it becomes common knowledge."

"I don't think they will yet," Hana said. "We'll have to talk to the mer representative when he arrives tomorrow."

I interjected before they could switch to another topic. "You're right that a lot of people on the outside are watching Wren's stream too. What if we used it as a platform to call for help? If there's a future where we try to evacuate all the people we can." My gaze landed on Auric, whose expression was cynical at best. "We cleared out the most dangerous creatures in Cerris City Library with the help of a couple unnatural hunters. They're competing, not trying to be 'heroes.'" I put up air quotes. "But there *are* people who will come help us if they know it's possible."

"I question the wisdom of dragging anyone else into this conflict, bright soul," Phaeron replied quietly. "The fewer supernaturals around for Myuna to corrupt, the better it will be for us. However a small river can help, it's not possible to comprehend her evils without firsthand experience."

"Fuckin' hell. The first thing you asked was if I brought reinforcements," Auric grumbled.

"Of *our* kind, who understand the magnitude of a soul's corruption," he said.

"Who says they won't come when they see the sudair fighting?" A sharp grin took over the blue dimensional's face. "I have an idea that will keep you away from sitting on your ass in a library. You just have to appear on camera."

"Back on Soiluire, we called this clearing a path," Phaeron said a little later, at the head of our armed group heading away from the hospital.

"We're not going to get very far on foot," Braza grumbled in my head.

We'd all kind of gotten what we wanted. Braza seemed the most disappointed, as she'd initially thought we'd be striking out on our own. It was the impulsive teenaged side of her, I thought. Traveling in a big group was much slower, but this way, we were present to keep Phaeron sane. In the same breath, he was here with me, and that seemed to put him more at ease than staying in the library.

"That's not the point of why we're out here," I replied. In a way, I knew we were being humored. We had one objective for this trip, and that was to free a torchbearer from Myuna's control. We had to see if Phaeron could do it.

Our group's spirits seemed high. Roe and her familiar, Tank, wore identical smiles, faces lifted toward the sun. Bianca and Grace were nearly attached at the hip, muffling the occasional laugh. Ben and Geo were doing much the same, actually, from where they flanked me. I was relieved to see Geo smiling again, even in gargoyle form.

There were a couple guardians and Crystal fae with us, all familiar faces who'd been assigned to the library. Absent from our group were Jordan and Auric, who'd both stayed behind to plan; Áine, whose magic was needed at the hospital; and Grant, who seemed quite shy of Wren's camera. The blonde stood at the center of our group with her phone panning the scene. More often than not, it was focused on Phaeron, a new star to the "small river," as he still didn't quite understand what a stream was.

As I hadn't wanted my hybrid status broadcast to the supernatural world, I'd left Wren's staff behind. She didn't seem to care much about its fate, still having the moon scepter tied to her hip. Walking next to her was Willow, also on her phone but for a different reason. She had our map and wore Grace's microphone to coordinate with Tish.

"We're taking a left two blocks from here," Willow said.

"Got it," Phaeron said.

Meanwhile, Wren narrated our walk and the information flashing on Willow's phone as the map refreshed in real time. "The survivors have ransacked everything of value from these stores already. This road will lead us to a location where several skirmishes have been fought against Myuna's creatures. They've wrecked enough cars here after dark…"

Phaeron shot an annoyed glance over his shoulder. I spoke up to distract him. "Just pretend she's not there. It's for the stream."

"Right. Where others can watch what we're doing," he repeated dubiously.

"A lot of others," Ben pitched in. "And they give us money for the cause."

"Well then. Once you receive your share, maybe you'll stop trying to spend my wages for me," Phaeron said.

Ben covered a surprised laugh. "Nah, Big P. I still think you need to buy a car."

"What use do I have for a car?" Phaeron put his palms up in exasperation. It was like they'd picked this argument up from where they'd left it before we were ever trapped here.

"Or a phone," Geo rumbled.

I held my breath when there wasn't an immediate reply. The dimensional flashed a smile toward me. "I've promised Cress to buy four of them. Though I still don't see why I need one."

"You do," the three of us said practically on top of one another.

"All right," he chuckled. "Perhaps our task will be brief and we can take a couple detours. I am in want of new armor."

I'd insisted on him donning a shirt for the sake of the stream. The hospital had a plain black one that fit him well enough. If he hadn't still been simmering from me suggesting he stay behind, he might've teased me about covering up. There'd been the glimmer of the idea in his eyes, at least, before he'd silently shrugged it on.

"If we can find a shop that still has something in stock," I sighed. As Wren had suggested, the storefronts we passed were completely looted. Most windows were smashed in, displays empty or turned over. We stopped at a corner mart to scavenge for crumbs, just to find a trio of ratlike unnaturals already in the process of doing just that.

We killed them without much issue, but Phaeron dragged their corpses out by their tails and lit the match to burn the pile of them on the sidewalk. "Leave nothing behind that she can consume," he muttered when Wren panned her camera from the spreading fire to his profile.

He turned away, beckoning for the group to follow him. "Now that we've encountered her creatures, we can be sure there are more nearby. Stealth is of the essence," he said.

"I'm great at stealth!" my handbook piped up next to my ear, startling me. It'd been so good on this trip until now.

I turned toward it, putting a finger to my lips. Together, we went "shhhhh."

"See, I know the routine," it squeaked smugly.

"Your shouting is going to get me killed one of these days," I whispered.

In reply, it alighted its spine on my left shoulder. "You love me, Cressie-poo," it replied, actually lowering its voice too.

Geo's wings opened with a scrape of rock. He cleared a small area and took to the sky, hopping from rooftop to rooftop above us as we headed for the place where our allies had had several skirmishes with the enemy. I knew it on sight due to the wreckage of a few cars sitting in the middle of an intersection. Judging by the number of lanes, this would be a busy thoroughfare if circumstances were different.

"Incoming," Geo announced. We bristled with spells and weapons, waiting for the space of a few quickened heartbeats before several humanoid figures poured out of a gaping car repair shop across the street, alongside many more unnaturals that used to be various animals.

I was merging with Braza's power all the while, clothed in her purple-black shadows and wearing a wolflike visage over my face. "We want to keep the people alive, if possible," Phaeron said before taking his own shadowborn form and leaping forward.

His shadows speared the nearest torchbearer, slamming him on his back and wrapping him in a layer of dark ropes. While struggling and gnashing his teeth, the man had his eyes wide open, staring at us. I could see why those who'd fought torchbearers thought they were zombies. His irises were bleached under a sheet of glowing white, unnatural and dead-seeming.

I cast Lux on my sword and joined the melee, warding away the bulbous birds dive-bombing my friends with a few swings of my light. The monsters were afraid as ever of my power, so I cast Luminaire with a warning shout, aiming to dazzle our enemies.

Monsters screamed, and torchbearers cowered, but words formed on their lips, dry whispers. "My lady," rasped one. Another begged for mercy.

I froze, my mouth hanging open for one dumbfounded moment. They thought I was Myuna?

"Shake it off," Braza warned. They quickly realized I wasn't the soul-eating goddess and stumbled back into the fighting. Something hit me from behind, and I fell face-first to the pavement, my sword clattering out of arm's reach.

A fist struck the back of my head, and stars danced in my vision. The same person who'd stunned me grabbed under my armpits and started to drag me away from the group. I recognized the first torchbearer's face. My light must have melted away the shadowy ropes that'd bound him.

Braza wanted to lengthen my fingers into talons and slash him, but I had an idea to try first. I called silently to my handbook, and it flew into my palm. I circled my fist in a figure eight and held it up, willing the Lux spell to pass through it.

The handbook flared open in my grip and emitted a spotlight of concentrated parchment-colored light into the torchbearer's face. He released me, and I stumbled back.

"Hah, take that! 'Tis I that is luminous now!" the book exclaimed.

A different figure nudged me aside. I saw the flash of Phaeron's sword, the attack checked just in time for the torchbearer's sake. He reached into midair close to the man's chest and went very still.

Braza's shadows flowed over my eyes, letting me see the knotted white ball he was pulling from the man. Phaeron passed me the hilt of his sword and took a deep breath. With both hands, he unraveled the mess of tangles the man's soul was tied in until it was a white globe being pushed back into his body.

The man collapsed in a boneless heap. I eyed him for a moment. "Did that work?" I asked dubiously.

"Later," Phaeron grunted.

The fighting was dying down around us, and he had a few more souls to disentangle. There wasn't much else for me to do except to gingerly grab one of the bird corpses by the edge of a wing to drag it toward the burn pile being formed on the street corner. Geo took it from me and lobbed it on top of the pile.

"Look, I'm a UFO!" my handbook exclaimed, hovering itself halfway open over a broken feather. A scorching ray emanated down from it, setting the feather's edges on fire.

My brows rose. "Well, that's useful," I said. I tucked the smoking feather into the burn pile for it to spread.

"Thank you. I pride myself on being *quite* useful!"

Braza cut off its Lux spell, to its great disappointment. With our merge, I didn't feel how much power my spells drew, but she shared how depleted my natural reserves would be just from having the handbook lit for a few minutes.

"This is why we don't set random tools alight," she said. I had the feeling she'd scold me if the effect wasn't so impressive.

I turned toward the stretch of street where Phaeron had laid out six people in total. He stood over them quietly while Wren filmed him, patiently waiting for him to say something. When I joined him, looking at them with Braza's soul sight, she told me, *"The bright white color of the souls within these supernaturals is highly abnormal."* No wonder Phaeron had such a dark look on his face.

"Do you see them?" he asked me.

"I do, but I'm not sure I understand what I'm seeing," I admitted.

He beckoned for me to kneel with him by one of the former torch-bearers. "Do you see the cracks?" he asked, switching to Soiluirian in a hush.

I nodded. If this person's soul was a piece of pottery, it'd been dropped from a low height and was barely holding itself together.

"That is soul damage. Myuna's work is crude. The process of binding this person's will nearly tore their soul in several places." He frowned, the picture of troubled.

"Does that mean they're going to die?" Braza spoke for me in Soiluirian.

"Probably. If they wake, it will be to great pain. All of these people will have died briefly and been reborn, so they are unnatural, Myuna's will or no. They will either succumb to their wounds or their hungers."

I thought of my sister with dread for her.

"If they are lucky, there's a small chance they will recover. In that case...we will have to study them before releasing them back into the community." When he looked over at me, I saw the serious prince, the man who'd led his people safely to another world. "Braza, we must contain them until we know where their fates land."

"Yes, my prince," she said.

"In the meantime, Myuna is probably improving on her soul binding skills. If she takes her time, the future torchbearers may have enough intelligence and presence to use their magic again," he said, shaking his head slowly. "If that happens, we will be overwhelmed."

He looked up at Wren and her camera, switching to English. "Our mission is successful. Cress and I will use shadow magic to take these people to a safe place, then we shall return to the hospital," he said.

23
CRESS

With the people we'd rescued resting in individual containment rooms and the sun setting by the time our group returned to the safety of the hospital, there was little to do but rest and wait for the next day.

Which started before five in the morning, practically a crime. Madigan flipped on the overhead light in my coven's shared room in the hospital and rapped her knuckles on her crystal-covered shoulder. "Up, all of you! We have a visitor," she announced.

We were having another odd slumber party crammed together in one room overnight. Well, most of us were. Phaeron had never settled, and Geo had remained in gargoyle form, going down to fight any creatures that sniffed around the grounds overnight.

"Mom," Roe groaned, covering her eyes with a forearm.

"A merman is asking for Willow," Madigan said.

That had the redhead's attention. Several of us moved quicker with the news and stole glances at our quiet friend. She seemed just as confused as I felt, though hope sparkled in her eyes as she murmured, "Maybe he will teach me something about how to control my magic."

"Do you know who he might be?" I asked her.

She replied with an exaggerated shrug. Oh joy...another surprise.

"We don't all have to see who it is," she protested a little belatedly when the rest of our coven was already heading downstairs.

"The sun's not even up, and he was important enough to wake all of us," Ben said, shrugging as he fell into step with Willow and me. "We'll all want to see what's up."

Madigan waited in front of the door to the boardroom we kept using for group meetings. "This concerns a matter of your identity. I'd be honored to sit beside you while you hear what this man has to say," she said to Willow.

"Of course. Everyone's welcome to be here if they want to be," she answered. She looked completely blindsided when she walked in first and the merman bowed to her from where he stood at the back of the room.

"Oh, um, hello," she said with a nervous laugh.

"Hey, it's that guy." Ben elbowed Willow, gesturing to the aquatic familiar she had bobbing over her shoulder in its own personal bubble of water. It was a cuttlefish, apparently, so skilled in changing its coloring on command that I'd never gotten a good look at it.

"You know him?" I whispered to Ben. We all filed in and had seats around the table, a full coven—plus Áine and Madigan—show of support for whatever this man wanted from Willow.

"He was at the familiar fair. You know, the one where she got a dude's number?" he whispered back.

Oh, yeah. Willow had blushed over the news of snagging a "totally cute" merman's number at the event. He was in his land form, wearing a damp wetsuit molded to his broad shoulders and carved muscles. Cerulean fish scales sparkled on his cheeks and forehead where skin met short navy-blue hair. Fins flapped in place of human ears.

There was a trident propped against the back wall. Unlike the delicate silver one Willow carried, this one was solid, built for skewering with a head marked by a few swirling runes. Mer magic.

Willow looked ready to crawl under the conference table. "Zander, what's going on?" she asked.

"I know this is going to sound unusual, especially with an audience," the merman said slowly. "Laiken, the Coral King, has sent me to find you, Willow. We strongly suspect you are his daughter."

Her mouth popped open. "What?" she gasped.

"Whoa there. On what evidence?" Madigan interjected.

He brushed a hand through his hair. "Okay, yeah, you all might be a little suspicious, and that's normal. The supernatural world watched the broadcast of the fight that led to most of the Crown Coven dying. At this point, every pixel has been scrubbed for information. The merfolk took an interest in you, Willow, and your sudden surge of power. By the abyss, even the gray color your scales manifested in the recording seems to suggest they belong to the royal line."

"Oh no," she whispered.

"It didn't take much digging to find your name and other important information. Your age and status as a half-mer are what really tipped off some of us that know the king. He tried to hide you from his enemies, but if we've found you, they have as well. For your safety, you need to come with me," he said.

She looked down at her hands. I thought she was ducking her head from the attention on her, but then she lifted her arm. Pinkish scales covered the back of it, along with a shimmery fin of the same color. "Does this match?" she asked. The moment her focus broke so she could speak, her mer side smoothed back into creamy, human skin.

"Coral red. Royal blood runs true through your veins...Princess," Zander said, bowing to her again.

"Congratulations, Willow," I said, the first to break the silence that followed, where most of us gaped between the two of them.

"Wait, no. This is crazy," she said, interrupting the belated chorus of congratulations that followed mine. Her palms hit the table. "For those of you who don't know, King Laiken is a demigod merman who rules from...well, all you need to know is that his territory encompasses the Coral Sea and a chunk of the Pacific. He doesn't have *kids*."

"That have survived to adulthood," Zander appended. "Whatever you've heard in school, the reality is far more gruesome. All of your half-siblings have been murdered, and you will be next without protection."

She breathed a disbelieving laugh. "I don't know a place farther from King Laiken's enemies than this pocket dimension. We have more to worry about than merfolk politics right now!"

"Really? Because merfolk politics is the only thing keeping Ocean Gate 438 open. We've been turning a blind eye when groups of unnatural hunters go in and survivors come out. All because the king is waiting for his daughter to return to safety," he said.

My mouth popped open at the implications. "All because of me?" Willow asked in a small voice. "But...if I go with you, he'll close it?"

"The moment you're through, Princess."

"What if the unnaturals realize it's open first?"

Zander quirked his lip. "If things here would grow too dire, I'm sure he would close it. But only if you refuse to leave and the evil goddess is heading for the gate."

Willow was practically sparkling as she turned to me. She gave me a meaningful look, one that promised she had an idea. "Cress," she whispered. "It's my time in the sun."

"I'd say so, Princess," I replied.

A flush didn't dim her toothy grin. "Thank you, Zander. I need some time to consider your offer and what to do next," she said to him. He hesitated, looking confused by her gentle dismissal.

"In the meantime, will you help me learn how to wield some of my magic?" she invited.

Willow remained with Zander, encouraging the rest of us to go back to sleep. I only left because she seemed to trust him and he was already holding a globe of water to begin a practice session she needed quite badly.

While everyone else filtered back to our shared room, I sat on the side of an upturned couch and closed my eyes, reaching for Braza over our soul tether. She'd left me when I'd fallen asleep, and my head seemed too quiet without her.

"Good morning, brightest of souls," she said.

"Hi, Braza. Do you want to come hang out?" The question seemed too casual, considering she was hitchhiking along in my body for this particular brand of "hanging out," but what else was I going to call it?

"Perhaps later. I sense you had an exciting morning."

I took a moment to show her the complete memory of the early wakeup and the merman's revelations for Willow. *"Do you know anything about the king they were talking about?"*

"I would ask a librarian, but..." After letting that hang for a moment, she laughed softly. *"I already know some. The affairs of mer didn't reach Moongrove Library often, but King Laiken is a particularly old figure. He was one of the last mer rulers to agree to relations with the greater supernatural community. His kingdom's wealth suffered for his decision. Such a thing breeds discontent."*

"Enough to have his family members murdered?" I demanded.

"Certainly. Up until now, he has been too powerful to kill. Not all demigod supernaturals are built the same. I can recommend some fascinating books on the lives and times of the truly godlike amongst us once we escape this pocket dimension."

"That sounds amazing." At this point, I'd even take a textbook to tuck into for an evening. I missed the escapism of reading.

"Phaeron is awake, by the way, and heading your way," she added. *"I gave him as much privacy as I could when he retired to the room you two shared the night prior."*

"Hopefully he slept," I said.

She withdrew from my awareness with a feeling of farewell. A few moments later, something tickled under my chin. Playful tendrils of shadow transformed into solid fingers attached to the Moihan dimensional who tilted my head up and leaned over to kiss me briefly.

"Do you need me to right this couch?" Phaeron asked. Though his eyes were lidded as if he'd just woken, purplish shadows were starting to color the hollows underneath them.

"Maybe if you lie down with me," I said seriously.

"Don't tempt me, bright soul. We are in public," he purred.

My breath hitched despite my concern for him, and I held up my index finger. "For a nap."

He lifted me by the hips and flipped the couch onto its feet with a twirl of his shadows.

"Showoff," I teased. The corner of his mouth lifted, but he didn't sit, not even when he placed me back down. "If you don't want to sleep, just resting for a while won't hurt. I'll tell you about the meeting you missed."

"Joy," he sighed but lowered onto the couch and held his arms out for me. He guided me so he was the big spoon, tucking my back to the line of his body. Our legs twined, and his breath ghosted over my ear. "You'll find that the older you get, the more meetings occupy your time."

"Madigan and Hana do seem to be in a lot of them," I said.

He hummed, nuzzling into my hair. I stifled a giggle at the sensation.

"Well, you might as well tell me why this one was different from all the rest," he murmured.

I told him of Willow's potential change in status as a mer princess, distracted quickly when he took the opportunity to pepper my earlobe on down to my jaw with playful nips. Hopefully this meant he wasn't angry at me anymore for yesterday's disagreement.

"I am not overly surprised," he rumbled close to my ear. There was no hiding my shiver, and I felt him smile. "Her mer side is powerful enough. Hybrid or no, it was impressive she nearly drowned several people upon unlocking that side of herself."

"Sure, but it's made her more afraid of what she can do. I hope Zander can teach her some control," I sighed. "In the meantime, you were in a different meeting and never told me the outcome."

"Which one was that?"

"You spoke with Geo and Ben privately," I prompted.

"Oh. I think you will be pleased."

"But, like, what did you all say?" I asked. "Did you get Geo to agree—"

He patted my hip. "Be right back."

His solid form turned to shadow, and he set me to sit upright rather than roll into the space he left behind. I sighed and rested my head back, taking my own advice and resting for the day ahead. Now that Braza had pointed it out, I recognized that he was going out of his way to change the subject.

Phaeron didn't take long to reform. His shadows tickled over my skin again before becoming firm fingers, tugging my hair to fall over the back of the couch. I sat up and glanced over my shoulder, seeing he'd retrieved a comb and a brush and something else coiled in his tail.

"Don't worry. They're yours," he said. He started brushing out my hair, gently teasing out the knots.

I flushed. "It's not that bad, is it?"

"Are Braza's memories still fading?" he asked in return. "You are my mate. It's my joy to care for your needs."

He brushed on, humming a merry but unfamiliar tune. When I tried to look back at him, he pressed his fingertips to my temples and steered my head to the angle he wanted. I tried to focus on what I remembered of Braza's life, some of the finer details slipping through my fingers like water. "You used to wear dark blue on your face and horns."

"A couple lifetimes ago, yes."

"If you want to teach me the symbols...I could try drawing them on your horns," I offered.

"Soon." He stooped to kiss my temple. "I am the definition of 'at war' right now and should not wear any adornments."

"But when Myuna is dead..."

He breathed a wistful sigh. "If you are comfortable observing this part of my culture, I would love to be marked as a mated male once more."

"Of course," I breathed, sensing this meant a lot more to him than he was willing to put into words.

I barely felt the plastic edge of the comb as he divided my hair into sections. "Though I suppose you would have to source gold stain for the task. But maybe I'm overthinking it. I'm not sure it will matter as much as it used to."

"Gold is for the king?" I guessed.

"First prince," he answered. "Paradoxically, my parents were able to wear whatever color they desired. And yet every day, they had servants paint their faces with white stain."

"Wait—"

"Hold still," he chuckled. He started braiding my hair.

"But you should be the king," I said. There was an extra tickle on my scalp from his shadows moving with his fingers. I had the feeling he was about to tie my hair into a complicated style.

"And yet I have no intentions of ever being a king. The nation that joined the tribes of my people was poisoned by Myuna's influence. I want nothing to do with it. Besides...the world has moved on while I was in stasis, and my people have too. There *is* no throne to take." He almost sounded happy about it, so I simply shrugged.

"If that's your decision. About your parents…" I bit my lip.

"I'll tell you anything you wish to know. Much of it is unflattering," he said.

"They were torchbearers?" I asked.

"Indeed. She did not turn them fully white like she did my brother, but they were the strongest followers she had. They shared animaris after an age of ruling to satisfy Myuna and earn her continued favor. The goddess was pleased to groom Endaeron, and they were quite happy to have yielded an heir and a spare on their first try. They pursued their own interests afterward."

"Does that bother you?"

"Not anymore. When I was a child, I longed for the love heaped on my brother and wondered why Myuna had overlooked me. But it makes sense now. If Endaeron had died before the Age of Decay, I would've taken his place as first prince and been corrupted by her magic in his stead. At one point, I'd have thought it an honor," he said with a scoff. "But without her blessing, I was never truly his rival when he lived. Now that he is a monster, it doesn't matter."

He was braiding the tips of my hair, so when I looked over my shoulder at him, he didn't move my head back a third time. "Still, you never should've been made to feel lesser."

He flashed a reassuring smile. "It is something I am at peace with. Almost done, by the way."

"Time for one more question?"

"As many as you desire," he answered in his effortless purr.

"What is animaris?"

"Ah." There was a wicked gleam in his topaz eyes. "As a rough translation, it is essence or life force, something my kind puts to use that yours does not. Males naturally have more than females due to how we reproduce. I know humans can get pregnant at most any time past puberty, but for my people, it is a conscious choice nurtured by both sides through a pregnancy. Animaris follows the lifecycle of the child. First, it's an aphrodisiac for the mother."

He released my braid and slid closer. I propped myself on my knees, turning to rest my arm on the top of the couch to face him directly. "How is it shared?" I asked, feeling a bit of warmth rise to my cheeks.

I'd given him a great opening to rest his fangs on my neck. His hot breath fanned over my exposed nape, and I stilled. Was this a test? Heat pooled between my legs as he drew his tongue over my skin, lips skimming my pulse point.

"Usually the same place as a mating mark," he answered. With a groan, he jerked away from me and shook his head.

He spoke while staring at my neck, which I covered with my fingers. "Anyway, once the child is made, both parents continuously share animaris to encourage growth in the womb. Since hybrids don't exist for my people, the baby usually takes after the father, as this is the stage where he's sharing energy while the mother shares nutrients. Once they are born, both parents are tethered to the child equally until they enter adolescence and their own soul and animaris is fully formed."

I beckoned for him to come sit with me, and he grew rigid, shuttering his eyes for a few long moments. "I just remember Braza was an unhappy child because of animaris," I said.

"Mmm, the lack thereof. She was small for being of the Iorsio tribe. We never had a chance..." He drifted off with a look of pain.

"Phaeron?" I murmured.

"Children can be adopted in such a way that blood ties do not matter," he continued.

"You can talk about her. I mean, you don't have to avoid your old mate's name for my sake," I said, though my heart was in my throat.

This time, he did come sit down and drew my hands into his. "Cress, talking about past mates is unkind. Anything I tell you will make you wonder if I am comparing you or if I still think of her."

"It would be cruel to expect you not to ever think about her or the daughter you had."

That look of pain sharpened. I didn't know if Phaeron could cry, but by the defined facets I saw within the glowing depth of his eyes, he was close. "I'm sorry... I shouldn't have mentioned..." I stammered.

"Keshora," he breathed out. "Ravai. And Braza. The family Myuna purposefully destroyed. *My* family."

I gave his hands a squeeze in sympathy. "It was a beautiful one," I said.

He wet his lips, considering me for a few moments. "You would have liked Keshora. She was a kind soul. What you didn't see from Braza's memories was how heartbroken she was when her application to adopt Braza was denied. I felt it halfway across a continent, fighting in one of my old nation's constant pointless wars. Keshora loved and desired children more than anything."

He hesitated, reading my face again. I smiled some in encouragement. "That's where she was very different from you. But she was well into her hundredth year when we met, while you're just getting started," he said.

"Does that feel weird to you?" I asked with a nervous quaver.

He leaned over to touch his forehead to mine. "You have incredible potential, bright soul, and that means you will be my equal. I just get the honor of helping you reach that pinnacle. My body recognized you as my mate, my True Light, immediately," he answered. I breathed out with relief. It seemed he knew exactly what to say to make my heart shimmer. "That is destiny and nothing less. What *is* weird to me is you wearing half of Braza's power. Having you both in the same body is..." He tisked lightly.

"She gives us privacy," I said.

"She is a powercore. There is no privacy," he countered.

I raised a brow. "Okay, she's your daughter."

"One who I have failed immeasurably," he murmured. He looked over at a group of defenders coming and going from the front entrance. It was a shift change, and amongst the Crystal fae was Geo in his gargoyle form. He spotted us and started for where we were sitting.

"What do you mean? She still adores you," I said. He just had to look at everything she'd done for him lately to prove it.

"I was not strong enough to say goodbye to her. I so desperately wanted her...to live..." Phaeron cocked his head, looking at Geo strangely.

I hardly noticed, though, standing and holding my arms out to Geo. His face lit up, and he took his human form before lifting and whirling me around. "Good morning, beautiful," he said.

"Safe and sound because of you." I shared a kiss with him once he placed me back on my feet.

I expected Phaeron to have disappeared, like he so often did when I took my eyes off him for a moment too long. Except this time, he was where I'd left him. "Take her away if you please. She must be getting tired of my stories by now," he said.

"Okay." After a pause, Geo reconsidered and added, "We will be at breakfast. Come with us and get your ration."

My astonishment must've been obvious, as Phaeron winked before Geo laced his fingers with mine and tugged me along to get some essential calories for the day ahead.

24
PHAERON

WE ATE breakfast in a waiting room with Cress's coven, as the hospital's tiny cafeteria was already packed full of defenders and staff members gulping down their rations before getting to work. The witches were quite excited. Breakfast was bacon and eggs.

Cress had gotten plenty of compliments for the formal braid I'd given her, with rows of tiny, hearty wildflowers tied just behind her ears. I was rather proud of my handiwork. She sat between Geo and me, taking slow, distracted bites while she chatted with Willow, who'd perched in a seat across from us.

"We can just announce that Ocean Gate 438 is open and ask for backup. I bet you people will come," Willow was saying. "My maybe-father won't close it unless I go through it, so why not get some help?"

"It would be unwise," I said in as gentle a tone as I could muster. I could see she was in delicate spirits, excited to contribute and help. "We need specific help. If you put a call out to the greater supernatural world, the first people to arrive through that ocean gate will be young glory seekers and a handful of demigods foolish enough to think they can take Myuna on directly. They will only feed her and make her stronger."

Willow's face fell. "But—"

"How will we even separate the help we want versus the help that arrives?" Geo asked.

"Easily enough. We don't ask for help," I said. Cress had been in the earlier meeting where we'd discussed this already and nodded tentatively. "The fewer living souls inside Cerris City, the better. If we truly wish to take advantage of Ocean Gate 438, we will evacuate the whole city, including the staff at this hospital. We'd scare the bounty hunters into returning to where they came from. No one remains except those absolutely necessary to our mission."

Dubious glances turned my way from every witch in earshot. I folded and crunched down a whole strip of bacon, waiting. The salt and fat exploded on my tongue just right, and I closed my eyes from simple pleasure. I could've eaten a whole side of bacon rather than the two sad strips each of us had been rationed.

"If all of our support leaves," Geo said slowly, "who will remain to take care of Myuna and her monsters?"

Roe, sitting close enough to pick up the conversation, pitched in, "There's no way everyone can be evacuated, no matter how far-reaching Wren's stream is. Too many people will die if you're thinking we leave too and collapse the pocket dimension behind us."

"I didn't say we flee. I'm not convinced Myuna can be erased so easily, anyway." I didn't hide the troubled twist to my mouth. "What if the fabric of Cerris City rips around her as it collapses? It will be the Age of Decay all over again, but *much* worse with such a huge population of unaware humans facing a hungry cosmic deity."

"We don't know that will happen," Roe said.

"We don't know it won't," I countered. "Auric et Vess has a plan to return Myuna to Soiluire. It will not require an army to carry out. All we have to do is get him close enough to her to manipulate the Void that clings to her like a second skin."

Willow stroked her chin thoughtfully. "Going back to getting as many people out of Cerris City as possible. We could use the stream for announcing a gathering point and avoid mentioning the ocean gate."

"Indeed. But we must be prepared to fight. We will face the majority of Myuna's forces, as the unnaturals will follow survivors or sense a big group of us and attack. When we win, we break up the flow of unwilling servants into her service and destroy what she's already amassed. She will be forced into the one thing she doesn't want to do…" I bared my fangs in a bloodthirsty grin. "To get up and fight for herself."

Cress worried her lip. "But if we lose…"

"We'd be completely fucked, right?" Willow murmured. "We'd deliver everyone left in Cerris City to Myuna's monsters."

"We won't lose. We can't," Roe said, punching her palm.

"We won't," I echoed, looking over Cress's head at Geo. He raised an eyebrow back. "We need to gather some resources before this fight."

"Such as?" he prompted.

"Armor, weapons, food, water. I would strike out on my own, but I need Cress with me," I said.

A dangerous rumble sounded from the gargoyle's throat.

"Which means you need to come too," I concluded.

"Count me in," Roe said. Not to be left out, as always. "Where are we going?"

I drew a folded map out of my pocket. I'd nicked one from a tourist display that was running low on them since most were pinned on the wall of the makeshift war room. Unfolding it, I pinched its corners with a few tendrils of shadow and floated it between us. "Highfall's Mall. Too far away for us to walk there. I know you want to help, Roe…but this is a mission for the three of us. If we run into danger, Cress and I can blend into the shadows, while Geo can fly."

"Hey, what about me?" Ben called. He sat with Wren, the two of them bent over a set of paper notes covered in basic celestial witch runes.

"And we carry Ben along to manage the stream," I added.

Wren narrowed her eyes, and Roe shifted uncomfortably at my suggestion. But we were simply too large of a group to cover the ground I wanted to see tonight.

"If you break my phone, I'll break you," Wren grumbled.

I chuckled. "We will bring back as many new phones as we can carry."

I reached down to take my other piece of bacon, and my thumb skimmed three. Cress stole a quick glance my way and covered her lips with her fingers, a subtle enough tell as to where they'd come from.

I curled my tail tip around her calf for a small caress. If only we had time for more than mere teases. *Soon,* I told myself.

Hopefully she and the other two men would be willing to go along with the rest of my plan once we were en route.

"Are you sure about this?" Cress asked, stealing glances upward. Myuna's foul bird creatures lined the roofs, watching our truck drive by with unblinking white stares.

Geo could've flown ahead of us and chased them off, but I needed him here to listen to my full plan. At my request, he remained in human form in the seat behind Cress. She drove. When our options were her or Ben, her caution was the preferable choice.

Our allies had lent us one of the largest flatbeds for what they thought was a supply run. Highfall's Mall was outside of the territory that'd been searched for survivors. It sat at the edge of the pocket dimension, a mega-sized structure sure to already be looted and occupied.

The truck hit a bump in the road, jostling us. I stifled a growl, already disliking the confines of this cabin. "Myuna has a special interest in you and me. If she is aware we have split off from the rest of the group, there's a higher chance she will send her strongest servant after us," I answered.

Ben said through gritted teeth, "*Garroway.*"

"You want to use me as bait again?" Cress asked dryly.

"We are both bait this time. If we are out after nightfall in a prominent public place, we can compel Myuna to send him," I said.

Geo's frown deepened. "I did not agree to this trip to put Cress in danger."

"Wait, Geo, put that aside for a moment," Ben said, turning in his seat to look at the gargoyle. "This is our chance to finally turn Garroway into ash."

The look of disapproval slowly morphed on Geo's face. He blew out a slow sigh. "As always, it seems I am the only one saying no to a reckless plan," he grumbled. "But I have wondered why we have not yet seen Garroway and the Hunger. They could decimate the survivors we've gathered in the hospital if given half a chance."

"They will once there are no easier options to steal and deliver to Myuna. She is still acting like her old, predictable self, going for the lowest-hanging fruit first," I said.

"Once we evacuate survivors through the ocean gate, there won't be many of those left," Cress said.

"Exactly. There is no better way to fight him than on our own terms."

And this time, I would snuff out the Hungering Darkness completely. I had hesitated too many times before, seeing it as the remains of my brother more than the shade that'd murdered and consumed hundreds of innocents. It was time I ripped its remaining soul in half...see how it failed to cope with such a devastating wound.

Cress smiled after a moment, saying in a two-toned voice full of forced levity, "Plus, if we have to wait for nightfall...shopping spree!"

"Everything left is free," Ben agreed.

Even Geo cracked a little grin. "Park the truck right by the doors to load it up."

And I will ensure no unnaturals disturb your fun, I thought.

Bella meowed at me, her eyes wide and concerned from where she rested belly up in the crook of my arm. "Everything's okay, baby," Cress cooed toward her familiar. The other two cats were in the back, napping with Ben's ferret. "Except...if I knew we were going after Garroway, I wouldn't have brought my familiars at all."

"We will keep an eye on them," I said. It was the only thing we could do, since Myuna was corrupting animals big and small to serve her. But they were more than just pets. They could help Cress and Ben fight by letting them borrow an ounce of feline grace or another attribute through the familiar bond.

With the help of Wren's phone, we arrived at Highfall's Mall in a short time. Ben placed a small device in his ear and tapped his thumbs across the phone's screen. "Hey, Tish, we're here," he said, speaking to seemingly no one. "No shit? The power's out in the whole building?"

"Don't turn the stream on until we know what we're dealing with," I said to him before ghosting out of the vehicle as shadows. I stretched as the others climbed out, and Ben muttered "showoff" in my direction.

"I've grown to master a proper entrance or exit in my time," I said.

"Proper? Try dramatic," he replied. "Well, this is your kind of place,

Big P. We're going blind into the dark. Tish can't find a single camera online to warn us of what's inside."

He pointed through a set of glass doors, where the insides of the mall were shrouded in darkness. "I'll do some scouting. Stay here," I said, turning to shadows before anyone could air a complaint.

I felt for the small tether of power connecting me to Braza. Neither of us had severed it, even once my free will was returned. It gave me a good idea of how far I could travel before my mind was susceptible to Myuna or Endaeron.

That thread grew taut before I was done scouting the whole complex. It was four stories of shops, play areas, and kiosks. The lights were out and the air stale. I'd expected survivors and detected none... but Myuna's creatures had infested the food court and restaurants, while her torchbearers shuffled along like sleepwalkers in the common areas. I unbound the souls of the two nearest the entryway, then dragged their unconscious bodies into my shadows.

Cress's eyes widened when I took form in the blinding sunlight and laid the former torchbearers in the bed of the truck. "Seems we have something to occupy our time after all," I said, sharing with the group what I'd seen.

"Once we take care of all the torchbearers, I could drive them back to the library?" Ben suggested.

"Perhaps. I don't like the idea of splitting up further," I said. The first batch I'd unbound from Myuna's will still rested in their containment rooms without waking. These victims had a similar level of soul damage, unfortunately. Early victims of the goddess's sloppy work.

Cress drew her sword and handbook and set the edge of her blade alight. It'd be a beacon for any unnatural the moment she stepped into the mall. Geo nudged his way in front of her after transitioning to gargoyle form, holding his tower shield and a mace made from his quartz spikes. And Ben announced he was turning on the stream, placing the phone in a sling over his chest.

"Yeah, I hear you," he muttered while he drew blood runes up his arm. "I don't need you chattering in my ear, Bianca... Uh huh, fuck you too. For those early watchers, hi, it's Ben. Today we're going extreme shopping."

I shook my head, bemused by the whole idea of streaming. "Ready?" I asked.

Cress, now wearing the purple-black shadows of Braza's power, nodded first. She wrapped a concentration of darkness around her blade to dim it.

I hissed toward Ben for quiet and pointed at the nearest shopfront. A sheet of what looked like chain-lengths covered up the entrance, except a huge hole had been ripped through the metal. Dozens of white eyes turned our way from the bowels of what'd once been a restaurant.

Geo charged, catching the first lunging rat-creature with a swing of his weapon. It died with a piercing squeal, and I hung back, hearing the death cry echo further into the enemy-infested mall.

Footsteps pounded their way toward us. I raised both hands, warping the shadows into grasping things. Three more turned supernaturals threw themselves into my snares. I made quick work of unbinding their souls and was about to carry them through the shadows to our truck when a flash of green brushed the back of my hand.

Stinging pain followed the line of a two-inch long cut. I swirled into the shadows, passing through a second shot of green magic while searching for the culprit. A verdant witch clutching a wand stooped just behind a counter, her white eyes roaming for where I'd gone. I reappeared behind her, and she froze as my claws tugged her soul free.

I clucked my tongue as I inspected the loose knot her soul had been tied into. Just as I'd feared—Myuna was figuring out how not to destroy her victims utterly during the binding process. We'd have to be more careful to weed out intelligent torchbearers. There were countless hiding spaces in this mall for ambushes.

The others were waiting for me when I returned with the verdant witch's unconscious body. *"Trouble, my prince?"* Braza asked privately.

I answered her aloud for the sake of the group. "Perhaps this location is too infested with Myuna's victims. That last witch still had access to her magic. Imagine if there are many more like her... We will exhaust ourselves clearing out the mall before nightfall."

"I think we should try it," Cress said. "Imagine if we gained control of the mall and used it as a rendezvous point for survivors."

I shrugged and gathered up the unconscious torchbearer to deliver her to the truck. In the meantime, Cress talked to Geo and Ben. The former expressed a desire for us to leave before nightfall, while the latter wanted a good fight.

The familiars were distracted by a game of chase around their witches' feet, with Flit outpacing them. He used me as an obstacle when I took a knee, scaling my leg and squirming when I caught him and placed him on the ground.

"I know you can understand me," I said. Four sets of eyes blinked up at me, quite keen for a set of animals. "Your task is to stay close to your witch and avoid capture at all costs."

Flit bobbed his head and moved to stand by Ben's feet. Bella purred and brushed my leg, tail up, while Jin meowed in response. "They're saying they understand," Cress translated.

"Let's see how we feel after a couple hours of this, then," I said, standing.

The beast of shadows and teeth hiding just under my skin relished the idea of a true fight. I would've eagerly taken on the challenge ahead of us on my own if it weren't for the hole in my soul and the consequences that came with it.

Cress lit the way for Ben and Geo while I prowled at the edges of her magic. I had to turn my head away from her radiance. It made my mouth water. Another reason to despise the Hungering Darkness, for infecting me with this desire to taste my mate's soul. It was truly relentless.

I pitched my frustrations into the intermittent fights that followed. It took less than an hour for us to travel to the top floor and clear it, though I spent a significant amount of time afterward forming a burn pile of slain unnaturals and filling the truck bed with unconscious torchbearers. One of us would have to return to the library sooner than expected.

Chill wind kissed my face, and I risked a glance at the sky as clouds skidded over the sun. An angry gray storm flowed toward us from the horizon, moving impossibly fast on magic-kissed gales. With that realization came a pricking sensation over my scalp. The ghost of white talons trying to burrow into my skull.

The Hungering Darkness was coming.

25
CRESS

"Totally chic, don't you think?" I asked Braza, eyeing the dress displayed on one of the last standing mannequins in a storefront. We were taking a quick break while Phaeron cleaned up the mess we'd made of the unnatural nests we'd stomped.

"You should try it on. Dark colors look nice on you," she answered in my head.

"Maybe if we get a chance to shop." I practically pouted. Maybe it was my entitlement showing, but I'd hoped the mall would've been relatively empty and untouched. A shopping spree in a mega mall with just my men and Braza? *Yes, please.*

"Are you talking to yourself again?" my handbook asked, fluttering in for a landing on top of my head.

"Quiet. There are still monsters," hissed Jin. I stooped to scratch her behind the ears, and she loosed a soft purr, leaning into my fingertips.

"Is the kitty mad at me?" my handbook asked in a loud whisper.

I put a finger to my lips, and again, we went "shhhh" at the same time.

Braza crackled with electric surety. *"Something's wrong."*

I lifted my weapon and spun, looking for the danger. Ben and Geo stirred nearby, alert within moments. Over the sound of my breath, I could hear the calls of unnaturals on the levels below us, plus the sound of claws on tile. "They're on the move," I murmured.

Phaeron took form from shadows just as I was smothering my blade's glow. A crazed glint flashed in his gemstone eyes, his teeth bared in a snarl. Braza reacted first, throwing out a wave of energy that suffused him within moments.

He flinched and grasped his head. With my weapon dimmed, he was nearly one with the dark mall around us. "Endaeron is almost here," he growled.

A winged shape dive-bombed us. The creature, a former seagull with a puffed-out chest like a water balloon, released a shrill scream. It exploded with a wet sound when Geo smashed it on the flat of his shield. "Myuna is not content to wait for nightfall," he rumbled.

"Much as I want to fuck up Garroway...we're outnumbered," Ben pointed out.

Thunder rumbled overhead. Rain began to aggressively patter against the ceiling.

"I moved the torchbearers we rescued to the entrance foyer," Phaeron said. I heard the rasp of his sword leaving its sheath. "It's too late to retreat."

"Then it's time we stood and fought." Despite everything, Ben smiled. There was a sound of glass cracking, and then he had purple liquid on his fingertips, using it to paint a bold eye symbol between his brows.

Geo took to the air with a heave of his obsidian body. There was an outraged series of shrieks that followed, accompanied by the sound of groaning metal. I encouraged Braza's shadows over my face, parting the impenetrable darkness to spot what he'd done. He'd dropped his considerable weight in the middle of the closest escalator, buckling it in half and stranding the torchbearers that were halfway up its stationary length.

Dozens of hands grabbed for the gargoyle, dragging him off balance toward the seething mass of unnaturals.

"He can handle himself," Braza reassured me. A split second later, he'd taken to the air again, shaking off a doskalo-like creature trying to cling to his ankle. It dropped for a hard landing a floor below.

Every prickling length of her shadows had gone taut with awareness, pressing into my skin with an electric sense of danger. The Hungering Darkness was somewhere close, its presence swirling over our heads in search of an opening.

"Go hide," I whispered to Jin, who scampered away but not too far, hunkering down with the other familiars. I could still feel my connection to her, the ferocity I could borrow if I needed it. Bella could grant me her enhanced senses, while Milo preferred to lend his feline grace. In a pinch, their contributions could change the momentum of a fight.

"Geo!" I shouted. We needed him here, with us. He was in the process of destroying the other escalator, set a few yards away from the first. It wouldn't stop the unnatural infestation below us, but they would have to find another route to the top floor.

White shadows took form right in front of me. Garroway moved like a blur, striking my sword right out of my hand with a full-strength snap of his own blade. The Lux spell sputtered out, throwing our surroundings into dim murk. The relentless gray storm overhead prevented any natural light from interfering.

Phaeron charged him with a shadowborn's roar, shattering the air with his fury and the ring of metal on metal. I sent out a tendril of Braza's shadows to retrieve my sword by its hilt and turned to Ben. The mark on his forehead glowed a faint purple. "Can you see with that?" I asked, pointing at it.

"Kind of," he answered.

"Good enough," I said, then leapt forward in full shadowborn form to join the duel of black and white shadows.

Phaeron had been edged back from the combination of Endaeron's power and Garroway's vampire strength and speed. He attacked with bladed shadows, distracting Garroway for a key moment. I slipped my weapon into the vampire's guard, spraying dark blood from a slash just above his ribs.

But the rip of flesh began to knit together. Skin and blood reattached before my eyes, a sickening sight that reminded me of how a blood witch healed from a mending rune. In seconds, all that was left was the blood on his skin and the rip in his clothes.

He'd turned to glare in my direction. "Cress, at last. How I've grown to despise you," he said in a two-toned voice. White shadow flashed in my face, forming thorny tendrils that bound my upper arms to my chest.

"The feeling's mut—"

His magic ensnared and moved me; I squeezed my eyes shut just in time, struggling out of his shadows. We'd traveled down a level, and I was a few feet above the ground when I freed myself of his magical grasp. I crashed to the unforgiving tile with my arms still pinned to my side, pain flaring through my hip and leg.

What felt like a hundred sets of eyes turned hot attention toward me. Unnatural creatures and torchbearers alike leapt the moment I landed. Panicking for a moment, I released a shout of alarm, only drawing more attention to myself. Braza took over to help and made shadowy claws over my fingers, which I used to cut through the bindings he'd left on me. They dissipated into white wisps before fading, leaving bright spots over my vision.

I stood and drew my sword, squaring up against an onslaught of monsters. As I debated fleeing, an obsidian figure swooped in for a landing and faltered, lost in the dimness of our surroundings.

"Light," he ground out. I cast a quick Lux on my sword, and the monsters winced. Geo kicked the closest raccoon-like creature away before it could sink its teeth into my shadows and flesh. He lifted his shield and spread his wings, blocking a handful of torchbearers and their grasping hands from reaching me.

A warning jolt of pain radiated down from my jarred hip when I moved to cover his back. *"I shall repair you. We must rejoin the prince before Endaeron tries to take his mind,"* Braza said with urgency. We both noticed the duel of black and white above us, occasionally punctuated by the flash of a silvery throwing dagger or a hint of Ben's blood magic infusing a strike.

No one was fighting alone, at least. I helped Geo with waves of light and shadow, shooting out darkness with many sharp edges to strike at the creatures surrounding us.

I cowed the torchbearers by blinding them with a flare from my weapon. They babbled, begging Myuna for mercy as they clawed at their eyes.

"Your goddess says stand down," I ordered with as much authority I could muster. A family of four—two adults and two kids of different ages—the nearest white-eyed people, dropped their hands and stayed in place, looking confused.

Geo hesitated before pivoting, showing no mercy for the twisted animals still throwing themselves at us. The blunt force of his fighting style crunched stretched bones and strained tendons. It left a graveyard around him, shattered bodies tripping the torchbearers that were still trying to get through him to me.

We could try to save them, unlike the animals. As long as Phaeron survived this fight, he could unbind their souls. "I'm going up! Come with me!" I shouted to Geo before falling into the shadows, letting Braza control the magic that turned us into particles.

In a blink, we cleared the guardrail one story up, just in time to see Garroway catch one of Ben's daggers and reverse its course, embedding it in his chest. I heard the sucking gasp he took as he fell backward.

"Stay alive a bit longer, little Benjamin. We have unfinished business," Garroway said in a two-toned drawl.

Ben bared his teeth with another gasping breath. He probed at the wound and wrote the rune for healing on his skin with a shaking hand. I placed myself between him and the possessed vampire, sinking into a guard stance.

"As do we, blood baron," Phaeron snarled.

He reengaged Garroway's attention, lifting his sword to check the vampire's next strike. Several new rips decorated his shirt, most over superficial wounds that leaked his fuchsia blood. The worst one was just under his armpit, where it would cause him trouble in an already difficult fight.

In life, he and Endaeron had been fairly evenly matched with swordplay and shadows. But in death, Endaeron had the advantage of Garroway's preternatural healing and other attributes to help him when he was outnumbered four to one.

I prepared to leap back into the fray. Braza pulled at my awareness, asking for a few more moments as I tested my wounded leg. Her power had turned the lingering ache into a smaller pinch of pain.

Garroway tilted his head. "Ah, yes. So we do. My lady is quite displeased to have you off your leash—"

Phaeron's attention drifted for a split second before he disengaged in a swirl of black shadows, which stirred in the wake of Geo arriving like a battering ram. He checked his momentum with stony wings and slammed shield-first into Garroway, sending him straight through a glass storefront.

I lined up just a step behind Geo as he and Phaeron faced the ragged hole together, forming a wall of muscle and rock. But the Hungering Darkness didn't emerge as a corporeal vampire, instead escaping as a curl of white shadow.

"Behind you!" Ben called in a strained voice.

I whirled around just in time to see Garroway's sword descending toward my head. He'd taken a page out of Phaeron's playbook of tricks to use his shadows to appear in a blind spot. The first to react properly was Phaeron, who caught the swing of the weapon with his own.

His shadowborn form bared its lengthened fangs. "You will not harm my mate," he snarled. "This is the end, Endaeron."

I called on Jin, borrowing from the core of fury she held for the creature that'd killed her first witch. That fierce desire for revenge filled me. I moved with sinewy grace to dance between them as the two men reengaged their stalemate. Phaeron pressed the attack, and so did I, wounding Garroway when he wasn't able to hold us both off at the same time.

When the vampire's sword strayed too close to me, he met the edge of Geo's shield or the swing of his mace. My stony protector moved with me rather than the two nimble swordsmen, covering any avenue that might lead to my harm.

Garroway's wounds were beginning to stick, his vampiric healing overwhelmed by his mounting injuries. It was a matter of time before he started slowing, bogged down by pain. He wasn't going to win this fight, even with Ben recuperating. A flash of understanding lit his blood-colored eyes before he turned to white mist.

"Is there any way to stop him from running?" I asked Braza.

"Patience, brightest of souls. Turn off Lux for a moment."

I did as she suggested, shaking the lingering light out of my weapon. Now that I wasn't actively fighting, Geo shouldered in front of me, shield raised for whatever came next.

"Lick your wounds, then. Coward," Phaeron spat, watching Garroway circle overhead, just beyond our reach.

"As I was saying." Without physical lungs, the dry rasp of a voice

speaking telepathically had to be the Hungering Darkness. *"Myuna desires your return. And she is practically salivating for the soul of the purple-haired witch."*

"She can have neither." Phaeron bristled with power, more and more darkness answering to his will. Without the light of my weapon in the way, he beckoned a wave of shadows. A tide of blackness swarmed over the curl of white shadow and dragged it back to the ground. Upon impact, it became Garroway again, struggling against several loops of inky rope binding his body and forcing its way into his mouth, nostrils, and eyes.

"Why must you struggle against the inevitable?" hissed the Hungering Darkness, independent of its host body's choking and writhing. White light flared around Garroway, and Phaeron staggered, clutching his head.

Braza forced a steady stream of power into him through the invisible tether between them. Geo spread his wings to block me from going to him, rumbling dangerously when Phaeron turned. White flared over the yellow in his eyes.

"You shall not harm her," Geo said.

"Just one taste." The psychic whisper was chilling when I realized Phaeron was compelled by it.

He echoed, "Just one taste."

Garroway was getting to his feet, shaking off the choking shadows. White shadows made extra fangs around his victorious grin as Phaeron evaded around Geo's wide stance, rushing straight toward me.

I backed away instinctively from the visage of a predator on the hunt. Before Phaeron could lunge through the remaining distance between us, Geo grabbed his shoulder, fingers digging in hard as the dimensional struggled and bit him, though his shadowborn fangs slid ineffectively off the gargoyle's stone arm. Already, his form softened at the edges, threatening to slip into the shadows and out of Geo's grasp.

"This isn't you. Come back to me." I was begging, fumbling for the mark of protection he'd left on my wrist. I touched it and breathed his name.

Phaeron froze, tilting his head. It was impossible to read his expression under the black shadows that made up his shadowborn form. The white shadows that blazed through the holes for his eyes flared brighter. Was that the Hungering Darkness digging in, forcing his will into my mate's skull?

I circled my thumb on his mark, breathy with fright. "Your True Light needs you."

A snarl of rage left his fanged maw. He drew on his magic for a burst of strength and ripped away from Geo. The gargoyle fumbled and cursed viciously, rushing toward me.

I lifted my hands defensively, shadowy claws out, and braced for impact. No matter how fast Geo was, Phaeron could relocate himself in a blink. But instead of going for me again, Phaeron had turned around and sunk his teeth deep in the white shadows over Garroway's shoulder.

There was no mistaking how he jerked his head to the side, tearing at the Hungering Darkness like an animal. My mouth dropped open in shock. "Oh, fuck," I whispered, fearing the worst for him.

A cloud of white magic enveloped Phaeron. He was a horned shadow crouching within the heart of it, unmoving.

Garroway staggered to the side, clutching his head and his blood-stained sword. He looked around and took in his surroundings, mouth twisting into a sneer. "Well, then," he muttered.

He turned and fled in a blur of speed.

PHAERON

I tore the Hungering Darkness down the middle, just like it'd done to Braza's soul so long ago. When I'd envisioned myself destroying it so utterly, I hadn't dreamed of using my teeth or swallowing a mouthful of the vapors that spurted from the wound like blood.

With that taste, I was damned. So many of my people had started an addiction to the rush of energy and memory within a soul with just one bite. It became a craving that couldn't be slaked except by death. There was no coming back from it once one of us has destroyed the soul of another.

I gave thanks that instead of drinking in the spice and sunlight of

Cress's soul, it was what remained of my brother's spirit tearing between my teeth. His memories suffused my mind as the white magic keeping him stitched together failed.

I would've expected him to taste of blood and grave dirt, as painful deaths were the only thing he'd wrought ever since the Age of Decay, but Endaeron was not an ordinary soul, not even when it was only a portion of him left behind. A smooth alcoholic taste suffused my mouth; it was Endaeron's favorite blend, something we'd left behind on Soiluire...akin to an aged whisky.

I felt my awareness fall deeper and deeper out of my body.

A jolt passed through my mind. I opened my eyes, finding myself in a distantly familiar room with that whisky taste on my tongue. And next to me, a figure I'd forgotten yet never could. Endaeron, alive, taller than me. He was ivory-white horns to feet, broad with icy wings shot through with silver blood in his veins. Gold stain limned his forward-facing horns and the angles of his face.

He was in his prime, the First Prince in his suit of white fabric, with the golden symbol of a shadowborn on the breast. Though technically, it was "lightborn" in his case, with his white shadows.

I stilled, and my breath caught. "Brother," I said, like this memory would turn to speak with me.

To my shock, he did. His face tilted down, his white-lined eyes meeting mine. "Brother," he echoed, deep and sure. "Our time is short and your needs are great, so I have selected this memory for you to witness before I fade."

I became aware of the scene around us in a blink, dropped into it as a bystander. Endaeron stood by Myuna's right hand, with me inserted on his other side. In this memory, she was in the form of an Iorsio tribe female, seated on a massive throne in one of her many private rooms. A Vrassorm woman knelt before her, her skin nearly as pale as the goddess from what she witnessed within a globe of black Void energy.

"Well? What does the Void whisper of my future?" Myuna asked in her awful multi-layered voice.

The woman was a Vess, with one cloudy eye and the other quivering with fear. "I need to consult with it f-further, my lady. S-Sometimes the Void can be so cryptic..."

A tight smile twisted Myuna's mouth. "I insist. Surely you do not doubt your goddess's ability to understand a prophecy?"

"My lady, it is unwise to probe the future out of fear," Endaeron said.

As a dimensional, her eyes glittered like diamonds as she swung her attention toward him. I tensed, but she didn't notice me. Of course not. This had happened on another planet, in another age where my brother still lived.

Even seated, she loomed over him. "Do I seem fearful to you?"

"Fear comes in many forms. It would be disconcerting if you were looking for any other reason," he answered.

She propped her chin on her fist, stirring a circle of light with her other hand. "So long I have known you, and yet there is still so much for you to learn. My ascension is soon."

He was the picture of happiness. "Yes, my lady."

With a flick of her wrist, that circle of light spun toward him, popping against his cheek like a soap bubble. "And you shall ascend with me. To ensure our success, why not harvest the Void? Why not have its greatest wielders tell me what could go wrong?"

She laughed, a great shriek of wailing souls. The Vess flinched, as did I.

"I didn't know what she meant, Phaeron." My brother's voice was in my head as the memory continued to play out.

"You were the one closest to her. You never asked for specifics?" I asked aloud. My voice echoed hollowly in the vault of his memory.

"Just watch."

Hands curling into fists, I did. The Vess had extinguished the Void in the room and gathered her skirts to kneel before Myuna. "Please, great goddess of light, spare me in exchange for the knowledge I have found for you within the Void."

"So there will be something to interrupt my ascension. Speak freely, my child. I will reward you for your candor." Myuna wove light between her fingers as she spoke, easing into her throne more. It seemed to put the Vess at ease.

She closed her eyes and spoke with the echoing power of the Void behind her. "A tide of souls will wash Soiluire clean."

Myuna's fingers froze for a moment. Her secret was there on the tip of this female's tongue...there for Endaeron to unravel.

So why hadn't he?

"You shall swell with great power and hold everything you desire in your palms."

Light pulsed under the goddess's skin as she leaned in, a grin spanning the pit of her mouth. "Go on," she purred.

"But this planet shall be your last." The Void giggled around the Vess. She bowed her head nearly to the ground as the pulse of Myuna's light heated the air. "Another shall ascend to rival you, and she will bring about your end."

The goddess wasn't pretending to be at ease anymore. She stared at the Vess with white-hot fury. "*Who would dare?*" she thundered with the voices of hundreds.

Dread tingled along my scalp as Endaeron whispered to Myuna, patting her lustrous arm. Of centuries of memories. *this* was what he'd chosen to show me...

"It's okay, my lady. You were right to ask for a warning. Now we can handle it," he soothed.

"Who?" Myuna whispered to the frightened Vess.

With a swallow, she forced out the rest quickly. "She who would mate the son of night and fight you alongside his daughter. She will defeat you before you have a chance to spread your influence on a new world."

No. It couldn't be, I thought. A sick feeling rose in my stomach as I eyed the patterns on Endaeron's horns. He'd worn these particular marks late in his life, with his last mate...around the time Keshora and I welcomed Ravai.

This was why Myuna had targeted my mate and daughters.

"And that is all the Void whispered?" Myuna asked.

"Yes, my lady."

With one intake of breath, Myuna had the Vess's soul in her mouth. The body slumped pitifully to the ground.

"Myuna!" Endaeron exclaimed, shocked. "She was only doing as you asked!"

The goddess's skin shimmered from the infusion of power. "As always, you shall breathe no word of this, as you yet live," she stated. "This Vess simply...disappeared." She lassoed the woman's discarded form with the rope of light she'd woven, consuming it whole to leave no evidence behind.

Endaeron stared at her in defiance. "Eating those who bring you bad news isn't going to solve your problems, my lady," he said through gritted teeth.

"You're right. There is still one problem I will have to preemptively consume," she simpered.

The scene smudged into darkness. Endaeron and I hung in the Void together, surrounded by shadows. "I did not know, at first, that she thought the son of night was you. I would've done more, I swear," he said.

"You could not speak of it," I replied sharply. In a tunnel of endless black, there was nothing to look at besides him. Nowhere for my bottled-up rage to go except for straight at him. "You stood by a goddess of entropy as her champion and helped her fool our people. How do you like your *ascension* now?"

"I was as much a victim as you were. Maybe more, if we must measure our suffering." He met my snarling with calm, his palms up. Though a human gesture, we observed it too.

I sensed that he was flimsy, just a memory of a memory. To scream and rail at him would be futile. He wasn't able to do anything about Myuna now. And he had willfully armed me with a piece of knowledge I needed time to chew on.

I drew back my claws and fangs. "Say what you will, then," I invited more quietly.

"Myuna groomed me from birth for something far worse than taking up a throne. She had two options, but she used to talk about how your darkness stung her when you were the babe she picked up first," he said. "She never forgot that you slighted her when you were minutes old."

My lips pulled back in a sneer.

"Your shadowborn soul was too pure for the seed she planted in mine instead. She made me...like her," he sighed.

"That is quite apparent from what you did as the Hungering Darkness."

"You don't understand. I was her seedling. The only soul she would take with her once she wiped out Soiluire completely." This vision of him was starting to fade around the edges, the sounds and colors of reality pressing in around us. He growled, baring a mouthful of teeth. "Stay with me a little longer."

"I'm trying." It was like straining to hold on to the edges of a dream. No matter what, my body wanted to wake up.

"As a nascent god of entropy, my remains will be built like her. There is a hollow within my core. Search it. Maybe you can do some good with what remains."

I swallowed past a lump in my throat, not trusting my voice. I simply nodded.

Sorrow filled his eyes, which gleamed like milky diamonds. "I'm sorry, brother. Even if I had years rather than moments to atone..."

"Endaeron, no." He was nearly gone, and my composure fell apart as I envisioned what would come next for him. What remained was too shredded and warped to find the next life. This was my last chance to speak to him at all before he became dust. "I—I forgive you! I only wish you peace."

"It would bring me great peace...to fix one thing I did wrong..." Fading in earnest, he extended to me a spark of bright white. "Take what is left, freely given."

I let him place it in my palm and drew him into a one-armed hug. The ghost of his wings closed around me before I was suddenly in the shopping mall, surrounded by the stench of blood. I knelt on the ground, my mouth still tasting of Soiluirian whisky.

A spot of warmth was now clenched in my hand. I turned it over and gaped. It was a teeny piece of a soul that was white with lightborn shadows. I sensed Endaeron within it, with no lingering hint of Myuna. Grief tightened around my eyes. "Is this truly all that remains of you?" I whispered.

Freely given, I could do whatever I wanted with it. I could snuff it out, warp it so the last part of Endaeron felt pain before it faded away. It wasn't large enough to exist on its own for long.

I waited to feel hunger, to salivate over consuming this soul energy. I'd bitten the Hungering Darkness, after all. The cravings were said to be immediate and life-altering. But there was nothing of the sort...

Only new mourning squeezing its way in with the old. That was

Endaeron, and he had given me tangible hope to dance on my fingertips. A patch for the hole in my soul. A way for a small portion of him to live on in me if I chose to accept it.

I pressed that piece of him to my chest. It attached to my soul like a magnet, flowing to the spot where it was needed to make me whole again. Tension bled out of my body on a wave of sheer relief.

The ghost of the best of my brother remained, and I felt it all: a hint of his confidence and savvy. His boisterous laugh, his optimism, his love for women and drink. There was even a bit of his strength, skill with a blade, and honor in knowing when to use it.

To turn *him* into a monster like her, Myuna had had to crush and destroy nearly everything about him. That was the true tragedy of Endaeron et Myudair, his only other remains the white residue scattered around my knees.

I rifled through it with my hands and senses alike, scattering husk-like pieces of souls sucked clean of their energy and color. The moment my claws touched them, they disintegrated. But one piece was larger than the rest, freshly torn away from its rightful home. Young, male, a hint of carefree emotion twined with blood witch magic.

I tucked it into a ball and held it protectively. Without a vessel to hold it, I needed to get it back to Lucas right away.

26

BEN

THERE WAS a particular look on Garroway's face. One that said he was going to bolt before he actually did, running full pelt away from the four of us.

Oh no you fucking don't, I thought, struggling back to my feet. The mending rune had made sure I wouldn't die from the sucking chest wound he'd given me, but that didn't mean I was ready to run him down.

"A little boost?" I asked Geo while Cress disappeared in a swirl of Braza's shadows to give chase.

Geo reluctantly turned his attention away from the vapor of white shadow still enveloping Phaeron. "Yes," he said, running at me with his wings flaring out. He lifted me by the hips, and I clung to him with my arms. We took to the air and gained ground on the retreating vampire.

"You want to double back for Big P?" I suggested.

"He can handle himself," Geo rumbled.

I wasn't so sure. But then again, he was an indescribably old being from another world, while I was squarely twenty with a deep grudge for the vampire trying to escape his rightful death, so I didn't argue.

Garroway snaked his way around some of the unnatural creatures and enslaved supernaturals. They had found another way to the top floor but had frozen in place, white-glazed eyes staring out at nothing. "Eerie," I muttered to myself.

Of course, when I could've wished for the monsters to attack someone and drag him off, they didn't bother.

"The Hunger must be dead," Geo commented.

But it wasn't a mission accomplished. Not yet.

Static crackled in my ear, and I nearly ripped off the tiny mic taped to my ear. Bianca, Tish, and Wren had spoken on and off during the less dangerous parts of our trip, just to go silent with the big battle. "...Ben? Ben, you there?" Tish asked.

"Oh, thank fuck. The stream is back," Bianca said a moment later. "You okay?"

"Mostly okay," I answered. The mending rune had closed the worst of the wound, leaving a raw edge of pain below my collar.

"Want to tell the audience what happened, then?" Wren prompted.

"Just...give us a few minutes," I said, flustered. If they'd missed *all* of that battle, then I didn't have the breath to explain it.

Light was starting to pour in from the dirty windows overhead, courtesy of a few gaps in the storm clouds. They appeared to be receding as rapidly as they came on...almost like they were magically created.

Below us, Garroway struggled within a trap of black and purple shadows. His ankle was caught in a thorny loop of them, and he bared his fangs in a frustrated grimace while glancing up at the sky. If the freak storm was fading, that meant he was stranded here with us and a whole bunch of monsters until nightfall.

Sounded like my kind of party.

Geo dropped lower to the ground and released his hold on me, giving me a running start. He flapped his wings hard before coming down on Garroway with his full obsidian weight. The vampire gave up trying to escape the shadow trap and rolled his ankle at a brutal angle to avoid getting crushed.

The snare disappeared, and Garroway straightened, favoring his broken foot. He came face-to-face with Cress, her head and hair bare of Braza's power, though the shadows curled around her hand and glowing sword. He recoiled and pivoted, but he was boxed in by Geo and me.

"Oh no. Nowhere to run," I mocked, flipping a dagger between my fingers.

"All right, I admit it," the vampire drawled, slowly raising both hands. "You've got me. How much will it take for us to part ways peacefully? A million each?" He flashed his most charming spider smile toward Cress. "Two, perhaps? I can have the funds wired to your bank account tonight."

Cress tilted her head, pretending to consider. "I think for many, Garroway," she said, tapping her chin with an elongated shadow claw, "your death is priceless."

Face morphing into a snarl, he turned and pointedly met my gaze. The force of his vampiric compulsion reached for purchase within my mind, but I was beyond used to his tricks after a lifetime of them.

"Fucking shank him already," Bianca muttered in my earpiece.

"With pleasure," I said, already in motion, signaling Geo. I snapped my fingers, casting a level-two celestial spell. A new trick just for him—a series of exploding stars right in his face. Geo clamped onto Garroway's upper arms to force him to take the brunt of the magic. Stinging burns broke out all over the vampire's exposed skin.

"The magic I was supposed to have," I said. I pictured the spiked rune that made the spell possible, about to snap my fingers to set it off again.

"You insolent—" Inky darkness slid over his mouth, cutting off anything else he might say. His eyes bulged in their sockets, and he thrashed, struggling in futility to break Geo's hold. Shadows had twined around and through his legs, rendering him completely immobile.

Geo nodded, and Cress gestured. He was all mine.

I sheathed my dagger. My fingers shook with the sheer force of my anticipation. "Doesn't feel good, does it?" I asked, daring to step into his space and stare him down properly. "To be silenced and held down. At the complete mercy of another person."

Something like fear lit in his bloody gaze, along with a pleading softness that said, *"Maybe three million?"*

"I don't want your blood money. I don't want your contacts or your resources or even your pocket dimensions," I told that expression, hoping to see that light of hope die when he realized he was about to pay for his sins.

His eyes widened, and he made a muffled shout. It wasn't until Phaeron spoke that I realized he'd snuck up on us out of the shadows. "There's one thing *I* want before you go on."

I nearly jumped out of my skin. "Goddamn, Big P. We've got to put a bell on you," I muttered.

"I would not wear it, Little B," he said.

I stepped aside for him, figuring he had a few things to say to Garroway after his time under the tender mercies of him and Myuna. Phaeron looked like he'd rolled in flour, something white and powdery smeared on his face, horns, and clothes. Otherwise, he seemed...fine? Maybe better than fine, with some new confidence in how he held himself. Cress eyed him closely, and he winked back at her before reaching for Garroway.

He unbuckled the sword strapped at the vampire's side with one hand and the aid of his shadows. More muffled sounds came from Garroway, along with a futile thrash of his whole body.

Phaeron fastened the sword to his belt and tipped his head my way. "Sorry to interrupt. Might I help? Though it looks like you all have it well in hand."

Well, that was the gist of my grand revenge speech anyway. I glanced up at the peaceful blue sky left now that the storm had passed. "He needs to greet the sun," I said.

"I'll carry him," Geo rumbled.

"And I'll keep him bound in shadows," Cress said in a two-toned voice.

I saluted them playfully, and together, they took him down to the bottom floor. Phaeron offered his free hand, the other curled in a loose fist. "Little B?" I asked.

"If you must call me something silly, am I not permitted to do the same?"

"I think..." I grinned up at him and took his hand. "I'm finally rubbing off on you."

"Frightening." He grinned back, baring his fangs, then turned into shadows slower than normal, giving me plenty of warning to close my eyes before we were jerked to another location.

When I felt tile below my feet again, I jumped back in surprise with a shout of "holy shit!" A massive rat-shaped unnatural scurried toward the doors we'd entered the mall through, joining a stampede of monsters and people alike. They hadn't bothered with the mechanism of the doors, instead going straight through the glass in the middle.

Cress, Geo, and a viciously struggling Garroway stood just to the side, while Phaeron and I had landed amidst a group of stragglers. I palmed a dagger, but these unnaturals weren't interested in fighting anymore. They ran like their life depended on it.

"She's taken control of them. She knows we'd kill them otherwise," Phaeron remarked. He casually grew shadow talons and ended the lives of a pair of rat creatures that brought up the rear. Whatever good cheer that'd come over him faded quickly as he dragged the corpses outside by their naked tails. "They took the torchbearers I unbound from her will. And the burn pile."

"Looks like we're not going to be invited to do another supply run anytime soon," I snarked.

Unfortunately, this was being recorded on stream, which meant Roe's mom was going to be *pissed*. The truck was destroyed—the wheels popped by ragged slashes, the doors and hood torn clean off. Truck guts littered the front of the mall. Here, a half-shredded seat; there, a chunk of metal that could've been part of the engine torn straight from the front.

"Roe is going to be so mad we didn't bring her," Cress whispered.

Phaeron had ditched the rats to help pick up and bind Garroway instead. He had the ankles in one hand while Geo had the shoulders. The vampire resembled a worm with how he was bound in two layers of shadowy ropes and reduced to squirming as the two men carried him out of the shade of the building.

"Right here's great," I said. They dropped him on the wet pavement, and I made sure he was face-up to greet the sun properly. His skin was already starting to redden as rays kissed his face.

"That looks like it hurts," I taunted the vampire, squatting by his head. Phaeron lingered close by, weaving shadows back into place when the sun threatened to fray away the ropes that bound Garroway.

"In your moment of greatest need, where is the goddess who declared you her right hand?" the dimensional added with a low chuckle. He was watching for Garroway's death nearly as avidly as I was. Did that make us a fucked-up pair?

I pulled the phone out of its sling, swiftly killing the stream and pulling the mic off my ear before Bianca could cuss me out. The public didn't need to see us gloating over this.

Black spots broke out over Garroway's face, the skin charring and becoming eddies of ash on the breeze. "I want you to remember how many people you killed like this. Burning in their own agony, often from the inside out," I said with a sneer.

The shadowy gag was wearing away, poorly muffling his screams. He jerked, trying to roll over and hide from the unforgiving sun. Obsidian hands seized his legs, slamming him back onto his back. Geo nodded toward us and backed his shadow away. He put his arm around Cress, who watched from a healthy distance, a concerned frown on her face.

I pinned the vampire's shoulders down, careful of any snapping fangs as the heat damage accelerated. "Better enjoy the coolest moments left," I said with malicious glee. "Hell is hotter still."

His skin and facial hair caught fire, his whole body going concave as he entered the last stages of burning to ash. Garroway's screams faded to one last moan of agony before only char remained of him and what he'd been wearing. The wind started to break apart the man shape left around the burnt clothing when Phaeron and Cress withdrew their magic.

I snapped a picture and texted it to Bianca. Instead of the stream of abuse I expected, she merely texted back, "Wish I could've seen it. :("

The excitement was fading about as fast as it'd been to kill Garroway out in the sun. "It was too easy for him," I texted back before pocketing the device. Any death would've been too easy, though. What would've really satisfied me, when he was the reason I'd lost my mom and childhood? When Lucas was still in a coma in a hospital we were about to evacuate.

There was an awkward silence between the four of us. Well, they had just helped me murder a man, no matter how deserving he'd been. I didn't know what to say after it was done, either.

"Shopping spree?" I suggested.

Cress breathed a disbelieving laugh.

"No," Geo grumbled.

"Stay if you wish. I need to borrow Little B," Phaeron said.

Cress covered her mouth, trying to contain a string of tired giggles. "You're really calling him that?"

"Yes, and I will bring him back shortly. I owe you all phones, after all." Phaeron glanced toward the wreckage of our transportation. "We'll need to steal another truck, I presume?"

I handed Wren's phone over to Cress. "Here. Call Bianca. She knows how to hotwire a car. I'm sure you can get tools from the mall somewhere."

Geo raised a stony brow. "And if the unnaturals return?"

"They won't," Phaeron said confidently. He rested a hand on my shoulder.

"Wait, you never told me why—" And we were off in a puff of shadows.

By the time Phaeron released me, I was about to throw up over his leather boots. We'd arrived in a hospital room in what felt like no time at all. Dizzy, I fell toward the nearest trashcan and fumbled it under my chin to dry heave until my stomach felt better.

"Sorry. Time is of the essence," the dimensional said. He offered me a hand up once I set the trashcan aside.

We were in Lucas's room. The steady hum of machinery beeped around his still form swallowed up in white sheets.

Phaeron turned toward him too. He leaned over my little brother, presumably staring at his soul. "Such a long possession by the Hungering Darkness has left him quite damaged. But he is the last victim," he murmured. "And a chunk of his soul remained in the belly of the monster."

I choked on a breath. "You're going to save him?"

"I cannot make any promises," he warned. "But my soul was just made whole, and the process was...easy. The missing piece knew exactly where to slot." He untucked Lucas from his hospital sheets and drew aside the collar of the gown. I went to the other side of the bed, watching with my heart beating erratically in my throat.

Phaeron opened his fist and placed his palm flat against the skin over my brother's heart. A jolt passed through Lucas. His fingers twitched; his legs shifted. He was waking up!

Above the ventilator strapped to his face, his eyes flared open. The irises were a shade of gray one small notch off from white and swam around in a panic as he spotted the two of us standing over him. "Lucas," I breathed.

He clawed the mask off his face and started screaming. Dragging his nails over his cheeks, he nearly scratched furrows into himself before I caught his wrists. "It's okay. You're in control. It's okay," Phaeron was saying.

"Look at me," I begged as Lucas continued screaming his lungs out.

The door into the hall slammed open, and in rushed Mama Rollins at the head of a trio of nurses. Thank fuck she was here—anyone else would've seen what was happening and immediately assume the worst.

"Use some magic. Check him," Cress's mom barked toward the fae nurse behind her.

Phaeron slipped into the shadows and reappeared at my side in moments, giving the green-skinned woman space to work. "Lucas, you're okay," I said, giving his wrists a shake. "You're in a hospital, and you're safe."

"You are your own person, free of the Hungering Darkness," Phaeron added.

The title seemed to catch his attention. Lucas relaxed back into the bed and looked around again in earnest. Green tinged his skin from the fae nurse's magic. She was quickly checking him head to toe.

"Ben?" Lucas rasped. He hiccupped dryly, his face creasing like he was going to cry. "Ben, I'm so sorry, I didn't mean to run off like that."

"Shh." I looped one arm under his shoulders, awkwardly bending down to hug him when he was still hooked up to several machines. "It doesn't matter. All I care about is that you're finally back."

I looked up at Phaeron. "Thank you," I said, properly teary for my brother and me both.

He dipped his chin in acknowledgment, a hint of something like grief and longing passing over his expression. "I'll give you some privacy," he said.

27
GEO

CRESS and I exchanged a glance the moment after Phaeron and Ben disappeared in a swirl of shadows. "I don't feel like committing grand theft auto right now. Do you?" she asked.

"No," I answered.

"How about this? I'm going to go find us something to eat in the mall, and then we can go back to the library."

"No," I said again. Her eyelids fluttered. "I shall come with you to find something to eat."

"But you can't see in the dark," she pointed out.

My shoulder blades ground together when I shrugged. "And you control light. You're not going back in there without me."

She tilted her head back and forth before unsheathing her sword and casting Lux upon it. With no need for us to hide anymore, the shadows she'd worn over herself like a coat seeped back into her skin.

With a surprised sound, she glanced down. "Oh, hi, Flit. Ben left without you, huh. You can hang out with us for now," she said to the ferret standing on one of her shoes. She lifted him with her free hand and placed him on her shoulder. He draped across the back of her neck and settled with a little huff.

"You'll have a lot more fun if you take your human form," she suggested to me before tiptoeing over the glass shards littering the way back into the mall. Her three cats stood clear of the wreckage, waiting for her.

I crunched straight through them, lifting her by the hips to set her outside of the destruction wrought by Myuna's creatures. She turned with a crease between her brows, undoubtedly to tell me to stop treating her like a doll, but I was already halfway through the process of shedding my wings and stone skin.

I swallowed her complaint with my warm human lips against hers. She sagged into me with a muffled moan.

Banding my arms around her, I cuddled her and rested my chin atop her head. "Why is it so important we retrieve some food?" I asked. She was tired and bloodstained, with rips in her clothing. I was sure she had wounds that needed tending.

My stone heart thrummed in my chest. I would ensure she received proper care with my own hands, even if I had to carry her out of this dark mall before she was ready to leave.

"I would give my left arm for some junk food, Geo," she said matter-of-factly. She removed her handbook from the holster on her hip. "*The Librarian Witch's Handbook*, scan for junk food that hasn't been spoiled."

"Aye, aye, Captain!" it squeaked, taking flight from her palm. It flapped away into the gloom ahead.

She took my hand and tugged me along, holding her gleaming sword in her free hand. "Are you sure about this?" I asked.

"I'm feeling okay. Promise. Besides, when was the last time I had you to myself?" She had a cheerful bounce to her step. "And it's always a treat to see you outside of gargoyle form."

"It's always a joy to be with you," I answered.

She ducked her head with a giggle. "Aw. I love you," she said.

There was no mistaking the rush of warmth that suffused me head to toe, loosening muscles and joints from their rocky stiffness. Those three words were more efficient than a full-course meal or any cup of coffee in reviving the man in me. "I love you too."

After a couple seconds' pause, I added, "We should locate your junk food quickly." The longer we delayed, the more likely one or both of her other men would return. I might've agreed to share her, but that didn't mean I wouldn't hoard every second of her undivided attention like the gold it was.

She smiled and led me to a directory, which helped us map out all the probable stores to visit. As we headed to the closest one, a shadow wound around her feet and released a rasping meow. "Okay, okay. Jin wants to take a ride on your shoulder," she said, motioning to the black cat.

I bent down, and Jin jumped the rest of the way, little razor claws digging into my skin. It was the most pain I'd felt all day, a fact that made me feel guilt over the bruises and scrapes Cress had sustained from her fight with the Hungering Darkness.

"Greetings, small feline," I said, nearly knocking her clean off my shoulder trying to pet her. She purred thunderously and dug in to remain in place, rubbing her face against my fingers.

Jin perched on my shoulder like a mini gargoyle as we started finding the kinds of things Cress wanted to bring back with her. The first store was dedicated to selling records and movies, with a small subsection full of chips, candy, and cans of soda in bright packaging. The unnaturals that'd overrun the mall had torn into some of them, but Cress's face lit up nonetheless when she realized there were a few rows higher up that were left untouched.

We left with two sturdy shopping bags full of junk. She had the biggest grin on her face, so I refrained from asking if this meant we were done. "Let's make a pile of loot," I suggested.

"Of what?" she giggled. "Did you hear 'loot' on the Internet?"

"Yes," I admitted.

"Well, I agree." She whisked away the two bags behind a still-sealed security gate in a swirl of shadows.

I don't know how long we spent in the gloom of the mall, combing several stores for their goods. We did not find any new phones to claim, alas, but by the time Cress and her familiars grew tired of walking, we'd amassed enough junk to ration some to everyone. Well, if Cress wanted to share. Once we gathered up all the shopping bags and boxes, the first thing she did was tear into a container of chocolate-dipped cookies.

She crunched down on one, and I watched the pleasure crease her expression at the taste of chocolate. She offered me the box, where the cookies stuck out like straws, but I only took one to commit its taste to this memory. It was sweet and crisp against my teeth, the chocolate studded with crushed almonds for that extra kick of flavor.

"Good, right?" she asked.

I smiled dreamily at her. "Fantastic."

We worked our way through the cookies slowly, as she relished each one. Only when she was down to the last one did she wave it around to punctuate what she said. "I was thinking I could take all of this and you back to the library with Braza's shadows."

I frowned. "I would be happy to assist you."

"Yes, but this way, you don't have to go back to gargoyle form. I'll drop the familiars back at their room and then..." She winked.

Hmm, now that was quite tempting. It wouldn't be a long flight, but I'd lose the certainty that I was a man, rather than a rock, with any time in my other form. I'd gotten a grip on my emotions and loosened my fingers enough to properly scratch Jin under the chin, two benchmarks amongst many that had to be achieved each time I became a man again.

So I said yes and allowed her to enfold me, the familiars, and our loot in a layer of black-purple shadows. There was a tugging sensation, and wind ran along my skin and through my hair before we arrived in a familiar room. Cress appeared next to me and sighed as the shadows flowed away from her body, disappearing like mist.

The familiars were no longer with us, so she must've released them from her magic before letting me go. "First, my feet are killing me, and I stink. Shower?" she offered.

I heard the weight of fatigue in her voice and resisted the urge to carry her there myself. "Only if I get the privilege of joining you."

"I thought that was a given," she said. She backed in that direction, shedding clothing as she went. My mouth went dry as I pursued her, also undressing along the way. Just the sight of all that soft skin had heat flooding to my groin.

She leaned over to turn on the shower and stood in a graceful arch, lifting her hips to jiggle the globes of her ass for my appreciative gaze. Shooting a coy smile over her shoulder, she stepped into the stream of water and then let off a less than dignified screech. "It's cold!"

A tentative laugh ground out of me. "Turn it up," I suggested.

"I did! Fuck," she sighed. "Guess there's no more hot water."

I stepped in behind her and drew the curtain. The water was punishingly chill, dampening my earlier excitement. Well, we both needed to wash, and she had cuts and scrapes on her body that I intended to clean before she leapt out of the tub. I pulled her into my body heat with one arm and grabbed the soap, lathering up my hands.

"I'll go quick," I promised before rubbing the suds into her shoulders and arms. As soon as both of us were soaked with cold water, I turned so my back took the brunt of the stream. Icy mist rolled around us.

Despite what I'd said, I found myself worshiping her body, hands molding to her curves and brushing tenderly over new hurts. I gave her breasts an admiring squeeze, and she leaned her head back on my shoulder, damp hair tickling my chest. "I was hoping we could..." she said tentatively.

"Soon," I rumbled. Definitely not here, while she was standing on aching feet and cringing away from the cold water. I knelt to finish cleaning her long legs and helped her balance for a quick scrub of her soles.

Her teeth clicked together when we switched places, and she slid the bar of soap out of my palm. "My turn."

I breathed out from her touch, which was as soft as she was. After being hard and unfeeling for so long, simply being touched was its own pleasure. I closed my eyes as Cress stroked the lines of my muscles in a path top to bottom. She was finished before I wanted her to be, shutting off the water with a sigh of relief.

She passed me a towel and tousled her hair with another. "You haven't relaxed like that in a long time," she murmured.

"That's the magic of your touch," I answered.

She hummed, drying herself off thoroughly with a few shivers along the way. "Geo," she said, tossing the towels aside and coming over to rest her palms on my chest. I rubbed her back, feeling the chill she carried on her skin. "I think you need to start taking longer breaks from your gargoyle form."

"My duty is to protect you." I answered without really thinking. "Well...you are my duty, of course. And I am the only gargoyle in this entire pocket dimension. Thanks to Phaeron's tempering of my stone, I have yet to be injured. While you..."

She glanced down at her body, touching the reddened skin around a set of scratches on her side. "This could have been much worse. What I'm saying is, it's okay to take a breather from constant vigilance. I appreciate everything you've done. But..." She leaned in to press a kiss above where my stone heart rested. "I need you like this sometimes."

A little tremor passed through me, a shockwave emerging from the brush of her lips. I couldn't deny the rightness of what she was asking. Her heart was big enough to encompass me along with her other two men, but I needed to occupy that space. In this, I needed to bend, to be flexible.

To be soft, when all I'd ever been was hard and unyielding.

"I need you, too," I murmured. "Touch me."

"Where?" she asked.

"Everywhere."

Her palms ran up to my shoulders, rubbing outward down the line of my arms. With a gentle nudge, she started walking me backward. "Everywhere, hmm? I'm going to take you literally."

I nodded. Good. I was always literal.

She traced new pathways over my body, taking her time without the obligation to hurry us out of a cold shower. I backed into the bed and lifted her to sit astride my lap. Her lips and tongue followed the trails set by her fingers, and by the time she was halfway down my chest, I was hard as obsidian, jutting into her hip.

One of her hands slipped down to cup my erection, and I held in a gasp. "I'll take care of you last," she promised before reaching over for Wren's phone resting on the bedside table. I watched her through lidded eyes as she scrolled through a music app and put on a slow and smooth instrumental that played a little tinny through the small speaker.

She used the pace of the music to slow down and leave no inch of me untouched. I slid my fingers through her damp hair, finding what I'd asked for had swiftly turned into the sweetest torture as she skimmed her attention around my cock. She kissed her way down my thighs. That was about all I could take. "Cress," I moaned.

Her brown eyes flashed to my face. She'd put on a playful expression, but she had to know. "I...I was not speaking literally," I said.

She covered her mouth with a hand, eyes creasing at the corners. "No?"

"No," I confirmed.

"This is a first," she said, skimming her palms back up my thighs. I throbbed for the touch she was so close to delivering. "Are you sure you want me to jump straight to the end?"

Her fingertips skimmed closer. "Yes," I practically begged.

While she didn't laugh, mirth danced in her eyes as she rose between my legs and licked her way up my shaft. She cupped my tightened balls, rolling them between her fingers. I moaned her name, grateful when she took the crown between her lips and sank me further into the heat of her mouth inch by inch.

She didn't hold back. Her mouth was torment and relief, keeping me in place so I could only reach her shoulders and back. I was possessed with desire for her, to caress her as she had touched me.

"Maybe not the end," I said, tugging on her hair. "Come join me on the bed."

A furrow appeared between her brows as she slid my cock back out of her mouth. I helped lift her up and lay her out on the bed, bracing myself above her to take in all that soft skin turned golden by lamp light. A body I was made for. My hands, shaped for her curves. I started at her hips, running up the dip of her belly to the swell of her breasts.

My lips, shaped to mesh with hers. I reminded myself to inhale as I kissed her, as her mouth so often stole my breath. Our tongues met in a heated tangle.

My stone heart, animating me to her service. It throbbed in my chest, full to bursting with the satisfaction of this moment. I cupped her cheek, meeting her gaze briefly. How had one person so efficiently become my purpose? I'd already changed for her, flexed when I didn't think I ever could.

Cress was my everything.

I was still kissing her when I ran my palm down her thighs, moving her leg to open her for me. Rubbing my cock between her folds, I reluctantly pulled back at the last moment to ask, "Condom?" I regretted that I didn't have one handy.

Her hands pulled me back, one at my hip, the other hooked around my neck. "No," she said.

I smiled, grateful I got to see her expression as I sank into her. My cock, formed to fit her perfectly. Her kiss-swollen lips hung open as I sank into her to the root. We communicated like how I used to. "Good?" I rumbled.

"Yes," she gasped.

"Okay." But it was more than merely *okay*. Being inside of her was simply *right*.

I braced my weight on one arm, still touching her, a gentle counterpoint to the way her body rocked with my thrusts. The texture of her skin, the way her breast jiggled in my palm; the muscles low on her belly shifted as she lifted her hips to mine; every piece came together to form the whole of her pleasure.

She came with a velvety clench on my cock, arching into me. I savored the brush of our sweat-slicked bodies together. As much as I didn't want this to end, I was close, and her leg twitched from taking my thrusts during that sensitive time after her peak. I let go, spilling in a rush of liquid heat and settling still hard inside of her.

It only took her a few minutes before she asked, "Again?"

And I answered, "Sure."

28

PHAERON

At the dawn of my life, a set of scholars had taught me what it meant to be a prince. A straight posture was a requirement; composure, a necessity. I had to achieve perfection. I'd caught glimpses of the ideal prince within me, though *perfect* was always an impossible standard.

Shadowborn were instinctively drawn to dark, quiet places. We'd evolved on a planet shaded by eternal night as protectors, there to eliminate unseen threats so the rest of our kind could thrive. I was meant to have a territory to patrol, unceasingly seeking out the next fight until my True Light called me home and into her arms.

There was also the rage, a trait inconvenient and inferior to my station. Yet it so often simmered under my skin, reminding me not to remain in one place for long. I'd tried to heed my tutors and snuff out its sparks and heat, but it remained part of my core being, the blame of its reoccurrence straddled somewhere between the instincts of a shadowborn and the inferiority of a second prince.

I hated when there were witnesses to when I lost control. I always sought solitude to hunt and exist without the judgment of society or man.

But first, while balanced on a knife's edge of self-control, I looked for Cress and found her scent lingering in Highfall's Mall, twined with Geo's earthen tang. She alone had the power to ground me.

But they'd left the mall by that point. I was the only living person in the whole complex.

Alone.

I took form far from the battlefield where the Hungering Darkness fell. My chest rose and fell in shallow gasps for air. I was too hot; my clothes and armor were too tight. And even with no man-made lights shining overhead, the numerous panes of windows high above made this mall too *fucking* bright.

Shadows erupted from my skin while I screamed a shadowborn's howl. Magic and power answered my call, and I wrapped myself in a cloak of night and became a destructive creature with a wolflike head and a trailing tail of spikes. My fingers lengthened into foot-long talons, shredding sidings and tile like ripping paper.

"Myuna!" I raged. Every uprooted sign and display could've been her, thrown, shredded, and ruined.

I pictured her paranoid expression, the rage and fear that'd twisted her face from the Void's wisdom: *"She will defeat you before you have a chance to spread your influence on a new world."*

But the narrow-sighted monster had set her sights on what was before her, not the scope of what the Void knew. A prophecy from a Vess was supposed to be taken with a cynical ear, for it was most likely the madness and the laughter speaking through them.

I continued my rampage, imagining tearing her throat out with my teeth. Did goddesses bleed? Or was she simply a hollow vessel, a stretched-out form of clay that would deflate from a mortal wound?

She'd trespassed against me personally, worse than I could've ever imagined. My wobbly memories conjured Keshora, and my pace faltered a moment. I squeezed a guardrail over the three-story drop to the bottom of the mall, leaving behind an impression of my hands.

Keshora, as I knew her, was a weaver and a mother. A proud but unlikely second princess. I'd returned from war to find that, in my absence, she'd given her heart to two girls, *Ravita* and *Brazita*. When I tried to imagine their nicknames in her voice, only the throbbing of my heartbeat filled my ears.

"She who would mate the son of night and fight you alongside his daughter."

I made a sound of pain low in my throat. It was ludicrous. Myuna thought the Void's prophecy would be crushed into dust as long as she killed Keshora and Ravai, two women who'd never been a threat to her.

"It wasn't referring to either of them," I mumbled, as if the truth would bring them back.

Unlike the wreckage I'd left behind me, I damaged the railing purposefully, creating a ledge for me to sit and dangle my feet and tail over the perilous drop. My power receded in tufts of smoke, exposing the rawness of my expression. What I thought was anger twisted and revealed itself as chest-cracking grief, which pounced the moment I acknowledged the truth.

My brother was dead.

My family was murdered.

My world was destroyed.

And my people were scattered and endangered, unlikely to unite as a kingdom again.

At the center of it all sat Myuna, gorging and laughing in her death knell of a voice. Fear and revulsion shuddered through my body. If the Void's prophecy was to be believed and her assumption of my identity as "the son of night" was correct, then I was a key figure to her end. But the one to wield the sword would be Cress, aided by Braza. I was two crucial steps from setting that destiny into motion.

I inspected my hands. Blood and smears of white-ish powder clotted under my nails and in the creases of my skin. One step would be easier than the other. I had no doubt Cress would agree to carry my mating mark, but I still needed to cobble together a proper gift for her.

And Braza... I cursed under my breath. I'd ruined that relationship with careless, unguarded thoughts. We'd had powercores on Soiluire, but she'd been the first I'd known before her transformation. Though she had become *other*, it'd been tactless to shout in my head that she wasn't the daughter I remembered and marvel at how strange she'd become upon shedding her body.

I couldn't remember the last time she'd called me Father, a consequence I deserved and one that would not be reversed with a simple apology. I would produce a grander gesture for her for the right reason. Not just to kill Myuna, but to give Braza back the life she deserved.

"Well," I said, scrubbing my cheeks to rub away the self-pity, "idleness is the enemy of progress."

I fixated on my new mission, becoming a spirit that popped in and out of being only to take what I needed. Clothes were last, for when I cleansed the filth of battle from my skin. First, I sought abandoned shops for rare spell reagents. The couple I found were already ransacked, most items of value taken.

No matter. I was chasing another memory, a ritual few supernaturals would remember and fewer still would approve of. I filled a box with powders and tonics that'd been overlooked on their shelves and tucked in a few potions of a vibrant hue of purple that matched Cress's hair. I'd noticed earlier that some of the strands were reverting to a dark brown, a sign she needed to renew the dye.

There was one reagent no shop would sell, and I found myself browsing the guardian witch sections of each one I visited, looking for a suitable replacement. The best I could find was the scale of an earthen dragon, and that was lucky, as it was hidden under something else in a nearly empty display case. It wasn't much on its own, just a matte disc the color of dried mud, but I felt the latent power within it as it sat across the length of my palm.

The most powerful supernaturals in this world were those that took a dragon's shape. As unlikely as this scale was for the task I required of it, it would do if I did not acquire a better alternative.

Evening was beginning to touch the sky as I considered what to find next. Traditionally, I should present Cress with a gift made by my own hands. But I didn't have time for that, not with Myuna breathing down our necks. I would make her something she'd cherish if we made it back to the safety of New Salem and Moongrove Academy.

In the meantime, I sought comforts for her. As night fell, I encountered more unnaturals stirring from their nests. They met a swift death as I emerged from the darkness with each sighting. It felt good to have two blades in my hands again, though most of Myuna's creatures required little effort to slay.

The occasional roaming torchbearer added hours to my quest, as each time I unbound a soul, I ended up with an unconscious body that needed to be carried to Cerris City Library. I felt Braza tracking me coming and going, though she didn't try to talk to me as I added a few people at a time to spare containment rooms.

Past midnight, there were no more unnaturals to kill. I sensed the wrongness of that fact when I dared take form in a beauty store. Chill dread creeped up my scalp while I busied myself with inspecting labels. There was a baffling amount of makeup products, lotions, hair care, and serums in this store.

I stilled halfway into my search and turned in the direction of timid footsteps. There was a soft gasp and a scuffle. Human sounds.

"Hello there. I won't hurt you," I said.

"That's exactly what a monster would say." She sounded young, and I caught myself rolling my eyes despite the circumstances.

"None of Myuna's creatures speak coherently. That's how I know you are not one. You may apply the same logic to me." I glanced down at myself and hoped she wasn't a shifter or vampire, able to see the state I was in through the dark. My shirt was in tatters, and I still bore the grime of battle, new and old. "Would you like me to take you to a safe place?"

"I thought I had a safe place." She was peeking around a display of nail polishes, and I caught a glimpse of her aura, that of a witch who hadn't picked an affinity yet. I drew a layer of shadows over my torso when I noticed she was aiming a phone light in my direction. "Oh! You're the dimensional from the stream. Are you here to rescue me?"

I tilted my head, bemused, and fibbed, "Yes." I would take her to the hospital no matter what. She needed to evacuate with the rest of the survivors we were protecting. "But before we leave, I need some advice."

The girl ended up being an employee who was living in the back room of the shop alone. She was more than happy to help me load up on things Cress probably wanted. I left with a couple heavy bags of various products and her in my shadows, plopping her on the front steps of the hospital and disappearing the moment she turned to thank me.

I returned to the library to deposit the bags next to the other items I'd found, finally turning my attention toward making myself presentable. First, a shower. I luxuriated in the cool water even though it ran off me in the various colors of blood and battle. I was cleansing my wounds a second time when the feeling of dread returned.

Power intensified in the air, and I clutched my skull, wailing from the pressure bearing down from all angles. It lasted for all of a minute before abruptly disappearing. I shut the shower off, breathing heavily.

There was no questioning that Myuna had done something awful. But what could it have been?

My thoughts strayed to Carly. I could only hope she hadn't harmed the girl further with whatever madness she was undertaking now.

Braza tentatively brushed my mind. *"I know you're probably resting…"* she said.

"My next rest will be when Myuna is dead," I replied.

She had a way of holding her silence in a way that felt disapproving.

"I shall come to you shortly." I didn't need her to be concerned for me, even though I muffled a yawn at the thought of sleep.

"I shall be ready," she murmured.

The fatigue I was running from threatened to catch up with me as I dressed in the set of too-tight clothes that'd been left here earlier and prepared what I was going to say in the mirror. I had to keep moving. Though I did pause by the bed to catch a breath of the scent lingering on the sheets. The perfume of Cress's arousal and my magic, intertwined.

My body ached for hers. I'd make her my mate on this bed now that my soul was whole.

I shook my head sharply and turned into shadows, leaving before I could fantasize about it further. Taking form in front of the domed powercore, I forwent the formality of bowing and asking permission to enter. Braza was already formed of black and purple energy in the middle of her small space, hands on her hips, tail flicking as she took a good look at me.

I didn't give her a chance to speak before I swept her off her feet and into a hug. Whatever she was going to say rolled into a squeak of surprise, then she hugged me back, curling her wings into a looser second embrace.

She fixed her luminous powercore eyes on me, a little furrow in her brow. She was undoubtedly searching my mind for an explanation, but the rehearsed words had evaporated away already. I was, perhaps, more fatigued than I expected. I held her more firmly, enough that her body dimpled and static tingled on my skin.

"I'm sorry," I said in the language of our people.

"About—"

"I'm sorry, Brazita," I corrected myself.

Her breath caught. Though I didn't think she needed to breathe, some gestures transcended death and ascension into a new form.

"Recent events have forced me to look at what I have become, and there is much I would change," I continued. "Starting with my failures as a father. I have much to apologize for, but I hope we can repair the damage between us."

Her smile echoed a brightening of our surroundings. The immediate joy and relief were unmistakable. "I would like that more than anything," she murmured. She angled her head, and I met her halfway, our foreheads touching. A sign of trust and affection for our race blessed with sharp horns.

There was an echo of Cress's chastisement in my ears, once uttered in this small space. *"The fact that she's* here *and that she made me Guardian of Moongrove Library was all for you."* Braza had been trying to reach across the gap this whole time.

"I want to apologize too, for holding you in containment for so long," she said.

I shook my head. "I've already accepted your reasoning and come to peace with the missing years. If I hadn't been contained for that period of time, how would I have met Cress? Your actions guided my destiny."

She wiggled, and I realized I still had her held up off the ground. I placed her on her feet, and she beamed up at me. "You're happy with her," she said knowingly. "It's time."

"Tomorrow." I was pleased at the approval I felt from the electric currents of her power. The tether between Cress and Braza made them close in their own way. No one was cheering on Cress more than my adopted daughter. "But first, I have to tell you something."

A hint of wariness touched her voice. "Okay."

It was easier to show her. I took her hands and closed my eyes, letting the memory of Endaeron's last moments float to the front of my mind. Reliving the Void's prophecy was no easier a second time, and it was tied up in other thoughts Braza undoubtedly skimmed from my mind.

Her energy-formed fingers were starting to feel warm in mine as she took from my body heat. She was silent for a while after witnessing what I'd seen and concluded about Myuna's actions afterward. I only hoped she'd picked up that I would've come around and apologized to her with or without this glimpse into the past.

When she finally spoke, it wasn't about the prophecy at all. "What you're planning to give me is illegal by supernatural law."

"But do you want it?" I asked.

She glanced away, lip caught between her teeth. "Every gargoyle forgets their past life," she said.

"A purposeful flaw, I imagine. Otherwise, the supernatural world would be flooded with witches chasing immortality." I squeezed her fingers, surer than ever that I wanted to try to do this for her. "I have Geo, who may allow me to study the spells keeping him animated, and an abundance of time. I would make the body perfect for you so you can have the life that was stolen from you so long ago. No human law will stop me from trying, only your word that you wish to continue on as a powercore."

She took in our surroundings, releasing a sigh weighted by centuries of unceasing service. If I thought I was tired, all I had to do was listen to her to know what true exhaustion sounded like. "I...I do want to be alive again. But how will we hide a female gargoyle? And who will power Moongrove Library?" she asked.

"We'll figure it out. Besides, you switched places with the power-core in this library, now empty save for temporary containment of torchbearers. There's never been a better time for you to go missing." I nodded slowly to myself, seeing it play out in my mind's eye. "We will blame Myuna, and this library will remain empty until another power source can be found. In the meantime, I'll hold your soul in a suitable temporary vessel."

I pulled the dragon's scale from my pocket, and she took it to inspect. "This isn't a purified fae crystal," she said skeptically.

"It is the best I could find for now. I have faith it will contain your soul long enough to give me time to source a proper gargoyle heart," I said.

In answer, she gestured overhead at the powercore above us. "All of this is my soul now."

I glanced up with a thoughtful hum. "Perhaps I should find you two. One for each half."

Though I'd never been involved in making gargoyles directly, I knew the magic-washed stones chosen for their hearts were selected for the lattice structure within. If I phrased the question correctly, maybe one of the Crystal Court fae would be willing to sell me two without realizing what they were for.

"I shall write down everything I remember about gargoyle creation. Between us, we can figure out the spells and materials. Once Cress and I defeat Myuna for good, we will have all the time in the world." The smile she offered was fragile with hope.

I'm sure mine was as well. "There are a few last things I need to retrieve from the city. Perhaps when I return, we could sit and talk for a while?"

"I'll be here," she said wryly.

29
CRESS

GEO and I took the luxury of a slow wakeup with Wren's phone between us, watching highly satisfying videos of molding kinetic sand and hydraulic presses at work. Then the device buzzed continuously and threatened to jump out of my hand. It was Ben texting in bursts from someone else's phone.

Geo groaned in denial, and I made a sound of agreement. The outside world was about to steal us both away; I knew it.

I pieced Ben's message together and read it in a frenetic pace in my head from how short the individual texts were. "Hey, babe, where are you? Have you seen Geo or Phaeron? You have to come to the hospital! My brother's awake! He's doing good, and I want to introduce you guys. Sorry, did I wake you? I've been waiting all day for you to steal a car and come back! You're okay, right?"

Someone had to teach this man to text all his thoughts in one message.

Wait, Lucas was awake? I gasped and reread that particular message. "We have to go!" I exclaimed.

"What? What's wrong?" Geo asked, sitting up at full alert.

I grinned and showed him the message. "We have to say hello to Ben's brother."

His silvery eyes widened. "That is quite remarkable," he murmured.

I stood to get dressed, reaching out for Braza in my head while I tugged on my clothes and attempted to text Ben back all at the same time. *"Good morning, brightest of souls."*

"Guess what," we said at nearly the same time.

She already knew my news, that some miracle had occurred to wake Lucas from his coma. There was a playful jolt to her energy today, as if she knew exactly how it happened and was looking forward to me figuring it out.

"I've spent the greater part of the early morning with my father," she said.

I didn't miss the change in title. My jaw dropped, then a delighted smile formed on my lips. *"You two made up."*

"We did. I'll let him know where you and Geo are going. But for now, we're catching up."

I knew all he had to do was set his pride aside and apologize. She'd wanted to repair their familial relationship so badly.

"I'm happy for you," I said while humming an upbeat tune out the door and to the elevator. Geo was just a step behind me, resting an arm around me while we waited.

"Thank you. By the way, did you feel the anomaly last night?"

"The what now?" I asked.

"Myuna's power surged for a short time last night. Perhaps if we'd been merged, you would've noticed it." She sounded troubled. *"I'm hoping you can speak with the seers to figure out if they know what she did."*

"Of course." I had a question for Hana, which meant I'd probably be pestering her with several of them to get a halfway decent understanding of her answer. Though I hadn't forgotten the very literal hint she'd given me about Phaeron's "slumber," which I'd completely overthought.

Without the convenience of shadow travel, Geo had to take his gargoyle form to fly us to the hospital. There were no signs of unnaturals on the streets, nor any white-eyed birds staring from signposts and rooftops. I rubbed my arms, more unnerved by the lack of Myuna's monsters with the knowledge that she'd done something big last night.

We could've had a leisurely late winter stroll free of threats and kept Geo out of his stone form. He shed it upon landing and took a moment to breathe and pinch the bridge of his nose. Once he'd recovered, he jerked his chin in hello to the bored-looking defenders on duty around the hospital's perimeter on our way inside. Several hellos were called back to him.

I hesitated between seeking out Hana or Ben first. The decision was made for me, though, as the dark-haired woman was sitting primly on a couch in the foyer, her signature secretive smile in place when we made eye contact.

"You have questions," she said.

"I do." I turned to Geo, brow raised curiously.

"Tell me if you figure out anything concrete," he rumbled. I wasn't too surprised, since he cared more about actions than possibilities. He took Wren's phone to return to her, and I slid onto the couch next to Hana.

She gestured for me to speak and stacked her hands patiently. Though she'd mastered the mysterious air of an augur, I wasn't sure if she knew the faces of the demons I wrestled with: the first time I'd come face-to-face with death. Her daughter Lanie's unseeing eyes, her motionless body sprawled in a pool of her own blood. And in the aftermath, Hana had gazed into the future for me...

"You told me once." I took a ragged breath, feeling myself get choked up. "You told me that I'd avenge Lanie."

"And so you have," she said. The knowing look hadn't left her face yet.

"But I didn't kill the Hungering Darkness. That was Phaeron," I said in a small voice.

"Ah. Didn't I tell you that I saw you vanquish a creature, standing over it with three men who adore you? That *did* happen." Her aura lit with gray, centered around her head. "I see it, even, but the monster you four watched die was the vampire, not the Hungering Darkness. Fairly accurate as far as a gaze into the gray is concerned."

I felt the chill of goosebumps. What she'd told me and what happened still didn't quite match up. How often had her augury been a shade off from reality?

"I see," I said neutrally.

She turned her dark eyes my way. They reflected with gray magic deep in her pupils. "In this, you have fully avenged my daughter. The blood baron's legacy is dust, and the unnatural remnant who attacked her is no more."

"What about my sister, Carly?" I leaned in, yearning for some hope. "Have you seen her future?"

She maintained her mysterious poker face. "I have. There are good outcomes and bad, as sure as everyone else's fate at present."

I wrung my hands. How intensely vague of her. "Will we cross paths before she ends up in a morgue?" I asked in a smaller voice. With everything that'd been happening, I missed Carly more than ever.

"You will," she confirmed, then cleared her throat and clearly picked another topic. "I see now that you are on the verge of discovering your potential."

I set my spine under that prophetic gaze, wondering what exactly she was seeing when she inspected me. "What should I do?" I breathed.

"The hour of our final confrontation with Myuna grows near. She has chosen a new champion and embedded a seed of entropy in their soul. In this, she has learned from us and plans to raise a larger force than ours. We must broadcast our evacuation plans before it's too late for the majority of Cerris City's survivors," she intoned.

I held my breath, committing every word to memory.

"Pool your resources, and you will find the key to our victory." She nodded slowly, and between one blink and the next, the gray magic left her. Her shoulders slumped, and she muffled a yawn. "And speak to Phaeron. We can spare you both for a day while the rest of us prepare."

"Fuckin' hell. That was a damn good prophecy." We both jumped when the gravelly voice spoke up behind us. Auric et Vess had appeared out of nowhere silently, just as Phaeron usually did. Maybe it was a dimensional thing.

Hana recovered first. "How long were you listening?" she asked.

"I heard the whole thing from the other side. The Void frothed up nicely for you. It speaks to you, hmm?" He was inspecting her closely.

"Augurs see the future," she corrected.

"Fascinating," he remarked. "Where I live, there are no human augurs. Only my kind." He tapped the angular cheekbone below his sightless eye meaningfully.

"Perhaps the madness would be less if you saw, rather than heard, its wisdom," she said.

"If only the whispering stopped that easily." He flashed a multi-fanged smile before his one good eye trained on me. "Hey. Resources are usually pooled in a circle, if you catch my meaning."

I felt my lips press together. If anything, it felt like he'd just said something random to confuse me.

"Eh. The sudair will know, if you don't figure it out." He made a dismissive gesture.

"Well, thank you both for your wisdom," I said, standing. I tucked away the tidbit that Hana had looked into *the Void* to see the future. I could wonder about the implications later.

Hana waved farewell while Auric said a gruff "Bye, kid" before turning his attention back to her. I went to Lucas's room first, but it was empty, the sheets on the bed in an untidy pile to the side. While I stood in the threshold, I caught a hint of Ben's laugh and followed it to a waiting room jam-packed with people.

My coven and friends were mixed with a group of healthy survivors. At the center of it all was Wren, phone in hand, interviewing a teenage girl.

Ben stood toward the edges of the gathering and waved me over. He had a hand resting on the handle of a wheelchair, where his brother sat, head lolled back. I was caught for a moment by Ben's big, carefree smile. It was rare to see him without that signature smirk, but he was obviously carrying on over some story for Lucas's benefit.

Geo was nearby, keeping careful watch as always. He flashed me a quick wink, and I brushed my fingertips up his arm on my way by him. The contact had him shivering with awareness.

"Cress!" Ben's teeth were practically sparkling. "Come meet my bro, Lucas."

"Hello, Lucas." I held my hand out for a shake, and he gripped my fingers loosely. His smile was slow and shy, and he looked me over with unusually pale eyes. We'd met before, though I doubted he remembered it, as he'd been deep within the possession of the Hungering Darkness.

The real Lucas peered up at me with slow blinks, as if he were still waking up. He was nothing like the young man I'd briefly met; his weakened body was lost in his hospital gown, and he looked like he'd been dipped in bleach from his ghostly skin tone and how platinum his overlong hair had become.

A little line of concentration marked his forehead. "It's a pleasure to meet you." He spoke slowly, almost stiffly. I wondered if it was difficult for him to talk after a monster had been speaking through him for months. "Ben has nothing but praise for his anam cara."

I felt a blush touch my cheeks. "We definitely complete each other," I said, sharing a glance with Ben before returning my attention to him. "How are you doing?"

"Better...I think," he said, speaking in short bursts. "It's frustrating. I'm not a blood witch anymore. There's no easy recovery ahead."

"Not a blood witch anymore?" I echoed in surprise.

"Yeah, blood runes don't work on him anymore," Ben confirmed. The shadow of troubled thoughts passed over his face. "Big P might be able to take a look at him and tell us what happened to his affinity, but earlier, he restored Lucas's soul and dipped. No one's seen him since."

He told me about the scrap of soul Phaeron had been holding after killing the Hungering Darkness. How Phaeron had pressed it to Lucas's chest and woken him when modern medicine hadn't done a thing.

"Oh, shit," I muttered. "Ben, he'd just killed what was left of his own brother. No wonder he disappeared."

He scratched the back of his head, lips quirked. "I know. The man needs a hug and a medal. Can you make him reappear so we can give him both?" he asked.

I touched the mark of protection on my wrist, drawing breath to say Phaeron's name when I noticed motion on Lucas's hospital gown. "Isn't that your shoulder mouse?" I asked. The cute little albino mouse was climbing up to perch on Lucas's shoulder instead.

"My brother's familiar, it turns out," he chuckled.

"Wow, that's—" I jumped at the sudden pressure of hands on my waist.

Phaeron's fingers seemed to form first, but it was unmistakably his presence behind me and his breath in my hair. "You called?" he asked. I felt a rush of warmth between my thighs from his smooth voice suddenly washing over my ear.

"You know, on second thought, wearing a bell won't save our girl from getting jump scared by you, Big P," Ben said casually. "Where'd you go?"

"Here and there," Phaeron answered, and the girl Wren interviewed suddenly pointed at him.

"It was him! He found me last night!"

The dimensional's presence behind me vanished the moment Wren turned her phone toward us. I waved awkwardly, as did Ben, and a moment later, Lucas too. Geo gazed stoically at the lens.

"Anyway," Wren said, rolling her eyes before focusing the camera on the girl again.

"Do you see her expression? In the dictionary under 'crestfallen,'" Ben quipped in a whisper. He started to wheel Lucas's chair toward the hallway, and Geo followed.

The moment we turned a corner, Phaeron reformed a pace behind us. "She was about to say where I'd saved her from. I've got to keep some secrets."

Ben raised a hand, wiggling his fingers. "Air of mystique."

I snuck a glance over my shoulder. Yeah, he hadn't slept again. But he'd washed the white residue off his skin and had found a black sweater and dark wash jeans that he looked comfortable in. He was relaxed, laugh lines creasing the skin around his yellow eyes. "Something of the sort," he agreed.

Once the five of us were in Lucas's room and the door was closed behind us, Ben turned the wheelchair toward Phaeron. "I was hoping you could take a look at his soul. Blood runes aren't working to help him heal."

"One should not expect another to walk through hell unscathed, Little B," Phaeron answered but crouched down to be on eye level with Lucas. The young man seemed to be mustering himself to speak while Phaeron tilted his head, inspecting his soul closely.

Ben edged closer to me and took my hand when I reached for him. Our anam cara marks brushed, setting off a spark of awareness, and I squeezed his palm. I missed him. Now that I'd had a night with Geo, I craved two more, and they had *Ben* and *Phaeron* written on them. My body hummed for more of Ben now that he'd shed the manacles of guilt over his brother's condition.

"Did you know there's a white streak in your...darkness?" Lucas's weak voice drew my attention back to him. He gestured vaguely in a circle.

Phaeron's pupils narrowed to slits. "You can see my soul," he remarked.

A white streak? How alarming. He met my gaze over Lucas's shoulder, eyes shining with pain for an unguarded moment before he schooled his expression. "Endaeron repaired the damage he caused me with the last bit of himself. I assure you, I am whole," he said.

Wow. When Braza reassured me that Phaeron was safe, she hadn't mentioned this. I couldn't imagine how difficult it was for him.

Phaeron crooked his finger at me, gesturing for me to squat next to him. "What do you see of her soul?"

Lucas blinked, his gaze going unfocused, before he flinched away from me. "Like…looking into the sun," he mumbled.

Phaeron smiled wide enough to show the edge of his fangs. "Perhaps we shouldn't blind the boy."

I took the hint and returned to Ben's side, leaning against him companionably.

"Well, I admit that this is unique. No human has seen my soul with their own magic," the dimensional continued. "While your soul, Lucas, is still taking a new shape after what you've experienced. It's said that extreme trauma can cause changes to a witch's affinity. What I see is that you've been altered by a minion of Myuna without becoming corrupted. Time will tell if you'll be able to find a way to draw on soul energy, as I suspect that is your new affinity."

Lucas breathed raggedly, looking moments from a panic attack. "I don't want to eat souls," he said between gulps of air.

Phaeron laid his hand over Lucas's, pitching his voice to soothe. "No one's eating souls here. Perhaps you will find a ghost willing to share if you help them move on to the afterlife, or no consistent source shows up. Witches channel magic through common origins that can be found most anywhere. You've simply been altered to draw upon a much more uncommon supply of magic."

"Well, fuck," Ben muttered.

"And when you're feeling stronger, I will teach you what I know of souls. I already have a few ideas of what you might be able to do. You're not alone, okay?" Phaeron continued, patting his hand when he earned a slow nod.

"You're in good hands," Geo said. I smiled to myself at the unexpected praise from him.

Lucas needed rest for the moment, so I flagged down a nurse while my men helped him back into bed. Mom answered the call button and drew me into a brief hug. "Thank God you're still all right. Did you know your demo—" She caught herself at the last moment. "Dimensional boyfriend is the reason Lucas woke up?"

"Pretty amazing, right?" All I could do was beam. Even with Lucas having an uncertain future with his magic, that was worlds better than being in a vegetative state. Phaeron had done this without any expectations of praise, which meant I needed to be the one to sing it for him.

He glanced over his shoulder like he sensed us talking about him. "One good turn deserves another." He crossed the room in a few strides and reached out to take my hands in his. "Now if you all will excuse me, there's something I need to show Cress."

I met his slitted gaze. "You don't mind if I steal you away, do you?" he purred more quietly. I had a feeling...well, a *hope*, I knew why he wanted a moment alone and agreed wholeheartedly.

30
CRESS

PHAERON WHISKED me away in an embrace of shadows. By the time I blinked away the dizzy spell that followed my sudden relocation, he'd placed me on the couch in one of the library's private rooms. It was his room at this point, with the tatters of the clothes he'd shredded off me still lying beside the bed and his night-air scent lingering around us.

I took a deep breath and released it in a happy sigh. That smell clung to his skin, magic and man combined.

It took me a heartbeat longer to realize there were bags cluttering the floor by my feet. Phaeron had an odd expression, something like chagrin tugging at his dark gray lips as he looked at them. He was about to apologize about something, so I stood and kissed him before he could.

He cupped the back of my neck and stroked down the sensitive column. His lips caressed mine at a slow, measured pace, at odds with the frenzy that usually lit in him at the brush of my mouth. It was such a small tell, but also an immediate neon sign that suggested something had changed. He was in control, just as he'd promised, his soul healed.

So that meant...maybe this really was the moment he'd claim me in the ways he'd promised. Pulling back, he met my gaze. Warmth danced in the topaz facets of his eyes, and I stood mesmerized by them.

"Can I tell you something?" he murmured.

He could tell me a lot of things with that voice of his. By his serious tone, I had the feeling this wasn't a sexy kind of something and sobered myself. "What is it?"

He smoothed his thumb down my cheek, tender despite the weight of what he was about to share. "My brother showed me a memory as he was dying. A prophecy of Myuna's fate that he bore witness to," he said.

"Was it an accurate prophecy?" I asked, huskier than I intended. The roughened textured of his callused fingers brushed featherlight down my jaw and the tender skin over my throat.

A hint of pain sparked in his gaze. "It was told by the Void, so it has the chance of being accurate one day. Listen to this and tell me if you think you know who it speaks of..." He took a breath and intoned it from memory. "Another shall ascend to rival you, and she will bring about your end. She who would mate the son of night and fight you alongside his daughter. She will defeat you before you have a chance to spread your influence on a new world."

There was a knot where my heart should be, beating erratically against my ribcage. "Wait...no," I said. He tilted my chin up so I would see the way he was looking at me. "It couldn't be me."

"It could be you," he echoed.

I considered the prophecy's wording again. There was one step I hadn't taken, one close enough that I felt my toes resting on the precipice, itching to take the plunge. My heart thudded. I *wanted* to be the one to kill Myuna. Why would I back away from my destiny just because a dimensional had seen it in the Void?

"Keshora and Ravai died because of that prophecy. Myuna has been sure of my identity as 'the son of night' before I even knew what Earth was," he continued, like he mistook my pause for doubt.

"It's a self-fulfilling prophecy. Myuna is causing it to come true because of her reaction to it," I said. If only he could feel how much I wanted to take care of her menace once and for all. Not only for my own sake, for things to go "back to normal," but also to give him the closure he so clearly needed because of this goddess who had ruined his old life. "She meets her death *here*, in a new world, at the end of my sword."

He released me and stepped away, working the buckle of his belt. Was he getting naked already? *He went for that fast!*

Phaeron pulled his sheathed swords free from his hips and sank to his knees in one graceful motion, laying them at my feet. He cupped my right hand with both of his, brushing a kiss over my fingertips. "Cressida Rollins Darkmore," he began. "From this moment forth, I swear my blood, blades, and magic to your service."

There was adoration in his gaze as he said this oath. I reminded myself to breathe, caught up in how special it was to see such a private glimpse of his culture. Of course he wouldn't immediately undress and take me to bed. He was an old-fashioned prince first, and I loved that about him.

"You have captivated me from the moment we met. For what is a soul but a manifestation of a person's core truth? How radiant you are, my True Light in the purest sense. I swear to be your Shadow, a loyal protector. The one to come running to fulfill your *every* need." He ended this with a suggestive lift of his brows, and I shivered with awareness.

But he wasn't finished speaking. He gestured to the pile of bags by the couch. "Though I have little by way of material wealth, I have found for you a patchwork gift. I hope you will accept a more proper offering that I will make for you by hand when we are again in a period of peace."

I wanted to say that he didn't have to give me anything, but this was a dance I was just learning the rhythm to. Perhaps all shadowborn made their mates custom gifts. Ah, shit. I didn't have anything to give him in return. "Phaeron, it's okay, I—"

"Let me finish," he whispered. "If you accept me as your mate, it would mean everything to me and my new life here. Your family and friends will be mine too. Your other mates will be my brothers. But you, Cress, shall be the only goddess of light I answer to. Will you wear my mating mark openly, without regret?"

He waited expectantly for my answer, and I bit my lip. I hadn't gotten him anything or prepared any fancy words. If I was going to be a good mate, at least I could try to offer the latter. Phaeron watched my expression and smiled wide enough to show his fangs, amusement creasing around his eyes. "A simple yes or no will suffice," he added.

"Yes," I rushed to say. "Of course it's a yes. I've wanted this since…" A dark containment room in Moongrove Library. I pictured the viciousness of his desire when he let it off the short leash of his self-control.

I would've walked out of that room as his mate if circumstances allowed, but there hadn't been a moment between us yet where he could fully trust himself. "You don't want to take a bite of my soul anymore, right?"

"Not in the slightest," he said. He took my free hand and pressed a kiss to the mark of protection on the inside of my wrist. There was a prick of pain, soothed by the brush of his tongue, and then that bit of magic was gone.

"Hey!" I protested.

"I will replace it with something better," he said. His hands moved to my hips, nudging me closer. A coil of his tail drew his weapons out of the way. "With the mating mark, I will always know when you need me, and in what way."

"Will it work the other way around?" I asked. He flicked open the button of my jeans, dragging the zipper down with the tip of his claw.

"I only know one answer, based on the experience with a different human mate. Shall we see what happens with us rather than look to the past?"

"Okay." Cool air hit the damp fabric between my legs when he nudged my jeans down, and I trembled with anticipation. It was finally happening. I could have Phaeron without fear of his control snapping at the wrong moment.

He hooked his thumbs through the thin straps of my panties. "I think I'll begin my worship of you here," he said, dragging them down ever so slowly.

"You should try me in your other form," I suggested. My cheeks heated as he paused and tilted his head, considering what I'd said.

Then a grin split his face. "Naughty witch. I know what you want," he teased. With a murmured word in his native language, his features shifted into the alien angles of Soiluire. He flicked his forked tongue out with a wink.

I nodded eagerly. When he'd been stuck like this, I couldn't help but wonder what he could do with that tongue and how the rest of his body differed under his clothes. Maybe he'd indulge my every wicked thought as soon as today.

Solid shadows unfurled around us, helping him angle and anchor my legs. His claws dimpled my skin where he held me spread open for him. He laved his way up my inner thigh and peppered the path with grazes of his sharp teeth. I was already moaning for him before he reached my aching center and delved between my pussy lips with one stroke of his tongue.

I nearly jolted off him from the shock of pleasure. That tongue was a lot longer than I expected, and its forked end fluttered over my clit just so. His answering growl vibrated through me, his grip tightening. I felt him mumbling, and it became English halfway through, "...Don't move, Cress. My horns."

He tilted his head an inch to the side, and the hard point at the end of his spiraled horn jabbed in a sensitive spot close to my ass. "I won't," I yelped.

He answered with a Soiluirian purr and tugged my thighs just a bit wider. Now I noticed the ridges of his horns against my skin and the occasional brush of the tips, but with me as still as I could bear, there were no more unwelcome pokes. Only the glide of his tongue and lips as he feasted on me.

I would've expected him to need a bit of time to get used to his old body since he'd been modified to be more humanlike centuries ago, but he used that tongue like he'd never been parted from its length and flexibility. By the time he wiggled it up my channel and stimulated every inch, I was trembling in place.

Shadows held my hips steady, and when he noticed how close I was, he circled his mouth to mimic how I'd chase the high of pleasure. His horns were the most natural handhold, so I clutched them with both hands as I came hard, back arching and toes curling.

He cleaned my pussy with slow, sure strokes and a rumble deep in his throat. It seemed he genuinely liked the taste of me, and I flushed pleasantly at the thought. When he retracted his magic and placed me back on my shaky legs, my bare soles hit the carpet, and I glanced down, impressed. He'd worked off my shoes and bunched-up jeans while I was otherwise distracted, leaving me bare from the waist down.

For the moment, he remained on his knees, licking the glistening remains of my pleasure from his face while adjusting the bulge that tented the front of his pants. His toothsome grin put his usual viciously pleasure-filled smile in context. This was who he was, the wolflike shadowborn that lurked below his princely manners.

"You're incredible," I told him.

He shifted, blunting his sharp alien features back into humanlike ones. "What was that?"

I pulled off my shirt and bra. "Come and get me," I invited instead.

His gaze brightened with predatory interest. It wasn't really that far from the couch to the bed, but I walked backward to the edge and sat while he prowled after me, shedding clothes on the way. He slid his arms on the bed and leaned in to cage me with his body.

I breathed in his presence, the earthy scent of night that clung to him like a cologne, and felt his soft skin and dense muscle as I caressed his chest. Several lifetimes of fighting scars patterned him, faded by time but still notable to the touch.

He was so close, the heat of him resting between my legs. "This is permanent, Cress. You'll wear my mark for as long as we both live," he said against my lips.

"Are you asking if I'm sure?"

Instead of a kiss, he rested our foreheads together, gaze soft on mine. "You must understand this is a lifetime of devotion I promised you. Some may find that…" He circled a hand, searching for a word. "… intense."

Maybe it was. By most metrics, our relationship had been a whirlwind, but I didn't need more time. No matter how unlikely our pairing was, we fit together. "We're meant to be, literally light and dark," I murmured.

He brushed a hand through my hair, breathing out his lingering tension. "You complete me, bright soul."

The next thing I knew, he was lifting me to carry me around the bed and laying out so I straddled him. His shadows reached for the bedside lamp. "Could you keep it on? I want to see you," I said.

"Not the request I expected." But he retracted his magic, his pupils slitted in the golden light. His hair pooled over one shoulder, dark and glossy as ink.

I ran my nails over his chest, earning a soft, approving hiss. "What *were* you expecting?" I caught his throbbing length between my cheeks, rolling my hips to tease him through my slick folds. One of the hard bumps that gave it unusual texture caught against my sensitive flesh, feeling like the press of a fingertip.

He bared his fangs in a grin. "I will fulfill anything you desire. You need but ask."

"Well, I was curious…" I drew out another stroke against him.

"If I've learned anything on Earth…" He rested his hands on my hips, nudging me onto the crown of his cock. "…it is that curiosity is utterly human."

I sank down onto him slowly, savoring how he stretched me. "Is your dick any different in your other form?" I asked.

He held me flush against him, head tilted at a coy angle. "Let's find out," he purred. In a few seconds, he'd transitioned to his alien form and rested lengthened claws ever so carefully on my skin. Something else had changed about him, but I felt it inside me as a slight thickening when he was already a snug fit.

I lifted and popped my mouth open with a shocked cry. The discovery was immediate, an unusual but intense starburst of sensation. He watched my reaction with a pleased expression as I sank onto him again for more. Like his vampire-like fangs were remnants of a whole mouth full of them, the few nubs on his length were a hint at the full texture he had in this form.

He stimulated every inch of me even on the way down, hitting that sensitive inner patch for a gush of liquid warmth. His shadows piled pillows behind him, and he propped up his shoulders, crooking a finger with a literal smolder in his eyes. I saw the Iorsio tribe in him, a hint of yellow flame, as if he didn't already have the most beautiful eyes on this world and the next.

I leaned in as he'd beckoned and felt him shift, taking control. His fangs grazed my lips, his kiss hungry but measured. With one hand, he helped me ride him as fast as I could stand without coming on the spot. He cupped the back of my head and ran gentle pressure down my jaw with strokes of his thumb.

My body tightened as I sped toward release…and then he slowed and stopped, holding my hips to his. Huffing out a frustrated breath, I wiggled, and that release slipped away one second at a time. "Phaeron," I groaned.

He took his time shifting back to his humanlike form. "I made you something like a promise before…this." He gestured to encompass the room.

"You did?" I couldn't think of anything. Not when he'd thoroughly scrambled my brain and was still nestled within me, hard as iron.

"Mmm. Perhaps it will come to you soon."

He caught my lips, this time hardly holding back with only two fangs to navigate. During that savage kiss, he started to move again, reawakening my body. But this time, I ached for that release I'd been denied and started to tremble as we approached it again.

I halfway expected him to stop again when I was close but breathed a vicious "Fuck!" when he did.

"Now, now," he teased, a growl edging his tone. He wasn't unaffected by his own game.

I worked my jaw, finding it harder to talk. "What was the promise?"

He shook his head minutely. "Trust me, you'll remember," he rumbled.

When he thrust again, the rise and fall of pleasure to frustration took even less time. "Please," I breathed. He wanted me to beg. Oh! He wanted me to beg him to bite me.

One day, you will carry my mating mark. You'll beg for it.

I felt his cock kick within me as he clamped down on his release too. He met my gaze and sighed, filtering a few locks of my hair through his fingers. Speaking Soiluirian, his cadence rose and fell in waves. Like music or poetry. Words of love. Words to soothe.

"I trust you," I answered. My tongue felt too big for my mouth. "I love you. I want to carry your mark forever. On my skin and my soul. I want to be yours. Please, Phaeron."

His hold on me tightened. When he lifted me and thrust deeply, I knew. We were speeding toward the end this time. He skimmed his lips down my neck, and I was wound so tightly even his hot breath was erotic as it washed over my skin.

"It will hurt, but you will barely feel it," he promised. He used his free hand to angle my head, placing his fangs in just the right place, in the hollow where neck and shoulder met. I was already unraveling, coming so hard my eyes rolled back.

He inhaled and then bit me. I screamed, pleasure and pain flaring and entwining for several heartbeats before he exhaled. He'd swapped a tiny piece of our souls, and I felt the pressure of memories that weren't my own all crowding in as my body surrendered to unconsciousness.

31
CRESS

Like when Braza created the tether between us, I experienced Phaeron's memories as if I were him. Yet a tug in my gut reminded me I wasn't a Moihan male, as if I wasn't quite sleeping under the layer of his recollections. I existed as a tagalong for the journey through his past.

The pieces of memory were snippets from a very long life. Yet what I saw defined who he was.

Shadowborn. Soldier. Prince. Lover. Father.

His earliest memories were of shadows, curling and billowing between his small hands. They were always there behind the beacons of a goddess of light otherwise present on a world saturated in a deep shroud of night lit only by distant, cold stars.

What he truly remembered of childhood were bits and pieces of an ancient whole. Finely tailored suits reduced to shreds because they fit too snugly. The shadowborn rage, overwhelming in a boy's body.

He associated his Iorsio mother with her disapproval; her pursed, white-stained mouth.

His father, however, let brief glimpses of sympathy through the cracks of his stony visage. Phaeron and his twin had taken after him, after all, beget of the strongest shadowborn to ever serve Myuna.

It was his father that'd put him into physical training early, and from there, he discovered his first love...a weapon in his hands.

The sword did not require manners or doublespeak, nor did it look at him with weighty expectations. It was straightforward, something to master. He learned with one, then two swords, moving through forms and stances until his fingers bled and it all became muscle memory. He honed himself to a fine edge of mastery made of blade and shadow.

Like any other weapon, he was put to use. His birth nation was constantly at war, conquering and expanding in the name of Myuna. The softness of his teenage years dulled as time progressed. One of the only constants he had was his brother. Early on, they would trade battlefields: from court to bloodshed and back. Phaeron preferred bloodshed at first, but he did his duty as a prince as was required.

The first half of his immortal lifetime was divided into eras, each corresponding with a different mate. Phaeron had shared his first female, Hisulet, with Endaeron. The royal family and courtiers viewed their relationship as perfect, as Hisulet was Vrassorm and a noble groomed for the tasks of royalty. She'd loved them both but had eventually bent to the whims of the court and carried Endaeron's heir, with a second on the way, when she'd taken a drink from a poisoned cup. Once she was buried, Phaeron sought cold-blooded revenge while his brother and nephew continued to mourn.

His parents shuffled him to war for a longer period of time, which suited him fine at first, especially when he crossed blades with his second mate, Baeri. She was shadowborn and Moihan too, a fierce warrior from a rival nation that'd played cat and mouse with him over the course of several battles. When they came together, it was not sweet and gentle, but a whirlwind of claws and snapping fangs. He carried the scratches down his back with pride.

Baeri woke something cruel in Phaeron. He took pleasure in his strength and skill, fighting for the end result of victory and his mate's approval. Together, they had a streak of victories that won Myuna uncontested control of an entire continent. Enemies began to lay down their arms when they saw him across the battlefield rather than risk having their immortal lives torn apart.

Baeri had died as she'd lived, suffering a truly violent and instant death right next to Phaeron. He returned to the capital alone, ready to receive accolades, but instead was handed orders to lead his army overseas for continued conquest. Eyes still burning from grief, he'd refused and drawn Myuna's ire, which reflected in the court's response to him, especially when Endaeron left to fulfill the goddess's wishes instead.

Phaeron met his third mate soon after taking to his old diplomatic role, marking the shortest time between losing a beloved and discovering another. Solirin was an Iorsio tribe debutant, young and doe-eyed, who trembled when he first tried to touch her. To have a female fear him was so strange that he'd taken another look at himself and his reputation. For her, he trimmed his claws and polished his manners, slowly coaxing her trust and affection with gentle touches, poetry, and flowers.

They spent over a century together. It was a time he remembered fondly, as it was the closest he'd come to retiring his weapons for good. Then they decided to have a child, and Solirin passed in the midst of a difficult birth. He'd gained a son, Sennvold, but lost his True Light. This would not be the last time he raised a child alone, and his son took after him in more than just looks. When Phaeron returned to the battlefield, his boy was his squire and eventually a full-fledged shadowborn warrior.

Now that Phaeron was older, he saw the rashness of youth in Sennvold and the exhilaration of the fight in his fourth mate when their paths crossed in a war camp. Theda was Moihan too, but not shadow-born; instead, she was an experienced axe maiden who'd fought for Myuna only because her country had been conquered. Their pairing was benefited by experience. His newest mate went to war for the challenge and glory, not to gloat over how many kills she could etch into the runes on her armor, as vicious Baeri had done.

They grew tired of fighting together after several campaigns. Phaeron spoke of retirement more and more, suggesting Sennvold could take up the mantle of general with a few more decades' experience. He was done fighting because Myuna told him to. If she did not accept his decision to retire with his mate, they would disappear. He knew where to take her.

Days before they were to return to the capital, Theda was assassinated, taking a blade that'd been meant for his back. He grew bitter with regret that she'd pushed him out of the way. There was no one else for an endless drudgery of years after her death, as if fate was saying that he'd outlived too many of the women in his life and did not deserve another.

His memories skipped ahead, coming back into crystal focus with the ringing of claws on metal. Phaeron rapped the ends of his swords, peace tied in their sheathes, as he waited one cold evening at the mouth of a cave. Not just any cave, but Shenmaw, an underground town and home to the secretive Vess.

Restlessness shifted under his skin. I felt a shade of his discomfort and the weight of darker thoughts and emotions. It felt like he was here because of the despair, loneliness, and heartache that filled him, though he longed to melt into the night as the passing seconds wore his resolve away.

He had announced to the Vrassorm male keeping guard that he was there to see Auric et Vess. The leader of the voidwhisperers was not usually one to be summoned casually, but Phaeron had minded their rules and kept to the line in the dirt he was not allowed to pass.

I was surprised when Auric arrived. He was nearly unchanged this far in the past, except he had two intact backswept horns and his navy-blue hair was long and woven elaborately into braids. The stain on his face glimmered purple, tracing jagged lines over his skin and horns.

He still had a spiked tail, tattooed blue skin, and a clouded eye, the other teal with a scratch-thin pupil. Phaeron tensed as the other male inspected him, tension threading the air between them.

Phaeron broke the silence first. "I have come to take you up on your offer." He was ready to disappear. Slowly, he inched his chin down in a show of respect for the elder Vess. Here in Shenmaw, Auric was the ranking male, practically a king of the tiny population he kept protected underground.

Auric also held a precarious political position as the leader of an order separate from Myuna's nation of worshipers. Shenmaw was within her territory, clinging to a technicality for its neutral existence. It was close to uninhabitable, reportedly close enough to a rip in the world that the Void's madness twined through the air like a physical force.

None of the devout wanted to experience the Void that way, and they weren't invited at any rate. As long as Auric sent a steady supply of Vess to predict the future for Myuna, Shenmaw was allowed to govern itself.

A smile broke across Auric's face. "About time, kid. Leave your goddess at the line and enter." His voice was also the same, a deep rumble from his barrel chest.

"Myuna does not dwell in my heart. I am no more than a tool to her, a blade," Phaeron said with venom.

Auric turned, motioning to the guard, who resumed his post in front of Shenmaw's opening. "Then you are welcome here. Come," he said over his shoulder.

Phaeron followed, and time blurred. I felt his surprise as he walked Shenmaw's spacious corridors for the first time. Many single-eyed Vess practiced their magic here, but there were others from all walks of life. The one thing they had in common, he knew, was they all spurned the goddess of light to live in the pitch-black depths of the earth.

I felt his loneliness deepen. There were families here, and the sense of loss within him grew more biting. "Will you look into the Void for me?" he asked.

"That's what I do, kid." Auric stole another glance over his shoulder. "But this is the first time you've asked. What are you trying to find?"

"Hope, perhaps," he murmured.

Auric grunted. "The Void contains little of that. Come eat with Geryn and me."

Phaeron resigned himself to the cross-examination about to occur with Auric and his mate. Later that evening, when their young children had been put to bed, he sat with them, nursing a cup of spicy-sour broth that was common amongst the seers. It helped clarify the sight and sounds of the Void, apparently. He couldn't stomach much of it.

He shared his news and his request. He'd only just buried Sennvold, the last of his family. It was an honorable death for his boy but an unbearable loss all the same. War had finally ruined everything he'd held dear, and he felt...so alone. He found it hard to say the words, gazing into the depths of his soup rather than meet their eyes.

Auric's hand on his shoulder was about as welcome as the sharp edges of shattered glass. But his only words of comfort were, "The Void cannot soothe your pain, nor will it give you an immediate answer. You would be better served by reaching for community rather than the unknown."

"A promise of future peace would be enough. I have been unmarked for so long now..." Long enough that he'd forgotten the relief of a True Light's soothing touch. He needed something to anticipate, something to hold on to. Desperately enough to truly anger Myuna, should she know he'd gone to Shenmaw and ducked into the one place her all-seeing light did not reach.

Geryn glanced toward Auric. She was also of the Vrassorm tribe, but not a Vess, her belly well rounded with child. "He could stay here for a while. We have the space."

"If it pleases you." Auric gave her a tender smile. He wouldn't invite another male into his mate's space unless she approved. She'd be bedding down soon to rest for the last months of her pregnancy, exhausted by the needs of the growing child.

Phaeron masked his discomfort with a sip of broth. "I don't mean to impose, especially not at a delicate time."

Geryn smiled warmly. "Nonsense," she said with a dismissive wave of her hand.

So, Phaeron stayed and eventually learned the peoples' many reasons for hiding from Myuna in Shenmaw. He let his own resentment of her fester, created by her wars and the thousand cuts of indifference she'd led her followers and his parents to inflict upon him.

Auric took Phaeron on days' worth of tours deep with discussions on magic and meaning. He showed Phaeron how easy it was to call upon his latent soul magic here, so close to a rip in reality, implying with his knowing smirk that he should practice with it. The Void must have informed him of a possible future where he needed it.

Soul magic was akin to a party trick on Soiluire, though Myuna took a shine to those who had true skill in it. Most of them became torch-bearers...except for Phaeron, ever the forgotten shadow to Endaeron. Still, he made a mental note to practice glancing deeper into others, stealing fleeting looks at their souls.

Long before he ever saw the rip in reality, his conversations with

Auric and Geryn steered him toward airing how deep his burden had become. "Without a family of my own making, I'm not sure of my purpose anymore," he murmured to his friends, who listened well. "I have grown weary of what I once enjoyed. Why fight and perpetuate the cycle of tragedy?"

He only wanted *peace*. The desire echoed back to me full definition. He yearned for it within himself.

When he finally accepted this truth and began to feel his pain ebbing, Auric took him to see the Void. It was in a cavern deep within Shenmaw, where the blackness of the Void leaked into reality. Their surroundings distorted in the narrow corridor, and Phaeron felt the chill of the space between worlds for the first time.

Its laughter immersed him, and he growled, swinging his head around, looking for the threats mocking him. He kept a leery eye out, fearful of the alien presence of the magic and how it dug into his senses.

Visions played across the walls. Faceless figures drifted in and out of focus, interacting with Phaeron's shadow in various ways. Creatures dying, spraying blood from a slash of his sword. Females laughing, giving him the charmed looks he once strived to earn. Laughter. Screeches. Demonic, warped noises that could've once been words.

He hunched and covered his ears as the whispers pushed in, too many to be understood.

"You have to ask it to focus on what you want," Auric advised over the cacophony. He took him by the arm and guided him to the site of the rift, where the visions and sounds were at their most real.

The Void responded to Phaeron's thoughts, a blessing when he'd have to scream over the echoes as they intensified in the small, cavernous space. He wanted to know there was a future for him, that the piercing loneliness he contended with each day would pass.

The chill in the air intensified, prickling over his skin like ice needles, and answered. Half or more was madness and distortion, but Auric was there to wave away the worst of it.

The future immersed him. Voices of all kinds spoke his name. Male, female...kind tones, needy ones, furious intonations. Auric and Geryn swirled in with them before stopping abruptly.

I didn't recognize any others at first, but woven into the tapestry of sound was Keshora and then Morgana. And...my voice. Ben and Geo were there too, and all our friends and eventually Auric once more. Phaeron didn't realize there was a change of worlds and languages. The Void presented us all as the same: those that would cross his path in the future.

Phaeron raised his head, letting his eyes slip closed. My voice had caught his attention, and his lips curled slowly. *Definitely a lover,* he thought, picturing me as a curvy Moihan female.

When he opened his eyes again, the Void showed him children. Delicately clawed hands holding an infant that could've been Ravai. A scramble of insanity that Auric quietly dispelled for him. Then toddler Braza shyly meeting his gaze as he placed her on a countertop.

Phaeron reached out, scalding his fingertips on freezing cold Void mist. He hissed and flicked his hand, only regretting that he'd disrupted that particular vision. He longed to hold them with a fierceness that was nearly painful.

The two girls reappeared, older. He watched them from the edge of a field, soaking in their laughter as they played within the shadows, using them to jump around trying to tackle one another.

Optimism for the future rekindled in his chest. Those were the only sweet laughs within the whole Void so far.

"It could be a turning of the millennia before this happens," Auric said. The visions became nonsense once he relaxed the fist he'd been holding at his side.

The scene was just changing. There was a third child, who he only caught a fleeting glance of. Phaeron ended up shrugging, embracing the knowledge that there might be more family further into his future. But I could've gasped, creating a dissonance that completely shifted the course of his soul memories.

TIME SPED BY. For the next age of his life, he'd stayed with the Shenmaw rebels until he became one as well, before returning to the capital to cross paths with a new mate, Keshora, and fitting ill at ease into his old life and the weighty expectation that he return to fighting in Myuna's name. He'd had a spell of contentment and a family he lost along with everything else in the Age of Decay.

I saw him with Morgana next, and yes, he'd loved her dearly. It wasn't as hard as I'd expected to watch them together after seeing him in love five other times. He viewed his first human lover as both fascinating and fragile. In their short time together, he'd figured out how to elevate her to demigoddess status just so they could be together into eternity.

Phaeron's memories jarred forward. He'd woken to a world changed, damaged librarian witch runes fading to black on the ceiling above. He'd been locked away for two hundred years by Morgana, a huge rift that betrayed the vows of their mating.

"Why?" he'd asked in a pained whisper.

The emotions were still real, as recent as an echo. He'd later stood before her ghost and heard her reasons, but her memory was tainted now, a complicated blip in time for him. She had picked him up at his lowest and helped him acclimate to a new world. Her presence in his life was once hope, a promise that he was not alone in this strange world, where his people were feared and hated. Now that she had found her purpose in death, he could wish her well and allow them both to move on.

But in sealing him in stasis, she had cut him off from everyone and everything that'd still mattered to him. He had essentially risen from his grave by waking up. That it was an accidental side effect from a blood baron's plot to unleash the Hungering Darkness made it worse. He could've been lost to time in that room.

My heart twisted as I watched him struggle, his stark retread of a lack of a *purpose* now a resonant note in his memories. When he wasn't blacking out from the Hungering Darkness's attempts to control him, he sat in an alley with a homeless man, sipping the cheap alcohol he kept in a paper bag. I barely recognized David, a bear shifter Phaeron had later introduced me to, under a layer of hair and grime.

The alleyway served as a resting place when he failed to find a sense of normalcy in the modern world. Lanie had just died, and he saw me in his mind's eye, all grief and ugly tears and incorrect conclusions.

He had no place on Earth. No people, no mate...nothing but the ear of the shifter next to him, who drank to muffle the pain of his soul damage. He spoke in depth about a place called Aurora Heights, where shifters rejected by their mates gathered for second chances.

"Why don't you go to this place?" he'd asked.

"I dunno, man," David slurred, knocking back the rest of a nearly empty bottle. He looked into its depths, and his expression darkened. "I guess I keep expecting someone from my sleuth to come find me."

"Your family?" Phaeron guessed.

"Yeah. Maybe they're just ashamed of me now. My perfect match rejected me...so there has to be something wrong with me." With a shrug, David placed the empty bottle aside and transferred the paper wrapping to a new one. He turned the cap toward Phaeron.

"While you yet live, there's nothing to stop you from finding a new path." As he spoke, he used his shadows to remove the cap with an effortless twist. His shadowborn abilities...reduced to a party trick.

Yet David barked a laugh. "You're like a fortune cookie, man."

His eyes narrowed. "What is a fortune...cookie?"

David just laughed harder. He seemed to think Phaeron was hilarious for some reason. They shared the bottle, and Phaeron cringed from the first few sips. Had distilleries not improved while he rested in stasis?

"You know, like from Chinese joints." Sometimes he took pity on Phaeron and tried to explain. "You break the cookie open, and it tells you your fortune. Sometimes they're all mystical like you are."

"The cookie tells... You know what? Never mind." He leaned back, his head full of fuzzy warmth.

There was nothing to stop him from treading a new path of his own. To become someone else again, continuing to adapt and grow even though it felt like the twilight of his immortal life. He saw me again when he closed his eyes, this time walking side by side with Lanie. We'd been dressed nearly identically, something my seer friend had done on purpose.

Phaeron was sure she'd been targeted because of me. My proximity to his release meant it was a miracle the Hungering Darkness hadn't immediately killed me and eaten my soul to soothe the edge of its starvation. But if it had a sniff of me, then it would hunt me tirelessly until it was my eyelids he was forced to close.

As the only one who could go toe-to-toe with his undead brother, he had a duty to try to protect me, even if I hated him in those days for assuming *he* was the monster.

I'D LIVED MOST of the memories that passed by next. Phaeron didn't find much purpose until he was kneeling in the dirt, bleeding out from protecting me and my friends from our ill-fated first fight with the Hungering Darkness. As Áine healed him back from the brink of death, he'd asked, "Do you see now that I am not a monster, bright soul?"

My shaky "yes" had meant much more to him than I'd ever expected. There was a chance we'd make amends, even become allies, now that it was understood that we had the same enemy.

He began to think of me as lovely and often triggered his other-worldly sight to see my form haloed by my soul. Light was anathema to a shadowborn...but not the kind I put off. My soul flickered around me like liquid gold, an eternally flattering light source that limned my cheeks and put a shine to my purple hair. My brown eyes turned honey-toned and sparkling.

He'd been admiring me for longer than he'd admitted to. I was soft and rounded compared to the females of his own species, confusing his attraction. Fate reminded him that it was my voice to bring him back from Endaeron's control twice, helping him shake off his cravings to bite into my soul since he admired it so.

As early as the evening he'd walked me to my dorm room, he'd known I was supposed to be his next True Light. From then on, he'd taken the duties of my Shadow and gladly stepped into the role of training and spending time with me and my friends. Tempering Geo's stone form and protecting Ben with his presence were merely a part of it.

With the tug of hunger in him every time he glimpsed my soul, his role as protector was all he felt he could offer. That didn't prevent the little touches and teases as both of our feelings deepened, but each was a test of his control. One slip, and he'd hurt me beyond repair...but he couldn't bring himself to stay away.

If I could've caught a breath, I would've at the feeling of yearning that deepened in him with time. He'd ached with unfulfilled need so acutely each time he denied both of us more. Enough to have a spike of shadowborn rage toward his oldest friend when Auric called me "a mate in name only."

I saw a closed-door conversation between him, Geo, and Ben; then the memories took a single step back in time from his diplomatic request for peace between my three men. "It is easy to love Cress" in a conference room became the soft slide of covers against his naked body and my slight form so close to his.

"I have missed you far more than words could convey." Underneath the tender whisper was the horror he'd barely staved off, the control Myuna had failed to fully exert over him. He'd refused to give in to her with me on his mind, my name on his lips. Knowing he would one day return to me sustained him and kept him awake, aware, and alive just long enough to save his life and soul.

I'd comforted him and run my fingers through his hair, blunted the disjointed edges that existed within him after his torture at her hands. But it was my reaction when he'd tried to pull away again that'd tilted his self-control straight to possessive desire.

I will not go quietly into eternity without lying with you, he'd thought.

That had truly been lovemaking in the dark. My skin glowed to his sight alone when I was surrounded by his shadows, and he'd touched my face, enamored by the sight and the utter trust I'd surrendered to him.

From that night on, I was fiercely *his* and the one to complete him in his new Earth life. I was his mate, his future, his purpose, and his much-longed-for peace.

32
CRESS

I woke feeling more loved than I could imagine, drifting on the safety of my mate's feelings through a rough return to wakefulness. My skin ached like I'd been sandpapered top to bottom, and I couldn't lift my head from where it rested under Phaeron's chin. The pain radiated from my shoulder like a pinched nerve.

Well, as he'd explained, we'd just swapped a tiny piece of our souls to create a permanent bond between us. Maybe this was a taste of what it'd feel like if he'd taken a bite out of my soul as he'd craved until very recently. His brother had given him a very important gift: the opportunity to start again without being impaired by soul hunger.

Phaeron was out cold underneath me, his breathing evening out to the slow and steady cadence of deep sleep. At some point, my memories must've transitioned straight to dreamland for him. I couldn't really be upset about it. Compared to the pieces of his life I'd seen, mine must've been brief and mundane.

No one could really rival an immortal prince from another planet for interesting life experiences.

Knowing he needed rest pretty badly, I moved off of his chest carefully. I'd been out long enough that my legs had regained most of their feeling. I tucked a layer of covers around him and took slow, measured steps toward the gifts he'd gathered overnight.

He'd known to raid a beauty store, and I could've wept when I saw moisturizers and makeup again, especially the expensive brand names I wasn't able to afford. But I put it all aside, shifting through bags of nice clothes and a box full of bottles and what could be random odds and ends.

For Braza's gargoyle form. I simply knew about it now and would help him do what it took to give her a new body. It was incredibly important to him... She was family.

He'd taken several different models of new phones and accessories as well. I fished out the one with the newest hardware and a sparkly case, putting them aside to set up soon. Ben and Geo were going to be overjoyed when they got new devices too, *and* they'd stop taking mine! Win-win.

Lying flat at the bottom of all this stuff was what I was looking for. "My precious," I murmured, pulling out a new, quality sketchbook and a premier pack of colored pencils. I thumbed through the blank pages and opened the pack as quietly as possible, stealing a glance at Phaeron's sleeping form to ensure I hadn't woken him.

I ran my fingers over the rainbow of pencils I'd freed and smiled to myself. It wasn't much, but I could give him something back. I gathered up the art supplies and laid a loose blanket over my naked body before propping the sketchpad on my legs and getting to work. I scribbled away with my tongue caught between my teeth, recreating something from Phaeron's memories before it faded and smudged like many of Braza's recollections had.

With him sleeping away, I had a chance to take my time. I hadn't drawn a portrait like this in a while, but I was a woman possessed. It took full form, and I was rubbing a cramp from my hand when Phaeron finally stirred.

The phantom sensation of panic gripped my chest as he shot up, looking around. When he found where I'd set up, he tilted his head. I realized I was feeling his emotions—in this case, his confusion. "I didn't want to wake you. You needed to sleep," I said.

"Silly female." He sounded groggy. He rubbed his face, glancing down at his clawed hand and flexing it. "All I need is you."

My heart fluttered. I quickly placed the pencils back into their slots and flipped the sketchbook closed, taking it with me. As soon as the blanket fell, the rising burn of his lust kindled across our mating bond, and my sex ached for him in response. I placed the sketchbook on the bedside table and let him pull me back into bed, though he cupped my stiff neck so we didn't jostle the place he'd bitten me.

When we lay face-to-face, he swept my hair back to look at the wound and blew cool air over it. "My mark is developing well," he said, proud. I realized I hadn't taken a moment to look into a mirror at it, and he responded like he knew my thoughts. "You can inspect it later, once it's set."

"How..." I drifted off when I realized that was the wrong question to ask. It was magic from his world, undoubtedly stronger on his end of things. "This really is intense, huh?"

He nodded. "It will fade some with time. But I will always know your needs so I can fulfill them." He stroked his thumb over the curve of my cheek, and I felt him admiring me. I could only mirror him, appreciating seeing him at ease. He really was handsome in a striking way, different yet familiar. Still a man despite every extraordinary circumstance.

"What did my soul memories show you?" I asked.

"A true understanding of who you are." He held me to his chest when he felt how that answer made me nervous for what, exactly, he'd seen. He spoke tenderly in my ear. "Relax, bright soul. I should be the fearful one, with how many terrible decisions I have had to make and live with. You probably saw the worst of me."

"With your shadowborn mate...Baeri," I murmured.

Pressing his lips together tightly, he nodded. "We were too young to understand the damage we caused. I am glad I am not that person anymore. You could say I've been someone different with each of my mates, versions of myself tailored to them," he said.

"I saw them all briefly. If you'd told me before this that you'd had six women before you met...I mean, you've lived so long..." I stammered, drifting to a stop when he pressed his fingers to my lips.

He took my breath away just by looking at me and pushing his tender feelings into my headspace. "They mattered to me in their time. The memories should have shown you that I've had to move on far more than I've wanted to."

"No one should have to bury so many wives," I agreed quietly.

"Each funeral was more difficult than the last. Fate seemed cruel for sparing me, yet it has led me to you. You've swiftly become someone I cannot live without." He took my hand, laying it over his chest and the steady beat of his heart. "I have no desire to exist on Earth without you. Whatever length your life shall be, I will be glad to go along with you when you depart for paradise."

"Phaeron," I said, shocked.

"Too honest?" He was completely serious. This wasn't just him expressing devotion, but a kind of world weariness I could barely wrap my head around.

I got a little teary. I'd just seen how much loss he'd endured and didn't want to picture a time where he was gone. Seeing my distress, he kissed me, slow and loving, while his hands traced my curves. "Don't worry," he said into my lips. "I will find a way for you to enjoy immortality with me first. I want a long, long time with you."

I wanted that too, as long as we could also have Ben and Geo with us. "I agree. I hope you can retire from fighting like you've wanted to for so long."

"Yes," he murmured.

"What do you want to do instead?" I asked.

The sparkle was back in his eyes as he imagined the future. "Mmm, I've found joy in teaching others. I would continue to pursue that and await the day you give me children to raise." He mentioned it casually, like a logical extension of our relationship.

"This is not to say I will hang up my weapons forever. Anyone who challenges our family will find my blades as keen as ever. Besides...most of your friends are unmated women, and I will continue to protect them as they grow into their powers. Maybe it's old-fashioned by Earth standards, but it is only right."

"There's my prince," I said with affection.

"Yes, yours," he purred. "But that's enough about me. You were wondering what your soul memories showed me."

The anxious butterflies took flight in my belly again at the reminder.

"First, I need you to understand that I am not 'more important' than you in any way. I am a prince of nothing and wish I never had the title since I've seen it has intimidated you. We are equals. Okay?"

"Okay," I answered. He rewarded me with another kiss.

"To put your mind at ease, I saw your early childhood and the abusive rages of a man your mother made the decision to leave. May I kill him?"

"What?" I practically yelped.

"I didn't think you'd agree to that," he said, sounding a little disappointed. "You survived growing up with very little, doing your best with what you had, and took a job early to support your mother and sister. Discovering that you're a witch was a twist of good fortune until it came with the baggage of political plots and assassins. One of your biggest regrets is misjudging me and my intentions at first."

That was an understatement. He kissed the apology off my mouth before I could say it, as I'd started to do with him. "I could have stayed and done a better job convincing you of the circumstances," he murmured.

"But you were depressed," I added.

I reached out and brushed my fingertips over his cheek. He closed his eyes, tilting his face for more. "Incredibly. Yet I found it within myself to go on," he said.

"I'm glad."

He breathed a soft sigh. "Me too."

"I saw you talking about it with David. Did you ever find out what a fortune cookie is?"

He cracked open one eye to squint at me. "He wasn't making that up?"

"No, he just explained it really badly," I said, muffling a laugh at his disbelief. "They're folded around a slip of paper that holds a generic statement about the future."

"Hmm. Would I do a good job making fortune statements?"

"I think so."

"David also thought most of the things I told him about my past were from video games." I got the distinct feeling his thought at the moment was *whatever those are* and had another chuckle over that. "Thank you for reminding me of him. I'll have to check on him when we return."

"Maybe he's moved on to Aurora Heights," I said.

He shook his head. "Wanting your family to wake up and see how they've wronged you is one of the strongest desires one can have."

"Spoken from experience." At this point, I was exploring the curl of his horn. It was built solidly, hard and smooth, thinning at the pointed end.

"They never saw me. I found more fulfillment in moving on and being the father I'd never had." He took my wrist and placed my hand on his cheek again, nuzzling against my palm.

"Speaking of which," we said at the same time.

"Jinx. You go first," I said.

He already had that uncanny way of looking right through me, and now I'd armed him with insider knowledge of the depths of my soul. "I think you will make a great mother. Your circumstances are going to be much different from your own childhood."

"I do want kids one day." But he'd touched on something that went deeper, which I hadn't said aloud to another person. "I've had a strong role model. My adopted mother is my hero."

"But you haven't known a positive father figure. You've been afraid of marrying a male like her ex-mate?" The concept seemed to puzzle him.

"It's a human thing. I don't want to give any kids of mine a father like that. And"—I held up a finger—"I realize it's a silly fear when I know now I'd make a dad of Ben, Geo, or you. None of you are like that."

"The babe would have three fathers. Practically tripping over us." He rubbed my belly with quiet longing.

"I have a little gift for you," I said, seeing that it was time to show him, before I could embrace any last-second doubts that he'd find it a meaningful mating gift.

He reassured those nerves. "You don't have to give me anything. You are gift enough."

"It's in the sketchbook. There was a memory... You looked into the Void," I said clumsily.

His pupils narrowed. "I have only done that willingly a handful of times. Was Auric there?" Shifting to lie on his back, he reached for the sketchbook.

"Yeah. It was the first time, I think," I supplied.

"Then the Void was as honest as it can be," he commented.

He flipped up the front cover and looked at the portrait I'd made. The kid was unmistakably Phaeron's son, I thought, if a shade like his mother too. Lighter gray skin; straight, dark brown hair, and slitted dimensional eyes cooled to orange embers. He could've been ten, with the points of his horns starting to emerge from his crown and a layer of baby fat that could give way to high cheekbones one day.

Maybe I was wrong and Phaeron had already met this boy and said goodbye to him without it appearing in his memories or regrets. But the way he froze with a sharp inhale, the phantom of his emotions cycling between surprise, realization, and yearning erased my doubts.

"Is this...?" He reached out to touch the paper.

"I think so," I answered in the same hush.

He set the sketchbook aside and rolled onto me, framing my face and peppering it with kisses. I felt his joy like my own but winced when he put me on my back. My neck was still quite tender. "Thank you," he said, touching foreheads with me. "I don't know how, but...it must be possible."

"We'll figure it out," I promised.

"Someday." He went for the mating mark next, licking the tender space and blowing another cool, soothing breath over it. "Would you like to try my animaris? It might overtake the pain of this setting."

"Sure," I said but swatted him when he bit me none too gently. *Ow.*

The new wound stung for a few seconds. "You're responding to it fast." He gave my hip a squeeze, watching my reaction closely.

Warmth replaced the pain and swiftly met my bloodstream, spreading from there. It hit my heart and radiated out from my chest. A pleasant flush was soon buzzing through me head to toe. He palmed one of my breasts and tweaked the hardened bud, grinning as I nearly arched off the bed. I felt so sensitive all of a sudden and tingled from the brush of his skin on mine. "Phaeron," I moaned.

He hardened against my thigh, responding to my sudden surge of need in kind. "Is this normal?" I asked breathlessly.

"Completely." Despite how he throbbed against me, he pinned my hip, making no move to claim me. "I only gave you a bit. It should wear off...about now."

I did notice it fading. I still ached for him, though, and that was all me, jumpstarted by his animaris. I touched my shoulder. The mating mark tingled with discomfort, but there were no open bite wounds. "It healed me," I said.

He nodded, saying, "I gave you a tiny amount of my life force. It'll fix up superficial wounds and bruises, but it's meant to excite you. Now that you know what it feels like, do you want more?"

I checked myself on agreeing enthusiastically, wiggling underneath him. "Depends. Are you going to deny me again?"

He lifted my hips and thrust with little preamble. Back arching, I moaned hard; it was a relief to feel him fill me again. "I have not the strength nor will to deny you anything," he growled.

"Then I want more. A lot more." I tilted my head, and he kissed his mark before biting down.

BEN

I drew the short straw to go find out where Cress and Phaeron had gone, to deliver a message. I was a bit grumpy about it, but they were probably fucking, and there were only a few safe places around to do that.

She'd been making bedroom eyes at me, damn it, and he'd stolen her away before I could. I was jealous. It felt like it'd been ages since we'd had some bonding time...and I didn't want Big P biting my head off for interrupting them with the news I had to share.

The run to the library was uneventful, though. I didn't have to worry about unnaturals. According to our spy extraordinaire, Grant, there were no more animal unnaturals because Myuna had eaten them all to cast a huge spell that was bad news for us. Because of it, the torchbearers seemed to be waking up from their zombielike state and practicing their magic again.

"Just knock," I told myself as I navigated the wreckage of the first floor and took the stairs down. "The worst that can reasonably happen is he tells you to go away. Again."

And I would not. We needed Phaeron in full tall, dark, and terrifying mode to help us plan the upcoming offensive, and the meeting was scheduled for tomorrow. He needed to know that before he got back to hoarding our girl in his shadow dungeon or whatever.

I didn't worry for long that he'd taken her someplace new. The scream I heard came from the same room where I'd last found them. As expected, it sounded like they were having a good time. I rolled my eyes and knocked.

No answer.

I tried again. *Knock. Knock. Creak...*

The door seemed to have unlatched and opened on its own. "It's Ben?" Cress was asking.

"I can wait for you guys to, uh, finish," I said, peeking inside anyway.

Shadows obscured more than their outlines, but the slap of skin on skin was pretty distinctive. My pants got tight fast from her breathy moan. "Ben," she called, sounding more than a little lust-drunk.

"You can be here if you help pleasure our mate," Phaeron added in a tight growl.

"Oh! C'mere, Ben," Cress cried out.

"Don't threaten me with a good time," I said, jolting into the room and locking the door again behind me. Phaeron retracted his shadows and helped lay Cress down at the foot of the bed. She was giggling and flushed, watching me strip avidly with eyes more dilated than normal.

He sat behind her, waiting with impatient flicks of his tail. But I didn't pay much attention to him, more worried about what was going on with her. "You okay, babe?" I murmured, bending down to kiss her.

"Better than okay. Touch me," she demanded, meeting my lips with open-mouthed passion. Phaeron also answered her need, running his palms up the back of her legs and squeezing her ass.

While I moaned and met her tongue for tongue, he said, "She's under the effects of my animaris. She consented to it."

I broke off the kiss with a, "Your what now?"

"An aphrod—"

"His sexy venom," Cress interrupted.

I felt my face light up. Oh, I was going to have fun with that. "Just full of tricks, aren't you, Big P?" I teased.

"An understatement, Little B," he replied in kind. "But enough talk.

Join us…or don't." He lifted her into his arms and kissed her with the same level of passion she'd hit me with at the door.

Like hell I was going to choose not to join them. I climbed onto the bed behind her, smoothing my hands down her back and leaning in to kiss her unmarked shoulder. There was a new pattern of dimensional magic on the other shoulder, looking like fancy scrollwork stretching a couple inches in a circular pattern around two points where he'd obviously bitten her. Maybe that was where the "sexy venom" thing came from.

His mark on her was a light gray, unlike the pair of black and purple bat-like wings over her shoulder blades, where Braza had tethered to her. The magic was dormant, the skin pebbling with goosebumps in the wake of my touch. I could get used to her being this responsive. I loved hearing how much she enjoyed having us both kissing and stroking her all over.

I'd gotten used to navigating around an extra pair of hands with how often she preferred to have Geo and me at the same time. Phaeron cheated, though, using his shadow magic to leave lingering touches on her legs and arms where we weren't concentrating much attention. I focused on stroking her hips and belly, feeling her quiver between us, almost like she'd come from touch alone.

My fingers dipped toward her overheated core. Fuck, she was already soaked. "Ben, wait," he said, cupping Cress's cheeks. "Look at me, bright soul. Ben's here now. You're about to have us both."

"Oh, yes," she said dreamily.

"Any preferences?" he asked.

She leaned back to look at me over her shoulder. "How do you want me?" she asked huskily. With those lidded bedroom eyes on me, I would've said any way she wanted, but it was clear she was offering it back to me since they'd been at this a while.

"You know I can't resist that pussy, babe," I answered.

Without missing a beat, Phaeron put in, "And you've made quite the mess of me."

"Oh no, we can't have that." She leaned back further into my arms, threading her fingers into my hair as our lips met for a hungry kiss. I took the opportunity to shape the familiar curves of her body with my hands.

As impatient as he'd been to have her again, Phaeron sat back and watched us with an approving growl. When she pulled away with a lingering graze on my bottom lip, he stood and helped her balance on her hands and knees, using his tail to prop her up around the middle. She moaned into his cock when I ran mine through her slick folds.

"Hey, Big P," I said, reaching for his tail. "Could I borrow this?"

With a wave of his hand, he made a cushion of shadows for her middle and held his tail at an angle for me to take. The bunch and flex of muscles under the skin suggested he could've done this for himself, but I was in the business of pleasuring Cress right now, so I teased her with him, drawing a few inches of tail over her pussy.

She moaned into his cock as it sank into her mouth. He cupped the back of her head, testing her with a couple shallow thrusts. "She's going to love this," I said, grabbing her hips and sliding myself home within her easily. She jolted and arched back to meet my hips, fists clenching on the bedsheets.

He waited to see what I was going to do, which was place the tip of his tail at the entrance of her ass. It was perfectly shaped for such a task. "Good." His usually smooth voice was little more than a rumble as he slid the first inch within her and twisted it. "Then she'll enjoy all three of us at once someday."

"How the hell is that going to work?" I asked. I was more focused on staying steady for her despite how she came hard, making me ache to spill early.

"I have a few ideas," he said.

"Of course you do."

"Jealous of something, Little B?"

"Yeah, actually. I wish I had a flexible tail for situations exactly like this one," I said. He was keeping pace with me with it, driving several inches of tail into her. If her mouth wasn't occupied, she'd definitely be screaming right about now.

"I have to have some assets to please her with, besides my wit," he said.

Cress breathed a distinct little "hehe," giggling like she did when I coaxed Geo into bantering with me in bed. Maybe whatever venom he'd given her was wearing off, as she was clear-eyed once he and I finished and lay out on either side of her.

Phaeron touched the mark on her shoulder. "More?" he asked.

"Wait, wait," I put in. "I came here to tell you two something."

"Can it hold on for a couple hours?" she asked.

I scratched the back of my head. "I guess?"

"Awesome, because I want to ride you both for at least that long before letting reality in again." She tilted her head for Phaeron. "More animaris, please."

33
GEO

I APPEARED on Wren's stream to deliver an important message. She'd wanted me in stone form, where my grinding tones and deadly serious expression would lend us credibility with the remaining survivors in Cerris City.

I looked into the camera and said, "We have discovered an exit to the pocket dimension that Myuna and her forces don't know about. All survivors and noncombatants will be evacuated through this secret exit in one week's time."

I listed the four new rendezvous points Ashbough Protective Services was opening up now that we knew Myuna had consumed her poorly shaped monster creatures. The seers had balanced out all possible futures for the evacuation and decided one week would allow us to gather as many of the dwindling population of survivors as possible while the twisted goddess would still be mastering the fine control needed for the unfamiliar magic of her torchbearers.

According to our changeling, there didn't seem to be any movement coming from Myuna's throne. She was deep in meditation alongside a handful of the most powerful supernaturals she'd managed to bring under her sway. We were still outnumbered three-to-one by her torchbearers, and that number could still grow before we moved a large group toward the operating ocean gate.

Hell, if we messed this up, her forces would grow *because* of us. I made it my new, temporary duty to help locate survivors and bring them to safety. For the rest of the day, I flew loops around the furthest reaches of the city as a scout and guard for anyone I came across.

It was my pleasure to serve. Cress would be happy I'd used my time wisely, and it helped me feel productive. I had no doubts Phaeron and Ben were, quite literally, fulfilling my primary duty, and...I came to terms with it on my long scouting flights. Logically, I knew I could not be with her all the time. There was work only I could do here and wouldn't if I had to choose between it and protecting Cress.

I glowed with the pride of a job well done the next morning, having personally saved a dozen survivors and left a single stray torchbearer in quartz cuffs and a medically induced sleep in one of the hospital's rooms. I stood in the foyer, waiting in human form, a few minutes before the big meeting when they arrived in a swoop of shadows.

Phaeron had transported them with his hands on Cress and Ben's shoulders. Her face lit up when she saw me. "Geo! I have something for you," she announced.

I found her elation to be infectious, cracking the first smile out of my recent stint in gargoyle form. "Oh?" I asked.

She took the back of my hand and placed a cool plastic box in my palm. "Your very own phone. Brand new." She beamed as I looked from it to her and released a single, grinding laugh.

"Now I will never break yours again," I said.

"Look, he's smiling. That's practically bursting with joy," Ben laughed, reminding me he and Phaeron were still there. The dimensional hung back a step, wearing an expression that could only be described as besotted as he watched Cress.

I nodded in approval and bent to kiss her. "Thank you," I said.

She lingered close, hands resting on my chest. "Of course. Ben's going to get us all signed up on a plan together, and then you can watch cat videos to your heart's content."

"Soon." I had a pang of regret to end this moment, but the meeting was about to start without us. I pocketed the new phone for the moment. "There is a lot that still needs to be done. Some decisions were made in your absence yesterday, and other things need an expert's opinion." My gaze flashed more deliberately toward Phaeron.

"I enjoyed my respite quite thoroughly," he replied. And judging by the lack of dark hollows under his eyes, it seemed he had finally rested. Good. He'd be ready for the tough challenges ahead. "After the meeting, perhaps I could trouble you for a moment alone, Geo?"

"No problem. I want to show you to a torchbearer that needs your attention anyway," I said.

He dipped his head and led the way to the meeting, which started up the moment we settled. Madigan stood over a spread of maps pulled down from the wall. Today, we were joined by the usual group of decision makers: the two Crown Coven members, Hana Graygazer, Auric et Vess, Madigan's husbands, plus Roe and Grant.

Auric greeted Phaeron in Soiluirian, who replied in kind, taking a seat next to him. I glanced over at Cress, who shrugged. Without Braza, we had no hope of knowing what they were actually saying, but Auric's guffaw and hearty slap on Phaeron's back seemed fairly universal.

"Fashionably later than me. Nice," Roe said, fist-bumping Cress.

"Hello, you all. Welcome," Madigan said at the same time. "We are gathered to plan our methods of attack. We've just set the hourglass over and have less than a week to evacuate civilians and noncombatants before it's too late."

"What do you already know of Myuna's recent actions?" Phaeron asked.

She mentioned the consumption of most of her unnaturals and the way the torchbearers were seeming to wake and use their magic at her direction. He nodded, speaking up at the end of her narrative. "I've come to understand that Myuna is not the only monster of her kind. She intended to create another being of entropy in my brother and planted a seed of corruption in his soul. It was why the Hungering Darkness was so exceptionally awful while also being like her.

"It is more than likely, with its death, she has chosen to ascend another, who is helping her control her torchbearers. Such an expenditure of magic would be quite difficult for her in her current state without a sacrifice." His yellow gaze cut to Grant. "Do you know who she ascended?"

"No. I just know she's sitting around with five of her strongest minions right now. It could be any one of them," he answered.

The others nodded. At some point, he must've shown his

changeling nature to everyone else in this room. Soon it wouldn't be much of a secret at all, if we survived the coming fights.

"If we can kill the ascended torchbearer, Myuna will be at her weakest. She will be so distracted by her hunger that we could bait her into a trap. Auric will manipulate the Void to send her back to rot away on the remnants of Soiluire," Phaeron said.

Hana's grave voice cut through his confident tones. "We will still need someone to stand toe-to-toe with her while he works."

He frowned, shaking his head. "Even weakened, she is still akin to a goddess…"

"A point we can come back to," Madigan interjected. "We have exchanged a few messages with the Coral King. He's willing to send his myrmidons to help us defend the ocean gate as long as Willow Frost is among the evacuees."

Cress shifted uncomfortably. "Has Willow agreed to this?"

Roe turned to her with a guilty little look. "Most of our people are leaving with her. She's going to be okay."

"Who is going to stay, then?" she pressed.

"Well, you, Ben, and me. Wren wants to stream the battle, but we want to avoid that. We're going to be using deadly force against the torchbearers. It's the only way we'll survive," the redhead replied.

Cress paled, while Phaeron nodded in grim understanding. With him as the only one capable of unbinding the souls twisted to Myuna's service, he could not physically save them all. With no further protests aired, Madigan finished outlining the rough sketch of our battle plan.

We would lure Myuna's torchbearers and chosen ascended to the lake where the ocean gate dwelled and fight to the bitter end to evacuate nearly everyone. Then, Auric would take the remaining fighters through the Void to Myuna's chamber directly.

"The smaller the group that remains, the less likely I lose someone along the way," he added.

"Comforting," our leader said dryly.

"He speaks in jest," Phaeron said, rolling his eyes. "His control of the Void is masterful."

"Why joke at a time like this?" I asked. Everyone but me seemed to turn to humor when up against such serious events.

"What better time?" Auric countered. "The hour of Myuna's death approaches, as foretold long ago, by a Vess as dear to me as a sister. She gave her life to tell the dread goddess she would be defeated by the duo of Phaeron's mate and daughter." His one good eye fixed across the table at her, glowing teal. "And now we have Cressida et Sudaira and her tether to the powercore, who, in life, was Phaeron's adopted daughter. She is only missing one thing. Have you figured out what you need to do next yet?"

Color touched Cress's cheeks as most everyone turned their attention her way. "It slipped my mind," she admitted.

"I believe the wording was…" he drifted off with a glance at Hana. "*Pool your resources, and you will find the key to our victory.* Right?"

She nodded. Phaeron seemed unsurprised, saying, "I remember now. I saw the conversation in Cress's memories and your heavy-handed hint as well. You believe a mating circle will truly be a solution here?"

Ben sucked in a gasp, while I felt as blank as Cress looked. I went ahead and asked the question for both of us. "What is a mating circle?"

For once, this room filled with all these big personalities was pin-drop silent. Ben was the one to break the silence, albeit with a nervous shake to his voice. "It's like marriage, but for a group, sealed with cupid magic."

Cress's eyes widened. "Marriage?" she echoed.

I drew breath to reassure her. The saying was that one could be married to their duty, after all. I wouldn't have minded binding myself to her forever at that moment.

"It is crazy enough to work." Phaeron disappeared in a whirl of shadows, taking form again behind Cress's chair. He rubbed her shoulders and bent to whisper something into her ear.

"It's a lot to ask of you all. We can find another way," Roe blurted.

"I would appreciate an opportunity to discuss this with my mate and her potential circle," Phaeron said, a steely edge to his voice. "Without an expectant audience."

It was Prince Orthus who responded first by pushing back his chair and standing. "For such a lofty request, it is the least we can do," he said, gesturing to the room at large. Madigan nodded and turned, going with him to be first out the door.

Soon, we were alone, and Cress was pacing the room. "Why is us all getting *married* such a big deal?" she asked.

I stood too, wanting to hold and comfort her while she balanced herself on the edge of panic. Ben did the same. "There's more to it than the marriage part, babe."

"Allow me to explain," Phaeron cut in, shooting him a warning look. "The point of a mating circle is empowerment. The more mates one person can bind into the circle, the more powerful they become. With us bound to you, Cress, you will be able to take from a pool of our magic, attributes, and resources. Imagine having my shadows and skill with a sword, Geo's impenetrable stone skin, and Ben's channeling ability. Plus your tether to Braza."

I imagined it, and judging by the way her steps faltered, so did Cress. "She would be unstoppable," I said with wonder.

"No wonder we're the plan," Ben said, running a hand through his overlong hair.

Cress shook her head slowly. "Is all that possible?"

Phaeron walked into the path of her pacing, cupping her face. "Yes, it would be possible," he said, stroking his thumbs over her cheeks. "And it would allow me to share my immortality with you, Geo, and Ben. It is the next step for our relationship anyway...merely so early as to scare you."

"I'm not scared," she said slowly. When he raised a brow, she blew out a breath. "Okay, maybe a little bit."

"Until this meeting, I was not sure how you and Braza would accomplish such a feat," Phaeron admitted. "But perhaps the four of us, plus the might of a full ancient powercore, can match a starving goddess. Before we decide anything, there is one huge downside I will remind you all of."

"It's permanent?" she guessed.

"Surprisingly, no. You could disband the circle once you have slain Myuna," he said. "It ties our fates together as one. If any of us die, so do the others." There was an odd note of relief in his tone.

"Victory or death," I said.

He grunted in agreement. "As it always has been. If we go this route, we will be the ones to distract Myuna while Auric weaves the Void to trap her and drag her back to Soiluire. I would not put you in such danger if there was any other way." There was a distinct *but* at the end of his statement.

There probably wasn't another way. None of us could fight Myuna alone without being consumed.

"Are you willing to do this?" she asked Phaeron.

Without hesitation, he said, "In time, I would have begged for the opportunity to share eternity with you. So what if it is a little early? I love you dearly enough to share you."

"I love you too," she murmured. She drew up to the tips of her toes to share a kiss with him before turning to me next. She took my hands, looking up at me. "What about you, Geo?" she asked.

"Now that I know it's possible, I want it more than anything. You can always use my magic to keep yourself safe," I said. After a couple moments, I thought to add something, and she waited with a knowing look until I did. "I already recognize you as my only love, my duty and devotion. This is merely a formality."

She started to blush again. "Even if you have to share me?" she asked in an undertone.

"At first, I found the others unworthy of your attention," I said honestly. "In time, they have become tolerable."

Ben, who waited a few steps away for his turn, scoffed. "Tolerable. C'mon, Geo. You can say we're friends at this point."

"We'll be family yet," Phaeron added.

"Even...more than tolerable at times, yes," I ground out. "I have bent for you, Cress, made myself flexible to change." For a gargoyle, it was akin to admitting the impossible, yet I was more than that now. I was a man because of her.

She reached up to kiss me next. "Thank you, Geo. I know it couldn't have been easy."

"Yes." An understatement. I released her, reluctant to see her turn away, but she needed to talk to Ben.

She met his eye, and he smirked. "Why'd I have to be last? Now I have to follow up what they said," he snarked.

Cress looped her arms around his shoulders, pressing closer to him and dropping her voice. "Because I think you're the only one as scared as I am over how big a step it is," she murmured.

As they put their heads together, Phaeron caught my eye and angled one horn toward the door. "Now is as good a time as any to give them a moment," he said to me. "Call to me when you have a decision, bright soul."

"Okay," she answered over her shoulder.

I led him out, heading for the room where the torchbearer I'd captured yesterday was resting. "I have a large request," Phaeron said once we were alone in the elevator.

I felt a sudden, oily surge of trepidation. "What is it?" I asked.

"I want to give my daughter a new life, and one of the only ways to accomplish that safely is through making her a gargoyle." He clasped his hands together. "Will you assist me?"

Though I was happy he didn't mince words, it was perhaps the boldest request he could make that didn't involve Cress. We arrived on the correct floor as I answered, "That is highly illegal."

He didn't say anything else until we entered the torchbearer's room. She lay on the bed, arms cuffed over her chest by my quartz, ankles tied to the bedposts. Though I was assured she'd be kept asleep until Phaeron could see to her soul, her eyes were open, unblinking, and glowing white from within.

Sitting by her bedside was none other than Lucas, who withdrew his hands from her arm when we came in. "I was just—"

The torchbearer lifted her head from its pillow at the sound of the door latching closed behind us. An overwide smile split her face. "Phaeron et Sudair." It wasn't a normal human's voice, but the screaming echoes of dozens of wailing souls all speaking in chorus.

That had to be Myuna speaking through her. But Phaeron didn't reply immediately, instead taking a ragged breath and stopping short with his eyes narrowing to tiny slits.

"You took something from me, Phaeron et Sudair. I felt you kill my beloved Endaeron," she continued. Lucas clapped his hands over his ears when she laughed, and that awful sound seemed to jolt Phaeron back to himself. He reached out with a lash of shadowy magic, lassoing it around the general shape of the torchbearer and pulling.

Myuna's laugh faded, and the woman's eyelids began to fall. "So I took..." Myuna rasped. "...something from...you."

She went silent. He took a rigid breath from between his teeth and noticed Lucas's attention, moving his hands slowly to untie what

Myuna had done to this victim's soul. Coming to her bedside, he reached down and returned it to her with a hand on her chest.

Then, in a tone laden with agony, he said, "I know who she ascended in my brother's place." Pressing his palms into his eyelids, he made a sound of anger low in his throat. "I should have been more like you, Geo, dedicated to duty over pleasure. I should have rescued her before..."

"Who are you talking about?" I demanded.

"Carly," he gritted out. "She picked her out of spite. Who has had time to impress Myuna otherwise?"

Tentatively, I laid a hand on his shoulder. "You can't be so sure."

"Myuna has little left to harm me with. And she meant harm, even with that threat." He dropped his hands, looking over at me with eyes that gleamed internally like yellow gemstones. His slitted pupils dilated with his surprise when there was a gasp from the bed behind us.

The former torchbearer was trying to sit up, looking around in a panic and thrashing against her restraints. "Where am I? Who the fuck are all of you?" she demanded.

We both turned to Lucas, who looked embarrassed. "Sorry, ma'am. I didn't mean to wake you. Uh, again," he said.

"What did you do?" I asked.

"Her soul is..." Phaeron scrubbed his eyes. "Young man, I think you need to come with me. All of you, in fact."

DESPITE HOW HE said her soul was miraculously stable, Phaeron still placed the woman in a stasis room and asked Lucas for an explanation. Ben's brother was less sickly today but still needed to sit down shortly after arriving in the library from the sudden jerk of the dimensional's shadows.

"I dunno. There were a lot of cracks in her soul. It felt like my magic could do something for her, and the next thing I know, she's awake and..." He pinched the bridge of his nose. "I'm dizzy."

I walked away and returned with an armful of Cress's beloved junk food and soda. Lucas looked like he could've wept when he saw what I was offering him. "Finally. Flavor," he murmured.

As he tore into a pack of chips, Phaeron drew me a few paces away. "He healed her soul. I've never seen anything like it," he whispered.

"His new affinity is powerful," I stated.

"Potentially the miracle we need, with all the torchbearers we have saved," he said. "However, a week is not long to master a unique power. Especially considering..." He gestured over at Lucas, who'd abruptly passed out with his hand in the chip bag.

He went to return him to the hospital, taking the junk food with them with a promise to hide it from the nurses. I waited with the patience of my stone form for him to return, knowing he would want to speak in more depth about what he'd revealed in the elevator.

I considered what I knew of Braza. A considerable amount, considering she was the powercore to my home library and tethered to Cress. She'd told me as much as she remembered of Braza's life after experiencing it close to firsthand. But did she deserve a gargoyle form and a second chance?

Did anyone? I was here, after all, first animated by an honored witch I was nothing like.

When the shadows writhed in front of me, I was already saying, "I do not know the secrets to my own making."

He answered as he took form. "The secrets are within you. I acknowledge that I am asking the world of you, but you are my only hope to make a gargoyle form for her possible. I need to study your heart and the magic that made you."

I stiffened. He'd taken my heart out before to say his goodbyes to Morgana, but this was something entirely different.

"I understand she means a lot to you," I said. By the shift in his expression, that was an understatement. "You realize she will not be the same person, yes? If you wish to pass her off as a gargoyle that has existed since creating one was legal...she will need the body of a man. There are no female gargoyles."

He blew out a breath, nostrils flaring. "I cannot make changes to the spells unless I see them first. Perhaps it is folly, but I need to see for myself if it is possible."

I considered whether it would be wise to aid him in veering so far from the right side of supernatural law. What shifted my opinion was knowing that Cress would approve. She did have a deep connection with the powercore and expressed her regrets that Braza's life had been cut short so traumatically.

Phaeron waited for me to come to some semblance of a decision. With a sigh, I said, "She could pass as a half-gargoyle if her body is formed with it in mind. One of my friends has a daughter, and she inherited some of his features and a temporary version of his stone form."

A smile started to tug at his lips, showing the edges of his fangs. "You would help me?"

"After we join Cress's mating circle, yes," I said.

He breathed out with relief and stepped forward, reaching out. "You will be as close as family on that day, if not sooner. Come, clasp arms with me, brother."

Now that was a change in tone from the hostile way we'd met. Cress had led me down this path, though, where I suspected he and Ben would both become my closest friends in time. Because of her, I had a future where I *had* friends.

We gripped one another's forearms with a new sense of kinship.

34
CRESS

After how intense Phaeron and Geo could be, it was nice to sit with Ben in the quiet conference room. We held hands, our anam cara marks brushing with the spark to remind us that we were connected. He'd left a mark on my skin too, but one first made of deep friendship that we'd turned into something more.

We chatted around the subject, calming down together, before he finally sighed and said, "I never thought the fate of anything would hinge on me getting married."

"Me neither."

He snickered, and I giggled, which snowballed into a laughing fit for us both.

"I don't even know where we're going to find a cupid for the ceremony!" he chortled.

"Imagine if we could make Dr. Aurina do it," I said, picturing her embittered face. That airbrushed bitch had tried to steal Phaeron's affections, and I was angry about it anew now that I'd experienced the intimacy of his mating bond.

On second thought, I didn't want her anywhere near him again.

"You know, Ben, we could do a lot with forever," I added more seriously.

He sobered up as well. "I know. But it could be about as long as one week if one of us gets eaten by Myuna. At the same time, it sounds like we will all get *homphed* by her if we don't make a mating circle."

"Homph?" I echoed.

He smirked. "Thought the situation warranted some onomatopoeia."

I laughed again and shook my head at the same time. My cheeks were starting to hurt in the good way from all the fun I'd been having within the last day. To think I could have this every day for the rest of a —hopefully—very long life with my men.

All I had to do was slay an interstellar dread goddess first. No pressure.

"I love you, Ben," I said. "Let's do this and see if it's so bad."

He squeezed my hand. "I love you too. And something tells me it's not going to be bad at all."

"If it doesn't work out, we can disband it after we kill Myuna," I continued, worrying my bottom lip between my teeth.

"Nah." At some point, he'd swapped the smirk he wore like armor for a more genuine expression. "It's going to be amazing. You kidding? First thing I'm going to do is steal your celestial magic and piece it together with mine. Maybe together we make one celestial witch."

I was a little surprised that was what he'd go for, but maybe he was right. He'd practiced and ended up with a better basic grasp of the spells than I did, and I was the one with the light in my soul. Come to think of it, my birth mother's ghost hadn't appeared much lately. I should've practiced harder with her.

"Good luck with that," I chuckled. "Should I get Phaeron and Geo to come back?"

"Nah. Let them figure some of their shit out first. C'mere, babe," he said, patting his lap. We cuddled together for a while, to my less than subtle sigh of relief. I'd definitely overdone the animaris yesterday. It'd healed most of the lingering soreness I'd otherwise have, but I was content to have my lady bits relax after sharing so much passion in a short time with him and Phaeron.

He took my device and worked on setting up a phone plan with four lines. I rested my head on his shoulder and watched him type in a card number straight from memory. "I always forget it's a 'Ph,'" he said, going back and fixing his spelling of Phaeron's name.

"You have this memorized?" I asked, raising a brow up at him.

"Yeah. You think he knew how to set any modern stuff up? I got him a bank account and credit card and made sure he paid all the bills for our place." He shrugged underneath me. "Now he's making our cell plan payment. We can change the name on the account later."

"Out of curiosity, do you know how much money he has?" I asked.

"Let's see." He navigated to a bank's website and logged in. Snickering, he added, "Nice."

Phaeron had $969.47 to his name. "Fuck, we're all broke," I said, covering my face. "You, Geo, and I have nothing."

"Maybe Wren will share that sweet, sweet stream revenue," he suggested. "People have been throwing money at her, and she doesn't know what to do with it. It's not like we need it right this moment."

"I'll get a job once we're out," I sighed. Much as I've started to consider Wren a friend, I doubted she'd be in a position to share much of her streaming money. Considering how we'd openly admitted we would have to start killing torchbearers and Myuna's new ascended, it would only be right to distribute the money to the families affected.

"No, no," Ben said. "We make Phaeron and Geo get jobs. What says eternal devotion better than working a nine-to-five for the two broke college students in your mating circle?"

I laughed, covering my face with my hand. "Oh, Ben, you're awful."

"I'm just saying!"

"I thought you weren't a student." I poked his belly where he was ticklish.

He tried to bat me away. "I am conveniently a student right now."

There was a knock on the door, swiftly preceding Auric poking his head into the room. "You kids done having your moment?" he rumbled. I sucked in a startled breath. "Good, because I brought you a cupid."

He held the door open for a woman to walk in. He'd said "cupid," but I wondered if he meant angel, as she had a set of feathery, off-white wings and the same kind of flawless face as Dr. Aurina. Her lips formed a perfect blood-red bow in a heart-shaped face, and her pink hair fell in ringlets down her back.

The only thing that made me think something might be off about her was the shapeless white robe she wore, along with a collar of blue lace. She held herself still like a frightened deer when he reached over to unhook the collar from her slender neck.

"You will be able to stay here once you perform the ritual for me. Don't worry, you're amongst good people," he told her in an undertone. It was the kindest I'd heard the old dimensional sound, other than in my secondhand memories of him with Phaeron.

With a nod, she made a shaky smile. "T-thank you," she whispered.

Ben and I exchanged a glance. "Well, go on," Auric said in his usual abrasive manner. "Call your mate."

"How are you so sure I've agreed to join a mating circle?" I asked. He gave me such an unamused look that I nearly regretted even that small challenge.

"I hate stupid 'what if' questions. Call your mate," he repeated.

I put my hand over the mating mark on my shoulder. It was already prickling with awareness, like Phaeron could sense how much I wanted him to act as a buffer between Auric and me. He was able to send me a feeling back, like a cheerful "Be right there!"

"I called him," I chirped. I made introductions with the cupid woman while we waited. She had a soft-spoken, musical voice and seemed to have little interest in small talk but told me her name was Crissina.

Phaeron and Geo arrived through the shadows after a few minutes, taking form behind where Ben and I sat. Phaeron ran his fingers over his mating mark, and I felt a streak of possessiveness in him flare as he squeezed my shoulder.

"Where did you come from?" Geo asked Crissina.

"I found her," Auric answered.

It was still a little disorienting to feel Phaeron's suspicions rise separate from my own. "She was in Cerris City?" he asked.

"No, but once she does me the favor of securing you lot into a mating circle, she's going to stay to be evacuated like she was here all along," Auric said. "Let's just say she is leaving a bad situation."

Phaeron frowned. "Ah. Well, thank you," he said to her before turning his attention to me. "You've both decided?"

"Let's get married," I said with a lot of cheer and a pinch of nerves for seasoning.

Crissina shifted her wings with the silvery sound of her feathers rubbing together. "Um. Do you have a private place to go afterward?" she murmured.

"We do," Phaeron said.

"Come along," Auric said, turning toward the door. "I went ahead and invited some witnesses to the establishment of your mating circle."

Something told me "some" witnesses meant it would be the whole hospital, and as I walked out hand in hand with Ben on one side, Phaeron standing on my other side, and Geo behind us, I saw I was right. The maze of upturned tables, chairs, and sofas had been hastily moved aside to make space for us in the foyer, and several friendly faces lined the second-floor landing, hooting and waving down at us.

Arrayed in a waiting semicircle was my coven and our closest friends, plus Mom, who looked like she'd just hastily pulled her mask off and changed into street clothes. She came forward and pulled me a step away from my men. "What's happening, baby? They announced that you're going through some kind of marriage ritual to save all of us?" she asked, one shade away from panicking.

"Relax. It is meant to be," said my birth mother's ghost as she formed next to Mom and sent tingles up my arm as she attempted to hold my other hand. Mom had no idea she was there, as only Phaeron and I could see her. And Lucas too, I supposed. He was with my coven, leaning against Roe heavily.

"That's right, Mom," I said, squeezing her hand. "It's...well, it is a big deal, but it's not a sacrifice. I love these three men."

Eris dabbed at her eyes with the corner of her sleeve. "One glance at you all, and I knew it would lead here eventually," she said.

I smiled briefly at Eris before meeting Mom's concerned gaze. She'd be worried about me being coerced into this or moving *way* too fast, and I wasn't sure how to convince her otherwise. Compared to me, she barely knew my men.

Well, there was little to do except tell her everything. "I'll be right back," I said, tugging Mom into a private nook behind where Áine was weaving branches and blooming vines together, creating a makeshift trellis of flowers. She beamed up at her creation proudly.

In the meantime, Phaeron snagged Eris's attention, coaxing her away for a few minutes of privacy for us. "Mom, I know this is going to sound crazy," I prefaced. The truth came out in a rush about mating circles, my tether with Braza, and our plan to defeat Myuna. It was a lot, and I'd had a bit of time to accept it all, while I left her reeling and holding the side of her head.

"Your sister's not here to see it," she said in a sad hush.

My heart hurt at the reminder. "I wish she was. But we can't delay until we find her."

Mom's expression twisted with worry. "If...if any of them don't treat you well after this, they have me to answer to," she said, drawing me into a crushing hug. "I understand why you have to do this, but it is *very* sudden."

"It is," I agreed.

"But you're going to kick Myuna's pearly white butt, huh?" She held me harder, enough to restrict my airflow.

"Yeah," I gasped out. "In theory."

She loosened her hold enough for it to become a normal hug. We swayed together for a few moments before she whispered, "Can I tell you something crazy too?"

"Of course."

"You know that fae man who keeps following me?"

"The really annoying one?" I asked.

"Yup. We finally had a conversation past him trying to 'protect' me," she said, making air quotes with one hand. "He believes I am his fated mate."

I sucked in a breath so hard it was a wonder my lungs didn't explode.

"And if you can...get magically married to three men...to save us all from a soul-eating goddess," she continued with a few rapid blinks, "then I think I just might accept his invitation to go on a date."

"Mom!" I practically shrieked, bouncing on the balls of my feet. Most of my coven and all of my men came running to see me clutching her with an open-mouthed grin. "Guys! Everyone! My mom is going on a date!"

They whooped, which caused our watching audience to do the same. A big blush overtook Mom's fair cheeks.

"I knew it," Ben said under the general din of the crowd.

"Is he a worthy male?" Phaeron asked. "Perhaps I should inform him I will rearrange his insides if he acts like her last partner."

"Maybe that is too extreme for a first date," Geo suggested.

Phaeron nodded slowly. "The second date, then."

I gave Mom one last squeeze. "I think it's time," I said.

"Wait! Promise me you'll have a normal...ish wedding in a couple years," she said, clasping her hands under her chin.

"Absolutely," I said. "You're going to walk me down the aisle, and Carly is going to be my maid of honor. We have it planned, remember?"

A hint of tears sheened her eyes. "How could I forget?"

She took her place in front of my coven next to Jordan, unknowingly having my birth mother on her other side, who was also holding back from weeping. "Right here," Crissina whispered, pointing to a place for me to stand.

She sprinkled magic around me, the sparkles matching the off-white of her feathers. She repeated the process three times, having Ben stand about a yard to my right, facing me. Phaeron went to my left, and she gave him a wide berth as she dispersed magic around his feet. I glanced over my shoulder to see her place Geo behind me.

"Are you four ready?" she asked.

"Yes," I said amongst a masculine murmur of agreement.

"Then let us begin." She raised her hands and spread her wings. The particles of magic around my feet danced to a personal breeze, spiraling upward slowly. She went to stand before me. "State your full name."

"Cressida Rollins Darkmore," I answered.

"Are you here of your own free will?"

"Yes."

She spoke with the familiarity of an old ritual. "From this moment forward, these three men will be bound to you upon their agreement and admission of free will. You will become the strongest member of your circle, its core figure. As such, you must protect and cherish those who have joined you on this path. I sense three is the limit of what you can bind to you at this time."

"That's fine by me," I said. I couldn't even imagine needing the intimacy of such a close relationship with any other man.

"Very well." A hint of some emotion touched her perfect lips before she went to Ben next. She had him state his name and agree that he was here of his free will as well. But what came after that was different for him. "Do you agree without regret to bind yourself to Cressida Rollins Darkmore's circle?"

He looked over at me, a shy sort of smile on his face. Gone was his usual smirk. "I do," he said.

She dipped her head in a brief nod. "From the moment of your binding, you shall be known as Benjamin Darkmore."

Then she repeated the process with Geo, seeming puzzled when he stated his full name as Geo, like she expected more. He accepted his new name, Geo Darkmore, without complaint.

Finally, Phaeron, who quietly told her his title before she could announce it. "Phaeron Darkmore et Sudair," she repeated at the end of his part of the ceremony.

"Humans have been trying to give me a family name for centuries," he murmured. "I am glad to accept yours, bright soul. Also...brace yourself."

Crissina spread her wings again, and the particles of her magic began to form patterns and loops midair. More sparkles leaked from her palms to fill in the gaps of the complicated lattice of cupid magic which connected us. She drew in a deep breath and began to sing in another language, the words flowing out of her like an angel's call.

"Body, heart, and mind," Phaeron translated in a low voice. "I bid these souls entwined."

The audience murmured in awe as the magic shimmered to the cadence of her words. There was more to the song, but I barely heard it as the binding portion began, and I forgot who I was in the sudden crush of power, magic, strength, and knowledge that flowed into me.

For however long it took, I knew what it felt like to be my handbook, stuffed as full of foreign facts and magics as I could take.

I was Ben: young, limber, and irreverent. His power tasted of blood in the back of my throat and felt like possibility. Anything a body was capable of, his magic could do.

At the same time, Geo: solid, focused, and steady. I had the sensation of my skin being cool rock, impervious to all but the slow weathering of elements.

And also Phaeron, but he was a reprieve on the edge of where I could've been overwhelmed. I'd already seen the depths of his soul yesterday, yet his magic felt like raw power in my veins.

Just when I thought I couldn't take it anymore, Crissina's angel voice dipped, and all I'd experienced and all that I was moved on through the circle. Ben knew what it was like to draw librarian witch runes with a silver sword. Geo clutched the strength of my emotions tight to himself. Phaeron focused on the skills he could glean, how to cut and sew and apply makeup like a modern human.

And just like that, the song was over, and the sparkling magic suffused us. While I figured I'd be sneezing cupid dust for days, a small portion of the ambient magic went to my three men. I squeezed my chest, feeling a heaviness that hadn't been there earlier.

"Ladies and gentlemen, the Darkmore circle," Crissina announced, and the foyer exploded with applause.

I looked around, dizzy and off-center all of a sudden. Sound was coming in and out, like I was hearing from one of my men's ears as well as my own. The clinical lighting around us seemed too bright. Geo put his arms around me to steady me as I wobbled.

"Smile and wave," Phaeron instructed in one ear. "We're leaving as soon as you blow a kiss so we can consummate the circle and stabilize its effects."

"Thank you for doing this for us," Ben said, probably to Crissina.

I did as Phaeron said, hoping I didn't make anyone concerned if they noticed my sudden disorientation. I found Mom and Eris and blew them the kiss, then closed my eyes to be whisked away into darkness.

35
CRESS

Phaeron placed me back in the same room we'd just been sharing with Ben. "I'll go get the others. Just rest a moment." He felt concerned for me, which was about as defined in my mind as if I were the worried one.

"Okay," I said.

He vanished back into the shadows, and it was a relief to be alone for a few minutes. I rested my head back against the couch, waiting for my ears to stop ringing. The dizziness would probably return when it was just me and my men, but I sure hoped it wouldn't be so bad after we consummated the mating circle.

I was a married woman now. Just thinking about it gave me butterflies. How'd I get so lucky as to have this experience, even if it was in the service of taking down a larger threat? Now that we were bound together in the same circle, I would not need to pick and choose my affections. I'd keep all three of them close.

Supernaturals often formed groups with multiple people, especially with notable someones like Dr. Aurina and her five partners or Madigan and her three husbands. It'd been on display during the Mabon feast as well, when family units had included children and multiple spouses to a single partner.

And I was that core figure now. Me, someone who, only a year ago, had no idea the supernatural world existed. Once we ended the threat Myuna posed, I would get to spend my days with three incredible men.

They arrived, and I felt the shape of their thoughts as I teetered to my feet. Ben reacted first, catching a hold of me around the waist before I could fall. He was wondering, *"Is Cress all right?"*

"I'm fine, I think," I said, though he hadn't spoken aloud.

Geo observed our surroundings and noted the bags of gifts and the fading smell of sex from the night prior. *"I knew it,"* he thought.

And Phaeron was considering how to change the mood in the room, noting how tense we were. *"My mate will not know peace again if we don't stabilize the circle. How can this be romantic if those two males keep standing there gawking at her?"*

"I was admiring her. She's shining," Geo said in a defensive tone.

I looked down at myself from their concentrated attention. "Oh *nooo*," I exclaimed, pulling at my shirt. "It looks like I drowned in a glitter factory!"

Geo and Phaeron exchanged a glance. They didn't understand, but Ben pulled a sympathetic face. "This is never coming out," I explained. "Is it in my hair? On my face?"

"No, and yes," Phaeron answered. "I believe we're meant to...smear it around. It's cupid magic." Though unsaid, I felt him imagining us skin to skin, the sparkles absorbing into us because of shared pleasure.

I flushed with heat at the thought. "Shall we see how much of me it covers?" I invited.

Judging by the arousal suddenly leaking from all three of them, that was a major *yes*. Phaeron had wanted to change the mood, and it seemed he had with one lusty thought.

Kind of like animaris, spreading through the bloodstream once it hit the heart. His gaze flashed with awareness, and he wondered if I wanted another bite. And while I did...no, it wouldn't be right for this moment to let my body take over.

He nodded. We'd just had a full conversation in the space of a few moments... How surreal. I toed off my shoes while Geo murmured, "What even is animaris?"

"Phaeron's sexy venom," Ben said.

The gargoyle's brow furrowed. "His what?"

Phaeron barely cracked a smile, but now I felt him using all of his impressive self-control not to die laughing.

I giggled for him, and that, plus the shimmy of my hips as I slipped out of my jeans, had their undivided attention. Ben started to help me. He'd gotten a thrill at hearing my *"sexy little laugh,"* and then all three of them were reaching to pull my clothes away faster. A few seams popped in the frenzy to get me naked.

"I think it's safe to say all of you sparkles," Geo remarked. I saw hints of creamy, glimmering flesh, but their mouths and hands were on me. Ben tilted my head up, our lips meeting, breath heating, tongues and teeth clashing.

Geo's broad palm splayed over my lower back, holding me steady. He tweaked one hard nipple between his fingers with practiced care, and that was him laving up the soft plane of my belly.

I knew it wasn't Phaeron, since the sharp edges of his fangs were working their way up my inner thigh. He braced my shaky legs as he snuck a taste of me, projecting a feeling of smug satisfaction.

Their emotions, thoughts, and desires came together for a moment. They gave, and I took, but I didn't just want them to please me. I tugged at the back of Geo's shirt and fumbled for Ben's pants, needing to feel their skin on mine, wanting to give back.

"Whatever you want, babe," Ben groaned once he pulled away from my lips.

Clothes hit the ground, and claws pressed into my skin in warning not to move. Phaeron dove in eagerly for a feast, suckling on my clit and sharing how I tasted with the other two men. That wasn't playing fair. Ben and Geo throbbed with need as they revealed their bodies—and a bit of cupid magic on their chests, I noted vaguely. I jolted with a moan when a smooth tail ran between my pussy lips, twisting to get the first few inches slick.

"Fuck," Ben said. There were grunts of agreement. "Your body is putting off 'fuck me' signals that I can feel now."

Phaeron maneuvered my legs around his horns after giving my clit one last lick. He lifted and shook his head briskly, focusing long enough to take us all in. "If you stay like this, Cress…"

He outlined a simple enough plan to account for all our limbs and their general bulk. Despite some crowding, it seemed like the soundest way for me to have all three of them at the same time. We agreed enthusiastically as a unit, and I coaxed Ben and Geo in closer with a shiver of anticipation.

Phaeron shaped the curve of my hips and ass, and I glanced over my shoulder when he reappeared there with an eddy of shadows. I thought, *"You're still wearing too many clothes."*

"Patience," he answered. The slickened tip of his tail brushed the edges of my hot core again before pressing into my ass with intention. My mouth opened on a gasp, and Geo took me by the jaw, turning my head toward where he stood beside me. His quicksilver eyes glimmered with love, and we kissed for a long moment.

Ben's hands were on me too, squeezing my breasts and gripping my waist above Phaeron's clawed fingers. His cock throbbed against my lower belly until I took it in hand, stroking my thumb through the slick at the tip to draw it over his velvety shaft. I soaked in the sound of his moan.

My lips left Geo's when he stepped away reluctantly and went to stand on the bed. I looked over, measuring the distance from my lips to his shaft. I was a little too short to do more than lick the underside, but that just might be perfect.

Phaeron's hands slipped under my ass, lifting me, and Ben caught my knees, guiding my legs around him. With the boost and some quick shuffling, I turned my head again and kissed Geo's blunt tip. Flicking my tongue out, I tasted his salty essence and started to take him into my mouth. The tail in my ass flexed, wiggling a little deeper to curl my toes, while Ben was rubbing against my clit and getting ready to slide inside of me.

If I thought being shared between two guys was intense, it didn't hold a finger to the focused attention of all three of my men. I sank into the feelings of their shared affections and desires, which only built as the tension between us pulled taut.

"Take her," Phaeron demanded. He trembled with desire, holding me to his now bare chest as he continued preparing my ass with slow pumps of his tail. The other two barely needed the invitation. Ben pushed the first few inches into me while I sucked more of Geo into my mouth. We moaned together when their pleasure was a separate sensation yet as bright as a starburst when mixed with mine.

The synchronized way they claimed me broke. Ben slammed home, his hard lower belly grinding my clit. Fingers threaded through my hair, Geo claimed my mouth with more care. I gripped what I couldn't fit my lips around and moved my head in counterpoint to the thrust of his hips. The echoes of sensation between us felt incredible but overwhelming, and yet I only wanted more.

They adjusted, finding a new balance that was insistent, gentle, and teasing all at the same time. Phaeron didn't use any shadowy tricks, not with three sets of hands making sure no sensitive skin went untouched. His claws left light scratches under my ass, a little pain to ground me in the here and now.

I was beginning to feel a tug of magic between Ben and me, stronger than the sparks of our anam cara marks. Little did I know that I was shedding cupid sparkles by the moment, a minor detail compared to how it felt to join with him. The snap of his hips drove me higher and made it clearer that a tether of sorts was forming between us.

I only noticed Phaeron was moving when his tail slid free of my ass, an absence quickly filled by the nudge of his hot length. He'd disrobed the rest of the way and hadn't jostled me a single time. His sudden entrance pushed me into Ben, my legs gripping him harder. When I came, it was like a detonation—no, an implosion. My eyes rolled back in my head, and I came close to losing consciousness.

Ben came with me, and *snap*. Something fell into place between us in the radiance of bliss. I could feel him in a magical sense, a presence woven with shades of maroon and gold and tied to me by fine strands.

With a jerk, I returned to myself and noticed a warm liquid rush between my thighs when Ben withdrew, panting hard. My legs had gone limp, but Phaeron held me up and pressed to him by the hips. *"Take her next, Geo,"* he thought.

Geo pulled free of my mouth, grunting an agreement. His eagerness pulsed within me like a second heartbeat. He wanted to step down from the bed and hold me, which he did, guiding my arms around his shoulders. He supported me under the thighs, helping Phaeron push me between them with effortless strength. *"A muscle sandwich. My favorite.*" It was a quick thought, but it didn't go unnoticed.

Phaeron chuckled close to my ear. "Is it?" he growled. He rolled his hips, pushing deeper into my sensitive ass. I'd have been weak-kneed if my legs weren't already jelly.

"Mmm, yeah," I moaned.

Geo settled himself in the circle of my legs, brushing the thick head of his cock between my slick lower lips. He took himself in hand and claimed me next. I could tell he wanted to take his time, yet it was difficult for him not to spill immediately from the tight, hot squeeze of my pussy.

Cupid magic smeared between us, bright against his dark skin. I watched it disappear as that feeling of connection built between us with each slow, powerful thrust. With my back pressed to a firm chest, my core rocked from his pace. My pleasure mounted to match his quickly, as Phaeron stroked into me the same way, following him like an echo.

Ben tugged my hair to grab my attention. With a little reach, we could kiss, and his lips were a gentle and soft counterpoint to my body's utter claiming. Unhurried compared to Geo's tightening hold and the couple body-shaking pounds of his hips before he came and I followed a moment later.

With a second *snap*, Geo and I connected, and his presence, glittering with multicolored shards like the quartz in his gargoyle form, slid into place next to Ben's. My eyelids sagged, and darkness clustered at the corner of my vision before I drifted back to full consciousness with the sensation of my mating mark sparking with warm sensation.

Phaeron suckled on the swirls of ink he'd left on my shoulder. *"Come back to me, sweet mate,"* he thought.

"I'm here," I croaked.

Ben had stopped kissing me to watch the force of that second orgasm. He helped hold me up when Geo had to stagger away to take a moment to recover.

The cock buried in my ass throbbed insistently. Phaeron's claws dimpled the skin around my waist, and he panted while he licked his mark. "One more," he said.

"One more, babe," Ben said.

I nodded, echoing them both. I could do one more, even though I'd never come so intensely twice in a row. Phaeron jerked at the end of his next thrust, growling like the roll of thunder.

Ben's clever fingers pressed between my thighs, thumb circling my clit. He curled his fingertips within my pussy, searching inside me by touch. I leaned into him to take the force of Phaeron's next push. Judging by the way he shook with restraint, he had one more left before he came.

Another pair of hands rejoined us, landing on my breasts to stroke and tease. Geo rubbed my painfully puckered nipples. I moaned hard— he nipped my free shoulder just as Ben found the ultrasensitive patch within me that lit up every inch of my sensitive skin.

My head fell back with Phaeron's last thrust before he came and I followed with a little extra coaxing. He was already there, like our mating bond intertwined with the tether of fine strands, ensuring his shadow-black presence was bound to me in both ways. The sensation of his pleased rumble followed me into the bliss that followed.

The cupid magic entwined us all together and faded out once Phaeron and I completed the circle. My men were all permanently connected to me now, and while I rode the high of my last orgasm, I felt like I *could* take on an eldritch goddess and win. I was an unstoppable force of blades, shadows, and obsidian.

But I was also loved by three men, who I equally adored. That sensation of affection and satisfaction hummed through our mating circle, shared by all four of us and made stronger for it. I could've stayed in the embrace of this feeling for days, if not longer.

I drifted down from this feeling far more slowly. When I came to, I became aware that we'd all moved to the bed at some point. All three of my men were touching me, waiting for me to stir. I blinked a few times, relaxing into the sensation of being surrounded by them, and not only in the physical sense.

Where I could reach into the depths of my librarian and celestial witch magic, there were now three more strands. Their magic orbited mine, just a little extra reach away. I could borrow shadows as easily as the piece of celestial witchery Ben held in his aura. They were contained and separate from me now that the circle was stable, and that was already better than the crush of their emotions, senses, and thoughts all at the same time.

"Welcome back," Geo said. He was propped on his side, still hard but patient about it, like he always was. I felt his arousal first, but it pulsed all around the mating circle. It seemed heightened emotions were still shared between us.

I wasn't going to leave this bed for a long while. Not that I minded.

36
CRESS

BEN SHARED that it was common for those newly tied in a mating circle to disappear for several weeks before rejoining polite society. I understood exactly why. I'd had all three of my men in every possible way, often all of them at the same time, and had lost track of when and where I was. Without sleep, hours passed in a timeless blur.

When we started wanting non-carnal experiences, we did so as a unit, with a collective "Shouldn't we be doing something else?"

As we prepared to get out of bed, Phaeron figured out how to borrow from me. I felt a tug on my magic from the strands that connected us and sensed a request coming from him. *"Can we trade eyesights and knowledge of technology?"*

I agreed and felt a shift between us, soon covering my eyes from the assault of the lamp lit right next to the bed. While lying next to me, he wove a tendril of shadow between my fingers, forming a blindfold of sorts. "You see why I expected to go blind on your world," he said.

I heard the rapid clicking of his thumbs on his new phone's screen as he set it up, then he turned the haptics off.

"Yeah. We're getting you sunglasses," I declared.

"Should've done that a while ago," Ben commented from the other side of the bed.

"We've been a bit preoccupied," Phaeron said. "Hmm. This was a lot easier than I expected." He gave me back what he'd borrowed, and I glanced over to see his pupils narrowing to slits as he looked at the phone screen he'd dimmed until it was nearly black.

"You should ask Geo for tips," I suggested. The gargoyle grunted from somewhere on the floor. He was retrieving clothes, the most determined of us to leave this room today.

Phaeron nodded, staring at the screen with utmost concentration. "Geo, why is the…" He seemed to wrack his brain. "…browser named after a hunting expedition?"

"It takes you on an adventure through the Internet," he answered.

"Ah, yes. An apt name."

Ben and I started to crack up in sync. The next thing I knew, tendrils of shadow coiled under my back and rolled me off the bed. I sprawled on the carpet with a squeak of surprise. Judging by the nearby thud and curse from Geo, Ben had been pushed off too, on top of the gargoyle.

"Let's get moving," Phaeron said, turning into shadows and reappearing at the foot of the bed, where he started to dress himself.

I reached out and plucked away Phaeron's sense of balance. There was a hint of resistance, but it seemed I didn't need to ask to take an attribute from him. One moment, he was shrugging on his shirt and looking for his pants, and the next, he was tripping over his tail and stumbling.

I gaped for a split second, then rose with his usual grace to my feet. "You're right. We should be practicing," I said.

He hissed a laugh. "Fair play, bright soul, but I need that back."

He already had his balance returned by the time he finished speaking. I didn't know how to hold on to it for long, as it was naturally his soundless predator's prowl instead of something I had practiced.

We dressed successfully without ripping the clothes right back off and relocated to the other room we'd claimed. We sat in a circle facing one another, our various weapons in the middle: my sun staff, Geo's crystal shield and quartz hammer, Ben's daggers, and Phaeron's swords.

"It would be ideal if we got to a place of trust where any of us could pick up these weapons and wield them like the original owner," Phaeron said.

"How do we do that without crippling someone else?" I asked. My mind drifted to how easily he'd blinded me with a taste of his usual photosensitivity. I was worried this would be more difficult than just taking attributes from one another. We still needed them to function.

"Practice," he replied. "And a clever mind, perhaps. Much as I would like to see you face Myuna carrying one of my swords and Geo's shield, there are factors at play other than skill."

I had a feeling I knew where this was going. "I can't lift his shield. It's too heavy," I admitted.

"Therefore, you will need to borrow some strength, as well as two separate skills from either of us," Phaeron said. "Three separate attributes to channel continuously from us to you. Lose your attention on just one of them, and everything gets fumbled. In the meantime, we will fight by your side and share what you don't need between the three of us. We'll all have to learn a fine balancing act."

I nibbled into my bottom lip before steeling my resolve. We hadn't joined a mating circle just for the hell of it. First, it was time for baby steps. We started borrowing from each other and testing what we could do while seated and relatively at ease. What we shared turned out to be more aligned to quirks of personality and small skills and attributes.

I worked up a headache concentrating, trying to hold on to a portion of Geo's stoicism. I'd quickly learned that something so integral to who someone else was was almost impossible to keep in full. But Geo had patience in spades, so I could borrow some without immediately losing a hold of it. Designating how much, exactly, was where I needed a lot more practice.

While I didn't have much trouble reaching out and plucking something from them, my men struggled more. They had to reach through my magic to one other, a process that was tedious for all of us. They were bound to me, though, so it made sense that I controlled the flow of the magic.

I was concentrating so hard that I missed a flash of emotion between Phaeron and Ben. The dimensional pinched the other man with little flickers of shadows and they glared at one another.

The next time it happened, Ben's arousal sparked through our bond, closely followed by Phaeron trying to resist feeling the same way. "I can't help it," Ben said, swiping at the shadows before he could get pinched again.

"Think about something else, then."

"Something unsexy," I suggested, picking up on the problem. "Like Myuna."

Phaeron's burst of hatred was strong enough that we all felt it. There was an echo amongst us, a shared distaste for the goddess who'd tortured him and threatened the lives of those we loved. I thought of Carly's uncertain future, worried for her continued absence, and Phaeron and Geo tensed.

This seemed to dampen Ben for a while, but it wasn't long until I felt his attention running up and down my form in appreciation. I was no longer holding on to a portion of Geo's steadiness, and while it was a relief to feel like myself again, I didn't need the sudden tingles of awareness when I was trying to focus.

Yet all three men had turned their attention toward me within a breath. *Here we go again,* I thought, sure we were going tumbling back into bed for who knew how long.

The next moment, Phaeron and Ben disappeared in a swirl of shadows. Some time passed without them, during which I kissed Geo and then pushed at his chest when he tried to draw me in closer. I murmured, "We really shouldn't."

He rumbled an "indeed" with great reluctance.

The dimensional returned sans Ben. "He'll rejoin us shortly, once he's cooled down," he said. I felt him tug on my magic in request, as he was practicing by borrowing bits of my knowledge to learn more about modern culture from what I knew. I sent him memes, and his nose wrinkled at that bunch of nonsense out of context.

"Where'd you put him?" I asked.

Phaeron shrugged. "A cleaning closet."

I had a hearty laugh before explaining what a horny jail was to him and Geo. "It's not usually a literal place, but I guess we've got to make an exception," I said.

It was a lot less funny when I got distracted by the flex of Geo's muscles that evening while we were still practicing and ended up the second member of the circle to go to horny jail. At least I knew where Phaeron had found a janitor's closet—on floor negative one behind a door that'd been locked earlier.

I spent maybe ten minutes breathing in the cleaning product fumes before deciding I was definitely, most assuredly not horny anymore. The guys had called it quits without me and greeted me with a scavenged dinner and their caressing hands and...yup, we were in bed again.

MADIGAN ARRIVED the next morning with her own mating circle in tow, and our real training began. "We gave you guys a couple days to get used to it. Sorry it couldn't be longer," she'd said.

Had it really been two days? I figured it had, considering how tired I felt when not in bed with my men. We definitely had not had enough time to get used to this, but by necessity, we had to move on.

Their arrival started the clock on four last days of practice before we would help escort a crowd of survivors to the ocean gate. The knowledge was like a bucket of ice water over my head. As much as I wanted my men, we were using up precious time, and a lot of lives would be on the line soon.

The first thing they did was separate us into different containment rooms for a one-on-one talk. I was with Madigan, face flaming when the first question out of my mouth was, "Will it always be like this?" She'd barked a laugh and hugged me, knowing exactly what I meant.

"Yes and no. It takes a while to get used to sharing strong emotions. But men outside of your circle will be entirely unappealing. And vice versa for your men. The stability of your shared relationships becomes quite comforting."

"That's a relief," I said.

She patted my shoulder reassuringly. "When I was just coming into my power and circle, another woman took me aside to teach me everything I could do as the core of a mating circle. If you think I got to grow my reputation as Mad Ash without a significant amount of my men's help, you'd be wrong," she said.

"Every circle is different, of course. The secret to my success is that the members of my circle specialize in similar magic. We all manipulate earth, stone, and crystal with strength-based runes," she explained. "Over time, we've figured out how my men can send me three different pieces of their magic and muscles so I seem unusually gifted in guardian witch spells.

"What I see in your circle is that you have one man specializing in each of the three measures of power level. If you can take something from each of them, it would boost your own power level significantly, to the point where you could hold off someone as strong as Myuna for a short time. It would take a lot out of all of you to maintain it for a prolonged battle, but we'll work up your endurance as much as we can."

We ended up chatting for hours, with my handbook floating nearby, recording every piece of knowledge Madigan shared. Milo curled up in her lap, purring, while my other two familiars spied on happenings around the library.

Bella had ended up in the room with Phaeron and Orthus, projecting happiness from all the belly rubs she was getting from the dimensional. I'd almost forgotten he liked cats and Bella in particular. There wasn't an equivalent pet from Soiluire, as far as I could tell.

Meanwhile, Jin had avoided the ongoing conversations and was watching the powercore ripple with shadows and the points of purple-black claws. She was fairly sure Braza was practicing with her shadow-born magic within the confines of her living space.

Armed with the knowledge of those who'd gone through this before, we rejoined one another in a large room on floor negative five, fully equipped with weapons and armor. Phaeron had acquired a new leather chest piece from his nightly wanderings, though it remained free of the runic etchings of his original.

A set of his gifts had been from the same store, and I wore them to get used to the weight and movement of the celestial witch robe partnered with a pair of dark pants built for my heavy librarian witch belt. It was an expensive ensemble due to the magic woven into the cloth, a concept that immediately fascinated the side of me that'd wanted to go into fashion design before meeting my men had set me on another path.

The stars and tiny crescent moons stitched into the robe formed celestial runic shapes, making it resistant to heat and light. When I donned the matching gloves and lifted the robe's hood over my face, I'd never get a sunburn again, but more importantly, they'd dampen a fraction of Myuna's light magic when we finally met to fight.

My men and I squared off against Madigan and her circle. "Hit me as hard as you can," she invited, fully encased in her red crystal armor and resting the head of her warhammer on the ground. "I guarantee you I won't break."

"None of us will," Orthus agreed.

Aaron, the less serious of the guardian witch twins, pointed to the shadowy claws lengthening over Phaeron's hands. "We do bleed, though."

"I shall be gentle," he replied. He'd drawn one of his swords and taken up a guard stance, opting not to use all of his combat skills for this fight. There was some reluctance in him that I immediately understood. He didn't want to harm our allies, even for practice.

I tried not to let his emotions into my headspace too much. First, we had to share magic. I looked toward Ben, who traded a part of his blood witchery for a portion of my celestial witchery. He carried his father's staff, Evening Guidance, intending to practice with it first.

I held out my finger for Phaeron to prick with one of his talons and winced before drawing the blood rune for strength on my arm.

"Not like that," Ben said, taking gentle hold of my hand to draw it a second time. With a squeeze on the pad of my finger, he drew out enough blood to etch the rune for energy right below it. There was a surge through my muscles, and I itched to use them, practically vibrating in place.

Geo offered me his shield. It was a massive slab of crystal, but I buckled it to my arm and lifted, amazed when it came off the ground smoothly with the help of the blood magic runes. He gave me a measure of his endurance, necessary for taking hits in the thick of battle and continuing on without tiring.

Lastly, Phaeron drew his other sword, offering it to me hilt first. "A weapon of two worlds, yours to wield," he murmured.

A sense of wonder that didn't belong to the circle suffused me. Braza slid into my mind, her electric presence further augmenting me in a way that felt as familiar as sliding my feet into a pair of shoes. Together, we admired the shining length of metal, polished to gleaming, with words in the dimensional language etched up the middle.

"He reforged his Soiluirian blades with Earth silver upon learning how deadly it is to unnaturals," she told me privately. *"This blade is Flame. It's the shorter of his two swords, made for his left hand."*

"Thank you. Your swords are named?" I asked.

He nodded, tapping the gemstone set into the end of the pommel. It was a gleaming yellow with orange undertones, shades I'd seen in his eyes countless times. The other had a red and black stone. "Shadow and Flame, to reflect myself," he explained. "As long as you have my skill to wield it, I believe Flame suits you better."

"And mine as well," Braza said through me, creating a two-toned echo to my voice.

"Between us, she will be unstoppable," he said. He lent me some of his considerable knowledge of swordplay, honed over endless years at war.

Madigan picked up her warhammer, slinging it up at the ready. "All right, let's see what you all can do," she said. With a grin, she swung the massive weapon at me.

For all the skills of others swirling in my head, I still panicked and held up the shield, taking the full force of the blow. The crystal rang and vibrated my arm, and there was dissonance in my head. Geo thought I'd done a great job, but Ben and Phaeron would've sidestepped, and Braza was annoyed, wondering why I'd taken such a slow attack head-on.

I lost control of the connections with my men just like that, and the shield tipped forward, threatening to take me toppling over with it. Several masculine shouts sounded as Phaeron caught me and Orthus did something with his magic to make the shield lighter.

"Let's try that again," Madigan suggested.

And thus began the first session of us practicing combining our skills under pressure.

PHAERON

We had little downtime as a unit from the moment Madigan and her mates started helping us train. My shadowborn side liked that—we were moving closer to our goal, even if we weren't leaving the library yet.

Cress's coven and friends moved back into their rooms by the second day of our training, many of them helping by testing Cress's concentration with their varied magics. She was figuring out how to channel for longer and flinching less when spells or weapons came her way.

I tried not to be too territorial when she spent much of the evening before bedtime in a communal area with her friends rather than her mates. She needed community and, sensing my mood, dragged me in to spend time with them too. As we chatted, she rested in the circle of my arms, where she belonged.

According to them, things were as silent as the grave up on the streets. But that meant Myuna was also practicing her magic, testing the bounds of her army's control through her new ascended.

"When will you tell her your suspicions?" Braza asked. Now that we'd exited the bedroom, she was privy to all my thoughts and worries again.

"I don't know." I still hoped I was wrong, but it made too much sense. Selecting Carly for ascension was akin to the twist of a knife. She was also the only target we'd hesitate to kill, making her the best strategic choice, as Myuna's control would falter with the death of her chosen assistant. *"There's one more factor I'd like to consider. Why present Cress with a problem and no solution?"*

Lucas was here. He was growing stronger by the day, and the unusual ripples that suffused his soul were flattening, smoothing into a new whole to represent who he was after his ordeal. I had to see what his new magic could do, and that would only be possible if I witnessed how he'd healed one of Myuna's victims. If his magic reliably mended the cracks and traumas that resulted from soul ties, perhaps he could help me remove a seed of corruption planted in Myuna's chosen ascendant, regardless of whether it was Carly or someone else entirely.

"Promise me you're not going to go after Carly on your own," Braza said, nervous.

"Of course not."

Grant was the only coven member not here. I intended to shake him for information on a certain blue-haired teenager once he returned from his spying.

Cress leaned her head back to look at me, and I took the opportunity to kiss her sideways. "Penny for your thoughts?" she asked.

Between our mating bond and our connection in the circle, she'd feel my restlessness without a doubt. Maybe even that I was having a conversation with Braza and plotting over some of the finer details before the coming confrontation. "Aren't pennies worthless?" I asked.

"Well, your thoughts aren't," she said.

I leaned in, whispering in her ear, "What if I was mentally undressing you?"

Braza's presence in my mind faded in an instant, and both Ben and Geo faltered mid-sentence to turn their heads our way. Blushing, Cress reached up and tapped me on the nose. "You know what this means," she whispered back. "Horny jail."

I tugged on her sleeve, exposing the edge of my mating mark. Giving it a lick, I felt her tense and bite her lip to cage in a gasp.

"Oh no, horny jail," I teased, stealing her away to the closet with me on a wisp of shadow.

IT WAS MUCH LATER that night when Geo and I sat at the base of the powercore and he allowed me to pull his crystalline heart free from his chest. I began the painstaking task of writing down the runes that encircled his heart, borrowing most of Cress's drawing ability to diagram it.

I hadn't had to ask for permission, since she was sleeping off our visit to the closet. It seemed the magic would continue working even if one member of the circle was unconscious. That could be helpful in a pinch.

I used her skill to write down and study the numerous chains of spell runes that led from the heart back into Geo's body next, noting them down on a separate page somewhere in the middle of Cress's sketchbook. Braza's electric energy watched over my shoulder. "Do these match what you can remember?" I asked her.

"They are animation spells. None concern the identity of the soul inside of the heart," she replied.

We both had the same translation spell, which made these human-made runes something I could read and understand. Unfortunately, she was right. At some point, I'd started copying down the same threads of runes—his heart was like a central nervous system while he was in gargoyle form, connecting to each limb, muscle, and tendon.

I manipulated these threads with care, relying on my shadows to keep from tugging one free of its connection by accident. They were intricately wrapped and would only unravel from each other so much before there was tension. The edge of a shadow brushed the strand of runes they were all wound around, and a fission of pain ran from it straight to my fingers and down my arm. I jerked away with a hiss. That'd felt like trying to grab a bolt of lightning.

"Let me try, Father," Braza said. Her powercore presence pressed into the gaps where I'd threaded my shadows.

In the meantime, I inspected my new wound that ran from fingertip to shoulder, branching in the patterns of an electric shock. I noted it at the bottom of a page. Geo wasn't entirely helpless even while his heart was exposed in gargoyle form. That magic had to be guarding the most important runes keeping him animated.

I flipped the notebook back to the first page while Braza hummed and shifted around the magic, murmuring to herself. The portrait Cress had drawn from my memories gazed back at me. Our son. She saw much of me in the boy, but in this quiet moment, I noted how he was human in his smile and the curve of his ears.

The Void had seen a future where he lived. I was struck breathless by hope, no matter how unlikely it seemed that a witch could carry a dimensional child to term. If we lived and Myuna died, he could exist. Perhaps Cress would agree to name him Teziel, meaning victorious. I had met many good males with that name in my time.

Braza tapped on my thoughts, and I glanced up. *"May I see?"* she asked politely.

"We have no other secrets. This is certainly not one," I replied.

She took in the drawing and squealed in delight. *"He looks just like you both."*

"He was foretold by the same vision that showed me you and

Ravai," I told her, faltering for a moment. "He is still an idea, a kind daydream before I remember I live in this unforgiving world now. I do not seek to replace you, Brazita."

Her tone implied a smile. *"I understand. You might have a future with both of us. I was able to inspect this."*

She pushed an image of the central link of runes connected to Geo's heart. I flipped back to my sketches and added these runes, heart thudding hard in my chest as she sent two more memories from different angles. It was a woven braid of several spells concerning control, identity, intelligence, duty, and the protective spell meant to electrocute anyone who tried to tamper with them.

I smiled to myself. Given time, I would unravel each of these runes into their component spells. My clawed finger followed the path of the identity spell, already spotting where it was written for the soul in the crystal heart to forget its past life and start again with a baseline of the duty that it was entwined with. There was a significant chance I could make this work.

Once I placed his heart back in his chest, Geo shuddered and shifted back into his human form with a grind of clashing rocks. He coughed up a plume of dust, then ground out, "Well?"

I clapped him on the shoulder. "I'll have my daughter back because of you. Words cannot express my gratitude...but perhaps you would welcome an idea that will elevate you in the eyes of our mate."

He straightened slowly, having spent this whole time hunched over with his heart exposed. "I'm listening," he stated.

37
BEN

"Tʜᴀᴛ ᴏɴᴇ ᴄᴀsᴛs Sᴛᴀʀsᴇᴀʀ, ᴀ ʟᴇᴠᴇʟ-ғɪᴠᴇ sᴘᴇʟʟ," Cress's handbook informed me when I held out one of the pieces of paper attached to Evening Guidance. My father had stored a trove of spells on the staff, and I was still trying to figure out which were useful. Most were priceless, spells I'd find nearly impossible to replace once they were used up.

At my core, I was still a blood witch, but I could still cobble up enough celestial witchery with Cress's help to channel these spells. Very few witches, even those in varied mating circles like mine, had the ability to switch between affinities. I was *rare*. But that didn't mean I was powerful, and I crammed every second I wasn't training with Cress or sleeping. It was the evening of our third day of serious training, with one more to go before we joined the push to save everyone we could.

"Starsear is commonly a spell for celestial witches with a star alignment. Like you, bub! It makes one gigantic star-shaped, uh, thing, that explodes," the handbook continued cheerfully in its squeaky toy voice. Now that it had identified the spell, it flew a curlicue over my head.

It then shouted a dramatic "*KABEWM!*" and flopped out of the air with the clap of its pages snapping closed.

I snickered. I couldn't help it. Ever since the mating circle ritual, I found it as amusing as Cress did.

She peered into the room I'd claimed for the evening, and my cock twitched just at the sight of her. *Down, boy.* Sharing lust with two other dudes was ridiculous. Especially when I was usually the first to get distracted and thus sent to the closet.

"Is everything okay?" Cress asked.

"Just demonstrating how devastating Starsear is," the handbook whispered from the floor.

She came in to pick it up and gave it a little toss so it would take flight again. "Everything's fine," I added.

"Well, good. I thought you might want to know that Phaeron is having Lucas experiment with his magic."

I clenched my fists. Lucas had barely begun to recover from his coma. There had to be a damn good reason he was being pushed to use his nebulous new magic, no matter how powerful Phaeron thought it might be. "Where?" I demanded.

We walked to the row of containment rooms for the former torch-bearers. One was unlocked, and inside were the two men, standing over an unconscious body resting on a narrow cot. Phaeron watched Lucas nearly as closely as my brother stared at the woman.

Lucas had his hands held palms out toward her until the door latched behind us loudly and he startled. He turned our way, then a wide smile split his pale face. "Hey, big bro! Guess what," he said.

An ugly gasp sounded from the woman he'd been working magic on. She leveraged herself to her elbows, looking around with rapid breaths causing her chest to heave. Phaeron nudged Lucas our way and bent to speak to her in soothing tones.

Lucas came over and dropped his voice to a whisper. "We've figured out how I can gather more energy for my affinity. It turns out that helping others with damage to their souls gives me the power to help more people." He beamed with pure relief. The idea of inflicting hurt to acquire soul energy had really triggered him.

I gave him a quick once-over. "And you're feeling all right?" I asked.

He considered himself, finger to chin in thought. His nod was slow in coming. "I think so. You know how it was hard to activate blood runes when we first took our affinity? It's like that. The more I practice, the faster and easier it is. And Phaeron's been a great teacher." With a glance over his shoulder, he shrugged. "Though he tends to disappear a lot."

The dimensional in question had left behind shadowy smoke in place of him and the woman Lucas had healed. I wouldn't be surprised if he'd taken her to one of our safe houses to wait for the trip to the ocean gate.

"Does he jump scare you when he comes back, or does he save that for Cress?" I asked.

"Oh, I think he reserves that for me," she said. "I'll just be minding my own business, and everyone else goes quiet. And I ask myself 'He's behind me, isn't he?'"

The shadows twitched behind her, taking shape into Phaeron. There was a mischievous gleam in his eyes. "He's not always standing behind you. That would be ridiculous," I said, biting the inside of my cheek to keep from giving him away.

"Yeah, well..." She drifted off and glanced over her shoulder, yelping when he took that moment to grab her.

Lucas made a *blech* face when their play wrestling turned into kissing, and I elbowed him. "Hey, she has a sister," I said in an undertone.

There was one benefit to the bleaching he'd gone through. He clearly blushed up to his ears when I embarrassed him. "Ben," he complained. "I'm some kind of soul witch now. I don't have time to think about girls."

"Pretty sure you'll be back to that in no time," I teased.

Phaeron cleared his throat as he pulled away from Cress. "I did have a goal for us to reach this evening," he said, gesturing for us to follow him. "We have containment rooms to clear, and then I have some news to share. Grant has returned with our last glimpse of information on Myuna's machinations."

"Oh, where is the spy extraordinaire?" I asked, following my brother and Cress as we all headed for the next containment room.

"At this hour, resting," he answered. Somehow, he also sent me a thought in my head through the magic of the mating circle. *"I'd prefer to tell our circle something privately. I've already bribed Grant to keep it to himself until tomorrow morning."*

"All right," I murmured. I'd have to ask him how he did that. He seemed to be figuring out what this magic could do a lot faster than Geo or me.

Cress's eyes narrowed, like she knew he'd done something, but she didn't comment.

"Anyway, these last few torchbearers are more recent victims. Myuna's power runs deeper in them...nearly embedded in their souls. I was able to remove her control, but her corruption remains," he said to Lucas. "I would be quite keen to see if you can help them."

Lucas squared his shoulders with confidence. "Leave it to me," he said.

I guessed I was turning overprotective, as I earned an annoyed look over his shoulder when I said, "Just don't overexert yourself, okay? I don't want you leaving this pocket dimension wheeled out on a hospital bed."

"I'll be fine. Trust," he said.

I stood aside with Cress, who watched them with shadows of black and purple flickering over her eyes. I'd seen it enough to know that Braza was lending her soul sight so she could watch what was going on.

"Their souls are still bleached." She leaned over to whisper to me, gesturing to the two unconscious people on either ends of the containment room. "I see the corruption as swirls of brighter white. Lucas is trying to get a hold of it to pull it out."

Sweat visibly beaded Lucas's forehead. He concentrated, flexing his fingers like he could grab and remove Myuna's influence as easily as pulling a weed. As the minutes rolled on, it was clear it wasn't that simple.

I ended up behind Cress, cuddling her to my front while she watched and updated me occasionally on how he was doing. His success was obvious from her gasp before she said, "He's holding the corruption separate from that person's soul. It looks like he's absorbing it."

"Is that safe for him?" I asked, looking between her and Phaeron.

The dimensional watched intently before nodding toward me. "In this case, it seems power is power," he said.

"A *lot* of power," Lucas murmured. "I don't even know what to do with it."

"How fortuitous, for I have a plan that hinges on that feeling," Phaeron said.

Blinking, Lucas moved on to the next person to remove their

corruption too. "I mean, sure. Whatever you want. You saved my life, after all."

There was a heaviness to his reaction and response. "We shall face many soon that we will not be able to save. But there is one person who we must, who is corrupted more dangerously than anyone in these containment rooms. After seeing how your magic works, I believe you are up to this task."

"Who?" Cress asked. The spike of dread from her hit me like a sucker punch.

"I suggest you gather up Geo and head to a private room. I will tell you the news and my plan as soon as we finish up here," Phaeron promised. "You will want to be sitting down for this, bright soul."

CRESS

Phaeron didn't hide the truth from me—he'd suspected for days that Myuna had ascended Carly. It hurt, but he'd had a reason to keep it private as he sought a solution for the situation first.

I could hardly breathe. Grant had spotted her commanding torch-bearers separately from the goddess while wielding a staff formed of white light. Carly was bleached more severely than Lucas, according to the changeling, overriding even the magical blue dye in her hair to render her fully white, like Myuna had once done to Endaeron.

"She is still alive, so there is hope we can pry the seed of corruption out of her before Myuna transforms her into a second Hungering Darkness," Phaeron was saying.

At some point, I'd tuned out, curling into a ball with my chin on my knees. Ugly tears and sobs ripped from me despite being pressed between Ben and Geo, who tried to comfort me with tender touches. "She picked my sister on purpose," I croaked.

"Indeed. She wanted to hurt us," Phaeron said more quietly. He stood apart, watching my breakdown, shame radiating from him. "Apologies will not suffice, I know. I failed her when she was brought before Myuna the first time and did not attempt to rescue her before... I did not know she was capable of turning your sister against us quite like this."

I sniffled, scrubbing at my face. "How could you have known?"

It was personal. It had to be. Myuna had to realize the prophecy she feared most was on the cusp of coming true. Phaeron's mate, assisted by his daughter, was coming to cut the bitch's head off. And like a cornered animal, Myuna had struck out in the only way she could. She'd put us in a situation where the easiest victory was closed to us. Neither Phaeron nor I would sacrifice Carly, but if we didn't, her torch-bearers would kill our defenders and friends with free access to their magic.

My grief twined quickly with a new burn in my chest, hatred blazing to life like I'd never felt before. There were few people I'd truly wanted to kill, but they were the villains of my life. Those who were now deceased, Garroway or Blaize Starsurge, for what they'd done to me, my family, or to others. But Myuna...I would commit any kind of violence necessary to ensure she joined them in hell.

Understanding seemed to glimmer in Phaeron's gemstone eyes. "Do you want to hear my plan to fix this?" he asked.

I nodded, and he shared it. We'd prepare one last containment room layered with librarian witch runes and powered by Braza. Lucas would remain behind in the room to await delivery of Carly, though he'd have a fallback in putting them both into stasis if removing her corruption was beyond his abilities.

Geo had already agreed to be the retriever. He didn't flinch when I turned a look his way. "You could've told me about this too, you know," I grumbled.

"My apologies," he said in that grinding way that suggested he'd been in gargoyle form recently.

"In the meantime, I will be storing the second half of Braza's power in this," Phaeron added, withdrawing a dragon scale from his pocket and handing it to me.

It was ringed with runes on its front and back, currently a dormant black. "It just needs a librarian witch's blessing before it can hold a soul and hook into the spells that would reanimate it in a gargoyle's body," he added.

"Wait, what?" Ben asked.

"He copied the runes from my heart last night," Geo supplied. "I shall explain the situation to Ben."

He drew aside a confused, scowling Ben to the other side of the room while Phaeron sat next to me to walk me through the blessing. It needed a kick of librarian witch power, something I did easily enough through drawing a rune over it with the tip of Flame, which functioned just as well as any of the other silver swords I'd used for spellcasting.

The scale crackled with power, each of its runes glowing from within with purple light. "I knew the scale could do it," he said. He picked it up and held it to my ear. It thrummed at a deep frequency, awaiting an occupant.

"What about the other half of her soul?" I asked.

"For right now, you will have to hold it within yourself. After we kill Myuna, I am assuming it will be a simple thing to acquire a crystal heart from our Crystal Court allies. Prince Orthus seems the sort who would give it freely, even if he knows what it's for," he said.

Though we were in private, Braza made herself known with a crackle of her electric presence over my shoulders. *"I assume you will have to draw upon a significant portion of my power to fight Myuna. If it all comes from the half attached to you, brightest of souls, you'll barely notice me clinging to you while you all seek a second heart."*

"Hmm. Who are we lying to, then?" I asked.

Phaeron dipped his head in acknowledgment of the unspoken intention. "Most everyone. The death of a powercore is a monumental event, nearly unheard of, but Myuna will be an easy scapegoat for Braza's disappearance. From there, it will take years to construct her gargoyle body with the proper intentionality that will be required to hide the suddenness of her second life from this modern world."

My brow furrowed. That would be nearly impossible, considering most everyone had a social media trail that started with their parents photographing them in diapers. "We should at least get Madigan and her men in the know. My coven, too. They're good at keeping secrets."

"Agreed," Braza said. *"I'll want some friends who know who I am."*

With a sigh, Phaeron rubbed his face and thought it over, replying after a while, "Yes, perhaps with the assistance of a fae deal. Grant's identity has been the only well-guarded secret amongst us."

"I'm sure Áine would help us with that."

I trusted her a hell of a lot more than Grant, even though he'd done nothing to earn suspicion other than exist as a changeling from a dangerous court. His scouting and spying had really come in handy, but sometimes I couldn't help but wonder what his ultimate angle was and who he served back in the Autumn Court. Áine didn't have that kind of potential baggage behind her intentions.

"She would. And while no plan is foolproof, I will do everything in my power to return your sister." He took my hand in between both of his and searched my face for forgiveness.

I smiled back sadly. It was clear he sought the kind of absolution I couldn't offer him. "Carly will forgive you when she's returned to herself. I'm sure she knows you were as much a victim as she is. Hell, judging by the other torchbearers we've encountered, this whole time may be as memorable to her as a long nightmare."

He brought my fingertips to his lips to kiss. "I hope so, bright soul. She is family now. The thought of her warped into undeath like my brother is unthinkable. I have to save her now, like I wish I could've saved him then." He released a ragged sound of pain.

"We will," I said. We had to. My sister deserved nothing less.

38
CRESS

My sister's fate had me throwing everything I could into our final day of training. I stood toe-to-toe with Madigan, the two of us brawling like juggernauts with the combined backing of all of our men. As evening fell, I covered myself in healing blood runes to recover from all my various hurts and spent what was left of the night before the battles ahead with my coven and friends.

We'd taken over the staff break room in the library, dragging in extra chairs from elsewhere to fit everyone. Roe was rolling a water bottle between her hands, looking pensive. Her moods were usually contagious, and considering she seemed concerned, tensions were high until one of the Furies, Grace, arrived and plunked a few wine bottles on the table toward the back of the break room.

"To take the edge off," she said, starting to rummage in the cupboards. "Surely this place has got some cups."

"Hey, not to spoil your fun, but most of us are underage," Grant said.

She shrugged and started taking down an assortment of plastic cups. "I won't snitch. It's the end either way. Might as well enjoy it."

The other Fury, Tish, was already set up in a corner of the room with her laptop. She glanced up from the screen and paused mid-typing. "Besides, that's about enough for one glass for each of us," she tittered.

Phaeron stood to help Grace pour and distribute. "On the eve of big battles, I'd drink with my men and discuss what we'd do *when* we'd win. It helps to focus on goals, not fears. We all have lives to return to once Myuna dies and we leave Cerris City at last," he said.

"That sounds like a good idea. Who'd like to go first?" Roe asked, accepting a cup partially filled with wine and taking a careful sip. She winced at its taste.

Bianca was the one to break the silence. "First things first, I am going to fight to the bitter end. I'm not running away through the ocean gate."

"You're not?" I asked, surprised.

"No way." She toasted me with her cup. "I haven't run from a fight yet, and tomorrow won't be the exception."

"There was that one time before Samhain—" Ben began to say.

"That was different," she interrupted. "I didn't actually want to fight you."

"Uh huh." He turned down a cup of wine. "You can have mine, Big P. You seem bougie enough to like wine." When Phaeron's brow furrowed, Ben added, "He doesn't understand slang, you guys. His translation spell is a bit literal."

The dimensional's eyes narrowed. "It translates intention well enough."

"Mating circle life. Yuck," Bianca said lightly.

"Fuck off," he answered her in the same tone.

"I'm going to, actually." She glanced away, fidgeting with her fingers for a moment. "I guess this is your official notice that I accepted a position with the Furies as their third member. I'm going to hunt unnaturals professionally with Grace and Tish." The mountain lion shifter nodded stoically, while Tish beamed.

Ben blinked in surprise. "No shit?"

"None. I can't stand the idea of going back to school, and that's where most of you guys are headed." She wrinkled her nose in distaste. "So, I'm going to go do what I'm good at—killing monsters."

I nodded. She'd been spending a lot of time with those two women. It only made sense that she'd join them. "Good luck," I said.

"Thanks. And best of luck replacing me, of course. Now that Wren's made our coven famous, there'll be tons of witches that will want to take my place," she said with a flip of her hand.

"Hey, she mentioned you by name, Wren. What's next for you?" I asked.

The blonde sighed into her cup. "Well, apply for college loans, first off." She laughed alone, a nervous chuckle. "I'm going to reinvent myself, maybe go off on my own like it's the old times to seek out a new experience to name myself after. I'll have to continue streaming something too, with all the followers I've built up."

"You don't have to be alone," Roe said.

Tish glanced down at her computer, clicking around. "And I'll help you with your stream. I'm having a blast being a mod. Your fan group is popping off right now!"

My brows rose. "You have a fan group?"

"Yeah, but they're going to get bored of me once Myuna's dead and such."

"Nonsense!" Tish chirped, to an echo of agreement around the room.

Wren loosened her shoulders from a rather un-Wren-like hunch. "You're right. It'll be fine…great, even. What about you…Roe?"

Now it was the redhead's turn to look nervous. "Well, I hate keeping secrets," she blurted out. "I made a deal with a fae a few months ago, and I, uh, I'm gonna have to take off for a while to back up my end of things."

Áine's deerlike ears pinned back. "I immediately do not like this. Who was the fae? What was the deal?" she demanded.

It looked like Roe was going to hold her breath until she exploded. Her gaze tracked across the crowded room to Grant, who opened and closed his mouth a few times before scuffing his foot on the floor.

"If I show you my true form, Áine, do you promise not to get too mad?" he asked.

She whipped her head around, nostrils flared. No one smelled a fae deal like one of the fair folk. "I agree," she stated slowly and watched as Grant melted away, replaced by his changeling form. Her mouth fell open in shock.

Áine hopped to her hooves, pointing at him. "Changeling!" she barked. "And to think I *trusted* you!"

"I can explain—"

She spoke over him, panning the room in disbelief, but it seemed the only ones surprised were her and the Furies, not including Bianca. "Did you all know about this? Every time he disappeared..."

"He was spying for us. Áine, please. I'm sorry you're learning like this." Roe got up and hugged the faun, who stood there trembling and not returning the affection.

"You made a deal with him?" she asked in a low voice. "An Autumn Court changeling, one of the *enemy*. Roe, how could you?"

"I can explain," she said, echoing Grant.

Áine pulled away, crossing her arms and taking her seat at an angle. "By all means," she said with gritted teeth.

"Well, we needed his help around Samhain, when Garroway and the Hungering Darkness went to ground," Roe began slowly, her voice shaking as she spoke to the faun's turned back. "He revealed himself first to a small group because he was tired of pretending to be boring-as-toast Grant Norwood."

"To be fair, my sponsor also wanted more information than I was gathering. He suggested that I be your friend," Grant put in.

"Yeah. So, the deal was of friendship," Roe said, nodding. "He would spy for us and do whatever we needed for free, and in exchange, I would visit the Autumn Court with him to compete with other fae nobility for the crown prince's hand."

Áine's cold shoulder thawed almost immediately. "What?" she asked, looking over her shoulder at Roe in disbelief.

Roe smiled sheepishly. "He said I didn't have to take it too seriously."

The faun turned a glare on Grant. "Well, *changeling*, how about you explain why you'd ask for something like that of my best friend."

I sensed that Ben wanted some popcorn. Most of us watched this play out, heads turning back and forth between the three of them. I had to admit, I was curious about the competition too. But the Autumn Court...helmed by a bloodthirsty queen who once sacrificed countless lives to the old Mother Tree that'd anchored the pocket dimension where Northern Supernatural University and the rest of New Salem resided. That was too dangerous a place for Roe to go alone.

"All right," Grant said, flicking his green and orange braid over his shoulder. "Long answer or short?"

Our friends shouted their answers, punctuated by Áine's eye roll and drawl of, "Tell me everything."

"Everything, cool. So, I'm Ambrose." He put a hand on his chest. "That's part of my true name, I mean. Before Roe and I shook on our deal, I told her the whole thing, so she can order me to dance myself to death if she wants. I'm the crown prince's body double and have spent most of my life learning how to be him."

"He's the mysterious sponsor," Roe said.

Ambrose sighed, his dragonfly wings shifting and layering over one another tightly on his back. "Prince Soryn asked me to seek out potential brides in the ruins of the Fall Court. Little did I expect to find it a bustling metropolis and for my cover story to tie me to the most important coven of witches in the whole of Moongrove Academy. I've been winging it for a while, pun not intended."

Phaeron felt badly for him, which echoed over our circle. "Your spying has been invaluable to us," he said.

"Well, thank you. I've been keeping Soryn alive for a few years, since I came of age and earned permission to impersonate his lordship. Believe it or not, I can't take the shape of folks above a certain power level threshold. I've never been Geo or Phaeron." He pointed at the two men with his thumb. "And trust me, I've tried."

"Don't try anymore," Geo grumbled.

"It's all good. I need your permission and blood to ever be able to," Ambrose said. "Anyway, there's a somewhat likely chance that Soryn is still alive without me. He doesn't actually want to get married, but he does want to end his mother's curse. Most of you are familiar with the old Fall Court's bloody past, I presume?"

Áine scowled. "I was the one who told most of them."

"Well, she made a deal with one of the Unspoken Ones long ago to have the power to augment her first Mother Tree with the blood of sacrifices. A side effect of that deal was true immortality. But she's kind of...rotting." Ambrose flinched as he said it. "Like, she has enough enemies that she's been assassinated a few times, but her body just gets back up and continues on. And as more time passes and she doesn't fulfill her end of the bargain, the more Autumn Court denizens get afflicted this way too."

Phaeron tilted his head. "Unspoken One…as in a death fae?"

"Yup. Thus, the undeath. He's getting impatient. Soryn is gathering allies for what we're calling Turning Leaf, a movement to remove both the Autumn Queen and the Unspoken One so our friends and family members can rest in peace and we can finally make amends to courts we've wronged." Ambrose nodded toward Áine, who seemed to finally be listening and accepting what he was saying. "In the meantime, Roe is considered royal fae by technicality, so I'm going to look like I'm doing my job by bringing her home to star in the next bridal competition the Autumn Queen puts on for Soryn. And there's your long answer, Áine."

"Hmph. I'm coming with you," she said to Roe.

"Wait—" she began to protest.

"I'll hide my Spring-ness, promise. If you're going to be in a bridal competition, you're going to need a fae you trust," the faun huffed.

"Sounds like a party. Can I come too?" Ben asked. Both of them said a quick no at him. "Okay, fine. But how is Roe fae anything? She's human. Right?" He eyed her as if waiting for her to drop a glamor too.

"The Crystal Prince is one of my fathers. Technically, that puts me in line for the Crystal Court throne," Roe answered. "But if the bridal competition is held in typical fae style, Prince Soryn shouldn't even look twice at me. I'll be in and out before you know it."

Ambrose glanced away from her. From his expression, he thought otherwise. He shook his head, schooled his face, and said, "And as for me, I'm hopping through the ocean gate wearing Willow's face tomorrow. Girl, if someone tries to kill me, you owe me twice over."

"Sorry. It might happen, given the history." Willow ducked her head shyly under the room's concentrated attention. "I, uh, wanted to stay and fight. My control has gotten better."

I raised a brow and glanced around. "Who here is leaving through the ocean gate tomorrow?" I asked. Only Ambrose raised his hand, though he'd shifted to look exactly like Willow. Her reedy form was engulfed by his clothes.

"Really?" I asked in surprise.

"Furies finish what they start," Grace said.

Roe held up a fist. "You know I'm not going anywhere. I got your back."

Wren held up her phone in echo to the redhead. "Someone's got to record you defeating a goddess. We just won't stream any fights with torchbearers if we can help it."

"You're all the best. I thought...well, I thought you'd want to be safe," I said. "But I guess none of us will be. Not even Ambrose. Would you go back to being yourself, please?"

He transformed to his changeling form and made a dramatic bow. "It's still Willow's turn to talk," he said.

"Well, what I do next depends on how much danger Ambrose finds. I might go find my place in my alleged father's city or hide from the mer if it turns out a lot of them want to kill me," she said, scratching the back of her head with an uncertain tilt to her lips.

"Play it by ear," Roe suggested.

"Yeah. I guess that covers everyone but Cress and her circle. What's next?" she asked me.

"Um..." For all my fantasizing about the white-picket-fence life with my three men, I couldn't imagine returning to my quiet dorm room with the empty bed where Lanie used to sleep. My life had grown too large and busy to fit back into that box, even though I knew I needed classes and a degree to eventually get an ideal job. "I'm going to debate whether to tell NSU that I'm a hybrid witch so I can learn more celestial magic. And hopefully move out into an apartment big enough for my circle."

"Staff quarters," Ben suggested. "You and Geo can move in with Big P and me."

Phaeron released a skeptical breath. "Implying I'm still employed at Moongrove Library. I intend to resign anyway, as I'd rather cut off part of my tail than work for Dr. Aurina any longer."

"While he searches for a job, I intend to be gainfully employed with the SPDI. I've been texting my old friend, Marl." Geo held up his own phone. "He's a fellow gargoyle who's served for decades. They're always looking for durable talent."

Amusingly, I felt a dissonance between Phaeron and Ben's reactions. The former nodded in approval, while the latter balked at the idea of Geo becoming a member of the supernatural police. But it suited him, I thought. Criminals would rue the day they crossed Officer Geo.

"Officer Darkmore," Phaeron whispered behind his hand, in response to my thoughts.

Right, they had my name now. I kept forgetting.

"Well, I'm going to be a student," Ben said. "Just throwing that out there. I'll major in something useful and even go to class."

"I'll believe it when I see it," I said, a sentiment most of the coven echoed.

I looked down at my cup of wine, left untouched where I'd rested it on my thigh. Most everyone had finished their taste of alcohol by now. Taking a sip, I recognized that it was a milder wine, both bitter and sweet notes mingling on my tongue. Kind of like this moment, a bubble of peace right before the uncertainty of tomorrow. Sweet, but bitter with the knowledge that we might lose anyone who'd chosen to stay with us until the very end.

39
GEO

WE WOKE early and traveled to the hospital to join a meeting of fighters. Those staying behind to battle Myuna and her torchbearers filled the foyer, where instead of gathering to witness a mating circle ritual, all attention was on Madigan explaining how the upcoming battle would go.

The acoustics of the room caused her hearty voice to echo up to the people lining the second-floor landing. "We want to stir up Myuna's forces and cause them to meet us at the lake where our ocean gate lies. To generate as much motion as possible, you have been divided into five teams to escort noncombatants from either the hospital or one of our four safe houses."

A few glanced my way as I gave a grinding nod. I was in my stone form, placed prominently behind Madigan as the leader of team four. While I flew there, most of the team would be driving, and then we would approach the battlefield on foot, as our assigned safe house was closest to the lake.

"You have full authority to use lethal force on any torchbearer you meet today. They will certainly be doing their best to kill us," Madigan continued. "We are outnumbered and outmatched if our intel is accurate and they are able to use their magic and wits against us."

A hush of voices followed her declaration, some astonished looks being passed around. Many of those staying were the Crystal fae and guardian witches of Ashbough Protective Services, who had been spending their time defending our territory until the recent lull in activity. They knew about as much as the handful of doctors and nurses who'd dressed themselves in distinctive colors for battlefield triage.

"However, we do have the element of surprise. King Laiken has promised to send myrmidons to help us defend the ocean gate. These will be fresh and rested merfolk right next to their element. The tide of battle may easily turn to our favor, pun intended." She paused for a moment, waiting for a few groans amongst the crowd.

"While we engage the torchbearers, our noncombatants will flee to safety through the ocean gate. I know it may seem counterintuitive, but we want as much torchbearer attention as possible while our civilian count dwindles. It's a bait and switch, folks. We will be teleporting using dimensional magic the moment the gate closes and the myrmidons leave." She glanced over at Auric, beckoning him over.

"We're not mentioning the Void?" Cress asked quietly. She held hands with Ben a couple paces away, where they stood with the cluster of their coven.

Ben shrugged. "I still don't think I understand what it is," he whispered back.

Phaeron wasn't present to attempt to explain it again. To get the last librarian witches to leave their posts at the library, he'd promised to personally defend Braza. He'd rejoin us with her powercore half safely secured in his dragon scale later on. The only person who would truly remain at the library was Lucas, awaiting a delivery of Carly in one last containment room.

Hopefully his unusual new magic could do something for her. Cress would never forgive herself if we lost her sister, especially this close to the end of everything.

"All right, listen up," Auric said gruffly, cutting through the crowd's murmuring. "Many of you haven't met a dimensional that looks quite like me. I specialize in, ah, teleporting. My magic will look like a heat mirage or sometimes blue and black mist. You will want to be ready to disengage from any fight and cluster up, else I'll end up leaving you behind. The actual relocation will take three seconds, if that, and you will feel an intense chill on your skin. Questions?"

He didn't pause. "Good. During the second half of our plan, I will drop us all in the audience chamber where Myuna has been sitting this whole time. She…teleported here from my old home world and left behind a hole, so to speak. My goal once we arrive is to send her back through that hole and sew it closed so she cannot return. It will take me a while to harness enough power to make it possible."

"What are we doing in the meantime?" shouted a Crystal fae from the second floor.

Madigan gestured up at him and answered, "We expect a smaller force of elite torchbearers will remain behind with their goddess. Those of us who choose to fight will hold them off from Auric as he works his magic.

"As for Myuna, no one is to engage her recklessly. Any attempts to do so may result in the consumption of your soul or the possibility of being turned into a torchbearer and against your friends. Only Cress Darkmore and her circle will approach her, and then it is only to distract. This way forward was seen as the most successful path by the Graygazers."

She turned to Cress, who flexed the powers Braza gave her to make purple-black shadows slide into being and dance and eddy around her when she raised an arm to wave. "Thank you for your bravery," Madigan said.

After a tense smattering of applause, Madigan opened the floor to questions. She went over fine details before dismissing the meeting for us to head off and put the plan into motion. I gathered team four, which mostly consisted of friends, both from Cress's coven and the defenders who'd helped us clear the library of its monsters.

"Madigan would like a few of our cars to whip through the city streets en route for maximum attention," I stated.

Ben and Bianca both lit up. "Race you," she said.

"You're on!" he exclaimed.

Cress raised a brow but shook her head rather than say anything. She'd probably been planning on carrying Ben in her shadows. Instead, she turned to Grant and Willow, making an offer to them in an undertone. They disappeared with her into the darkness, and as the rest of us finished coordinating transportation, the merman who'd originally come here for Willow walked up to join us.

It took me a moment to remember his name. Zander. He was dressed in what I assumed was a myrmidon's battle armor, gleaming plates interlocking over his chest like oversized fish scales. One over his heart was etched with a symbol of jagged coral. Those plates continued over a leather kilt that looked like it was designed to wrap around the weak point where fish tail met man's torso in his aquatic form.

He carried along his heavy trident, using its blunt end like a walking stick. "Where's Princess Willow?" he asked, eyes narrowing as he took in our group.

"She's taking a safe route to meet us there," Ben answered for me. He knew I was practically incapable of uttering direct lies in my stone form.

"Is there such a thing as a safe route?" the mer warrior asked skeptically.

Ben smirked. "Let me put it this way. It's less dangerous than Bianca's driving."

She shot him a venomous look. "We'll see about that. I'll meet you on the road." We split up, most of the team following them when they headed off to claim a vehicle, while I emerged into the early morning through the front doors and spread my wings. Flying might've been slower travel than the maximum speed of a car, but nothing could beat the feeling of soaring across the sky.

I knew the way from my trips scouting or performing search and rescue. The safe house was a dance hall, where an overflow of healthy noncombatants had been living ever since Myuna had consumed her unnatural creatures. The survivors were now out in the parking lot, many clustered in family groups. Some of them held suitcases or sacks of belongings; others had the clothes on their backs and clutched weapons, ready to fight for their freedom.

Spotting Cress's purple head of hair, I came in for a landing nearby and checked my momentum with heavy strokes of my wings to land without cratering the asphalt. "Willow?" I asked the brown-haired girl next to Cress, who ducked her head too readily.

"Nope," replied the changeling in his voice before switching to speak in her usual wispy tones. "She's wearing a set of Crystal fae armor over there. I assume she'll take some of it off before she gets in the water and sinks like, well, a stone."

I glanced in the direction he pointed. Her thin outline was bulked out by the hard facets of the armor, and it did look too heavy for her.

"Oh, I put a glamor over her trident," Ambrose added. The graceful weapon seemed to resemble the kind of hammer a guardian witch would wield. If anyone checked her aura, the deception would fall apart, but no one would be looking in the midst of battle.

"Did she make a separate bargain for such services?" I asked.

"Curious?" he countered with a lift of a brow. "As a matter of fact, no. I want to see King Laiken's palace and politics for myself. It seems like a shoo-in for a hellhole worse than the Autumn Court, but maybe I'm biased."

"Perhaps," I muttered.

"I mean, there shouldn't be undead there," Cress pointed out.

Ambrose smacked his lips. "Guess it's hard to get worse than that."

We lapsed into companionable silence, some of the survivors around us drifting close enough to eavesdrop. Ambrose practiced some of Willow's typical poses and expressions as if he were limbering himself up for a performance as her for the foreseeable future. I wondered what he planned on doing when he was asked to demonstrate her powerful water magic.

Well, a problem unrelated to the challenges ahead. While I pushed away any squirmy feeling of nerves with ease as a gargoyle, Cress tugged some of my stoic calm to wrap her own emotions in a dampening blanket to keep from bouncing on the balls of her heels or pacing as we waited.

The sound of wheels screeching on pavement had all of us looking up. Two cars came zooming into the parking lot, engines purring as they came to an abrupt stop and fighters piled out. "Incoming!" shouted a guardian witch coming from one of the vehicles.

A third truck struggled along, its side gouged by massive claws. I loaded a quartz spike in my right arm, lifting my palm and waiting to sight the creature that'd done such damage in one long swipe.

Weapons unsheathed, and magic ignited around me. We all heard it coming, the *thump thump thump* of heavy paws.

A shifter in full grizzly bear form charged into our midst with an ursine roar. Its tiny, round eyes blazed with Myuna's white power, and spittle ran in rivulets from its open jaws. Each stride was punctuated with its pants and grunts.

It noticed Cress mid-stride and changed course to head straight at her. The same guardian witch jumped in the way and raised a portion of asphalt to serve as a shield. With agility that belied its bulk, the bear edged around the chunk of road to slam its paw into the witch. He crashed to the ground with the crack of his stone armor hitting concrete.

Shadows wrapped around Cress, making her a purple and black version of Phaeron's shadowborn form, complete with tendrils trailing after her to emulate a pair of wings and a tail. She stepped forward to meet the bear shifter at the same time I fired my primed spike. It cut into its thick hide, emerging through its shoulder.

Left arm failing to take its weight, it skidded to the ground. An ordinary shifter would've bellowed in pain, but it was eerily silent as it struggled to its paws and accidentally shoved the spike further through its body. Several spells ripped into it as it lurched forward, gaze still focused on Cress with murderous intent.

She hesitated when it fell again nearly at her feet. "You have to do this," she said in a two-toned voice, but I had the feeling it was Braza speaking.

"He's crippled. We could still save him when Phaeron arrives," she said in response to herself.

The bear used its back paws to launch at her, stretching out in one last-ditch effort to tear out her throat. I moved to shove her aside, and my hand met shadows when she reflexively turned to vapor and reappeared a couple feet away. Its bulk hit me, staggering even my gargoyle form. I dropped my shield and caught its head, ending its life with a harsh twist to save her from the task.

The bear dropped, head rolled askew. In death, it shifted back into the limp form of a naked man, his body covered in the same wounds he'd sustained as a bear.

"Let's get moving," I rumbled to get attention off the body.

Eyes averted slowly from him, back to me as I issued instructions. The survivors moved into a cluster as I told them to, with fighters forming a protective ring around them. I picked up my shield while consolidating my quartz into a club for the fight ahead and walked at the front of the group. Cress and Ben moved into place a step behind me.

We took a back road, circling around the bulk of an abandoned strip mall. The ground sloped downward, and we ran into a fence that bordered this side of the lake.

It was a mer-made thing, crystal-green water rimmed by imported sand. There was no visual sign of an active ocean gate from here. It would be in the middle of the lake, where the water was deepest, connected to a network of similar gates for aquatic folk to move through freely.

I looked for any hint of movement on the lake past the placid ripples from a breeze. The myrmidons had to be scouting the area, awaiting us. We were relying on them, after all. There would be no reaching the ocean gate without the help of an oceanic witch or one of the merfolk.

Another team emerged from the tree line several yards away and headed toward us. Now that our allies were arriving, weapons were drawn, defensive lines were established, and traps were set around the perimeter from pointed stones to sand stirred into a mire.

Civilians were placed behind the wall of defenders, backs to the lake. We wanted to look helpless to draw out the torchbearers in force, but Cress and Ben shared a feeling of unease that infiltrated our circle as more and more people joined us. All was quiet, save the murmurs that built as we waited for some sign of movement from the lake.

"The hospital's team hasn't gotten here yet," Ben commented.

"Do you think they're taunting torchbearers?" Cress asked in a two-toned voice.

He exaggerated a shrug. "Hurry up and wait to find out."

Wind stirred the crystals that formed my hair in gargoyle form. It would've been a beautiful spring day, the sky clear and blue, if this calm lakeside wasn't about to become a battlefield. Even the trained Crystal fae and guardian witches started to shift and rub at their armor as time passed.

There was a splash of water, and many of us turned to look. A dark-skinned mermaid emerged from the lake, dripping streams of water from her armor and a battle trident clutched in one maroon-finned hand.

"Is the princess here?" she demanded. The coppery fish scales on her cheeks caught the light when she turned to Zander and Willow emerging from the crowd. "Good. Let's go. King Laiken is expecting her."

The real Willow, still concealed in heavy armor, turned to stare meaningfully at the changeling that was taking up the center of attention as her. "Um," Ambrose said, scuffing his foot. "Everyone else first. I won't go through the gate unless you help all these people."

Willow nodded in agreement behind him.

The mermaid bared her teeth in a bloodthirsty grin. She snapped the butt of her weapon underwater, a swirl of bright blue magic emerging from it as a ribbon that sped away deep into the lake.

I wanted to say the surge of relief within me was from the mating circle. Cress breathed out with it as figures breached the water's surface. Merfolk of all kinds were here. I recognized the finned and sharp-toothed horses as shapeshifted kelpies, along with the long, sinuous form of a single sea dragon shifter.

The combined power of the mer began to part the lake, creating a narrow path that led deeper and deeper through the silt at the bottom of the lakebed. It revealed the ocean gate, a pair of columns carved from cerulean stone with a sheet of magic that looked as thin as a soap bubble stretched between them.

The dry path expanded wide enough for two people to walk side by side, and that was when the maroon-scaled mermaid nodded toward the fake Willow. "It is safe. Send your people through, and I will remain at your side to protect you, Your Highness." Her warmth faded as her eyes landed on Zander. "Good job finally doing something useful for our kingdom," she added to him tightly.

His gruff response was drowned out by Madigan and others shouting, "Form a line!" With her arrival, heading up the group that'd traveled here from the hospital, the trap was fully set. The first survivors rushed to the safety promised by the ocean gate, disappearing the moment they touched the gate's bubble of magic.

A handful of guardian witches helped maintain calm and stopped the shoving that resulted when most of the survivors saw the truth: salvation was real and in sight. That didn't stop several screams, most shrill with the panic of children, when a less friendly shifter announced itself with a roar, followed by the howls of several wolves.

These shifters were sighted first, each torchbearers with flaming white eyes that prowled the line of the fence, growling. "There are so many," Cress muttered.

They came from sidewalks and backstreets, forming a crowd in minutes. While our guardian witches fired volleys of sharpened stones toward them, Myuna's turned guardian witches nullified the rocks into dust and crumpled lengths of metal fence like balling up paper.

I had to acknowledge that she and her chosen ascendant had practiced well. These torchbearers moved like they were in charge of their own bodies and actions, though many faced us in torn and stained clothes, wielding makeshift weapons. They may have the numbers, but we were more prepared to fight.

As they fanned out and the shifters prowled looking for weaknesses in our defensive lines, each of the torchbearers began to speak at the same time. In the past, when Myuna wanted to talk to us, she used her discordant voice straight through her victims. These men and women used their own voices, forming a monotone chorus.

"Where is the son of night? All this trouble, and Phaeron refuses to face me?"

"Release your hold on these people, Myuna!" Madigan shouted back at the crowd. She flashed a quick look over her shoulder, where survivors were still fleeing through the ocean gate, now a coordinated line with fighters and mer placed at regular intervals to shove civilians along.

A flat chuckle sounded from the chorus. "It seems we have not been properly reintroduced. Myuna has sent me to crush you in her stead," they said. The crowd tremored and parted for a petite figure.

Cress gasped, and I felt her vertigo secondhand before Ben steadied her and murmured in her ear. Across the short stretch of beach stood Carly, a white apparition standing ramrod straight. Myuna's light glowed from her irises, a subtle difference to set her apart from the blank white stare of the torchbearers who surrounded her. She held a length of pure white light in her hand as if it were a celestial witch staff.

"Carly!" Cress screamed.

It was so unusual to see Carly turn such a hateful look toward her sister. But as Phaeron had said, this wasn't her, but a twisted version with any good qualities sanded away. Myuna's ultimate vision was to turn her into another soul-consuming monster, and with that came the death of who Carly used to be.

"My lady has seen potential in me above all others. I am an ascendant now, the one who commands the goddess's legion." Though Carly's lips moved, it was the torchbearers who spoke for her. "However, we do not need to fight. Surrender Phaeron and Cress to the lady's mercy, and the rest of you may run to safety." The crowd gestured dismissively as a unit.

"Carly, this is crazy! You're the one who should surrender to us. We can help you," Cress called. Tears clustered in her eyes even as the shadows around her stirred, ready for the fight ahead.

"I don't need your pity anymore. I am more powerful now than you could ever imagine."

"I've never *pitied* you! You're my sister, no matter if you're a supernatural or not. Come with us, and we'll get the corruption out of you." She shifted to the side, shouting around the bulk of the fighters who moved into position, bracing for a fight.

A cold smile crossed Carly's face. "Look at you. Now that I have power, here you are begging me to let it go." She lifted her staff of light, and the torchbearers shifted, preparing to fight. "If you will not surrender, I will take you to Myuna by force."

"There is no sense in arguing with her while Myuna is treating her like a puppet," I gritted out. With a nod, Cress called upon the shadows, letting them wrap around her and releasing an unearthly howl.

In answer, Carly pointed with the staff, and her people surged forward, meeting us fist for fist and spell for spell. I flared my wings and took up a defensive stance in front of Cress, assuming rightly that several white-eyed shifters would be going for her throat directly.

She threaded her shadows around my bulk, striking at vulnerable openings as a pair of wolves and a tiger shifter tried to maneuver around the shining surface of my shield and the swing of my club. They learned I was a living wall. No force Myuna had called up could get past me to hurt my love.

But for every enemy we downed, two took their place. Ben fought at

Cress's back, relying on his old combat training with daggers in hand and blood runes drawn. Cress channeled some of my durability into him, trading back to me some of his agility.

If the torchbearers showed any hint of emotion, they might've been surprised at the speed I countered attacks and swung back, or how spells designed to gouge and burn flesh only grazed Ben.

I tuned out the screams of the dying and of panicking civilians as our allies were inched backward under the onslaught of the torchbearers. It was only when the possessed guardian witch that'd crossed weapons with me twitched and spoke did I take a moment to listen.

"Too cowardly to fight, son of night?" The torchbearers were everywhere, speaking slightly off sync mid-combat.

I didn't bother trying to find Phaeron, knowing he'd be an elusive curl of smoke until it was time for us to trade places. The librarians must've finally passed through the ocean gate for him to have revealed himself.

When he'd first suggested the plan we were about to engage to save Cress's sister, I hadn't thought Carly's corruption would run so deep that she would seem to willingly turn on us. But he'd told me everything to expect. That name, *son of night*, was all Myuna. There was every possibility Myuna was watching and manipulating this fight through her ascendant, which meant the tirades and threats would begin now that she'd noticed Phaeron's presence.

"Did you know I used to look up to you? I thought you would save me when Myuna first held me," Carly continued, the confession too raw to be anything but her own. "How foolish of me. Like any shadow, all you're doing now is tiptoeing around. Look at what happens when you pick the light."

A ray of white radiance blasted from her direction at the back of her forces, reflecting off the lake's surface. It appeared to be a direct hit, as Phaeron slipped out of his shadow form and crashed into the water. He emerged, sputtering, on the back of a nickering kelpie.

I caught a glimpse of the dwindling number of civilians. The other side of the battlefield was full of the drowned corpses of torchbearers who'd crossed the maroon-scaled mermaid and her forces. But instead of pressing their advantage, they began to retreat toward the water with changeling Willow at the back of the procession of noncombatants.

I fought on. Though the mer had helped, they wouldn't stop the onslaught of possessed aiming for Cress. It did not take long for Phaeron to emerge at my side, drawing his sword. He was soaked through, looking pissed but unharmed.

"Go," he said. Black shadows swarmed down his arms, forming talons over his fingers.

"You don't want to do the honors?" I confirmed.

"You are better suited for the task. I will make amends with the girl when she is back to her senses."

I nodded and sucked my quartz club back into my arm, reforming it into the tool I needed. I flared my wings further, careful of where my allies were standing, and lifted off the ground with a heavy flap. Phaeron moved into the place I'd been after a second flap took me airborne and sailing over the heads of the combatants.

Carly realized what was happening when I landed with a thud before her, letting the force of impact knock her off-balance. She bared her teeth and turned the staff toward me, shooting out a superheated wave of light. My obsidian body sizzled and heated as it absorbed the magic, but stone could be heated hundreds of times without sustaining any damage.

I took a step forward, and she scrambled back. Whipping the staff, her next attack was a spinning disc of white light, which I deflected with a lift of my shield. "You cannot harm me. I was tempered to fight the Hungering Darkness, whom you are not," I rumbled.

Her breathing quickened, a glimpse of the scared teen girl under the overwhelming influence of Myuna's magic. "Get away from me," she yelped, this time without a monotone echo.

"It is for your own good," I answered, grabbing her wrist and smacking the staff out of her hand with a bash of my shield before I purposefully dropped it on the sand.

A set of quartz handcuffs emerged from my hand, sealing around one wrist. We wrestled for her other hand before I managed to grab and secure it. Carly screamed at the top of her lungs when I seized her and took to the sky.

The screaming faded as the air thinned. I sped through the sky as fast as my stone body would allow, pumping my wings with urgency. My destination: a single containment room and the young man waiting to see if he could do anything to help her return to herself.

Carly whipped her head around suddenly, hitting an unnatural angle that caused her neck to crack. "*Unhand my chosen ascendant now,*" she said in the fully wailing cacophony of Myuna's rage-filled presence.

I met her glowing white eyes. "Or what?" I asked.

"*I flood her with my power,*" Myuna answered. A flourish of light pulsed from Carly's body, lighting up her skeleton to shine through her skin for a moment. "*To your simple mortal mind, she will die. She will become something greater than Endaeron ever was, capable of consuming even your rock-encased soul.*"

She inspected my expressionless face, the threat hanging between us. Here was the moment Phaeron admitted he was not strong enough to face.

So, I did it for him, saying, "Bullshit."

The answering bellow was deafening. "*Do you not care for this girl at all? Would you not mourn if she died?*"

"There's no need for mourning," I stated. "You are not powerful enough to do more than bluster."

"*Hmm. The prophecy only concerned the son of night, his mate, and his daughter. It never mentioned a man of stone impervious to magic. Who are you?*" Myuna asked.

"My name is Geo."

"*Geo. I look forward to consuming you whole.*" Her presence left Carly, who fell into a limp faint in my arms.

40
CRESS

When Geo carried Carly away and she screamed, so did the torchbearers. It was the scene of a horror movie, with the gore washing into the lake as the water flowed over our feet. The mer had retreated with who they thought was Willow and closed the dry stretch to the ocean gate. Eddies of pinkish foam splashed over the battlefield.

When the echoes of screaming faded, the torchbearers dropped weapons and spells, eyes glazing over to blank, zombielike stares. Phaeron placed his sword aside and grabbed the soul of the nearest one, untying it from Myuna's control.

"Do you see what to do?" he asked in Soiluirian.

Braza answered affirmatively from my lips.

"Madigan!" Phaeron shouted. The woman's red-clad head turned his way. "Carly's lost control!"

"Arms down," she shouted. Her fighters echoed the order and took the cue to stop fighting, watching with unease as the torchbearers that were still alive went limp and some collapsed bonelessly with the one controlling them gone.

I let Braza take control for now, and she turned on her soul sight. I was disoriented by the sudden double-images overlaid behind everyone, their souls appearing like auras except larger and with more vivid and varied colors. But she knew exactly what she was looking at and what to do. While she worked, my suppressed thoughts came back up from where I'd buried them during the battle.

That'd been my sister saying those awful things. I couldn't get her hate-filled stare out of my head, aimed directly at me. Even though I knew, logically, she was as much a victim as the torchbearers we'd had to kill, it hurt. She'd suffered and become this shade of herself…a servant brainwashed to believe Myuna's side was just.

"If we can remove the seed of corruption planted in her soul, she will return to the girl you know," Braza said privately.

"That's a big if." Though Lucas had been able to save the less afflicted souls, who knew if he was powerful enough to erase the full and malicious intent behind Carly's deep corruption.

Phaeron had been able to confirm that Lucas had rescued those people from unnatural status and returned their souls to the state they'd been in before encountering a dread goddess. There were no others with magic twisted into a new form, like Lucas, but also none so severely changed as Carly. *"If she remains unnatural, then what?"* I asked.

Braza sighed deeply. *"Another big if. She may have to be contained in a library, depending on if she develops a hunger for souls. Otherwise, she would be monitored for the rest of her life and fed bits of powercore energy to stave off any possible cravings. In the best possible scenario, Lucas removes Myuna's influence completely, and Carly becomes fully human again."*

After the pain of having her soul warped by Myuna…well, I hoped my sister would be okay to return to her normal self. *"Now that I have power, here you are begging me to let it go,"* she had said. But I didn't know if that was her deepest wish twisted by corruption or a true reflection of how she felt within.

"While there is no harm in speculation, we have one last fight ahead of us," Braza said, cutting into my thoughts. Our allies helped move the unconscious torchbearers we'd saved first, dragging them away from the lake. Then came the dead, pulled out of the water before they could sink into the waves.

Though many of us had been hardened against such a sight after the awful fights that'd occurred with countless unnatural creatures over these long months, fighters and medical personnel alike wept over several of the fallen. The air had changed. We were all that was left in the whole of this pocket dimension, other than Myuna. And I was afraid more would be sacrificed to see this through to the end.

I looked around for my men, coven mates, and friends. Phaeron was a few feet away, wringing water out of his hair. For a few moments, I saw him with Braza's soul sight and paused. *Son of night* became a lot more literal all of a sudden.

Phaeron's soul was a rich, velvety black, with a flicker of white that arched toward the top. The patch of Endaeron looked like a crescent moon at the right angle, and I'd expected the piece of my soul we'd swapped with his mating bite would look the same way. Yet instead, my light came through in pinpricks, making it look like his soul had been carved from a starry night.

I blinked, and the sight was gone. He'd noticed my stare and tilted his head. "What has you so spellbound, my heart?" he asked.

"I've never seen your soul before now." I searched for a way to describe it other than *pretty*, considering how he could wax poetic about my own. "It's like a peaceful night. One I could get lost in."

There was a flicker of interest in his expression before he pressed his lips together tightly. "Tell me more soon," he said, edging closer and showing me the rune-etched edge of the dragon scale. Braza shivered within me in recognition of the holding place for the other half of her soul. Her emotions felt a lot like anticipation and hope for her fresh start.

He slipped it back out of view as Auric approached us, growling. "The more time we spend dawdling, the more prepared Myuna will be for us," he snapped in Soiluirian.

"I told you. I don't want to go until Geo is with us," Phaeron said.

"This is not what we agreed to. You told me we were killing the ascendant, not trying to save her."

I glanced away from them, pretending not to understand. I looked around again for all my friends. They'd come together, everyone alive if a little scuffed. Ben had his back turned to Bianca, who was applying a healing rune for him on a gash over his shoulder blade.

Phaeron spoke to Auric much more patiently than I would have. "Plans change. We did not expect to save any lives today, yet we have. Peace, old friend. Myuna will be rotting again on the planet she destroyed before you know it."

"She deserves to die a true death. Her soul ripped to shreds, unable to enter any semblance of the next life," Auric said in a tone of pure acid. "I wish I were strong enough to do it."

"You will still be responsible for ending her reign of terror here before it begins. We could not send her through the Void without you."

"That still does not bring back Geryn. Fuckin' hell, even if Myuna dies today, that does not give Geryn or any of the other lost souls a single ounce of rest," Auric muttered.

Phaeron rested a hand on his shoulder, and his sympathy and understanding flowed across the mating circle to me. They remained that way for a few minutes, until Madigan and her men checked in with us about the plan. "Geo should be back any minute now. Once he is, we will empower Cress and be ready to go," he said.

Madigan nodded to me, and nerves fluttered in my belly. They intensified with every beat of my heart as it sank in: this was truly it. Either my circle held off Myuna long enough for Auric to send her through the Void, or we all died. Not just my life and those of my men were at stake, but also the lives of almost everyone I cared about.

"It'll just be like what we practiced," I murmured to myself.

My friends came over to cluster around me. Ben seemed to pick up on my headspace immediately and wrapped his arms around me for a quick hug. "Just think. In a few years, we're going to be talking about that one time we fought a goddess," he said.

"And won!" Roe exclaimed, staggering me with a slap on the back.

I looked around at them all, still amazed everyone had stayed to fight, other than Ambrose, who'd engaged in a different kind of battle halfway across the world in King Laiken's undersea court. Willow had shed the heavy armor disguise and stood in the lake up to her knees. Water wove around her delicate trident, forming spheres that rotated around her body like moons to a planet.

I felt such an overwhelming surge of gratitude seeing even my most gentle friend ready to fight with us. "You all are the best," I said, swiping under my eye. "We're going to do this... We're going to get through this together."

Ben reached out and squeezed my hand, static brushing our anam cara marks. "Together," he agreed. I managed a tense smile for him.

When Geo landed a few minutes later, he found me between Ben and Phaeron, his discarded shield gleaming at our feet. I met his quick-silver gaze with anticipation, and he shifted into human form to cup my cheek in a warm hand.

"How is she?" I whispered.

He pressed a kiss into my hair. "She is with Lucas now. Though Myuna blustered, she didn't do anything to harm her," he said.

I flung my arms around him, sighing with relief. "Thank you."

He hugged me back, squeezing gently. I looked up to see a meaningful glance pass from him to Phaeron. "What did Lucas say?" the dimensional asked.

"That Myuna's corruption is very distinct inside her soul. He promised to do his best to remove it," Geo answered.

"Once she is gone, his task may be easier," Phaeron mused.

An impatient noise nearby had Geo stiffening and turning to glare at Auric's darkening face. I put a hand on his arm. "It's all right. We should get moving," I said to my men, who nodded.

After days of practice, we had found a pattern of sharing our magic and abilities that worked best. First, Ben and I shared our witcheries, with him taking my celestial side and me taking his blood runes. I cut myself on my sword and lifted my sleeve to paint the runes for strength, agility, and speed on my skin before putting a tiny healing rune over the cut to close it fast.

Next was Phaeron, whose knowledge of swordplay mixed with Braza's shadows and magic to lend me the skills of a shadowborn.

And finally was Geo, who changed back into gargoyle form and gave me as much of his endurance and stoicism as possible. He bent and offered me his crystal shield.

"We're ready," I told Auric in a two-toned voice.

He grumbled in his native tongue as word traveled through the group of fighters. We gathered in a tight semicircle at his direction, and the weight of many expectant gazes seared into my back. *I can't mess this up. I won't.*

When he raised his arms, shimmering magic in shades of sapphire and gray spread from his feet, flowing around us. It moved like mist, getting under the layers of my clothes to chill my skin. I stayed by Phaeron's side as the Void closed in around us. He'd done this before, walked the endless nothing for what could've been an eternity, and come out on the other side okay.

It was over in the time it took to blink twice. We went from a bloodied beachside to the remains of the audience chamber where Myuna sat upon the dais, towering over us in her glowing white splendor. When we first came here before the Crown Coven, I'd thought the chamber was beautiful, with the artful display of the seven affinities of witch magic. It'd been built to impress all seeking an audience with the highest coven in North America.

The battle and resulting occupation by a ravenous goddess had wrecked it. Auric had dropped us in the middle of the long path that led to the dais. Instead of a placid pool with splashing sculptures to our left, there was a crater littered with shattered cement debris. Dried blood stains turned much of the sides brown.

To our right, the carefully cultivated soil with its verdant display of flowers and herbs was turned over, finger-shaped furrows marking where huge hands had combed all living matter free of its home. The domed roof overhead had long lost all of its glass, with the metal frames hanging and looking like they could fall at any moment.

Myuna wasn't the only one here. A dozen figures stood below the dais, their heads jolting up as she noticed our sudden appearance. Her shocked gaze moved unerringly to Phaeron and me standing together, and she opened her mouth to scream. Though Braza quickly plugged my ears with shadows, everyone else covered their ears to block out some of the unholy sound.

"*You stand before Myuna the White, the reaper of worlds!*" she shrieked. Her voice shook me to my core, resonant with power, madness, and countless souls crying out through her cavernous open mouth. "*Throw down your weapons and prostrate yourself for my mercy, or face the end!*"

Despite Geo's steadiness grounding me, my heart still thumped hard against my ribcage as I stepped forward, raising Flame until its tip pointed at her chest. "Myuna!" I shouted. After the deafening force of her, my voice felt like it was emerging through water. "I, Cressida Rollins Darkmore, challenge you to a duel!"

My arm trembled as Myuna observed me with a sneer. I only had to keep her occupied for a few minutes, long enough for Auric to do what he needed to. Strains of laughter danced in and out of my ears, a chorus of disembodied, mocking voices. The mist of the Void seeped and spread in freezing eddies toward the dais. Bluish mist rolled over our feet, gathering in the pits and valleys of the broken concrete.

Braza flared her power, wrapping me in shadows of black and purple when Myuna eased off the dais, standing to her full height. "It is *you*. No matter how much I tried to twist fate, this moment has arrived all the same." She reached toward the sky, harnessing a beam of light and holding it, shimmering and pulsing, in her hand. "It seems I must destroy you myself to be free of this wretched prophecy. I will fight you, she who would mate the son of night. And to keep all of these friends of yours busy, they will fight my followers."

Each of the men and women behind her had flares of cold white light in their eyes. Most dashed past Myuna at a full run, weapons lifting. One, a near-naked man, rippled with a shifter's transformation and expanded rapidly. Crimson scales coated his elongated neck, and ridges grew over his back. He spread leathery wings and roared, blasting a superheated wave of flame directly at me.

Myuna smirked, firelight flickering over her milky eyes. "Oops," she said. I felt her attempt at being playful in the headache that rushed through me when I became shadows and reemerged a few yards to the side.

We hadn't come here to fight fair, so I wouldn't expect Myuna to either. It was in her very best interest that I get "accidentally" turned into a smear of ash. I raised the crystal shield, shouting, "Let's see if you have better aim than him!"

For a moment, her gaze was unfocused. Sounds of battle raged around us, and I waited tensely for what she'd do next. *Just keep her attention. Don't let her get any closer to souls she could consume.*

"I got it!" I heard Roe announce. She ran as fast as she could in her orange crystal armor, intercepting the dragon shifter's head. As he inhaled to breathe another gout of fire, she nailed his jaw in an uppercut, and Myuna stirred, her mouth gaping when the dragon bared his fangs.

She took a step toward me, and I retreated, facing her back to the rest of the group. I would soon be pinned between the dais and the far wall, but my breath was turning to smoke with each exhale. The Void was so close I could practically taste the madness and its taunting words hanging just out of the range of hearing. The mist was thickening up, turning the air gray and dense. It muffled some of the sounds of combat around us, making it truly seem like it was just Myuna and me locked in a duel to the death.

Myuna flipped the ray of light around her arm, its point now forming a spear that jabbed at my face. Braza's power blew away from my body when I leaned to the side, feeling the sear of intense light so close to my skin. When I whipped a set of sharp shadow tendrils toward the goddess's exposed arm, they dissipated into nothing moments from contact. Braza cursed in my head. *"Her power is a counter to mine. Try using Flame."*

I flowed into the first form of a fighting style that'd barely seen the light of Earth. When Myuna jabbed for my heart, I deflected her light and shoved with my shield, following through with Flame to cut a jagged line into her forearm.

To my horror, her skin split open in bloodless, hanging chunks, as if she were made of papier-mâché. I caught a glimpse of her hollow, black insides before the rip closed on its own, the skin flowing back together in moments. There was no sign I'd hurt her at all, not even a grunt of pain.

"Do you see now what it is to face a goddess?" Though she'd pitched her voice to whisper, it still boomed over me. She grabbed her spear in both hands and drove it downward toward my skull. With the sear of light so intense, I barely gathered enough shadows to move sideways and reappear a few feet from the impact of her impossible weapon.

She checked the momentum and swung to the side, hitting me against the shoulder. My robe took some of the blow, but white-hot agony burnt and crisped my skin underneath it.

My hold on my men's powers wavered when I needed them most. Phaeron's fighting techniques slipped from my fingertips, leaving his weapon feeling awkward in my hand. *"Focus, my love,"* he said over our mating circle. A moment later, he pressed the lost knowledge back into my head.

"Keep moving," Braza urged. There was no way to easily paint a healing rune on myself, given the location of the wound.

I took to the shadows before Myuna could try to skewer me again, regrouping up on the dais. God, it stank up here, like fear, piss, and rot all smeared in a ghastly mix.

"We just need to disarm her. That spear is too intense," I said, hoping she'd get angry when she saw me standing so close to her throne. Her legs had left indents in the tile and metal from sitting there for so long.

In one way, I was lucky. Myuna was uncertain of where I was for a moment, her white eyes roving points through the Void mist. When she spotted me, she hurled her weapon at me, and it disappeared in a burst of sunlight when I ducked aside.

"What is the meaning of this Void magic?" she boomed.

I groaned in a mix of agony and dismay when she held her arm toward the sky and a new shaft of light began to form in her palm. She swept it in an arc, clearing away some of the mist that'd been creeping in to surround her. Through the cold gray buffet, she approached me with her hand still raised, the weapon in her hand sputtering in and out of existence.

That was it. She couldn't get unfiltered light with the interference of other magics. "Phaeron!" I screamed, unknowing of how he was doing in the fight below. He read my intentions and responded immediately, creating a thick cloud of black shadow to blot out the encroaching sun.

The only light in the chamber now was from Myuna herself, her sickly white radiance doubling in intensity when the sunlight faded from her hand completely. She clenched her fist with a furious bellow. "If you insist on interfering, then I will have every head in this room in addition to hers," she announced.

Her body warped, arms stretching out of their sockets first. She became longer, thinner, a towering eldritch horror with sharp talons of light erupting from her fingertips. Black slits opened in her torso, over her arms and legs and even her forehead and cheeks. Mouths. Countless sucking mouths.

"Oh god, oh shit," I said under my breath. I lunged forward and dove into the shadows, emerging inches from her grasping hand as it tried to close around the nearest ally—a doctor helping a badly burned guardian witch. They stood back at what they'd thought was a safe distance before she proved that whatever she was made of was stretchy enough for her to reach anywhere in this chamber.

Her hand bounced off my shield, which rang with a discordant note.

I slammed into the doctor and rolled off him, cracking my head against the floor. With a groan, my gargoyle-enhanced endurance fled, and my body erupted with pain all over.

I looked over in dismay at Geo's crystal shield where it'd landed a yard away. It vibrated intensely enough to spread a web of cracks through the inside of it. If I was lucky, it could take one more blow before it shattered into crystal confetti. But first...I reached for Geo across the mating circle and felt him meet me halfway with the endurance I lost.

Bolstered by him, I stood and felt a shiver wrack my figure. It was *so* cold all of a sudden, turning my sweat to ice against my skin. Auric stood behind the wall of our fighters, which I'd crossed violently with Myuna's slap. His brow was knitted with concentration, his mouth forming whispers only heard by the Void. The densest gray and blue mist unspooled from his hands as he seemed to will it into existence, plucking it from beyond.

His one good eye met mine, and the mist parted for him so I could read his lips. *Bring her over here.*

In the freezing presence of the Void, only the burn on my shoulder remained a throbbing, angry patch. It twinged as I raised Flame and took up a guard stance. Myuna lumbered toward me even now, her massive body seeming slower than it was. She lashed out a hand to grab me, and I stepped aside, only to spear her hand into the ground with Flame as the stake.

She howled in fury and pain, shaking the whole complex. A chunk of metal fell from the ceiling, landing amidst my allies with a deafening crunch. I didn't have time to worry if everyone was all right—she leapt and snapped her stretchy body to rubber band to the location where her hand was pinned. She grabbed me with her free hand.

Hopefully Auric could deploy that trap fast, as the sucking mouths along her body were dangerously close to everyone else. Myuna loomed over me, black mouth gaped in a victorious smirk. Her booming voice shook me further as I gasped for air in her crushing grip. "You see now that you cannot win." Black spots crowded the edges of my vision when first Geo's magic slipped from my grasp, then Phaeron's and Ben's.

The shield slipped out of my nerveless fingers, shattering with the delicate tinkling of small pieces of glass. I *did* see the nothingness of the

Void enveloping us both in its freezing embrace, the gray and blue mist condensing into a bubble over her head. She was too busy gloating over her impending victory to notice the precise moment we slipped into the space between worlds.

"No prophecy can spell the ending of a goddess such as I." Without the acoustics of an audience chamber, her many voices rang hollow. "How foolish I was...to believe..."

My vision was fading. I gasped for air, and painful prickles coursed over my skin head to toe as I just couldn't find any to fill my lungs. Myuna squeezed me instinctively now as she turned her gaze to the Void, a dark nothingness in all directions.

"This cannot be!" she thundered.

In one last act of defiance, Braza spoke to her, mind to mind. *"Soon you will know only the rot of Soiluire, and I hope you choke on it."*

Her pale irises refocused on me, the prize she crushed in one hand. "You insolent—no. I shall know the taste of you *first.*"

Myuna lifted me, and I fell face-first into her mouth's pit.

41
PHAERON

Familiar shadowborn rage coursed through my body as Myuna's minions rushed us. Eleven supernaturals, all possessing strong magic or powerful, enchanted weapons. And the last of the dozen... I fixed my gaze on the dragon shifter that'd tried to incinerate my mate.

And on Roe as she recklessly ran ahead of our defensive line to punch said dragon in the face. I swore under my breath and burst into shadows, racing after her. With Cress occupying Myuna's attention, it was my duty to nullify the second-worst threat here.

The dragon raised a taloned foot to crush Roe, flinching at the last minute as my shadowy claws punched through the scales over his sole and loosed streams of blood. While fire dragons ran hot, his blood shouldn't have steamed as much as it had under normal circumstances.

Insane chatters of laughter accompanied the Void's chilling touch. Its mist surrounded me gleefully, frosting the dragon blood I flicked off my shadows as I regrouped next to Roe.

"Defensive magic, now," I ordered her. All we'd done was annoy the massive shifter, who, to our luck, was moving much slower than he should, dragging under Myuna's control.

"Got it," she said. Luckily, there was plenty of debris lying around that answered to the magic of a guardian witch. She cobbled together a wall of cement, rocks, and tiles.

Our opponent turned one blazing eye my way, sucking in a deep breath to feed the inferno at the back of his throat. I disappeared into shadows when he was already breathing out, to keep the gout of fire away from Roe.

Reappearing by his hindquarters, I lashed solid shadows into knotted ropes between his legs and tail. "Hey, ugly!" Roe shouted, accompanied by the sound of rocks cracking against scales. *Fuck.* The bold female had a death wish.

And I was acting on Cress's wishes too much, trying to ensnare the shifter to lead him into a moment of weakness, to save him and his soul. She'd taken much of my sword skills, and it seemed I'd gained her empathy. A dangerous emotion, given the stakes. I should've shoved my sword through his skull and been done with it.

Instead, I ripped my weapon through the wing membrane looming nearby, which flared with his shift of attention. I accompanied it with a shadowborn's roar of challenge, hoping he would realize Roe was not the opponent worth his flames. He swung his head on his long neck, lifting his wings and looking at me over his shoulder.

That's right. Come this way.

I shifted my stance, suddenly more confident with the sword in my hand. Cress had lost the skills she'd borrowed from me, which created a ripple over our circle and mating bond. I closed my eyes for a critical moment. *"Focus, my love,"* I encouraged, sending her back what she needed from me.

A solid force slammed into my waist. I was thrown several yards from the impact, only seeing the dragon's turned hindquarters and the tail he'd struck me with. I cushioned my landing with shadows, skidding to a stop and making an exaggerated groan to tickle his prey sense.

Light exploded in the chamber, filtering through the gloom of mist starting to surround Myuna. Someone screamed, though it echoed a hundred times with the rest of the voices the Void wanted us to hear. Still lying on the ground, my gaze flashed to the dais, where Cress crouched behind the crystal shield, her face turned to the ceiling.

"What is the meaning of this Void magic?" the goddess boomed, swatting the mist aside. I bared my fangs. As powerful as she was, she couldn't do much more than hold Auric's magic at bay. The Void had never answered to her command.

She was gathering rays of light, her hand held in that direction. "Phaeron!" Cress screamed, reaching out to our mating bond. She needed my darkness, and I gave her nighttime, reaching upward too and blasting all the shadows over my form and every ounce of magic I could muster to block out the sun and cut off Myuna from its power.

The goddess's furious bellow resonated with ghostly laughter. "If you insist on interfering, then I will have every head in this room in addition to hers," Myuna thundered.

I was sure she would turn her wrath on me and hissed, welcoming it. The dragon was in motion again, lunging at me, a crimson blur with a snapping, ember-filled mouth. With my power occupied helping Cress, I didn't dare try to dive into the shadows to avoid him.

I rolled to my feet and leapt, sinking my claws into his scaled neck and climbing. He tripped from the snare I'd tied through his back legs, his bulk going down. The jarring impact of his body hitting the ground nearly unseated me, but I remained clinging on his neck.

"Are you okay?" Roe shouted.

"Fine! Hold his head if you can," I called back. I searched him frantically with soul sight, locating the aura of his soul between his shoulder blades, where his wings met prominent flight muscles clothed in plate-like scales. It did not encompass his whole body, remaining the same size as it would be if he were in his human form.

I dove for it as he started to stand. There was an abrupt jerk of his head and neck; Roe's grunt of effort was eclipsed by the sound of flame igniting. I had moments before he incinerated her and so I hooked my claws into his soul and heaved for all I was worth. It didn't want to come free, emerging nearly torn from my efforts.

When I had his knotted soul between my hands, he slumped to the ground, drooling burning liquid. I tisked under my breath as I got a good look at it. No wonder it'd been a challenge to remove. Myuna had tied it into two knots, a sign he hadn't gone to her control easily.

My hands were shaking. It was cold, bitterly so. The Void's presence made it nearly impossible to untie both knots, and it took all my focus to do so for a few crucial moments.

Cress's alarm and pain tore through me. I gasped for air, dropping the soul back into its body.

Myuna had my mate in her hand, crushing her with overlong fingers. The Void swirled around them both, forming a dense bubble of blue-tinged mist that closed into a cage while the goddess gloated.

And then they disappeared together.

My mating bond intensified with agony, urgency, and distance all at once, a shrill tone at the back of my head. Sunlight returned to the chamber as I ripped my power back, appearing where Myuna had stood and pulling Flame from the ground.

There were a few torchbearers still standing. They'd gone limp without Myuna's presence, staring around at us with blank white eyes.

I took my shadowborn form and let my shadows hold my swords. With one leap, I was before Auric. I grabbed the front of his suit, dragging his stout body up so we were face-to-face. "Send me after her," I snarled.

"It's too la—"

"Right now!" I shouted at him.

"She's already halfway to—"

Pain flooded down my back, and my fingers clenched, tearing his clothes. He slipped out of my grip as I bent over, breathing heavily.

Cress!

My bonds to her pulled taut. Energy flowed from me into the endless nothing, a tether of pure life force. Something—*Myuna*—guzzled the power greedily on the other side.

"If you've ever valued our friendship," I rasped, "you will open the way."

Figures crowded us. "I'm going with you," Geo rumbled.

Ben helped support me upright. His face was dangerously wan, but his tone brooked no argument. "Me too."

Instead of wasting his breath, Auric drew the Void's presence back. Cold mist enveloped his fingers, and it was the work of moments to open a rip in reality and expand its yawning black mouth wide enough to fit us one at a time. "I will leave you in the Void if there's any sign of Myuna returning here," he said, deadly serious.

"Fine," I said. I flexed my hands, and my magic retracted, placing my sword hilts in my palms.

Auric shouldered between the rip and me. "I will reverse part of the spell so you can find her."

"I'll find her. No one should follow, though," I growled. He nodded and stepped aside for Geo, Ben, and me.

On the other side, the rip was an oval of brightness in a world of encroaching cold and nothingness. "Whoa," Ben murmured, bending to try to touch a ground that wasn't there.

"Stop fucking around. Follow me, and stay close," I snapped, following the call of my mating bond. Ben recoiled, shocked, but did as I said.

I'd be able to find Cress even in the endlessness of the Void. Nothing, not even the whisper of voices and visions, would stop my forward charge.

I didn't dare disappear into shadows to move faster, considering the other pieces of Cress's heart ran to keep pace behind me. Without me, they'd be lost here in minutes and then reduced to laughing echoes. If one of us died, we'd all haunt the Void for eternity.

Instead, I spread my magic, forming a shadowy bubble of relative safety from the Void's madness. The visions and whispers were held at bay from its radius. As long as Ben and Geo didn't listen too closely or stray to chase a vision, we stood a chance of making it to Cress in time.

"What is this place?" It was Roe's voice. I flinched at the sound and glanced over my shoulder. It was the real her. She'd retracted her crystal armor into its pendant and sprinted to join us alongside Wren and Áine.

My blood ran as hot as liquid flame. "You should not be here," I said harshly. "I thought I made it clear that *no one should've followed us!*"

Roe puffed along, shrugging off my anger. "Cress is my coven mate, and I wasn't about to leave her behind...no matter where the hell we are." She had a chipper enough tone, like a run through the Void was a Saturday morning jog and not a dip into a location of near-guaranteed insanity and death.

"Don't worry." Wren's voice was a lot more labored. "The blue dude cut everyone else off. It's just us."

I grunted. It was the least he could do after banishing my mate to the Void with the likes of Myuna. If we survived this, he'd be lucky if I didn't gut and fillet him for the oversight.

And if we didn't...

"Phaeron," called a voice from the Void. I didn't turn my gaze, knowing an apparition would be there to try to tempt me from my path.

"Come back to bed." A whisper of Soilurian from a long-lost lover.

A couple of my companions startled and made confused sounds. "Ignore everything you see and hear. It's all fake," I advised over one shoulder.

Easier said than done sometimes. I saw a small figure at the edge of my vision, a gray-skinned boy. His orange eyes glowed in the darkness, and he waved for my attention. He was a smiling, happy kid dressed in human clothes. Gritting my teeth, I turned away from him. As much as I desired a family, he was only a manifestation the Void thought would distract me.

Nothing would prevent me from getting to my mate, though. I felt the currents of magic around us shifting and Cress's presence coming toward us as Auric reversed his spell, as promised. She was no longer halfway to Soiluire, where she'd perish long before we'd manage to find her. In fact, we were drawing close enough to hear the echoes of distortion from what had to be Myuna's voice.

My pace faltered, and I nearly tripped to fall into nothingness. Between the numbness brought on by the cold and the suction of magic and life force, I was fading faster than expected. Geo and Ben had to be faring similarly...but we would limp to Myuna if we had to. She could not have the considerable power of our mating circle, plus the half of Braza's soul Cress carried.

Still, we slowed, and there was some relief between Ben, who *was* limping, and Wren, whose breath sawed as she clutched her side. I strode unerringly toward the glow of white light marking the first landmark in this place of nothing.

Myuna was thrashing around, occasionally screaming in her chorus of agony shriek. At first, I thought it was from a Void feeding frenzy, but her belly bulged and roiled, jerking her hollow body around as if she were a ragdoll.

It looked excruciating. I grinned, finally speeding ahead of the group when the rest of the way forward was obvious. My boot met her shoulder, knocking her prone on her back. "Indigestion?" I sneered.

My mating bond tugged straight downward, toward her stomach.

Cress was in there, fighting back. Before Myuna could consume me next, I drew one of my swords down her middle, splitting open the gaping blackness within her.

From the nightmare of her guts, human fingers emerged. I grabbed my mate's hand to lift her free, gasping in shock when I got a good look at the light blazing from her.

CRESS

Myuna's guts were like a portal to another world. Braza and I fell and fell and fell like we were on our way to some kind of twisted Wonderland.

"Good going, getting us eaten," I thought to her irritably. Without the crushing grip of the oversized goddess, I'd begun to breathe again and consider whether it'd be possible to condense into shadows to escape from between Myuna's lips.

But Braza was not responsive, nor were her shadowy powers. I was leaking a trail of black and purple and began to fear the worst when I saw it. Was it Braza's lifeblood? Were both of us already dead and I hadn't felt it?

Eventually, I landed face down on a soft heap, and intense pain ricocheted through me. *Fuck, definitely not dead yet.* I hurt all over, especially over my burned shoulder. My clothes fell right off me when I moved my arms to lift up to my knees. That expensive robe, reinforced with magic, disintegrated into threads before my eyes.

My naked skin blistered and reddened, and it was excruciating to experience. I'd taken an acid bath somewhere on the way down—Myuna was *digesting* me. "Well," I said from a raw throat. "Hell of a way to go." I took heart in knowing Myuna would die eventually, starving to death on the planet she'd already destroyed. My sacrifice wouldn't be in vain.

But my *men*. When I died, so would they. I wished I knew how to sever the mating circle so I could do it here and now. If only they could keep going, to escape Cerris City and enjoy a blissful, Myuna-free life.

Phaeron wouldn't go on without me even if I figured out how to save him, though. I felt him like he was still with me, the mating mark on my shoulder pulsing with flashes of hot and cold prickles.

Maybe someday, someone would discover the dragon scale he carried with the other half of Braza's soul. She could live on... I mean, I didn't know for sure about that. Could half a soul as big as a powercore continue to exist without the other half? It was an unheard-of situation. She'd be the first and only one to attempt it.

Shadows sputtered around me, lacing into two thin wraps for my breasts and hips when I gestured. *"Braza?"* I projected hopefully.

"Cress," she answered. Her voice was faint. *"Touch the souls."*

What? There was nothing here but us. I looked up first, seeing the white-lined layer of Myuna's stomach. Then down...ugh. What did I think I'd landed on? Those were...souls, I guess. Parts of them, sucked dry of everything except for a paper-thin layer.

There were heaps of souls everywhere I looked, mountains of the remains of the dead who'd passed the same way I was about to. My gorge rose, and I gagged, swallowing down the taste of vomit before it could burn my throat any worse.

Fuck, that's disgusting. Still, I did as Braza commanded, putting my palms down beside my knees. The ribbons of her leaking magic reversed course, flowing downward and out like a wave.

The nearest souls twitched. Each caught a spark of magic from Braza, and their colors quickly shifted from black and purple to skin tones. Souls inflated with new purpose, glowing from within and erasing major features with an internal shine.

These husks turned into souls once more. *Ghosts.* Hundreds, then thousands, and then more, all of the damned turning eyes limned with light toward me, the only one still alive amongst us.

"Um, hi," I said to the nearest person, a human man who must've died quite recently. He stared at me without any comprehension. Most of those around us were tall and horned, similarly blank, but further back in the crowd were smaller, furry shapes and others with scales and spiky fins. Just how many worlds' worth of different people had Myuna consumed?

"Make way," said a female voice. She spoke in Soiluirian, but some vestige of Braza translated her words. "That is my daughter! Make way!"

The souls murmured, a sound like a distant crowd, but parted for the liveliest one. A glowing gray figure pushed her way to me, her red eyes like liquid rubies. "Brazita...no. You are not her."

Keshora et Sudaira's kindly face fell with disappointment. Something broke between Braza and me in that moment, and she flowed free of me, standing beside me in shades of black and purple. "It's me," she answered.

By some miracle, I understood, and tears pricked my eyes when both souls crashed together for a strong hug.

A third figure piled into their embrace with a girlish laugh. "Braza!" Ravai exclaimed, her voice high, on the cusp of breaking to the deeper tones of adulthood.

"Ravai! Wait, how are you here?" Braza asked. She looped an arm around her sister, holding both of her lost family members close.

For a moment, Ravai looked baffled by the question. "I...oh. Uncle took my soul and carried it to the goddess to eat." She looked around at the silent audience of souls, blinking twice. "I guess I've been here ever since."

My heart broke for her and everyone else who'd formed mountains of husks within Myuna's stomach. There had to be billions of victims here. The foundation under my feet was shifting as more and more souls stood back up, briefly reanimated to bear witness to this reunion and my eventual death. *Think, Cress.* There had to be a way to escape.

"She's been using your power as her own," I said, mostly to myself. Thousands of eyes blinked. Ah, shit. Most of them were from Soiluire and had never seen a human in their lives. I tested the thread of connection between Braza and me and tried to repeat myself in their language.

Keshora was the one to answer. "That's right. I watched for an age as more and more of my people came here before the true end came..."

Cutting herself off, she released Braza and stepped toward me. Her pupils narrowed as she lowered toward my shoulder, inspecting the mark there. "You have mated my male. Who are you?" she asked suspiciously.

"Oh...ha haaa," I stammered. Maybe Myuna's stomach acid didn't have to kill me. Keshora, for all that I was promised that she was nice and gentle, looked ready to tear my throat out.

Braza put her hand on her arm. "Mother, please," she coaxed. "You have been dead quite some time. This is Cress, his new mate from the world we traveled to."

"It's nice to meet you. I've heard…well, I haven't heard much," I said, apparently deciding to put my foot further down my mouth. "Braza speaks well of you. And Phaeron had a very difficult time overcoming your death."

Keshora's eyes gained facets as she made a sound of pain deep in her throat. A set of hands seized mine, feeling as soft and pliable as jelly. "What about me?" Ravai blurted. "How is he? I've missed him so much!"

"He's…" I didn't know how to answer her questions, considering my impending death.

"Take a look at her soul," Braza whispered to their mother in the meantime.

I squeezed Ravai's hands. She had infectious energy, and I wished I had more time to get to know her. "Your death is something he still can't bring himself to talk about. I think he's missed you just as much as you've missed him."

It seemed I was here just to cause his old family pain, as she made the same dimensional noise I associated with their way of crying. She pulled me into a hug while she wailed. "I'm sorry," I said, squeezing her tight.

"Thank you for bringing him comfort. And for being a good friend to my sister." She glanced toward them. "She wouldn't speak up for just anyone."

At this point, Keshora and Braza were deep in conversation. It seemed the older dimensional was relaxing, at least, listening and nodding as Braza fell into the tones of explaining something as quickly as possible.

When she was done, Keshora breathed out slowly and squared her shoulders. She turned to me. "You are still alive," she stated. "Your soul is made of light, just like the creature I once revered as a goddess. For the ages I have rotted here, she has used up every bit of what made me who I was. I had no choice in this because there wasn't a choice."

She stepped forward, putting her clawed hand over my marked shoulder. "But now there is one, and I choose you." When nothing happened and we just blinked at each other, she put pressure on my skin. "You may be a strange being yourself and not a goddess, but you may use what is left of me all the same. Make me anew in your light."

The spark within her dimmed a fraction, while I started giving off a hint of a glow. I glanced down at myself with a gasp.

"Oh, me too!" Ravai exclaimed, putting her hand on my other shoulder. "Make me anew in your light!"

Another soul's hand landed on Keshora's shoulder, and she flinched. But power flowed from her into me. Yet another soul joined him, and then a dozen more, and then a hundred, a chain reaction spreading through the lost souls as they gave me what they could in the name of salvation.

I filled from within with light, growing stronger and stretching the limits of my magic to find it a well filling itself with pure power. These people gladly fed me what they could. It wasn't that they knew me, but as a unit, they decided I was better than Myuna and worthier than the monster that'd originally consumed them.

I became strong enough that my skin healed of its burns and blisters. "We have to get out of here. And the only way out...is through," I said, pointing at the wall of Myuna's stomach. The chain of souls moved with me, all of us beginning to hammer at her from within. The material of her skin stretched and morphed around our fists like wet clay.

A force slapped the other side of her belly, sending me tumbling backward, and many others went flying. That must've been her hand. So, she felt us in here. I hoped it was painful to have a roiling sea of spirits hitting every wall of her stomach. The Iorsio tribe souls even took flight and slammed into the sloping roof of this inner chamber.

A terrible, distorted noise vibrated her skin. She must've been saying something, but for once, those she'd damned did not scream out through her mouth, but hit her with more ferocity than ever.

The only thing that stopped us momentarily was when the whole chamber rolled. Myuna must've flopped onto her belly, as she pitched all of us forward. The spirits weighed no more than a feather each, but I still felt crushed by the sheer number of them until they started regrouping and hitting her again.

Soon she was rolling around constantly, churning us in a whirlpool. Many spirits brushed past me, only adding their magic to mine in the process. I caught glimpses of more alien souls than I ever thought existed, nameless creatures of races long snuffed out by Myuna. Their power and sorrow filled my magic to overflowing.

There was no pain when I was flung into one of her stomach's walls anymore. The material was bound to tear eventually under our onslaught. Legions of souls rose to join us, stretching the limits of her insides in our revolt.

My marked shoulder itched intensely. I felt Phaeron when I touched it... He was close? But that was impossible. Auric would've sealed the way behind Myuna, not risking any chance of her returning.

With our next onslaught, I had the sensation of movement. We could've been curving Myuna's spine or tugging her around or...I don't know. There was nothing to see in here but the countless furious spirits now given the freedom to do something against their murderer. All I could tell for sure was that she was *definitely* screaming.

We were flung one more time. I got up and launched myself at her again, just to see the tip of something sharp breach the top of this chamber and drag down. There was a sheen of darkness between us and...more darkness beyond. But a pulse of urgency in my chest had me reaching through the darkness for the spray of cold beyond the humid depths of Myuna's guts.

A leather-clad hand wrapped around my own and pulled. I drew in a breath of chill Void air and met Phaeron's gaze. He was in full shadowborn form, practically vibrating with the fury that came along with it. The sudden surge of my mating circle's heightened emotions hit me like a punch to the gut.

They were all here, and a few of my friends besides, all gaping at me as I emerged like the sun, fully naked and blazing with light from within.

42
CRESS

Souls fled out from behind me, a gilded flood of them. One, darker than the rest, kept to my side. It was a relief to see Braza, even though it was strange that she and I were only tethered by the merest thread. She reached into Phaeron's shadows while he stared at me in disbelief, retrieving the dragon scale and diving back into Myuna's torn belly without him seeming to notice.

"How dare you. She was delicious," the goddess grumbled. She probed at the slash across her midsection, pushing the flaps of skin together, but they did not sew into a seamless whole like the last time I'd wounded her. Souls held the wound open, and thousands of them escaped by the second, flowing into my body. I felt their presence like a pressure within, my form stretching to accommodate so many different pieces of others and the power they wished to lend me.

Finally, Phaeron gathered his wits. "Cress, are you all right?"

"I think so." I had the voice echo now, the power of thousands or more coming through me. "You might want to step back."

He hesitated before turning to Roe and the others, herding them with shadows and gestures. I flexed my hand, willing my new power to give me a sword to match my new stature. A hundred souls surrendered part of their energy for me to have one form for me, the hilt perfectly matching my enlarged hand. The blade was made of pure celestial magic, glowing golden.

Myuna stumbled to her feet and gathered her own magic, creating the shaft of a white-glowing spear and flipping its blade up. She straightened with a wince. "You have...stolen from me. It is no matter. We will still end it here, in these moments past the prophecy. You defeated me..." She coughed up a dribble of black tar, smearing it across her white cheek. "And now I will defeat you."

All the while, the flood of souls from her stomach did not abate. As I grew, she diminished, my light dwarfing hers. "Big words. Let's go," I said, lunging at her. Our weapons caught and rebounded. She stumbled backward, wailing in earnest and stirring up the Void to scream with her.

I clenched my teeth and tried to block out the awful cacophony. Amidst the wailing were voices I recognized. Roe called my name in desperation, and I pivoted, only seeing darkness from where the shout originated. The Void wasn't going to watch this battle quietly, it seemed.

I struck out at her again, opening a wound in her side that closed itself quickly. Now it was obvious she drew on the life force of those within her to mend so fast or to strike so hard. A dozen souls had to give up their power to help me heal just as swiftly when the next thrust of her spear jabbed its point through my thigh.

Our gazes met. We were of the same size now, meeting somewhere in the middle of her impossible stature and my ordinary human frame. There was a new emotion there, something I don't think Myuna had felt for a long time.

Fear.

She attacked in a flurry of blows, all the while stoking burning rays of light from the holes of several mouths that formed on her torso and arms. Inspired by her changing it up, I summoned a ball of concentrated light and threw it at her, shaking the Void with the resulting explosion and knocking Myuna off her feet.

The Void echoed the explosion with a set of gleeful cackles.

"Ka*bewm*," I whispered for my handbook, which was hopefully flying in distressed circles somewhere on Earth, awaiting my safe return.

I swung my sword downward, intending to lop off her head. But it was still me, and I wasn't borrowing anyone else's sword skills. The blade dug into her back and shoulder blades, creating a cut that seared itself open with blackened edges. The dark matter that seemed to hold her together internally was exposed.

"No," Myuna groaned, lifting up and grabbing a huge handful of glowing souls that'd escaped when she hit the ground. She ate them again, struggling to swallow with several painful gulps as their fists made round outlines against her throat.

I kicked her weapon out of her hand, and it disappeared into wisps of light. Holding the tip of my sword to her neck, I echoed her with a smirk. "Do you see what it is to face a goddess?"

Her lips spread across her gaping mouth in a grimace. "You are no goddess," she thundered in her loud but diminished voice.

"I'm starting to realize that you never were one to begin with," I replied, lifting my weapon for one last strike to end this.

"You are no goddess," the Void trumpeted.

Myuna launched herself at me, her mouth stretching even wider and sucking hard. I felt an obscene tug on the souls within me as she knocked us both to the ground. We grappled, her punching, me trying to stab her, and rolled a couple times before something lassoed her around the neck and dug in with ebon hooks.

It looked like shadows and vines braided into one massive rope. At the other end heaved Phaeron and Áine, plus Ben, Geo, Roe, and Wren anchoring behind them. But further back, feeding shadows to make the rope as sturdy as possible, was a team of horned spirits.

I pushed Myuna and watched with a grin as the vines grew new tendrils to encircle her neck completely, with shadows following their path to reinforce them. She gripped the rope with both hands, gasping and thrashing, still leaking more and more spirits. For once, she was quiet, and my ears rang as I stood over her with sword in hand, wondering where to stab her to truly end her awful existence once and for all.

"You are no goddess," the Void echoed again, quieter this time.

"Shut up," I muttered, my brow drawn in concentration.

I opted for the heart, thrusting my sword downward clear through her chest. With one last jerk, she went limp, save for the flaps of her stomach, where her victims continued to escape. I gazed down at her still face. "It's over," I said with the relief of a destroyed world's worth of souls.

The rope around her neck faded, the vines withering away to brittle stalks in an instant. I was reaching down to tear her belly open further when her body flared with white light. A white figure emerged and lifted up, floating inches above the corpse.

I jumped backward and faced it, sword raised. It looked like a soul and perhaps Myuna as her original race, a spiky-finned creature with a mouthful of razor teeth. Her clawed hands darted out, catching my wrists.

"It is the turning of an eon. You are worthy where I no longer am," she said, putting something in my palm.

It was massive and white, pulsing with power and a slimy feeling. *Hunger.* It looked like she'd shoved her heart, stabbed straight through the center, in my hand. It was fleshy and ribbed with swollen veins and, impossibly, still beat outside of its body. Ichor slowly dribbled from its underside in a slimy trail.

"When I cut out Stalvos the White's heart at the end of my own world's destruction, he gave me this. A mature seed of power." Myuna's soul still spoke all languages simultaneously, but her voice was garbled by the flaring gills along her neck.

The Void played out the scene as she narrated it. A different pair stood next to us. A male creature rendered in white, offering this same heart to a living Myuna, who was covered in fish scales that glimmered teal and green. Her battle armor was covered in greasy white blood, and her alien spear dripped with it.

"*I accept,*" her apparition said, swallowing the heart in one bite.

In a blink, the memory was gone. Myuna's soul said, "It is yours. *You* are the goddess now, the one to own all the power in the universe. The souls you need are already within you. Consume them and rise."

Some evil power in the heart called to me, whispering to do it. To swallow it and ascend, to become the next reaper of worlds. I could still return to Earth and finish what she'd started.

The many souls within me clamored, screaming, their terror filling my every pore. I jolted and shook my head sharply, my stomach turning with disgust.

"Power…so delicious. It is the way of things," she whispered, leaning forward with anticipation when I lifted the heart.

I stared at it, astonished that I'd been tempted for a moment. How insane, to willingly become a soul-eating monster for power.

"Myuna," I stated. I met her bulging fish eyes to watch her reaction when I filled my palm with light, pure and searing, and coated the seed in a white-hot bath of magic. It crumpled to dust, drifting into fine particles the Void absorbed. "The answer is *no*. Go to hell, where you belong!"

The white apparition's mouth dropped open, despair clearly etched over her alien features. She released the opening strains of a scream of denial before the Void ripped her apart with tendrils of gray magic, dragging her back toward her corpse for a feast that would only leave her voice and memories behind to haunt its depths forever.

I breathed out with relief to see her dead for good, then looked down at myself and wondered, *What now?* Because I was full of unknown magic and half again as tall as I usually was. The internal glow hid my nakedness at least, as it did for the souls now climbing out of Myuna's husk and standing in a clump whispering and looking around.

I walked over to my friends and mates, feeling like I was lumbering with my change in stature.

"That. Was. Amazing!" Wren declared loudly, clapping with each word. "I got it all on film, don't you worry. The whole supernatural world is going to know about this!"

A smile split my lips out of sheer disbelief that she'd been filming the fight. "There's no internet in the Void, Wren. There's no way you streamed any of it," Ben corrected.

She fixed him with an impatient look. "I *recorded* it. Now we have video evidence that Myuna is, like, majorly dead, so we can get out of godforsaken Cerris City."

"Good thinking," I said, wincing at the boom of my own voice. "Um, I need to be de-goddessed now."

Pretty much everyone turned to Phaeron. He'd released his shadow-born form and was talking quietly with a Moihan tribe male until he felt our attention on him. "How exactly did this happen?" he asked, gesturing up at my face.

"Well, you see...I think Braza's energy gave the souls left within—"

Phaeron's eyes dilated, and he whipped his head around. "Where's Braza?" he demanded.

"The last I saw her, she—oh shit." I turned toward Myuna's corpse. "She was grabbing the other half of her soul from you and diving back inside Myuna."

In a blink, he was next to the corpse, pulling open the rip in her belly and sticking his head in to look inside. He released a muffled howl and fished in her stomach, removing something and turning to show me when I loomed behind him. It was the dragon scale...cracked into two uneven pieces. The runes on it flickered with the last vestiges of energy.

"There's almost nothing left," he said, looking at me with new realization. "All of the energy she gathered as a powercore went to awakening the souls of Myuna's victims."

A bolt of dread thrilled through me. This couldn't be. She was an ancient powercore, the venerated protector of Moorgrove Library. And the other half of her soul was tethered to me...a shiny little thread still connecting us to my awareness. Yet I had no idea where she was.

"I-I'll just give some of the magic back to her. T-that's possible, right?" I stammered, reaching for the broken scale.

He jerked away from me, his breath growing shallow. We were both panicking, feeding into a feedback loop that was no good for either of us.

Geo inserted his steadiness between us, both physically and emotionally. That loop of negative emotion broke upon his stone form, even as he laid an obsidian palm on Phaeron's shoulder and my arm. "Braza is a being of shadow, and right now, you are glowing like the sun," he rumbled. "Undo this magic, and perhaps she will show herself."

"Well said," Phaeron sighed, scrubbing at his face. "All right, Cress. Try again to tell me how you became like this."

I did, leaving no detail out, not even flinching away from the fact that it was his deceased mate that kicked off the whole change that had led us all to freedom.

"Make me anew in your light," he repeated slowly. "No..." He switched to Soiluirian, which I didn't understand without Braza's presence. "Clearly, you must release all these souls that have bound their last vestiges to you. But we are still in the Void. What will become of them afterward?"

The spirit he'd been talking to stepped forward again, asking Phaeron a question. They spoke for a minute while I shifted with nerves. "My father claims to sense the way forward to the next life," he eventually translated.

My jaw dropped. He was being really casual about having his father right there. But they were both standing rigidly, avoiding eye contact. It had to be a matter of pride at this point. "So, once I release these souls, they will be able to go too?" I asked.

Phaeron wore a troubled frown as he considered. "In theory. It would be for the best to release them and have them try, at least, my bright mate. It is not right for you to hold on to them for much longer."

I completely agreed. So, I took part of his knowledge of Soiluirian along the mating circle and repeated the phrase he guessed would do the trick. "I have made you anew in my light, and now I release you from your vow."

The pressure within my body released like a deflating balloon. It was a near-immediate flood of souls, countless spirits fleeing the confines of our temporary pact. Many winked out of existence immediately, especially the older ones that'd been consumed before the fall of Soiluire.

Phaeron confirmed with his father that they'd gone on to the next life rather than been consumed by the Void. "He claims it has little power over them. Less than over us...but that may be because the Void has Myuna to feast upon for the moment. You may notice that it's gone suspiciously quiet," he said.

I hadn't noticed it'd shut up, but that was probably because I was feeling like a limp spaghetti noodle as I quickly lost the power of numbers that'd made me a "goddess." My inner glow winked out, and I slumped into his arms. Phaeron glanced down at my bare skin with brows rising, having accidentally cupped my belly. His cool shadows enveloped my modesty.

Actually, everything felt super cold all of a sudden, except for his body heat. I snuggled into him for more of it, and he snuck a gentle nip on my ear. "Glad to have you human-sized again," he murmured.

"I thought being taller than you was the best part of all of this," I sighed.

He whispered in my ear, "I'd get on my knees for you in a heartbeat." Phaeron was nuzzling into my hair when the last two souls emerged from me...Ravai and Keshora. It was only my stiffening that had him look up.

I still had that basic grasp of his language that I'd borrowed, so I understood Keshora saying, "So it is true."

And Ravai bulldozing straight past the awkwardness with a cry of, "Father!"

He gently nudged me aside and caught her when she flung herself into his arms. They spun and touched their foreheads. "My Ravita. How blessed I am to see you again," he said tenderly.

I met Geo's eye, tilting my head in suggestion. They deserved some privacy.

Keshora intercepted me before I took more than a couple steps. "Wait. Braza spoke highly of you...Cress. She's not with you?"

"I'm going to go looking for her," I said, hitching my thumb in the direction I felt our fraying tether pointing. With a nod, she fell into step with Geo and me.

It wasn't a long walk, but I kept shooting glances over my shoulder, knowing from some hazy secondhand memory that it was a death sentence to stray too far from others in the Void. Keshora kept me occupied with questions, fitting in some pieces she'd missed by dying before the Age of Decay.

She keened with pain when I told her how Braza had died and of the desperate decision made to sustain her by making her a powercore. "She sacrificed herself for us. No wonder I felt her the moment I woke... It was a fraction of her magic that revived me," she said.

My eyes filled with tears as we closed in on where Braza was and spotted her lying there. What had once been a hearty connection bolstered by her nearly endless pool of energy was nearly nothing because the half of Braza I'd carried was *literally* half of her now.

The Hungering Darkness had bisected her messily, cutting her soul from hip diagonally to her opposite shoulder. She had one wing and one arm like this. Her soul was still black and purple shadows, the jagged wound less ghastly with the details obscured. *"You came for me,"* she whispered in my mind.

"Oh my god, Braza," I said in English, sinking to my knees beside her. "I'm so sorry. I had no idea you were sacrificing *everything.*"

"Would you have stopped me if I told you?"

"Yes! At least, I would've told you to save some for yourself. Anything but this." I took her hand in both of mine. Hot tears trickled down my frozen cheeks. "Let's get you back to Phaeron. He has the other half of your soul...maybe there's a chance..."

"Allow me," Geo offered, bending slowly and offering his steady arms for the task. I clued a distressed Keshora in on what we were doing, and she helped me lift Braza into his hold. He carried her while I tried to calm her mother with reassurances I wasn't sure were true.

It seemed pretty certain that Braza was fading. Her black shadows were looking more like gray vapor, and the purple was sparsely intertwined with it.

Sensing my distress, Phaeron met us halfway with Ravai and the broken scale. Ben tagged along as well, rushing to hold me to share body warmth. After rubbing my arms, he shrugged off his shirt for me to wear. He was nearly too hot to the touch... I must've been more chilled than I realized.

"The scale is in two pieces. Could it hold both halves of her?" I asked desperately.

Phaeron tapped the larger piece of scale. Out flowed the bottom half of her, in the same drained state. Worse, actually, with her legs and tail flickering in and out of sight. "If Lucas were here..." he muttered. "She just needs some energy to stabilize her."

"Can anything be done for her?" Keshora fretted.

"It is my time. But I cannot feel the next life..." Braza whispered. She watched souls winking out of sight around us.

Phaeron answered Keshora with, "She gave away too much. All of these souls moving on around us do so with her energy. She'd need at least a spark returned. But that will deny a soul the power to move on to the next life."

Ravai gasped, exchanging a glance with her mother. "It has to be me."

"Ravita, no," Phaeron said immediately. "After everything you've been through, you deserve paradise."

"Mother, he told me he has a plan to return her to life. To living, breathing life. I could do this for her. She sacrificed so much for everyone else..." She looked past him to her, clasping her hands together.

"What's happening?" Ben whispered.

I explained the argument in English as Phaeron grew more dismayed. Keshora was nodding, moved by Ravai's plea. "There's no way for you to go to the next life if you do this," he put in.

"I'll do it," Keshora said firmly.

"There's no way for them to move on to the next life," I echoed.

The air stirred beside me in a way I was intimately familiar with by this point. My birth mother took form, and Ben gasped. I guess in the Void, all spirits were visible, as he'd never seen her before this moment. "Is the problem that they don't have someone to show them the way?" Eris asked, uncharacteristically solemn.

"It's a matter of energy, Mother," I said.

"Well, I have plenty of that." She smiled over at me, distinctly bittersweet. "It is time I moved on, dear one. I could think of no better way to go than in helping others...if they will let me." Keshora was eyeing Eris with suspicion.

Phaeron and I spoke at the same time. He invited her over to try, while I blurted, "Are you sure?"

In reply, Eris hugged me. I stepped away from Ben, letting my birth mother hold me as an adult for the first and only time. More tears leaked out of the corners of my eyes.

Eris said, "You are the core of a mating circle. I watched you defeat a goddess. Yes, I would say I fulfilled my purpose here...to help you."

"Thank you for everything, Mom," I murmured. When I let her go, she gave me one last look and nod before heading over to the ghostly dimensional family. At Phaeron's direction, she held Keshora and Ravai's hands, while they each grasped a hand attached to one of Braza's halves. They were both donating their spark back to Braza.

With a glance my way, Phaeron said, "I beseech my goddess for a miracle." He wove shadows and soul magic, feeding energy from Eris to the two dimensionals. They glowed with a new infusion of power before a portion of it passed into Braza.

Her shadows darkened considerably, but I continued to hold my breath, not feeling my connection to her grow any stronger. Phaeron blew out a tense breath and held out the two pieces of the dragon scale. Braza's bottom half went into the larger shard without trouble. He chanted a new spell and held the smaller shard toward her head.

With a wrench I felt down to my own soul, he cut the connection between us permanently, and Braza's top half turned into curls of shadows that absorbed into the smaller shard. The mark along my back burned and tingled, making an unpleasant crawling sensation.

He tilted both shards to inspect the steadily glowing runes on them. Satisfied, he lashed them together with a tendril of shadow. "It is fortunate the scale broke. I believe she will be okay," he said. His eyes shone with a mix of grief and relief as he drew in first Keshora for a hug good-bye, then Ravai. My understanding of their language disappeared, tugged away by him for a few private words to them both.

Eventually, the two spirits turned to Eris and took her hands again. Together, they faded to nothing, heading off to the next life together.

I hiccupped a sob. It hurt a lot worse than expected to say goodbye, and Phaeron echoed that feeling. Even though he'd come to peace with their deaths long ago, it was hard to have them back for such a short visit.

"Maybe you could see them again on Samhain," I suggested quietly.

With a sigh, he adjusted his swords and sat. "Perhaps." He began unlacing his boots and passed them to me. Though they were far too big, they enveloped my icy-soled feet in much-needed warmth.

We watched the last straggling souls wink out of existence and the Void break down what was left of Myuna's corpse. Soon, it was just us, the living, and Áine came over, scuffing her hoof. "I know this was intense and all...but shouldn't we be heading back?" she asked.

Phaeron quirked his lips. "You all may as well be sitting for this news." He waited, and everyone but Geo had a seat around him. "I don't know the way back."

"What?" Roe spluttered.

"I sense my mate like a second heartbeat and led you straight to her due to that alone. But wayfinding in the Void is impossible to all but the

Vess," he explained, putting his palms up in apology. "If we try to go back without assistance, we will only become hopelessly lost."

Ben scowled. "What the fuck, Big P?"

"If Auric knows what's good for him, he'll rescue us!" Phaeron shouted up at the Void's sky. "He owes us for sending Cress here in the first place."

I looked at him in astonishment. "You came after me without any guarantee you'd return?"

"To clarify, Ben, Geo, and I did." He slanted a look in my three friends' direction.

"No." Ben held up a finger. "To clarify his clarification, I did *not* know that was what I was signing up for."

Geo cracked a smile in his stone form. "I would do it again," he rumbled.

I propped my chin on my fist, shivering head to toe. "I love you all so much," I said. Ben snagged me to pull into his lap to share more body heat.

Wren rolled her eyes, warming her fingers by rubbing her hands together. "*Please* stop there before you start kissing."

Áine and Roe exchanged a glance. "I'd do it again too. That fight was fucking awesome, and it was even cooler that you all saved so many souls," the faun said, with Roe nodding emphatically in agreement.

Some of the good cheer faded from Phaeron's face. He ran his thumb over the cracked dragon scale he still held before slipping it into his pocket. "We may as well make something of our time while we wait." He laid out on his back. The lengths of his sheathed swords sank into the Void's ground like it wasn't there.

He spoke sternly at our surroundings. "All right, Void. We've delivered you a feast today. How about you provide a boon in return for Myuna? As you will have my most dire enemy's memories and voice forever... this is the last time I shall visit you with any semblance of willingness."

Moments passed in silence before Roe asked, "What are you doing?"

"Shh." He pointed upward. "Look."

I exchanged a glance with Ben, who shrugged, and settled onto his back. I lay on top of him, observing the swirling mist far above us. It patterned the sky with tones of blue, gray, and black, rolling like a muted aurora.

Those colors became a backdrop when the Void started showing us pieces of our possible futures; whole and coherent scenes, though they were split between all of us evenly. It was a rare moment of kindness for the darkness between worlds. I began to smile, seeing happiness in each, no matter whose future it was.

"Remember, it could be ages before any of this comes true, if it ever does," Phaeron murmured. But his eyes glimmered like topazes from the last vision the Void shared, and the slow leak of grief from his side of the mating circle turned on its head so intensely that my heart felt full.

The Void showed us an apple tree covered in autumn leaves. If I wasn't looking closely, I'd have missed the trio of kids sitting on its lowest boughs.

My breath caught as I noted a few details. The girl, who was maybe nine, sat with her back to the trunk. She ate an apple slowly while thumbing through a book. Her little lopsided smile as she giggled over something she read was so familiar that I nudged Ben, and he pressed a kiss to my crown.

Meanwhile, the two boys shared the bottom branch. Geo's son was the second eldest and could've been all of seven years old, but he was a little protector already with his arm around his brother. He'd plucked a pair of apples from the next branch up and shared one. *"Here you go, Tezzy."* The dimensional boy was too young to have gotten onto the tree on his own and had his tail wrapped around the branch underneath them nervously.

It ended there, to an aggrieved sound from Geo and a softer sigh from Phaeron. "Ages? I hope it's soon," the gargoyle said. At some point, he'd shifted back to human form, and though he was frustrated at the brief vision, he wore an optimistic smile with his gaze fixed on the sky.

Me, too, I thought.

Auric showed up soon after, just as I was starting to shiver even in Ben's hold. "So *I* owe *you* hmm?" he grumbled. He and Phaeron snipped at each other in Soiluirian before the Vess opened a new rip in reality that radiated much-needed heat.

43
CRESS

It took us a week to convince the governing supernatural councils and covens of the world that Myuna was, in fact, dead and that Wren's video wasn't heavily doctored footage. But eventually, we were released from Cerris City and allowed to go back to normal life.

Whatever "normal" was.

A day after our return to New Salem, I was in a familiar office in the center of a semicircle of five chairs facing the cupid woman behind the sandy wood desk. The other chairs were filled by my men and my sister. Dr. Aurina was as flawless as ever, resplendent in a green dress that offset the candy pink of her flowing hair and the gleam of her rose gold wings.

"Rowena Ashbough sent me to represent A Little Wicked Coven in her place. She's in the Crystal Court right now, recovering with her family," I said as soon as small talk faded.

It was a bit of a white lie. Yes, Roe was in the Crystal Court, but she was preparing for her visit to the much more cutthroat Autumn Court with Áine and Ambrose. She'd texted to tell me that the changeling was more than a little disgruntled. His undersea stay as Willow had included one test of magic he'd had to fib his way out of and two assassination attempts.

The real Willow was happily ensconced in my dorm room as my

unofficial roommate, though she'd soon have the room to herself. We planned to hide her comings and goings for now, until the attention on her identity as maybe-royalty faded.

For now, it was spring break, a real slap in the face after losing track of time for so long in an otherworldly situation.

"Of course. From what I hear, you're quite the celebrity," Aurina simpered. She opened a folder on her desk and shuffled paper. "But you are also a scholarship student who's missed over two months of coursework."

"Surely vanquishing an ancient eldritch goddess qualifies for an exception," I replied.

When Aurina laughed, it sounded like the tinkling of bells, high and sweet. "Oh, it does! It is so exceptional, in fact, that I don't know what to do with you and your friends except reenroll you all for a summer semester. You will still have access to your dorm room and campus services if you need to speak with anyone about your ordeal."

Through our mating circle, Phaeron made me aware of Aurina's emotional magic slowly filtering into my mind. She was projecting sympathy and kindness, but now that I was aware of it, she simply seemed tired and a little bored. As important as this meeting was for us, it was just another Tuesday for the University President.

"Thank you," I said, grateful for her generosity anyway.

Aurina nodded, picking up a pen. "Are any of your coven mates interested in changing their major? Now would be a good time to make it official."

It was Ben who spoke up. "Yeah, I want to go into Criminal Justice."

"A bold choice, Mr. Cross," she replied, scribbling something down.

He flinched at hearing his old alias from his Garroway days. "And an opportunity to update my file would be great, too," he added.

She hummed in agreement and continued writing as I listed the other change. I was going into Occult Studies with Wren, the two of us minoring in our witcheries now. It'd be fun. My former nemesis promised to give Ben and me access to all the notes and lectures from her celestial witch classes so we could continue practicing on the sly.

"There's one more thing I was hoping you could do for my coven. This is my sister, Carly."

I rested a hand on her ghostly white arm and gave her a little squeeze. Carly turned her head with uncanny slowness to look at me. It'd taken five bottles of magical hair dye, but the bleached color of her hair was transformed into a shiny teal with only a few white highlights showing. We'd fit her with contacts to make her eyes appear blue, but she forgot to blink them still. Under the guise of scratching my cheek, I tapped the side of my lips.

Mechanically, she smiled. Ah, god, we needed to work on this. On the bad days, it seemed like she'd forgotten how to be a person.

"You may know that one of my coven mates died during the slaughter used to summon Myuna to Earth. His name was Heath Storm," I continued, turning back to Aurina with one last pat of Carly's arm. "We would like to keep his spot open to honor his death. We didn't get the opportunity to do that for Lanie Graygazer, so you would understand that it would mean a lot to us."

Aurina's pen halted for a moment. "Of course. Unfortunately, your coven leader will still receive applications for that spot until it's filled. And given your fame, the application pile will only grow."

I lifted a shoulder. Roe could handle it. "Carly will be coming to NSU in the fall. We plan on holding the spot for her."

There was a whole intricate plan for her, in fact, including forging high school graduation information for her and Lucas so they could both live on campus starting next school year. She was always a person around Lucas, who was still trying to mend the damage done to her soul despite not having the best understanding of his own magic.

Unlike everyone else twisted by Myuna's control, Carly was still an unnatural, her soul and body stained by death and corruption. Though Lucas and Phaeron had saved her from a fate worse than death by pulling the seed of entropy from her soul and destroying it, she had a long, hard road of recovery ahead.

"I don't see any problem with that." Aurina spared Carly a smile before glancing away in discomfort. Though she wouldn't know why, she'd find my sister unsettling.

I met Phaeron's eye and nodded, turning the floor over to him. "About the matter of my employment," he said. He hadn't wanted to talk to her, finding Aurina's presence barely tolerable. If I weren't happily mated to him, I'd have bristled by the way his voice had her beautiful feathers rustling.

"You are welcome in Moongrove Library in your old position, of course. If there is any professor turnover at the end of the semester, you'd have no trouble getting promoted, Prince Sudair." Her pink brows jumped with a purr of his title, which she used as a surname since she didn't know better.

"Darkmore," he corrected.

"Pardon?"

He raised his left hand. On his ring finger glittered a black band with a stripe of shimmery gray crystal. "Prince Phaeron Darkmore et Sudair. Did we fail to inform you of our mating circle?" He smirked, enjoying the way her mouth popped open as the rest of us flashed our rings, gifts courtesy of the Crystal Court.

Geo's was the heaviest, a platinum band inset with a shiny crystal that matched the multicolored glimmer of his quartz. It was made to flex for his shifts into gargoyle form. Ben wore a gold ring, his crystal yellow with veins of red and orange. And mine was a traditional style for the core of a mating circle, a single gold band with a triangle-cut diamond and three smaller crystals set along each edge, their colors matching what my men wore.

"Well...wow...congratulations," Aurina said grudgingly.

He nodded. If she understood dimensional culture, she'd have realized he was mated earlier into the conversation. He'd gotten his hair cut and accepted adornment, gratefully acknowledging that he was at peace after an immortal lifetime of war. I mourned the loss of his longer hair but loved running my hands over the silky black feathers that framed his horns and sharp ears.

As for his makeup, I'd dusted his eyelids and cheekbones with shimmery black, an understated modern style that wouldn't get him second glances. Though I was still learning the markings that should decorate his horns, I'd convinced him to let me paint them in yellow edged with gold. They popped against his usual monochromatic outfits.

"Many thanks. So...my position. I would like it back once we return." This, he said with the same level of reluctance as she'd displayed. He'd give it five years, long enough to get Carly through college and comb through the library's resources for any mention of gargoyle creation. Though we had the help of Geo and now Madigan and her men, who called Braza a silent hero for what she'd done, there was much we didn't know about the process. Especially since Braza was a split soul housed in a questionable vessel.

It'd put Phaeron at ease to put both halves together on the shelf of a stasis room in Moongrove Library, where she would sleep without pain until we figured out what to do to bring her back properly.

Geo put in, "We will all start our lives again after our honeymoon." He still had the tickets in hand, fanning them with an excited half smile.

I don't think I imagined the jealousy that flashed in the cupid demigoddess's eyes as she read the name of the supernatural-friendly cruise company. They were another incredible gift that'd arrived today and hadn't left Geo's grip since. Generously paid for by the Ashbough, Evenstar, and Graygazer families...our honeymoon. Two blissful months, just the four of us, with no expectations other than to have fun and solidify our mating circle properly.

Everything else was taken care of for now. I'd be placing Carly's hand in Lucas's after this meeting was finished. They'd live in the Crystal Court for now, under the watchful eye of Madigan and Mom, who'd officially become an Ashbough Protective Services medic, complete with an apartment in the peaceful court. She was within walking distance of her maybe-boyfriend, if she would ever admit whether she actually liked the fae male who followed her like a forlorn puppy.

Pushing to my feet, I waved to Aurina and held my arms out to help Carly to her feet. "If you'll excuse us," I said with a brilliant smile. "We do have a plane to catch."

"Wishing you all the happiness in marital bliss," Aurina replied. She watched us leave and jotted one last note down on a new file marked with Carly's name.

We passed by a moderately full waiting room, pausing as Lucas glanced up from his phone and scrambled to join us. He looked like any ordinary kid now, dressed in a hoody with his hair shaved on the sides and permed on top. "How'd it go?" he asked Carly, taking her hand.

She blinked slowly before lighting up. "Good, I think. I'm joining Cress's coven in the fall. Hey, do you want to get something to eat? I'm *starving*..." We descended the stairs ahead of them, in a hurry where they were not.

"Now kiss," Ben murmured. He made no secret of how he thought they looked good together.

Phaeron rolled his eyes, slipping on a pair of sunglasses that'd been pinned to his collar. "Give them a few years to mature, Little B."

Geo echoed the gesture. "Not everyone needs to be shipped," he said in agreement.

"On the contrary, G Man." Ben held up a finger. "It is the law that two people who help one another heal should get together."

The gargoyle attempted to stare at him stonily, but he was also fighting a smile at the new nickname he'd finally approved of. We'd vetoed Hard G, Gigantic G, and It's Just Geo until Ben had finally come up with something the big man liked.

"You're going to be a terrible policeman if you keep making up laws," he rumbled.

As they continued their back and forth, Phaeron offered his arm, and I took it. The sunglasses were doing a world of good for his eyesight, but I already missed his otherworldly smolder. "Let us be off to experience this...plane," he said, still highly suspicious of modern air travel.

"We're flying first class. You might have some knee room," I said, lifting to my tiptoes to kiss him. The moment we were finished, I turned to see Ben and Geo lined up for their kisses. My heart swelled for all three of them and the uninterrupted time we were about to have.

I kissed them too, then we walked out into the sunlight to go enjoy our new life together.

BONUS EPILOGUE: GOLDEN HOUR

CRESS

IF TIME COULD BE COUNTED by the fall of sand in an hourglass, then I swear someone was tampering with its neck. I'd once fought the self-proclaimed reaper of worlds, Myuna, and counted the moments of my survival breath by breath. The individual motes of sand dropped ever so slowly when each second was a matter of life or death.

Compare that trial to an all-expenses paid cruise with my mates for a well-deserved vacation. The floodgates on the sands of time opened up. A month passed in the blink of an eye. I barely noticed it leaving at first, too busy exploring the bonds of my mating circle. With no pressing reason to leave our cabin, we solidified that magic skin-to-skin, rocking with the rhythm of the ocean's waves.

My morning was Phaeron's night. Given the opportunity, he'd become mostly nocturnal, sleeping when the sun was at its peak. The only time he'd emerge during the day was to watch the sun set. Every single day. No matter what we were doing, he'd announce the sun was setting and disappear in a whirl of shadows to go watch it.

It was a vigil of sorts. A few minutes of stillness before he indulged the shadowborn urge to patrol his territory and protect the innocent.

With our mating bond, I sensed it all and his restlessness growing stronger with each passing day.

Though he wasn't pushy about it, he liked company as we viewed the horizon. I'd joined him today, the two of us standing at the railing facing the oncoming sunset. Golden light bathed his gray skin, gleaming off his spiraled horns. He wore sunglasses so dark I could probably wear them and stare directly at the sun without blinding myself.

Seabirds called to one another, many coming to roost around us for the evening. A light, saltwater-kissed breeze blew over the waves. This space was the nearest thing we had to privacy outside of our cabin, as many of our fellow vacationers were indulging in the distant sound of live music on another deck.

My mind drifted. Phaeron had caught my calf in an affectionate coil of his tail and toyed with a lock of my purple hair. "Why haven't you asked me what's on your mind?" he eventually asked.

I was trying to figure out *how* to ask without seeming rude. Mating circle life had proven tricky, as there were no secrets between us all anymore. For better or for worse.

I twisted my lips before just saying it. "I noticed you might be bored of this trip. Is it too long? We could see about disembarking early...or something." A hint of nerves wove through the words, betraying my worries.

Ben, Geo, and I had found plenty of things to do. Even as the newly bonded urgency faded, we were often occupied by each other. And as much as Phaeron participated too, he was still the one who paced the ship at night like a caged tiger exploring the boundaries of his prison.

"Bored," he echoed thoughtfully. "I am not bored with you, bright soul, nor of my new brothers. But of late, I've found myself without a purpose."

He read my confusion and inclined his head. "I know I'm on vacation," he said to my unspoken thoughts. "Consider that I have not had a vacation since..."

As he blew out a wry chuckle, I suggested, "Ever?"

"Ever," he agreed. "There was always another war to fight or a goddess to slay. Myuna's dying scream still echoes in my ears. I *relish* it.

But...what now? I have not stood still like this since before the Age of Decay. It does not suit a shadowborn to be aimless."

I didn't really have an answer for him. I'd thought he was tired of viewing supernatural culture as an outsider. He'd struggled to parse out the humor in our visits to the comedy club or the movie theater. Or... worse, I'd worried the honeymoon of our mating was already over. But this was something different, a challenge more difficult to fix.

"Life is going to slow down a lot. It's not like there's another goddess we need to slay. I mean, I *hope* there's not another," I said, shuddering.

"I know. Soon, we'll be back at the university, and I'll have my miniscule job training young librarians. I'll be okay." He flashed a smile. "In the meantime, Ben has been listening to my old war stories. There is much of my glory days I'm glad to leave behind. And Earth, as strange as it is, has instances of great beauty."

He leaned down and kissed me, pulling me close. My heart leapt at what he'd implied, my skin tingling with awareness. His tail teased its way further up my leg. I'd put on a breezy skirt in part to tempt him, because he couldn't resist his teases. "I hope you still feel welcome. Even if some of the people around here are super rude."

As the only dimensional on board, he'd received his share of gawking and stupid, intrusive questions. He made a dismissive wave. "No matter the age, I will still be a visitor. Or, as Ben says, an alien. It is what it is."

"Is it?"

He responded with a noncommittal hum and straightened, facing the sunset. Shades of orange lit the horizon, spreading through the water and turning it into molten gold. "Soiluire never had a celestial body so majestic as a sun, nor as poignant a moment as a sunset," he murmured. "Do humans feel hope when it rises again to banish the dark?"

I considered as the shades of evening darkened around us. "When we stop going about the motions to notice it, yes."

"That is how I feel when it sets." He took the sunglasses from his face and pinned them into the neckline of his shirt. As the incoming night settled around us, his shadowy magic stirred around him in eddies of black mist. I admired him, but not just for his otherworldly looks. He saw the world so differently as a visitor, and that was beautiful in its own way.

Phaeron skimmed my cheek with his fingertips. "Shall we—" he'd begun to say, only to cut himself off with a growl. An unexpectedly frigid gust blew over us. He faced the intrusion, putting himself between me and a rip in reality that carried the chill of the Void.

I shuddered violently as the rip of magic parted for a familiar figure, then knit closed as if it'd never been there. Phaeron relaxed, though he freed his tail from my leg to whip it irritably.

He spoke to the newcomer, Auric et Vess, in the hissing tones of Soiluirian. I no longer had any hope of understanding their conversation without Braza, a reminder that sobered my mood more swiftly than the bite of the Void's chill. I missed her dearly.

Auric switched to speaking English first. He made a shallow bow, a stiff motion in his tailored suit. "Good evening to the Sudair and the Goddess Slayer. The Void suggested this was a good time to drop in. Considering you're both clothed, looks like it was right."

Phaeron rolled his eyes. "What do you need?"

"I'm here to call in the favor you owe me."

My mate tilted his horned head. His thoughts whirled as he tried to pinpoint which favor his friend was here to call in.

"For saving us from the Void?" I guessed.

Auric turned his good eye my way. Despite the darkness around us, it still had a pinprick of a pupil within a glowing teal iris. "That would be the one," he said, smirking.

Phaeron bristled. "No. That is a debt *you* owe *me* for sending my mate into the Void in the first place." A hint of shadowborn power deepened his voice. Auric didn't so much as flinch as the night stirred around us, the shadows bending to Phaeron's will.

I reached through his magic to pat his arm, trying to calm him down before he brought extra attention to us. The shadows rubbed harmlessly against my skin.

"It turned out well," the other dimensional remarked. "I have a task that requires a male of the Sudair's capabilities."

Some of Phaeron's menace faded. "Are you saying..."

A flicker of a wince crossed Auric's face. "I need your help. One of my projects has gone awry," he muttered.

I exchanged a glance with Phaeron as a glimmer of excitement kindled at his end of our mating bond. "He needs my help," he echoed. He smiled with gloating energy, flashing his fangs.

After feeling his reaction, I wanted to smile too, though I cast a worried glance at Auric first. "Wait. Is this, like, a dangerous project?" I asked.

He made an "eh" noise amongst a scoff, waving me away. "A little danger only makes it more fun, Goddess Slayer."

Phaeron was practically beaming at this point. "He's right. Will it take long?"

"A couple days at most."

"Give me a few minutes to grab my swords." He whisked me away into the shadows with him, and we emerged into the privacy of our cabin and the quiet of the bedroom. Ben and Geo weren't here since they were expecting us for dinner.

I crossed my arms. "You don't even know what he needs you to do."

"Auric is a dear friend. He wouldn't interrupt our vacation if he didn't need me." He bent to rest his forehead against mine. "I will be safe, bright soul. I promise."

He reasoned away my worries until I relented and helped him pack for a short trip. With a last, lingering kiss, he disappeared into his shadows.

THAT WAS A COUPLE DAYS AGO, and I tried not to dwell on it. Phaeron was impossible to reach since he'd left his phone behind. Not that he ever turned it on or used it unless he absolutely had to. But it would've been *nice* if he'd chosen to communicate with it this time. I just had to hope Auric's project wasn't too perilous.

One afternoon, a heavy rain drove us indoors. It pattered on the roof high over our heads as I chewed my way through a handful of popcorn piece by piece. Multi-colored light played out over Geo's face as the indoor theater shook with a bass noise. He was watching the movie, and I was mostly watching him. The gargoyle had the jumbo popcorn bag in his lap and chewed through it to the pace of the film.

This was a supernatural-friendly cruise, which meant they showed films I'd never even heard of. Most of the effects were real magic. Ben had already seen this one and rated it "so bad it's funny," but that wasn't how Geo saw it.

The movie was almost done, but it'd just revealed a plot twist I'd started anticipating maybe twenty minutes in. Geo was rapt, complete with a whisper of, "Did you *see* that?"

I'd leaned my head on his shoulder, cozy against him. I whispered back, "Yup. Pretty crazy."

For a man who'd become addicted to browsing the internet and watching highly satisfying videos, before this vacation, he'd never seen a movie. Okay, technically, he'd seen *one* that time he'd escorted Ben and me on one of our first dates. But he'd been in full gargoyle mode then, without the emotions to properly appreciate the story playing out on screen.

Now he knew what he was missing. Everything about movies was new for Geo. The quotes were fresh, the twists were mind-blowing, and every genre was a unique twist. So far, he seemed to prefer the action flicks.

He tried daily to catch a movie either on the indoor screen by day or out on the lido deck by night. I joined him when I could. It gave me the opportunity to witness his enjoyment with pride for how far he'd come. Even this less-than-good film had him on the edge of his seat for a nail-biting, popcorn-crunching climax as the heroes saved the day at the last possible second. He breathed a sigh of relief alongside the characters on screen.

He finally noticed me admiring him and turned a grin my way. The mating circle wouldn't hide how I basked in the radiance of his emotions, fully formed and so *human*. "Did you see that?" I echoed him playfully.

"How could I miss it?" He leaned over to kiss me as the hero finally smooched his love interest on screen. We made out as the credits rolled, heartbeats falling into sync in the now-familiar way our bond shared strong feelings and sensations.

I was the one who drew back first. "Someone promised me pizza. If you've got any room after all that popcorn," I teased.

"I paced myself."

"Uh huh." I'd gotten a few handfuls to snack on this time. He was kind of getting better about sharing the bag. "I think you're making a memory of this cruise and popcorn."

He'd shared the wisdom of his friend and fellow gargoyle, Marl, with me. Every special moment he experienced, he went out of his way to tie a scent or a flavor to. It'd later help him make the transition from stone to man when he inevitably had to take gargoyle form again. *"To prompt me to remember what's most important. That I'm alive,"* he'd said.

"That wouldn't be so bad," he mused now. We joined the small group leaving the theater, his arm slung around my waist. "The pizza here is one of a kind."

My belly rumbled in agreement. Before this vacation, I hadn't known how competitive cruise lines were with their pizza. It made the greasy pies I was used to pale in comparison. The ingredients were incredibly fresh, preserved by...well, magic.

"Whatever works for you. As long as I get you back when you have to shift," I said.

We followed a carpeted path to one of our favorite restaurants. The occasional window high overhead revealed the overcast sky. The sun was starting to emerge from between sets of gloomy clouds as they released their last drizzle of rain. Light gilded the planes of Geo's face, drawing out the bronze tones under his dark brown skin.

He smiled back at me, revealing a flash of the perfect teeth he'd been sculpted with. "You'll always get me back. Loving you is my only duty," he murmured.

I brightened. It'd never get old to feel him mean it. "I love you too," I answered.

We got our pizza slices and ate amongst a crowd of fellow vacationers, discussing the movie we'd just watched, interspersed with moments of thoughtful silence. He spoke more than he used to but was still introspective, exploring the depths of his thoughts and emerging with the occasional kernel of knowledge. He listened attentively and lingered over our bond, content in the feeling of *us*. I learned how to do the same thing from his lead.

We were at the end of our meal when my phone buzzed. It was a rare single message from Ben, asking if we'd be returning to the cabin soon. I checked my time zone app and hummed. "We might be able to fit in a call home if we head back to the cabin," I told Geo.

He nodded and stood, offering me a hand up. "Maybe Roe will have an update on her situation," he said.

"Hmm, we could call her too. The start of the bridal competition was almost a week ago." The last time I'd called my mom in the Crystal Court, we'd had an opportunity to wish Roe and Áine luck. The competition began with a ball in the treacherous Autumn Court. I swallowed past a lump of nerves for my friends. "We *should* call her too," I amended.

I texted that we were on our way back, and my device buzzed with one of Ben's customary fragmented responses. I glanced over the string of messages and chuckled, then put my phone away as we took a leisurely path back up to our cabin.

Ben had left the door unlocked, and we entered, calling out a hello. We'd been given a suite, which constituted multiple rooms with a private balcony. Saving the world did give us a few perks.

"Hey! I figured it out!" Ben crowed from the direction of the bedroom. He poked his head through the doorframe.

He'd shaved—after teasing Phaeron relentlessly for his old-fashioned speech, he'd been on the receiving end of the same for attempting to grow out a beard. His facial hair had become thick and bushy in record time, but now he was back to his smooth-faced good looks. All the better to see his perpetually lopsided smile.

Over his shoulder flew my handbook. "Welcome back," it said in its squeaky toy voice. I hadn't packed it—it'd snuck itself into my luggage.

"What is it you've figured out?" Geo asked.

"She didn't tell you?" Ben gasped. "I know how old Phaeron is!"

The gargoyle muttered something that sounded like, "This again?" I rolled my eyes playfully and went over to share a quick kiss with Ben.

"Did you ask *The Librarian Witch's Handbook*?" I whispered.

His eyes darted. "Uh, *nooo*."

The handbook flew a loop-de-loop over our heads. "Hehe! Of course he did. And I have the answer for you! But first..." It hovered midair and attempted a more serious voice. "I'm insulted you didn't ask me first, Cressie-poo. I'm the authority on everything, remember?"

I smiled and shook my head. This silly thing. "It's Ben that cares about this, remember?" I echoed.

"Oh, yeah!" it squeaked. "So, does that mean you don't want to know the number?"

"I didn't say that." I cast a curious glance over at Ben.

He was still smirking, satisfied with his new knowledge. "One tho—"

The handbook zoomed over, flapping in front of his face. Ben sputtered and tried to bat it away, but it evaded the swipe of his hand.

"Let me tell you my *very scientific process* for figuring out this impressive number!" it exclaimed. "A Soiluire day is approximately 31.66 Earth hours long. If you add how old he was when—"

Ben caught it by the spine and closed its pages abruptly. He held the struggling book closed by its front and back covers. "Let's stop before it goes on for hours about Phaeron's various life goals, like it did to me. The number is 1,741 Earth years," he said. The handbook's binding sagged in defeat.

"Whoa," I gasped. Holy shit, that was old.

"I *know*!" Ben exclaimed.

Geo gave a thoughtful hum. "Is that adding in his time in stasis?"

Ben nodded. "Of course. You've gotta add in the stasis."

"Wonder if that's the right age," I mused, mostly to myself.

Phaeron alleged that he knew how old he was but wouldn't admit to it, something that'd driven Ben nuts. That shockingly large number didn't seem real, and yet, I believed it. He had the kind of world-weariness sometimes that spoke to a life stretched nearly to its breaking point.

"What's next, now that you've figured out his age?" Geo asked, cutting into my thoughts.

"I was thinking that I start informing Big P of random facts from the year 1741. There are websites for that, you know." Ben held up his phone. "You guys ready to call Mama Rollins?"

"Yeah. Let's call Roe too," I suggested. We sat on the couch together, with me in the center, holding the phone as we put in a video call to Mom first.

After several long rings, my sister answered. She wasn't wearing her contacts, so her bleached and unblinking eyes stared holes into the screen. I shifted uncomfortably.

"Who is it?" a young man asked just off screen.

He rested his hand on her shoulder, and her face relaxed, then lit up as she took in the three of us crowding into frame. "It's Cress, Ben, and Geo," Carly said.

Lucas leaned into view and waved. "Hey, you guys."

"Little bro!" Ben exclaimed.

"Calling to tell us about all the fun we're missing?" Carly giggled. She reached up to take Lucas's hand with a shy smile over at him. The camera shook as they started walking.

Ben gave me several little nudges with his elbow. While he was still rooting for them to get together, they just seemed like friends to me. They were often together by necessity. So much so that Mom had practically adopted Lucas.

"You know it," I answered. "How are things going with you?"

"I'm getting a little better every day," she answered.

Lucas nodded. "We'll have all the bad stuff out before you know it."

They entered a new room, judging by the change of lighting and the murmuring of several new voices. "Cress and her circle called," Carly announced.

She turned around and lifted the phone to show several familiar faces. There were a bunch of hellos and waving. We waved back, and my face stretched with a grin. They were in a dining room together. It looked like they'd just sat down, as the place settings weren't even put out yet. Roe and Áine were there, along with Madigan and her men and their gaggle of kids.

I also spotted Mom's maybe-boyfriend, a Crystal fae named Evander. She was still undecided about him and his pronouncements that they were fated mates. But, as promised, they'd finally gone on a date.

When I'd asked how it went, her expression had softened, a reaction I'd never seen her have over a man. The fact that he was at this gathering was a good sign. At least, if he wasn't welcome, I knew Madigan and Roe would've tossed him out, no questions asked.

"Looks like you guys are about to eat dinner? We don't mean to interrupt," Ben said.

"Nonsense!" Madigan was the one who answered.

The phone screen bounced as it passed hands until Mom's face was in frame. "We were just catching up. How are you, baby?"

We checked in and traded some stories of the last week. She told me how my familiars were doing, as she was cat sitting for me and also watching Flit, Ben's ferret. I relaxed, resting between my men as she updated us on the last week and what little she could say as a freshly minted Ashbough Protective Services medic.

When it was our turn, I was about to tell her about Phaeron's absence when curls of black smoke leaked into our room from the balcony. I made an excited gasp as the dimensional took shape from the shadows.

"Auric alleged that my arrival will be perfectly timed." His teeth were a flash of white amidst the distinctive fuchsia of dimensional blood sprayed across his face. More of it soaked his shirt. He had a bag slung over his shoulder and his swords sheathed at his hips.

My mouth hung open mid word as I gaped at him. It was all I could do not to scream and startle everyone.

Phaeron's cheer faded as he felt the whole circle's reaction. My shock mingled with the protective reflexes of Geo, who tensed to jump between me and danger. Phaeron put up his hands. "The blood's not mine," he whispered.

"Go clean yourself off," Geo rumbled.

I tried to mask a nervous laugh, turning back to the phone screen as Phaeron flowed back into the shadows.

"Well, give me the phone. You guys should hear about how the ball went," Roe said from off camera. Mom twinkled her fingers at us before her phone was passed around and aimed up at Roe's face. Áine squeezed into the frame, squishing her cheek against the redhead's.

Phaeron rejoined us, now shirtless and damp from a quick scrubbing. And free of any blood or wounds, thank goodness. He took form out of the shadows in a low seated position, leaning his back into my legs. The majority of his bulk rested under the bolted-down coffee table. I didn't angle the phone down, since he wouldn't look into the screen anyway. Too bright.

"Sorry for the delay. I'm here," he said.

The folks on the other side of our call paused to say hello to him before Roe cleared her throat. "All right, I settled my end of the deal that got us Ambrose's friendship. He and Áine escorted me to the ball. I was the last announced out of a lineup of stunning fae women all dressed in these fluffy gowns that were supposed to represent their court or something. You'd have loved it, Cress."

I was already in my head, imagining what those gowns could've looked like. You could take a gal out of the fashion design major, but looking nice would always be in style.

"And then there was me, wearing a day dress and some leggings. I think the Autumn Queen sneered at me. Kind of hard to tell, with the whole dead thing she had going on."

"She's really undead?" Ben asked.

"Yeah." Roe pulled a face. So did I. "She was all shriveled up and dry. Her skin looked like a stretched piece of parchment paper. I didn't, like, talk to her or anything. All she really did was sit on her throne anyway, once the party started."

"We didn't give her a hosting gift, either. Big breach of fae etiquette," Áine added.

"I was also rude to Prince Soryn for our one required dance. There's no way they're going to want me to continue the bridal competition." Roe flashed a thumbs-up. "One and done. Ambrose hasn't come back, though. I think Prince Soryn needed him to do his actual job as a body double."

Áine's brows lifted and she looked over at the redhead askance. "You haven't told them the best part."

Roe covered her hand with the opposite palm as she forced a laugh. "Oh. Um. So, a big group of undead came out of nowhere and swarmed the ball."

"*What?*" I demanded. She should've led with that!

"That's not even the part I was talking about," the faun giggled.

They turned to one another and murmured together while I exchanged anxious glances with my men. "Oh! She means when I danced with the Unspoken One," Roe said.

My eyes widened another fraction. Phaeron leaned up, looking into the screen for as long as he could stand it. "You don't look undead. How did he touch you and not kill you?" he asked.

"Who cares? There was a zombie attack," Ben blurted. "Talk about that!"

The dimensional slanted a narrowed look at him. "The touch of a death fae is anathema—"

"I don't have time to figure out your five-dollar words right now, Big P—"

My eye twitched. "Would you guys—"

"Stop," Geo cut in. "She's trying to tell us what happened."

Roe had her free hand popped under her chin, lips pursed in amusement. "The Unspoken One was wearing gloves. All of him was covered. He was wearing this elaborate mask too, and I had no idea who he was. But the plan was to be a terrible guest, so I told him that he was at the wrong party, since the ball wasn't a masquerade. I may have also told him his mask looked silly."

"Insulting a death fae," Phaeron muttered.

"He told me it was a jackal's visage and that he always wore it. And that no one here was brave enough to look at the face of death. It kind of hit me like a clue-by-four, but he disappeared before I could apologize. Didn't see him again." She shrugged, unconcerned.

"Did you make him mad? Was that why there were zombies?" Ben pressed.

"No, no," she said, waving the concern away. "I mean, I thought so at first. There was a lot of screaming when they first arrived. I pulled this mace away from a suit of armor they had on display and went ham on the undead while all those prettily dressed fae watched. I was back in Cerris City for a moment there, you know?"

Though she couldn't see him, Phaeron was nodding with a grim sort of understanding.

"I didn't stop until I swung hard enough to send a zombie's head flying. He laughed." She shook her head in disbelief. "And as his head disappeared into the tree line, he called 'nice shot!' I stopped and looked around. All the Autumn Court fae were looking at me as if I'd sprouted a second head. The other competitors and the fae from their courts were the ones screaming. I guess it's pretty normal for the undead of the court to want to party too? And I kind of massively overreacted?"

"I think you're right. It's safe to say they're not going to want to see you again," Ben remarked.

"Yeah, exactly. Worst guest *ever*. They're still reassembling the body parts." She forced a brighter tone. "So, that's what happened. Can't wait to see you all in person! I'm already planning a big Midsummer bash that you're going to love."

"Can't wait," I said, speaking up before Phaeron could air whatever had darkened his thoughts. His tail flicked alongside a sense of unease that rolled from his side of our mating bond to mine.

"Take it easy, eh?" She smiled and passed the phone along.

We had a shorter visit with the others at the table. As soon as we said our goodbyes, Phaeron disappeared into his shadows, muttering something about a shower. He turned the water on a couple moments later.

"I'm glad things worked out for Roe," I said. Ben and Geo murmured in agreement. It was one less thing to worry about. The prospect of Roe interacting any further with the Autumn Court and its cursed undead was enough to make me sweat.

I stood and stretched, intending to go question Phaeron on where he'd been and why he'd arrived covered in blood. Ben caught my hand and tugged so my back was flush against his muscled chest.

"I have an idea, babe." He whispered it in my ear, and I muffled a laugh and nodded in agreement.

We'd come up with a new game somewhere between the creation of our mating circle and now. I was always eager to play it, entertained regardless of the results. I turned to Geo and shuffled into the bedroom, motioning for him to follow with a come hither gesture through the threshold.

Despite our generous accommodations, the bedroom was still little more than a bed and a closet. I stopped at the foot of the bed and faced my mates, inching up my shirt to expose a sliver of my midriff. Geo bit his bottom lip, while Ben watched me with hunger already gleaming in his eyes. Neither made a move toward me as I loosened my clothes, showing a hint of shoulder here, a flash of my hip there.

The game was simple. Two of my three men appreciated the show and shared their growing arousal over the mating circle. We'd see how long it took for the absent mate to come around looking to join in.

I had a different approach for luring each man. Ben operated on FOMO. If he thought he was missing out on something, he would sprint over. Geo required a touch of pleasure from the mating circle—not the burn of lust. He appreciated an invitation with that level of directness.

And Phaeron? Well, he had an immortal's sense of patience, preferring a slow burn and the fleeting edges of teasing. He always showed up ready to go if we started slow and lingered with the heavy petting. With him just in the shower, I didn't expect it to take long.

Once I stripped off my shirt, Ben replaced my fingers with his, cupping my breasts through my lacy bra. We kissed almost leisurely. He pinched and teased my nipples despite the fabric covering them, giving the left and right equal, slow treatment.

Geo came up behind me, his touch caressing up my thigh. I tilted my head with a soft gasp when his teeth found the curve of my neck. He touched the spaces where my clothes were loose and slid fingers into the juncture between my legs, rubbing the intimate spot dampening my shorts.

I pulled my lips from Ben's and paused, waiting for any kind of reaction over the mating circle from Phaeron. He was probably trying to ignore us, as I heard him singing softly. Cool mist drifted from the cold shower turned on full blast. I turned around and kissed Geo next. He met me with more passion, our tongues brushing.

I tugged at Geo's shirt, ready for it to be gone. He and Ben teamed up to made short work of my clothes first. They removed my bra to fling it to one side, and I stepped out of the rest so my shorts and panties could swiftly following it. With their hands working together to cover my curves, their clothes didn't follow as fast.

I freed Geo of his shirt and spread lingering touches over his skin. His stone heart thudded back against my fingertips, as alive as the rest of him. As I stripped him down, he presented himself, chest lifted, proudly ready for his duty as my mate. He lingered in our mating circle, taking in the feeling of my loving admiration of him.

With a last, lingering kiss, I switched my attention to Ben again. He'd started to disrobe without me, so I skimmed my fingers over the scars on his side. Eyes lidding, he made a tender moan. The site of the blood rune was shockingly sensitive. It'd once been used to spread pain through his whole body, but we'd repurposed it for pleasure.

The scars were starting to fade, and while the ugliness of

Garroway's evil would always remain on him, his body was slowly cycling away the black and crimson marring his skin.

I appreciated the texture left behind—a sign that he'd survived despite his hellish upbringing—and flicked one last glance in the direction of the shower. Still on. And Phaeron was still singing. I guessed he didn't want to join us after all, and his emotions finally shifted as he must've sensed my disappointment.

He sent a nudge back over our mating bond, as if to say *go ahead*. A trace of amusement escaped his ironclad self-control. Two could play this game.

"I don't think he's coming," I whispered to my other mates.

"If he doesn't get out of that shower, he sure isn't." Ben smirked at his own joke, while I groaned and bounced my palm off my forehead.

"Well, if you two want to, you'd better get on that bed," I said.

"Yes, ma'am." Geo was first on it and held his arms out to help me down. He helped arrange me facing away from him. This position was an old favorite at this point, making it easier to share me between them. Geo guided my hips back until my lower lips kissed his crown. Ben was on his knees, offering his erection to my mouth.

Ben adjusted forward as I sank down on Geo's cock, my lips parted in a moan. I opened my mouth further to accept Ben's length, flashing a loving look up at him as he stroked my hair. We found a rhythm together, the three of us moving as one. That was, until the shower shut off and Phaeron appeared with a whoosh of shadowy magic.

"Holy shit!" Ben exclaimed, nearly falling off the end of the bed. I helped catch him before he took the rest of us down with him. His cock popped right out of my mouth with the sudden motion. "Can't you give some warning?"

I looked over at Phaeron. He was seated just past the foot of the bed, the loose towel over his lap doing little to hide the tenting of his arousal. Had he unbolted a chair? Most of the furniture on board was secured.

He flashed his fangs. "No. And I have assembled my own cuck chair from my shadows, bright soul," he said in answer to my thoughts. I sputtered in surprise. "Yes, I definitely learned that slang from Ben."

"Even I knew what that meant," Geo mused. He'd paused, holding my hips flush with his.

"That's because you are terminally online, as the humans say," the dimensional remarked. "Fuck our mate, gargoyle. I'm content to watch."

I held up a finger to contest the terminally online comment, but my mouth was watering for more of Ben, so I let it go. He offered himself again, and we resumed what we'd started. Once the shock of Phaeron's sudden appearance wore off, he had a fistful of my hair and was pushing as much of his cock into my mouth as I could fit. I trembled from secondhand pleasure. Our mating bonds were full of pleasant echoes.

Geo shook his head and thrust at about the same time, drawing a muffled moan from me. My toes curled from the force. We found the rhythm we'd lost, but this time, Phaeron's enjoyment joined ours. He stroked himself and watched the show.

"Hey, Big P, guess what," Ben said, breathless and panting.

The dimension arched a brow. "You wish to have a conversation *now?*"

As a matter of fact, *I* did. While he was unoccupied, he could tell us about Auric's project for him. Not that I was fully listening as I circled my hips and chased my pleasure with increasingly high-pitched cries.

"He knows how old you are," Geo grunted with effort.

Phaeron sighed. "By all means, remind me of the number."

Ben didn't, but only because we shared a high of physical pleasure, coming at nearly the same time. My bliss joined the echo from my two mates, drawing a shiver through my body at the intensity of our release. Once I went limp with bliss, I just wanted to do it again. A sentiment we all shared.

Ben caught me before I could collapse on jellied limbs, shifting me to sit upright against Geo's side. I drifted in the fuzzy warmth of an afterglow. Phaeron's gaze was soft on me when I refocused on him, still seated and waiting, hands folded over his towel.

"1,741 Earth years," Ben said proudly once he caught his breath.

Phaeron simply said, "No."

"What do you mean, no? Book! Get over here."

There was a scuffle of pages from the other room before it squeaked, "It's *The Librarian Witch's Handbook* to you. And are you all engaging in coitus? I will have you know, I don't want to see that."

"I thought you were nearsighted," I teased it.

"You asked the handbook," Phaeron said, chuckling. He switched to his native language for a short conversation with the wispfly that animated the handbook, shaking his head all the while.

"*Oooooh!* 1,241," it said in English.

"Congratulations. You know how old I am, if we are counting the stasis," the dimensional added. His sigh held a lost world's worth of weariness.

Ben's mood started to drop. "It's not quite as old as I thought?" he offered.

"About a millennium less than I always assumed," Geo added with an attempt at a delicate tone.

"You don't look a day over thirty," I put in.

The hint of loneliness shading Phaeron's eyes vanished. He cracked a fond smile at the three of us. "As I have told Cress, there have been eras of my life marked by the influence of a mate, or a lack thereof. This is merely the start of my last era. A chance to be thirty again." He winked in my direction. "You all make me feel young."

"N'aww," Ben said under his breath.

I thought that was sweet, but judging by the discomfort coming from my other two mates, it was perhaps also too much for them. "Could one of you make sure the handbook doesn't come in here?" I asked.

Geo hopped to his feet with a grunt of agreement.

"Hey, book," Ben called. "Don't come in here unless you want to see some freaky shadow sex."

There was another scuffle of pages as the handbook released a startled "eek!"

"That's what it gets for sneaking into our vacation," he muttered, getting up too. "You've got maybe five minutes before we rejoin you, Big P."

The dimensional inclined his head in acknowledgment. Amusement radiated off of him. "See you soon."

As soon as Ben was out of the room, I said, "Okay, you've got some expla—"

Phaeron swept me up in a rush of shadows. I blinked and was pinned against the wall, with him holding me up with his hands and magic alike. He pressed his forehead to mine in dimensional affection.

"I was safe," he murmured. "I shall tell you of my adventure…later?" He coiled his tail up my leg, rubbing its tip over the swell of my ass. With tendrils of shadow acting as extra limbs, he was supporting me without my lower back flush to the wall. I was practically cocooned in darkness, with Phaeron's topaz eyes seeming all the brighter for it.

I quivered with anticipation. "Not too much later." I didn't think I could wait much longer to hear why he'd been covered in blood.

He accepted with a nod and a fanged grin. The muscled length of his tail rubbed between my legs, gathering slickness from its tip to the first few inches. He cleaned the rest away with the textured brush of his towel.

"I missed you. I missed *this*." He skimmed his lips over the pulse of my neck. After discarding the towel, he stepped closer so I could anchor my legs around his waist. The heat of his pulsing cock nestled between my pussy lips. With a jolt of need, more precome came to replace what he'd wiped away.

"I missed you too." I ran my fingers down the strength of his chest and the swells of muscle he was slowly rebuilding with time and dedication.

He cupped my cheek. "I know. Your longing called me home, my True Light. It seems if I am to have adventures, I should bring my mate."

"Yes, you should." My response was practically a grumble.

He kissed me, and the darkness closed in around us. With his eyes closed, there was no light to see by, making the feel of him against me all the more important. His other hand plucked and teased my nipple— or was that the stroking pseudo-touch of a shadow?—while his tail uncoiled from my leg to tease the rim of my ass while I trembled. With how it tapered, he was often in charge of preparing me to take more back there.

I stroked his tail close to the base, where it was thickest. His answering otherworldly growl vibrated through me, and his lips traveled from mine to the mating mark on my shoulder. Just a simple kiss from him there sent a shockwave of pleasure through me.

"Phaeron, please," I said breathlessly.

His lips parted with his next kiss on the mark, pressing the sharp edges of his teeth without breaking skin. It was an invitation, but also a decision. If he spiked my lust with a dose of his animaris, we'd be dragging Ben and Geo into more group sex too. Something they'd never minded before. I tilted my head to give him better access, and he sank his fangs into me.

Warmth kindled from my core out to my limbs, deepening from a light tingle to a singular, burning need to have him inside me. He slipped his tail into my ass first, just the flexible tip. It wasn't enough. I grabbed him blindly, trying to pull him closer, and he eased forward with a satisfied chuckle.

He sank his cock inside me at just the right angle. One of the hard nubs on his shaft brushed the ultra-sensitive patch within me, and I lost my mind a bit. "More," I groaned, lust-drunk. "*More.*"

To his credit, he gave me more, pulling me into the drive of his hips, and sank his tail deeper in my ass, one little coaxing wiggle at a time, before thrusting with it as well so I never had the sensation of being empty.

And when I was on the cusp of a screaming orgasm, he stopped. Fucking *stopped.* I called out in frustration, my nails sinking into his skin as the sensation of release slipped away. He hissed and arched into my fingers and the bite of pain they delivered.

"Peace," he murmured, sounding a room away when my mind was soaked in animaris-fueled desire.

Phaeron drew back the shadows around us like opening a curtain, revealing Ben and Geo standing in the bedroom with their arms crossed, exuding lust and impatience.

I practically moaned their names as I reached for them. "Geo. Ben."

"How quickly five minutes pass," Phaeron mused. "Let's share her."

Music to my ears. "Oh, yes…" And this tumbled me into hours of loving with all three of my mates. We explored and solidified our mating circle again, just because we could.

SOME TIME LATER, we were in a satisfied pile on the bed. I lay on top of Ben, playing "guess the rune" by tracing random runes from the blood and celestial witcheries on his bare chest. Phaeron stirred, waking up from a catnap.

"The sun will set soon," he murmured.

"You got an internal clock in there somewhere, Big P?"

The dimensional glanced over at Ben, brows drawing together. "I don't have machinery in me."

Ben laughed. "Not a *literal* clock."

"I can sense the lack of shadows. Cress calls this time of day the golden hour."

"Great for pictures." I stretched my arms over my head. I needed to find some clothes, because I wanted to watch the sunset too.

Phaeron sighed playfully. "Yes, the beautiful time where my magic is at its weakest."

"That sounds like a personal problem," Ben said.

As the two of them continued to go back and forth, Geo helped me out of the pile and to my feet. "I think I'll join you today," he said.

I went into the closet to pick out something comfortable and emerged with a swimsuit top and skirt. I had a coverup tossed over my arm, just in case it got chilly tonight. Geo eyed what I was wearing and put on swim trunks.

"I'll go too if we walk like normal people," Ben was saying.

Phaeron disappeared into wisps of shadows and appeared in the same place a few seconds later wearing a pair of swim trunks as well. "'Normal' is a social construct, Little B," he answered.

Rolling his eyes, Ben got to his feet last and kissed me on his way by. He read the room and dressed similarly, with the addition of a hooded jacket he left unzipped for now. It mostly covered the sight of his blood rune, and he could zip it up if it got too windy outside.

I paid a quick visit to the bathroom to run a brush through my hair, and then we were off. I walked with Ben's hand in mine as we headed up to the deck. "Do you think Phaeron's ever going to tell us where he disappeared to?" he asked.

"Probably," the dimensional answered behind us. Ben startled and whipped his head around. "What? You were the one who wanted to walk."

Phaeron was behind us on the stairs, with Geo bringing up the rear. Some habits never left, as the gargoyle kept a watchful eye on our surroundings.

"You know what? This is good. Better than your usual disappearing act," Ben said. On cue, the dimensional turned into misty shadows. My anam cara shook his head. "Anyway, babe, let's get some dinner after this."

"How about some Italian?" Geo suggested.

"You just had pizza," I pointed out.

He chuckled. "And?"

"Pizza does sound good," Phaeron mused.

Ben jumped a second time, breathing a low curse, as the dimensional reappeared a couple steps behind us. "You were there the whole time."

"Yes, it's normal for me," Phaeron teased.

I smiled to myself. *This* was pretty normal for us, all things considered. No threats to solve. No pressing worries past what our next meal would be. We emerged on deck, and the diffuse light of golden hour washed over us. It gleamed off Ben's blond-brown hair, the glint of silver in Geo's eyes, and the rim of Phaeron's sunglasses as he slipped them on.

We were earlier than usual. The sun wouldn't set for several minutes yet, and we found an empty section of railing to stand and wait.

Phaeron dropped his voice to keep what he said between us. "Not to bore you with dimensional politics," he began. "But perhaps you all should know a bit about them, considering I am being roped into a facet of them through Auric."

"Uh oh," Ben replied.

Phaeron nodded. "There is a fae court, far from here, where an old rival of mine settled. She believed in our kind's superiority from the moment we were decried as demons here on Earth. While I chose to befriend humans and see them as equals..." His face pinched with concern.

"We split what remained of our people and went our separate ways. While I've been in stasis and most of my people scattered to the wind, she's mated a fae king and declared herself and her followers 'demons' during this time."

"Uh oh," Geo said, a deeper echo of Ben as we all watched the dimensional, worried for what he'd say next.

"Auric lives in her court now. He is—eternally, it would seem—a rebel and an underdog. A role I enjoy as well." Phaeron's teeth flashed briefly in wry amusement. "His project was to save a rare kind of supernatural that is treated the most poorly by these demons, cupids who have manifested their wings. There's a sense of...enjoyment"—he wrinkled his nose—"they take in pulling the feathers off the closest thing to angels."

"Oh, that explains the cupid he took to Cerris City," I said mostly to myself.

Phaeron nodded. "And another one who was in an unforeseen situation just earlier today. Auric needed me to take her to safety in my shadows, which I did. But I couldn't resist returning and dispensing a little justice to those who thought to enslave her. Thus, the blood."

"So, are you going to need to help the creepy, err, friend with cupid rescue more?" Ben asked.

Phaeron shrugged, not seeming attached to the idea. "Rarely, but I wouldn't turn down an opportunity to be useful. It would cause quite a stir if I were recognized. Besides, I have a job and a mate to protect." He shot me a fond look, which I returned. "I suspect we will be saving Roe from danger when our vacation is done as well."

"What, from the Autumn Court?" I asked.

"Where else, bright soul? She acted out of the norm in front of a death fae. It's the sort of thing that could stir an immortal's interest."

My lips were parted on a reply when a stranger called, "Excuse me." It was a middle-aged witch, with a teenage girl behind her who was engrossed in something on her phone. The older witch looked between us and smiled. "Are you in a mating circle? I see you four together all the time."

"Yes, ma'am," Ben answered.

Her smile widened. "Would you like a picture together? The sky is just so pretty this time of day."

Why not? I thought. I gave her my phone to take the picture and put my coverup behind us. Phaeron placed his sunglasses atop it, squinting as his slitted eyes adjusted to the sunlight.

We clustered together, and the motherly witch snapped several pictures. I'd later thumb through them and pick out my favorite: when another breeze kicked up to stir our hair. Phaeron was distracted by the luster of my purple locks and caught several strands between his fingers. Geo posed on my other side. A side effect of being a gargoyle: he knew exactly how to hold a stance. And Ben angled himself just right as well, his hair molten gold in the sun. He wore the rarest of his smiles, a truly carefree one.

"Enjoy the rest of your vacation," the witch bid in farewell as she dragged her teen further up the deck to watch the sunset too.

Phaeron put an arm around me as we watched the sun sink into the waves. "There's plenty to look forward to, bright soul. Things to do, places we're needed. It's the golden hour of our lives."

"Hopeful," I agreed.

"Beautiful," Ben added, joining us at the railing. The sun turned the water orange across the horizon.

"And something to be protected," Geo put in, flanking my anam cara.

Ben nudged him, smirking. "You would say that, G Man."

"It's my duty," the gargoyle deadpanned.

Phaeron shook his head. As early evening colors lit the sky, his gaze slipped back to me. "We're going to be listening to this for the rest of our lives," he murmured. But he wasn't speaking in judgment. If anything, he was grateful for this moment together.

I nodded in agreement. Only a year ago, I had no idea the supernatural world existed. Now I was mate bonded to three incredible men. My heart was light as I said, "I wouldn't have it any other way."

Artwork made by Janenajla Arts

ABOUT THE AUTHOR

Ella Hendricks is an author of romances with dark roots and steamy twists. She loves getting lost in fantasy worlds, especially if the monsters are naughty and the lady saves the day in the end. When Ella is not writing about swoon-worthy men, she's off collecting video game achievements. She holds a master's degree in journalism and lives in Texas with her family.

Find out more about her books at: www.ellahendricks.com